Sorcerer's Moon

By Julian May

Voyager

Sorcerer's Moon

THE BOREAL MOON TALE:
BOOK Three

JULIAN MAY

HarperCollins*Publishers*

3295392

Voyager
An Imprint of HarperCollins*Publishers*
77–85 Fulham Palace Road,
Hammersmith, London W6 8JB

www.voyager-books.co.uk

Published by *Voyager* 2006
1

Copyright © 2006 by Starykon Productions, Inc

The Author asserts the moral right to
be identified as the author of this work

Maps by Richard Geiger

A catalogue record for this book
is available from the British Library

ISBN-13 978 0 00 712324 7
ISBN-10 0 00 712324 8

Typeset in Meridien by Palimpsest Book Production Limited,
Polmont, Stirlingshire

Printed and bound in Great Britain by
Clays Limited, St Ives plc

All rights reserved. No part of this publication may be
reproduced, stored in a retrieval system, or transmitted,
in any form or by any means, electronic, mechanical,
photocopying, recording or otherwise, without the prior
permission of the publishers.

This book is proudly printed on paper which contains wood
from well managed forests, certified in accordance with
the rules of the Forest Stewardship Council.
For more information about FSC,
please visit www.fsc.org

Mixed Sources
Product group from well-managed
forests and other controlled sources
www.fsc.org Cert no. SW-COC-1806
FSC © 1996 Forest Stewardship Council

BARREN LANDS

ICE BEAR CHANNEL

WESTERN OCEAN

BLAZING ISLES

DAWNTIDE ISLES

STORMLANDS
MORNAIN
DONOR VALE
BLUE TARN
WHITE TARN
TARNHOLME
WHITERIME MTS.
GREEN MORASS
DIREWOLD CASTLE
ELDERWOLD
CASTLE TERMINAL
TWEENWATER
DISMAL HEIGHTS
GREAT FEN
CASTLE FENGUARD
MALLTHORP
HOLT MALLBURN
REDBERN

SEA

SINISTRAL MTS.
DEXTRAL MOUNTAINS
BEOBROOK HOLD
ZETH ABBEY
WESTKEEP
DEMON SEAT
VANGUARD
SWAN
BRENT
BRE

BOREAL

STORM ISLES
WESTERLEY
CALA BLENHOLME

TO EASTERN MAINLAND

VIGILANT ISLES

DOLPHIN CHANNEL

NIS-GATA
NIS-BRAL
R.G.
OWNABEDA
MAKAILE
KLOMKOILE
AKAL
STIPPEN
NIS-MOEN
NIS-TILLAN

ANDRADH
FORAILE

CONTINENTAL MAINLAND

HIGH
BLENHOLME
ISLAND

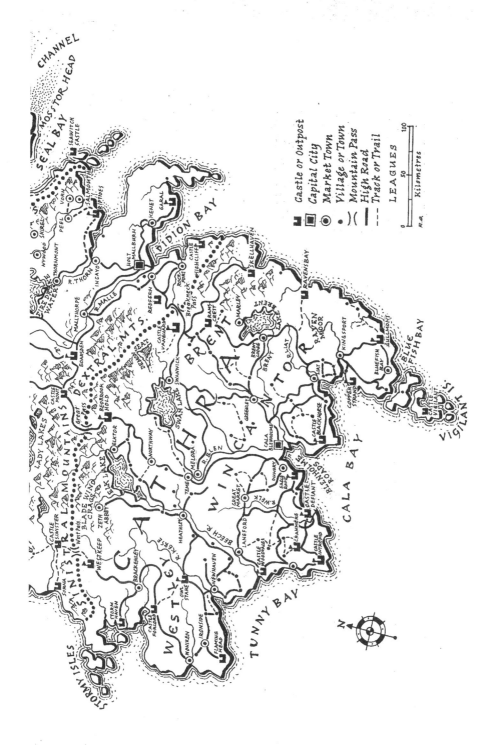

As our valiant warriors proceed inland in the conquest of High Blenholme Island, I command that all inactive moonstone amulets discovered on the dead bodies of our Salka foe be smashed into dust and scattered to the Boreal Winds, for the sorcery they conjure is an abomination and a mortal danger to all thinking creatures – be they human or nonhuman.

– BAZEKOY, Emperor of the World

PROLOGUE

The Royal Intelligencer

With evening, the incessant warm rain that had plagued us for three days stopped, the sky cleared at last, and I caught a glimpse of the rising moon. Its position confirmed the fear that had haunted me since morning. We were traveling in the wrong direction, going north instead of south. We were lost.

Even worse, I was now positive that something was stalking us. It was very large, clever enough to stay hidden in the thick brush along the shore, and it betrayed itself only rarely by unnatural movements of the greenery or a slight sound –

Like that! The faint crack of a broken stick.

I stopped paddling and the skiff drifted to a halt. I peered into shadowy undergrowth a dozen ells away and cupped a hand about my ear, straining to listen. There was no wind. The waters of the lake were flat calm. Save for the faraway wailing cry of a black-throated diver bird, the silence was absolute. My normal senses perceived nothing. Once again, I tried without success to summon my talent, but my uncanny abilities were still too weak even to scry through the flimsy barrier of reeds and shrubs into the boreal forest beyond.

Yet instinct assured me that the stalker was there, watching us.

The sky overhead had turned to deepest blue, with a few scattered stars beginning to appear. On my right hand the full Harvest Moon rose, brilliantly white, through the raggedy ranks of spruce trees that topped the ridge alongside the narrow lake. I looked toward the opposite shore and beheld a wonderful thing in the sky above it – a great arc of pearly light spread across the retreating bank of rainclouds in the west.

I must have exclaimed at the sight of it, waking her. Induna stirred in the bottom of the boat, uncovered her head, which had been shielded from the rain by blankets and an oilskin cloak, and lifted herself painfully on one elbow.

'Deveron?' Her voice was low and anxious. 'Is something wrong?'

For the moment, I dodged the question. 'Look over there. It's a moon bow.'

'How beautiful. I've heard of them but never seen one before. They're supposed to portend great good luck.'

I thought: We have sore need of that, beyond doubt!

Even as we watched, the marvel began to fade. It was gone almost as soon as it had appeared. I took up the water-flask and bent over the woman who should have been my wife sixteen years ago, who had already given up so much for my sake and who now might be rewarded only with gruesome death. Induna lay with her head pillowed on a pack. She had been asleep for hours, still recovering from the sacrifice made shortly after our arrival in this forsaken wilderness three days earlier.

I said, 'Take some water, love. I'll help you to sit up.'

The boat rocked as we shifted position. It was a flat-bottomed skiff of the unique Andradhian style, made of tough sheets of thin bark, pointed at both ends. The Boatwright I'd bought it from had intended it for the jungle streams of the distant Southern Continent; but being lightweight and easy to portage, it was also the perfect craft for voyaging among the bewildering maze of bogs, rivers and chains of lakes that comprised the forbidding Green Morass of northern Didion.

Induna drank only a little before sinking back onto her improvised cushion with a sigh. 'I feel stronger. The sleep did me good. I think I'll be able to eat something tonight. Will we be going ashore soon? My poor bladder is nigh bursting.'

I pointed to a small wooded island that lay off the bow. 'We'll camp there, rather than on the mainland. I . . . think something might be following the boat along the shore, keeping out of sight.'

Her eyes widened. 'Is it an animal?'

'Perhaps not. It tracks us very slyly. It's best that we not take chances.'

'So you can't oversee what it might be?'

I began to paddle again, digging briskly. 'My wind-sensibilities are still useless, even though my physical strength now seems completely restored, thanks to you.'

'How long has this creature been trailing us?'

'God only knows. I became aware of it this morning, shortly after we embarked from the last campsite, but it might have been pursuing us for longer, hidden by the mist and rain. It's a sizable thing, probably much larger than a human being. I pray it's only a curious brown bear or wandering tundra-lion. I can fend a beast off easily with a few firebolts from my crossbow.'

She spoke hesitantly. 'Could it possibly be a Salka? You recall that I told you that the forces of the Sovereignty believed that the monsters' main force was massed many leagues to the north of here, around Beacon Lake. But they might have sent out scouts.'

'I think not. The amphibians move clumsily on land, as this thing does not. And Salka would be more likely to follow a small boat by swimming underwater. Our pursuer is something else.'

Induna and I both suspected what it might be. But neither of us wanted to name the dire possibility aloud, nor did we voice the uncomfortable thought that we might have been under observation by the supposedly extinct Morass Worms almost from the first disastrous moment of our arrival.

Like most citizens of Cathra, I'd known almost nothing of the giant horrors until I came to live in Tarn. Induna's mother had told legends of them as we shared the folklore of our disparate homelands during long winter nights in the Deep Creek Cove manorhouse. No Tarnian had laid eyes on a Morass Worm for at least three hundred years, but their memory lived on through grisly tales relished by the simpler people of the northlands. The storytellers could not even agree upon the fabled creatures' appearance, describing them variously as huge fanged eels, scaly serpents, slime-covered salamanders, or even colossal centipedes with writhing multiple limbs. Like the Salka, the Green Men, and the Small Lights, they were said to be prehistoric inhabitants of the island who were driven into the waste lands by invading humankind. The worms were intelligent, not mere animals. Supposedly they were able to appear out of nowhere and kill their prey by breathing fire. The hardheaded Didionite foresters who dwelt in the far northern parts of High Blenholme mostly scoffed at the old tales and were certain that the worms no longer existed – if they ever had. But then, humans almost never ventured into the trackless depths of the Green Morass . . .

After an interval of tense silence, during which I paddled as strongly as I could, I said to Induna, 'In the tales your mother told back at our manorhouse, she said that the Morass Worms and the Salka were deadly enemies in ancient times. Would the amphibians dare to invade Blenholme from the north coast if their old antagonists still lived in the region?'

'Perhaps the Salka leaders also believed the worms to be

extinct,' Induna said. 'After all, their Eminent Four are natives of the Dawntide Isles, unfamiliar with Blenholme's remote interior.'

It was something worth pondering, but we spoke no more about it, for we had finally reached the lake island. As the hull of the skiff grounded on the muddy bottom, I hopped into the shallow water and lifted Induna's slight form in my arms, carrying her ashore. She insisted she was now able to walk. After she made a discreet detour into the bushes, we traveled a short distance inland until we reached a clearing among the trees that I deemed safer for a campsite than the beach. I planned to surround it with numbers of the magical turquoise warning-pebbles that I carried and make several large fires as well.

While she sat resting on a rock, still wrapped in the oilskin cloak, I snapped off deadwood from the lower trunks of the spruces until there was a sizable heap a few feet away from her, then set this reasonably dry small stuff ablaze with several tarnsticks from my waterproof belt-pouch. I was still incapable of summoning fire with magic.

Induna gave a sigh of satisfaction and held out her hands to the warmth. The flames emphasized her pallid skin and dark green eyes. Her hair, normally a lustrous red-gold aureole, had turned to dark tendrils from the prevailing dampness. She still suffered the effects of her soul's diminishing, but her ability to walk and sit upright now without assistance seemed hopeful signs.

'I'll bring larger pieces of driftwood from the shore and build a better fire as soon as I get the boat out of the water and unload the packs,' I said. 'Will you be all right here alone for a few minutes?'

'Don't worry, Deveron. I'm really feeling much stronger.' She smiled at me. 'And I'm still very glad that I came with you.'

Her words sent a pang of guilt through my heart. 'You should not have taken hold of me as I conjured the sigil,' I muttered. 'Who knows what will become of us now? The unknown thing that follows is only one of the dangers besetting us. We're lost, Induna! The overcast skies and tangled waterways, combined with the quenching of my talent caused by moonstone sorcery, have muddled my wits completely. I have no notion where the castle might be. All we can do is reverse direction and travel southward in the morning, and pray that my abilities recover enough for me to scry the place out and conjure effective magical defenses that will get us there in safety. My Andradhian pebble-charms and other weapons can't protect us for long against thinking adversaries – whatever their shape.'

'All will be well. Remember the moon bow!'

Her attempt at good cheer only made me feel worse. Anger as well as dread rose like a hot tide in my soul and I could not help the bitter words that burst forth. 'Moon bow luck is only a fairytale spun for gullible children, sweetheart, as you know very well. This venture is a failure before it has scarce begun, and I curse the Source for dragging you into it – for using you as the bait to lure me back into his demonic conflict. He knew very well that I'd be convinced by no one else, that my love for you had only strengthened after all the years spent apart and I'd do whatever you asked. The Source reunited us – but small joy we'll have in one another! We'll likely die in this cursèd Green Morass, while he and his immortal cohorts will live on and find more effective human pawns to fight their battles among the stars.'

She responded with spirit. 'I'm no pawn, Deveron Austrey! No one forced me to bring the Source's message. I enlisted in the New Conflict freely – as you once did. And it was my own free choice to accompany you to the morass in spite of your protests. Perhaps I was a fool to come. But what would have happened had I not been at your side to release you from Subtle Gateway's pain-debt after we arrived here? Without me, your drowned body would now be lying on a riverbank, with wolves and swamp-fitches gnawing your bones.'

'True,' I agreed wretchedly. My eyes welled up at the loving fervor in the voice of this woman I had abandoned so many years ago, whose fate was once again linked inseparably with mine. 'I *am* glad you're here.' I strode to her and clasped her to my breast. 'How could I not be? Somehow, we'll survive. And return together to the Barking Sands.'

She murmured a few words, lifting her face to be kissed. But even as I bent to comply she went stiff in my arms, and from her parted lips came a soft moan of terror. 'Deveron . . . behind you.'

Still holding her tightly to me, I swung about and saw a huge thing looming amongst the dark spruces. Its sinuous body was thicker than a barrel and gleamed wet and smooth in the dancing firelight, appearing to be at least five ells in length. It had approached us without a sound. As we gaped, too stricken to move, it reared up and revealed strong limbs armed with scythe-like claws. In its own hideous fashion, it was quite beautiful. The gemlike green eyes set into its grotesquely ornate head shone with an inner radiance that betokened talent as well as intelligence. It opened its mouth slightly, showing yellowish fangs as lucent as topaz, and gave a soft hiss as it glided toward us, fraught with elegant menace.

The Morass Worm matched none of the trite descriptions of the old tales. Its glossy, longnecked body was apparently clothed in sleek wet fur or dark feathers rather than scales, and its exhalations, while fetid enough, lacked the hot sulphurous taint of its mythical namesake. It was no fire-breather, but rather a creature of flesh and blood. During my long exile in southern Andradh, I'd heard sailors from the Malachite Islands sing songs about such fearsome predators, giving them another name. The creature menacing us had no wings, unlike its Andradhian counterpart, but its frightful conformation was almost identical.

It was a dragon.

It spoke, and we heard it not with our ears but with our minds.

I command that you shall not move. I command that you shall not use the Salka moonstones, nor conjure any other sorcery against me.

Its windvoice was silken-soft, almost languid, full of arrogant confidence. Induna and I were helpless, incapable of fight or flight. I was aware of an awesome talent inspecting us as though we were novel and unsavory specimens on an alchymist's bench.

'We mean no harm,' I managed to say. 'We are only lost travelers, trying to find Castle Morass –'

Silence!

The great neck arched downward and the talons reached out and seized both of us. We clung tighter to one another and prepared to die. The creature pulled us toward its opening mouth. Its eyes were like blazing emeralds with central pools of darkness that grew to enormous proportions and then swallowed us whole.

In the earlier volumes of this Boreal Moon Tale, I told of my first years of service to Conrig Wincantor, nicknamed Ironcrown, High King of Cathra and Sovereign of High Blenholme Island. I, Deveron Austrey, was born with powerful uncanny abilities that were strangely imperceptible to the Brothers of Zeth, who examine small children for such traits and compel the windtalented to join their Mystical Order. One of my gifts, which I hardly understood during my boyhood, enabled me to detect magical potential in others.

At the age of twelve, when I was a lowly apprentice leatherworker in the Cala Palace stables and Conrig was Prince Heritor of Cathra, I chanced to look into the royal youth's eyes as I helped him mount his horse. There I recognized the faint but unmistakable glint that marks a person possessing magical talent. Not knowing its importance, I blurted out my discovery to the appalled prince. Fortunately for me, no other person was near enough to overhear. So instead of having me killed, Conrig made me his personal snudge (or spy) and called me by that name.

I kept his secret, which would have disqualified him for the Cathran kingship even though his talent was very meager. In time, with a good deal of assistance from the powerful sorceress Ullanoth of Moss – and, I must admit, from me – Conrig inherited his father's throne.

After winning a war against the forces of Didion, Ironcrown declared himself the Sovereign of Blenholme. A few years later he fulfilled his ambition to unite the four quarreling states of our island into a single nation. But this was to be only a first step toward Conrig's ultimate objective: to emulate his ancestor, Emperor Bazekoy the Great, and conquer the rest of the known world.

Conrig Wincantor was a brilliant politician and a warrior of immense valor. Nevertheless he possessed a ruthlessness and an icy expediency that often troubled my over-tender conscience; but in spite of these misgivings, I served him faithfully throughout my adolescence. When I entered manhood at the age of twenty, Conrig knighted me, named me his Royal Intelligencer, and almost immediately entrusted me with a crucial new mission.

I was sent to the land of Tarn to search for the king's vengeful divorced wife, Princess Maudrayne. Believed to be drowned, she had reappeared after four years and posed a unique threat to the Sovereignty. Not only had she covertly given birth to

Conrig's eldest son – who by law would take precedence over the king's heirs by his second marriage – but she also knew that her former husband possessed weak magical talent. If she revealed his secret and convinced the Lords Judicial of Cathra that she spoke the truth, Conrig would lose his throne. Even if she were not believed, her mere accusation might fatally undermine the already wavering loyalty of the vassal states of Tarn and Didion and plunge the island into chaos.

Ironcrown was adamant that I should do whatever was necessary to guarantee Maudrayne's silence, as well as eliminate the dynastic menace posed by her young son Dyfrig. I balked at the obvious solution – assassination – and conceived a plan that I hoped might save the lives of the princess and her little boy while still satisfying the king.

As I undertook the difficult task of finding the pair, I discovered that the stability of Conrig's reign had a more overreaching importance: High Blenholme Island was about to be invaded by a horde of Salka monsters. Incited by the young sorcerer Beynor ash Linndal, deposed ruler of Moss and brother to his successor Conjure-Queen Ullanoth, the enormous amphibians intended to take back the island from which most of them had been expelled over a thousand years earlier by Emperor Bazekoy.

Both Beynor and the Salka planned to use moonstone sigils, instruments of sorcery empowered by the supernatural Beaconfolk, to bring about the reconquest. The auroral Beacons, who were also called the Great Lights, comprised two opposing factions that were embroiled in a mysterious New Conflict of their own. I had been drawn into it against my will – as had numbers of other humans who are also part of this Boreal Moon Tale – but by the end of the mission involving Princess Maudrayne and her son, I mistakenly believed I had escaped the Lights' thrall.

*   *   *

The mission itself was both a success and a failure. With the help of loyal companions – and my reluctant employment of two moonstone sigils, which the 'good' Light called the Source had compelled me to accept – I rescued Maudrayne and her child Dyfrig from a strange captivity. I was able to convince the princess to recant her spiteful revelation of Conrig's secret to the Sealords of Tarn. In turn, the High King agreed that young Dyfrig might be placed third in the Cathran royal succession, behind his twin sons Orrion and Corodon, born of his marriage to Risalla of Didion. The boy was to become the adopted son of Earl Marshal Parlian Beorbrook, a Cathran peer of uncompromising honesty. To assure the child's loyalty to the Sovereign, Dyfrig would never see or communicate with his mother again.

Unknown to me, Ironcrown was too cynical to trust his former wife's promise not to publicly reaffirm his secret talent. After having agreed that Maudrayne would be allowed to live in quiet exile with her Tarnian relatives, he arranged for her murder by poison, which was passed off as suicide. I was so disillusioned by the king's perfidy that I left his service without permission. I fled to a remote region of western Tarn, accompanied by a young woman named Induna of Barking Sands, an apprentice shaman-healer who had earlier saved my life and also assisted in the rescue of Maudrayne and her son. For a few months I lived with Induna and her mother in a tiny village near Northkeep.

In the best of romantic endings I should have married Induna and made a new life for myself, secure from the Sovereignty's tumult and intrigues as well as from the more subtle machinations of the Beaconfolk.

The reality was messier.

Shortly after my abrupt resignation from the intelligencer post, I sent a message to Conrig via his elder brother Vra-Stergos, Cathra's Royal Alchymist, who had been friendly toward me during my years of service to the king. In it I apologized for my affront to the regal dignity (but gave no reason for my dereliction of duty), swore that I intended to continue guarding Conrig's secret with my life, and said that I wanted only to be left in peace. I also returned the considerable sum of money vouchsafed to me by the Crown when I was granted knighthood.

There was no reply to my message, and none of my later attempts to windspeak Lord Stergos were successful. He and Conrig were occupied with more urgent matters. The king's domestic enemies, Cathra's Lords of the Southern Shore, had demanded that he defend himself against persistent Tarnian accusations that he possessed magical talent, was thus not the legitimate High King of Cathra, and therefore was unworthy of Tarn's fealty.

The official inquiry was as brief as it was dramatic. No member of Cathra's Mystical Order of Zeth could swear that they detected talent in the king. (The scrupulously honest Vra-Stergos was saved from having to condemn his brother because of the precise wording of the oath, even though he knew well enough that the accusation was true.) Maudrayne was believed dead and unable to renew her denunciation, and I was shielded by sorcery and refused to testify. Since there were no other witnesses against Conrig who had status under Cathran law, he won his case easily.

The Sealords of Tarn cursed all lawyers and grudgingly continued to pay the heavy taxes imposed by the Sovereignty. The wealthy Lords of the Southern Shore did the same, thwarted in their attempt to put Duke Feribor Blackhorse, their ringleader, on the Cathran throne in place of Conrig.

In the devastated little kingdom of Moss, far from the tranquil cottage on the edge of the Western Ocean where I dwelt with Induna and her mother, the Salka hunkered down in the lands they had overrun and pondered the next big step in the reconquest of 'their' island. They owned numbers of minor moonstone sigils which they had already successfully used as weapons, and hatched plans to obtain others that were more potent. Conjure-Queen Ullanoth, who had ruled Moss before the Salka invasion, was believed by most people to have perished through imprudent use of her sigils. Her scheming younger brother Beynor had dropped out of sight after quarreling with the victorious monsters, his former secret allies. No one knew (or cared) what had become of him.

With the security of the Sovereignty now his primary concern, Conrig garrisoned troops at crucial points along the Dismal Heights from Rainy Pass to Riptide Bay, supposedly making a land invasion of Didion by the Salka impossible. At the same time the formidable Joint Fleet of the Sovereignty, equipped with tarnblaze cannons, patrolled the waters off the island's eastern coast in a show of strength designed to keep the amphibians in check. In spite of the blockade, the monsters made several waterborne forays against coastal settlements of Didion and Cathra. But finally, in a single decisive battle, the Salka stronghold in the Dawntide Isles was completely destroyed by the Sovereignty, and an interval of peace settled over High Blenholme.

As for myself, Induna and her mother Maris, a much-admired shaman in Tarn's coastal Stormlands, had invited me to stay with them indefinitely in order to learn the healer's art, since I no longer had any taste for spying. Using part of the fortune she had inherited from her late grand-sire, the renegade wizard Blind Bozuk, Induna purchased a fine manorhouse and lands that lay in a pleasant place called Deep Creek Cove, backed by grasslands. For my sake the manor was fortified with ingenious magical defenses. Rumors persisted that High King Conrig still thought I was even more of a threat to his Iron Crown than Maudrayne had ever been. Induna and I both feared he'd eventually send someone to eliminate me, and we resolved to be ready.

Maris was a kind person endowed with singular wisdom, who helped me to a deeper understanding of my uncanny abilities. (Up until then, I had been entirely self-taught in magic.) She also gave me valuable advice concerning the two moonstone sigils, Concealer and Subtle Gateway, that were still in my possession. I yearned to cast those soul-destroying tools of the Beaconfolk into the deep sea so I'd never again be tempted to use them; but Maris counseled against it. In one of her trances, she'd had a puzzling vision concerning me and the stones and an enigmatic black creature bound with sapphire chains who dwelt beneath the icecap of the Barren Lands. Maris had no notion of the dark thing's identity – although I had! – but she was certain that my destiny involved both the creature and the two sigils. When Induna added her pleas to those of her mother, I finally agreed to keep the moonstones.

Induna . . .

She later admitted that she had loved me almost as soon as she first saw me lying senseless in a rock shelter on the Desolation Coast, at the point of death after having rashly used the Subtle Gateway sigil to transport me and my companions and all our gear to the place where Maudrayne and Dyfrig were imprisoned. Induna realized at once that my mortal illness was the result of Beaconfolk sorcery. The terrible beings of the Sky Realm were feeding on my pain, and no groundling remedy could heal me.

So she shared with me a small portion of her own soul, in a manner that only northland shamans are capable of. It left her diminished even as it cured me. Later, she performed the same mystical operation once again, shortly before I decided to renounce my fealty to King Conrig. Her selfless acts of generosity did not immediately inspire my love. On the contrary, I was left with vague feelings of discomfort and indebtedness that only melted away during the long months when we worked together and began to really know one another.

I was amazed when it finally occurred to me that life without her would be unthinkable. The emotion I felt toward Induna at that time was no overwhelming passion: I was then, as I am now, a man plagued by an aloof and calculating nature. But she was my best friend, my teacher, and my comforter, and if I did not yet love her as wholeheartedly as she loved me, I still wanted none other for my wife.

We were solemnly betrothed according to Tarnian custom, and planned to marry in the summer of 1134, in Blossom Moon, when I was one-and-twenty years of age and Induna was eighteen. But the Cathran warship arrived in the waters off Deep Creek Cove three weeks before that, and our happy plans came to nothing.

Commanded by Tinnis Catclaw, the same debonair but unscupulous Lord Constable who had agreed to murder Princess Maudrayne on Conrig's orders, the vessel carried a coven of mercenary Didionite wizards. Six of the disguised magickers came stealthily ashore and combined their talents to overpower Induna and Maris while they were beyond our home's magical defenses, visiting the byre of a local smallholder to attend the difficult birth of a foal. I myself had been working with them, until I was sent back to the manorhouse to fetch a special physick to soothe the suffering mare. I was there when the wizards announced their ultimatum.

I was ordered to row out to the warship lurking just beyond the cove's northern headland and surrender to the Lord Constable, who carried the Sovereign's warrant for my arrest . . . or else scry my womenfolk as they were burnt alive in a tarnblaze holocaust that would leave behind nothing but a heap of charred bones.

The horrific tarnblaze chymical was impervious to any sorcerous intervention I might have attempted, nor had I any hope of reaching Induna and Maris before it could be ignited. I had no choice but to comply.

I left the place that had become my only true home and allowed myself to be shackled and hauled aboard the Cathran man o' war. Lord Catclaw awaited me on deck, an oddly apologetic expression on his handsome countenance and his long blond hair tied in a tail. Two armed seamen gripped me. He ordered a third to slice off my clothing and footgear with a keen varg sword, using great caution. When I stood stark naked, the constable smiled in satisfaction as he saw the moonstone sigil called Concealer hanging on a thin chain around my neck. Properly conjured, it would render me invisible. Conrig knew about it, of course. I had used it in his service.

'Don't think to call upon your devilish Beaconfolk amulet,' Catclaw warned me, 'or I'll have this fellow here bespeak the other wizards on shore to ignite the tarnblaze.' He beckoned to a black-robed magicker standing nearby, who held a golden goblet and a pair of nippers. 'You! Get the sigil off him. I've been told it cannot be conjured unless it's next to his skin. Be very careful not to handle it yourself, except with the cup and tool. The High King himself has warned me of its perils.'

The wizard eased the translucent small pendant into the goblet, then severed its chain. Had he touched the moonstone with his own bare flesh, he would have been hideously burned. Concealer was bonded to me, and no one else could use it or even handle it with impunity.

'Where is the second sigil?' Catclaw demanded. 'The one called Subtle Gateway, which transports a person instantly from place to place? I have been commanded by the King's Grace to seize both amulets from you and bring them back to him.'

In spite of all my warnings, sigil sorcery obviously still held an unhealthy fascination for Conrig.

I responded in a near-whisper, which was all I was capable of without betraying myself. 'I threw the thing into deep water months ago. His Grace knows full well how much I abominate moonstone magic. Concealer is a minor sort that causes only insignificant discomfort to the user, but Gateway was one of the so-called Great Stones. Conjuring it induced an appalling agony and put my very soul in peril to the pain-eating Beaconfolk. When I rescued Princess Maudrayne and completed my mission, I had no more need of it. I was glad to get rid of the thing.'

I was lying. But Catclaw was not about to find that out until I learned what he planned to do with me – along with Induna and Maris.

One of the ship's officers stepped forward. 'Shall we go ashore and search for the stone in his house, my lord?'

'Why bother?' I told the Lord Constable. 'The sigils are worthless to the High King, whether he realizes it or not. When I die – and I presume my fate is sealed – any sigil owned by me becomes inactive: a worthless piece of rock. I learned how to use them only by a lucky accident. No one knows how to bond them to a new owner save the Salka who made them in the first place. Once, Queen Ullanoth of Moss and her lunatic brother Beynor also knew the secret. But she's dead and he has disappeared.'

Tinnis Catclaw frowned and appeared to be considering the matter.

Emboldened, I asked the all-important question. 'Do you now intend to kill my betrothed and her mother as well as me?'

The constable waved a dismissive hand. 'The threat was only a bluff, a ploy to bring about your capture. Not even the Sovereign would dare harm a well-known shaman-healer such as Maris of Barking Sands, nor her daughter – who is an anointed Sealady of Tarn, albeit one of minimal rank. Such

deeds might provoke the touchy Tarnian leaders beyond
endurance. At this moment the girl and her mother are harm-
lessly sleeping off their enchantment, lying in the straw beside
a mare and her newborn colt. The hireling wizards have
followed my orders and scattered to the four winds. All they
care about is how they'll spend their bags of Cathran gold.'

I sighed in relief. The only persons that I had ever taken
to my heart would be safe now from Conrig's revenge . . .
but only if I abandoned them.

'How do you intend to dispose of me?' I asked.

Catclaw pulled himself up in a dignified huff. 'Your just
punishment will be meted out strictly according to Cathran
law. Once this warship rides the high seas, you'll be tried for
treason. Your disavowal of fealty meets the legal criterion.
As Lord Constable, I have the judicial authority to order your
summary execution. You'll hang from a yardarm.'

'But do you solemnly swear to me that Induna and Maris
will be spared?'

'I've already said so,' Catclaw retorted testily, 'and I'm a
man of honor.'

'Oh, yes?' I hissed. 'Did Princess Maudrayne find you
honorable?'

His face drained of color. He gave a sharp command to the
seamen who held and surrounded me. 'All of you – move
away from the prisoner! Draw your swords and stand ready,
but step back. Farther yet! If he stirs, slay him where he stands.'

The astonished men retreated a good eight feet away.
Catclaw stood very close to me and his voice would have
been inaudible to the others.

'Since you are to die within the hour, I'll tell you how I
dealt with Princess Maude. I was indeed commanded to kill
her. I confess that I wrote her suicide note. It stated that she
could not bear to live if she would never be allowed to see
her son Dyfrig again, as the High King had decreed. I offered

her poison . . . but gave her instead a potion that rendered her senseless and slowed her heart. She lay cold and still as a dead woman on the deck of my frigate, which was docked at Donorvale Quay, ready to return to Cathra with the boy. The Tarnian authorities bore witness to the sudden and tragic demise of the princess. Her body was placed in a lead coffin and kept in my own cabin, covered with a blanket of roses, until it could be buried at sea. This was High King Conrig's command, following my own suggestion. Poor little Dyfrig was devastated by his mother's suicide and could not bear to watch the ceremony. But the coffin my crew consigned to the depths of the Western Ocean was empty.'

I nearly choked upon that which I held inside my cheek. 'Alive?' I gasped.

'She was the most beautiful woman I'd ever known,' Tinnis Catclaw said. 'Conrig Ironcrown cast her off when it seemed she could not bear him a son. He declared her an archenemy of the Sovereignty and commanded her death. But I had long loved her from afar. I still do – even though I am now able to visit her only on rare occasions in my hunting lodge north of Swan Lake, where she willingly remains hidden for the sake of Prince Dyfrig. Maude is a proud and spirited soul. But she is . . . kind to me. And kings do not live forever.'

'Great God,' I murmured. 'You are as much a traitor as I.'

He smiled. 'And yet, I don't believe you'll use your wind-speech to reveal my secret before you die.'

'No,' I agreed. It was the farthest thing from my mind. 'Conduct your trial, my lord. Prepare the rope. But I ask a favor, as one turncoat to another. Dress me in decent clothing beforehand, restore my knight's belt and purse, and forgo shackles. I swear I'll behave with dignity. And as I go to my death, let your wizard stand a few ells away holding the chalice with my sigil. It would give me a melancholy comfort to have it near me.'

He agreed.

Later, while the great ship sliced the waves on its southerly course, and those members of the crew who were not on watch gathered in solemn ranks to witness my dispatch, I mounted the improvised scaffold unfettered.

'Do you have any last words?' the Lord Constable asked me.

'My lord, I bear you and the King's Grace no malice,' I told him. Tell Conrig that. And now, farewell.'

He stepped back to accommodate the hangman. I lifted my arm and cried out, 'Concealer – to me!'

The sigil flew out of the cup and into my waiting hand. A roar of surprise rose from the astounded crew. But before a man of them could move, I intoned the brief spell that conjured the tiny door-shaped carving called Subtle Gateway, hardly larger than a thumbnail, which had been concealed in my mouth since I quit the manorhouse.

Agony smote me like a thunderclap. I knew that it was going to last for a long time, disabling me profoundly – perhaps even fatally – and this time there'd be no respite vouchsafed by Induna. The Great Lights would eat their fill of my pain without hindrance.

But if I survived, I'd open my eyes in the southernmost region of the continental nation of Andradh, over two thousand leagues away, far beyond the reach of Conrig Ironcrown, Sovereign of High Blenholme Island, and perhaps even beyond that of the Beaconfolk themselves.

I did survive.

And dwelt in Andradh among the Wave-Harriers for the next sixteen years, until Induna came knocking on my door and, against all odds, convinced me to become the Royal Intelligencer once again.

ONE

It was a kind of daydream that overcame High King Conrig Wincantor at inconvenient moments, snatching him from the real world into a fantastic . . . elsewhere. Without warning, he would find himself in a cramped chamber, dimly lit and stifling, surrounded on all sides by a hostile mob.

The adversaries howled and darted at him like malignant phantoms, clutching at his crown – his priceless Iron Crown. They reached out with hands and claws and tentacles, howling curses and filthy insults, trying to rip the symbol of Sovereignty away from him, saying he had no right to it.

'I do!' he bellowed. 'It's mine. I earned it and defended it. Leave be! Go away!'

He fought them with all his mortal strength and with all his secret uncanny talent as well, smiting with his longsword and smashing and blasting the foe with magical bombards. Some of the raging attackers were human, persons that he'd loved who gave only hatred and malice in return; some enemies were rebellious vassals flouting his rightful authority; some were dim-witted grotesques trying to pull down the great edifice he'd built, in a pathetic extirpation motivated only by envy and spite.

Enemies all!

He'd fought them for years. He'd never surrender.

'I won't give in!' he cried, holding tight to the crown. 'I'll rule this island and rule the world.'

'No,' they roared. 'Never!'

'Yes! I shall conquer. I shall!'

Always, as those last defiant words rang out, the frantic tugging weakened, yielding to his superior strength. The grasping tangle of limbs fell away from the prize, leaving him in sole possession. He crowned himself anew with the dark metal circlet and felt the old joy ignite within him, banishing all doubt and fear. Thwarted, the mass of enemies melted away, while his shout of triumph echoed in a vault of sunlit clouds.

'My foes are many, but I crush them all. I bow to no power in the Sky or the Ground Realm. I reign. I rule!'

It was the simple truth . . . So why didn't his enemies understand that and let him be? Why did they keep returning over and over to trouble him with these unquiet waking dreams?

Why?

It was maddening.

Orrion Wincantor, Prince Heritor of Cathra and unwilling bridegroom-elect, felt a need to stop and take stock of the situation before climbing any farther. He dropped behind his older brother, Vra-Bramlow, and his twin, Prince Corodon, and paused to catch his breath and stare up at the looming bulk of Demon Seat in morose silence.

Why did I let Bram and Coro talk me into this? he asked himself. Scaling a mountain in order to perform forbidden sorcery! The notion was idiotic . . . and damned dangerous as well. Coro might easily have broken his leg when he lost his footing and took a tumble back at the torrent, and he himself was rock-bruised and aching. But they'd nearly reached the top now, and it was probably too late to suggest they turn back without seeming to be craven.

Was it also too late to disavow the magical tomfoolery? Might he yet find a way to laugh off the venture after they'd gained the summit, claiming that he'd never intended to ask the Sky Demons for a blasphemous miracle and had only made the ascent to distract himself from his heartache?

But that would be a lie.

The view of the surrounding Cathran countryside was stupendous. From the ledge where he rested Orrion could see most of Swan Lake, the distinctive spiky crest above Beorbrook Hold, the isolated monolith of Elktor, and even a faraway twinkling to the east that had to be the famous crystal window of Castle Vanguard. Below him the steep ridges of the mountain's south flank, thrown into prominence by bright sunlight, resembled notched axe-blades. The glacial ice lying between them was grubby from leftover ash that had been deposited by eruptions of Tarnian volcanos two decades earlier. A few pink and gold alpine wildflowers bloomed in crevices nearby. The summit rocks above showed patches of brilliant white, dusted by the first light snowfall of approaching autumn.

Summer that year had been uncommonly warm, melting more snow than usual from the Dextral Range. Even Demon Seat, the loftiest peak on High Blenholme Island, had lost most of the shroud that ordinarily softened its grim contours. The unusual sight of those bare slopes, visible to the three royal brothers from Swan Lake, had been the inspiration for this adventure. Orrion had yielded to the others' urgings on a fatalistic impulse. It was a last resort. Why not chance it?

He bowed his head in misery. 'Oh, Nyla,' he whispered, 'if only there were another way! Dearest friend of my childhood, everyone at court knew that I had chosen you for my bride. Even Father gave tacit consent – until that bastard, Somarus of Didion, murmured against the Sovereignty. And now, Nyla, our only hope lies in dark magic.'

Magic, that bane of the Wincantor family . . .

Prince Heritor Orrion had a profound distrust of uncanny powers. His study of certain Didionite documents, reluctantly provided by his mother Queen Risalla when he insisted on knowing the truth about the fall of Holt Mallburn, had convinced him that his father Conrig had made use of illicit Beaconfolk sorcery to establish his Sovereignty, thus committing a terrible sin against the Zeth Codex. Beyond doubt Conrig Wincantor had schemed with Ullanoth of Moss to conquer Didion's capital city through foulest magic. He had also relied on the Conjure-Queen's moonstone sigils to win the Battle of Cala Bay, forcing Didion to become the vassal of Cathra.

Over the years, the Lords of the Southern Shore had kept those shameful allegations of sorcery alive, just as they continued to stoke the fires of calumny hinting that Conrig himself was besmirched with windtalent. Now, with the latest Salka threat, Duke Feribor Blackhorse and his fellow conspirators openly speculated that the Sovereign was preparing to use Beaconfolk magic once again, to counter the monsters' massive invasion of northern Didion.

But so what if he does? Orrion asked himself. Am I any better than my flawed sire? At least his sin might save our island from the Salka, whereas the deed I contemplate committing is motivated only by a selfish desire to escape a loveless marriage.

The brothers had begun their melancholy journey from Cala Palace to Boarsden Castle in Didion, where the betrothal ceremony was to take place, over a tennight earlier, allowing ample time for a side trip to Swan Lake. The two royal princes were each accompanied by six Heart Companions, young nobles who were close friends. Vra-Bramlow, the novice Brother of Zeth, had no retinue, as was fitting for one belonging to the austere Order.

Prince Orrion was a keen salmon angler. (Sportfishing with an artificial lure was now all the rage, having been newly introduced from Tarn.) His brothers hoped that a few days on the beautiful body of water would lift Orrion's depressed spirits. The three princes and their entourage had been invited to stay at a rustic lodge owned by Count Swanwick, a trusted ally of the royal family. But the fish proved elusive and the diversion was turning out to be a failure.

It was Vra-Bramlow who conceived the audacious scheme to resolve his brother Orrion's predicament once and for all. Before revealing his idea to the twins, he windspoke one of Castle Vanguard's young alchymists, who had been a fellow student of occult science at Zeth Abbey, to verify that an ascent of the currently near-snowless Demon Seat would be feasible. A Vanguard resident would know if anyone did, since the peak was part of that dukedom.

Vra-Hundig reluctantly conceded that daring men might be able to climb to the top of the mountain, using trails that in other years were deeply buried in snowdrifts. A couple of madcap young fellows had scaled the peak some sixty years ago for the fun of it, but one of them perished of exposure during the descent. Hundig described the likeliest access routes in detail and wondered who among Vra-Bramlow's friends would be lunatic enough to attempt such a useless feat.

No one, the royal novice had reassured his former class-mate. No one at all. The inquiry was only intended to settle a bet made with his twin brothers.

The next morning, as the princes and their companions broke their fast in the fishing lodge's hall, Bramlow quietly told Orrion and Corodon about a certain ancient tract he had recently come upon in the abbey library. It contained convincing accounts of miracles worked atop Demon Seat in days long gone by. Why shouldn't Orrion seek a miracle of his own on the mysterious mountain?

'I know the possibility's a slim one,' the novice alchymist admitted, 'but the manuscript said that the demons grant favors to petitioners who are *worthy* – and who is worthier than you, Orry? One day you must take up leadership of the Sovereignty, the heaviest burden in all of Blenholme. It's not right that you should be deprived of your one true love, merely to strengthen the weak reed of Didionite loyalty.'

Corodon smirked. 'What a pity King Somarus rejected my hand for his daughter in place of Orry's. I'm so much better looking!'

'But you aren't the Prince Heritor.' Bramlow's dark brown eyes flashed with anger. This was no matter for levity.

'I can't see how magic could change the mind of Somarus,' Orrion said, looking dejected. 'Not with that villain of a chancellor making decisions for him. I suspect Kilian Blackhorse was the one who thought up the marriage ploy in the first place. God knows what sort of convoluted plan that traitor has in mind for me and Princess Hyndry, but his malice toward Cathra has never flagged.'

'If *I* wore Father's Iron Crown,' Corodon said, 'I'd put down Kilian like a mad dog! Then I'd depose that insolent fat rogue Somarus and replace him with a less surly kinglet.'

'Easier said than done,' Orrion said. 'Didion is a patch-work realm – a rabble of mistrustful barbarian chieftains, clannish timber-lords, and greedy shipbuilding magnates and merchants who control the true wealth of the land. At present, none save Somarus seems able to keep the lot stitched together. Should Didion fall apart and be unable or unwilling to continue helping Cathra and Tarn fight the Salka, then all of Blenholme is likely doomed. If my marriage to Princess Hyndry can keep King Somarus loyal to the Sovereignty, then I have no choice but to submit. I thank you for proposing that I seek a miracle, Bram, but the notion is too outlandish to take seriously.'

'Orry, don't be such a lily-liver!' Prince Corodon exclaimed. 'Is your love for Nyla so tepid and gutless that you'd renounce her without a fight? I'd move heaven and earth if I were in your shoes, even though the odds for success were long. Listen: Bram and I will climb the peak with you. It'll be a rare adventure!'

'Our Heart Companions will think we've lost our minds,' Orrion protested, nodding toward the long table where the young noblemen were chattering noisily. 'And what if they gossip, and Father finds out how I tried to flout his command by calling upon demons?'

'We could let the men accompany us for part of the way, to the base of the mountain,' Bramlow said. 'Then the three of us can try for the summit together. We say nothing of our true intent. Instead we tell them we intend to plant the flag of the Sovereignty up there on a tall staff, where anyone with a good spyglass may see it and be astounded. It's a silly stunt, but we could say it was Coro's idea.'

'Yes, blame me!' the daredevil prince crowed. 'Why the hell not?'

'Because we might suffer injury,' Orrion said, 'or even fall to our deaths.'

'My friend Vra-Hundig at Castle Vanguard told me that the trail up the mountain is not especially difficult,' Bramlow said. 'What usually makes the summit inacessible is the heavy snow – which has melted this year.'

Orrion could feel his opposition weakening. 'Bram, tell me true: do you seriously believe these so-called demons might exist and be willing to help me?'

Vra-Bramlow took hold of the silver novice's gammadion,

emblem of the Zeth Order, that hung on a chain around his neck. 'By my halidom, I do. Dearest brother, we all know other improbable myths of this island that have a basis in truth. I admit that this one strains credulity to the bursting point – but recall our dying grandsire and the oracle of Bazekoy's Head. It seemed ludicrous that the oracle should have spoken the truth: yet it did. So what say you? Shall we dare the demons? Decide now, for it will take us at least a day to reach the mountain's foot, and another to make the climb. We have not a moment to waste.'

And here I am, Prince Heritor Orrion thought sadly. Grasping at the most puny of straws, putting my two brothers at risk, ready to commit a horrendous sin. But I would do anything, even forfeit my life, if I might thereby wed my darling Nyla, rather than the barbarian princess chosen for me by my heartless sire –

'Orry! We're waiting for you. Stop gawking at the scenery and get moving!'

He felt resentment at the sound of his twin brother's strident voice echoing among the crags. It was not Coro's place to give orders to the Heritor. Nevertheless Orrion rose to his feet, adjusted the baldric that supported his leather fardel of food and drink, picked up his iron-shod staff, and resumed his ascent of the steep, zigzag trail.

A couple of hundred ells above him, Corodon and Vra-Bramlow stood side by side, watching the toiling figure.

'He's finally coming,' the younger prince said in exasperation. 'Too bad Orry's legs aren't as long as ours. The climb's been hard on him. If nothing else, this day's work might pare a few pounds from his belly and let him cut a better figure in his court raiment. Then we won't have wasted our time scaling this rockpile, even if the poor wight fails to conjure his impossible miracle.'

'Don't tell me you're skeptical about magic!' Bramlow lifted a teasing eyebrow. 'You, of all people? Orry would be disappointed to hear it.'

Corodon turned about and seized his older brother's shoulders. 'Bram, you promised! Never even hint of what you know about me to Orry or to any other person. If you do, I swear I'll cut your tripes out, even though it be sacrilege to harm a Brother of Zeth!'

Chuckling, Bramlow pried the clutching fingers away easily and took tight hold of Corodon's wrists, rendering him helpless. The brawny young alchymist used no talent in the subduing, only main strength. His features were pleasant and bland, as usual.

'I said I'd never betray you, Coro, and I won't. Not unless you do deliberate harm to Orrion. But your mean-spirited insults are becoming tedious.'

Corodon relaxed and gave a nervous laugh. 'You know I was only joking. I love my twin with all my heart! But if he found me out, his bloody great sense of honor would make him spill the beans to Father. I'd have to join you as a celibate in the Order – and living such a life would kill me.'

'It's not so bad. We have spells to calm the urgings of the flesh.'

'Oh, wonderful.' Corodon rolled his eyes. 'And many simple joys of wizardhood to take their place, no doubt! But I'd never become a mighty Doctor Arcanorum as you will. My talent is so piss-poor that the alchymists can't even detect it. I curse the day I let slip my stupid jumping coin trick and betrayed myself to you. If you turn me in to the Order, I'd be lucky to be nominated to the Brother Caretakers! Do you want me to spend my life mopping abbey floors or raking chickenshite?'

'Then learn to control your spiteful tongue and stop teasing Orry. You resent that he's Prince Heritor, rather than you, and that's only natural. But you must give him the respect he deserves. God help you if you make mock of him when we reach the summit and he conjures the demons. This is a deadly serious business to him.'

'I know. I'll do as you say. Only let go of me – he's coming.'

Corodon tore loose from Bramlow's grip. He slid a short way downslope to greet his twin heartily and offer him wine. Orrion accepted the flask and drank a little for the sake of politeness. The two of them rejoined Bramlow and stood arm in arm.

Both princes were eighteen, two years younger than the novice, short of their majority and the belt of knighthood, but old enough at last to fight at their royal father's side, should the Army of the Sovereignty ever snap out of its indecisive funk and attack the Salka invaders. Corodon was the younger by less than an hour's time, taller even than Conrig's six feet and with his father's striking good looks. He had the king's shining wheaten hair as well, which he wore overlong, and his mother's sapphire-bright eyes. His public demeanor was both charming and fearless, and he was well regarded by many of the important lords at court. But Prince Corodon conspicuously lacked the level-headedness of the other royal offspring, even including their solemn little sister, Princess Wylgana, at sixteen the youngest child of Conrig and Risalla and presumably the last. Corodon's brash and often foolhardy behavior had caused certain members of the Privy Council to secretly thank heaven that he had not emerged from his mother's womb ahead of his nonidentical twin.

No such cloud hung over Orrion, although some suspected that his eventual reign would be competent rather than outstanding. The Prince Heritor was shrewd, well-read, and only slightly pompous, a plain-featured youth of middle stature, solidly muscled rather than overweight. His newly cultivated moustache and his hair were the indeterminate pale color of dry sand, and his eyes were more grey than blue. He had long since outgrown the bodily weaknesses that had blighted his early childhood and now enjoyed good health. His fighting prowess was much less flamboyant than Corodon's, but he wielded both the two-handed longsword and the lighter varg blade with acceptable skill – as an aspirant to Cathra's kingship was legally obligated to do.

Vra-Bramlow said to the others, 'It's time we were going. We must reach the summit within a couple of hours, or give up hope of returning to the Heart Companions before nightfall. Sleeping rough on the mountainside tonight might be very disagreeable. See those mare's-tail clouds streaming out of the northwest? They mean that the weather could change for the worse.'

So they resumed climbing, with Bramlow taking the lead and using his windsenses to search out the best route among the confusing masses of rock. None of them had spare breath now for conversation, so each labored alone, occupied by unquiet thoughts.

There really was a Demon Seat.

Orrion had insisted that it was his right to be the first to stand on the mountaintop and Bramlow agreed, so Corodon had no choice but to give in, muttering resentfully. While the others waited below, the Prince Heritor climbed the last few ells on all fours, then pulled himself upright on a kind of broken-walled natural terrace that comprised the summit. What he found caused him to shout in astonishment. 'Bazekoy's Bones! I don't believe this. Come up and see, lads!'

Bramlow and Corodon scrambled to the top and the three of them stood huddled together in the brisk wind. The nearly level area was partially covered with a thin layer of snow. The most abundant variety of rock round about them was grey granite; but there was also a sizable outcropping of nearly translucent mineral, bluish-white in color. Some large chunks of this had broken apart and fallen in a heap that bore a rough resemblance to a chair or throne.

Corodon gave a whoop of delight. Before the others could stop him, he plumped himself down on the unusual formation. 'Futter me blind – it's real! A Demon Seat! What say all three of us beg a miracle? I know what I'd ask: Let me be Prince Heritor in place of Orry. I'll gladly wed Princess Hyndry. They say she's a fine lusty wench for all that she's a widow, and older.'

'Coro, you prattling fool!' The novice dragged his brother down and flung him into the snow. Corodon uttered a half-hearted curse.

Orrion helped his aggrieved twin back onto his feet. 'Let him be, Bram. He meant nothing by it. It's only his bit of fun.'

Vra-Bramlow knew better; but he swallowed his indignation and growing sense of unease and squinted up at the clouds. They had thickened and the sun had dropped halfway to the horizon, resembling a disk of dull white vellum against a murky background. 'We can't stay here long. Do you still want to do this, Orry?'

The Prince Heritor drew in a breath. 'Yes. Tell me how.'

While Corodon crouched in a sheltered niche, munching sausage and drinking from the wine flask, Bramlow explained the simple conjuration procedure.

'Stand by the seat and place one hand on it. Close your eyes. Try to clear your mind of all distracting thoughts. Assume an attitude of childlike humility and reverence, as a worthy petitioner of the Sky Realm should.'

Corodon gave a muffled snort of laughter.

'Be quiet!' Bramlow barked. 'Another sound from you, and I'll make you wait downslope.'

'What then?' Orrion demanded. 'How shall I summon the demons? Do I simply state my wish: *Let me be able to wed Lady Nyla Brackenfield?*'

'Don't call them demons. They might be insulted. If you must address them, say Lords of the Sky. The ancient writings were unclear as to the wording of the petition. I'd say, first name yourself, then speak out your plea naturally but briefly. Avoid any tinge of fear or disrespect. These beings must decide for themselves whether you're worthy of their miracle.' He folded his arms about Orrion in a brief embrace. 'Good luck, my brother.'

'And so say I also,' Corodon called gruffly. 'May you receive your heart's desire.'

Vra-Bramlow withdrew a dozen paces, dropped to his knees in the shallow snow, and bowed his head.

Orrion approached the seat as if he were a man half-asleep. A sudden gust of cold wind hit his face like a knife-cut. He removed his gloves, placed his right hand upon the irregular milky slab that formed the back of the natural throne, and closed his eyes.

'Great Lords of the Sky!' He spoke firmly. 'I beseech you to grant me a favor – if it should be your will, and if you find me worthy.'

For a long time nothing happened. Then he felt a slow-growing warmth beneath the hand that rested on the frigid rock surface. One of his brothers gave a soft gasp of mingled fear and amazement. Orrion dared to crack open his eyelids for the merest instant and saw that the entire Demon Seat formation was aglow with an interior luminosity, at first dim as a will o' the wisp, then increasingly bright. The heat beneath his right hand gradually increased. Before he could think what to do next, he felt a sudden thrust of pain smite his brain. Then there were voices speaking in unison, deep and inhuman, questioning him in an oddly hesitant manner.

Orrion knew instinctively that they spoke to his soul and were inaudible to the others.

WHO . . . WHAT . . . WHY?

He tried to keep panic from his response. 'Great Lords of the Sky, my name is Orrion Wincantor. I'm here to beg a miracle of you, if you please. I – I ask your help because I have nowhere else to turn.'

HOW DO YOU KNOW ABOUT US? HOW DID YOU KNOW TO COME TO THIS PLACE?

'My older brother read an ancient tract. It told how you had granted miracles to others many years ago.'

YES . . . SOME OF US FREELY GAVE BOONS TO HUMANS. WE REMEMBER NOW. WE HOPED TO GAIN AN ADVANTAGE OVER THE EVIL ONES. THOSE WERE STRANGE TIMES IN THE SKY REALM AND ON THE GROUND. THE TACTIC WAS NOT VERY SUCCESSFUL.

The demonic ramblings made no sense to Orrion. His hand, resting upon the stone, was beginning to feel uncomfortably warm. 'Do I have your gracious permission to ask my favor?'

WELL . . . AT LEAST YOU ARE WORTHY, AS ARE THE OTHER TWO WHO COWER NEXT TO OUR CRAG . . . WHAT DO YOU WANT, ORRION WINCANTOR?

'Great Lords of the Sky, if – if you will, grant me a miracle. Let me be able to wed my true love, Nyla Brackenfield, daughter to Count Hale Brackenfield, Lord Lieutenant of the Realm.'

There was silence. His right hand grew ever more painful, but he dared not lift it. Finally the inhuman voices spoke again, seeming puzzled.

WHY DO YOU REQUIRE A MAGICAL INTERVENTION MERELY IN ORDER TO MATE WITH YOUR CHOSEN PERSON?

'I – Great Lords, I'm the High King's son, heir to the throne of Cathra and the Iron Crown of Sovereignty. My father

Conrig has picked another wife for me, in spite of my wishes. I must obey him for the sake of my princely honor.'

The demons fell into a silence that seemed endless.

Orrion forced himself not to cry out. The burning sensation in his hand continued to grow and was fast becoming unbearable. 'Great Lords, if my request cannot be granted, then I humbly beg your pardon for having disturbed you. My brothers and I will depart from your mountain forthwith.'

WE THINK THE REQUEST IS NOT IMPOSSIBLE. IT IS HARD FOR THE SKY REALM TO INTERACT WITH THE GROUND BECAUSE IT UPSETS THE GREAT BALANCE OF POWER, BUT WE ARE WILLING TO HELP YOU. YOU WILL PAY A GREAT PRICE FOR THIS FAVOR. ARE YOU ABSOLUTELY CERTAIN THAT YOU WANT IT?

'Yes. Please.'

THEN LIFT YOUR RIGHT HAND FROM THE MOON CRAG AND HOLD IT ALOFT.

For a moment, Orrion didn't understand. Then he realized he was being told to let go of that awful piece of hot rock. 'Yes! Oh, thank you!' In a paroxysm of gratitude, he thrust his arm heavenward and dared to open his eyes.

He saw blackness around him, and abundant diamond-sharp twinkling stars, as though night had inexplicably fallen and he hung suspended in the heavens high above the earth. A formless drift of multi-hued Light, that slowly took the shape of many mournful faces, shone among the familiar polar constellations. Then a blue flare blinded him as it engulfed most of his uplifted arm like a blast of silent lightning.

He fell from the sky into nothingness, feeling no pain.

'Orry! Orry, my poor twin, are you alive?'

'He breathes. I can feel his heart beating. Draw closer to shield him from the elements.'

Slowly, Orrion Wincantor, Prince Heritor of Cathra, opened his eyes. A folded cloak pillowed his head and another covered his body. He was chilled but not otherwise uncomfortable. A cold drizzle was falling. His brothers knelt beside him.

'Take a sip of this brandy,' Vra-Bramlow urged, lifting him so he could drink. The fiery spirit burnt his gullet, then settled in a glowing pool in his belly. 'Can you move?'

'Yes. Help me to sit up.'

They assisted him. Orrion looked about and realized that they were still at the summit of Demon Seat and it was yet daytime – although the louring grey clouds now hung so close it seemed a man might reach up and touch them. Corodon was strangely excited, while Bramlow's face was stiff with shock and his eyes red from weeping.

Orrion managed a reassuring smile. 'Have I been senseless long?'

'Perhaps half an hour,' Bramlow said. 'We – we were very worried about you. The change in weather came very quickly. It might snow. We were wondering how to carry you to a more sheltered place when you finally came to yourself – thanks be to God!'

'Well, I'm quite all right,' Orrion said. 'It seems I've survived my encounter with the demons.'

'What were they like?' Corodon asked eagerly. 'We saw nothing of them, only a sudden dazzling light, and then you were lying on the rocks.'

'After I begged my boon, I found myself afloat in a dark sky. I saw a multitude of ghostly faces glowing among the stars –'

'Zeth save us!' Bramlow exclaimed. But he bit off the words he would have said next, not wanting Orrion to know that he'd very likely conjured the evil Beaconfolk, and said only, 'Were they fearsome things?'

'Not really. They seemed almost bewildered that a human being would call upon them. But I stated my request boldly, as you advised, and they asked if I was sure I wanted it. I said I did. There was a great flash of blueish light, brighter than the sun, and I remember nothing more.' He sighed. 'I suppose there's naught left to do but wait to see if my miracle will be granted. Just help me to my feet, lads. We should get going.'

'Are you in pain, my brother?' Corodon asked.

'Not at all. I feel healthy as a horse.'

'Orrion –' Fresh tears sprang into Bramlow's dark eyes and he gave a wordless cry before turning his head away, unable to speak further.

'What's wrong?' the Prince Heritor said in alarm.

His twin regarded him with a strange expression. 'Brother, your miracle has already occurred, but not in the manner that you might have wished.' Slowly, he pulled open the blanketing cloak so that Orrion's body was exposed.

The Heritor looked down at himself and felt his heart lurch.

Impossible! There was no pain – indeed, he felt as though nothing at all had happened. The sleeve of his heavy leather jerkin and the woolen shirt beneath had been burnt away to a point just below the right elbow; his lower arm and hand *felt* as normal as always . . . but they had apparently been rendered invisible. When his left hand probed the anomaly he felt a smooth stump of healed flesh and bone at the end of his truncated right arm.

'Gone,' he murmured, transfixed. 'Yet it seems as though it's still there. I've heard of men losing a limb in battle experiencing a like phenomenon. Odd, isn't it, lads?'

'His mind wanders,' Corodon said. 'Poor devil.'

'Don't you understand what the cursèd demons have done to you?' Bramlow cried in a voice choked with horror. 'They have taken your sword-arm, Orry! By the laws of our kingdom – and Didion as well – such a wound makes you ineligible for the throne.'

'You're no longer Prince Heritor, twin brother.' Corodon's face was suffused with a terrible exultation. 'I am.' His gaze flickered and he looked sidelong at Bramlow. 'Not our royal father, nor King Somarus, nor anyone else can deny me. Isn't that right, Bram?'

The novice said nothing.

Corodon turned back to Orrion. 'You and Nyla are free to wed. I offer my heartfelt felicitations and wish you every happiness.' He paused with a judicious frown. 'It would be best, I think, if we explained matters to Father and King Somarus face to face, rather than breaking the news at long distance. What do you think, Bram?'

The reply was curt. 'I dare not windspeak such incredible tidings. No one would believe me.'

On one level of his mind, Orrion felt an eerie detachment, as though he were watching some fantastic drama enacted by the palace players that had nothing to do with reality. On another level he was coolly rational. The ramifications of the demons' action were clear and irrefutable, just as Coro had said. There could be no waffling on King Conrig's part, no talk of Orrion learning lefthanded swordplay to evade the restriction.

Corodon must be named Heritor.

Coro? Impetuous, happy-go-lucky Coro become heir to the throne? The notion had never occurred to Orrion. The miracle he'd hoped for would have simply changed his father's mind, so that he might marry Nyla and in time make her his queen. But now . . .

Vra-Bramlow stood close to him. 'I shall never forgive myself for this, Orry,' the novice muttered. 'Never.' And he thought: What am I to do? If I tell Father the truth about Coro's talent, the crown will pass out of the Wincantor family

– to Beorbrook's adopted son Dyfrig, or even to our wicked cousin Feribor Blackhorse!

Orrion climbed slowly to his feet. His expression was still strange, even though his voice sounded calm. 'I was willing to pay any price for my sweet love. I've paid, and I shall accept whatever penalty Father metes out to me – even banishment. All the blame is mine, Bram. You have nothing to reproach yourself for.'

Vra-Bramlow shook his head. 'Not true,' he whispered, but could say no more.

'We can never tell Father the exact truth of this affair,' Orrion said. He was staring into the distance, as if contemplating some faraway event. 'He's a hard man, and I'll not have him revenge himself on either one of *you*. We three must agree on a suitable fiction to explain my loss, and we must swear never to deviate from it.'

'Of course,' Corodon exclaimed warmly. 'Bram's the cleverest. He'll think up a proper yarn for us to spin. And let's not forget to plant the banner before we leave, as we planned to do.'

'Oh, for God's sake, Coro,' Bramlow groaned.

'I'll do it for luck, if for no other reason.' Corodon opened his pack, shook out the scarlet silk pennon of the Sovereignty with its four interlocked golden crowns (Conrig still claimed the overlordship of Moss, even though the Salka had conquered it), and began tying it to his own climbing staff. Bramlow and Orrion watched as he built a cairn of rocks behind Demon Seat and set about fixing the royal banner atop it.

Orrion spoke quietly to Bramlow. 'Can you bespeak a message to the Zeth Brethren in Cala Palace for me, or are we too far away?'

'At this great height, I should be able to do it. No natural barriers impede my windspeech. What do you want me to say?'

'The message is to be given to Lady Nyla. In my name, beseech her to hasten to Boarsden with all speed and meet me there, for the sake of our love. Ask that she also bring her parents, and that they travel with the greatest possible secrecy.'

The novice frowned. 'Orry, are you sure about this?'

'She and I must be near one another as I confess my transgression to Father. If he spares my life, I mean to wed Nyla immediately. This is why she must bring her parents.'

Deeply troubled, Vra-Bramlow said, 'It might be better if we first meet Nyla and the Lord Lieutenant and his lady elsewhere than Boarsden Castle, so you have an opportunity to . . . prepare them beforehand.'

'You're right. Perhaps near the border, at Beorbrook Hold in Cathra?'

Bramlow shook his head. 'You'd never be able to conceal your disability from the earl marshal's alchymists. They'd insist on examining the arm if we try to pass it off as a climbing injury that I'd already treated and bound up. We'll be able to fend off your Heart Companions that way, but not real physicians . . . I have it – we'll meet the Brackenfields at the Castlemont Fortress hostelry just across the pass in Didion. No one there will think it amiss if Cathran travelers keep to themselves. And it's only a day's ride from the fort to Boarsden.'

'Very well. Bespeak the message, Bram, before Coro finishes.'

A few minutes later, Prince Corodon climbed down from the moonstone outcropping, took his twin's good left arm, and draped it over one of his shoulders. 'That's done. If any windsearcher should scry the mountaintop, the banner will confirm that we were here. Now lean on me, Orry, and we'll start down.' He offered a reassuring smile. 'Don't be downhearted. Everything will work out for the best. This happenstance is strange beyond measure, but we can't deny that it gives both of us our heart's desire!'

She had obtained a sheet of vellum scraped so thin it was nearly transparent, that might be folded into the most exiguous of hiding places and kept safe. From the desk drawer she took a silver inkwell and a crow-quill pen with a fine nib, so that her writing might be minuscule and take up the least possible room, yet still be be legible. These things she laid out just before midnight, after long hesitation deciding that the time had finally come.

It was the most important letter she would ever write. If it were intercepted, it would surely be her heart's death, though no man laid a hand on her. But if it reached its intended recipient, all her years of suffering would have been well spent.

My dearest Dyfrig!

This missive comes to you after what must have been a perilous journey, undertaken by my most faithful friend. I pray you to reward her and shield her from the retribution that would fall upon her if her rôle in carrying the letter to you were discovered by the Sovereign or his agents.

The one who writes to you is your mother, Maudrayne Northkeep, once wife to Conrig Wincantor and former Queen of Cathra.

I know you thought me dead, and there were many times when I despaired of my life's continuing, so bleak has been my existence, deprived of pouring upon you the maternal love you deserve. How I longed to see and know you, to watch you grow and thrive, to share your joys and comfort your hurts as a natural mother should! My only solace was knowing that you had been given into the care of good people, and this enabled me to hold fast in spite of all hardship.

I could not write to you earlier, whilst you were still a child. It was necessary to delay until you were an adult man grown, strong in health and mature in mind and character, able to understand and make wise use of the secrets I now entrust to you.

I am informed that you have achieved your twentieth year and a man's estate, and have earned knighthood, and are esteemed by your adoptive parents and all who are close to you. It is time for you to know the truth about your heritage and decide how it may shape your destiny in years to come.

You are indeed the legitimate first-born son of Conrig Wincantor, Sovereign of Blenholme, by virtue of Cathran law. I was ever faithful to my royal husband, even though he betrayed me with another woman and has encouraged rumors vilifying my honor. He did not know that I carried his child when he divorced me for expedient reasons of state. My heart was so wrung with anger and grief at his earlier betrayal of me with Conjure-Queen Ullanoth and his subsequent willingness to set me aside so he could marry the Didionite princess that I withheld information of my pregnancy from him. Sinfully, I attempted to end both my life and your own by casting myself into the sea.

When my friend, the Grand Shaman Ansel Pikan, rescued me and took me away to Tarn, I was at first grateful. You were born in the isolated steading of a sea-hag called Dobnelu, whom you perhaps remember kindly. She and Ansel were both servants of a supernatural being called the Source of the Old Conflict or the One Denied the Sky. It was some years before I discovered that the loyalty of these so-called friends was first to this inhuman creature and only second to you and me.

High King Conrig learned of my survival and of your own existence. He sought to kill us because of the threat we posed to his heirs by Risalla of Didion – and for another reason, which I shall disclose to you anon. But the assassin he sent, one Deveron Austrey, who was the Royal Intelligencer, proved too virtuous and compassionate a man to do the king's bloody work. Instead he engineered what he thought would be a compromise that would save both our lives. I was to live quietly in Tarn, and you would be adopted by Earl Marshal Parlian Beorbrook as a putative royal bastard of mine. The king accepted, then broke this agreement, secretly sending Tinnis Catclaw, Constable of the Realm, to kill me with poison and feign my suicide.

This Lord Tinnis, for a mercy, was one who had long loved me hopelessly from afar. After I pledged to keep silent and remain his secret captive and leman so long as I would live, he falsified my death. I was transported to a hunting lodge of his called Gentian Fell, situated high in the Dextral Mountains, some thirty leagues east of Beorbrook Hold. Here I have abided anonymously for sixteen years, together with my dear friend Rusgann Moorcock, who was once my personal maidservant. She will, I pray the God of the Heights and Depths, place this letter in your hand.

Make no mistake: Tinnis has been as devoted and lavish a captor as any poor prisoner could hope for. My quarters are elegant and comfortable, for all that they are in a remote place. I have the best food and drink, books and music. During the calm moons of summer and autumn, before winter snows close the mountain tracks for weeks at a time, a few trusted female relatives of the Lord Constable visit me with their young children and vouchsafe the mysterious 'Lady Mayda' diversion and educated companionship. Under guard, I am allowed to walk the alpine meadows and even go a-hawking, a diversion close to my heart.

I freely confess that four or five times a year, for short periods, Tinnis Catclaw himself is here in residence and shares my bed. He is a kindly man in his way, ever gentle with me, and I have a lonely woman's needs which you, my dear son, will one day understand and forgive. I thus fulfill my part of the pact I made with Lord Tinnis in exchange for my life.

The Salka invasion in Didion has made it impossible for him to make his customary visits this summer, since he must attend the ongoing Council of War at Boarsden. The consequent lapse of discipline among my guards here emboldened me to contrive a plan for Rusgann's escape and, I pray, her transport of this letter to you. She will first seek you in Beorbrook Hold amongst your foster family, where I pray she may find you, since the journey is not long. If you are not there she will proceed to Boarsden Castle.

Now I will attempt to explain the darker reasons for Conrig's enmity towards you and me.

Dyfrig, my son, we live in a world awash with sorcery. High Blenholme Island is no mundane human habitat as is the Southern Continent. Before Emperor Bazekoy dared to subdue it, this land was a domain of inhuman entities that fought viciously amongst themselves, using every manner of magic. The most abundant race, the Salka monsters, were linked in an unholy symbiosis with the Beaconfolk, those Great Lights of the Sky Realm, who channeled uncanny power to the ferocious amphibians through moonstone amulets.

After Bazekoy's conquest and banishment of the Salka, which I have been told was accomplished while the Beaconfolk were distracted by quarreling amongst themselves, certain human settlers dared to mate with the Green Men of Blenholme, a race of very small nonhuman people, secretive and dangerous, who have large emerald eyes but other-wise resemble us closely. Like the other prehistoric island dwellers, the Green Ones possess inborn magical abilities. These they pass on to their part-human descendants, even through many generations.

I do not have to explain to you the longstanding Cathran mistrust of magical 'talent'. It dates to Bazekoy's day and reflects his justified fear and antipathy toward the Beaconfolk sorcery used by the Salka as a weapon. The Didionites share a similar ambivalent attitude toward magickers, but the other two human nations of Blenholme are more broad-minded. In Tarn, the talented shaman-healers opted to focus their uncanny powers on activities that were mostly worthy and helpful. The land of Moss was a more sinister kettle of fish – a hotbed of malicious wizards who oppressed their untalented human fellows mercilessly until the celebrated Rothbannon whipped them into line and established the Conjure-Kingdom.

Moss retained a sizable population of Salka who largely shunned mankind. Rothbannon chose to live

peaceably with the monsters rather than oppress
them. He even became friendly with the Salka of the
Dawntide Isles. After a time, the creatures so trusted
this stern but scrupulously fair human ruler that they
unwisely handed over to him their most cherished
relics – a set of inactive moonstone amulets or sigils
that became known as the Seven Stones of
Rothbannon. These things were nothing less than
physical channels of Beaconfolk sorcery. They gave
tremendous power to the human user at the price of
pain – and sometimes his very soul.

I do not have to reiterate the depressing history of
Rothbannon's descendants. They lacked his prudence
and wielded the sigils in ways that often called down
the wrath of the Lights. Your natural father's para-
mour, Conjure-Queen Ullanoth, used moonstones to
aid the establishment of the Sovereignty and further
her own lust. The accusations made by Didion and by
Cathra's Lords of the South against Conrig and
Ullanoth are shamefully true: the union of High
Blenholme was built upon a foundation of unholy
magic and adultery.

This was made possible by the fact that Conrig
himself has inherited a small and nearly indetectable
portion of magical talent, which gave him a fatal
affinity with the beautiful Mossland witch. Even more
dire, Conrig holds his Iron Crown under false pretenses:
by law, no talented man may be Cathra's king.

You, my dearest son, have no stain of talent whatsoever. I was assured of this by both Ansel Pikan and
the sea-hag Dobnelu. Thus you are the rightful
Sovereign of Blenholme, and no one – human or
inhuman – may deny you your heritage . . . if you
should choose to take it up.

There is one credible witness who may attest to
your freedom from talent and to Conrig's attainting.
He is the same Deveron Austrey who resigned from
his post as Royal Intelligencer after his conscience was
sickened by Conrig's treatment of me. I am told that
he was convicted of treason but escaped to the
Continent, where he has lived in obscurity for long
years. Whether you seek him out and use his testi-
mony to your advantage is up to you.

My beloved child, your future is in your own
hands. If some day you ascend to the throne of
Cathra and I still live, I hope we may be united on
this earth. If this is not to be, I look forward to our
eventual reunion in paradise and assure you of my
prayers.

I am your mother,
MAUDRAYNE, Princess Dowager of Cathra

She sanded the parchment, took scissors and trimmed the
sheet to its smallest possible compass, folded it, and sealed
it with three tiny drops of unstamped wax. It was now a
thing scarcely an inch square.

From her jewel case, filled with valuable baubles bestowed
upon her by Tinnis Catclaw, she took a flat golden locket
just large enough to contain the letter. Her desk yielded a
small tin of cement, a sticky substance that dried hard and
waterproof, used by the lodge's guards to refasten loose
fletching on their arrows. She had begged it from one of the
kinder men, saying she wished to use it in binding a book.
But instead, she carefully daubed a thin line of the black
stuff around the edge of the locket, sealing it shut. No harm
would come to the letter now, no matter how wet its
messenger became.

Rusgann would decide where to hide the locket on her

person when they met at breakfast and completed plans for the escape.

Maudrayne snuffed the candle on the desk and slowly rose. The only light now came from a low-burning oil lamp on a night-table beside her tester bed. Outside, the wind moaned and sleet rattled faintly against the heavily shuttered windows.

She began to disrobe for bed, standing before a long pier glass. The doughty noblewomen of Tarn scorned the hovering bodyservants of more effete southern ladies, and she was accustomed to deal with her own garments and hairdressing except when some special occasion necessitated elaborate attire.

She was two-score-and-four years of age, tall but fine-boned, and of unusual strength thanks to her love of walking, riding, and bow-hunting. The skin of her face was still creamy, unlined save for a faint crease between her brows. This imperfection, together with her dark-circled green eyes, like forest pools forever shaded from sunlight, were permanent legacies of her suffering.

She unfastened her opal necklace and golden plait-clasps and put them on the dressing table, then doffed the myrtle-green wool surcoat and girdled gown of apricot silk, arranging them neatly upon wooden perches. After removing low-cut houseshoes and gartered stockings, she let slip to the floor her sleeveless linen underkirtle and drawers and stood naked before the mirror, unbraiding her abundant copper tresses. Her breasts were still high and firm and her belly was unmarked by the stress of childbearing. Her shield of womanhood was as blazing bright as the hair of her head.

'You are still comely, Maude,' she whispered, gazing upon herself for a long moment before the reflection was blurred by an upwelling of tears as sharp as acid. 'Your besotted gaoler adores you and showers you with every gift save liberty. So why does the memory of *him*, and him alone, still heat your blood, even though you try to crush and deny it? Is there no way your heart will ever escape his thrall?'

She went to the bed, drew up the covers, and pinched the lamp's wick with moistened fingers. In the darkness, warm beneath a swansdown comforter, she found no comfort.

She thought: The letter will bring an end to it. Surely it will! I'll be rid of this perfidious bond, this shameful yearning that should be revulsion, this love for him that should be hatred. It'll be over. Dear God, let me forget Conrig and be at peace . . . else I'll have to go to him.

And do what I must do.

TWO

Ansel Pikan, Grand Shaman of Tarn, who lay dying from injuries suffered in the Battle of the Barren Lands, started up from his pillow with a loud groan. Sweat poured from his body and his heart thudded as though it would leap from his chest. 'Thalassa . . . Wix . . . Come to me!'

The door to his chamber flew open. A buxom woman of impressive mien, wearing threadbare robes that had once been rich and costly, swept inside. She was followed by a sturdy little old man with eyes like jet beads and bushy white hair. The pair hurried to the bedside and ministered to the stricken shaman, assisting him to swallow two kinds of physick and a beaker of water. Then, working deftly together, the two of them changed Ansel's damp nightgown and bed linen, and replaced his down comforter with another that hung warming at the hearth on a wooden rack. As they bent over him, checking the dressings on the terrible injuries to his hip and left side that would likely be the death of him, Ansel tried to relate what he'd dreamt. But his speech was nearly inaudible.

'The Source . . . a dream of deep import . . . might endanger our great plan for Conrig.'

'Wait until the medicines ease your pain and we have made you comfortable again,' the sorceress Thalassa Dru urged him. 'Be still for a few minutes, and you'll make more sense.'

'A strange thing,' Ansel murmured, falling back onto the freshened pillow. 'So strange.'

'Your feet are like ice,' said the man called Wix. 'Let me put these wool booties on you. You should have a warming stone as well. I'll get one from the kitchen.'

'I'll need you to bring something else.' Thalassa fingered the pulse in Ansel's emaciated neck for a few moments. 'Fetch the phial of aqua mirabilis from my stillroom, along with a cup of warm milk.'

'Yes, my lady.' The old fellow trotted out, closing the door.

She found a chair, put it next to the bed, and took Ansel's skeletal hand in her own warm, plump one. The candle-light showed her how sadly the Grand Shaman had declined since she had visited him earlier that evening. He would not live much longer. God only knew how he'd reached the Tarnian mainland after traveling from the Barrens in his small boat, finally finding help at Cold Harbor. The local magickers bespoke Thalassa when Ansel cried out her name, and she had spirited him away through subtle magical corridors to her secluded retreat in the western foothills of the White Rime Mountains.

'Now, my old friend,' she said to him, 'save your breath. Use windspeech to tell me what the Source revealed in your dream.'

'He conferred with the Likeminded Remnant of Lights, who told of a unique thing that happened this very day. A portentous thing. An unprecedented thing. On Demon Seat Mountain, no less!'

'Well, well. How very curious. I've oft wondered about that place. Pray continue.'

'The three young princes of Cathra ascended to the summit together. The Heritor, Orrion, begged a boon of the Sky Realm while touching the second Moon Crag formation, which lies on that very mountaintop. Who'd have thought it was there? And what a strange coincidence it was found by those lads, after our own fruitless windsearching.'

'Most peculiar, I must agree. What happened to Prince Orrion? Did the Lights strike him dead for insolence?'

'Nay. Fortunately, the Pain-Eaters completely ignored his irregular attempt at conjuring. And so the Likeminded ventured to answer the boy themselves, almost without volition. In some way, they channeled their power to the Ground Realm through the crag, and thence to Orrion. It was little more than an experimental exercise to the Likeminded, and they were much surprised that it succeeded.'

'God of the Heights and Depths,' Thalassa whispered. 'Then the Likeminded Remnant are no longer impotent! The scales of fate may be tipping in our direction at long last.'

Ansel Pikan's cracked lips widened in a smile. His wind-voice was as clear and incisive as ever, although it would not have reached beyond the bedchamber had he tried to project it.

'Our dear Source's chains of blue ice have weakened slowly over the years, as we gathered scattered sigils and brought them to him for destruction. And ill-fated though my own enterprise in the Barrens was, I did manage to deny the Salka most of the first Moon Crag. That has to count in our favor.'

She pulled the comforter more snugly around him. 'I prayed it would, though the Source himself seemed uncertain . . . What did you mean when you spoke of our plan for King Conrig being endangered? Is it put at risk somehow by the Demon Seat episode?'

Ansel set forth the basic facts of the arranged marriage

that had driven Prince Orrion to his unwitting conjuration of the Lights.

'The consequences of Orrion's loss will enfuriate and trouble the king, leaving him more vulnerable than he can possibly know. Long years of opposing the Salka, as well as contending against his human enemies, have turned him harsh and unyielding. Conrig sees his hope of extending his Sovereignty beyond this island fading away. He has always been a difficult New Conflict participant – all the more so because he doesn't know he's been enlisted! He'll be harder than ever to control once his scheme for his son Orrion lies in ruins.'

'Do you think the Source's plan for influencing the Sovereign through Deveron Austrey might now be impossible?'

'We must trust that the former spy can still find a way to regain his old master's friendship. Conrig cannot defeat the Salka invasion through human military efforts alone. Convincing him of that will not be easy.'

'Perhaps Cray will think of something,' Thalassa said, 'as she did so fortuitously in the matter of the worms!' She considered for a moment. 'I shall have to go to her at once. We two must soul-travel beneath the Ice and consult the Source together on these matters.'

The dying shaman gave a prolonged sigh. He spoke aloud in a voice as faint as rustling leaves. 'How I wish I were able to go with you! At least tell the Source that I beg forgiveness for having defied him. I had no choice but to go to the Barren Lands and destroy the first Moon Crag.'

'Of course I'll tell him, even though I'm certain he already knows and agrees you did the proper thing. He tried to dissuade you because of a premonition that you would not survive the mission and an understandable desire not to lose you. As a Sky Being, albeit one trapped in a body of flesh, he sometimes fails to understand our stubborn groundling self-righteousness. To say nothing of our foolish courage and need for direct action.'

Ansel Pikan began to laugh, but broke off in a fit of painful coughing. Thalassa Dru held his head against her ample breast until Wix came with the new medicament. Two drops of the elixer in milk were sufficient to bring relief to the shaman, after which she placed the heated, flannel-wrapped rock at his feet.

'And now I must go through subtle corridors to the Green Folk. I'm loath to abandon you, my dear, but I have no choice. I leave you in good hands. Wix will stay at your side this night, and his mistress is as good a physician as I am.' Thalassa kissed Ansel's brow.

He spoke to her voicelessly on the wind. 'I know my life is nearly over. I'm content with what I have accomplished. Don't fret about me. Save your energies for the Conflict. We'll win out. I'm certain of it.'

'And so am I,' the sorceress said with as much confidence as she could summon, even though a lump of cold doubt weighted her heart. She stayed at his side for a few minutes more, until his eyes closed in sleep. Then she snuffed all of the candles save one and rose from the bedside stool.

'Wix, build up a fire in here and see to the shutters. The wind is rising outside the lodge and there will be sleet very soon. I must set out on my journey without delay, and I've no time to give you detailed instructions. You must care for our dear friend as best you can.'

'Don't worry, my lady. I'll see to everything. Shall I wake my mistress and tell her you've departed?'

'She needs her rest. I believe Ansel will sleep quietly for some hours. But don't hesitate to fetch her if there should be a need.'

'Yes, my lady. May your magical journey be swift and safe.'

Thalassa Dru sha Lisfallon, elder sister of the late Conjure-King Linndal of Moss and the aunt of Ullanoth and Beynor, smiled at the little old man. 'I only hope the weather is better at Castle Morass.'

It was Master Shaman Kalawnn, second of the Eminent Four of the Salka monsters and guardian of the Known Potency, who first found out what the Likeminded Lights had done on Demon Seat.

He was deep within the bowels of Fenguard Castle in Moss, the new center of the Salka Authority now that the Dawntide Citadel had been destroyed by the vile humans, supervising the lapidary workers. They were preparing to cleave yet another fragile piece of mineral gleaned from the debris of the shattered Barren Lands Moon Crag. All previous attempts had ended in failure as the flawed moonstone disintegrated.

Suddenly Kalawnn felt a warning tingle from the minor sigil named Scriber that hung around his neck. This was followed by a severe pain deep within his brain.

'Ahroo!'

The shaman clasped his neck with both tentacles and flopped away from the cutting bench as the vision crashed into his mind like a storm-surge. For a moment, he was blind to all else. A second low-pitched howl escaped his maw. He subsided onto the floor of the cavern, an enormous amphibian creature nearly twice the height of a man and more than four times as bulky, helpless as a beached whale.

'Eminent One – what's wrong?' Several artisans crowded about him, head-crests erect and great red eyes goggling with dismay.

'Wait . . . wait,' he managed to say. 'A windsensed revelation! I must comprehend it fully.'

Nonplussed, the other Salka stood away from his quivering body. Those who wore strength-giving sigils conjured supportive power and channeled it to the Master Shaman. The others could only focus their healing talent and murmur prayers.

'Look at his neck!' a gem-carver exclaimed. 'The skin covering his gizzard glows crimson. The Potency within is active! Perhaps it disapproves of what we were about to do. Perhaps it's angry with us for trying to work poor-quality material into new sigils.'

The others picked up the portentous word and repeated it anxiously. 'The Potency! The Potency –'

'Silence!' Kalawnn bellowed. The eldritch seizure that had so abruptly afflicted him was over. He rose to his full majestic height, eyes wide open and agleam like balls of fire. 'There is no need to be anxious. The Potency is not angry. It had nothing to do with my vision.'

'But, master!' one of the lapidaries protested. 'We saw the glow within your crop, where the Stone of Stones is hidden –'

'I have just received a most surprising piece of information from the Great Lights,' Kalawnn said. 'I must leave you now and share this news with the other three Eminences. I command you to carry on cleaving the piece of raw moonstone. Bespeak me at once with the results of the operation.'

He slithered out of the workroom with surprising rapidity and made his way to the castle's Chamber of Audience – formerly the Conjure-Queen's throne room – where his colleagues were in conference. Almost all traces of human occupation had been eradicated from the Mossland fortress of Fenguard by its new inhabitants. The doors were now enlarged to allow ready access to huge bodies and the windows were smaller to conserve the delightful boggy ambiance favored by Salka sensibilities. A coating of black mold softened the harsh stonework of the stairways and passages; rusting iron wall-sconces that once supported torches or oil lamps now held amber globes full of luminous marine organisms; the floors of the public areas were carpeted with decaying reeds and sedges from the fens, while the private rooms and the Chamber of Audience had more desirable floor coverings of fragrant kelp and other algae.

The erstwhile royal dais, lit by pendant bowls of glow-worms, had been enlarged to contain the seaweed-heaped golden couches of the Eminent Ones. These were pushed to the very edge of the platform so that the reclining Salka leaders could study a large map laid out on a low table crafted of whalebone. The map, a three-dimensional work of art depicting High Blenholme Island in relief, was an ingenious mosaic of sea-unicorn ivory, pearl-shell, and many-colored amber. Its rivers and bodies of water were indicated by shining bits of turquoise or lapis, and the salient features were labeled with small gold plaques. Golden figurines of miniature warriors – some Salka, some human, and some mysteriously shaped – were scattered about the map surface. Model ships, as intricate as fine jewelry, clustered in separate flotillas on the lapis sea.

As Kalawnn entered, the four persons bent over the map lifted their great heads. The aged Conservator of Wisdom looked vaguely startled, the First Judge bestowed an ironic smile of greeting, and the Supreme Warrior, mighty Ugusawnn, seemed even more truculent and grouchy than usual. The fourth Salka, a sage of middle rank who had been pushing the tiny figures about the map with a golden pointer and lecturing the Eminences, bowed his head to Kalawnn and stood in a respectful pose. The Master Shaman recognized him as Peladawnn, a military strategist.

'You may leave us,' the shaman commanded. Peladawnn nodded and wriggled off.

'Well, colleague,' the Supreme Warrior rumbled, 'it's high time you condescended to join our little planning session. I was just about to explain my new idea for breaking the impasse at Beacon Lake.'

Ugusawnn had returned from the encampment a tennight earlier when it became evident that the army's advance was hopelessly stalled, leaving his subordinate generals to manage the tedious holding action.

'I'd be most eager to hear your plan,' the Master Shaman said. 'But first, I must give you tidings of the utmost importance. The Great Lights have bespoken me a message.'

'Ahroo!' cried the other Eminences. Such a direct communication was virtually unheard of.

The rotund First Judge took a hasty gulp from a golden chalice. 'What did they say?'

Before answering, The Master Shaman inserted one tentacle into his gaping mouth and pulled the Known Potency from his craw. He lifted it high and it glistened with his own body fluids, a small moonstone carving of a ribbon twisted strangely into a figure-eight that had only a single side and a single edge. Kalawnn held it delicately between four clawed tentacle digits. Its soft glow pulsated slowly.

'The Potency reacted in a strange manner to the message. Therefore, I will temporarily remove it from my person.'

The Conservator and the Judge murmured apprehensively. The Supreme Warrior said, 'Just get on with it, Kalawnn!'

'Humans have discovered the second Moon Crag.'

'*Ahroo!*'

'It is situated atop the immensely high mountain known as Demon Seat,' the Master Shaman said, 'just south of the Didion frontier, near Castle Vanguard in Cathra. The Great Lights once again became aware of its location when the detestable Likeminded Remnant used the crag to channel sorcerous Sky power to a human petitioner.'

'You believed that, Kalawnn?' The frail Conservator of Wisdom spoke in a labored wheeze. 'More likely, the Lights have known all along where the second crag was. Only their Likeminded enemies' unexpected discovery and use of it has prompted this warning to us.'

'Who cares why they saw fit to finally tell us about it?' the Supreme Warrior trumpeted. 'Now we know! And perhaps this second crag has a better grade of mineral than the pitiful crumbling stuff we were able to salvage in the Barren Lands.'

'At such terrible cost,' the Conservator lamented, 'only to find that it is virtually useless for creating new Sigils of Supreme Power.'

'Perhaps not as useless as you think,' Kalawnn said. 'My workers are cleaving the best piece at this very moment, seeking to free a small perfect portion of mineral from the worthless matrix. If they are successful, we'll be able to make at least one new Great Sigil. We shall have to decide which one is the most appropriate. For practical reasons, it should be a type that is not too difficult to carve.'

'A Destroyer!' Ugusawnn cried. 'A simple wand. What could be easier than that? And what is more appropriate than the deadliest moonstone weapon of them all?'

'Recall that Destroyers are also the most perilous to those who wield them,' the Conservator said. 'During Bazekoy's invasion, numbers of our bravest warriors perished when they tried to conjure Destroying power in a manner that the Lights deemed presumptuous or excessive. The sigil acquired a dire reputation amongst our ancestors for that very reason.'

The Judge said, 'Even the wily human villain Rothbannon was reluctant to make use of the Destroyer he tricked us into giving him.'

Kalawnn inclined his head. 'We should also keep in mind the heinous fate that befell Queen Taspiroth of Moss, Rothbannon's descendant, when she tried to use the sigil wrongly. Her husband King Linndal, my friend and colleague in sorcery, was driven mad by horror and grief after the atrocious tortures wreaked upon the queen's body before her soul was consigned to the Hell of Ice.'

'What in the world did the wretched woman attempt to do with the sigil?' the First Judge inquired with clinical interest. 'Knock the Moon out of the sky?'

'Worse,' Kalawnn said. 'She was angered by certain – um – activities carried out by the Salka bands inhabiting the Little Fen. So she commanded Destroyer to kill every one of our people then dwelling on High Blenholme Island.'

'Ahroo!' the other Eminences exclaimed, aghast.

'If such a terrible deed had taken place,' the Master Shaman continued, 'the minor sigils worn by those Salka would have died with their owners, depriving the Great Lights of the pain-energies they crave.'

The elderly Conservator of Wisdom digested this piece of information with a thoughtful frown. 'But how are *we* to know which commands are safe to give this deadly sigil? I rccall no guidelines for Destroyer's use.'

'There are none,' Kalawnn admitted. 'Whoever was chosen to use the Great Stone against the enemy would put his own life and soul at risk, in addition to suffering a tremendous pain-debt. We would require a daring and selfless volunteer . . . or even several of them, if the worst should happen. Of course, we might abolish the Lights' control of the Destroyer by means of the Known Potency, as we originally planned. But then the limitation would prevail.'

'A single abolished Destroyer,' the Judge said, 'even when used to best advantage, might not suffice to win back the rest of our island.'

'It would grease the skids of victory,' the Master Shaman said, 'terrify the foe, and give our troops needed encouragement. Later on, if we manufacture more Destroyers from this second Moon Crag, the limitation will no longer be a serious factor.'

'First, we must *reach* the second Crag,' the old Conservator pointed out.

'Quite right!' said mighty Ugusawnn. 'Our valiant prospecting force was decimated before attaining the Barren Lands Crag, thwarted by arctic elements, harsh terrain, and the withholding of the Lights' favor. At the very threshold of success, our warriors met catastrophe at the hands of a single Tarnian witch-doctor!'

The Conservator spoke with reproach. 'Are we seriously considering a new expedition to Demon Seat in Cathra? Only look at the map laid out before you, colleagues . . . How can even the best and bravest of our people hope to penetrate this well-guarded region of enemy territory? They would have to fight every inch of the way from Skellhaven on the coast, then crawl up a colossal mountain peak.'

'Humans climbed the mountain.' The Judge selected a juicy mollusk from a bowl of refreshments and popped it into his mouth. 'Kalawnn said so. Why can't our warriors do the same?'

'Humans are more agile than we,' the Conservator said. 'The very puniness of their bodies works to their advantage, and –'

The Supreme Warrior had been scowling ferociously, deep in thought. Now he interrupted without apology. 'Colleagues, listen to me! Most of our seasoned fighters are fetched up in the Green Morass of northern Didion, unable to advance further. Only untested reserves are available to us here in Moss. To attack Demon Seat now would require an army of many thousands – virtually all the troops we have in training – and there is no certainty of success. The terrain is rough, with few suitable waterways to ease our passage to the mountain. It would be impossible for our warriors to travel over it quickly. I cannot recommend that we move upon the second Moon Crag. Not until we are much stronger . . . and the humans much weaker.'

'What *do* you recommend?' the First Judge inquired.

The Supreme Warrior said, 'We should carry out the strategic action that Peladawnn and I were in the process of explaining when Kalawnn joined us.'

'What is this plan?' the Master Shaman asked.

The Salka general took up the golden pointer left behind by the military strategist and began to indicate features on the map.

'I propose that we immediately abandon our unsuccessful push through the Beacon River Valley. It was an excellent scheme, but it has failed for reasons we could not anticipate. I propose that the regular army should now withdraw to the north coast, feigning a return to Moss. However, the force will actually set out to circumnavigate Tarn – thus! – moving north around the Lavalands Peninsula and then westward, using the greatest stealth to ensure that our warriors are not detected by human ships. Meanwhile, our keen young reserves will swim *southward* from here in Moss, past Didion and Cathra, into the Dolphin Channel, where they will turn west. At the Western Ocean they will proceed north to Terminal Bay near the disputed frontier between Tarn and Didion. There the united army will regroup and launch a new offensive.'

'But the time factor –' the Conservator protested.

'It will take no more than half a moon to get both forces into position,' Ugusawnn said. 'Plenty of time before the really severe winter weather rolls in. We'll vanquish all human settlements on Terminal Bay in short order – even without using a Destroyer. Then, while the reserves hold the bay secure, our regular army force invades Didion via the Dennech and Shadow Rivers and the Tweenwater marshes.'

'I like it!' the First Judge enthused.

'The pirate strongholds of Terminal Bay have fleets of well-armed gunboats and a few fighting frigates,' the Warrior went on, placing tiny model ships into position by way of demonstration. 'They'd have to be vanquished promptly before they were reinforced by the enemy fleets based at Tarnholme and at Yelicum in the Firth of Gayle. But observe how constricted the entrance to Terminal Bay is.'

'Ah!' breathed the other Eminences.

'Once the bay is secured by our warriors, it can be readily defended from attack by sea – a situation which the local human pirates have taken advantage of for centuries!'

'How much opposition might we expect as we move inland?' Kalawnn asked. 'Unlike the Green Morass, the region seems to have numerous castles and settlements.'

'But most are very small,' Ugusawnn said. 'The fortified town of Dennech-Cuva would be bound to put up a good fight, since it is the ducal seat. We should probably beleaguer and bypass it, leaving the inhabitants to starve. The castles deeper within the Great Wold are pitiful things – barely more than strongholds for brigands. The region's rivers are deep, providing excellent corridors for troop movement, and the swamps are much more congenial to swift Salka progress than the terrain of the Green Morass, even though the distance to be covered is greater. There should be plenty of aquatic food for our warriors along the line of advance. We'll build a string of garrison lodges in suitable spots for hibernators. However, most of our army would spend the winter in a state of alertness in Terminal Bay. It doesn't ice over and it's full of fish.'

'How far do you think we might penetrate this year?' the Judge inquired eagerly.

'With luck, we'll get as far as the Wold Road before bad weather stops us. That's the main land route connecting Tarn to Cathra and Didion. If we control it, we own the heart of High Blenholme Island!'

'Audacious,' murmured the Conservator of Wisdom, studying the map. 'Too bad we didn't choose this course in the first place.'

'Beacon Lake would have been faster,' the Supreme Warrior growled. 'If we hadn't encountered *them*.'

'Even if we don't reach the road this year,' the Judge said, 'we'd surely be able to get there by late spring, wouldn't we?'

'Beyond a doubt,' said the Warrior. 'And with high mountains protecting our position on two sides and the bay secure at our rear, it would be difficult for the enemy to outflank us. Their main body of troops would have to come at us *along the Wold Road*. We could cut it at many points – not just one – by demolishing bridges and causeways through the wetlands.'

The Conservator blinked his feebly glowing eyes. 'Is there any alternative to this proposal?'

'Only an ignominious retreat to Moss,' said the Warrior, 'with a renewed assault in spring. This is what the foe will expect us to do, of course. But they will be taken completely by surprise if we strike from the Western Ocean this year.'

'Do we have the resources to accomplish this?' asked the Master Shaman.

'We do,' Ugusawnn stated, 'if we act without delay. And this new scheme also enables us to reclaim the element of shock that was lost when we stalled at Beacon Lake.'

'Well thought,' said the First Judge. 'Shall we agree to put this plan into action?'

The others concurred unanimously. The Warrior displayed a frightful smile of triumph and began to gather the map figurines into a golden box.

'Before we disperse,' the Conservator of Wisdom muttered,

'I must return to Kalawnn's earlier news of significant import. What was the nature of the sorcery channeled by the vile Likeminded Lights to the humans who climbed Demon Seat?'

'I'm not certain, Wise One, but I believe it was a fairly insignificant display of power,' the Master Shaman said. 'A mere trifle. You must understand, colleagues, that the truly remarkable thing is the fact that the Defeated Remnant had the ability to channel sorcery at all! One wonders whether the struggle between the two factions of Lights might be entering a new phase.' He studied the enigmatic sigil called the Known Potency, which he still held in his tentacle. 'Perhaps the Great Lights would tell us what happened if I inquired.'

The Warrior gave a thunderous snort. 'We'd do better to ask them whether the human who used the Moon Crag's magic had any notion at all what he was doing!'

'True,' the First Judge agreed. 'Find out who this person was. Was he sent by the One Denied the Sky, who is called the Source by humankind? What favor was obtained? Do humans now intend to create new Sigils of Supreme Power from the second crag to oppose our conquest?'

'I will attempt to ask the questions –' Kalawnn began to say. But almost simultaneouly a call came to him on the wind. 'Colleagues, be patient while my associates bespeak me concerning their work on the Barren Lands mineral.' He closed his eyes, then almost immediately reopened them. 'Ahroo!' he roared. The force of his breath blew away several of the map's miniature ships.

'What?' the other three Eminences demanded.

'The lapidaries have cloven the chunk of raw moonstone successfully, making not just one flawless blank, but *two*.'

'Congratulations, Kalawnn!' said the First Judge. 'A notable feat!

The Master Shaman continued. 'The first piece of raw stone

is much smaller, a mere wafer. We must decide which sigil it is best suited for – but I incline toward a Subtle Gateway, even though that particular Great Stone is quite difficult to carve.'

The Conservator inclined his head in approbation. 'If we possessed one of those, we would have easy access to the Demon Seat Moon Crag and all the raw mineral we could possibly use!'

'How long will it take your lapidaries to make the two sigils, Kalawnn?' the First Judge asked.

'The Destroyer, twelve or thirteen days. The Gateway, a few days less – if the supremely delicate sigil doesn't shatter during manufacture, as is all too likely. Two teams of carvers will be working separately. The most experienced will be assigned to the Gateway project.'

'We must have a contingency plan,' the Supreme Warrior said, 'in case of failure. Two new sigils won't reconquer the whole island. We need more – and we need them soon. Perhaps the Lights can advise us on this matter, as well as answering the Wisc Onc's inquiries about the humans who climbed the mountain and the nature of the magical boon granted to them by the Likeminded.'

Kalawnn said, 'I will attempt to bespeak them now.' His eyes closed.

The other three Eminences waited: Ugusawnn reining in his impatience, the First Judge seeming to be interested only in a fresh snack, and the venerable Conservator doing his best not to nod off.

At last the Master Shaman re-opened his eyes. 'I am told that three sons of High King Conrig ascended Demon Seat together. They were not sent by the Source and knew little of the second Moon Crag's potential, save that it might grant a miracle to a worthy petitioner. They know nothing at all about sigil-making.'

'Ahroo!' The Supreme Warrior vented a sigh of relief.

'What favor was granted?' the Judge asked, picking a bit of prawn shell from his back teeth.

Kalawnn cocked his head-crest in bemusement. 'The Prince Heritor of Cathra asked that he be spared from mating with a princess of Didion, since he did not love her.'

'What?' cried the others.

Kalawnn shrugged. 'It's hardly believable, yet this royal tadpole was silly enough to beg such a mundane boon – and the Defeated Ones complied in the only manner possible. They burnt off his sword arm. A prince lacking that appendage is deemed unworthy to inherit the throne of either Cathra or Didion.'

The other Eminences fell about laughing at the eccentricities of humankind until Kalawnn brought them up short. 'I asked the Light who responded to me one other question. The most important of all, I think: *What is the best possible way for Salka to obtain raw moonstone from the Demon Seat Crag?*'

'The answer?' the Conservator demanded.

Kalawnn lifted both tentacles in a helpless gesture. 'Colleagues, the Light spoke only two words: *Ask Beynor.*'

'Are you absolutely sure you remember how to say the spell, Jegg?' the sorcerer asked.

'Oh, yes, master!' The servant lad's coarse features were ruddy with excitement. A north wind had risen, carrying the first fat drops of rain from the darkening sky. The two of them stood on a stony slope a dozen ells below the cave where Gorvik had been ordered to wait.

'Let's go over it one final time. I'll ask the questions the Great Light will put to you in the Salka language, and you answer in a loud, gruff voice.'

Jegg did as he was told. His accent was still a little off, but it would do.

'Very good.' The sorcerer opened his belt-pouch. He placed one moonstone on the ground and offered the other one to the boy. 'Now hold out your hand. It's time to put on the power-giving sigil.'

'I can't believe it'll really happen,' Jegg gushed, staring at the simple ring of carved mineral that had been placed on his right index finger. Its name was Weathermaker. 'I'll be a magicker, too – better'n Gor, almost as great as you! The ring'll let me command rain and snow and sunshine – even whirlwinds and lightning!'

'It will all come true if you perform the ritual properly and are steadfast in enduring the necessary pain.'

'Oh, master, I will!' The servant boy was twelve years old. He believed everything that Beynor of Moss had told him.

'Now we're ready. I'll go up to the cave and wait there with Gorvik. You count to one hundred, then begin. Kneel down and press the ring to the moonstone disk lying there. Remember – no matter what happens, you must keep the two stones together.'

The sorcerer hurried to the cleft in the rockface, a disused bear's den. The Didionite hedge-wizard Gorvik Kitstow lurked just inside the entrance, eyeing him in shifty silence.

Beynor thought, Yes, you know what I'm doing, and why! But it doesn't matter anymore –

The abrupt blaze of emerald flame and the thunderous concussion made both men flinch.

'Frizzle me fewmets!' Gorvik cried. He took a few unsteady steps out of the cave, but the entire area was swathed in malodorous smoke and nothing could be seen clearly. The rustic magicker muttered more obscenities under his breath.

Beynor ignored him until the cleansing wind had done its work. Then he returned to the scene of the experiment with Gorvik trailing after him. All that now remained of the un-fortunate Jegg was a heap of foul-smelling ash lying on the hillside amidst scorched remnants of gorse and heather. Slow rain extinguished the last burning bits of vegetation.

'Not even a bone left!' Gorvik wagged his uncouth head in disbelief. He had the physique of a blacksmith and a face that looked as though it had been well and truly smashed, then re-molded into an approximation of human features. 'Nary a scrap o'cloth or bit o' shoe-leather. The poor li'l sod's vanished off the face o' the earth. That's some terrific sorcery!'

'It's Beaconfolk sorcery, the greatest there is – and the most dangerous.'

Beynor drew Moss's magnificent Sword of State, the only relic of his aborted reign as Conjure-King, and stirred the gritty ash with its tip. After a few moments he uncovered the ring carved from moonstone, together with a thin disk of the same material, narrowly framed in gold, that was less than a handspan in diameter. He stooped and retrieved them, and after wrapping each one carefully in cloth, slipped both objects into his wallet. He cleaned the sword against his bootcuff and replaced it in its scabbard.

'Didja know Jegg 'uz gonna die?' Gorvik asked offhandedly. 'I heard ye tell 'im the Coldlight Army'd put power into the ring if he spoke the spell ye taught 'im. But sumpin' went way wrong, di'nit?'

The rain fell harder. Beynor started back up the slope toward the shelter of the den, where the three of them had camped out during the final summer of searching. 'So you eavesdropped on us.'

'Nay, master. Just caught a few words by chance, like. And wondered why ye'd let a simple knave like Jegg do conjurin' for ye, steada doin' it yerself – or givin' the job to a born wiz like me.'

'It was a test,' Beynor said shortly. 'One that was regrettably necessary. And whether you realize it or not, the test was a success.'

The hulking Didionite grinned, revealing a mouthful of stained broken teeth enriched by a single incongruous gold incisor that gleamed like a bright coin lying on a dungheap. 'Not a success for Jegg, I'm thinkin'! Still, he weren't much of a servant to ye, and none back in Elktor will miss 'im. What went wrong? Why'd the Lights smite 'im with their thunderbolt?'

Beynor re-entered the cave, not bothering to hide his impatience. He had not borne the long years of frustration easily, and his gaunt frame and sunburnt narrow features framed by sparse platinum hair made him look much older than his seven-and-thirty years. Once inside he doffed his wet cloak and hung it on a peg pounded into a crevice. He was attired in a grey leather hunting habit, well made but worn from rough usage and badly scuffed about the knees. After removing his sword belt and hanging the heavy weapon from a second peg, he put more fuel on the smoldering fire and sat down on a flat stone opposite the flow of acrid smoke. The vagrant wisps that threatened him he diverted with his talent.

'Fetch me a double dram of spirits,' he commanded Gorvik.

'There's only a wee bit left, master,' the wizard protested. 'I was savin' it for –'

'Pour it out, damn you! There's no need to stay here any longer. Don't you understand that our endless searching in this miserable place is done? I have the three Great Stones. It matters not if there are lesser ones still lying about somewhere. I'm leaving. I won't return.'

'But the magical book –'

'The bear who scattered the contents of the bag originally hidden in this cave obviously left the book in an exposed place where it was destroyed by vermin and the elements. That moonstone disk you found this morning in the ravine is all that remains of it. The disk was once fastened to the book's cover.'

Gorvik's piggy eyes gleamed in sudden understanding. 'Ah! Then it's the *disk* you needed to conjure yer three sigils – not the book itself.'

'Using the spells written down in the book would have been much safer. But, yes: the stones can be brought to life in another way with the disk. A more perilous way, as young Jegg discovered.'

The big magicker took the jug of liquor and two dented pewter cups from the rocky shelf that held their nearly depleted supply of food and drink. He was dressed in a ragged fustian tunic and cross-gartered leggings, and had only a short hooded cape of ill-tanned goatskin to keep off the elements. He thrust a half-cup of malt into Beynor's outstretched hand, then poured a generous noggin for himself and sat down on another rock, mumbling under his breath.

'What did you say?' Beynor asked sharply.

'I said ye killed that lad on purpose, master. Or rather – ye let the Beaconfolk blast 'im to ashes and soot. I'm wonderin' why. What good are magical moonstone amulets if the Lights slay the one who uses 'em?'

Beynor stared at the fire and sipped his drink. Almost absently, he said, 'They only slay persons they consider *unworthy*.'

'And Jegg was?'

'Yes. Obviously.'

'But ye di'nt know that aforehand?'

'Not really,' Beynor admitted with peevish reluctance. 'I hoped he would survive but was almost certain he would not.'

Gorvik nodded in slow satisfaction. 'And that was the test. I see. Now I unnerstand.'

Beynor lifted his head and shot a glance like a steel dart at the big man squatting near him. Yes, the cunning rascal had almost certainly guessed the truth . . .

Beynor had searched for the three lost Great Stones of Darasilo's Trove and the book that accompanied them for sixteen years, combing the region around the bear's lair in the high moorlands east of Elktor in Cathra where he knew the trove had disappeared. Sigils, even the inactive ones he hunted, could not be perceived through windsight; they had to be sought using the naked eyes. He made a map of the area, drew a grid of squares upon it, and set out to search each square, patiently lifting every rock and bit of vegetation that might conceal a small amulet.

He labored throughout the temperate months of each year, then retired to lonely rooms in Elktor City during the winter, when snow and severe cold made spending long hours outdoors impossible, occupying himself by windwatching his foes and trying to invade their dreams.

During the early years of his search Beynor had hired sturdy dullards such as Jegg to assist him in his fatiguing work, men or boys he was confident would not understand the value of the things he sought. But the kind of helper he really needed was a fellow-adept – not a brilliant magicker, but one he could dominate and use as a cat's-paw, thus circumventing the curse laid on him by the Beaconfolk.

Long years ago, when Beynor lost his throne, the Great Lights had told him that he would be cast into the Hell of Ice if he attempted to activate and use any moonstone sigils. He still possessed powerful inborn magical talents, but these were inadequate to raise him to the lofty position his twisted ambition craved.

A scheme of his to neutralize the Beaconfolk's curse with the help of the Salka had fallen apart on the day the huge amphibians invaded the Conjure-Kingdom of Moss and discovered that Queen Ullanoth's collection of sigils, which Beynor had promised to turn over to them, was inexplicably gone.

In the months that followed, the sorcerer had lived furtively, outlawed by Somarus, King of Didion, whose Lord Chancellor had once been Beynor's co-conspirator and was now his mortal enemy. The faint hope of finding some of Darasilo's lost sigils and using them to bring down two kings – and his nemesis Kilian Blackhorse as well – then became Beynor's principal motive for living.

He knew the remains of Darasilo's Trove had been hidden in a rocky den on the high moorlands east of Elktor in northern Cathra. But soon after reaching the place, he made the heartbreaking discovery that a cavebear had chewed up the leather fardel holding the precious items and scattered its contents about the hillside. Beynor slew the animal by flinging a magical fireball into its wide-open jaws. Then he began what he feared would be a futile search for the sigils and the magical book.

Luck was with him, however. After only a few weeks, he recovered the first missing Great Stone.

It was a sigil named Ice-Master, a moonstone pendant shaped like an icicle the size of a man's little finger, lying in plain sight on the bank of a stream below the mouth of the cave. Of course the stone was inactive, not bonded to any groundling person and so unable to draw power from the Beaconfolk. The Ice-Master was only a bit of carved rock, as harmless to Beynor as it was worthless . . . for the time being, at least. Until he chose a loyal and amenable person to conjure the sigil for him, who would only use its sorcery as he commanded.

That encouraging first discovery had to sustain Beynor throughout nine more weary years of searching, when he finally found the second important moonstone, a finger-ring called Weathermaker. When he was Conjure-King of Moss he had owned another Great Stone of this type, and it had been his undoing. He had used it in a manner that the capricious

Beaconfolk disapproved, and they'd snatched it from him, called down the curse, and driven him from his throne into exile among the Salka.

Now he possessed a second Weathermaker and an Ice-Master as well. Only a single major sigil from the depleted trove – Destroyer, the greatest of them all – remained to be found, along with the ancient book written in the Salka language containing spells for activating and controlling all manner of Great Stones. At that point, Beynor began thinking seriously about recruiting the necessary cat's-paw who would enable him to evade the Lights' curse.

He was almost – but not quite – certain that the puppet would have to possess windtalent.

Magickers not affiliated with the abhorrent Brothers of Zeth were uncommon in the nation of Cathra. But Elktor, Beynor's base of operations, was close to the Didion border, and now and then an itinerant conjurer of that country would pass through the city. Those that Beynor encountered early on in his long quest he had deemed unsuitable for various reasons. Gorvik Kitstow, who had shown up in Elktor late the previous winter, was different. He was mildly talented, sharp as a bodkin in gulling the yokels out of silver pennies, yet not possessed of deep intelligence . . . or so Beynor had thought.

He decided to take Gorvik partially into his confidence, tell him something of the sigils' background, and determine whether he might make a suitable collaborator. Meanwhile, the burly hedge-wizard could assist in the search, along with the boy Jegg.

Beynor resumed his labors in spring and was satisfied when Gorvik worked diligently and without asking inconvenient questions. Near the end of Blossom Moon the hedge-wizard found the innocuous-looking little stone wand called Destroyer, which Beynor believed was the key to supreme power. And then, on the day before yesterday, Gorvik also located the moonstone disk that was formerly affixed to the cover of the missing magic book. It was the last part of the trove Beynor needed to carry out his plan.

But should Gorvik Kitstow still be part of that plan?

Beynor now had serious doubts. If it were possible for an untalented, biddable lout such as young Jegg to use sigil magic, then far better to play it safe and bond the moonstones to him.

But the calamitous test had settled the matter decisively. The cat's-paw must of necessity be a person of talent. But if not Gorvik, then who?

Out of nowhere, as he sipped his cup of spirits, stared at the leaping flames, and pondered the dilemma, a marvelous new idea came to the sorcerer. Why not make a more daring choice of creature – a man needing more subtle forms of control, who might nevertheless help Beynor achieve his goal far more quickly . . . ?

Gorvik had been speaking for some minutes while Beynor was lost in thought. Now the man's words became ominously clear.

'All yer high and mighty plans, master, that ye tantalized me with while we hunted – I admit I was a wee bit skeptical anything'd come of 'em. Ye hafta admit the idee of almighty Beaconfolk sorcery channeled through moonstones was unlikely. But seein' what I seen today changed my mind. Ye tried to bond a sigil to young Jegg, who lacked talent as much as he lacked brains. The Lights rejected 'im. It's clear ye need a man with talent. So let's get on with it. Bond the things to me. I'm not afeered.'

'What makes you think that I might do such a thing?'

Gorvik Kitstow gave a knowing chuckle. 'Well, 'tis obvious that ye don't want to try conjurin' a sigil yerself. Else ye'd never have risked turnin' over a powerful magical tool to a

dolt like Jegg. Ye'd have made the thing yer own right off
the mark if ye could. But maybe ye can't! Maybe the Lights
won't let ye. Am I right?' He winked.

'Yes,' Beynor said calmly. 'You've hit on it exactly. I know
how the Great Stones work, the way to conjure them. But
I'm banned from using them myself. I require a faithful assistant – one possessing innate magical talent, not a normal-
minded wight like Jegg – who will stand at my side as I drive
the Salka into the sea, destroy the Sovereignty, and bring
the human population of Blenholme to its knees . . . Do you
believe you're the man for it?'

Gorvik tossed down the last of his drink and rose to his
feet. His head nearly grazed the roof of that part of the cave
and his great knobby hands flexed. The gold tooth flashed
in the firelight as his smile widened.

'Well, I been thinkin' on that. I did overhear ye tell Jegg
the spell that conjures the moonstones. So I reckon it
wouldn't be that hard to use 'em, once I called 'em to life
meself.'

'You think that, do you?' Beynor sat very still. For a time,
there was silence except for the drip of rainwater and the
snap of burning wood.

'So I do,' said Gorvik. There was no longer any trace of
servility in his voice, only evil self-assurance. 'Don't be
lookin' to yer sword, nor reachin' for yer dagger neither. Ye
know how quick I be. And strong.'

'Yes,' said Beynor.

Gorvik began to edge closer.

'Just keep yer hands resting on yer knees, unnerstand?
Don't move.'

'I won't.'

'Ye were once a king, so y'say, and a great sorcerer. But
now ye're neither and the magical moonstones are no good
to ye. So think how matters lie and decide if we two might

make a diff'rent sort o' bargain – with me the master and ye the man! Hand over the sigils now and keep yer life. What d'ye say?'

Beynor shrugged. 'All right.' He removed the small pouch holding the stones from his belt and held it up for the shabby wizard to see.

Then he tossed it into the fire.

Gorvik gave a bellow of rage. But before his hands could close on Beynor's throat, the Mossland Sword of State hanging on the cave wall flew from its scabbard and transfixed his neck from side to side just below the jawbone. A great jet of blood spurted from the magicker's open mouth, just missing Beynor. Gorvik toppled into the fire like a felled oak and smothered the flames.

Beynor rose to his feet and stepped back. He waited until the writhing body was still, drew out the sword, and wiped it on the dead man's tunic. Then he hauled the corpse aside and retrieved the wallet, which was only slightly scorched. He dipped it into a rain puddle, poured the sigils out onto the stone seat very carefully, and inspected them.

They were unharmed. The disk, Weathermaker, Ice-Master, and the all-important Destroyer were not even warm to the touch.

'To think I was foolish enough to consider bonding these to a lowborn blockhead,' he murmured, 'when the proper candidate has been awaiting me all these years!'

Beynor had made a near-fatal mistake with Gorvik, letting him overhear the spell of conjuration. That blunder would never happen again. The new cat's-paw he had in mind was infinitely more intelligent (and dangerous) than the hedge-wizard, but he was also a man ruled by unbridled ambition.

Confiding in him would be a great gamble on Beynor's part. The safer course by far would be to look for a more pliable magical assistant. Any large city in Didion would have numbers of impoverished wizards inhabiting its underworld that he could pick and choose among. He had already been forced to postpone his great scheme for sixteen years. Why act hastily now?

There was an answer to that: after a long period of relative inaction broken only by a few ineffectual coastal raids against humanity, the Salka had invaded northern Didion in force. The Sovereignty was gravely imperiled.

Beynor had scried the monsters' Barren Lands operation earlier in the year from a high point in the Sinistral Mountains. He knew that the Salka had managed to bring a small amount of mineral from the devastated arctic Moon Crag to Royal Fenguard. Their shamans would be doing their utmost to fashion more Great Stones from the meager sample, especially Destroyers. If they succeeded, they would possess powerful weapons to use against humanity. There was a time when Beynor had encouraged Salka aggression. Might it still serve his own purposes – but in a very different way?

He hadn't attempted to windwatch the monsters' military activities closely since beginning this summer's work. The moorland where he searched for the lost trove lay immediately below the southern slope of the great rocky massif that divided Blenholme, a formidable barrier even to his remarkable scrying talent. While on occasional supply trips to Elktor, he had heard news about the stalled Salka incursion far to the north. Thus far, the great army mobilized by the Sovereignty had made no serious attempt to engage the inhuman enemy host.

It was a situation ripe with opportunities.

Beynor decided that his first move should be to cross over the mountains into Didion and see whether hostilities had fizzled out altogether, or whether the amphibians were only biding their time before resuming their southward advance.

One by one, he lifted and caressed the small moonstone carvings resting on the rock: a miniature icicle, a translucent ring, and a fragile wand incised with the phases of the moon. So much power! If only he could tap into it safely.

Outside, daylight was fading. The cave was a two-hour ride from Elktor, which lay to the west. But he'd left nothing of value in his rooms there. If he followed the track directly eastward instead, he could reach the great frontier city of Beorbrook by midnight even in the rain. After spending the night at an inn, he could head out for Great Pass and Didion in the morning. Conrig Ironcrown, King Somarus, High Sealord Sernin Donorvale, and all of their battle-leaders and high-ranking advisers were gathered in a Council of War at Boarsden Castle. They'd twiddled their thumbs up there for weeks, apparently unsure of how to proceed against the Salka invaders.

I could survey the situation, Beynor told himself. Make my final decision about approaching the candidate after studying the possibilities. The journey to Boarsden would take only three or four days.

He replaced the inactive sigils in the blackened leather pouch and stowed it securely inside his shirt. Then he buckled on Moss's Sword of State and hurried to the cave mouth to bespeak the horses. Both of them, along with Jegg's pony, had fled in terror when the Great Lights' green thunderbolt struck the boy dead. But the animals would return readily enough at the irresistible summons of his magic.

THREE

In the dragon's devouring abyss, darker than night and shot through with giddy red sparks, Induna of Barking Sands waited passively for death. Meanwhile, she dreamed of the time she had finally found Deveron.

The tropical night had been well advanced when the three-masted clipper ship tied up in Mikk-Rozodh and she was allowed to disembark. It was not the most propitious hour for a respectable woman to be wandering the docks in an unfamiliar port city. The Andradhian captain of the speedy merchantman, a grandfatherly sort who had treated her with unfailing courtesy during the long voyage, offered to have his third mate escort her to decent lodgings; but she declined with thanks, asking only to be directed to the nearest place where a small boat might be hired. Even though she was bone-weary and hungry, she knew she could never rest until she passed on the message she had come so far to deliver.

'You'll find punts at yon waterstairs,' the captain said, 'beyond the last slip, along the canal where the four torches flare. But are you sure you want to travel the backwaters of Mikk-Town so late at night?'

No female shaman had anything to fear from ordinary men. 'I'll be fine. Thank you again for your great kindness.'

Induna descended the gangplank, cloaked and carrying her embossed leather fardel on a strap secured over her shoulder. The canal was only about a hundred ells away. Nautical loiterers on the quay snickered and elbowed each other as she passed. One called out insolently, pretending to admire her red-gold hair, which was uncommon in the south, and asking what a Tarnian wench was doing so far from home.

It was a good question, she thought, but one too late to worry about now.

The Source had told her the name he was using and said that anyone in the Andradhian city of Mikk-Rozodh would know how to find him. She studied the small group of men gossiping at the foot of the waterstairs and selected the oldest, a thickset greybeard neatly attired in green canvas breeches, stout sandals, and a curious mesh shirt that revealed the silver hair on his chest.

'Goodman, I would like to hire a boat. Do you know the dwelling of Haydon the Sympath?'

He stepped away from the others, smiling good-naturedly, and touched the wide brim of his hat, which was woven of black straw. 'Aye, mistress. He's a Tarnian – as you are yourself, I'm thinking. But he's well thought-of in these parts in spite of it.'

The other boatmen guffawed. Tarn and Andradh were ancient foes, even though their people shared the same Wave-Harrier blood. An Andradhian invasion of Tarn nearly two decades ago, beaten back only with the help of Ironcrown's navy, had finally forced the proud Sealords to join the Sovereignty.

'Is Haydon's home far from here?' Induna asked.

'Not even an hour away. But it's late and he's a prickly sort, not to be approached after dark except for good reason. Does he know you?'

'Yes, from many years ago.'

'Then let's be off. My name's Momor and here's my punt. The trip will cost four silver pennies of Tarn, if you've none of our coin.'

The price was exorbitant but she had no choice. He helped her to board and settle herself, then stood on a stern platform and poled the slender craft along the canal and into the heart of the city. The clipper's crew had informed her that this region of southern Andradh was a low-lying collection of inhabited islands, most of them joined by humpback bridges, heavily populated along the shores and blessed with lush soil that supported rice farms and plantations of tropical fruits. These commodities, much valued in Tarn and elsewhere on High Blenholme, had formed the outward-bound clipper's cargo. On the voyage home it had been loaded with casks of dried salmon, salt cod, whale oil, opals, and gold. Induna had been the only paying passenger traveling the more than two thousand leagues from Mesta in Tarn's Shelter Bay to Mikk-Rozodh.

Once Momor's punt left the harbor area, with its tall-masted ships, sturdy warehouses, and bustling taverns and brothels, the buildings along the canal changed in character. At first the dwellings were grand, constructed of fine timber and imported stone, with balustered steps leading down to well-lighted landing stages. She saw only a handful of people moving about on the shore. A number of other punts and the occasional private barge or paddle-scow moved up and down the waterways, but most of the citizens seemed to have already retired to their homes.

Further along, the canal narrowed and began to wind sharply. Momor turned into a side-channel where the houses became meaner and more closely crowded, although still neat enough. They were made of pole and thatch, set on stilts in the mud, and often connected to one another by board walkways. Tiny watercraft were tied to laddered pilings below them. A multitude of feebly glowing lamps shone from unglazed windows, screened from flying insects by cloth or bead curtains. She saw people moving about within the houses, heard laughter, crying babes, music, and the night-cries of frogs and birds. The odors of exotic cooking and human waste vied with the rich perfume of the flowers that filled ornamental containers on almost every rickety balcony.

Induna unfastened her heavy cloak and folded it on the thwart beside her. Beneath it she wore a simple russet-colored linen gown. Momor said, 'That's right, mistress. You won't need a wool mantle here in Mikk-Town. Our weather's a far cry from that in Tarn. Nice and warm year-round. Overwarm during the rainy season, if you want the truth. You planning to stay long?'

'I don't know,' she said wearily. The message was all that really mattered.

During the voyage, she had tried to visualize her reunion with Deveron countless times, but without success. In truth, she didn't know his heart, his true self, well enough to speculate. Their time together before he was forced to flee had been too brief. Even after they were engaged to marry he had not opened his mind to her as windtalented lovers were wont to do. He was unfailingly gentle and considerate, but always on guard. They had kissed and caressed and laughed together but had never joined their bodies. It was not the custom in Tarn to swive before wedlock – although one honored more in the breach than the keeping by many young couples. But Deveron had respected it.

'Does he know you're coming, lass?' The boatman's bantering voice had turned compassionate.

'No.'

'Is he a relation?'

'In a manner of speaking. We – we were once betrothed,

but unhappy circumstances caused us to part. It's been many years.'

'Oho! So that's the way of it. And now things've changed for the better and you're come to tell him the good news, eh? Well, Haydon the Sympath has no wife or regular doxy here. He keeps house for himself. So mayhap you're in luck.'

She said nothing, having no illusions about her upcoming reception. If Deveron had wanted her to join him in his exile, he would have found a way to get word to her long ago, although Tarn was far beyond windspeech range, even for persons as highly talented as the two of them. But he had not sent for her. She knew that he had escaped from Conrig Ironcrown's agents sixteen years earlier; but whether he lived or not had been a mystery that was solved only when the Source bespoke her and sent her on this improbable journey.

'Your man's done well for himself in the years spent away from home,' Momor was saying. He had stowed his pole in the boat and installed a sculling oar at the stern when the waters of the canal became deeper. 'Even the rich folk consult Haydon, since they know he keeps his mouth shut. Was he also a sympath in Tarn?'

'We call them shaman-healers. Dev–Haydon was one, and so am I.'

Her reply inspired a drawn-out account of bodily miseries suffered by the boatman and his family, along with requests for free medical advice that lasted until the punt finally drew up at an isolated dock. Two small craft were tied there – a wooden dinghy and a peculiar elongated skiff fashioned from sheets of some thin material resembling treebark. The house served by the dock stood alone on an island that was otherwise densely forested with strange tall trees having narrow trunks crowned with mops of feathery leaves. One of the dock-pilings was adorned with a large carving of an owl, hung about with garlands of snail-shells. Another bore a brass ship's bell on a bracket and a lantern with a guttering flame.

'The sympath's sign,' Momor said, indicating the nightbird's image. 'Both an invitation and a warning. Owls are rare in this part of the world, omens of wisdom because they see in the dark . . . but also of sudden death because they swoop to kill on silent wings. Haydon's not to be trifled with, either.'

He sculled his punt up to the dock and tied the line to a cleat, then helped Induna to climb out. 'Will you want me to wait, mistress? I'll have to charge triple. My own bed's waiting.'

'No. You need not stay.' She gave him his fee. 'Am I supposed to ring this bell?'

'I'd recommend it.' Momor gave a laugh without much humor in it, slipped the line, and glided briskly away. In a few moments he was lost to sight around a bend in the canal.

Induna studied the owl image for a moment. The bird had been Deveron's heraldic cognizance and this was certainly his house. Unlike most of the flimsy dwellings she had seen, it was well-constructed of squared logs, Tarnian-style, with a covered porch surrounding it. Its roof was slate slabs, steeply pitched to shed rain, and the chimney was of stone. The windows that faced the canal were not large. They had been fitted with storm-shutters and were curtained by what looked like straw matting. Slivers of lamplight penetrated them, casting golden quadrangles on the ground. The front door was made of iron-bound planks. If he wished, Haydon the Sympath could turn his house into a rather tight little fort.

And that's why you never sent word to me, Induna said to herself. Deveron had not wanted to risk her life, should Ironcrown's assassins hunt him down.

She stood irresolute for a few more minutes, quite certain that he knew she was there, not wanting to disturb the gentle jungle sounds with the brass bell's clangor. Finally, with the

folded cloak tucked under one arm and her fardel under the
other, she walked down the dock and along the stone-
bordered path to the porch. Then she knocked on the door.

It opened almost immediately. He *had* been waiting.

He wore an unadorned tunic and trews of dark green
camlet, well worn and not especially clean; but his belt was
finely tooled and had a golden buckle. Around his neck a flat
gold case engraved with an owl hung from a handsome chain.
There were new lines at the corners of his vibrant blue eyes,
and his mouth had grown thinner and tighter. He had a short
beard and a neat moustache. His nut-brown hair was touched
with grey and cut shorter than she remembered, combed over
his forehead and ears like a close-fitting helmet.

'Welcome, love,' he said quietly. 'Come in and be at home.'

In the dragon's devouring abyss, darker than night and shot
through with giddy red sparks, Deveron Austrey waited
angrily for death. Meanwhile, he dreamed of the time Induna
finally found him.

She came with tentative steps into the house's sitting room,
which was separated from the apotheck workbenches and
shelves at the rear by a long counter with a half-door set
into it. The fireplace against the lefthand wall held a small
nest of glowing coals in its grate. A steaming teakettle hung
from an iron crane and a covered stoneware crock stood on
the warming-hob.

She seemed at a loss for words, still carrying the folded
cloak and the leather case. Her smile was almost fearful and
her eyes remained fixed on his face, as if comparing it with
another long remembered.

'Give me your things,' he said gently. 'Be seated in the
cushioned chair by the table. Is this all you have with you,
or did you leave more baggage in town? I can have it sent
for.'

'There's nothing else. The fardel holds everything I needed for the voyage. I only just arrived this evening on a clipper ship. I – I came directly to your house from the harbor.'

'I see.' He hung her cloak on a wallhook and placed the carrying case beneath it. 'Have you eaten?' When she shook her head, he fetched a bowl and a spoon and ladled out a generous portion of lamb pottage from the crock on the hob.

'I have herbal tea steeping in the pot – chamomile, lemon, and valerian to soothe the mind. Shall I pour you some, and perhaps add a splash of good Stippenese brandy? I was going to have some myself before retiring.'

'I'd like that,' she said. 'The stew is delicious. I was near starving. The ship's mess was served early in the afternoon, and I was too nervous to eat much, knowing we were approaching your home.'

'Help yourself to as much as you want. I usually break my morning fast with supper's leftovers, but I'll make us something much better tomorrow morning: buttered eggs with cocodrill sausage.'

He filled two plain pottery mugs, placing hers on the table and taking his own to an armchair that he pulled out from the wall.

'Cocodrill? What manner of meat would that be?' she asked.

'The tail portion of a huge lizard that dwells in our jungle waterways. I make the sausage myself. Smoked and well-peppered, with onions and herbs, it's fit for a king's banquet.'

'A king . . .' She lowered her eyes to her food, then continued to eat in silence.

'Is there still a price on my head?' he inquired lightly.

'The notices were taken down years ago.'

'Ah. But I daresay the reward still stands, doesn't it?'

'I hope not,' she murmured.

He paused in sipping his tea and leaned toward her. 'Why? What do you mean?'

She shook her head and would not meet his gaze, so he left off asking questions, content to wait for her to explain herself in her own good time.

When she finished her meal he refilled their mugs and led her outside to the covered porch facing the canal. Several sturdy sling-stools with leather seats were set about a low stand, which held three little clay pots. Using his talent, he struck a finger-flame and touched it to the pots' contents; fragrant smoke arose.

'The resin's smell keeps biting midges at bay most effectively. I wish we'd had it at our Deep Creek manorhouse.'

They sat side by side, drinking tea and listening to the night creatures. He had put out the lamp within the house and aside from the stars, the small lantern down on the dock gave the only light. She took a deep breath and reached for his hand. It was cool and rough with calluses.

'I came to you for a reason, Deveron. I was sent by the Source.'

He said nothing, but his fingers tightened on hers.

'He bespoke me some three weeks ago at the manor, giving me an urgent message for you. I left immediately. Tiglok's sons carried me south to Mesta in their sloop, and there I took passage on an Andradhian clipper.'

'This is the only reason you came, then.' His voice was toneless. 'You were compelled by that black manipulator. The One Denied the Sky has pulled you into his inhuman game. And now I suppose he seeks to re-enlist me as well.'

'The choice to come here was my own, Deveron. I can't deny how my heart leapt with joy at the prospect of seeing you once again, after so many years of not knowing whether you were dead or alive. The message . . . it's vitally important. But once the Source told me where you were, neither the powers of heaven nor hell could have kept me from coming. Since you left me, there's been no other. There could never be. But if – if it's what you want, I'll leave after saying what I must.' Her eyes overflowed.

He took her in his arms. 'Duna, Duna, don't cry. I had to go away. It was the only way to keep you and Maris safe from Ironcrown's evil minions.'

'I know.' She wiped her face on her sleeve and sat up straighter. 'And here is the Source's message. Make of it what you will. He asks that you return to High Blenholme with the utmost speed and stealth, using the Subtle Gateway sigil. You must go to Castle Morass in Didion and there take counsel of your – your twice-great-grandmother, after which you are to present yourself to the Sovereign of Blenholme and offer to serve and guide him as Royal Intelligencer once again.'

For a moment Deveron was rendered speechless. Then: 'It's a cosmic joke! One of those tricks the cursèd Beaconfolk are so fond of. What is the Source, save one of *them*? A renegade Light who now thinks to send me to my doom to serve some dark purpose –'

She touched his mouth with her free hand, cutting off the tirade. 'Nay! Not so, love. He told me you would be welcomed. That your special services are sorely needed. That the New Conflict now enters its final critical stages, and its outcome depends upon the defeat of the Salka as well as the evil Lights who empower them. You can help bring that about.'

He drew away from her with a violent motion and rose to his feet. 'I know almost nothing of the political situation on the island nowadays, save for the fragments of news that reach Mikk-Town and are gossiped about by my clients. Throughout this exile, I've deliberately avoided any attempt at scrying Conrig's court – not that it would have been easy, from this great distance. I didn't want to know what was happening in Blenholme. I still don't want to know!'

'Would you allow the island of your birth and all the human folk living there to fall prey to the Salka?'

He said nothing, turning his back to her and staring at the canal. His loud outburst had silenced the calls of the birds and frogs.

'If you wish,' she said with shy eagerness, 'I can tell you much of what's happened there. And once you've arrived in Didion, your great-great-grandmother –'

'There's no such person. My aged grandsire, who raised me after the death of my parents, never spoke of her. Even if she were alive, she'd be over a hundred years old. What use could such a feeble crone possibly be in a war against the Salka monsters?'

She rose and went to him, laying a hand on his shoulder. 'That's what you must discover, Deveron. You *must* return to Blenholme. Not for Conrig's sake – he's a tyrant unworthy of your love – but for the sake of the people he rules. For all his faults, he's a strong Sovereign. He's held the Salka in check this long, but only because the creatures have never taken full advantage of their sigil weaponry.'

'What are you saying?'

'Do you know that the Salka leaders have activated the Great Stone known as the Potency? The Source told me that it's a crucial tool of the New Conflict. Among other things, it can abolish the pain associated with sigil sorcery. Thus far, the monsters have made little use of it, perhaps for fear of offending the Beaconfolk and losing their magical weapons altogether. The minor sigils they now possess cause bearable pain, which they willingly endure. But lately the Salka have begun trying to fashion new sigils: not minor ones, but rather Great Stones like those once owned by their ancestors and by the rulers of Moss. If the monsters succeed in making these things, and then defy the Lights by abolishing the pain that limits the stones' use, they'll be unstoppable.'

'Unstoppable,' he repeated. 'Yet Conrig Ironcrown is supposed to stop them. With *my* insignificant help. I'm only a healer, Induna!'

'One who cannot be scried from afar by any sorcerer.'

'The Lights can see me. I'm only beyond their reach here. That's why they had to send you.'

'You have other wild talents that exceed those of most professional magickers. And you have the two sigils that the Source compelled you to keep in spite of yourself, the ones you used to escape Conrig's men. Are the stones now enclosed in that golden case hanging round your neck?'

He gripped the pendant in one fist without answering.

'Subtle Gateway will transport you to Castle Morass in the blink of an eye,' she said, 'just as it enabled you to travel from Tarn to this place. And with Concealer you'll be able to move about with complete invisibility at your destination. No other person has these advantages.'

When he replied, his voice trembled with an anger not directed at her. 'In the sixteen years I've dwelt here, I've never used these accurst moonstones. They imperil one's soul, as you already know. They seduce the user with the promise of more and more power and make him believe that the price is worth paying . . . Duna, I've *wanted* that power.'

'The Source knows that, love. He also knows your strength. You can turn the sigil magic against the Pain-Eaters if you choose to. You can help end their ability to enslave and harm persons living in the Ground Realm.'

'Let others fight this New Conflict! Why must I do it?'

'You know why. Accept the mission, Deveron, if you've ever loved me. If I could relieve you of the burden, I'd take it on myself in an instant. But I can't do this thing. Only you can.'

He gave a great sigh. 'It means so much to you?'

'On my life – it does.'

'Then how can it mean less to me?'

Her face lit up. 'You'll go?'

He nodded. When he spoke, his voice was sad. 'But only for your sake . . . as the Source knew well enough when he sent you.'

It took him the rest of the night to prepare for the journey.

Besides questioning Induna at length, he consulted maps and reference tomes before deciding on the supplies he would need. The Source's choice of Castle Morass as his destination was puzzling. The place was a primitive, ill-situated little fortress above the Wold Road, owned by old Ising Bedotha, one of Didion's most intransigent robber-barons. It was the last spot likely to be chosen by Conrig as a staging area for a strike against Salka pushing south along the Beacon River corridor toward human settlements surrounding Black Hare Lake.

Induna explained to him that, for unknown reasons, the shockingly swift Thunder Moon invasion by the monsters had come to an abrupt halt just three weeks after it began. Now, at the start of Harvest Moon, the Salka were still massed some fifty or sixty leagues north of Black Hare, in the heart of the Green Morass. If their advance remained stalled in that desolate wetland forest much longer, the onslaught of the bitter northern winter would force them either to hibernate or to retreat into the Icebear Channel. But there were disquieting rumors that the Salka were considering a new plan of action. Not even the Source knew what it might be.

Deveron decided he must be prepared for both rainy and cold weather. Leaving Induna to collect and dispose safely of the potentially harmful chymicals and herbal substances he would have to leave behind in the apotheck, he embarked for the city center in his dinghy. He had no furs or heavy leather garb of his own, but such things would be readily available from ship-chandlers he could roust out of bed at Mikk-Town quay . . . along with other merchants selling more unusual wares he had long since eschewed.

Dawn was breaking by the time he returned home. The dinghy was laden almost to the gunwales. Induna was surprised to see him unload it, then haul a second, lighter craft ashore and begin restowing almost everything inside it.

'I'm taking the skiff with me to Didion,' he explained. 'It'll be useful for getting around in the Green Morass. I don't dare transport myself directly to the near vicinity of the castle. Who knows what's waiting there besides my alleged twice-great-grandma? I'll ask the sigil to set me down in a safe place a few leagues away, then scry out the situation before presenting myself.'

'That's wise,' she agreed. 'It's such a long journey, though. You'll probably suffer severe pain-debt on your arrival.'

'Another excellent reason for not going straight to the castle. If my uncanny trip from Tarn to here was any indication, it'll be at least three days before I recover enough to function – even marginally. But I won't be struck down helpless the moment I arrive. There'll be a very brief interval during which I'll be able to move about and find shelter.'

'When you used Gateway to transport you and your companions on the search for Princess Maude, you were smitten nigh unto death.'

'I overreached myself. Asked the sigil to carry me too far with too many companions and too much baggage. And I did it again, having no choice, when I carried all of us to safety from Skullbone Peel to Donorvale. This time the power I demand will be much less.'

'Still . . . Perhaps you should take me with you. I weigh very little and I could make myself useful. I've hardly had time to tell you anything of events in Blenholme while you were away.'

'I'll learn soon enough,' he muttered. 'You are *not* going with me into the middle of a sorcerer's war. It's bad enough that you had to make this long sea voyage alone.'

'But you might have great need of my healing arts or magic.'

'You're staying here.'

'What if you should arrive badly disabled?' she cried in growing desperation. 'If I were there, I could once again share my soul's substance with you. It would cure you at once –'

'At the cost of your own wellbeing!' He took hold of her upper arms, drew her close, and kissed her hard on the lips. When he finally broke away, she saw there were tears in his eyes. 'Twice you made that terrible sacrifice for me, shortening your own life God only knows how much in the process. You won't do it again. I won't allow it! We must both face the fact that this journey is likely to be one that I won't return from alive.'

'No!' She clung to him. 'The Source wouldn't be so cruel. And he never forbade me from accompanying you to Didion. How do you know what kind of place the capricious Lights will set you down in? It could be next to a tundra-lion's lair!'

'And you'd rescue me from the ravening beast?'

'Yes! Why not?' She broke free and suddenly held a small ball of crackling flame in her hand. She flung it with a powerful overhand lob into the dark waters of the canal, where it was quenched with a loud hiss.

He showed her a small smile. 'You've learned new tricks, I see.'

'Deveron, take me!' she pleaded. 'I love you so much. We've only just found one another again.'

'Do you think I want to leave you? It's for your sake that I go! For *you*, Duna. Don't ask more of me.'

Replying not another word to her continuing entreaties, he finished loading the skiff, lashing down both a sheathed broadsword and a crossbow to the packs wrapped in oilskin. When he finally spoke again, his face was haggard and grim.

'Do you have gold enough for your voyage home?'

She touched the purse at her belt. 'More than enough.'

'Later in the day, a victualer's scow will make its weekly stop at my dock. You can get a ride back to town from him. Stay at the inn called the Golden Cocodrill. Mention my assumed name, Haydon, to the landlord. He'll see you safely aboard a ship sailing north. And now I must go into the house and change my clothes.'

'Deveron.' She held out an imploring hand. 'Is there any hope, before you leave me forever . . . if you could but find it in your heart . . .' She looked away. 'It's not for a Tarnian woman to ask such a thing.'

'What is it? If there's anything I can do to ease our parting, then tell me.' He took her hand and drew her close, but as the heavy golden case holding the moonstones pressed against the flesh of her bosom she pulled away with a small cry.

'If we could only . . . But no, it would be an unfair request with you facing such a dreadful ordeal. Go, put on your traveling clothes. I'll wait here and pray for us both.'

'I could prepare breakfast –'

He didn't understand and she could not tell him. She hung her head and the tears began again. 'I have no appetite for food.'

'Nor have I.'

He went into the house, emerging later clad in stout hunting gear, with a dagger at his waist and gauntlets tucked into his belt. The Great Stone called Subtle Gateway, which was actually a very small and delicate carving of a door, now hung naked on its chain in the open neck of his wool shirt

where he could grasp it easily and pronounce the incantation.

'But where's the Concealer?' she asked. 'Won't you make
yourself invisible before departing? Wouldn't it be safer?'

'No doubt – but using both sigils together would also
prolong the period of agony and helplessness.'

'I see.' She was still kneeling beside the boat. Sunrise lit
the sparkling canal and tropical flowers were blooming on
every hand. To a native of subarctic Tarn, the scene might
have been one of paradise; but Induna's eyes were too full
to see anything but his blurred features looking down on
her with a doleful smile.

He embraced her as a brother might, kissing her on the
forehead. Then he climbed into the beached skiff and knelt
on the bottom, bracing himself. He had organized the packs
so there was plenty of room in the elongated craft, and three
paddles were well secured beneath the thwarts so they would
not be lost.

'Farewell, Duna,' he said. 'We'll meet again.'

'I'm sure of it,' she replied in a strange soft voice.

Taking hold of the moonstone, he pronounced the incantation and gave instructions on where he desired to go. But
as he uttered the last words and the stone flared green she
flung herself into the boat on top of him, clutching his neck,
and they disappeared together in a soundless annihilation.

She dreamed of that crashing downpour of rain, the deeper
roar of the boreal river in flood, the gale-lashed willow
saplings like stinging whips flailing her face. The skiff lay at
an extreme angle, trapped among rocks and tilted nearly on
its side, atop a gravel bar in the midst of a foaming brown
torrent. She had been thrown clear onto muddy stones
among the dwarf trees; but Deveron was still in the boat,
caught between the thwarts and the oilskin-covered bundles

of cargo, with his eyes closed and uttering piteous groans. The Gateway sigil on its chain blazed like an emerald star against his throat.

Bruised over half her body, hampered by sodden skirts and the spiky willow thicket, she crept toward him on her hands and knees. When she was clear of the wretched little trees at last, she pulled herself to her feet and stood swaying, buffeted by wind and rain. She was already beginning to shiver, even though the air was not very cold.

What had happened to them? How had the magical transport gone wrong? It almost seemed as though the skiff had been flung onto the gravel bar from a considerable height. Had the Lights only reluctantly provided the sorcery, because it was somehow against their best interests?

The heavily wooded banks of the river were nine or ten ells distant on each side of the islet. The water was opaque and swirling. There was no way to tell how deep it was, but the current flowed with ominous swiftness, carrying all manner of broken vegetation and floating branches. The gravel bar itself was spindle-shaped with pointed ends, perhaps four ells wide where they had landed. Most of the willows that had taken root on it were already partially submerged. She'd fallen into the last patch that stood above water.

'Deveron!' she cried, taking hold of the front of his jerkin and shaking him. 'Can you hear me?'

He only moaned. A trickle of blood seeped from beneath his woolen cap. She pulled it off and found a large lump and an oozing scalp cut. Cautious probing of the skull on either side of it reassured her that the bone was yet solid and the wound superficial, for all the bloody mess. The pupils of his eyes were of the same size and he was not feverish. She hoped that he had only been stunned.

But should he remain partially conscious for much longer,

the sigil's pain-debt would overwhelm him. He would be helpless for three days or even longer . . .

If anything was to be done, she'd have to do it. It seemed obvious that they'd have to get off the gravel bar. It was too small and barren to be a satisfactory camping place. The predatory animals of the Green Morass would smell Deveron's blood and not hesitate to swim out and attack. Her magic and his weapons might fend the beasts off during the daytime, but what would happen when she fell asleep? The small willow trees wouldn't last long as firewood, even if she managed to ignite them.

No, there was no helping it. She would have to drag the skiff into the river and paddle to a safer place.

She pulled her wet skirts forward through her legs and tucked the cloth into the front of her belt, making it possible for her to move about more easily, then set about trying to tug and push the long narrow craft toward the water's edge. But it was much too heavy, besides being securely wedged in place by several large rocks. With a sinking heart, she realized that it would have to be unloaded.

The rain was falling harder than ever and the rushing river made a great noise. She felt confused and on the verge of panic. Her bruises and facial cuts ached and an insidious chill stiffened her hands. She considered pulling Deveron out of the boat, but he was not a small man and she feared she'd be unable to get him back in again. She'd do better to remove the packs, but they were large and heavy, covered with oilskin and firmly lashed down. Poor Deveron was lying in a pool of blood-tinged water that would have to be bailed out. But what to do first? . . .

Despondency suddenly overwhelmed her like a crushing wave. Furious words burst from her lips as she screamed up at the sky. 'It's your fault, Source! You told him to use the damned Gateway sigil. It was supposed to transport him to a safe place – I heard him command it. Is *this* what you call safe?'

The anger invigorated her and restored her right-thinking. She set about rigging an improvised tent over the entire boat, using a large oilskin along with rawhide cord that had tied down the packs. The three paddles served as poles and heavy stones substituted for tentpegs.

Her fingers were going numb and she was shivering badly by the time she finished. She would have to find more suitable clothing quickly or risk collapsing from exposure. Deveron had packed plenty of extra things, and the third pack she opened contained what she required. She stripped to the skin and put on woolen trews that she rolled to fit her short legs, two pairs of stockings, waxed-leather buskins that were only a trifle too large, a heavy tunic, and a fleece vest. One of the smaller oilskins served as a raincape. She found knitted fingerless mitts and a long scarf to wrap around her neck, and pulled a fur cap over her ears. After covering Deveron with a blanket and wrapping his wounded head in a shirt, she rested for a while beneath the meager shelter before beginning the hard work of shifting the packs.

Even though most of her clothing was already damp, she felt much warmer. A delicious languor spread through her body. She heard the crashing river and raindrops rattling on oilskin. Through slowly closing eyes, she saw a black wall of spruce trees on the shore, undergrowth tossing in the wind, and a sudden gleam of – *what?*

Was there something out there?

Fear jolted her awake. She struggled to her feet, used her talent to search the dark forest, but relaxed again when she scried no living thing. She and Deveron were alone in the wilderness. Alone on a tiny river island that was empty save for a patch of stunted willows –

She stiffened as her gaze swept over the little trees. Brown water now covered the base of every thin trunk. The river was rising. Without her noticing, the gravel bar had shrunk to half of its previous length.

Source! her terrified mind shrieked on the uncanny wind. *What am I to do?*

There was no reply.

Working frantically, she dismantled the shelter and returned the paddles and all of the unloaded equipment to the skiff. Then she surveyed the tilted craft. What would happen when the water rose under it? Would it capsize?

Not if you get in and weight it on the high side.

She gave a great start and almost lost her footing in the slippery mud. Then she gave a shrill laugh. 'Thank you for the reassurance, Source! Just make certain we don't flip in the rapids or go over a waterfall after we float free. I really don't know how to paddle this thing.'

He does. It's time to revive him, Induna. Do it now while there's still time, before the Pain-Eaters begin to feed.

'Source, do you mean –'

But she knew what was meant.

Cautiously, she levered herself into the skiff so they were lying face to face, then fastened their belts loosely together. Whatever happened would happen to both of them. She tucked translucent oilskin over their bodies to fend off the worst of the rain, enclosing them in golden gloom. It was almost cosy, she thought.

With the utmost caution she unfastened the chain of the sigil called Subtle Gateway and eased the moonstone into his wallet, which she reattached to his belt. Then she opened the front of both their shirts.

A tremendous clap of thunder exploded overhead, shaking the very earth and causing the grounded skiff to lurch.

'So you Lights disapprove, do you? Then rage and howl and shake the stars from their courses if you can! But know that I'll free him from you again, just as I did before. Your feast is over before it begins.'

She chanted the invocation with one hand resting between her breasts. The damp skin softened and became as yielding as bread dough. She reached through soft flesh and bone into her own beating heart and drew forth a tiny thing no larger than a finger-joint, a pearl-colored female image that was alive and moving. Her entire body shuddered and seemed on the verge of dissolution, then regained its mortal solidity. But she was diminished, deprived of a significant portion of vital energy, and she knew that this time the sacrifice would take a toll much greater than it had before.

Will I recover? she wondered. But it didn't matter. He would.

Her eyesight was beginning to fade as she pressed the shining little homuncule into his breast. It vanished and so did his agony. He was free. She heard him crying her name on the wind.

Induna!

In her dream she was content, smiling as the dragon pulled her down and down and down, into the black abyss.

The darkness brightened. Rainbow reflections shimmered on a quicksilver mirror. She saw again the awful gaping jaws and gemlike eyes of the Morass Worm, and watched that ghastly visage melt and metamorphose into a familiar human face.

His.

She woke.

He sat beside her, holding one of her hands. She lay in a warm, comfortable bed in a small room where wan sunlight shone through a leaded window of pebble-glass. Two women stood on either side of Deveron, smiling down at her. One was tall and fairhaired, dressed like a common serving wench, but with a bold and commanding bearing for all that she was still in the first blush of maidenhood. The girl's left wrist was bound in a splinted dressing. The second woman was much older but very comely. She was a tiny person who stood less than five feet tall. Enormous green eyes dominated a sweet unlined face. Her hair, of mingled silver and gold, was done up in two long plaits.

'The worm,' Induna whispered. 'The devouring worm!'

'Nay,' Deveron said, wiping her brow with a cool cloth. 'It rescued us, love. Unaccountable as it may seem, the dragon somehow brought the skiff with us inside to the very destination we originally sought: Castle Morass. You are resting in a village nearby.'

'We had been expecting you, my dear,' the very small woman said. 'The Source told us you would be coming.' Her smile was mischievous. 'I admit your manner of deliverance was unexpected. You were brought by Vaelrath, one of the few of her ferocious ilk who sometimes condescends to deal with my people.'

The tall girl said rather brusquely, 'How do you feel, Induna? You've lain senseless for over a day while the healers worked on you. Your man was frantic with worry – and with good reason. Did you truly donate a portion of your soul to save his life? Great Starry Bear! Never have I heard of such a thing.'

Induna pulled herself up on the pillows, discovering that she was wearing a finely embroidered linen nightgown. 'It is an uncommon piece of magic, rarely performed by Tarnian healers. And I now feel well recovered. But who are you two ladies, that you have familiar congress with such a dread creature as a Morass Worm?'

Deveron said, 'Where are my manners? Let me present Her Majesty, Casabarela Mallburn, daughter of the lamented King Honigalus, and rightful Queen Regnant of Didion.'

The fairhaired wench grinned. 'My Uncle Somarus, that murdering swine, calls me Casya Pretender. He'd pay ten thousand gold marks for me, dead or alive, but I have a temporary safe refuge here at Castle Morass, among secret friends, while my broken wrist heals.'

Deveron said, 'And may I also present Mistress Sithalooy Cray, who is a leader among the race of Green Men . . . and my newly discovered great-great-grandmother.'

'You must call me Cray.' The little woman held a cup to Induna's lips. 'Drink a little of this. It will strengthen you. Then we must discuss urgent matters, for our poor world is in a state of turmoil unknown since the days of that upstart human, Bazekoy. And *we* have been chosen to put it right – if such can be done.'

Deveron said firmly, 'But first, Eldmama, before we deal with such momentous things, we will talk of a wedding.'

The tall, rawboned woman dressed in a dusty black magicker's cloak and a broad-brimmed hat approached Beorbrook Hold with her heart full of hope – and feet that hurt like blue blazes.

It had taken Rusgann Moorcock two days and two nights, walking without stopping save for brief periods of rest, to negotiate the steep downhill track that led from Lord Tinnis Catclaw's mountain retreat to the civilized regions of northern Cathra. Her witch's disguise, coupled with her daunting height and fierce scowl, had warned off the few shepherds and other high-country denizens she'd met along the way. They had eyed her warily and kept their distance, wanting nothing to do with what appeared to be a wandering conjure-wife of Didion.

No one seemed to be pursuing her. Thanks to the cleverness of dear Lady Maude, it was probable that none of the guards up at Gentian Fell Lodge yet realized she was not lying sick abed. The weather had stayed fair and the lopsided moon had shone bright as day as she trudged through alpine meadows and valley forests with long and tireless strides. Finally, on the morn of the third day, she approached the gates of Beorbrook Town, above which towered the enormous Cathran fortress that guarded the approach to Great Pass. It was also the home of the Earl Marshal of the Realm, the Sovereign's most trusted general, and his adopted son Prince Dyfrig.

She was too exhausted to go much further without a long sleep and good food. But if the prince was in residence, she was determined to pass on the secret letter from his mother as soon as possible. She'd have to tread cautiously to avoid raising suspicion, however; it would never do to simply approach the barbican of Beorbrook Hold and demand an audience. Lady Maude had cautioned her that more subtle means were called for. First she must make discreet inquiries. Then, if Dyfrig was at home, she would contact him by sending a note to the earl marshal's daughter-in-law, Countess Morilye Kyle.

Rusgann stepped aside into a copse of alders, opened her pack, and set about altering her appearance. She tied her straggling grey-blonde hair into a neat bun, exchanged her black hat and cloak for the bright red head-kerchief, fancy knitted shawl, and white apron of a north-country peasant woman, and rearranged her plain features into a more amiable expression.

Keeping her gaze lowered and her manner unobtrusive, she moved among other common folk through the eastern city gate into a lower-class commercial quarter with open-air market stalls purveying fresh produce, poultry, and a wide variety of other inexpensive wares. She soon came upon a likely tavern situated next door to a stable. Sitting down with two other congenial-appearing female patrons who turned out to be an elderly mother and her buxom grown daughter, she ordered a hearty meal of chicken pottage with leeks and parsnips, rye bread, apple tart topped with clotted cream, and brown ale. Even before the food arrived, she and her table-companions were gossiping like old friends.

Rusgann pretended to be a mountain dweller from a remote steading, whose husband had recently died. Rather than endure a harsh winter alone in the highlands, she said, she'd sold off her goats and sheep to a neighbor and was on her way to join her sister's family in a village far to the south, near Teme.

'I've never visited a big city before,' she admitted with naive enthusiasm. 'Coming here is like a dream come true. What a wonderful market you have! A person could find anything her heart desired in such a place.'

The old woman cackled dismissively. 'Why, this piss-poor little clutch of stalls is nothing compared to the grand market square over near Beorbrook Hold. Now *that's* a market! Lords and ladies shop there for silks and jewels and fine wines from the Continent. And orn'ry bodies like us can buy real steel needles, and thread any color of the rainbow, and pastries and sweets good enough for a royal banquet.'

Rusgann's eyes widened with simulated awe. 'Might one see Marshal Parlian Beorbrook himself thereabouts? And his son, Prince Dyfrig?'

'Nay,' said the younger woman, speaking with her mouth full of meat pie. 'They're both up in Didion, fighting the Salka monsters with the Sovcreign's army – and so are most of Beorbrook's warriors. Don't tell me you didn't hear about the invasion?'

'Invasion!' Rusgann gasped, feigning dismay. 'Saint Zeth preserve us! I heard nothing about this. My steading is so far up in the mountains –'

'Now, don't be all in a flowster, dearie,' the oldwife said

soothingly. 'The great slimy brutes aren't anywhere near here. Back in Thunder Moon they bogged down someplace way up north in the Green Morass. Just came to a screeching halt for reasons nobody can fathom. Good thing, too – since it gave our Sovereign time to muster troops from all over the island. There's a whackin' great mob of fighting men gathered up around Boarsden on the River Malle, ready to smash the red-eyed fiends if they start to move again.'

'Thank God,' Rusgann exclaimed. 'I suppose the earl marshal and Prince Dyfrig are with the troops.'

'Where else?' the pie-eating woman said, reaching for her cannikin of ale. 'At Boarsden Castle, likely, where the great Council of War carries on wrangling.' She lowered her voice to a conspiratorial whisper. 'It's said the yellow-belly Diddlies refuse to march into the morass after the foe, and High King Conrig can't shift 'em. The Cathran and Tarnian warriors are left twiddling their thumbs!'

'Oh, my,' said Rusgann. 'So the Sovereign's army just sits and waits? That doesn't sound very wise.'

A potboy came up with her meal on a platter and demanded payment. She took coins from her well-filled purse.

'Without Diddly guides, it'd be suicide to go into the morass,' the oldwife observed with a sniff. 'It's not for the likes of us to second-guess kings and war-leaders.'

Rusgann grunted and fell upon the chicken stew like one starving. Her companions finished their own food and drink, and the beldame said, 'Well, it's time my daughter and I were off. Good luck in your journeying, lass. Be glad you're going south, away from Didion and the horrid Salka.'

'Well,' Rusgann said with a wry grin, 'I can only hope that my sister's children don't turn out to be monsters of another sort. Farewell!'

The two women smiled at her and left the tavern.

Rusgann sat back, sighing, and took a long pull of ale as she studied her surroundings. The place was clean enough and reasonably quiet. She'd seek a bed and get some sleep, then buy a strong saddle-mule from the adjacent stable. It would take her at least three days to reach Boarsden via Great Pass.

FOUR

After several days of hard slogging afoot through the dense forest above the western 'ear' of Black Hare Lake, the five-man reconnaissance party led by Prince Dyfrig Beorbrook reached the Raging River. At that point their Didionite guide, a fur-trapper named Calopticus Zorn, took the prince aside, nodded toward the opposite bank of the watercourse, and drew one finger across his throat in an eloquent gesture.

'I go no farther,' he stated.

'You mean the Salka control the country beyond the river?' Prince Dyfrig's skepticism was obvious. 'Have they truly penetrated this far south? That's not what the Didionite wind-searching team at Timberton Fortress told me.'

'I go no farther. Too dangerous.'

'You agreed to guide us to the Gulo Highlands,' Dyfrig said to him in a low, furious voice, 'and this you shall do! Our mission depends upon it.'

So did his own self-respect, for the prince was the one who had proposed this risky enterprise, hoping to prove his valor to his true father the earl marshal – and to the Sovereign, who was someone else.

It was still a source of astonishment to Dyfrig that

Ironcrown had so readily agreed to let him go on the scouting mission. All the High King had said was, 'What will you need?' Dyfrig had asked only that he and his equerry be accompanied by the best scrier and the best windspeaker available, and that he be granted sufficient funds to hire a Didionite guide who was not afraid to venture into the Green Morass. Calopticus Zorn had seemed to be sober, experienced, and reliable – up until now.

'Tell me what you're afraid of,' Dyfrig demanded of the man.

'I seen bad signs.' The trapper sat down on a moss-covered boulder, pulled a strip of smoked elk venison from his pack, and began to gnaw on it. The other members of the party, the prince's equerry Sir Stenlow Blueleaf and the two Zeth Brethren, exchanged puzzled glances.

'Signs of the Salka?' Dyfrig persisted. 'Why didn't you show them to us when you came across them? What kind of signs are you talking about?'

The guide shook his head. 'Very bad.' He was a lanky man some two-score years of age with a long jaw and slitty eyes, who wore greasy buckskin clothing and an incongruously splendid cap made of mink fur, with lappets that would have dangled on either side and behind had they not been tied to a bone button on the crown.

Vra-Erol Wintersett pursed his narrow lips. 'The rascal is lying, my lord prince.' The senior Brother of Zeth on the expedition, he was a man who did not suffer fools gladly and was much aware of his position as Chief Windsearcher in the Army of the Sovereignty. Unlike the other Cathrans, who were dressed drably so as not to attract attention, his hunting garb was of the finest plum-colored leather, cut to show off his muscular limbs and broad chest. His face was angular and deeply tanned. 'I never perceived any Salka windtraces nor any other indications of the amphibians' presence – and I've been alert for such things since we left the villages at Black Hare Lake. I think this fellow regrets having agreed to guide us and hopes we'll be frightened into turning back.'

'Zeth knows it's been miserable going,' remarked the second Brother, Vra-Odos Springhill. His specialty was long-distance windspeaking. A tireless older man of less than medium stature and sinewy build, uncomplaining up until now, it would be his job to report the findings of the recon-naissance party directly to Lord Stergos and the Sovereign, bypassing the Didionite wizards who usually gathered and relayed intelligence concerning the Salka horde to the Council of War based at Castle Boarsden.

'We can't turn back, Cal,' Dyfrig said to the guide, striving to hold his temper in check. 'If you force us to go on without you, I'll order Brother Odos to bespeak tidings of your bad faith and cowardice to King Somarus of Didion himself. You could be severely punished.'

'Huh.' The threat did not seem to upset the taciturn trapper. 'The king is far away and the north woods is big. But you better listen to what I say, prince. So far, the bad ones only been watching us. We cross this river, they're maybe gonna attack. Sign says so.'

'Who? The Salka?' Dyfrig demanded. 'For God's sake, man! Tell us plainly what you're afraid of.'

'Not Salka. Something worse.'

'What can be worse than Salka monsters?' asked Sir Stenlow. Dyfrig's equerry was a stalwart, rather solemn knight with raven hair and pale blue eyes. A few years older than the prince, he served as both bodyguard and confi-dential assistant.

'Come look, all of you.' Zorn climbed to his feet and strolled downstream, searching the muddy riverbank while still chewing. If the trapper was afraid, he didn't show it. The prince went after him, trailed by Stenlow and the two alchymists.

'Bear prints, lynx prints, reindeer and small animal prints galore,' Vra-Erol pointed out, not bothering to hide his irritation. 'We've kept the wild beasts at bay with our gammadion magic thus far, and we'll continue doing so. What's the bloody fuss?'

Calopticus Zorn peered over his shoulder, smirking. His greenish-yellow teeth were clogged with shreds of tough meat. 'How 'bout this?' he inquired with vulgar relish, pointing to the sodden ground at his feet.

'Bazekoy's Bowels!' Dyfrig crouched to study the sign, and the Brethren did as well, murmuring in astonishment. 'No Salka made these tracks.'

'It looks as though a big log was dragged across the mud into the water,' Sir Stenlow ventured. 'Perhaps by a bear?'

'Not unless the log was flexible,' Vra-Erol said quietly, 'and had clawed feet on either side. See? Here and here and here. These are not bear prints. They're too narrow and the claws are too long.'

'Codders!' whispered the dumfounded equerry. 'What manner of brute could it be, then?'

Dyfrig gave Zorn a stern look. 'Stop playing your silly games, Cal. What made these marks?'

'Worm.' A grimace of morbid satisfaction. 'Morass Worm, supposed to be dead and gone nigh on three hundred year. But maybe not, eh?' He chuckled.

'That's ridiculous!' the prince expostulated. 'I've never heard such bullshite. Worms are tiny things –'

Vra-Odos cleared his throat pedantically. 'The word was used in ancient times for larger mythical beasts.' He looked embarrassed. 'Er – dragons, to be specific. During our sojourn in Didion, I've perused volumes of their old tales that contain mention of intelligent Morass Worms. The creatures are given varying descriptions and no one seems to know –'

Zorn broke in. 'Back at camp, when we start out this morn, I seen claw-scrapes on tree trunks. More than one worm.'

'Well, *I* saw nothing of the sort!' snapped Vra-Erol. For all his off-putting and haughty manner, he had proved to be an expert in every sort of woodcraft.

'Didn't look high enough,' said the trapper smugly. 'Marks were four, five ells up a buncha big trees next the creek. Way too high for bear scratches.' He tipped his head toward the opposite bank of the strong-flowing river. 'They're yonder. I can smell 'em. The claw marks were a warning.'

Vra-Erol sniffed the air elaborately. 'I smell naught save river mud and conifer sap – and perhaps a whiff of carrion.'

Prince Dyfrig stared at the strange trace with an expression that mingled bafflement and frustration. He was twenty years of age and stood four fingers over six feet in height, having a slender build and quiet manner that belied his considerable physical strength. His hair was tawny and the eyes set deeply in his sun-browned features were an unusual deep brown verging on black, very much like those of the Sovereign. No one who saw the two of them together could doubt Dyfrig's parentage, but to speak openly of the resemblance was to risk the full weight of Conrig's wrath.

Dyfrig believed that his mother Maudrayne was dead, and by law and by love considered himself to be Parlian Beorbrook's son and heir. His being named third in succession to the throne of Cathra was inferred by him and many others to be a mere sop to the Tarnians, his mother's people, subject to annulment at any time by royal decree. Dyfrig had hardly given thought to the matter of his true parentage while growing up far from the court at Cala Blenholme; nor had he sought to impress the aloof king who was obviously his natural father. Up until now.

'Cal,' the prince said at last, 'I've decided that we'll stop here for a time while you do your best to find further signs of these strange creatures. I need better evidence than your tale of claw-marks and a churned-up mass of mud if I'm to report this to Lord Stergos and the Sovereign. None of the wizards at Count Timberton's fort mentioned giant worms amongst the beasts we should beware of.'

'Most wizards don't know,' Zorn said. 'Those that know, don't believe. Gang of fools.' He cocked his fur-capped head. 'Mind you, worms were all supposed to be dead.' He pulled off another chunk of dried meat and champed it noisily. 'Guess I'll take a hike along the riverbank. See what I can see. Should be safe enough. But don't any of you lot go wandering off into the trees.'

He ambled away.

'Insolent whoreson,' Vra-Erol muttered. 'Wonder if he could be right about the dragons?'

'I've also kept alert to our surroundings,' Vra-Odos said. 'I detected no creatures save the wildlife we might expect to find. If the Morass Worms do exist, I can only conclude that our windsenses and the gammadion sorcery of our Order are inadequate to disclose their presence.'

'You could be right, Brother,' Erol said. 'They might possess uncanny shielding talent of their own, as do some of the Salka.'

Sir Stenlow gave a slow whistle. 'Then . . . if there be numbers of the things lurking in this wilderness, it could explain the great mystery of why the Salka advance has stalled!'

The others stared at him for a long moment, speechless.

Dyfrig clapped the knight on the shoulder. 'Well said, Sten! You may have hit on it exactly. Our guide thought the worms died off centuries ago. Perhaps the Salka invaders believed the same thing – until a throng of the bastards popped up out of nowhere and gave battle around Beacon Lake. And won.'

'We must be absolutely certain this is true,' Vra-Odos cautioned, 'before passing the information on to the Sovereign. Even then –' His mouth twitched.

'There is a problem with credibility,' Dyfrig conceded with a sigh. An idea came to him. 'Vra-Erol, you were unable to scry anything of the Salka position from our previous camp-site. But since then, we've come over a high ridge into more level country. Might it be possible to oversee something useful from here, provided there's no intervening high ground between the river and Beacon Lake? You might catch some sort of glimpse of the Salka and their presumed antagonists.'

'One could try.' The veteran windsearcher was dubious. 'The overview, if there is one, would be indistinct. Perhaps useless to our purposes. We had hoped to discover whether the Salka plan to hibernate near Beacon Lake and resume their march in spring. Signs of that would be too subtle to ascertain at this distance. We are still over thirty leagues from their estimated position, nearly at the limit of my percep-tion. Any landform blocking the line of sight would muddle the wind-picture significantly.'

'Please try anyhow,' the prince urged.

'To increase the chance of success, I could climb one of the taller trees.'

Sir Stenlow regarded the dignified alchymist with surprise. 'You'd be able to manage such a thing, Brother Erol?'

A disdainful smile. 'I work for the army. I've climbed more trees than you've had hot dinners, boy.'

Dyfrig and Vra-Odos laughed. The prince said, 'Speaking of food, we're overdue for our own cold lunch.'

They found reasonably comfortable rocks to sit on and opened their packs. By the time they finished a brief meal of hardbread and ham, Calopticus Zorn had come back into view, trotting at a fair pace. They were relieved to see that nothing seemed to be following him.

The prince rose and called out. 'Ho, Cal! What did you find?'

Maddeningly, the trapper slowed to a deliberate walk. His long face wore a superior smile. As he drew closer, they could see that he was carrying a good-sized bone.

'More worm sign,' he declared, handing his evil-smelling trophy to the prince, who accepted it without demur. 'See them teeth marks? This is a big brown bear's upper armbone. Found a stripped carcass by following the carrion stink. Skull crushed like an egg to suck the brains.'

'But couldn't the bear have been attacked by a tundra-lion?' Dyfrig peered doubtfully at the deep gouges. The bone was at least several days old. 'I admit these wide-set marks are persuasive, but –'

'That don't convince you, lord prince?' Calopticus Zorn rummaged in his capacious belt-wallet. 'Maybe this will.' He held up an object that gleamed in the afternoon sunlight like a thick dagger-blade smoothly carved from topaz. 'Bastard broke it off in the bear's skull. Hardheaded beasts, bears.'

'God's Truth!' Vra-Erol exclaimed, seizing the thing from the trapper. 'Look at the size of it! Half a foot long or I'm buggered, and bits of tissue still clinging to the cracked root.' He turned to Dyfrig. 'No man can gainsay this. We have our proof, and we must hasten back to Boarsden to show it to the Sovereign and his generals.'

'Not before you climb that tree,' the lanky prince said. 'Give the tooth to Brother Odos – and come stand on my shoulders.'

The Sovereign of Blenholme and his most trusted adviser rode side by side along the crumbling dike track of the River Malle below Boarsden Castle. They were accompanied by two knights from the household of their host, Duke Ranwing.

The Didionite nobleman had done his best to dissuade his guests from making the excursion, pointing out that the bridge at Boar Creek had been destroyed and portions of the dike itself washed away by a powerful spring flood. Repairs were still incomplete because so many of the dukedom's ablebodied men had been called to arms against the Salka. Unsaid was the fact that the troops, along with over thirty thousand other warriors of Didion, Cathra, and Tarn, had cooled their heels at a vast encampment near Boarsden for over a moon because no one knew what the invaders were going to do and the leaders could not agree on defensive strategy.

'Surely Your Grace and Earl Marshal Parlian would better enjoy a boar hunt in the marshes,' the duke had urged. 'It would be my honor to accompany you –'

'No thank you, my lord,' Conrig said in a tone that was courteous but brooked no argument. 'I've no stomach for pig-sticking today. My old friend Beorbrook is all the company I need, and you yourself are no doubt occupied with preparations for tomorrow's great reception and betrothal feast. We'll go out by ourselves and view the historic spot.'

'But you must not ride alone, Your Grace,' Ranwing Boarsden protested. 'The dike track is dangerous.'

He would have given them an escort of a dozen knights, but Conrig insisted that only two would be permitted. With one warrior leading the way and the other trailing, and both well beyond earshot, the king and the earl marshal set out to see the spot where the infamous tragedy had taken place so many years earlier.

It was now mid-afternoon on the day before Conrig's three sons were scheduled to arrive at Boarsden for the betrothal ceremony. The sky was overcast and mist already rose over the marshy bottomlands below the castle's knoll. The air had turned chilly, although the autumnal equinox was still several days away, and dew hung heavy on the seed-plumes of the reed beds. A few small flocks of buntings and ducks took wing as the horses passed by. Out on the wide River Malle, covered barges laden with corn, the stoutly built flatboats of fur-traders, and narrow rafts of timber were being guided downstream to the populous valley settlements and the ship-building cities of Didion Bay.

'See over there, sire,' Beorbrook said, pointing ahead, 'where the rivercraft have pulled up along the opposite shore? That's where the great whirlpool lies. Boats and rafts must go carefully around it, then negotiate the long stretch of rapids below, one at a time.'

Conrig guided his mount across a rock-strewn cut. 'The track is in better shape than I thought it would be from the duke's warning. I think he had other reasons for not wanting us to ride out here.'

'He knows you'll want to talk about the disaster when you return, and King Somarus won't like that. The topic is an uncomfortable one to the king and his family – most especially now that the young Pretender has declared herself.'

'Ah, yes, Casya the Wold Wraith! We'll have to send someone capable to check her out. Or at least try to. Somarus's intelligencers haven't had any luck locating the wench's boltholes. I've heard that some searchers who went into the Great Wold after her never came out again.'

'It's wild country,' Beorbrook admitted. 'Parts of it are said to be even worse than the morass, with impenetrable scrub in areas once burnt over by wildfire, as well as treacherous sucking bogs.'

'Do you think there could be any validity to the girl's claim to Didion's throne, Parli?'

The earl marshal shrugged. He was a stocky, still powerful man of nine-and-sixty years, with hair and beard gone

snow-white while his brows remained black, giving startling emphasis to eyes that glittered like blue glacier ice.
'The body of the infant princess was never found. Of course,
neither were those of over half the victims of the attack on
the river, including King Honigalus and Queen Bryse. The
Salka monsters devoured them flesh and bone. The two
little princes drowned, poor lads, but their bodies came
down the rapids almost unscathed. There have been whispers about Princess Casabarela's survival for years. The
Vandragora clan – the late Queen Bryse's people – would
unite in a heartbeat with the great timberlords and certain
discontented barons to pull down Somarus if this Casya
Pretender looked at all legitimate.'

They rode in thoughtful silence for a few minutes. Then
the Boarsden household knight ahead of them reined in,
turned his horse to face the river, and removed his plumed
hat.

Conrig urged his own mount forward and came up beside
the man, who only pointed wordlessly to the broad expanse
of water. In a moment, they were joined by the earl marshal
and the knight who had been riding in the rear of the party.

'Where did the Salka ambush the royal barge, Sir Vargus?'
the Sovereign asked.

The first knight lifted his head, which had been bowed in
prayer. He was balding and jug-eared, with rugged features,
at least two decades older than his companion. 'Just upstream
of the great eddy, Your Grace. The action was very cleverly
planned. The oarsmen of the royal barge were weary after
having come upstream through the rapids, but they easily
avoided the vortex by keeping to the far shore. When the
boat returned to midstream and the approach to the castle,
the monsters rose up out of the water, smashed the oars and
rudder, and began swarming aboard. The royal barge drifted
helplessly in the current and was sucked down into the whorl

and smashed to bits. Nearly a hundred souls perished besides the royal family of Didion, including an aunt of my own who was a lady-in-waiting to the queen.'

'What a hideous tragedy,' Conrig said. 'And there were no survivors?'

Sir Vargus hesitated, whereupon the other knight, a thin, hard-faced young man whose name was Gansing, exclaimed, 'No one at all! And those who say otherwise are liars.'

Parlian Beorbrook interposed smoothly, 'It's been long rumored in Cathra that the Salka were incited to commit this heinous crime. A human sorcerer, Beynor of Moss, who was once Conjure-King, is said to have sought revenge against the royal family of Didion for some alleged insult.'

'I've heard the rumor,' Sir Gansing said. 'The best-informed persons at our court think it ridiculous. It's well known that the Salka despise all human beings. Why should they have done the bidding of Beynor? The notion is laughable.'

Sir Vargus stared out at the river and spoke in a voice full of suppressed tension. 'Those of us from the Firedrake country think otherwise. When Archwizard Fring Bulegosset was on his deathbed in Thornmont Town, he confessed that Beynor had admitted responsibility for the atrocity in a wind-spoken conversation with him. Fring also said that certain other persons of high rank knew that the attack would occur and did nothing to warn the king and queen.'

'Codswallop!' Gansing scoffed. 'Treasonous drivel! You should know better than to talk of such rubbish to the Sovereign.'

'Did this dying wizard name the other conspirators?' Conrig asked Vargus.

The knight's reply was reluctant. 'If he did, no one in Firedrake country will admit to knowing. I myself have no idea who they might have been.'

'Perhaps I can ask King Somarus when we dine tonight,' Conrig said, eyeing the earl marshal obliquely.

'Please don't, Your Grace!' Vargus's face had gone ashen. 'The rumors are very vague, and the tragedy took place many years ago. Our king would be distressed if he were reminded of it on a night when the mood should be one of joyful anticipation.'

'Oh, very well,' the Sovereign said. 'I suppose it would be bad form to speak of such sad things just before a betrothal. And as you said, Sir Vargus – it happened a long time ago. Let's go back to the castle. I've seen enough here. You and Sir Gansing ride well behind us. I wish to speak privily with the earl marshal. We are well aware of the track's hazards now.'

Both of them trotted off ahead of the Didionites. After a while, Conrig slowed and let Beorbrook draw up beside him. 'What did you think of the byplay between the knights, Parli?'

'It only confirms what we already know, sire. Didion is split into rival factions that would be at each other's throats – and ours as well – if the Salka threat didn't keep them united.'

'No, there's more,' the king said thoughtfully. 'The ambush on the River Malle was never satisfactorily explained. The Salka monsters hadn't ventured so far inland in centuries, and there was no easy way for them to have known about the annual progress of the royal barge upstream – unless a human confederate told them. Beynor certainly had a hand in the affair. He was exiled to the Dawntide Isles and had the opportunity to arouse the Salka. But revenge on his part seems a weak motive for slaughtering the entire royal family of Didion. There had to be a link with Somarus. He was the one who benefited, and I find it significant that he declared Beynor to be an outlaw after the fall of Moss. But what did *Beynor* hope to gain by killing Honigalus and his wife and children?'

The old general shook his head. 'Power of some kind. We may never know the truth of it unless he resurfaces. If Beynor had hopes of using the Salka to take back Moss from his sister Queen Ullanoth, he miscalculated badly.'

'I never heard the tale of the dying archwizard before,' the king remarked. 'Fascinating – Fring and Beynor and Somarus conspiring together, using the Salka to pull off a stupendous coup.'

'The Archwizard Fring was once a crony of our old nemesis Kilian Blackhorse, you know. And *he* restored his lost fortunes very handsomely when Somarus took Didion's throne.'

'Kilian, that silver-tongued whoreson!' Conrig growled. 'It's a good thing he's kept out of my way during these strategy meetings at Boarsden. I realize he's kept Somarus from flirting with rebellion. Still, I don't think I could control myself if we two were in the same room.'

'As Didion's Lord Chancellor, Kilian Blackhorse may well show up for the betrothal feast,' Beorbrook said. 'If so, you'll have to swallow your bile and put a cool face on it, sire.'

'Don't tell me how to behave, damn your eyes!'

But Conrig knew that his friend was right, and the knowledge made him sulky. Mulling over Kilian's spectacular treason, he was distracted from thinking further about Beynor and the Salka ambush; and so the Sovereign of Blenholme and Earl Marshal Parlian Beorbrook rode on together without speaking further of that matter.

For over three hundred years, the distinguished Beorbrook family of warriors had held Cathra's most critical frontier castle, which guarded the only reliable route between Cathra and its northern neighbors. The marshal's two elder sons, both able warriors, had lost their lives in the Edict of Sovereignty massacre, leaving only the third son, Count

Olvan Elktor, in line to inherit Beorbrook Hold and the vital duties that went with it. Though goodhearted and stalwart, Olvan was acknowledged to be too slow of wit to assume the important office held by his father. The earl marshal had been resigned to having the honor pass out of his family upon his death, when the shocking reappearance of Maudrayne Northkeep, along with her son Dyfrig, changed everything.

To the surprise of many, Conrig declared that he would be magnanimous to his divorced Tarnian wife, even though she had accused him of possessing windtalent. The king refused to acknowledge Dyfrig as his son (there was no proof his mother had cohabited with another, but neither was there proof that she had not); but in a great compromise intended to placate the Tarnians while preserving the dynastic status quo, Conrig decreed that whatever Dyfrig's heritage, he would be accepted into the ranks of Cathran royalty, placed third in the line of succession, and styled prince. The boy was to be adopted by Parlian Beorbrook and would inherit the office of Earl Marshal of the Realm if he proved competent.

It was an ingenious bargain that had defused several potentially ugly situations – including the ambitions of Duke Feribor Blackhorse, who was thereby demoted to fourth in the succession. But the bargain was also one that Conrig subsequently came to regret with all his heart and soul.

Prince Dyfrig Beorbrook was now an adult in Cathran law and the apple of his adoptive father's eye, while Conrig's feelings toward the young man were clouded with dark misgivings. He knew well enough that Dyfrig was his own first-born son, conceived while Conrig was still wed to Maudrayne, and the legitimate heir to the throne in spite of the royal divorce. But the king had only found out about the boy's birth four years after marrying Risalla Mallburn of Didion. The twin sons born to her were already named first and second in the royal succession when Dyfrig's existence became known. To have placed Risalla's sons behind the son of Maudrayne, when Dyfrig's parentage could not be officially verified, would have affronted hotheaded King Somarus beyond all endurance. (He was Risalla's full brother, while his more rational predecessor Honigalus had only been her half-brother.) The compromise placing Dyfrig third in the succession had been intended to strengthen the allegiance of Didion, while still appeasing Maude's uncle, Sernin Donorvale, the powerful High Sealord of Tarn.

In recent years, as Dyfrig matured into a young man of conspicuous intelligence and courage, Conrig became all too aware that certain influential persons in both Cathra and Tarn considered Beorbrook's adopted son to be a much better candidate for the Iron Crown of Sovereignty than either Orrion or Corodon: the Prince Heritor was thought to be worthy but colorless, while his younger twin was a hare-brained roisterer. The earl marshal's loyalty to the Sovereign was absolute and he swore that he had inculcated Dyfrig with the selfsame virtue. However, Beorbrook was an old man, with no aspirations other than service to his liege. The king brooded about what would happen when his faithful friend died and young Dyfrig became the principal military leader of Cathra, second only to the Sovereign himself.

Conrig Wincantor was only six-and-forty years old, in robust health despite the spiritual corrosion occasioned by fending off his many enemies. Once the Salka were soundly thrashed and sequestered in the unimportant corner of the island they'd earlier overrun, he intended to turn his eyes to the Continent. The nation of Andradh, lacking a strong central government, was in his opinion ripe for the taking.

But only if the Sovereignty of Blenholme remained firm under his leadership.

Only if *all* of Conrig's domestic enemies, real and potential, were neutralized.

The opportunity to solve the irksome problem of Dyfrig had come unexpectedly to the king a sennight earlier, following a particularly acrimonious meeting of the Council of War. The Cathran and Tarnian battle-leaders, whose idle forces were chafing for action, wanted to launch immediate attacks against the entrenched Salka horde from both land and sea; while the Didionites, who better understood the perils of fighting pitched battles in the awful Green Morass, insisted on holding back so long as the inhuman foe advanced no farther this year.

Conrig was being pressed for a final decision but knew he lacked important facts about the monsters' situation. *Why* had they stalled? Were they waiting for some new magical weaponry before advancing? Had numbers of them fallen ill? Were they expecting reinforcements from Moss? There were too many unanswered questions.

At this point Prince Dyfrig had approached the Sovereign in private and proposed leading a hazardous but well-thought-out scouting expedition into Salka-held territory. Since ships of the Sovereignty's Joint Fleet, sailing along the north coast of the island, were too far from the concentration of monsters to obtain useful intelligence through scrying, Conrig's strategists had been forced to rely on vague reports from overly cautious Didionite scouts and the weak-talented oversight of that country's wizards. Earlier attempts by sizable Cathran reconnaissance teams to penetrate the morass had been total disasters. The men had fallen victim to wild animals and hostile terrain, and the few survivors had no useful findings to report.

But now Dyfrig volunteered to try something different. He wanted to lead a small, elite group that would travel very quickly and secretly to a vantage point in the Gulo Highlands overlooking the Beacon Valley, a rugged region that the clumsy, water-loving amphibians were unlikely to have occupied. Once the little band gained the heights, its powerful windsearcher would be able to oversee the enemy position in relative safety; intelligence could then be windspoken directly to Lord Stergos without relaying it through the biased Didionites.

Instead of scoffing at the bold idea, Conrig seized on it. If the mission succeeded, the Army of the Sovereignty would obtain invaluable firsthand news about the enemy. If it failed, Dyfrig would either be viewed as an overreaching young fool – or a dead hero.

Conrig had authorized Dyfrig's scheme without consulting the earl marshal. Only the king and his trusted brother Stergos, the Royal Alchymist, knew the true goal of the mission was direct windtalent oversight of the Salka invaders. Everyone else, including Dyfrig's adoptive father, believed the prince was traveling only to Timberton Fortress, near Black Hare Lake, where he would personally question local informants about the movements of the enemy.

'Sire, there are riders coming from Boarsden Castle to meet us. Two of them, at a rather brisk clip.' Parlian Beorbrook still had the eyesight of an eagle, and a moment later he added, 'One of them is a local knight and the other is your royal brother.'

'I hope nothing's happened to delay those boys of mine.' Conrig's tone was sour. 'If we have to postpone this damned betrothal ceremony and magnify Somarus's resentment further, I'll wring their necks!'

The king put the spur to his mount and Beorbrook galloped after. But when the four riders met in a cloud of dust, Conrig was relieved to see the Royal Alchymist's beardless face alight with happiness.

'My liege,' Stergos cried, 'I've received important tidings on the wind! From Prince Dyfrig!'

'Then let's you and I and the earl marshal speak of it privily,' the king said in a pointed manner. The disappointed Didionite warrior backed his horse away.

'Is my dear son well?' the earl marshal inquired.

'Oh, yes!' Stergos was fairly hopping out of the saddle with excitement. 'He and his men have learned that the Salka are withdrawing – streaming northward in vast numbers.'

'God's Blood!' the Sovereign cried. He managed to supress his inappropriate consternation just in time. Not only had the young wretch survived his feckless adventure, but it seemed as though he had improbably covered himself with glory as well.

Stergos rushed on. 'Vra-Erol Wintersett, the army's Chief Windsearcher, was able to scry the huge host of monsters at Beacon Lake. His oversight was not crystal clear, but the direction of the Salka troop movement was unmistakable. They're retreating toward the sea.'

'The Brother scried this from Timberton Fortress?' The earl marshal was incredulous.

'Nay, my lord.' The Royal Alchymist's exuberance faltered. 'Prince Dyfrig led his party into the morass as far as the Raging River, deep in the wilderness. They were only about thirty leagues from the Salka position when they made their reconnaissance.'

Parlian Beorbrook groaned. 'Zeth save us – the young fool!'

'The Brother windsearcher is absolutely certain of this retreat?' Conrig demanded.

'He is. And there's more.' Stergos hesitated. 'It seems almost unbelievable, now that I think further about it. But – well –'

'Speak up, Gossy!' the king said harshly. 'Stop your damned dithering!'

The Royal Alchymist blinked. His brother's temper had grown increasingly short since the start of the massive Salka invasion. Unlike the earlier forays by amphibian forces against human coastal towns, it had caught the Sovereignty completely by surprise and shaken Conrig's heretofore invincible confidence. Stergos had tried not to take the king's emotional explosions personally, and he now spoke as calmly as he could.

'Dyfrig claims that he knows why the monsters halted at Beacon Lake. It seems there are other inhuman inhabitants of the Green Morass that the Salka were unaware of. That were unknown to the Didionites as well – save as half-forgotten legends. The mysterious creatures are said to be huge and very ferocious. Dyfrig believes that they attacked the Salka host, wreaked havoc on them, and stopped their advance.'

'Bloody hell,' Conrig murmured. 'And the prince and his men actually saw these things with their own eyes?'

'Not exactly,' Stergos admitted. 'They encountered strange tracks supposedly made by one of the creatures, and claw marks high in the trees. They also found a huge bear that had been torn to pieces and devoured by an unknown predator – and in its skull was one of the attacker's broken teeth. It's nearly the length of a man's hand and almost resembles a Salka tusk – save that it's golden-yellow in color, like a sharpened topaz gem, rather than glassy clear.'

The earl marshal said, 'But can they be sure that the bear wasn't brought down by others of its kind, or by some human hunter? This so-called tooth might be naught but a primitive weapon of some sort, made of something like obsidian.'

'The expedition guide is a Didionite fur-trapper,' Stergos said, 'the most experienced man Prince Dyfrig could hire in Timberton, where men of that stripe congregate. This fellow is adamant that the bear was killed by something called a

Morass Worm, a sort of dragon without wings that was thought to have gone extinct centuries ago. The worms are intelligent – and they possess talent, just as the Salka do.'

Conrig let loose a sharp obscenity. 'Giant worms? Dragons? Have they all lost their minds? Are we supposed to believe a tale spun by an ignorant Diddly stump-jumper?'

'Sire,' said the earl marshal, '*something* caused the Salka army's lighting advance to slam to a halt over a moon ago. It wasn't the terrain. They had a clear corridor through the morass: wetlands and rivers and lakes, perfect for such creatures. They could have reached the valley of the Upper Malle if they'd kept moving, and would have caught Didion's forces flatfooted before troops from Cathra or Tarn could reinforce them. Luckily for us, the brutes stopped dead in their tracks. We've speculated about some unknown disease decimating their ranks. But they didn't withdraw at the end of Thunder Moon, when they first stalled, so that explanation doesn't hold up. Dyfrig's does.'

The king's jaw muscles worked. He said, 'And you, Gossy? What do you think?'

'What Prince Dyfrig says is logical,' said the Royal Alchymist. He added with enthusiasm, 'And what a wonderful stroke of fate it is! The Salka are all but defeated. We won't have to fight them in that hellish bog country. You can announce the great news to Somarus and the generals and the Tarnian Sealords at supper tonight. Our warriors – all of the Sovereignty's warriors – can go home for the winter.'

Conrig thought: And I shall not lead Blenholme's army against the inhuman foe after all! The momentous battle that might have solidified our uneasy political unity is once again postponed . . .

Aloud, he said, 'The Salka withdrawal must be verified before we allow the troops to disperse. This apparent retreat might be only a feint. I'll announce that the findings of Dyfrig's party are only preliminary – but very hopeful.'

Beorbrook sighed. 'I suppose that's wise, sire.'

'If numbers of Salka are retreating into the sea, the fact can perhaps be confirmed by a Tarnian sloop or two carrying windsearchers along the north coast. The High Sealord must order boats out from Ice Haven at once.' Conrig addressed the Royal Alchymist. 'Gossy, I want you to contact the wind-speaking Brother who accompanies Dyfrig. Order the expedition to return to Boarsden immediately.'

'They're already on their way. But even coming at break-neck speed with little sleep and many changes of horse, it might take them four or five days to get here.'

'They are to bring with them both the Didionite guide and the alleged tooth, along with whatever other evidence they may have collected concerning these Morass Worms.'

'My talent isn't strong enough to bespeak Vra-Odos directly right away,' Stergos said to his brother. 'Even though I am a Doctor Arcanorum with a fair windspeaking facility, Prince Dyfrig's party is too far distant to hear my unfocused wind-hail. I must wait until they are closer – or until Vra-Odos calls out to *me* on a narrowly aimed thread of mental speech.'

'Then see that you keep your mental ears well pricked!' the king said curtly. 'Let me know just as soon as you're able to pass on my orders. And add another, which is even more important: Dyfrig is to make certain that the Didionite is closely guarded and tells no one about the presence of the Morass Worms. This charge I lay upon the prince with the full weight of my authority. It goes without saying that the Cathrans in the party will also be sworn to absolute secrecy.'

Beorbrook was puzzled. 'But, sire! Why?'

'Fighting Salka monsters in raids along the shores of our island in recent years has tested the courage of our warriors to the utmost,' Conrig replied. 'Think, Parli! The Didionites, especially, are terrified of the moonstone sorcery wielded by the great trolls and their habit of devouring their foes slowly, while yet alive.' A cynical smile twisted his mouth. 'Who can tell what our worthy allies might do if they learned they might now also have to battle dragons to save our beleaguered homeland?'

'Who can tell,' the earl marshal said somberly, 'what any of us would do?'

FIVE

'TO YOU, GIVER OF OUR MOST VALUED GIFT, FROM THOSE WHO REVERED YOUR LATE FATHER, WE SEND GREETINGS ON THE WIND AND ASK IN ALL FRIENDSHIP THAT YOU RESPOND.'

There was no reply to the combined bespoken hail of the Salka Eminences. Their previous fifty-odd windshouts, sent out at regular intervals throughout a very long day, had been equally futile. The Four were gathered on the highest turret of Fenguard Castle in Moss. The sun was sinking into a billow of fiery clouds on the horizon above the Little Fen.

'I think the depraved sea-squirt must be dead or gone away to the Continent,' the Supreme Warrior said. 'There's been no news of him for years. We've blanketed the entire island with generalized windcalls and the accumulated pain-debt is giving me a hellish headache. I'm ready to pack it up.' He twiddled the minor sigil that hung about his neck on a golden chain. The moonstone was a Longspeaker, and Ugusawnn and his colleagues had been using it jointly to channel their cautiously phrased salutation toward the human sorcerer Beynor, wherever he might be.

'The Great Light was specific,' the First Judge reminded

the others. 'Beynor is our best hope for gaining access to the
Demon Seat Moon Crag. Would the Light have said this if
the groundling sorcerer were dead?'

'Who knows?' The ancient Conservator of Wisdom had
slumped into a heap on the parapet, spent by unaccustomed
pain. 'Colleagues, if you intend to continue, you must do it
without me.'

'Beynor may be alive and well,' Master Shaman Kalawnn
said, 'but unwilling to speak to us for reasons of his own.
He and Ugusawnn hardly parted in cordial circumstances.
And the disappearance of Queen Ullanoth's sigils from
Rothbannon's tomb before Beynor could turn them over to
us as he'd promised must have been a terrible disappointment to him.'

'As it was to us!' growled the Warrior. Several of the
queen's sigils had been Great Stones, which the Salka coveted
because they had none of their own – save for the paradoxical Potency.

'Furthermore,' the Master Shaman said, 'if Beynor has
been able to windwatch our activities over the years, he
might well know that we were able to activate the Stone of
Stones without his help – even though he cannot scry the
sigil itself. He has thus been deprived of both of his most
crucial bargaining assets. No doubt he believes that there can
no longer be a fruitful business relationship between himself
and the Salka –'

'And now, when we call to him on the wind after ignoring
him for so long,' the Conservator interjected, 'he might think
we're up to no good. Is this what you're implying, Kalawnn?'

'Precisely, Wise One. I believe we must modify our hail if
we hope to get an answer: make it plain from the start that
we have something to offer aside from empty protestations
of friendship.'

The Supreme Warrior said nothing, while the First Judge

grunted in assent and refreshed himself with a cup of viscous ambergris cordial and a fat, lively crustacean.

The Conservator of Wisdom said, 'What do you suggest, Master Shaman?'

Kalawnn touched his throat with a tentacle digit. The sigil inside his crop sent out a brief pulse of light. 'The offer must be very appealing. Irresistible, in fact. Perhaps his own choice of several dozen useful minor sigils, first touched by the Potency to abolish their pain-link.'

'Ahroo!' the Supreme Warrior bellowed in outrage. '*Several dozen* stones? Once he learns of the limitation, he'll demand scores of the things! Even hundreds! We already have too few lesser sigils to ensure a decisive victory over the humans.'

The Judge said, 'Let's not tell Beynor about the limitation on abolished sigils. Let him discover the catch when it's too late, as the other human sorcerer did.'

'I don't like that idea at all,' Kalawnn said. 'What if he demands a demonstration before agreeing to work with us? No . . . honesty is the best course. If we can convince him of our good faith.'

'We return to the thorny issue of trust,' the Conservator said. 'Why should he believe that we'll keep our word this time – after Ugusawnn's earlier mistakes? Realistically, I don't see how we can make this plan work.'

'There *is* something else we might offer Beynor,' Kalawnn said. 'Prior to the destruction of our Dawntide Citadel by the tarnblaze bombshells of the human warships, I studied a certain archival tablet – the one that Beynor was so interested in himself. While my scholarship was interrupted by the battle, I did manage to glean some interesting bits of data before we were forced to evacuate. To make a long story short, I believe that the Greatest Stone might be capable of annulling Beynor's curse directly, making it possible for him to use sigils once again in the normal way. He might already know this!'

'A lengthy logical jump,' the First Judge observed, frowning. 'And one the groundling conjurer might prudently hesitate to make.'

'Not if he already knows the proper conjuration procedure,' said Kalawnn. 'It might well have been written down on a portion of the tablet that I was prevented from reading by the tumult of battle.'

'It's worth a try,' the Judge said. 'We could at least make the offer. What can we lose? Beynor might not even be alive . . .'

'Oh, very well.' The Warrior spoke in a resigned rumble. He took a firm grip on his Longspeaker sigil. 'Let's unite our talents again.'

'I'll join with you for one last attempt,' the Conservator said.

After a brief consultation to get the wording right (for there was always a chance that such a broad outcry might be overheard by the wrong persons) the Four closed their enormous glowing eyes and sent forth a generalized shout on the wind.

'TO YOU, GIVER OF OUR MOST VALUED GIFT, WE SEND GREETINGS AND OFFER THIS SINCERE PROPOSAL: ASSIST US IN A CERTAIN MATTER, AND WE WILL GRANT YOU FREE ACCESS TO THE GIFT, WHICH WE BELIEVE IS CAPABLE OF LIFTING YOUR DOLEFUL BURDEN. WE WILL ALSO GIVE YOU OTHER ITEMS OF GREAT VALUE AS A TOKEN OF OUR GRATITUDE AND ESTEEM.'

The Eminences disengaged their minds and waited.

Master Kalawnn found that he was holding his breath. Beynor *was* alive. He was certain of it. Over the years a feather-light, distant presence had invaded his sleep from time to time in the winter months – scrutinizing his dreams, asking him questions, attempting to exert subtle coercion that would carry over into his wakeful life. The Salka shaman had fended off the dream-intruder; but he knew it must have been Beynor, who had been an expert in that rarest of natural talents.

'So answer us!' Kalawnn broadcast his own silent entreaty to the strange, tormented human being who had almost been his friend. 'We need one another, Beynor, and this time there will be no double-dealing, rudeness or condescension on our part. We will treat with you as an equal and share the power of the Known Potency if you play fair with us. At least let us explain what we want and show you what we have to offer.'

Kalawnn listened, as did the others. And just as the sun descended behind the clouds, a gossamer thread of wind-speech seemed to emanate from the vanishing solar orb itself.

Hello again. If you have anything to say, be quick about it. I'm very busy.

Before the advent of the Sovereignty pacified the unruly interior of Didion and made safe the Wold Road leading from Cathra to Tarn, Castlemont Fortress was the only reasonably comfortable refuge for travelers between Great Pass and Boarsden. Its guest facilities had once been primitive: a stonewalled enclosure at the foot of the fort's knoll accommodated pack teams and their drivers, while simple bedchambers and a modest dining area located in the keep above served more fastidious guests.

When Somarus Mallburn assumed Didion's throne and accepted vassalage in the Sovereignty, the robber-barons and brigands who had infested the Wold with his tacit approval were largely put out of business. Traffic over the pass multiplied tenfold. As a consequence, the hostelry at Castlemont also expanded, welcoming ever-increasing numbers of travelers. Its shrewd castellan Shogadus, now elevated to the rank of viscount, became famous for his hospitality and grew exceedingly wealthy. It was his custom to greet personally and oversee the settling in of illustrious guests who were willing to pay a premium price for luxurious accommodations.

Among these, arriving late on a certain afternoon in Harvest Moon, was a solitary wayfarer who claimed to be Master Lund Farfield, a lawyer journeying from Cala City to Didion's capital of Holt Mallburn. He was a tall, slightly stooped man with hooded eyes and gaunt features that were sun-damaged and deeply creased. Silvery hair gave him a misleading appearance of middle age. Beneath the inevitable patina of mud and dust, his riding attire was sumptuous. He was also girded with a sword fit for royalty and rode a blood horse with a silver-studded saddle and bridle. The viscount and his chief steward Crick decided that the alleged lawyer must be a high-ranking Cathran nobleman traveling incognito – perhaps a court official on his way to the great ongoing Council of War at Boarsden Castle.

'I would like the best quarters in your dormitorium,' Master Lund said in a peremptory manner as he was greeted by the noble host. 'Price is no object.'

'Alas, messire!' Viscount Shogadus was regretful. 'Our finest suite has already been reserved for the three royal sons of the Sovereign of Blenholme, who are expected to arrive later this evening, along with their retainers.'

Well, well! thought the guest, doing his best to preserve an expression of well-bred vexation. He said, 'Most disappointing, my lord.'

'However, we have another chamber, even more splendidly appointed than that reserved for the princes, even though it be a trifle smaller.' Shogadus gave an ingratiating smile. 'Since you journey alone, Master Lund, perhaps you'll find it suitable. It is near to the rooms occupied by the Lord Lieutenant of Cathra and his family – high above the bustle of the inner ward and having a fine view of the countryside and the sunset.'

'Show me,' the visitor commanded. He thought: More and more intriguing! Why are all these distinguished Cathrans breaking their journey here on the same day?

Accompanied by a house varlet who carried his saddlebags, the man who called himself Master Lund followed Lord Castlemont and the steward Crick to a chamber in the west tower of the fortress. It had glazed casement windows, a fireplace, thick Incayo carpets on the floor, a tester bed with down pillows and comforter, and its own private jakes.

'It will do,' Lund decided, then tipped the steward a silver mark and inclined his head politely to Castlemont's owner. He ignored the varlet, who scuttled out after opening the window.

'How long will you stay with us, messire?' Crick inquired.

'One night.'

'There will be an evening meal for special guests in the great hall at the eighth hour,' Shogadus said. 'Or if you wish, a repast can be brought to you here.'

'It will be my pleasure to join you at table, my lord. Thank you for all your courtesy.'

Beynor locked the door when the others were gone, opened one of his bags, and took out a flask and a gilt cup. He had acquired his fine new mount, several changes of clothing, and accoutrements suited to his taste while passing through the great Cathran city of Beorbrook. As a sorcerer, he had no need to worry about money. It had been necessary for him to live modestly during the long years of searching for the lost sigils, so as not to attract unwelcome attention from officials in Elktor, but the time of deprivation was over. Things would be very different from now on.

He sipped mellow old apple brandy and watched the sun descend in the hazy, yellowish sky. The Salka had finally

stopped their incessant wind-yammering at him. Stupid
brutes – apparently too chickenhearted to use the Potency
to abolish sigil-pain even after Kalawnn had managed to activate the Greatest Stone. Perhaps they feared the Lights would
exact some terrible vengeance if they were deprived of their
vile treats!

How much had their Master Shaman learned about the
enigmatic sigil over the years? Obviously, Kalawnn was still
ignorant of some of the stone's secrets (as was Beynor
himself). The sorcerer's imperfect oversight of Kalawnn's
dreams had confirmed that years ago – along with the inconvenient fact that the Salka's greatest shaman now kept the
Potency secure inside his own gizzard. Kalawnn thought that
it had bonded to him alone, just as other activated sigils did,
and could be touched by no other person.

But Beynor knew that the stone had *not* bonded to the
Salka Master Shaman. The Potency was unique in many
ways. Once it had been brought to life, it was immortal and
it bonded to no one; any person who knew its manner of
working might handle and command it. The one who had
made it over a thousand years earlier had intended it as a
tool for good; but he had never activated the Stone of Stones,
since he came to realize that it could just as readily be used
for evil.

As Beynor was well aware, even though he'd long since
given up hope of getting his hands on it.

He had been mildly curious when the Eminent Four began
calling to him on the wind earlier in the day, but not so
curious that he would have risked a reply. Kalawnn, for one,
was adept enough to follow a bespoken windtrace back to
its source. Beynor was not sure whether any Salka could
scry him at long distance and read his lips. He doubted it.
Still, it would be unwise to let them know his whereabouts
until he found out what they were up to.

He had scried their army in Didion as soon as he crossed
Great Pass and the overview of the Green Morass became
more or less clear to his superlative windsight. The sight of
the monsters' precipitate retreat puzzled him even more than
news of their earlier invasion had. Although the Salka were
very effective water-fighters (being able to breathe through
their skins as well as through lungs, they could remain
submerged indefinitely), Beynor had not thought them
capable of such a large-scale military action on land. Piddling
border raids or coastal smash-and-grabs were more their
style. Those had been going on sporadically for years.

But somehow the Salka had chosen an ideal strike route
for this attack. It should have carried their force of nearly
fifty thousand warriors straight into Didion's heartland. Their
abrupt halt and belated withdrawal left Beynor mystified.
Would they go back to Moss now, or had they another plan
in mind?

It was a matter he'd have to mull over. But first, a survey
of the fortress's inhabitants – and then an overview of the
three Cathran princes, who had not yet arrived.

From his room, Beynor scried Castlemont for other adept
practitioners he might need to beware of. He found two
Didionite wizards of modest talent who were probably
members of the viscount's staff, and an elderly Brother of
Zeth taking his ease in the inner ward's walled herb garden
in the company of two Cathran noblewomen. Reading their
lips as they conversed, Beynor learned that the ladies were
Countess Orvada Brackenfield, wife of Cathra's powerful
Lord Lieutenant, and her daughter Nyla. The Brother was
their household alchymist Vra-Binon, who had accompanied
the family to a secret rendezvous with Orrion Wincantor.

Interesting . . .

None of the magickers inside the fort seemed likely to be
able to detect the windtraces of Beynor's scrying, so he began

to search the highroad between Castlemont and the pass for
the cavalcade of the Cathran princes. He found them still
more than an hour's journey distant. Knowing little of the
young royals, he spent some time watching them. His vision
was mute (only a Subtle Loophole sigil, such as the one once
owned by his sister Ullanoth, evinced an oversight with all
sounds attending) and the faces of the royal youths were
hidden for much of the time by their wide-brimmed hats,
inhibiting lip-reading; nevertheless he was able to identify
each prince and gain a slight understanding of their characters.

Prince Heritor Orrion was the most interesting. He had
apparently suffered some wound to his right arm, which was
heavily wrapped and held in a sling. His manner was one of
feverish excitement and he kept urging his companions to
hurry, even though their mounts were jaded and drooping
after what obviously had been a long day's ride.

I wonder why the Heritor is meeting the Brackenfield
family on the sly? Beynor asked himself. The gossip in Elktor
was that Orrion was to be betrothed to Princess Hyndry
Mallburn, the widow of Duke Garal's son. But the winsome
Lady Nyla seemed to be in a state of twittery anticipation.

As Beynor considered the implications of this, the final
hail of the Salka Eminences came faintly into his mind. He
muttered an obscenity. So the monsters wanted a favor of
him, did they? And nothing small, considering what they
offered in return! From his own studies of the Salka archives,
Beynor was virtually certain that the Potency *would* abolish
the Lights' curse on him; but the sigil had seemed hopelessly
out of reach.

I can't ignore them this time, he decided. I must take the
risk of answering.

He spoke on the wind: 'Hello again. If you have anything
to say, be quick about it. I'm very busy.'

The precisely directed response came from Master Kalawnn, his old mentor.

Beynor, I greet you after long years of silence and hope you are in good health.

'I am. Let's not waste time in pleasantries.'

We presume you know about our recent military incursion into Didion.

'I also know that your army is now fleeing like woodrats before wildfire and plunging headlong into the sea.'

All part of our strategy, dear friend. We withdraw from one position only to renew the attack even more fiercely in another.

'Ah. I see . . .'

What you may not be aware of is that earlier in the year we sent an expedition to the Barren Lands, where we located one of the two lost Moon Crags that provide raw material for the manufacture of new sigils.

'I know your warriors had a fight up there with the Grand Shaman of Tarn. He whipped your arses with his sorcery, and the crag was mostly pulverized during the ruckus. Too bad.'

We salvaged a small amount of useful mineral. As a matter of fact, our lapidaries are fashioning two Great Stones from it even as we bespeak one another. We intend to employ them as weapons in our intensified attack on the Sovereignty.

'Good luck. But what do you want of me, Kalawnn?'

We have just discovered the location of the second Moon Crag. It lies on a mountaintop in Cathra. We were informed by the Great Lights that YOU are the appropriate person to climb the mountain and bring us more sigil-making mineral from its summit.'

'Me?!'

If you agree, we invite you to come to Royal Fenguard as soon as possible. I myself will use the Potency's sorcery to free you of the Lights' curse before you set out to fetch moonstone specimens for us. When you bring us the raw mineral, we will reward you with a goodly number of minor sigils to advance your own ambitions. A Strength-Giver would be useful, wouldn't it? And maybe a Shapechanger or Concealer to disguise you from unfriendly observers? We are prepared to be very generous.

Beynor was stunned. The slimy imbeciles had no notion of what they were offering. Minor sigils? He'd take them, of course, to augment the Great Stones of his trove . . . and thus enable him to steal the Potency itself from Kalawnn!

But what if the Stone of Stones didn't abolish the curse? The Salka archival tablet he'd studied had given tantalizing hints, but no certainty. Moonstone sorcery ultimately derived from the Beaconfolk. If the curse still held, using even a sigil rendered pain-free by the Potency might bring down the wrath of the Lights upon him.

There's no simple solution to this dilemma, Beynor realized. Yet –

Do you understand our proposal? the Salka shaman asked.

Beynor said, 'We attempted to strike a bargain and work together years ago, Master Kalawnn. Regrettably, the collaboration fell apart due to Ugusawnn's hostility. If I agree to work with you again, there must be solid guarantees. And your Supreme Warrior will have no part in the operation.'

The Warrior repents his crass behavior, and we other Eminent Ones are willing to be magnanimous. In our earlier alliance, it was agreed that the Salka would take back High Blenholme Island, our ancestral home, using sigil magic. We would then assist you to conquer the nations of the Continent. Does this scenario still meet with your approval?

'It does.'

So are we agreed? You will help us to obtain fresh sigil-making materials?

'I can do nothing for you until I finish certain urgent business of my own. Even then, the terms of the new agreement must be clarified to our mutual satisfaction. I tell you here and now that the gift of a handful of minor sigils is totally inadequate.'

This can be negotiated.

'Where is this Moon Crag mountain? Is it difficult of access?'

It lies in the range you call Dextral, above Swan Lake, and would not be hard for a human to approach and climb. I won't be more specific until we speak face to face and come to an agreement.

'I don't intend to discuss your proposition further until I'm satisfied that I won't endanger my life or liberty by meeting with you.'

I can assure –

'Look here, Kalawnn. I said that I was busy with other matters. Consult your fellow-Eminences. Work out a scheme whereby you and I and one other Eminence – excluding Ugusawnn! – can at least meet safely to hammer out the terms of the agreement. It will have to be a generous one. Bespeak me again with a general hail two or three days from now, around sunset. Needless to say, I won't be staying long in the place where I am now.'

I understand. I will develop a plan acceptable to all of us. Farewell.

The windthread snapped, but Beynor had already traced it along most of its course. It led directly toward Fenguard in Moss. If the second Moon Crag was situated in the eastern Dextrals, the Salka leaders could gain access to it only through a full-scale invasion of Cathra. Even then, their amphibian physique was unsuited to rock scrambling. Using a trust-worthy human confederate was the only reasonable option.

That the Great Lights seemed to have recommended *his* services to the monsters was peculiar and perhaps even ominous, given that they had imposed the curse on him in the first place. It would be the height of folly to act hastily in this matter.

Beynor sipped brandy and watched the sun go down, until

he caught sight of a train of torch-bearing riders approaching the fortress from the southwest. It had to be the sons of Conrig Ironcrown.

'I ought to find out more about these princes,' he decided, 'since their father must play a crucial rôle in my plans.'

He set aside the cup and left his room, intending to get a good look at the three young men upon their arrival.

Prince Orrion followed his brother Vra-Bramlow from the Castlemont keep to the herb garden within the outer ward. It was surrounded by stone walls seven feet high on all sides in order to trap sunlight and shield the valued plants from cold winds, and had a sturdy oaken gate, which the royal novice unlatched.

'She awaits you within,' Bramlow said. 'There are lanterns lit to dispel the twilight gloom and to . . . assist you in your revelation. Certain rooms within the keep overlook the garden, so I'll remain outside and conjure a spell of couverture to defeat anyone who might try to spy on you. You'll have half an hour with her at most before we are to dine privately with her parents.'

'I understand. Thank you for arranging everything, Bram.' Orrion slipped into the garden and closed the door behind him.

A medley of rich odors hung in the evening air – lavender, hill-thyme, tea-sage, melilot, some sort of mint, even the perfume of late-blooming musk-roses. The herb beds were neatly organized, separated by narrow paths. Nyla had been sitting on a bench beneath a small apple tree heavy with nearly ripened fruit, head bowed and hands folded in her lap. She wore a pale blue gown with a cloak of fine white wool. As the latch clicked she jumped to her feet and ran to him with a glad cry. Her long unbound hair, the color of cinnamon, flew behind her like a banner gleaming in the lantern-light.

'Orrion! Oh, love, I thought we'd never see each other again.'

'Nyla –' His voice broke and his eyes filled. He embraced her with both his whole arm and the truncated limb, which was now free of its sling but still disguised with a grain-stuffed gauntlet simulating the missing member. 'My dearest, my darling love.' They kissed and clung together until finally he released her and said, 'We have only a little time before we must join the others. I have so much to explain – including why I asked you to meet me here at Castlemont. And I must also show you something and ask you an all-important question.'

'Of course.' She sensed the unease in his voice and the joy faded from her face.

He took her hand and led her back to the bench, seating himself near one of the iron lanterns. 'I feared you would not come. That your parents would forbid it.'

'Father resisted my entreaties. But I told him I'd never take food again if he and Mother ignored your urgent summons and prevented our meeting. My heart told me that something tremendous had happened, and there might yet be a chance for us . . .' She trailed off into silence.

He took a deep breath of the scented air. 'There is. Listen now without interrupting, sweetheart, for what I must tell you is difficult and frightening. Yet if you can accept it bravely, I will be the happiest man on earth.' He pulled off the glove and began to unwind the disguising bandages from his right arm. 'An improbable turn of fate has rendered me ineligible for the Throne of Sovereignty. I have been injured. I have lost my sword-hand and lower arm.'

'Oh, no!' She burst into tears.

'Hush. There is no pain. If you can summon the courage, you must look upon the wound. It is no ordinary one. May I roll up my sleeve?'

Her face was white as chalk and tears still flowed from her eyes, but they were wide open. She sat up straight. 'I will look and not swoon. I promise.'

'The sight is not so terrible, for the injury is entirely healed through magic, even though it happened less than a week ago.' He showed her the stump of the arm with its clean pad of skin and flesh showing only faint reddish lines of scarring.

'But how can this be?' she gasped. 'And you say it doesn't hurt?'

'Not at all. Listen: what I tell you now you must reveal to no one, not even your parents. I climbed a high mountain with my two brothers, intending to petition . . . certain supernatural beings for a miracle. I asked them to let it be possible for the two of us to marry, thinking that if they answered my prayer, my hardhearted father would relent from tearing us apart and cancel my betrothal to Princess Hyndry. The uncanny creatures at the mountaintop warned me that my miracle would require a heavy price. I told them I'd pay anything for you. I admit I did not expect to lose my lower right arm! But I renounce it gladly if – if you can find it in your heart to accept a mutilated man for your husband. A man who can never be king.'

Tenderly, she enclosed the stump in both of her small hands. 'I love you and want you, Orrion. It matters not a whit to me that you have no sword arm.'

'The Sovereign may condemn me to death,' Orrion said, 'or cast me into prison or banish me to some distant place. Even if he spares my life, he might forbid our union.'

'But if he does not?'

'This is why I asked you to travel here with your parents. If they will agree to it, I intend to wed you. But my honor demands that I first present myself to my father at Boarsden. There I must relinquish the title of Prince Heritor to my brother Corodon, while submitting myself to the king's mercy. You and your parents can wait here for Father's decision.'

'Surely you don't plan to tell the High King that your wound was caused by sorcery?' She was calmer now, contemplating their future.

'My brother Vra-Bramlow has thought of a plan. If it succeeds, the king and everyone else save you and my brothers and possibly Lord Stergos, the Royal Alchymist, will believe the loss of my arm was an accident, caused by my own rash misadventure, rather than the result of a magical bargain. Thus far, I've managed to conceal the severity of the injury from my own Heart Companions and from Coro's. I intend to continue the subterfuge until we reach Boarsden, so that no advance news of it will be transmitted on the wind. I'll seek the help of Lord Stergos, who has always been a kind friend to me, to hide the true nature of my wound and to plead mercy for you and me before the High King.'

Confusion clouded her features. 'And what if he forbids us to wed?'

'I don't think Father will be so cruel – or so wasteful.' Orrion's smile was mordant. 'I can still serve the Sovereignty well as a court official, even one-handed, and give you children of royal blood. As for Princess Hyndry, my twin brother Coro will happily wed her. And even more happily take up my role as Prince Heritor.'

'I – I'll pray for such a fortunate outcome.'

'Now we must go to your parents.'

They kissed, then left the walled garden. Vra-Bramlow joined them in the courtyard and all three went to dine with Count and Countess Brackenfield in their private rooms.

Beynor of Moss, whose peerless scrying ability had easily penetrated Bramlow's inexpert spell of couverture, had read the lips of the lovers and learned one of the Prince Heritor's secrets. Now, loitering unobtrusively near the staircase leading into the keep amongst a few other guests, he discovered a second, even greater secret – one that Orrion himself was unaware of.

As the prince's gaze momentarily met that of the gaunt stranger, he gave a pleasant nod of greeting and passed by –

Leaving Beynor stunned. For the sorcerer recognized what Cathra's Brothers of Zeth had evidently been unable to discern: like his father Conrig, Orrion Wincantor possessed a minute portion of uncanny talent. Its spark was unmistakable within the prince's eyes. It was evident that the young man knew nothing of his magical ability, nor did anyone else. He was doubly ineligible to inherit the throne of Cathra!

But what of his twin?

Prince Corodon would now inherit the throne. Suppose that he, too, unwittingly carried the taint? It would be easy enough for Beynor to learn the truth. All he need do was look the prince in the eye. And if both father and son were magically talented –

Beynor's plan to influence Conrig had been constrained by the king's intractable personality. He would be hellishly difficult to control, since Beynor could think of no coercive advantage to use against him. But Corodon, that shallow-minded fool, could well provide the much-needed leverage – one way or another.

If only the prince had talent . . .

'Messire?'

Beynor's stream of thought was broken by a polite voice. A castle footman had approached him. 'If you please, a fine dinner is about to be served to the guests in the great hall. Would you care to partake?'

'I would indeed,' Beynor exclaimed, clapping the fellow on the shoulder. 'Lead me to a good place at table, and I'll give you a generous token of my appreciation.'

'With pleasure, messire.'

The two of them ascended the stairs together, chatting pleasantly of inconsequential matters. Beynor showed disappointment when he was told that all three Cathran princes would dine privately, rather than with him and the other privileged guests. But there would be plenty of time tomorrow to make their acquaintance.

On a secluded hummock of dry land near Castle Morass stood a village inhabited by the uncanny small folk called the Green Men. On that night their meeting hall was brightly lit and adorned about the eaves and doorway with green boughs and late-summer flowers. Inside, a band of musicians played flute and syrinx, dulcimer and lute, hand-drum and woodblock, accompanying a chorus of high voices singing a nuptial anthem.

Crowned with purple and white asters, Induna and Deveron danced together, surrounded by a circle of well-wishers witnessing and celebrating their union. The wedding rings on their fingers were made of a shining transparent material resembling topaz. The village headman Cargalooy Tidzall, who pronounced the humans man and wife, told them that the rings were carved from the discarded teeth of Morass Worms, following an ancient Green tradition.

SIX

The suite in Boarsden Castle assigned to Somarus Mallburn, Didion's king, was situated in the huge North Tower at some distance from the rooms set aside for the other dignitaries, so that when His Majesty suffered one of his all-too-frequent drunken tantrums, the rest of the ranking guests attending the ongoing Council of War would not be disturbed.

After prudent questioning of the royal attendants, Kilian Blackhorse, Lord Chancellor of Didion, learned to his relief that tonight for a change Somarus was tranquil as well as wide awake. At the eleventh hour after noontide, when most of the castle had already retired, Kilian was admitted to the royal apartment by Kaligaskus, the Chief Lord of Chamber. Prudently, he waited near the door while being announced, in case he was refused an audience.

The monarch sat at a small table in his bedroom, clad in a nightshirt of white lawn and a shabby old sable-trimmed robe. Rain now hissed drearily on the tower's leaded windows and the air was rather chilly, but Somarus seemed not to notice, so engrossed was he in the task he'd assigned himself. Candlesticks backed by mirrors gave him bright light in a room otherwise dim. Spread out on the worktable was a collection of small boxes, tools, and other objects, along with a flagon of plum brandy and a golden goblet.

Using tweezers, Somarus lifted a dripping dead insect from a clay dish holding water. After scrutinizing this repugnant thing closely, he set it aside and began to fiddle with a small vice clamped to the table edge.

'Your Majesty?' The hushed voice of Kaligaskus caused the king to lift his head.

'What? Can't you see I'm busy, man? Go away.'

The attendant bowed. 'Lord Chancellor Kilian is here to confer with you, sire. He says the matter is urgent, else he would not have disturbed you.'

'Oh, very well,' Somarus muttered. He took up a bent piece of thin steel wire – actually a sewing needle that had been daintily modified by Duke Ranwing Boarsden's black-smith according to the king's own instructions – and fitted it into the brass-and-wood vice, tightening the jaws. 'There!' he whispered. 'Ready!' He quaffed spirits from the goblet and rubbed his hands in anticipation.

'I bid you good evening, Your Majesty.' Kilian Blackhorse had crept up with his usual sneakiness, giving the king an unpleasant start.

'I'm in the midst of something and I don't intend to set it aside,' Somarus grumbled, not bothering to look at the court official. 'And I'll not share my lifewater with you, either. Ranwing's cellar is running short, what with all the guests. If you want a drink, ask Kaligaskus.'

The Lord Chancellor snapped his fingers in irritable summons. He was a man spare of flesh and fine-featured, six-and-seventy years of age but still imposing in spite of increasing frailty of body. He had deep-set suspicious eyes and habitually kept his lips tightly shut, as if reluctant to let his thoughts escape his mouth. His will was indomitable and his store of patience huge; even so, King Somarus's fluctuating moods often tested him sorely.

'As you please, Majesty. I must say I'm surprised to see you working with your hands, like some common artificer.'

The royal reply was sweetly given. 'It soothes my mind to do so, my lord. If that makes me common, then sod you and be damned for a friggin' snot.'

Kilian winced. 'I beg your pardon. I meant no disparagement.'

'No? Well, it doesn't matter.' Somarus continued his careful adjustment of the captive piece of wire. His fat fingers were very steady. Unlike many other Didionites, he held his liquor well, even the notorious distillation of plums that was the national cup of cheer.

'Majesty, I wished to speak to you about the betrothal ceremony tomorrow, and also of the Sovereign's unexpected announcement at supper tonight.' Kilian lowered himself onto a chair brought up by the attendant. He accepted a crystal cup of red wine and took moderate sips while Somarus continued his finicky labors.

'I'll wager you can't guess what it is I'm making,' the king said, sounding like a cagey schoolboy.

Kilian breathed a sigh of longsuffering. 'Something very ingenious, one presumes.'

'Damned right. Watch me. You might learn something.'

The King of Didion was a year younger than the Sovereign, and once had been a man of striking, leonine appearance and hardy build, a celebrated fighting leader who owned a temper to match his once-fiery (now faded ginger) hair and beard. But he had not aged well and had grown corpulent and florid from excesses of meat and drink. Not a man of high intelligence, he was nevertheless both canny and alert, and at his best had a manner that was affable, generous, and leavened with bonhomie. At his worst, he was subject to bibulous rages and fits of melancholy. These had become more numerous since the painful death of his beloved wife Queen Thylla, who had succumbed to a breast canker four years earlier.

As a second son, he had come to his throne unexpectedly after the slaughter of his elder brother Honigalus, together with all of that unfortunate man's family who might have inherited the crown of Didion. The late royals had been atrociously done to death by Salka monsters, and many believed that the fierce amphibians had been abetted in some inexplicable way by Somarus himself, perhaps with the help of the Mossland sorcerer Beynor . . . and Kilian Blackhorse.

Whether this rumor was true or not, it soon became plain to certain powerful peers of Didion that while Somarus might once have been a successful warlord, defying his late brother by preying upon Wold Road caravans, he was a lamentably inexpert king – and no match at all for his brilliant liege, Conrig Wincantor. Factions in the Didion Grand Council who opposed Somarus would have long since pulled him down had it not been for Kilian's skill in rebuffing them, as the king himself grudgingly admitted. Somarus needed Kilian, and Kilian also needed Somarus.

At least for the time being . . .

The insidious chancellor was a powerful wizard as well as a consummate politician, and had a murky past. Although of royal Cathran blood, he could never legitimately rule that nation because of his magical talent and had been compelled to join the Zeth Brethren when still a boy. Kilian had served the Sovereign's predecessor, King Olmigon Wincantor, as Royal Alchymist and chief adviser – until ambition led him to overstep himself. He was caught plotting against his nephew Conrig, then Cathra's Prince Heritor, and was convicted of high treason for his pains. Kilian only escaped beheading after a plea for mercy by his sister, Queen Cataldis.

Locked up in Zeth Abbey to repent his sins, he audaciously decided to mend his shattered fortunes by organizing the theft of a collection of inactive moonstone sigils known as the Trove of Darasilo, which he and Beynor of Moss planned to share. Unfortunately, the purloined stones appeared to have been lost by Kilian's accomplices as they fled from the High King's agents.

Unfazed by this disaster, the one-time Royal Alchymist escaped to Didion with several other criminal associates, where he took advantage of the tragic demise of King Honigalus to insinuate himself into the court of his successor, Somarus. Within a short time Kilian made himself indispensable to the unsophisticated new monarch and was appointed Lord Chancellor.

Now, after sixteen years, he was firmly entrenched in Didion's quarrelsome Grand Council, rather like a tenacious mat of ivy whose tendrils hold together an unstable castle wall that might otherwise totter and collapse. Even Conrig Ironcrown unwillingly conceded his maternal uncle's expertise in statecraft – while forgetting nothing of the chancellor's earlier treachery.

Kilian Blackhorse was a shrewd political realist; he championed Didion's vassal status in the Sovereignty because only a united Blenholme could hold off the threat posed by the Salka monsters, while still allowing lucrative trade with the Continent.

But King Somarus Mallburn eventually rejected this point of logic. As years passed, he yearned to rule independently as his forebears had, without being subject to an overlord. It mattered not to the stubborn, fiercely patriotic king that Didion was better off within the Sovereignty, as Kilian maintained. Somarus clung to a more simple principle in his bluff warrior's heart: For nearly a thousand years, his nation's forests and heaths and boglands had been free . . . and now they were not.

Because Kilian was so adroit in smoothing the bumps and pitfalls of his uneasy kingship, Somarus had long since pretended not to notice the wizard's more blatant manipulations of him – the latest being the betrothal of his daughter Princess Hyndry to Prince Orrion. But one day, when fate smiled, Somarus vowed he would rid himself of both his irksome Lord Chancellor and the yoke of Ironcrown's Sovereignty. Until then he intended to bide his time, calming the towering resentment aflame within his bowels by means of the wonderful and soothing new pastime recently introduced to him by a congenial Tarnian visitor.

It was called 'angling'.

Kilian leaned forward and broke the drawn-out silence with some impatience.

'Majesty, earlier today I was reproached once again by the Duke of Dennech-Cuva, your bosom friend, for promoting the marriage of Princess Hyndry and the Cathran Crown Prince. Some of the duke's stated objections bordered on treason against the Sovereignty. You should caution him. I realize he's disappointed that the Princess Royal will not marry his own son –'

'Azarick Cuva is my staunchest supporter. He's free to voice his opinion. Anyhow, why shouldn't my daughter wed Count Egonus? They'd make a fine couple. Both widowed and childless, both randy as minks!'

The chancellor spoke patiently, as if repeating a lesson point to a dullard pupil. 'A second Didionite marriage tie with Cathra, in addition to that of your sister Queen Risalla, Conrig's wife, strengthens the bond of solidarity between the two nations and quenches dissension and animosity amongst the common people. We must think of the future.'

The king took a smallish brass bead from a box and held it to the light. 'Do you know what I think, my lord? I think

you envision Didion and Cathra becoming one single
kingdom after my demise. And *you* the Prime Minister over
all. If my son, Crown Prince Valardus, should perish through
misadventure, Hyndry would ascend the throne of Didion.'

'What an appalling thing to say!' Kilian cried.

'Such melancholy things have happened before, as we both
know.' Somarus took a spoon holding black stuff and warmed
it in a flame. 'Here is spruce gum mixed with charcoal, very
sticky and waterproof. I dab the least possible portion upon
that part of the wire closest to the loop held in the vice's
jaws. Then I slip this bead onto the wire so it meets the glue.
It will become the shiny head of an artificial insect, just so.'

Kilian's autocratic features twisted in bafflement. 'Insect?'

'That is what I am making, my lord.' Somarus nodded at
the dead thing floating in the dish of water. 'A simulation
of that creature.'

The chancellor rolled his eyes and drank a bit of wine, then
leaned forward to try again to engage the royal attention.
'Well, the betrothal is settled to the Sovereign's satisfaction.
In time, both you and the duke will no doubt see the wisdom
of it. Now, to change the subject: You know I have absented
myself from meals at Boarsden's high table whilst His
Sovereign Grace and the military leaders have dined with
you. I did this so as not to excite the ire of the High King . . .
who is, as you are aware, no good friend of mine. But I've
just been told that His Grace announced startling news this
night – the Salka invaders are supposedly in retreat. Is this
report true?'

'So it would seem.' Somarus took another generous pull
of brandy.

'And?' Kilian prompted.

The king's smile was glassy. Kilian began to suspect that
he was already very drunk. 'High and mighty Ironcrown
revealed something else that was interesting, too. Only Sernin

Donorvale and I yet know of it. I wonder if I should tell *you* about the dr –' He caught himself and grinned. 'Maybe not!'

Chuckling playfully, Somarus picked up a piece of rabbit-skin. He used tweezers to pull out both stiff guardhairs and fluffy undercoat fur from the leather, making two separate small piles.

'The Sovereign related news of something other than the Salka retreat?' Kilian was taken aback. His secret high-table informant had mentioned no other item of significance. 'Please share the news with me, sire.'

Somarus's countenance tightened obstinately. He took up a bobbin of fine silk thread and began to wind the filament round and round the steel wire, covering it evenly to the point where the shaft made a wide bend.

The chancellor assumed a more wheedling tone. 'I only wish to be able to advise you properly, Majesty. I beg you to trust me with whatever information of import you may have learned.'

'I don't mind telling you more about the Salka retreat. The tidings came from that young blade Dyfrig Beorbrook. It seems he didn't simply confine himself to questioning the usual backwoods sources about Salka activities up north, as he'd been expected to do. Instead, he personally undertook a perilous secret spying expedition deep into the Green Morass! Plucky little whoreson, eh? His windscryer oversaw the monster horde withdrawing from its encampment at Beacon Lake. The buggers are streaming north to the sea. Abandoning their invasion.'

'But, that's wonderful news!' the chancellor exclaimed. 'Did Prince Dyfrig discover why this is happening?'

The king paid no attention to Kilian's question. He spoke slowly and with precision. 'Now keep a close eye on me, wizard. I take a sparse clump of the stiffer rabbit guardhair, hold it in place against the wire just at its bend, and wind thread about

the hair to fasten it in place. Behold! The artificial insect now
has a wispy tail as well as a head.'

In spite of himself, Kilian peered at the king's handiwork.
'What the dev – what exactly is it that you are making, sire?'

'Didn't I just tell you, you clodpate? I am dressing this
angle to become a mock bug: a simulacrum of the dead creature here in the dish, which late was crammed into the belly
of a huge brown trout, along with several score of its deceased
kin.' The king poured more spirits into his goblet and took
a satisfied swig.

'You're dressing *what?*'

'This bent wire, called an angle, is in truth a fish hook.
No wonder you are surprised, for it hardly resembles the
crude things made of bone customarily used by our simple
fisherfolk. A large steel needle is heated red-hot in charcoal,
then the eye is nipped and tweaked to form a barb. The
needle's pointed end is turned into a loop where the fish-
line may be attached, and the entire thing then curved round
a tiny anvil, again while red-hot, into the proper hook shape.'

'But . . . why make such a thing, when bone hooks work
well enough and are so much cheaper? Our people have
used such from time immemorial.'

'Fool,' growled Somarus. 'Bone hooks and gorges do *not*
work well! Ask any village lad who sits all day on a river
bank, only to glean a stringer of panfish – mere tiddlers. He
has hardly any chance at all of capturing an enormous brown
trout or a salmon using impaled maggot or worm or
grasshopper. The noblest freshwater fish, unlike those in the
sea, will almost always craftily nibble off bits of bait rather
than swallowing it whole along with the unnatural-appearing
bone hook.'

'I didn't know that.'

'You're a clever man, Kilian. But perhaps not so clever as
you think. An angled steel, dressed to look like the trout's

natural food and played artfully in the water in imitation of a bug's movement, is far more effective than sharpened bone with bait, dangling limply from a bobber. Even better, such play makes fishing a *sport* as challenging as hunting the stag or grouse! This novel pastime was demonstrated to me some weeks ago by Sealord Yons Stormchild. It is all the rage in Tarn, and some of the younger Cathran nobility also now esteem it.'

'Very interesting, Majesty. But if we may return to more important matters –'

'I deem *this* important.' The king's tone was smooth and faintly menacing. 'Fashioning an artificial bug and scheming how I might outwit some venerable finny patriarch is immensely soothing to the troubled soul.'

'Mmm . . . just so. I'm sorry you suffer disquietude, sire.'

The king unfolded a bit of parchment and drew from it a strand of glittering golden tinsel. 'If you studied the dead thing in the dish intently, you would see that it has a metallic sheen. I propose to add such to my creation, first fixing the end of this short length of gold to the hook shank with additional turns of thread and letting it hang loose.'

'If the Salka are truly retreating,' Kilian persisted, 'it means we can disband the standing armies, at least for the winter. Get the Tarnian and Cathran troops out of Didion, You know they've been eating us out of house and home.'

Somarus shot a meaningful look at the chancellor. 'Once the Salka are gone, and Ironcrown and his arrogant gang are quit of my country, I mean to concentrate all my energies on getting rid of *her*. The Wold Wraith. I want you to put your mind to the best way of doing it.'

'Her. You mean the shadowy lass who calls herself Queen Casabarela? But sire, this deluded chit is no true threat to your throne. How can she possibly prove her claim?'

'She need not do so, my lord. Nay – she need only exist,

and act as a magnet for the discontented of my realm! We must find her before Conrig Ironcrown does.' Somarus's voice fell to a whisper. 'And kill her . . . Now let's fatten the insect's body.'

The king took up fuzz from the heap of rabbit undercoat and spun it deftly around the still-attached thread by twirling, until the once-fine strand resembled yarn. 'See? I coat a length of unbroken thread with fur, then wind this fluffy bit round and round the hook shank to simulate the body of the insect. More fur on the thread nearest the head for a fat thorax. Lower on the shank, a more meager winding to simulate the thinner abdomen. In water, it will seem alive.'

Kilian allowed himself a superior simper. 'Alas, sire. The creation looks not much like an insect to me, especially with that dangling bit of tinsel. Would a fish really be fooled?'

The king's massive head lifted. His eyes, sunken in fatty folds, nevertheless had clear whites and gleamed with cunning; he looked more than ever like a ravaged but still menacing lion. 'Tell me, Lord Chancellor. What do you think might happen if Conrig Ironcrown chose to acknowledge little Casya Pretender as royal heir, rather than my own son, Crown Prince Valardus?'

'He would never dare!'

'So you say. And you are so much wiser than I . . . Or are you?' Somarus let loose a raucous guffaw.

Kilian sat back and took refuge in his cup of wine. What in Zeth's name had got into the king? He'd always been fairly tractable before, even in his cups – a valiant barbarian not overendowed with wits, content to let most knotty matters of state be dealt with by his betters. Had Duke Azarick Cuva planted this all-too-plausible doubt in the king's mind? Were the peer and his cohorts finally attempting to undermine Kilian's influence?

Somarus said, 'Now observe: I wind the gold tinsel about

the bug's abdomen in wide turns, investing my simulacrum with splendid gleaming bands. The end of the gold I tie down with twists of thread, then move on to the final touch of authenticity.'

'Sire, again to the point. You mentioned that another piece of information was confided to you at dinner by the Sovereign –'

'To hell with the Sovereign!' Somarus blared, surging up suddenly from his chair, eyes ablaze and great flabby body quivering with pent-up rage. Kilian was now certain that the monarch was pissed as a newt. 'And to hell with you, too, wizard, who dare try to play me like a farthing whistle! You think I'm an untutored savage, thickheaded and led as easily as a bull with a ring in his nose. But you're wrong, and soon I'll no longer have to put up with your chivvying and false-hearted blandishment. In my dreams, I've seen a great change coming. I've seen Didion free!' He began to tremble more violently and his engorged features turned nearly purple.

Kaligaskus rushed up. 'Majesty, Majesty – be calm, lest you damage the handiwork you've so nearly completed! It's going so well. One of the best angles you've ever made.' He took firm hold of the king's thick arm and pressed him back into his seat with surprising strength. 'Now then. Breathe deep, take a sip of the water of life – then back to the task.'

Somarus relaxed and the lurid flush faded from his face as Kilian sat frozen in place. *Dreams?* What dreams? Great God, had the royal dolt's mind finally come unhinged, or was something more sinister afoot? In either case, action would finally have to be taken . . .

Kaligaskus was obviously well able to cope with his master's seizure. After helping him to drink and blotting the royal lips with a silk kerchief he withdrew, leaving Somarus huffing slowly with his eyes shut. In a few minutes the king came to himself once again and spoke in a voice as calm and rational as before the attack overcame him.

'Hmm. Yes. It's time to finish up and retire. Observe, wizard! With these scissors I snip a bit of stiff feather from a goose-quill. I lay it over the furry thorax, behind the bead-head, and bind it down with more turns of thread. When trimmed short, thus, the feather simulates the cape-like wing case of the waterbug.' He pushed the dish containing the dead insect toward the chancellor. 'See for yourself.'

'The thing is half-decayed,' Kilian muttered in distaste. 'I cannot discern –'

'Not decayed, but partially digested by the fish. I told you, the insect was taken from the belly of a brown trout. And *this* is the very essence of the new angling: to discover what the large fish truly eats, not proffer it any old thing and hope to catch it by chance. A trout of noble size doesn't savor balls of cheese or bits of bread. Such regal swimmers may sometimes take worms or other soft bait, but they are not its preferred food, only what thoughtless man thinks to offer. This dead bug in the dish, so loathsome to us, lives in obscurity on the floor of streams and pools and is only rarely seen by human beings. Yet we can be certain Lord Brownie thinks it supremely delicious.'

Rather unsteadily, Kilian Blackhorse rose to his feet. 'Majesty, perhaps we can speak again tomorrow.'

Somarus's smile was beatific and his eyes seemed focused upon another, better world.

'So I complete my small, satisfying task, making three knots in the binding thread and snipping it off neatly. My artificial insect is done, a perfect fish's breakfast. With it, a man may truly match wits with a worthy prey. True, the great brown trout may be more easily netted – or even snagged in the flesh with cruel gigs. But conquering him with this dressed angle that I myself have fashioned . . . what a simple joy.

What a triumph of duplicity!' He began to giggle softly. 'Do you doubt me, Lord Chancellor? Come a-fishing with me on the morrow, and I'll prove my point.'

'Thank you, Majesty, but I am called to more pressing matters.' And Kilian thought: God's Blood, was ever a schemer in high places given less likely regal clay to mould?

They bade each other goodnight, and the one who slept most sweetly was the half-mad king.

The rain pelted Castlemont's lower fortified enclosure, where wagon-train drivers, pedlars, and other wayfarers of low estate found shelter for the night in a barnlike guest-hostel at the foot of the knoll crowned by the main keep. The building had a central stone hearth that provided warmth and a means whereby travelers might cook their own food, but few other amenities. Saddle mounts, draft animals, and livestock belonging to guests were hitched to ranks of posts or confined in large pens open to the elements. The beasts were furnished with mangers of cheap hay and troughs of water that now overflowed in the relentless downpour.

Rusgann Moorcock squatted at the edge of the fire, sparing a brief sympathetic thought for her drenched mule, and finished her supper of toasted bread, sausage, and dried apples. Rain falling through the roof's chimney-opening was beginning to quench the middle section of the heap of burning pine logs, producing choking billows of smoke. Some of the other guests were already coughing and shifting to more salubrious positions.

Sipping from one of her flasks of cherry brandy, she thought wistfully about her comfortable bedchamber back at Gentian Fell Lodge. Even though she had plenty of money, she hadn't dared to seek better accommodation in Castlemont's famous keep. She would have been too conspicuous. Here inside the dreary hostel, no one paid

any particular attention to her and she was finally beginning to relax . . . in spite of the fact that the hunt for her
was definitely on.

She was certain now that her escape from the Lord
Constable's hideaway had been discovered and her movements
traced to the tavern in Beorbrook Town. Earlier in the day,
when she came to the summit of Great Pass, the border guards
were questioning travelers about a tall woman wearing a red
headcloth, a many-colored shawl, and a long white apron,
who traveled afoot. Her description had undoubtedly been
broadcast far and wide by Vibifus, the unsavory hireling wizard
who resided at the hunting lodge and served as its windvoice.

Fortunately, before purchasing the mule, Rusgann had
once again put on her magicker's disguise. (It had also earned
her a small discount from the superstitious stable owner.)
On the way up the pass, she'd attached herself to one of the
many trains of supply-carts headed for the Sovereign Army
encampment, telling the teamsters she was afraid her mule
might go lame and strand her on the steep road. The men
offered to see her safely to Castlemont if she'd conjure good
luck for them. She promised to do that, for what it was
worth, and shared her brandy and repertoire of naughty
songs with them as well.

Later, when a suspicious soldier at Great Pass garrison chal-
lenged her and demanded to know her business, she slumped
in the saddle and gabbled senselessly and sniveled until one
of the carters stepped up and claimed she was just his batty
old grandma, heading home to Didion. The guard had
shrugged and waved her on . . .

'All to bed now!' declaimed the hostel keeper, who had
begun to shoo away the few people still gathered about the
hearth. He frowned at Rusgann and said, 'Will you hire a
pallet, mistress? Two farthings.' He held up a limp tube of
sacking, skimpily filled with straw.

And no extra charge for the fleas! she thought. All the same, she paid for the miserable mattress and carried it into a far corner. She pulled off her stout boots, unrolled the good woolen blanket she'd brought from the lodge, and lay down with her head pillowed on her saddle. On one side of her was a snoring cattle-drover who stank like he hadn't bathed in a year; on the other was a young peasant couple with a softly whimpering baby.

If she left very early tomorrow, she might reach Boarsden by evening. The friendly carters had told her that both town and castle would be in a state of turmoil because of the great gathering of nobles, warriors, and hangers-on. As yet, she had no notion of how to find Prince Dyfrig without giving herself away.

I'll think of something, she thought. I won't let my lady down.

In a brief moment of apprehension, she wondered how Maude fared back at Gentian Fell. Lord Tinnis had to know of Rusgann's flight by now. The report of it, bespoken by the wizard Vibifus, would have been passed on to the constable at Boarsden by one of the staff windvoices. But surely Tinnis would never punish the Princess Dowager for the escape of her lowborn friend. The man loved Maude to distraction.

No, Rusgann reassured herself. There was no danger to her dear lady – only to herself, as she'd known from the beginning and freely accepted. But she'd see the precious letter placed in Prince Dyfrig's hand or die trying.

She pulled her damp hat down over her face and closed her eyes. Something half-remembered nagged at her mind like a mouse nibbling maddeningly inside a wall, out of reach; nevertheless it was no time before she drifted off to sleep.

Over by the dying fire, the hostel-keeper stood with hands on hips, staring thoughtfully in her direction.

*   *   *

For Tinnis Catclaw, Constable of the Realm and chief enforcer
of the laws of the Sovereignty, there would be no rest at all
that night. He stood at the window of his tower-room in
Castle Boarsden, and his unseeing eyes streamed with hot
tears.

It had finally happened, as he knew it must one day. The
runaway wench could have only one purpose: to effect
the release of her captive mistress – probably by carrying some
appeal to the Princess Dowager's son Dyfrig, who was now
an adult and a belted knight with legal status before the law.

Perhaps Rusgann Moorcock would be captured before achie-
ving her goal, but Tinnis could hardly count on it. The woman
might already have passed on the secret to someone – perhaps
when she stopped in Beorbrook Town. If the earl marshal's
people went up to Gentian Fell to investigate, they *must* not
find Maudrayne.

Tinnis Catclaw's lofty position, his fortune, and his very
life depended on it.

'I must order it done,' he groaned, 'even though the very
thought tears the heart from my body.'

Wiping the tears from his face, he opened the door leading
to the corridor outside his chamber and shouted for his
captain of the guard, Sir Asgar Beeton, to fetch his chief windspeaker at once.

Deep in the Green Morass, alongside a wilderness game-trail
that led from the Raging River to Black Hare Lake, Dyfrig
Beorbrook felt himself come suddenly wide awake. His
companions still slept like dead men, huddled together for
warmth.

Earlier, thickening clouds had blotted out the light of the
stars and forced his party to halt their forced march back to
civilization. Vra-Erol Wintersett, the resolute military windsearcher, had wanted to press on regardless, using his

farseeing talent to lead the others through the pitch-dark forest. But the trapper Calopticus Zorn stubbornly balked at walking blind with only a hand on another man's shoulder to guide him; and Stenlow, Dyfrig's equerry, was nursing a bad heel blister. So they'd made a simple bivouac beneath an oilskin lean-to, intending to continue when the sky cleared or at daybreak, whichever came first.

Dyfrig had fallen into a profound and dreamless slumber almost instantly. None of them had rested properly since leaving the Raging River, so anxious were they to reach the lake villages where they might obtain horses and hasten their journey to Boarsden and the Sovereign.

The prince was unsure of what woke him. The boreal woodland was silent, enshrouded now in dense mist, but not quite dark. Off to his right, spruce trunks were faintly silhouetted against a fuzzy greenish glow, like the foxfire of rotting wood or the corposants of marshlands. As he studied this phenomenon in perplexity, another insubstantial shining cloud sprang suddenly into being on his left hand. Then a third appeared out of nowhere, immediately in front of the open lean-to. All three of the radiant patches were about a stone's-throw distant.

Could they be spunkies?

He felt his skin crawl. The intelligent nonhuman beings properly named the Small Lights were not normal denizens of the morass, but frequented areas further south, and eastward into Moss. Long years ago, Conjure-Queen Ullanoth was said to have summoned enormous legions of the tiny bloodsucking fiends to assist Prince Heritor Conrig in his daring land assault on Didion's capital city.

But spunkies glowed gold or white, not green.

With each passing moment the shining enigmas brightened. Soon he could discern that within each nimbus were two distinct sources of illumination, paired orbs of emerald, slowly coming closer, growing larger.

Three sets of huge eyes glowing in the mist.

Dyfrig's heart leapt with terror. He opened his mouth to cry out and rouse his companions, but found he could make no sound.

You will not speak aloud. You will not move. You will answer our questions soundlessly, through your thoughts. Do you understand?

He couldn't help it: a raspy cry escaped his lips.

BE SILENT, HUMAN! Speak through your thoughts. Are you too stupid to understand?

'No.' He said the word and heard himself say it, but knew that it had come mutely, from his mind. 'I understand, and I'm not stupid. You're a Morass Worm, aren't you!'

The creature did not answer the question. *Why have you dared to invade our lands? Who are you? Are you allies of our ancient foe, the Salka?*

The prince saw one pair of shining eyes rise slowly. The sinuous body of an enormous creature materialized as it approached, reared up, and finally halted some four ells away, looking down at him from more than twice the height of a tall man. Its head was ornamented with webbed frills and mobile tendrils, triple-crested, perhaps covered with close-fitting feathers or oddly marked fur. Its profile was wolfish rather than froggy like that of the grotesque Salka; but its teeth were equally huge, glassy daggers nearly six inches in length. It squatted on powerful hindlegs while holding its forelimbs at its sides with the sickle-sharp claws turned inward, as if indicating that it intended no harm. Because of the swirling vapors, Dyfrig could not see how long the creature's body might be; but it seemed to have a thick tail, rather like a lizard.

Or a dragon . . .

Answer me, human. Who are you and why are you here? Have you come from her who made the promise to us?

'My name is Dyfrig. I am a prince of my people. I'm here with my four companions seeking information about the Salka invaders. They are our enemies – just as you say they're yours. The Salka want to kill all humans and seize High Blenholme Island for themselves.'

All of it? The entire island and not merely this part? The worm seemed surprised.

'Yes. It's their stated intention. We've been fighting off Salka attacks for years along the coast. Their latest invasion from the north almost caught us by surprise. We gathered a great army of warriors to oppose them. When their advance suddenly halted, our leaders were puzzled. They didn't know if the monsters had suffered some disaster – or if they were only biding their time before moving ahead again.'

The worm's long tongue, forked and black, emerged from its mouth and flicked its lips.

WE were the disaster that befell the Salka! This foolish horde had apparently forgotten that we dwelt in the morass, and shared the island with them and with certain other entities in the time before the Old Conflict. It was pointed out to us that we could overwhelm the Salka if we fell upon them in a certain way – and so we did. Now we have driven them back into the sea. We presume we will now be allowed to live in peace, as she promised us.

Dyfrig managed to grin. 'We found a track made by one of your people, and a broken tooth, and wondered if you were responsible for the Salka retreat.'

You know the truth. So leave this morass and never return. This is part of the agreement.

'You have my solemn word, as a prince of my people, that we will go away. All of my race owe you a great debt of gratitude for stopping those evil brutes. We might not have been able to defeat them and their sigil sorcery if you hadn't intervened.'

The worm threw back its terrible head and uttered a

voiceless howl. *We spit upon sigil sorcery! We spit upon all abom-*
inable users of sigils! We spit upon the Great Lights who tempt
Ground beings to exchange pain for power!

Taken aback, Dyfrig could think of no response. What was
the creature talking about? But before he could put the
question, the Morass Worm abruptly dropped to all fours,
extended its neck, and uttered a soft vocal hiss.

But that will be resolved in the New Conflict that is to come. For
now, I command you to quit our lands and never come back. Do
you intend to obey me?

'I've said I would.' The prince replied with dignity. 'We were
already hastening to leave – but darkness and fatigue forced
our halt. My friends are tired and sore. If you'd be kind enough
to let them sleep until daybreak, I'd count it a courtesy.'

The fierce head inclined graciously. *They may sleep. So may*
you.

Dyfrig's smile was rueful. 'I'll probably lie wide-eyed.
You've frightened me half to death, you know.'

Sleep, the Morass Worm insisted. *And farewell.*

The creature who had spoken and its two companions,
visible only as disembodied pairs of emerald eyes, vanished
like blown-out flames. A strange sensation came over Dyfrig.
His mind seemed caught in a dizzying whirlpool of stars that
carried him down, down, into a place where there was only
darkness and quiet. A last question hovered in his mind:
Who had convinced the worms to attack the Salka in force?

But it was of little account, so long as the monsters were
gone. Prince Dyfrig forgot the matter and slept.

The false dawn of a new day greyed the sky of Tarn. It was
the final, bleakest hour before sunup when human vital energies are at their lowest ebb and the mortally ill and the frail
elderly cling most precariously to their hold upon the Ground
Realm.

Ansel Pikan's grip was finally failing. But he fought to stay alive with stubborn tenacity, and as he endured, he cried out.

'So many enemies swarm about, threatening him,' he raved, his voice stronger than it had been for days. 'Enemies – and he himself is likely the worst of them all. Source! You know that if Beynor's wicked scheme succeeds, the world falls down to ruin. Can you hear me? Use me one last time! Source, let me help Conrig Wincantor. Warn him, at least! He's Blenholme's only hope and he's doomed and I don't know what to do. Help him, Source!'

'Hush,' said the woman at the Grand Shaman's bedside. 'Help will come. Cray and Thalassa have bespoken me that the wild-talented Deveron Austrey is safe with the Green Men near Castle Morass. He is to provide assistance to the Sovereign. Our two good friends have gone entranced beneath the Ice to try to clarify the man's mission. The Source will advise them.'

'But does the Source *know* what must be done?' Ansel whispered. 'Does even the Remnant of the Likeminded know or care? They use Conrig! They used poor Maude and her child. They used you! They and the Source of the Conflict use all of us poor groundlings and then cast us aside. Ah, God have mercy –'

His words dissolved into a moan of anguish and she began to weep, knowing her charge was beyond the help of any physick or healing magic. She could only hold his hand now and pray he would soon pass.

For a time, the shaman subsided into gentle delirium, mumbling incomprehensibly until he fell silent and she thought that he was slipping away in his sleep. But his body stiffened suddenly, he took a deep rattling breath, and his eyes opened wide. They gleamed with marvelling triumph even as his windvoice spoke plain and calm to her mind's ear.

'Oh, my dear! Listen to me! We mistook the Source's meaning in his earlier message. Deveron Austrey is indeed sent to aid the Sovereign of Blenholme during the New Conflict . . . but that Sovereign is *not* Conrig Wincantor! Tell Deveron. And when you call out to him with a general wind-hail, as you must since you don't have his signature, you must use the name that the Beaconfolk know: call him Snudge.'

'Snudge? But that's no name at all. It's an epithet – what you call a snoop. A sneak.'

Ansel gave a crooked smile. 'He's all that – but much more as well. Do as I say. Pass on the message. And now farewell, daughter. The crucial Sky battle approaches. Be strong as you play your own part in it. Be strong!'

'What do you mean?' she cried. 'Ansel! Ansel!'

But the spark of talent was already fading from his eyes, along with all evidence of life. She released her pent breath in a great sigh. 'Voyage safely beyond the stars, dear friend, into peace.'

She kissed his brow, then sat back pondering the troubling things he'd said.

Had he suffered a deathbed delusion or was he favored with a last revelation of truth? By rights, she ought to relay his words first to Thalassa Dru, down in the Green village near Castle Morass. But the entranced sorceress would be absent from her fleshly body for heaven knew how long. Her visit to the Source might take days, and beneath the Ice she was far beyond the range of human windspeech.

What Ansel had said about Deveron Austrey hardly made sense. She had some memory of her former lover's Royal Intelligencer and recalled that Conrig had given the man an odd nickname. But Aunt Thalassa had told her nothing of Austrey's mission in the New Conflict.

And how could Conrig *not* be the Sovereign this person was sent to aid?

'Moon Mother mine!' she exclaimed in vexation. 'I suppose there's nothing else to do but bespeak this Snudge. Let him pass along the puzzling message to Thalassa when she returns to the Ground Realm.'

Ullanoth sha Linndal, once Conjure-Queen of Moss, for long years isolated from the outside world of her own free will so she could atone for her heinous misdeeds, pressed shut the eyelids of the dead man and drew the sheet up to cover his wasted features. She debated calling Wix, but decided to wait. Her devoted old retainer would be up and about soon enough. She needed time alone to settle her nerves with a strong cup of tea before attempting to bespeak the onetime Royal Intelligencer across the barrier of the White Rime Mountains.

Dawn backlit the range and turned its glaciers to a pale rosy hue by the time she finished her hot drink and went to the unshuttered kitchen window. No birds sang around the house. They had already sensed the approach of winter at this high altitude and flown away to the warmth of the Continent. The back garden of her aunt's retreat had been hit by a black frost a week or so earlier, and the recent sleet storm had turned it to a melancholy sight; only the toughest plants remained unblighted. Soon enough heavy snow would fall in the highlands of Tarn, and the house on the Upper Havoc River with its thick walls and rock-weighted roof would be cut off from normal human contact until spring.

But not from the uncanny byways traveled by Ullanoth's paternal aunt, Thalassa Dru . . .

The sorceress who was one of the principal agents of the One Denied the Sky had been granted unique gifts by him. Perhaps the most remarkable was the ability to move through what Thalassa called 'subtle corridors' – invisible passages criss-crossing the Sky and Ground worlds that enabled instantaneous transport as did Gateway sigils, but without the concommitant pain-price owed to the Great Lights. Wix had been carried to Thalassa's lodge in this way shortly before the Salka overran Fenguard Castle in Moss. Ullanoth herself had come there through the corridors somewhat later, after a sojourn in an eerie limbo that she could recall only dimly.

At the time when she lay dying from the debt incurred through excessive use of her Great Stones, she renounced the Lights and agreed to serve the Source in the New Conflict. Her soul's essence had been reduced to a tiny emerald sphere to save it from the Pain-Eaters who would have devoured it. Neither alive nor dead, she was imprisoned within the Ice of the Source's own otherworldly prison. Other souls were there with her – a few of them contrite power-seekers like herself, but most of them persons who had been rescued from the thrall of the Lights or from impending death while serving the One Denied the Sky. One of those prisoners, an aged Tarnian sea-hag named Dobnelu, had accompanied Ullanoth back to the Ground Realm at the Source's command, to act as her tutor in repentance. In the house of Thalassa Dru, the souls of the two women were reunited with their bodies, whereupon Ullanoth's years of true atonement began.

In time, Dobnelu passed on to eternal peace; but before she died the sea-hag whispered a secret to her pupil.

I know this strange new life of yours has been hard. You are discouraged, wondering if there is any purpose to your suffering and hard work. But persevere! If you do, your appointed task in the New Conflict will bring about the war's final resolution – through the death of the Potency.

Ullanoth had no idea at all what Dobnelu meant. Neither did Thalassa Dru.

But the old woman's words had been intended to comfort her. And so Ullanoth sha Linndal did persevere, for year after year after year, with loyal old Wix lending what human solace he could. And now it seemed that the long battle between good and evil Sky beings was about to reach its climax, and her own rôle in the drama would be revealed.

The rising sun crested the mountains and suddenly blinded her. She covered her eyes with her hands and sent out the windhail to the man called Snudge.

But there was no answer.

SEVEN

Zolanfel Kobee, the new Grand Shaman of Tarn, sat stiff as a plank on one of Stergos Wincantor's solarium chairs in Boarsden Castle. His eyes were glazed and his lips pressed tightly together as his mind soared on the wind, seeking important information from one confrere after another in far-distant parts of his native land.

He was a compact man with long silver hair and a flowing beard, who usually wore a rather sad smile, as though he'd seen a surfeit of worldly wickedness and hurt during his long years as a healer and magical adept in the High Sealord's court. This afternoon, anticipating the evening's betrothal festivities, he had donned his finest clothes: a tunic and red-gartered trews of burnished walnut leather, topped by a long vest of sealskin trimmed with golden embroidery and sea-ivory beads. Tucked into his belt was an ivory shaman's baton inlaid with precious metals, and over one shoulder he wore a baldric having pouches that contained charms and philtres and other small items used in thaumaturgical practice. On his chest hung his badge of office, a pectoral of gold encrusted with huge Tarnian opals. Ansel Pikan had left it in the care of Sernin Donorvale before undertaking his fatal mission to the Barren Lands. The High Sealord had invested the new Grand Shaman with the pectoral just that morning, after news of Ansel's death was bespoken to Boarsden by an anonymous female apprentice of the sorceress Thalassa Dru.

The Royal Alchymist of Cathra played an anxious game of solitaire while his Tarnian colleague remained entranced, seated opposite him at a round table. Stergos was losing – but it never occurred to him to cheat.

There came an urgent scratching at the door.

Stergos rose up quickly, poked a hole in the spell of couverture he'd erected to shield the room from spies, and used windsight to identify his secretary, the alchymist Vra-Dombol. He whispered the words that would uncover the door completely and cracked it open. 'What is it, Domby? I really cannot be disturbed.'

'Nor would I have done so without good reason, my lord,' the other Brother of Zeth murmured. 'But it seems that the three sons of the Sovereign have just ridden into Boarsden . . . and oddly enough, they beg immediate audience with you!'

Stergos frowned. He was a man of pleasantly youthful appearance in spite of his one-and-fifty years, dressed for the upcoming occasion in fine crimson vestments and with a little red-and-gold cap on his curling halo of fair hair. 'Did they say why they wanted to consult me?'

'Nay, my lord, save for swearing that the matter was most urgent.'

'Very well. Tell them I will see them as soon as possible, if they will be so good as to wait.'

'Yes, my lord.' Vra-Dombol withdrew and Stergos resecured the door, wondering what business the royal youths might have with him when they should be occupied fully with other matters. The eldest boy, Vra-Bramlow, whom he knew best, was a promising novice in Zeth's Mystical Order, who might one day appropriately assume Stergos's own

office. But the Royal Alchymist was not at all close to the
Prince Heritor and his twin brother. Throughout most of their
lives, Stergos had kept his distance from them because their
very existence was a reproach to his scrupulous conscience.

On a portentous day in the past, Stergos Wincantor had
stood anxiously at the side of the Sovereign while the
sorceress Ullanoth tested Queen Risalla's unborn babe for
both gender and talent. Both royal brothers already knew
that the twin princes Orrion and Corodon carried the same
minute portion of uncanny ability as did their father. Like
Conrig, they would be barred from the throne if their secret
was uncovered.

As it happened, the fetus carried by Risalla was indeed
free of magical taint – but being female, it was ineligible for
the Cathran crown. Since the queen could have no more
children after giving birth to Princess Wylgana, the High King
believed that he had no choice but to conceal the princes'
disqualifying talent, as he had his own.

Stergos was a reluctant accomplice in the great deceit, but
only insofar as he would never be required to perjure himself.
Adroit evasions and legal technicalities had thus far enabled
the alchymist to avoid confronting the perilous issue head-
on. Nevertheless, he feared that he'd not be able to walk the
tightrope forever. One day he would be forced to choose
between his own sacred honor as a Doctor Arcanorum and
the legitimacy of the Wincantor succession.

'Gossy . . . water, if you please.'

A croaking plea recalled Stergos to the presence of the Grand
Shaman of Tarn. He caught up a silver ewer and a beaker and
hurried to the other man's side. With soothing words, he
helped Zolanfel to moisten his dry mouth. Windspeaking long
distances sorely taxed both body and mind.

'Can you hold the cup, Zol? Good! I'll fetch some wine
and biscuits. They'll help revive you.'

When the shaman was more composed, Stergos asked, 'How did your people respond?'

'Things in Tarn go as well as can be expected.' Hazel eyes peered almost shyly from beneath Zolanfel's tangled grey brows. 'Sealord Tammig Bandyshanks of Ice Haven, on Havoc Bay where most of the Joint Fleet has stayed during the past moon awaiting orders, has disguised two racing sloops as fishing smacks and put aboard each a pair of topnotch scriers. These shamans can windsearch at least a short ways underwater, which most magickers of Cathra and Didion cannot. At this minute the sloops are hellbent for the mouth of the Beacon River on fair winds. They should arrive some time late tonight. I've warned their captains to be cautious and not to get too near the coast. The monsters usually swim only a league or two offshore because in the open northern sea, they may become the prey of fierce grampuses or unicorns, or even krakens.'

'And these shaman-observers will farspeak you their tidings?'

'No, they must relay through Ice Haven using a special code for safety's sake. We'll receive the news via a specially trained windvoice who is adroit at tight focus. The Salka might otherwise trace the thread of windspeech to Boarsden, realize they were being spied upon, and attack the sloops.'

'An excellent precaution.'

'Gossy, I've done one other thing on my own initiative that the Sovereign didn't command. Some distance north and west of Ice Haven lies Fort Ramis, the fief of the valiant Sealady Tallu and her husband Ontel, a shaman who was cousin to the late Ansel Pikan. Ontel is a noted weather-wizard and he's no slouch as an undersea-scrier, either. I've asked him to keep a sharp watch up in his part of the world . . . just in case the Salka *aren't* paddling back home to Moss as we've so blithely assumed.'

Stergos nodded in approval. 'Very prudent of you, Zol. Did you feel a presentiment of Salka guile?'

'Not really.' The shaman rubbed his temples, fending off post-oversight headache. 'But the great slippery fangers aren't really as stupid as we humans would like to believe. There are still nearly two moons of fair weather for them to wreak mischief elsewhere, now that their Beacon Valley thrust has turned to a balls-up.'

'Do you think they'd dare go to the west coast? Perhaps swim up the Firth of Gayle and attack Donorvale itself?'

'There are other possible objectives besides the Tarnian capital that are less well defended. I just think we should remain alert for any contingency. Advise your royal brother that Sealady Tallu is one of our most astute mariners. She has to be, since she's responsible for law and order along the entire Desolation Coast. If the Salka try to slip past her, she won't do anything so stupid as engaging them in combat. She'll find a way to follow circumspectly, guided by the longsight of her husband Ontel.'

'I'll inform Conrig. Now go and rest.'

The shaman rose and stretched. 'Yes. I could use a few quiet hours before the feast.'

Which is more than I shall probably have, Stergos thought, for my every instinct tells me that those royal pups, my nephews, are in some sort of trouble!

He ushered the Tarnian to the door, lifted the shielding spell, then bespoke Vra-Dombol and told him to bring in King Conrig's sons.

Beynor had contrived to follow not far behind the Cathran princes' entourage as it traveled from Castlemont to the fork in the highroad leading to Boarsden Castle. There he separated from the unusually somber party of young men and turned north to ride toward the town, where he intended to seek accommodation for the night.

His suspicion that Prince Corodon, like his twin Orrion,

possessed secret talent had been soundly confirmed, putting
him in a mood of almost giddy elation. It was all coming
right at last! When that silly young whelp Coro became Prince
Heritor, he'd be easy prey, a fish in a barrel readily caught,
cooked, and served up for Beynor's delectation.

And through the son, Beynor would ensnare the father . . .

The day had been a fine one, with the stormclouds that
had lingered earlier blown away by a brisk southwest wind.
As Beynor rode toward Boarsden Town in the mellow afternoon sunlight, he passed entire makeshift villages of gaily-
colored knightly pavilions and the leathern or grey canvas
tents of soldiers and attendants, set up in anticipation of the
great defensive battle in the Green Morass that would now
be indefinitely postponed.

The encampments had become squalid during fruitless
weeks of waiting, and his windsight discerned idle and restless warriors and their leaders hanging about in desultory
groups, gaming or drinking or quarreling or loafing near the
cook-tents in hopes of cadging food. Overseen at close range,
the once-proud banners and pennons displayed among the
shelters were faded and tattered by summer thunderstorms
and hot sun, and the conical stacks of pikes and lances were
filmed with rust. Dispirited war-horses stood droop-headed
in malodorous paddocks, tended by bored grooms.

Beynor knew that similar military camps occupied the
countryside on both sides of the River Malle. Each one,
whether the troops there were Cathran, Didionite, or Tarnian,
had at its entrance a huge flag on a tall staff: the scarlet
banner of the Sovereignty of High Blenholme with its four
golden crowns.

Four crowns.

So the whoreson Conrig Wincantor still claims the fealty
of Moss! the sorcerer thought, with a brief pang of fury. Little
did he know that the true Conjure-King rode but a few

leagues distant from him, carrying the Sovereignty's down-fall in a fine new belt-wallet . . .

Beynor entered Boarsden Town at its South Gate and began inquiring for rooms at superior inns – only to be met with polite regret, indifferent shrugs, and outright derision. Even the more modest places were full. Every bed in every hostelry was taken by the hangers-on who catered to or battened upon a great army: purveyors of food, drink, fodder, clothing, and hardware; itinerant entertainers and gamblers; pedlars of quack nostrums and sundries; and every manner of whore from elegant perfumed courtesans who might grace the bed of a lord to sad and aging drabs who had knocked out their front teeth in hopes of selling low service to the undiscriminating.

'Well, here's a pretty state of things,' Beynor murmured, riding slowly along the River Road after seeking in vain a bunk aboard one of the vessels moored at the docks. 'The mighty sorcerer arrives ready to subvert the government of the realm. But it seems probable that he'll have to spend the night rolled up in his fine new cloak in the yard of a rat-infested dive, fending off vermin and unwelcome bed-fellows with his naked Sword of State! Of course, I could smite some poor devil with my magic and force him to yield up his bug-ridden palliasse. Or –'

His longsighted gaze lifted to the Didionite fortress that loomed at the bend of the river. The red flag of Sovereignty flew from Boardsden Castle's highest towers and turrets, signi-fying that Conrig Ironcrown was in residence. Surrounding it on lower staves were the argent banner of Didion with its rampant black bear, Tarn's quartered ensign of azure and snow-white, emblazoned with longships, and the tusked-boar standard of the castle's owner, Duke Ranwing.

'But not a trace of my poor nation's moss-green pennon and golden swan,' Beynor observed, caressing the heraldic bird whose wings embraced the great emerald enclosed within the gilt pommel of his sword. A slow smile spread over his face. 'But perhaps my invitation to the betrothal ceremony only went astray! I think I'll go and find out.'

Turning his horse, he retraced his route to the city gate and set out for the castle.

Vra-Dombol ushered the three Cathran princes into Stergos's sanctum, quietly set out wine flagons, pitchers of ale, and platters of bread, cheese, and fresh fruit, then withdrew.

'Lord Stergos, venerable Doctor Arcanorum and dearest uncle, our fond greetings.' Vra-Bramlow bowed low, clasping the gammadion amulet that hung from his neck in a gesture of ritual respect while the twins hung back with uncomfortable smiles. 'On behalf of my brothers, I thank you for agreeing to see us privily, even before we pay our respects to the King's Sovereign Grace and our dear mother.'

'Please, please, boys – be at ease.' The anxiety of the Royal Alchymist was all too evident. 'Doff your cloaks and hats. Toss them anywhere. There's water and a laver if you wish to wash your faces and hands. And for God's sake, take a little to eat and a sup of wine or ale.' He frowned as he studied Prince Orrion more intently. 'Nephew – what's wrong with your arm? Why is it in a sling?'

'I'll tell you all about it, Uncle. But first, some of your wine. I'm dry as ashes after our long ride.'

Corodon declared, 'As for me, my back teeth are afloat with a more urgent need! Which way to the necessarium?'

There were laughs as the royal youths relaxed and made themselves at home, eventually sitting together with Stergos at the round table and making nervous small talk.

But finally Orrion rose to his feet, shedding the sling that had supported and concealed most of his lower right arm.

'Uncle, let's get to the heart of the matter with no more ado. We're here because of a woeful thing that has befallen me.'

He began to divest himself of the disguising gauntlet and the bandages beneath it. As Stergos uttered an involuntary cry of horror, the prince displayed the now well-healed amputation.

'Oh, merciful God,' the alchymist moaned. 'How did you suffer such a terrible loss?'

'We three will swear it came about through misadventure whilst climbing a mountain,' Orrion said, with a pointed glance at his brothers. They nodded. 'But the truth – which is known only to us and to the dear woman I love with all my heart and soul, Lady Nyla Brackenfield – is more awful. I leave to your judgment whether the King's Grace should be told the whole of it.'

He went on to narrate at length the ill-starred scaling of Demon Seat and the motivation therefor, finally pausing to take a swallow of wine at the point where he began to beg a miracle of the Sky beings.

'This scheme was irresponsible beyond belief!' Stergos cried. He turned to Bramlow. 'Didn't you realize that these so-called demons must surely be none other than the Beaconfolk?'

'No.' The novice Brother of Zeth hung his head. 'Not at first. I was an ignorant fool, my lord, thinking only that the magical favors supposedly vouchsafed to others on the mountaintop might possibly have happened, and if Orry petitioned the demons, he and his sweetheart might somehow be able to marry.' He looked up with haunted eyes. 'I confess that I suspected the truth about the uncanny forces he was about to invoke when we first saw the actual Demon Seat – the throne formation made of moonstone. I am aware, of course, that sigils carved from that mineral are used to channel Beaconfolk sorcery. Yet . . . I couldn't bear to discourage Orry from seeking his miracle.'

'And it was granted,' the Prince Heritor said evenly. 'Bram
is not to blame. The fault is mine, for being determined to
flout Father's command and my princely duty. And I solemnly
declare, Uncle, that I would do it over again even if I knew
the consequences.'

Stergos heaved a great sigh. 'Tell me in detail what the
demons said to you, and everything you remember about
the vision.'

Orrion obeyed, emphasizing the non-malignant aspect of
the Sky beings and their apparent hesitation and confusion.
'They even tried to dissuade me, warning that I'd pay a great
price.'

'Beaconfolk did that?' Stergos was taken aback. 'But –' His
expression changed to one of wild surmise. 'I wonder. Oh,
yes, I wonder! I'll have to consult with – with someone wiser
than I in high thaumaturgy to be sure of it. But it may be
that your demons were not members of the evil Coldlight
Army at all, but rather other supernatural Sky dwellers who
are their enemies. Great Zeth – this is extraordinary!'

Bramlow frowned. 'I don't understand.'

Orrion broke in. 'Forgive me if I say that it matters not
who the demons are, at least for now. What we've come
here for is help in breaking this terrible news to our father.'

'We can't have him tossing poor Orry into durance vile,'
Corodon said with a merry chuckle. 'Or banishing him to
some lonely exile on the Continent. My brother must marry
his Nyla – while I assume his duties as Prince Heritor and
wed the roundheeled Widow Princess of Didion.'

'Damn you, Coro!' Vra-Bramlow exclaimed. 'This is no
matter for jest!'

But the prince only helped himself to ale and a piece of
cheese.

Orrion said, 'My twin speaks the truth. I would wed Nyla
at once, if the King's Grace permits it. She and her parents

remain at Castlemont Fortress, awaiting word of my fate. But I fear Father's rage at having his plans for me baulked might lead him to vindictive action against them as well as me. Do you see any way, Uncle, that the king's temper might be softened?'

'I must think,' Stergos muttered. 'Oh, lad – you've put a dreadful burden on me. But I love you. I love all of you as though you were my own children! Let's spend some quiet time while I think matters over. Then I'll leave you here and see what sort of mood my royal brother is in, and perhaps lay the groundwork for your confession. This is the hour when the king customarily takes his ease after conferring with his advisers. I'll do my best for you.'

'Thank you, Uncle,' said Orrion. He slumped in his chair. 'If you are able, tell Father that I throw myself upon his mercy and acknowledge my sin and unutterable foolishness. I'll accept whatever penalty he may demand.'

Silence fell. It was broken at last by Corodon, whose face lit up as a sudden thought struck him. 'All this dreary talk made me forget that I have a small gift for you, Uncle!' He rummaged in his belt-wallet and extracted a wadded silk kerchief, which he carefully unwrapped. 'I neglected to mention to you lads that I brought back souvenirs of our venture – proof that we didn't imagine the entire mad escapade.'

He placed two small objects on the table.

'Bazekoy's Blazing Ballocks,' Bramlow whispered.

Speechless, Stergos stared at the roughly walnut-sized chunks of translucent moonstone mineral gleaming dully amidst the leftovers of food and drink.

'One for you, Uncle,' Corodon crowed, giving the smaller of the specimens to the alchymist, 'and one for me. Taken from the near vicinity of the Demon Seat itself!'

'These could be very dangerous, Coro.' With haste, Stergos

thrust the gift into the depths of his robe and held out his hand. 'You must let me keep yours locked away in a safe place as well. I'll return it to you whenever you wish, of course.'

The prince's blue eyes twinkled roguishly . . . and also revealed a fleeting glint of something else altogether, which the Doctor Arcanorum was all too aware of. 'Oh, I think not, Uncle. I bethought me to have the court jeweller polish and make a cap-bauble of the stone, or perhaps inset it into the hilt of a fine new dagger. Anyhow, I must keep it as a memento of a miracle. For who knows when I might require one of those myself?'

Still beaming, Corodon looked from one appalled face to another. 'What?' he said in puzzlement.

'He says he's *who*?' the Sovereign muttered testily, glancing up at his agitated host, Duke Ranwing Boarsden. Barefoot and dressed only in linen smallclothes and a light wrap, Conrig had been reclining on a longchair in his warm sitting room perusing a many-paged report. More sheets of parchment lay scattered on the carpeted floor, together with several leather document cases. The low sun of late afternoon shone through an open casement window straight into the face of the duke, making the droplets of sweat on his high forehead glisten.

'The man at the castle gate identifies himself as Conjure-King Beynor of Moss, unjustly deposed by his late sister Queen Ullanoth. According to him, he was exiled to the Continent for a score of years and only recently was able to make his way back to Blenholme. He lays claim to the vacant throne of his kingdom and asserts his right to declare himself your loyal vassal.'

'Futter me blind!' murmured the High King. 'What manner of fellow is he?'

'A thin man and tall, who perhaps was once very handsome of face. His features are now ravaged by the elements and deeply lined, but I think he may be younger than he looks. His hair is white and his eyes are black and piercing. His garb is travel-stained but very expensive, and he rides a fine blood horse with a magnificent saddle. But the thing that might best confirm his pretension is his two-handed sword – a kingly weapon if ever I've seen one. Its hilt is lavished with gold and inset opals, and the pommel is a golden swan enclosing a whacking big emerald. The blade is engraved with the names of every Mossland ruler from the fabled Rothbannon to Beynor himself, along with mottos and the like, written in our own language and also in another arcane tongue – which the fellow declares is Salkan!'

Conrig grunted. 'I never met Beynor face-to-face. I only know he schemed to deprive me of my crown, along with the traitorous whore's-twatling who was once Cathra's Royal Alchymist and who now serves as your kingdom's Lord Chancellor.'

Ranwing's eyes slid away in embarrassment. 'For what it's worth, my liege, there are many in Didion who likewise have no great love for Kilian Blackhorse.' An unpleasant little smile touched the duke's lips. 'Now including, I believe, King Somarus himself.'

The Sovereign's expression had gone darkly pensive. 'As I recall, His Majesty of Didion attended Conjure-King Beynor's calamitous coronation while yet a prince, along with his late brother Honigalus.'

'That is so, Your Grace.'

'Does King Somarus know about this strange new arrival?'

'Not yet, sire. I tried to inform him, but he had given orders not to be disturbed. Our king is napping, gathering strength for the betrothal feast tonight.'

Conrig uttered a harsh bark of laughter. 'Too futterin' bad about his beauty rest. Duty calls!'

He climbed to his feet and shouted for his Lord of Chamber.

'Telifar! Fetch me a more impressive houserobe and slippers and get rid of these documents. I'm expecting royal guests in a few minutes.' And to Ranwing: 'As for you, my lord duke, present my Sovereign compliments to King Somarus and tell him that I require his presence at once and will brook no refusal or delay. Explain what's happened. Then go to my Royal Alchymist, Lord Stergos. Tell him to hasten here with all of the highly adept Brothers of Zeth he can muster, along with whatever magical apparatus is needed to fend off the most powerful malign sorcery.'

The duke's mouth dropped open. 'Your Grace, I don't –'

'Just tell my brother what I said, curse you!' Conrig bellowed.

'Yes, my liege. Anything else?'

'Bring this Beynor up here. Treat him well but keep him under guard in one of my anterooms – and for God's sake don't let Kilian Blackhorse or any of his lickspittle minions get near him. As soon as King Somarus arrives in my apartment, bring the mysterious visitor in to us.'

Perspiring even more profusely, Duke Ranwing bowed and left the room.

Viscount Telifar Bankstead, Conrig's longtime personal attendant and Lord of Chamber, approached with a robe of scarlet-and-black samite and matching soft footgear. 'Shall I send for refreshments, sire?'

The Sovereign snatched the robe and slippers and began putting them on. 'Not bloody likely . . . But wait! Just to be on the safe side, in case this knave is who he claims to be, roust out the castle seamstresses and have them whip up a Mossland flag as fast as they can. It must be ready before tonight's feast. Nothing small, mind you, but a big silken banner with gold fringe, to match the other royal standards above the dais in the duke's great hall. The flag is not to be put up until I give the command.'

'I understand, sire.'

'And tell the duke's steward we may require another goodly chair at the high table tonight.' Conrig's mouth quirked in a satiric smile. 'Maybe not *too* goodly a chair . . .'

Around noontide, the little maidservant Chelaire had appeared at the door of Maudrayne's sitting room carrying a cloth-covered tray. It contained food that she began to set out on a table near the west window.

'I'm ever so sorry, Lady Mayda! But Master Vibifus commands that you be served your midday meal in your chambers today. And I know how much you were looking forward to your ride on the fells today, but I've been told to lock you in until sunset. There's some sort of urgent business afoot. I can't say what, I'm sure! House-carls are running about like scalded curs, packing coffers and panniers, and a squad of guardsmen went off down the track to town before first light, armed to the teeth. I asked Captain Grallon what was happening, if Lord Tinnis was finally coming for a visit or what, but he only called me a rude name and said I'd know soon enough, and then –'

'Very well.' Maudrayne broke into the maid's chatter. 'Do me a great favor, though, Chelaire: come and whisper through the door to me when you do discover what the rumpus is about.'

The girl bobbed a curtsey. She was only thirteen, the youngest of several orphan girls from Beorbrook Town taken into service at Gentian Fell Lodge. The other house servants were mostly married couples, while the guards were drawn from Tinnis Catclaw's home fief many leagues to the south. The warriors lived in a small barracks adjacent to the lodge.

They were handpicked by the Lord Constable for trustworthiness. But living in such isolation was a hardship for lively men, and with Lord Tinnis's long absences this summer, discipline had faltered, allowing Rusgann to slip away. No one in authority had yet questioned Maudrayne about her friend's mysterious three-day absence, which struck her as ominous . . .

'I'll come at once if I learn anything, Lady Mayda. Is there aught I can fetch for you before you're shut in? Books or more wine, perhaps?'

Maudrayne shook her head, glancing at the ample repast. 'No. I have all I need.'

When the little wench was gone and the key turned, the princess left the table and the untouched food and went to her bedchamber, which overlooked portions of the winding track leading south toward the massive border fortress of Beorbrook Hold and the large town around it. Nothing unusual was to be seen out there on the rugged slopes – no riders coming or going. Unfortunately, the lodge's walled courtyard was out of sight from any of her windows, as were the stable and the barracks.

'The guards who left at dawn must have gone after Rusgann,' Maudrayne decided, frowning. 'Captain Grallon probably forced the door to her room at long last and found her gone. And if the wizard Vibifus personally commanded my confinement without a stated reason, he can only have acted on the orders of the Lord Constable himself.'

There was nothing particularly unusual about Maudrayne being locked in her room. During her years of exile at Gentian Fell, she had become used to being sequestered whenever supply-trains from Beorbrook or certain visitors arrived at the hunting lodge. But explanations had always been given freely before, and the length of her detention seldom exceeded a couple of hours.

'Well, all I can do is wait,' she said to herself, returning to the sitting room and the dinner. 'And pray that my dear Rusgann is still free to carry my letter.'

After eating, she read until mid-afternoon. Chelaire did not return. Feeling ill at ease, the Princess Dowager stood for some time at an open window, listening. Indistinct sounds of speech came to her on the breeze. She heard a farrier hammering a horseshoe, and mules squealing – which probably meant they were being heavily loaded. Once there was a harsh male voice shouting filthy curses as a female wept piteously.

Shaking her head, she returned to her book, a favorite devoted to the natural history of the Dextral Mountains. It had been her pleasure during the sixteen years of her stay at Gentian Fell to gather specimens of every herb and wildflower in the vicinity, press them dry, then mount them on sheets of vellum with careful descriptions of their seeds and fruits and the sites where she'd found them. The book contained drawings of numerous plants; but Maudrayne had discovered many new ones, given them fanciful names, and attempted to group them with similar species.

When she died, her last testament directed that her herbarium collection go to the Brethren of Zeth Abbey, who esteemed such things.

When I die . . .

Up until this year, when Dyfrig came to man's estate, she had been content to remain silent in her exile at Gentian Fell, knowing that her good behavior assured her son's safety. Conrig would stand by his bargain, reluctantly made with the Tarnian High Sealord, if he believed she was dead and Dyfrig beyond her influence; and Tinnis Catclaw would preserve her life so long as she assuaged his illicit desires.

But the situation could not remain static. Once Dyfrig became an adult, he deserved to know the truth and mould his own destiny. He was the first-born male, with a claim superseding that of Conrig's other sons. Knowing his birthright, he must be allowed to claim it if he chose. She had debated with herself long and hard before composing the letter. Even now she had lingering doubts about the wisdom of entrusting it to Rusgann rather than trying to carry it to Dyfrig herself. But she was closely watched, while her friend was not –

Hist! Was that a muleteer's command for his animals to go forward?

She hurried to the bedchamber window and gasped at what she saw. At least fifteen mules – all that had come up to the lodge only a few days ago loaded with provisions, plus the two or three beasts kept for work about the place – were proceeding down the track, carrying huge packs and canvas-wrapped coffers. When they were out of sight, people on horseback appeared: the steward and his wife, male and female servants riding pillion, with stuffed saddlebags and bundles hung about their mounts. Some looked back over their shoulders as they departed and more than one woman was weeping.

'God's Blood!' Maudrayne whispered. 'They're abandoning the place. All of them.'

The mercenary Didionite wizard called Vibifus proudly sat his fine grey mare, cowled in black. The remaining guardsmen, their weapons and shields glittering, brought up the rear of the cavalcade. The only person who seemed to be missing was the Captain of the Guard, Grallon Haytor, a burly fellow with a forbidding mien, whom Maudrayne detested because he killed hares, marmots, and other small game profligately with his crossbow, then left them where they lay.

Swiftly, she went to the door of her apartment and began to pound on it with her fists, shouting for someone to let her out. When nothing happened, she took an oaken foot-stool and smote it against the door, making a great racket no one could fail to hear.

This proved fruitless as well, so she dashed to the window and began to scream. 'Help! Don't leave, I'm still here! Come back!'

Most of the riders were out of sight. A few guardsmen at the rear of the train seemed to cringe at the sound of her voice but continued on without looking back.

Then she saw Grallon riding away. He lashed his horse about the head with the reins trying to hurry it, even though the steep track made anything but a walking pace hazardous.

'Grallon! Stop, you filthy whoreson!' she howled. 'Am I being left to starve? Stop, I say!' But in a few moments he had disappeared.

Furious and frightened, she began to gnaw her fingernails. Now what? Her rooms were in a wing of the timbered lodge that overhung a seventy-foot drop onto jagged rocks. There was no other exit but through a window. So that was the way she would go!

What might serve as an improvised rope to effect her escape?

There were silk brocade draperies at both windows, and silk, she seemed to recall, was extremely strong. Tester hangings on her opulent bed were fashioned of the same material. And she had silk sheets. The fabric would have to be cut into strips, then firmly knotted.

'Curse it!' Her tableknife, the only blade they let her have, was a dullish thing without a point, fit only to cut cooked meat and soft fruit. It was useless for slicing the heavy silk. 'I'll have to use my embroidery scissors,' she said to herself, 'although they're tiny things and it'll take forever to do the job. But I *will* get out of here! I'll walk the thirty leagues to Beorbrook Hold. If Dyfrig's not there, I'll find sanctuary with

Earl Marshal Parlian's widowed daughter-in-law, Countess Morilye. Being Tarnian herself, she never despised me as the court ladies of Cathra did.'

She fumbled for her sewing basket, a thing she rarely used, in truth, because most womanly arts were not to her taste. The small scissors were there, with blades only an inch long but quite sharp. She climbed onto the stool and began to haul down the first pair of drapes.

'Faugh! So much dust –'

And then she stopped, frozen. *What was that smell?* The brocade slipped from her fingers. She hopped off the stool and approached the stout outer door, eyes wide with dread.

Thin wisps of smoke seeped from beneath it.

'Damn you to the Hells of Fire and Ice, Tinnis Catclaw!' she cried, then burst into tears of rage.

It made no difference whether Rusgann was still free or not. The Lord Constable had clearly decided to take no chance that the identity of his secret prisoner might be revealed. Above its sturdy stone foundation, Gentian Fell Lodge was built mostly of wood. If the iniquitous Captain Grallon had done his work efficiently, the place would burn to the bedrock. Not even her bones would remain intact after the inferno.

'I won't despair,' she whispered, wiping her eyes on her sleeve. 'I'll fashion the rope before –'

A sharp metallic click.

'God!' she breathed, taking hold of the latch handle and pulling, hardly daring to hope.

The iron-bound portal swung open, key still in the big lock. The little servant-wench Chelaire stood there, red-eyed and coughing in the murky haze, her garments torn and filthy. One of her eyes had been blacked, there was a great purple bruise on her brow, and her mouth bled where she'd lost a tooth.

'Lady Mayda . . . when I overheard what he planned to do, I . . . but he struck me and I fell down the outside stairs and lost my senses. I think they thought I'd died. They left me . . . Oh, hurry!'

'You blessed child!' Maudrayne embraced the girl. 'I'll find some way to repay you.'

Ideas flooded into her mind, notions that might save herself and the little maid once they were quit of the burning lodge. She was already wearing her opal necklace and golden hair-clasps. Swiftly, she pulled a woolen cloak from its peg and flung it onto the floor. Hauling open a coffer, she tossed out hunting boots, knit stockings, and her largest raincape. From her nightstand came her silver beaker, a half-burnt candle, and a tinderbox. Her dressing table yielded a little ivory casket of jeweled baubles and rings, presents from Tinnis Catclaw. Last of all, she seized from a nearby shelf the portfolio containing her precious herbarium, then bundled everything up in the cloak and thrust the improvised pack at Chelaire.

'Hold onto this tightly!' She scooped up the little servant in her strong arms and began to run down the west-wing corridor.

The flames had not yet reached this upper floor of the lodge, but when Maude reached the head of the main stair-case, she saw to her horror that the steps and bannisters were already on fire. The ornate vestibule below, and the great hall with its carved beams, tapestries, and mounted animal heads, was a raging inferno. As she hesitated, wondering whether it might be possible to dash through to the front door, a thick cloud of spark-laden smoke billowed up at her, sending her reeling and nearly causing her to drop the girl.

'My lady!' Chelaire screamed. 'The back stairs – we must go that way, down through the kitchen!'

Maude turned about, blinded and half-suffocated, then

staggered back the way she had come, finally reaching the east-wing stairway used by the lodge servants. The smoke was less dense up at the top, so they were able to breathe more easily. But someone had closed the door at the foot of the stairs and it was too dark to see what lay below.

'I can't carry you down,' Maudrayne gasped to the girl. 'It's too narrow and steep. Can you walk? Here – give me the bundle of things.'

Chelaire slipped out of her arms and scuttled downward. 'I'll see if it's safe. Wait there!' In a moment she gave a jubilant squeal and flung open the lower door, filling the stairwell with light. 'Come ahead, my lady! There's no fire here and almost no smoke.'

Clutching her awkward burden and murmuring a prayer of thanks, Maudrayne descended, followed Chelaire through the deserted kitchen and scullery, and emerged into the lodge's courtyard. The two of them stood still for a moment, gazing back at the elaborate timbered structure from which they'd just escaped. The lodge's entire western wing – including the apartment that had been Maude's own – was a roaring conflagration. Flames leapt from every window now and the roof was already beginning to collapse.

Chelaire burst into wild sobs. 'They wanted to burn you alive. Alive!'

'But they failed,' the Princess Dowager said, 'thanks to you. Now come away with me, dear child. We must be well away from here and find a safe place to sleep on the mountainside before darkness falls.'

Six guards led Beynor from the gatehouse to the Sovereign's quarters, where he was sequestered for over an hour in a stuffy little closet that was apparently used as an office by one of the ducal secretaries. It was furnished only with a bench, a writing desk and stool, a tall press stuffed full of

rolled parchments, a bookcase, and an oil lamp in a wall
sconce – lit because the place had only a narrow glazed loophole for a natural light source.

To preserve a modicum of dignity when they came for
him, Beynor sat down at the bare desk, thinking about what
the guards in the barbican had told him upon his arrival,
while he awaited Duke Ranwing's inspection. The men had
admired his mount and sword (although they seemed astonished that one so splendidly accoutered had arrived unat-
tended), and peppered him with questions in the egalitarian
manner of the Didionite lower classes.

Beynor had responded cheerfully, admitting his identity,
telling a tale of exile in faraway lands, and inquiring about
his devastated country as though he knew little of what had
transpired there during the past twenty years.

The guards winked and nudged each other, understandably
skeptical of his claim, but they continued to treat him with
hearty courtesy. Much of what they related was old news; but
Beynor was interested to learn that numbers of Mosslanders,
especially those dwelling in regions remote from Royal
Fenguard and the once-populous eastern seaboard, had escaped
the ravening Salka invaders and made new homes for themselves in Didion. There were now good-sized Mossy enclaves
in the city of Incayo and around Riptides Castle in the Thorn
River Estuary – humble folk for the most part, with a smat-
tering of ruined nobility as well. The guards knew of no important conjure-lords or members of Moss's once-powerful
Glaumerie Guild among the refugees. But one man allowed as
how such gentry were likely to keep quiet about their former
status to avoid provoking the jealousy of local magickers.

I must investigate these settlements of my countrymen,
Beynor said to himself. He would need human followers –
as well as a source of real money. Sorcery could accomplish
only so much.

Other thoughts and questions filled his head as he waited, speculations about the Salka Eminences' reaction if he should be accepted as Moss's legitimate ruler, even plans that might let him maintain a foothold in Ironcrown's court if his claim were denied. And then there was Beynor's slippery one-time ally Kilian Blackhorse, architect of the theft of Darasilo's Trove from Cala Palace as well as fellow-instigator of the massacre on the River Malle. How long would it take the cunning old bastard to begin wondering whether Beynor had finally found those missing moonstones?

I'll have to deal with Kilian first of all, the sorcerer decided. But before he could think further about it the door to the little room opened and Duke Ranwing stood there, backed by a dozen of his household knights. All of them wore full armor and held naked swords.

'Be so good as to come with us,' said the duke. 'Our Sovereign and His Majesty King Somarus have granted you an audience.'

Beynor inclined his head and rose from the desk. 'Certainly, my lord.'

'And you must entrust me with your weaponry, messire.'

'Very well.' Smiling, the sorcerer gave over his two daggers, his table-knife, and the Sword of State, which the duke accepted with a respectful nod. Ranwing Boarsden took the lead as the group proceeded to the High King's private chambers, carrying the great blade horizontal in his mailed hands. Beynor came after him, flanked and followed by the knights. The door to the royal sitting room swung open and the duke motioned for Beynor to enter ahead of him.

The place was crowded with at least twenty men wearing hooded crimson robes, doctors of the Mystical Order of Zeth wearing golden gammadion pendants. Each held high a different kind of sorcerous implement – crystals, charms and amulets wrought of many substances, wands, boxes with mysterious contents, and objects unidentifiable – as though they were gifts presented in salute.

Or talismans elevated to fend off encroaching danger.

The Royal Alchymist stepped forward to confront Beynor as soon as he was admitted. Stergos raised an ornate reliquary that contained one of Emperor Bazekoy's famous blue pearls and intoned: 'All harmful spells avaunt!'

Beynor was dazzled by a great flash of white light. But since he had attempted no conjuration or other magical activity (and the sigils in his wallet were not yet activated), he was unfazed. Assuming an expression of dignified forbearance, the sorcerer doffed his hat and made a formal obeisance to two men who were almost lost in the mob of alchymists. One of these was tall, blond and stalwart, wearing a red houserobe trimmed with black. The other was grossly overweight, attired in a worn-out gown with a moulting sable collar and cuffs.

'My heartfelt greetings to Your Sovereign Grace and to Your Majesty of Didion. I am Beynor of Moss, once a brother monarch of this island, long exiled but now returned to claim the vacant throne of my nation and offer fealty to the Sovereignty of Blenholme.'

'We'll see about that,' Ironcrown said, pushing through the Zeth Brethren without ceremony. He stood, fists on hips, surveying the smiling sorcerer from head to toe and back again.

One of the knights smote Beynor on the shoulder with his open hand. 'On your knees before the High King, varlet!'

Beynor stood as unyielding as a stone statue. His gaze was locked upon that of Conrig. 'It would not be proper,' he said mildly, 'since I am also an anointed king.'

'Let be!' said the Sovereign, surprising himself. The supplicant's manner bordered on insolence, but Conrig found himself unable to take offense. There was something about this man that inspired trust and good will – and another, more puzzling emotion as well. The High King beckoned to Somarus, who lumbered up and gave the visitor an intent glare through narrowed eyes. Conrig said, 'Put our guest to the test, Majesty, in the way we agreed upon.'

Somarus cleared his throat and declaimed: 'At the time of the real Beynor's coronation, when the arriving royal guests from Didion came in procession up the main street of Fenguard Town, several outrageous events occurred. The result was that my late father King Achardus ordered the parade to halt. Then he and I and Crown Prince Honigalus went up to the castle together to demand an explanation. King Beynor offered a plausible excuse. He said his jealous sister Ullanoth had used magic to embarrass him. Then he summarily condemned her to death and offered to let us watch the sentence carried out. The three of us agreed. But first, we said, we wanted to take care of another matter. *What was it?*'

Beynor's lips twitched with repressed amusement but he spoke gravely. 'As a result of Ullanoth's cruel trick, you three royal personages were splattered from helmet to heel-spur in the ordure of seagulls. You wished to clean off the bird-shite before viewing the evil witch's come-uppance.'

Somarus turned to Conrig with a short nod. 'He's got it. And only Beynor and my father and brother and I shared that conversation . . . This fellow looks like Beynor, too, given adjustments for serious wear and tear and the passage of long years. Although he seems not nearly as obnoxious and arrogant as the boy-king of yore.'

'Wear and tear and exile,' Beynor observed, 'tend to round off the sharp edges of the personality. I'm older and, I hope, wiser.'

'And are you still a sorcerer?' Conrig asked. His tone was neutral. 'I've heard that you were cursed by the Great Lights.'

'The rumor is not entirely accurate. My arcane powers
have been diminished by hardship, but I am still capable of
exercising moderate talent.' He nodded pleasantly at Stergos.
'The Reverend Doctor Arcanorum is undoubtedly much more
powerful than I. And perhaps certain others here in the castle
also.'

King Somarus hoisted a single eyebrow. 'Such as my Lord
Chancellor, Kilian Blackhorse?'

'That I cannot say.' Beynor turned back to Conrig. 'As I
approached this castle, I noted that your Sovereign banner
bears four crowns, not three. In your own heraldry, the
Conjure-Kingdom of Moss still lives. So – will you accept my
legitimacy and my avowal of fealty?'

Conrig glanced at the King of Didion, who gave a minimal
shrug and said, 'It's him. I'd bet my goolies on it. But who
can say whether the pitiful survivors of his devastated land
will accept him? If they agree, it might be prudent for the
Sovereignty to do likewise.'

'No,' said Conrig Ironcrown softly. 'If *I* accept him, then
his erstwhile subjects must!' He turned to the duke, who still
carried Beynor's Sword of State. 'My lord, give the great
blade to me.'

'Sire.' Ranwing handed it over.

Conrig flourished the glittering weapon. Admiring murmurs
came from the assemblage. To Beynor, he said, 'Kneel!' And
then: 'Do you vow fealty to the benevolent Sovereignty of High
Blenholme and accept its High King, Conrig Wincantor, as
your liege lord?'

'I do.'

Conrig tapped the kneeling sorcerer on each shoulder with
the flat of the blade. 'Inasmuch as a former ruler of Moss has
already acknowledged vassalage in the Sovereignty, it pleases
me to affirm you, Beynor ash Linndal, as lawful Conjure-
King of that nation, which is now occupied by Salka invaders.

In the fullness of time, the Sovereignty will see these vile interlopers vanquished and cast out of Moss. On that happy day, when you return to your kingdom in triumph, may you reign justly and prosperously.' There was a brief patter of applause. 'You may rise.'

Beynor climbed to his feet and accepted the return of his sword, which he sheathed with care. Both Conrig and Somarus embraced him with a certain reserve, after which the High King said, 'We're having a feast tonight. The betrothal of my son to Somarus's daughter. Do you want to come?'

A polite nod. 'It would be an honor and a pleasure, my liege.'

'You should know that it's our custom to come unarmed to formal dinners,' Conrig said, 'save for personal table-cutlery. You should also know that the incantation pronounced earlier by Lord Stergos will continue to nullify any harmful sorcery you may be tempted to use.'

'I understand.' Beynor was perfectly at ease. 'Please accept my heartfelt assurance that I come here in peace.'

'Most gratifying.' Ironcrown then raised his voice, silencing the murmuring throng of alchymists and knights. 'This audience is now at an end. My lord duke, your men will form a guard of honor for our new royal guest. Let them make certain that His Majesty the Conjure-King is well accommodated. My Royal Alchymist, Lord Stergos, will join them to escort King Beynor to the betrothal ceremony at the proper hour.'

Boarsden smote his breastplate in salute, formed up the knights with a sweeping gesture of command, and led Beynor out of the room.

When they were gone, Conrig beckoned to Stergos, speaking low. 'You're certain that Mossbelly villain will be unable to harm any of us with sorcery?'

The alchymist opened the precious reliquary and gave his royal brother another glimpse of Bazekoy's blue pearl. 'This is the most powerful quencher of evil spells in Saint Zeth's arsenal. You may recall how it defeated our treasonous Uncle Kilian when we came to arrest him. The pearl has limitations, of course, which I didn't think fit to mention to Beynor. But so long as he remains within these castle walls, he can perform no sorcery with a purpose that is manifestly evil.'

The High King laid a hand on his brother's shoulder. 'I'll rely on you to keep a close eye on him, Gossy – especially at the betrothal feast tonight. I'll have other things on my mind.'

'As to that, Prince Heritor Orrion has arrived at the castle. He begs permission to confer briefly with you.'

'God's Teeth! If he thinks to plead with me to change my decision at this late hour –'

'That's not what's on his mind at all,' Stergos said in a soothing tone. 'Talk to him, Con. It's very important.'

'I'll give him fifteen minutes,' the king said ungraciously. 'And now I'll thank you to leave me alone so I can sort out my thoughts.' He jerked a thumb at the throng of Zeth Brethren, who were still engaged in animated discussion of Beynor's reinstatement. 'And take this lot of jabbering magickers along with you!'

Far to the north, where the Beacon River flowed into the Icebear Channel separating High Blenholme Island from the Barren Lands, the retreating army of the Salka emerged from the river delta into the sea and split into two divergent columns of swimmers.

The first and smaller contingent turned eastward, staying near the surface and close to the rugged Didion coast with little attempt at concealment. As the great amphibians traveled, they greedily snapped up the saltwater fishes that had been missing from their diet during their tedious inland sojourn, littering the surface of the water with leftover bits of flesh that attracted hovering flocks of noisy seabirds.

The second group, which outnumbered the first by over two hundred to one, swam more rapidly and stayed deep beneath the waves. After heading directly north into open waters for nearly fifty leagues, with keen-talented rangers patrolling the route and warning of predatory animals or human ships, these Salka altered their course in a westerly direction toward the Lavalands Peninsula, the first leg in their long journey to Terminal Bay.

They swam steadily but without undue haste and expected to arrive at their destination within two weeks . . . or less.

EIGHT

The three princes waited for Stergos to return to his rooms.
They had no idea why the alchymist had been summoned
so suddenly by the High King, save that it had nothing to
do with them.

Orrion had rewrapped the end of his truncated arm in
bandages in preparation for the hoped-for audience with his
father. He stood apart from the others, staring out of the
solarium window and wondering whether he would ever see
Nyla again. Vra-Bramlow sat at the round table with
Corodon, studying his brother's moonstone souvenir with
his deep-scrying windtalent.

'I detect nothing remarkable about this rock of yours,' the
novice Brother said. 'It's not even flawless.'

'The chunks and slabs of the stuff that formed the Demon
Seat throne weren't flawless, either,' Coro reminded him,
'yet they glowed with a weird radiance and summoned the
Lords of the Sky readily enough when Orry touched them.
I'll wager this bit of mineral could do the same.'

'If you think to do silly experiments with it,' Bram said
matter-of-factly, 'then give up your hope of being Prince
Heritor, and be prepared to look up from the Hell of Ice to

see Dyfrig Beorbrook named heir to the throne – or else our depraved cousin Feribor Blackhorse, if young Dyfrig is unable to keep him at bay! The moonstone sigils have killed persons who make frivolous requests. Conjure-Queen Ullanoth died merely because she used sigil sorcery too often. Her mother Taspiroth was tortured to death and sent to hell for misusing one of the stones – no one knows how! The Beaconfolk won't stand being trifled with.'

'I'd never trifle in matters concerning my future crown.' Corodon picked up the mineral, wrapped it again in his kerchief, and put it away. 'I'm not such a fool as you may think.'

'Just remember that the demons ask a terrible price for their magical favors, little brother. Be sure you're willing to pay it.'

The younger prince cocked his handsome head. 'I could ask the price first, then decide whether the favor was worth it. Orry was satisfied with *his* bargain!'

The novice shook his head. 'Coro, you're talking like a child. How can I make you understand –'

The door to the solar opened and the Royal Alchymist entered. 'Nephews, I've just come from the Sovereign's chambers. Something quite bizarre just happened. Conjure-King Beynor of Moss has reappeared after dropping out of sight for nearly two decades. He came to the gate of Boarsden Castle, cool as a dill pickle, and declared himself. Both your father and King Somarus decided to accept him as legitimate after putting him to the test.'

The princes began to ask excited questions.

Stergos waved his hand to silence them and addressed himself to Orrion. 'The High King will be greatly distracted as he considers the implications of this event. We may hope that his anger towards you will be diminished as a consequence. Come along with me now, lad. I've told your father that you wish to discuss a weighty matter but said little else.

He agreed to see you' – the alchymist's shrug was apologetic – 'for a quarter of an hour.'

Prince Orrion burst into bitter laughter. 'I suppose it's plenty of time for him to decide whether I'll live or die!'

Bramlow said, 'And what about Coro and me? We'd hoped to stand at our brother's side, since we share a portion of the blame –'

'Speak for yourself, Bram,' Corodon said. 'I wasn't the one who told Orry about Demon Seat in the first place.'

'No,' the novice shot back, 'you only goaded him to climb the mountain, implying that he'd be craven and. unworthy of Lady Nyla if he held back!'

Orrion's face had gone pale. 'Brothers, don't quarrel. I must confront Father by myself – and I intend to maintain that you two were in no way at fault, that you even tried to prevent me from committing the folly that deprives me of the throne. I can say nothing else. Your reputations and your future must not be jeopardized by my misfortune. Coro will be king one day – and you, Bram, might serve as his Royal Alchymist and privy counselor.'

Stergos addressed the pair with unexpected formality. 'Vra-Bramlow, Prince Corodon, you will both stay in this room until you're sent for. And you'd do well to pray harder than ever before in your foolish young lives.'

When the Prince Heritor and the Royal Alchymist arrived at the Sovereign's apartment and were admitted by the Lord of Chamber, they found Conrig in his dressing room attended by two valets, a barber, and his confidential secretary, Mullan Overgard. The High King was simultaneously having his fingernails buffed, trying on different pairs of ornate footgear, getting his beard trimmed, and dictating an edict which restored to Beynor the dominion, authority, and regal honors attending the Conjure-Kingship of Moss.

'"Pursuant to the above, I hereby command all persons residing within that nation or claiming citizenship therein to render promptly to Beynor ash Linndal the oath of fealty" . . . et cetera, et cetera. But there's to be *nothing* in this edict about renewing the annual stipend we paid to the late Queen Ullanoth. Let Beynor finance his own comeback.'

Lord Mullan stifled a chuckle. 'As you please, sire.'

Conrig caught sight of the arrivals. 'Finish the thing properly and have the scribes use plenty of illuminated initial letters with gold flourishes when they draw it up. I'll sign and seal it tomorrow. The damned edict is only pro forma anyhow, since the Salka monsters own Moss down to the last frog, bog, and quagmire. But it'll make Beynor happy and it might impress the expatriate Mossbellies over in the Thorn Estuary.'

The secretary stoppered his ink bottle and began to pack up his small portable desk. 'I'll have it ready, Your Grace, along with the other relevant documents.'

Conrig said, 'Good.' He eyed his son with a certain wariness. 'Do you require complete privacy for this discussion, Orrion?'

The prince said, 'If you please, sire. Except for my dear Uncle Stergos, who is here only out of kindness.'

The Lord of Chamber herded everyone else from the room and then withdrew himself, closing the door.

'Fifteen minutes,' Conrig declared, pointing to a graduated hourglass on the dressing table. He picked up a silver-gilt hand-mirror and began to smooth the fair hairs of his moustache. 'And I warn you, Orry, I don't care a mouse-turd for wild rumors about Princess Hyndry and Count Egonus Cuva and the other men she's supposedly bedded. You and she must marry whether or not –'

'Father.' The prince let his cloak fall to the floor, took off his doublet, and thrust forth his right arm with the shirt-sleeve pushed above the elbow. The stump was neatly bandaged but the nature of the injury was all too obvious. 'I have suffered this grievous wound through my own fault, losing my sword hand and most of the lower forearm.'

The High King leapt to his feet and dropped the mirror with a loud cry. The glass shattered on the oaken floor, flinging bright shards in all directions, but Conrig seemed not to notice. His body had gone rigid and the blood drained from his countenance. After an interval of silence, he whispered, 'How?'

Orrion spoke as calmly as he could. 'As my brothers and I made our way northward from Cala Blenholme with our companions, we undertook a side-trip to Swan Lake to try the new style of fishing. Then I decided to climb one of the nearby mountains for the fun of it. Bram and Coro came with me, albeit with reluctance, but the rest of our friends remained behind. There was a rockslide and I took a bad fall. My lower arm and right hand were crushed beneath a great boulder. It seemed I would bleed to death where I lay. But Bram did what was necessary to free me. His healing talent and medical skill saved my life . . . for what's it's worth.'

Conrig said nothing. He had closed his eyes and stood unmoving with both fists clenched.

Orrion continued. 'I realize that my injury renders me incapable of ever leading our armies in battle. I can no longer be Prince Heritor of Cathra. With your gracious permission I will relinquish this honor to my twin brother Corodon, who – who is worthy to assume it.'

'Coro?' The king's harsh voice was incredulous as he emerged abruptly from his state of shock, dark eyes blazing with fury. '*Coro?*' he shouted at the top of his lungs. 'That scapegrace inherit my Iron Crown?'

Orrion pressed on doggedly. 'As for myself, I accept whatever penalty you think my foolishness deserves. My liege – dear Father – I ask for your mercy.'

With head bowed, the prince sank to his knees, oblivious of the bits of broken mirror that sliced through the thin leather of his riding habit like tiny knives.

He waited.

When Conrig finally spoke, it was as though each word were forced from his throat. 'I sentence you to death.'

'Oh, no!' Stergos cried in anguish. 'You can't –'

'Silence!' the king bellowed. 'You have nothing to say in this matter, Brother!'

Orrion lifted his head. He was calm and his eyes were dry. 'I deserve the penalty, Father, and I accept your judgment.'

Conrig's gaze shifted from the face of his son. 'Who else knows of this injury besides your brothers and Lord Stergos? Your Heart Companions?'

'Nay, sire. Because of the portentous nature of the wound, and my desire that news of it should not be spread abroad prematurely, I took care to conceal its true gravity from the men of my retinue and Coro's as well. They know the arm was hurt, but not that the hand was lost. I kept the stump well concealed – first in heavy bandages and later in a padded gauntlet and sling. On our journey from Swan Lake to Boarsden, we were careful not to stop at any place where officious Brothers of Zeth would demand to examine me.'

'Hmm. So no one else knows . . .'

Orrion hesitated. 'May I beg to know when my life will be forfeit, sire?'

'I suspend your sentence of death,' Ironcrown said. 'Instead I intend to banish you from my presence for as long as it pleases me. I'll decide later where you shall go.'

'Thank you! I –'

'Be still, damn you! This rash action of yours may have wrecked a delicately wrought stratagem of mine. A plan of supreme importance! If King Somarus now refuses to give the hand of his daughter to Corodon – and Zeth knows the fat bastard was already reluctant to have her wed *you* – the longterm prospects for Didion's allegiance to the Sovereignty are put at terrible risk. As is my own grand plan for the expansion of our hegemony to the Continent once the Salka threat is dealt with.'

Orrion was unable to conceal his surprise, but he made no comment. The Royal Alchymist could not help but murmur, 'Great Zeth, Con! You still dream of empire?'

Conrig turned to his older brother, pretending not to have heard the words of reproof. 'Tell me, Gossy: do you think Somarus will accept madcap Coro in place of this more worthy twin?'

'The dynastic advantage is the same,' Stergos replied stiffly. 'But we both know that the ultimate decision rests not with Didion's king but with his puppetmaster Kilian. Who may well *prefer* a royal son-in-law of Corodon's . . . special disposition.'

Conrig uttered a hollow laugh. 'You mean a malleable young idiot! Well, we'll find out at tonight's feast, won't we?'

Orrion ventured to say, 'I presume you would prefer me to absent myself, sire.'

'On the contrary. You will attend, as will both of your brothers, and this is what I expect you to do.' He explained in detail. 'Have I made myself clear?'

'Yes, sire.' The prince paused, thinking: Shall I tell him about Nyla? If I hold back and he learns that she and her parents are staying at Castlemont awaiting news of my fate, he might suspect that I contrived the injury!

'Get to your feet, boy,' the king ordered. 'You are dismissed. Go with your brothers to the suite of rooms prepared for you. Be sure to do exactly as I've commanded this evening – or I'll rethink my decision about your fate.'

Orrion could not help but flinch with pain as he rose. Flesh wounds from the broken mirror leaked blood through the knees of his trews and caused kindly Stergos to give a cry of consternation. Conrig looked away, grimacing in disgust.

'Truly, Uncle, the cuts are less severe than they seem,' the prince said. 'Don't be concerned.' And after taking a breath, he said to the High King: 'Sire, you inquired if any other person knew of the loss of my hand. I have not yet answered. There is only one more who knows, and she is Lady Nyla Brackenfield, the woman I once hoped to marry.'

Conrig whirled about with a curse, but Orrion continued resolutely.

'As my companions and I traveled down the road from Great Pass, we chanced to meet Nyla and her parents at a hostelry. I confess that I revealed the amputation to her. You see . . . I had to know whether she could still love a one-armed man.'

Conrig's dark eyes narrowed. 'So! And what did the lady say?'

'That her heart was steadfast. And if in your mercy you would allow me to live, she would willingly be my wife. I am to send word to her –'

'Where is she?' the king demanded.

'Lodged at Castlemont Fortress with her parents.'

'I'm gratified that you saw fit to tell me about her,' Conrig said in a voice of ice, 'even if somewhat belatedly.' He turned to Stergos. 'With changes of horse there's still plenty of time for the Brackenfields to get here in time for the betrothal feast. Gossy, bespeak the Boarsden wizards and have them pass on my command to the Lord Lieutenant and his family at Castlemont. They are to attend us tonight.'

Orrion was stricken with dread. Were his sweetheart and her parents to be publically humiliated because of him? 'Sire, Nyla and I –'

A fleeting dark shadow crossed Conrig's face. 'Orrion, you'd do well to remember that no person of royal blood – not even one who has been debased – may marry without the permission of the Sovereign. To do so is treason.'

'Yes, sire.'

'Don't mention this subject to me again. Not until one year has gone by. By then – who knows? The dangerous situation may have mended itself. If it has not, then God help you. And your Nyla.'

The High King moved to a sideboard where ornate caskets containing finger rings and other jewels stood open awaiting his choices, together with the official regalia he would don for the night's celebration. Also there, resting on a red velvet cushion and looking rather out of place amidst the glittering splendor of gold and gems, was a simple circlet of blued and polished dark metal. Once it had served as the head-hoop of a discarded cask of tarnblaze explosive on a Cathran man o' war. The ship's crew had used it in good humor to honor a sick old king who had left his proper royal crown behind when he came aboard to direct a crucial sea-battle from his deathbed.

Conrig Wincantor lifted the Iron Crown of Sovereignty and turned it slowly in his hands. His expression had become remote and he seemed to have forgotten that Orrion and Stergos were there.

The prince opened his mouth as if to speak, but the Royal Alchymist shook his head imperceptibly, then said, 'Your Grace, is there anything else you require of us at this time?'

'No,' the king replied, without looking at either of them. 'Go away. Tell my Lord of Chamber that no one is to enter until I give permission. No one – on pain of death.'

Holding high the flapping skirts of his black robe, the wizard Niavar Kettleford, an aging little man whose unprepossessing body and crossed eyes helped disguise his formidable intelligence, dashed down the corridor to the chambers of the

Lord Chancellor of Didion. The two guards who stood at the main door of the royal official's apartment in the Wizards' Tower snickered as he slid to a halt, gasping for breath, and almost collapsed at their feet.

'Quickly,' Niavar gasped. 'Open up at once! I have urgent news for Lord Kilian.'

'Whoa, there, master!' The tallest guard grasped Niavar's arm and steadied him. 'The chancellor gave orders that he wasn't to be interrupted for any reason. Doing a tricky bit of magical work he is, along with his other two assistants.'

The small man almost screamed. 'You must let me in! Or at least call Master Cleaton or Garon Curtling to the door so I can pass on the tidings. This is vitally important, I tell you!'

'So's the good health of our thumbs,' muttered the second guard, a sullen-looking bruiser. 'And that's what we'll get hung up by, if'n we disobey the chancellor's orders.'

Niavar's choler faded, leaving his features set and pale and his eyes reduced to slits. With his squint now imperceptible, he seemed a different person altogether – and dangerous. He backed away from the men, lifting both arms in a gesture of conjuration, and shrilled, 'You fools leave me no choice.'

'Oy!' the first guard cried in alarm. 'No need to get –'

An abrupt *snap snap!* – not very loud.

The men's eyes rolled back in their heads and they fell to the floor senseless in a crash of armor and weaponry. Niavar seized one of their halberds and began to hammer on the stout oaken door. It was protected by a shielding spell, of course, or he would have been able to conjure the lock open or at least windspeak those inside. He regretted causing an uproar – open-mouthed servants and a handful of junior magickers belonging to Duke Ranwing's cadre of house-wizards were already gathering at a safe distance at the opposite end of the corridor, staring at him – but the situation demanded drastic action.

Finally the door opened. The hulking form and pinched, swarthy countenance of his longtime colleague Cleaton Papworth glared down at him in outrage. 'Bloody hell, Squinty! What do you think you're playing at?'

'Let me in, Clete! I've unbelievable news! Beynor of Moss is here in the castle!' He pushed past the other wizard, who had been the Hebdomader or Prefect of Discipline for the Zeth Brethren of Cala Palace during Kilian's tenure as Royal Alchymist of Cathra, while Niavar himself had held the even more exalted post of Keeper of Arcana. Both men had shared their master's downfall and endured years of imprisonment with him. They now served as the Lord Chancellor's closest confidants.

'He's in a deep windsearching trance,' Cleaton said, motioning for Niavar to follow him into the inner rooms of the large apartment, 'trying to learn whether the Salka army is actually retreating to Moss. He's got to come off the wind soon or risk shriveling his brain. This is the third long-range scan he's done this afternoon. He also overlooked Prince Dyfrig and his scouting party and made an unsuccessful attempt to scry out the Wold Wraith.'

'You mean Casya Pretender? The girl who claims to be Didion's lost queen?'

'The same.' Cleaton's incongruously small mouth assumed a sour smile. 'King Somarus has commanded the master to find her and kill her. High time, if you ask me! But the bitch is under the protection of the Green Men, so tracking her down won't be easy . . . Now what's all this about Beynor?'

'I must inform the master first,' Niavar said primly.

Cleaton hissed in exasperation. 'Well, come along then.'

The two wizards entered a dimly lit chamber that seemed part thaumaturgical laboratory and part library. In the far corner was the tufted leather longchair used by Kilian during his more strenuous conjuring activities. He reclined on it, wrapped from head to toe in a black hooded cloak that concealed his face. The Lord Chancellor was a vain man, and an adept riding the wind was sometimes not a pretty sight.

Seated on a wooden chair at Kilian's side was a very good-looking blackrobe who appeared at least two decades younger than his associates. His name was Garon Curtling, and like the others he was a defrocked Brother of Zeth who had thrown in his lot with Kilian. Unlike Niavar and Cleaton, Garon had not served his master in Cala Palace or abetted his treason. Instead, he was the person who had enabled Kilian and his confederates to escape from Zeth Abbey. A member of a highland clan, Garon had guided the others over the rugged Sinistral Mountains to an eventual safe haven in Didion.

Garon Curtling had broken his vows and joined the fugitives because he could no longer abide the closely regulated, celibate life required of Cathrans possessing talent. In Didion (Kilian had informed him) magickers could enjoy feminine company without shame. They could even practise their craft independently and for profit if they chose, without being forced to join some repressive Order. Should Garon choose to remain with Kilian and the two other loyal associates while they wormed their way into King Somarus's confidence, there would be ample opportunities for all of them to make a lot of money.

Kilian had prospered mightily in the service of Didion, and so, in a more modest way, had Niavar and Cleaton. But Garon, who had gone directly from his family's isolated croft in the uplands to the novitiate at Zeth Abbey, was much less adept at soliciting bribes and kickbacks from supplicants at the court of Somarus in Holt Mallburn. Garon also spent more on women, strong drink, and gambling than his older colleagues, with the result that he accumulated no savings and finally had to be placed on an allowance by Kilian like an improvident son . . .

'I think he's waking up.' Cleaton bent over his recumbent master. 'Garon, prepare a tray with small beer and some honeycakes. He'll be weak and thirsty and require something sweet to restore his strength.'

The younger wizard nodded amiably and went off into an adjacent room. Cleaton fetched a basin of cool water and a cloth, lifted Kilian's hood, and began to bathe his livid, emaciated face. The elderly chancellor uttered a broken moan and his eyelids fluttered.

'What did the master learn about Prince Dyfrig and his men?' Niavar asked his colleague in a whisper. 'Was there any hint of that other mysterious discovery they supposedly made – the one only Conrig and Somarus and High Sealord Sernin were told of?'

Cleaton shook his head. 'Lord Kilian oversaw the reconnaissance party approaching the southern boundary of the morass above Black Hare Lake. They must have pressed on at an extraordinary pace in order to have covered ground so rapidly. Whatever the other discovery is, Prince Dyfrig is in a rare hurry to pass it along. But neither he nor any member of his party discussed it in a way that the master could discover through lip-reading.'

'Did he estimate how long it would take the group to reach Boarsden?'

'They won't reach a village with horses available until tomorrow. After that – with many changes of mount, and if the weather stays good and their stamina holds up – they could well arrive here in a couple of days.'

Both of the older wizards fell silent as their younger colleague returned with food and drink for the recovering Kilian. Cleaton lifted the chancellor to a sitting position while Niavar held a cup of beer to his blue-tinged lips.

'I'd – I'd rather have white wine,' the alchymist said in a cracked voice. 'Will you please fetch some, Garon?'

'But I'll have to go all the way to the buttery, my lord –'

'Then do so at once,' Cleaton snapped. 'And see that you re-secure the spell of couverture as you go out the door!'

Garon gave a negligent bow and sauntered away.

'You should not be so harsh with him,' Kilian murmured.

The former disciplinarian's brow was thunderous. 'He shouldn't question your orders, master. Nor mine and Niavar's, for that matter. But he does. Also, he's getting slip-shod and lazy in the performance of his regular duties and discontented with his allowance. The town doxies have upped the price for their favors.'

Kilian pinched the bridge of his aristocratic nose and screwed his face up briefly in pain. The strain of windspeaking had left him looking even older than his six-and-seventy years. 'Enough! Don't vex me with your petty squabbles. I'll take the beer after all, Niavar. I need something right now to moisten my throat after that last futile bout of scrying.'

The little wizard presented the cup again. 'So your survey of the Salka was disappointing, master?'

'There was little I could ascertain of their army's move-ment once the creatures entered the sea. Whilst swimming they are almost beyond my ken. I did scry feeding activity along the coast just east of the Beacon River, but it seemed to involve relatively small numbers of the monsters. One wonders if the tricksy wretches are really heading for home.'

'You believe they seek to mislead windwatchers?' Cleaton said.

'It's quite possible . . . I did spot two disguised Tarnian sloops approaching the area, keeping well out to sea. No doubt they've been sent by High Sealord Sernin to reconnoiter. If the vessels carry competent scriers my own oversight of the area may be redundant.'

'How so, master?' Cleaton wondered.

The chancellor sighed. 'I'd hoped to confirm the Salka retreat and announce my findings at the feast. I'm rather badly in need of a boost to my prestige, lads! When I talked to King Somarus last night, he was in an ugly mood. Not inclined to accept my good counsel at all. It seems His Majesty has had presaging dreams – of a free Didion, no less, shed of the yoke of Sovereignty! I didn't know what to make of it.'

Niavar gave a great start. 'My lord, I – I may have an explanation. Something unexpected has occurred, which may bode no good for our own secret objectives. Beynor of Moss has turned up. He's here in Boarsden Castle: an honored guest!'

'What?' Kilian sat bolt upright. 'Tell me everything!'

Niavar said, 'I heard rumors of a newly arrived nobleman from the servants, and also learned that Lord Stergos and his clique of senior magickers had been urgently summoned to wait upon the High King whilst this visitor was given a hearing. The audience chamber was secured by couverture and it was impossible for me to oversee the meeting itself; but afterwards I sought some of the Zeth Brethren out, keeping myself concealed, and listened to their gossip.'

He narrated a second-hand account of Beynor's meeting with Conrig and his ultimate affirmation as the legitimate Conjure-King of Moss, then concluded: 'So the scoundrel will sit at the high table at tonight's feast along with the heads of Blenholme's other vassal states.'

'And there is no doubt of this upstart's identity?' Kilian asked.

'King Somarus recognized Beynor, my lord. And the fellow carried Moss's Sword of State. The Zeth Brethren I eavesdropped upon are fully convinced that this man is the deposed Conjure-King. They said his aura was one of a powerful sorcerer, although his demeanor was mild and conciliatory. He claims he's been in exile on the Continent for the past two decades, after losing his throne to his sister Ullanoth. We know this to be false – he was with the Salka for some of that time – and one might suspect that High King Conrig also has his doubts. Yet he gave Beynor the royal accolade. Dubbed the whoreson with Moss's own Sword of State!'

'Ironcrown is up to something,' Kilian said. 'He would not have welcomed this landless knave to the inner circle of the Sovereignty lightly.'

'He hasn't quite done that yet,' Niavar pointed out. 'The Zeth Brethren said that the fellow is being hedged about with magical safety precautions. The Royal Alchymist even performed the "All Harmful Spells Avaunt" ritual over him, using one of Bazekoy's blue pearls. It'll hold good so long as Beynor remains within the ambit of Boarsden Castle.'

'Well, well!' Kilian's eyes gleamed with speculation. 'That's a useful thing to know.'

Niavar went on. 'When you spoke of King Somarus having strange dreams, I thought immediately of Beynor's peculiar talent. He could have been attempting to influence the sleeping king before presenting himself at court.'

'God of the Depths! That would imply that Beynor was situated reasonably close to Didion during part of his term of exile. He would not have been able to perform dream-invasion from a great distance.' The chancellor frowned at his henchmen. 'What about you two? Was there ever any hint that he encroached upon your slumber?'

'Nay, my lord,' Cleaton said. 'If he even made an attempt on me, I would have known.'

'As would I,' Niavar said. 'Each night before retiring, both of us conjure the somnial defensive screen you taught us long years ago. Not, I must confess, because we feared Beynor

– but rather to repel any possible assault by Salka mind-meddlers. Since the monsters activated the Potency sigil, we've been wary of what mischief they might attempt.'

'Beynor invaded the dreams of Somarus years ago,' Kilian recalled, 'to prepare him for the assassination of his brother Honigalus. I wonder who else he might have targeted? Not me, certainly. Not Stergos Wincantor or any other highly talented adept. But there are so many others without talent who are vulnerable, including even the Sovereign himself . . .'

Cleaton said, 'My lord, forgive me if I presume, but I believe this Conjure-King is a serious danger to you personally and to the great goal we've all worked so long and hard for.'

'You may be right,' Kilian said wearily. 'Yet keep in mind that he will be no easy mark. Beynor's natural talent is tremendous, even though he still carries the curse of the Great Lights.'

'Can we be sure of that?' Niavar said.

'No,' Kilian admitted. 'We can take nothing for granted where the capricious Beaconfolk are concerned.' He was silent for a time. 'And if Beynor spent his years of silent exile on High Blenholme Island rather than on the Continent, *what was he doing?* And why has he chosen to resurface here and now in this blatant – even irrational – manner, knowing that I'll deem him a mortal threat?'

'Clete spoke the truth, my lord,' Niavar said. 'We must find a way to kill him. Tonight, if possible.'

The chancellor sighed. 'Pull up some chairs, friends, and let's consider our options.'

The presence of Moss's green banner, in company with those of the other states of the Blenholme Sovereignty above the high-table dais, caused an undertone of shocked amazement during the processional entry and the seating of the guests at the lower tables. The handful of persons who knew the why of it spread word that Beynor the Conjure-King was back – reinstated by the Sovereign himself in spite of the fact that his kingdom had been overrun by man-eating monsters.

Extraordinary!

A flourish of trumpets rang out from the music gallery. The gorgeously attired royal personages and privileged guests began to enter, led by Duke Ranwing Boarsden and Duchess Piery. As befit his latecomer status among the vassals, Beynor followed the host and hostess. Cathra's Royal Alchymist came half a pace behind the Mossland sorcerer, smiling wanly and keeping his folded hands up the sleeves of his formal robes as though he were carrying something secretly. Then came the High Sealord of Tarn and Head of the Company of Equals, Sernin Donorvale, along with his adult sons Simok and Orfons; the new Grand Shaman Zolanfel; and Tarn's Field Commander, Sealord Yons Stormchild. Accompanying King Somarus of Didion was Crown Prince Valardus and his wife Princess Elyse; Duke Azarick Dennech-Cuva, who was Didion's Commander-in-Chief, and his wife Duchess Vyane; and the Royal Chancellor Kilian Blackhorse. Last of all to assume their seats were the Sovereign and his wife High Queen Risalla, accompanied by their oldest son Vra-Bramlow, Earl Marshal Parlian Beorbrook, and Cathra's Lord Lieutenant, Hale Brackenfield, with his wife Countess Orvada and their daughter Lady Nyla.

Two high-table chairs immediately to the left hand of Conrig Ironcrown remained empty.

The Sovereign, garbed in cloth-of-gold and black samite, rose with both hands lifted high. The throng of over two hundred peers, knights, and noble ladies waited in hushed eagerness for his announcement.

'My friends!' Conrig's voice, while carrying to every corner of of the great hall, had an oddly flat and ironic timbre. 'You were invited here tonight to witness and celebrate a ceremony of betrothal between my son, the Prince Heritor of Cathra, and Her Royal Highness, Princess Hyndry of Didion. A certain difficulty has arisen ... However, it is my fervent hope that the betrothal shall proceed as planned.'

Bewildered whispers and exclamations were suppressed as the High King turned and beckoned – first to the curtained vestibule on his right, and then to the one on the left. 'Let our beloved children enter.'

Orrion and Corodon, a thickset youth and a tall one, wearing simple gold coronets on their heads, came from the right, moving in front of the dais. They were dressed alike in white brocade with full-length crimson cloaks that concealed most of their upper bodies. Their faces were emotionless.

The Princess Royal, wearing a gown of Didion's heraldic silver and sable, emerged more tardily from the left. She was not very tall, but moved with the grace and confidence of a dancer. Her low-cut bodice and spectacular diamond necklace did nothing to distract attention from her admirable breasts. Hyndry was one-and-twenty years of age, widowed for two years after being married at sixteen to an elderly timberlord whose loyalty Somarus had been anxious to ensure. She had not yet given birth, so her waist and hips were still as lissome and shapely as those of a girl. Her hair was dark, worn in an elaborate coiffure of multiple braids topped by a diadem decorated with glittering rays of platinum. Her face was comely rather than beautiful, with a sharp nose and chin, and thin lips stained rosy pink.

Hyndry Mallburn stopped short when she saw *two* Cathran princes approaching her. Her blue eyes widened in perturbed surprise; but an instant later she regained her composure and stood with the twins before the Sovereign. Orrion and Corodon bowed to their royal father and Hyndry made a deep curtsey. Then they stepped back, made polite obeisance to one another, and again faced the High King.

'My dear daughter Hyndry,' Conrig said, 'you are plainly astonished – as are most persons within this hall – at the sight of two prospective husbands rather than the one you expected.'

'Damned right she is!' King Somarus surged to his feet, upsetting several goblets on the table before him; fortunately, they were still empty. 'What kind of a game d'you call this?'

'Be at ease, Your Majesty,' Conrig said, 'and all will be made clear.' He paused while the Didionite monarch sank back heavily into his seat, then addressed his sons. 'Orrion. Corodon. Please remove your cloaks and extend your arms.'

There was bedlam as the princes obeyed and the truth of the Heritor's condition became obvious. Gasps and groans of sympathy and revulsion came from many, along with furious roars amongst some of the warriors of Didion, who seemed to regard the revelation as an affront or even a misguided prank. Somarus emitted a howl that was almost triumphant, while poor Queen Risalla, Orrion's mother, fell back in her chair in a swoon, prompting the noble ladies at the high table to rush to her aid.

Princess Hyndry stood transfixed, her face turned to a mask devoid of emotion. She mouthed a single word inaudible in the tumult, which made Corodon's brows lift.

Earl Marshal Parlian picked up a great silver ladle intended for the serving of soup and banged it on the high table. 'Silence, all of you!'

The cries and babbling died away. Ironcrown continued in a tone that was unnaturally calm. 'My son Orrion has by doleful mischance lost his sword-arm and hand whilst hunting in the mountains. By our law he is now ineligible to become High King of Cathra and Sovereign of Blenholme. With my permission he abdicates in favor of his twin brother, Prince Corodon.'

In a manner obviously rehearsed, Orrion dropped to his

knees and kissed his brother's hand. After this he rose, approached the table, took off his coronet, and gave it into the outstretched hand of the Sovereign.

Conrig nodded and said to his son, 'Carelessness on your part caused this disaster. Therefore you will be punished.' He turned toward the right end of the high table. 'Hale Brackenfield, Lord Lieutenant of the Realm of Cathra, arise and approach.'

Looking mystified, Brackenfield did so.

Conrig once again addressed the entire company. 'I decree that Orrion Wincantor is here and now reduced to the rank of Knight Bachelor, forfeiting all honors and revenues attached to his erstwhile royal position. He is further banished from my court and commanded to take up residence in Castle Stormhaven, in the County of Westley and fiefdom of Brackenley, where he will remain subject to my pleasure. To this end, I place him in the charge of my Lord Lieutenant, owner of that castle, who will at dawn convey Sir Orrion thence by the fastest means possible.'

'Very well, my liege,' Brackenfield said. 'And is Pr – Sir Orrion now subject to my authority?'

'I name you my deputy in this matter,' Conrig replied, 'and command that you keep my son secure and safe. Please remove him from the hall immediately and keep him under close guard until your departure.'

'I will do so, Your Grace.' Brackenfield led Orrion away by grasping his good arm. Countess Orvada left her place at table, accompanied after a few moments by Lady Nyla, who had tears streaming unheeded down her cheeks. The countess retrieved Orrion's cloak, beckoned to her downcast daughter, and followed after her husband and Orrion.

When the four of them were gone, Princess Hyndry drew herself up, looked Conrig boldly in the eye, and said, 'That's all very well, sire! But what about *me*?'

'Hold your tongue, girl!' King Somarus growled.

'The man I agreed to marry is degraded and banished,' the princess persisted. She flipped a dismissive hand at Corodon. 'I won't be given casually to his twin brother like some outgrown garment handed down to a younger child! Orrion was at least a person of gentility and intelligence, with whom I was acquainted. I don't know *this* man at all, and what I've heard of him does not impress me.'

Corodon laughed aloud, and so did some seated at the low tables; but High King Conrig stood impassive.

'The law of Didion cannot compel a Princess Royal to take a husband against her will,' Hyndry declared in a voice that rang from the walls of the hall. 'I won't marry Corodon Wincantor.'

Most of the minor nobles and knights of Didion gave a great cheer and pounded their knife hilts on the tables until Somarus surged up again, face gone red and apoplectic, and shouted, 'Enough, damn you!'

Kilian the Lord Chancellor, who sat beside his king, now addressed him in urgent whispers. When Somarus nodded peevishly and took his seat, Kilian rose and bowed to the Sovereign. 'The reluctance of a spirited young woman to accept a husband without knowing more of his true character is quite understandable. Perhaps an interim period of courtship is in order, Your Grace, during which the new Prince Heritor and the Princess Royal can take the measure of one another. We may then hope that certain misunderstandings will be smoothed away –'

'No!' Hyndry said, turning her back on Corodon and pouring the full measure of her scorn upon the blackrobed wizard. 'I let you pressure me before with your crafty appeals, my lord. I won't make that mistake again. I'll choose my own second husband.'

'It *is* her right, you know!' The Duke of Dennech-Cuva

spoke up with unconcealed relish. The others at the high table recalled that the duke's son Egonus – diplomatically absent from the feast – was the swain favored by the princess.

Kilian shot Cuva a malignant glance. King Somarus looked guileful and toyed with his table-knife. More roars of approval came from the Didionite warriors, while certain Cathrans responded indignantly to what they perceived as an insult to the new Heritor. Corodon favored his partisans with a shrug and a sad smile that pretended hurt feelings, as if to ask how a woman of sensibility could reject one so handsome and charming as he.

Earl Marshal Parlian spoke under his breath to Conrig. 'They'll be fighting in another minute.' He banged the soup-ladle again, commanding silence.

'No decision on this matter will be made tonight,' the Sovereign declared. Sighs of relief and frustrated mutterings came from below the salt. 'I command that you, Princess Hyndry, and you, Prince Heritor Corodon, now join us at the high table. Come along! No pouting! Since we cannot cele-brate a betrothal tonight . . . I intend to provide us with another reason for happiness and good cheer.' He paused, casting his gaze about until all of those present realized that something momentous was about to be revealed. A vast still-ness prevailed until Conrig spoke again.

'Minutes before we entered this hall, I was informed by Duke Ranwing's chief windvoice that there is no doubt that the Salka are in full retreat.'

The hall erupted in a thunderous roar. Conrig waited a few moments and then resumed. 'Tarnian sloops with highly talented shamans aboard have confirmed that the monsters are indeed withdrawing to Moss, as we hoped. Their invasion has been abandoned. The threat of all-out war is over. Our troops will soon be able to return home.'

Jubilant shouts shook the stones of Boarsden Castle. At

Duke Ranwing's signal, pages and other servitors rushed into
the hall to fill every cup and carry in bowls and platters of
food. And so the great feast commenced, and the tribulations
of Hyndry and Corodon (and Orrion as well) were forgotten.

After a time, Kilian Blackhorse excused himself, telling
Somarus that the excitement and noise and rich food and
drink were giving him a liver attack. Rather to his surprise,
the monarch commiserated and urged him to seek a little
fresh air before getting a good night's sleep. Somarus even
beamed with kindly satisfaction as Azarick Cuva helped the
wizard to rise. When Kilian was gone, the two old friends
put their heads together in earnest conversation.

At the other end of the high table, the Royal Alchymist
Stergos was beginning to show the effects of consuming a
bit too much of his favorite Stippenese vintage. He was glad-
dened and relieved that the many stressful situations of that
long day had been satisfactorily resolved. Beynor was
behaving impeccably and there had been no need to call
upon Emperor Bazekoy's blue pearl again. The prospect of
peace on the island and an early return to his own quiet
sanctum in Cala Palace seemed worthy reasons for Stergos
to celebrate, so he overindulged in wine and eventually fell
into a doze, thus failing to notice when the seat next to him
at table was suddenly vacant.

Nor did anyone else take note of Beynor's disappearance.
The spell he cast was entirely benign, designed to work in
concert with the effects of ardent spirits and a surfeit of fine
victuals upon those enchanted. Using windsight to track
Kilian Blackhorse out of the castle hall onto the long battle-
ment overlooking the River Malle, the Conjure-King slipped
away after him.

The Lord Chancellor had already coerced the sentries
patrolling that section of the curtainwall to move off and

give him privacy. He was not really ill, only weary of verbal fencing with Somarus and his crony Cuva. Both of them had been elated by Hyndry's rejection of Corodon and flatly unwilling to consider Kilian's suggestions for changing the wilful widow's mind.

The very situation that Kilian dreaded was coming to pass: Somarus was thinking seriously of disavowing the Sovereignty. His surly manner tonight proved it. With the Salka horde in apparent disarray, Didion no longer had desperate need of Cathra's military support. Prospects for the royal marriage Kilian had counted upon to solidify the union between the two nations were in ruins.

'And so are my own ambitions,' the old schemer said to himself. 'Well, I'll think of something else . . . Or is it finally time to give up on intrigue and manipulation and living dangerously, take my accumulated treasure, and sail away to some warm and pleasant land?'

He began to pace slowly. Quitting the court of Didion and retreating to the Continent might be the best possible solution. Beynor's appearance boded nothing but mischief. What if he was still in league with the Salka? The scoundrel must be hatching some sort of convoluted plot, else he would not have approached Conrig so audaciously –

'Kilian Blackhorse!'

The wizard froze as he heard his name spoken.

This part of the castle's massive northern rampart was lit by fire-baskets; but they were far enough apart so that large areas of the parapet lay in deep shadow, especially the niches used by sentries for shelter during inclement weather. It was within one of these that the invisible man stood, only calling attention to himself after Kilian walked by, so that the wizard had to turn about to see who had called out softly to him.

But he knew it could only have been one person.

Beynor revealed himself in an eyeblink, standing with legs apart and arms folded nonchalantly. His smile was almost apologetic, so compelling and unthreatful that Kilian found himself holding back the magical thunderbolt he'd been about to fling. After all, Beynor was incapable of using harmful sorcery – and the Sovereign had accepted his pledge of fealty. One might as well find out what the rascal wanted.

'Have you been waiting long, Your Majesty?' Kilian inquired.

'No time at all, Lord Chancellor. Actually, I followed you out of the great hall unseen. What business we two must conduct won't take long. I'll have to return before I'm missed. The spell of misdirection I spun over the company won't last indefinitely.'

The Conjure-King was only a little taller than his former partner in crime, magnificently dressed in borrowed finery but without his Sword of State or anything resembling a crown. His narrow face with its frame of straight silvery hair was almost skull-like in the faint light, and his eyes were perceptible only as flame-sparks within dark orbits.

He vanished again. A moment later the wizard experienced the most frightful pain he'd ever known. It emanated from behind his right collarbone and was so appalling that he was rendered incapable of moving or uttering a sound. He would have collapsed from the shock, but a strong invisible hand cupped his chin from the rear, forcing his head back while the arm spanned his chest and held him precariously upright. Probing fingers dug again into the supersensitive spot. With his jaw held fast shut, Kilian's shriek of agony was muffled.

'Please don't move or attempt to use sorcery on me,' Beynor said. 'I'd rather not kill you. I'm going to let you talk to me, but if you cry out for help, you're a dead man.'

The grip on his chin relaxed. 'It hurts!' Kilian moaned.

'Stop pressing that nerve in my shoulder, for the love of God!'

The excruciating clavicular pang eased off. But Kilian, who had been trained as a physician in the Order of Zeth, knew it could be renewed again in an instant. The merciless fingers were still in place.

'I didn't think the strictures of Bazekoy's pearl would stop you for long,' the chancellor gasped. 'But . . . physical violence?'

'Sometimes the old-fashioned ways are best! Now tell me, my one-time friend: have you had any contact with the Salka Eminences during the years we were apart?'

'The Master Shaman Kalawnn and I bespoke one another a few times rather early on – not long after I became a close adviser to King Somarus. Kalawnn wished to discuss the Known Potency. He'd not yet learned how to activate it, you see. Ironcrown's navy bombarded Dawntide Citadel and destroyed the relevant archival tablet before the monsters finished studying it.'

'So you told Kalawnn about another source of information?'

'Two, actually,' said the former Doctor Arcanorum, 'written in the Salka language, of course. One lies in Zeth Abbey. I discovered that volume during my imprisonment there – a thing of mysterious provenance, purported to be a copy of a book written by Conjure-King Rothbannon himself. It was quite inaccessible to the Salka, of course. Unfortunately, there was no way I could get my hands on it, either.'

'And the second source was the original book, kept in the library of the Glaumerie Guild in Fenguard Castle,' Beynor stated. 'You only suspected it might be there, but your guess was a good one. I'd told you often enough about how Rothbannon got hold of his Seven Stones but forbore activating the Potency out of prudence. The rulers of the Conjure-Kingdom, myself included, have always known how to bring the Potency to life. The great mystery involved the Potency's operation. No one knew what it would do, save that it was likely to be mortally dangerous. Rothbannon himself was too cautious to activate it. Only when I deciphered the Salka archival tablet did I learn details of the sigil's functions.'

'I was not fool enough to tell Kalawnn about Rothbannon's book without demanding a reward,' Kilian said. 'I was promised five minor sigils of my choice, activated and then touched by the Potency so that I'd be able to use them without paying a pain-price to the Lights.'

Beynor laughed. A familiar bargain! 'Which did you choose?'

'An Interpenetrator, a Concealer, a Stunner, a Longspeaker, and a Wound-Healer. As agreed, I sailed to Fenguard in a heavily armed man o' war. My two most trusted associates, Niavar and Cleaton, accompanied me into the castle. A third man of mine, Garon Curtling, remained aboard the ship, which was moored in the Darkling River estuary with its port batteries aimed at the city. The captain had orders to bombard the castle and its environs with tarn-blaze munitions if an alarm was bespoken by me to Garon, or if I and my companions failed to return within two hours.'

The chancellor went on to describe what happened next. He and his underlings met the Four Eminences in the strangely remodeled throne room. A golden box holding the promised minor sigils, already glowing with uncanny life, was displayed to the humans. Five subordinate Salka, who had activated the stones and were thus bonded to them, demonstrated that the magical tools were in working order.

At this point, Kilian decided to trust Kalawnn, since there seemed to be no motive for treacherous dealing. He explained his hypothesis of the Guild library probably containing Rothbannon's original book about the Seven Stones.

The Eminences thought the idea was promising, but pointed out that the library had been sealed for safekeeping ever since the Salka invasion, since the paged books kept there would not stand examination by slimy Salka tentacle-digits. The place would have to be searched by humans – and the two-hour time span might not allow enough time for the task.

A problem easily solved: Kilian extended the deadline.

Within three hours the book was found. While Niavar and Cleaton held it open, Master Shaman Kalawnn intoned the lengthy conjuration that finally brought the Known Potency to effulgent life . . . inside the Salka leader's own gizzard.

Kilian and his companions were struck dumb with terror when the monster's throat glowed crimson, thinking that some catastrophe had occurred and Kalawnn was being consumed from within by astral fire. But the other Eminences only uttered ear-splitting contrabass chuckles.

The Conservator of Wisdom explained the unusual method of safeguarding the Stone of Stones. Then Kalawnn took up the golden box, opened wide his gigantic fanged maw, and dumped the box's contents down his gullet with a single neat flick. There was a brief bright flare, and then the glow in the Master Shaman's throat died away.

He spat out the minor sigils without ceremony and prof-fered them in their box to Kilian, who stared at the things dumfounded. They glowed softly green beneath a coat of slimy ichor – still alive, and presumably now free of any pain-debt to the Lights. But weren't they still bonded to the Salka who had originally activated them?

'You're understandably reluctant to take them up,' the Conservator of Wisdom said gravely. 'I have summoned a volunteer to demonstrate that the stones may now be handled safely by one who is not bonded to them, as was stated in the part of our archival tablet that we managed to decipher.'

The tall doors to the throne room swung open and two very large amphibians wearing the golden gorgets of military officers entered. They escorted a third Salka of woebegone aspect, whose tentacles were manacled with chains that seemed made of clear crystal.

'Krevalawnn, the test has been explained to you,' said the venerable Eminence. 'Pluck forth these sigils from their box and place them on the table.'

Trembling like a colossal blackish-green pudding with saucer-sized red eyes, the prisoner obeyed. When nothing at all happened to him, he exclaimed, 'Then I am free?'

'You are,' the Conservator affirmed. He gestured and the chains fell to the throne-room floor, their clatter muffled by the half-decayed layer of kelp that formed an odoriferous carpet.

As the officers led the volunteer away, the Conservator replaced the five minor sigils in the box himself, closed the lid, and handed it to Kilian. 'Our bargain comes to a satisfactory conclusion. And now you and your companions must make haste to board your ship before the tide turns. It would be dangerous for you to be caught in the Darkling Estuary at the ebb.'

'I have a final suggestion,' the Master Shaman said to Kilian. 'Even though these stones of yours are no longer connected to the pain-channels of the Sky Realm, they still partake of its powers. It would be prudent to use them circumspectly – only for serious reasons.'

*   *   *

'I agreed, and that was that.' The Lord Chancellor's voice had grown faint and raspy. 'Would you please consider releasing your hold on me now? Even without the nerve-pinch, being constrained in this fashion is very uncomfortable for one as old as I.'

'In a moment,' Beynor said. 'So you sailed home with the liberated sigils in your possession?'

'Yes.'

'And where are they now?'

Kilian began to laugh, a sound more dismal than mirthful. 'On a dusty cabinet shelf in my laboratory, where I relegated the accurst things after discovering the truth.'

'The . . . truth? You mean, they were useless? The Salka lied?'

'No, the monsters may have acted in good faith. They might not have known that an active sigil touched by the Potency will work only *once* after being rendered pain-free.'

'Once?' Beynor was incredulous. His own researches had hinted at no such thing. If it were true, his strategy would have to be changed.

'It's only logical, after all,' Kilian said. 'When the Beaconfolk discover that the stone no longer feeds their hunger, they refuse to empower it further.' He bit back another cry of pain. 'And now, Conjure-King, I've told you all I know about moon-stone sigils. I beseech you. Have pity on me!'

'Of course.'

The voice of the invisible man standing behind him was gentle. His grip on Kilian Blackhorse's chin eased and hope surged in the old alchymist's heart. But before he could conjure an attack-spell he felt the crook of an arm scissor his throat and a mighty blow strike his head at an oblique angle.

His neck snapped, and all thinking and scheming came to an end.

*   *   *

After consigning the body to the castle moat, from whence it would be carried into the river, Beynor returned to the feast, where no one had noticed his absence.

It was the best meal he'd had in twenty years.

NINE

High King Conrig went to bed alone that night, curtly rejecting the well-meant suggestion of his wife Risalla that she join him for mutual consolation. His tactless dismissal sent the queen away resentful and with hurt feelings; but he scarcely noticed, so infuriated and distraught was he at the defeat of his plan for the betrothal of Orrion and Hyndry.

Not even confirmation of the Salka army's retreat eased his mind. With the monsters now withdrawing, Somarus's loyalty would become more shaky than ever. He and Cuva had been thick as thieves during the feast, no doubt cooking up some fresh trouble. Hyndry's scornful dismissal of Corodon had played right into the Didionite king's fat hands.

Damn her for a pigheaded quiff! Damn Coro for . . . being what he was.

There seemed small chance of changing the mind of the headstrong Princess Royal through the courtship tactic proposed by Kilian. More likely, an unsuccessful public wooing would demonstrate to the entire Sovereignty what most members of the Cathran court already knew: that the new Prince Heritor was a poor second-best to his older twin.

How in God's name could such a handsome, empty-headed booby ever be worthy of the Iron Crown?

Burning with anger and frustration, awake and yet not awake, Conrig thrashed and turned until he sank at last into the strange half-conscious state that had plagued him for months – the nightmare of enemies.

The illusion this time was more vivid and fearsome than ever before. Once again he was trapped in a dim chamber with phantom adversaries on all sides, shrieking and jostling and vying with each other to tear the crown from his head. He laid about with his sword, hewing them to pieces, but no sooner were they hacked limb from limb than they rose up again, whole and stronger than ever.

Enemies. Everywhere.

Salka with clutching tentacles, blood-sucking spunkies, malignant bright Sky beings that tried to drink his pain, a scheming demonic creature, black and blind and immured in ice. And human foes! So many who hated and resented and feared him, persons alive and dead that he'd crushed or oppressed in order to keep that precious Iron Crown.

And now his own son had joined the evil host.

Not wretched Orrion; he was no threat. The enemy was another son, poised to snatch the crown away before any of the other foes realized that he was one of them. But who was he?

He had no face!

Conrig struck a heroic blow with his sword, severing the blank-featured head of the traitor-prince from his body, only to have another head grow up instantly to replace it. The unknown prince and the entire crowd of phantoms closed in, howling in a frenzy of rage and loathing.

Swinging the useless blade, Conrig screamed, 'Why won't you die? Why won't any of you die and leave me in peace?'

Because you are using the wrong weapon.

'Who spoke?' the High King cried in desperation. 'Is there help for me after all?'

There is. I'm here, bringing you what you need: the solution to all of your problems, the defense against all who hate you and would seize your crown.

At the end of his strength, Conrig caught sight of a tall thin man standing at the edge of the mêlée. He was holding up a small object, a wand of some sort carved from pale stone. *This is what you need to conquer.*

'Do I know you?' Conrig asked in bewilderment.

The man smiled. He and the enemies vanished. The nightmare ended as suddenly as it had begun, and the Sovereign of Blenholme slept dreamlessly until morning.

Deveron woke with Induna nestled against him. They lay on their sides under a warm coverlet, alone together in Eldmama Cray's borrowed cottage. The soft red-gold hair of his wife's head pressed against his lips and his arm caged her breasts gently as they rose and fell with her slow breathing.

Married for almost a day and a half! He thought about it and smiled as he remembered her shy confession on their wedding night: How desperately she had wanted him when they were finally reunited at his house in Mikk-Town. How she despaired when it seemed he'd make the magical journey to the Green Morass without her. More than anything in heaven and earth she had wanted to lie with him at least once before they separated forever. But a Tarnian woman would never take the initiative in such a private matter. It was against all custom for her to voice her desire. Instead she had flung herself into the boat with him as the Subtle Gateway opened, not caring what might happen to her so long as they remained together. In truth, she had not acted for any rational reason. She only wanted him and *would* have him, even if it meant defying the Source himself and the terrible Beaconfolk who empowered the Gateway sigil.

She had concluded her confession as he carried her to the marital bed for the first time. 'And now there's no need to ask the unaskable question. No need to explain.'

Nor was there. Both of them were persons of talent. With tacit permission freely given, they could speak wordlessly mind to mind as they consummated the love that had endured for sixteen years.

A night and a day and another night alone together. No one had been able to disturb them. Before departing with Thalassa Dru for the conference with the Source, Cray the Green Woman had taught Deveron how to shield her cottage with an invincible spell of couverture – a special wedding gift to her newfound great-great-grandson and his bride . . .

His arm tightened on Induna's body as the need awakened again within him. She woke smiling, turned and drew his face close to kiss his lips. Not a word was spoken. All that they did was perfect and sweet and complete. When it was done they lay apart, hand in hand.

'I wish we could stay here forever,' she whispered. 'In this little house, among these friendly people, in a world without brutal kings and wars and monsters and black sorcery.' She turned to look at him and her hand tightened in his. 'But we can't stay. You have your mission and now that you've recovered your strength you'll have to carry it out. But what will become of me?'

'We'll do the work together, of course.'

'What – what if the Source forbids it?'

Deveron laughed and took her in his arms. 'Let him try. Let *anyone* try to separate us now.'

They lay in a quiet embrace as the grey dawnlight intensified. The room was chilly, so he used his talent to kindle a fire in the wood already laid on the hearth, then scried beyond the cottage walls to see what kind of weather prevailed.

'There's fog this morning,' he observed. 'Dense as milk out in the morass, a little thinner here on the higher ground. Impossible to scry through. I wonder if we're in for an early autumn?'

She sighed. 'I suppose you ought to lift the spell of couverture. We should find out what's been happening in the outside world. But let's stay in bed until the fire warms the place up.'

'I can do that with my talent, too,' he pointed out.

She giggled. 'Use it to a better effect, my dearest, and I'll use mine as well.'

By the time they finished it was full light. They arose and dressed. While she collected bowls and cups and found tea to brew and eggs to boil and meal for griddle-cakes, he sat in a dim corner of the room and cancelled the cover-spell. Then he let the wind bring its messages to him.

The most urgent and astounding one came from a woman he had thought to be long dead. Ullanoth of Moss addressed him as Snudge, and seemed most annoyed that he had been unreachable for such a long time. Not even Cray and Thalassa, who had returned from beneath the Ice during the small hours of that morning, had been willing to breach the privacy of the newlyweds.

'Your Majesty! Is it really you? I thought you'd succumbed to the pain-debt of your Great Sigils many years ago. How do you know that private nickname of mine used by King Conrig?'

Obviously I am alive, Sir Snudge. And you need not style me as queen, for my younger brother Beynor has once again usurped the throne of Moss, thanks to your former master.

'Beynor is back?' Another amazing surprise.

Yes. The honored guest of the Sovereign in Boarsden Castle, where the battle-leaders of the realm are gathered in a Council of War against the Salka. As to your peculiar alias, I was reminded of it by Ansel Pikan, whom I attended on his deathbed –

'God rest him . . . What happened to the poor old fellow?'

He died two nights ago of wounds suffered in service to the Source, the One Denied the Sky. I also serve the New Conflict now, after atoning for my many evil deeds, and I know that you do as well. I bespoke you as Snudge because it is – and is not – your true name. This fact gives you a measure of protection from the worst caprices of the Great Lights, since you introduced yourself to them using it. Ansel bade me give you a message, one that's rather puzzling, concerning your new mission to the Sovereign of Blenholme.

'What is it, my lady? I know that I am to assist High King Conrig to carry out his own rôle in the New Conflict –'

The Sovereign who requires your assistance is not Conrig.

'What?! But that's –'

I can only tell you what Ansel said. A deathbed revelation came to him. And perhaps not vouchsafed by the Source at all. I've already discussed the matter with Cray and Thalassa, who wonder whether the information may have come from those mysterious allies of the Source who are called the Likeminded Remnant. As I understand it, these are 'good' Lights who were defeated in the Old Conflict but not confined beneath the Ice as was the Source. You will have to ask the others about this. I'll take up no more of your time, for I know they are anxious to bespeak you.

'Lady Ullanoth – wait! How am I to serve a Sovereign other than Conrig? As far as I know, such a person does not exist.'

Oh, he does. In the future if not in the present, and you must safeguard his life at all costs. Farewell, Sir Snudge.

Baffled, he sent out a windcall to his great-great-grand-mother. She responded at once, summoning him and Induna to the longhouse on the opposite side of the village, where the Green shamans had their workrooms and chambers for special ceremonies.

The situation is changing, Grandson, and not for the better. Come with your wife as soon as possible. I'll see that you're fed.

When the windthread snapped Deveron went to the hearth where Induna was at work. 'Hold off making our breakfast, sweetheart. We've been invited to eat with Eldmama Cray and Thalassa Dru. They're back from consulting the Source and have important tidings.' He lifted his shoulders in an apologetic gesture. 'I suspect our honeymoon is over.'

She swung the kettle away from the fire and kissed him. 'Never mind. So long as we can stay together, I'll be content.'

They had swooped down on the wagon-train not long after dawn, when it was barely five leagues out from Castlemont, a lightly armed company of Cathran warriors wearing the badge of a wildcat's paw. Their commander, a stout-bodied knight with a drinker's red nose and a cruel, thick-lipped mouth, wasted no time ordering her to dismount and doff her cloak and hat.

'She's the one!' he proclaimed in triumph, after studying a sheet of parchment that held a sketch. 'Her ugly face and the beanpole height of her are unmistakable . . . Rusgann Moorcock, you are under arrest for grand theft. Our Lord Constable, Tinnis Catclaw, commands that you be conveyed to Boarsden Castle and confined, awaiting his judgment.'

'You're mistaken!' she shrilled. 'I'm an honest herb-wife of Broadmead near Timberton, and my name is –'

Casually, the knight leaned from the saddle and smacked her across the face with the back of his gloved hand. 'Shut your gob, you smelly old besom, and climb back onto your mule. Larus! Trozo! Tie her wrists together and lash her feet to the stirrups.'

Two men-at-arms hastened to obey. The frightened drivers in the supply train sat mute on their wagons, helpless to save her. When Rusgann moaned at the tightness of her bonds, the brave carter who'd defended her from the border guard began to open his mouth. She eyed him and shook her head. When she was securely tied, the men remounted. One of them took the mule on a lead, and the entire troop of warriors wheeled about and headed for Boarsden.

Deveron and Induna put on wool cloaks against the morning dampness and made their way to the shamans' longhouse, greeted by smiling Green Folk going about their morning chores. A light drizzle began to fall, thinning the mist. Through a gap in the trees the partially ruined bulk of Castle Morass could be seen a scant half-league distant. Lighted windows shone in one of its broken towers.

'Do you suppose we'll get to meet the old robber-baron who owns the place before we go about our business?' Induna asked her husband. 'The village people only shook their heads when I asked about Ising Bedotha earlier. They said he's dotty as a mistle thrush. But I confess I'd love to know why he supports Casya Pretender and allows the Green Men sanctuary in his lands. Most Didionites fear the little people.'

'It's probably simple hatred of Somarus. The king was once an outlaw himself, you know, preying on Wold Road travelers with his gang of brigands until he took the throne and reformed. Since then, he's crushed most of the free-spirited barons of the backcountry without mercy – even those like Ising, who'd been his friends in the bad old days. I was told by Cray that royal troops battered Castle Morass for weeks, but the baron dug in his heels until Somarus finally called off the fight in disgust. The castle is really too remote from trade routes to be strategically important. Laying siege to it turned out to be prohibitively expensive.'

They walked together up the path leading to the long-house, which was a low building thatched with a deep layer of swamp grass. It had four chimneys and shuttered windows. The sheltered entry-way was adorned with the skulls of many small wild animals, strung into macabre garlands and hung from pegs. The door opened before they could knock. The Mossland sorceress Thalassa Dru emerged and immediately folded them both in her enormous soft embrace. She smelled of wild roses.

'Induna! Deveron! I was so sorry to miss your wedding. You must tell me all about it.'

'Perhaps later, Conjure-Princess,' Deveron said. 'We ask that you first recount your visit with the Source, and let us know what special duties he has planned for us.'

Cray, who had been almost hidden behind the voluminous robes of the larger woman, popped out smiling. 'Welcome, children! Come inside and you can eat as we talk. Everything's ready.'

The house had a central corridor illuminated by oil lamps, with many chambers opening on either side. In most of them nonhuman little shaman-crafters were at work on mysterious projects. They looked up and smiled briefly at the sight of the human visitors. Cray led the way to a larger room at the far end of the building, a kind of refectory and meeting-hall with several tables, chairs and benches, and a large fireplace holding a brisk blaze.

She seated Deveron and Induna at a low table near the hearth where two place settings waited, opened the warming oven, and removed a crock of oat porridge, two spit-roasted quail, and a dish of hot apple-bilberry compote. An adjacent pantry yielded honey, clotted cream, butter, and half a loaf of barley bread. She set out the food and poured four cups of mint tea, after which she and Thalassa Dru joined the newlyweds at the table.

'Won't you eat with us?' Induna protested.

'We broke our fast hours ago,' Cray said, 'when we

emerged from the trance state after dwelling subtly beneath the Ice visiting the Source. We let you two sleep in as long as we could.'

'One doesn't experience hunger or thirst while traveling entranced,' Thalassa explained. 'But when the soul and mortal body re-unite, one is ravenous!' She stirred a spoonful of honey into her tea and settled into a sturdy chair that had obviously been provided especially for her. 'Hmm. Perhaps I'll have just a bit of bread and butter!'

'Before you summoned us this morning,' Deveron said, 'I was bespoken by Lady Ullanoth. She said she had already told you of the strange statement made by Ansel Pikan as he lay dying – that our mission in the New Conflict is not to assist Conrig Ironcrown, but rather another Sovereign of Blenholme. Can you clarify this?'

'In good time,' Thalassa Dru replied. 'But first, tell me what you already know about the *Old* Conflict.'

'Very little,' Deveron admitted, while helping himself to the roast quail. He was also extremely hungry. 'At various times, the Source and Ansel spoke of a great battle between good and evil Lights that took place long ago and now is about to be resumed.'

Induna put cream on her porridge and mixed in some of the luscious stewed fruit. 'My mother Maris told me that the good Lights were defeated during the time that Emperor Bazekoy's invasion took place. Their leader was imprisoned beneath the Barren Lands icecap. Mother said that certain assistants – including herself – have worked throughout the centuries to liberate the leader, who calls himself the Source of the Conflict, and help prevent the Beaconfolk from extending their depraved dominion to humanity. The work of the helpers has mostly involved collecting inactive moon-stone sigils that were left scattered about the island by the Salka who fled Bazekoy's host.'

Cray nodded. 'We Green Folk also serve as helpers. Each time one of those recovered sigils was annihilated by the One Denied the Sky, he regained some of his lost strength. But let Thalassa tell the tale in an orderly fashion.'

It began in distant prehistoric times, when the Great Lights were a group undivided and incorrupt, only somewhat bored with their tranquil aetherial existence in the Sky Realm above the northern part of the world.

A certain Light conceived a great game. Its rules are unimportant – and indeed are rather incomprehensible to corporeal beings, except insofar as the game-pieces are concerned. For the inventor of the game used self-aware nonhuman creatures living on High Blenholme Island as unwitting pawns. First the Salka, and later the Small Lights, Green Men, and Morass Worms were drawn into the contest which was, in its early stages, almost entirely harmless to the game-pieces.

Each Great Light playing the game was alloted a number of pawns, who were subtly encouraged to choose one moon-stone sigil from a collection of many different kinds. The sigils were supernatural conduits that channeled Beaconfolk sorcery from the Sky Realm to that of the Ground. Some of the stones vouchsafed fairly inconsequential benefits to the user-pawn, while others were virtually miracle-working. The pawn was obliged to pay a price of physical discomfort in exchange for each magical deed performed with its sigil: the greater the magic, the more intense the discomfort.

The Light whose pawns were brave enough – or foolish enough – to rack up the greatest debt during a measured time period was declared the winner of that contest.

As time passed, the game changed character. While the spunkies, the Green Folk, and the Morass Worms eventually became wary of the insidious appeal of Beaconfolk sorcery and declined to participate any longer, the slower-thinking Salka grew more enthusiastic. Many were so eager to enjoy the magical rewards of the game that they manufactured their own sigils and clamored to become pawns.

Encouraged, the more unscrupulous players among the Lights created ever more powerful moonstones that demanded a genuinely painful – or even a deadly – price. In a terrible paradox, certain Lights began to revel in the torture that the Salka inflicted upon themselves. They learned to feed on the foolish amphibians' pain and became addicted to it. The original purpose of the game became perverted into a contest of sadistic gratification.

The Source realized too late the sinful thing he had done. He prevailed upon Likeminded Lights who were also dismayed by the burgeoning tragedy to help persuade the player-Lights to abandon their activities and close the channels that carried both power and pain. This effort was a failure. The Source then took on the material form of a Salka and entered the Ground Realm, where he hoped to end the game by convincing the amphibians that they were being shamefully exploited.

When most Salka refused to listen to him, the Source devised a unique sigil – the Potency – that he hoped would abolish the pain-debt associated with the moonstones and in time close the conduit. But when it came time for him to activate the Stone of Stones, he held back, not knowing for certain how the Potency would work. What if it made the situation worse, by enabling the Salka to use the sorcery of the Lights without any restrictions or consequences?

The pain-eating Beaconfolk were infuriated when they learned what the Source and the Likeminded had planned to do. They formed a Coldlight Army and initiated a mortal Conflict that spread throughout the Sky Realm and eventually affected the groundling inhabitants of High Blenholme as well.

The Likeminded were outnumbered and finally over-whelmed. Their selfless effort to save the Salka from the conse-quences of soul-destroying magic failed and they faced being extinguished. To spare his associates, the Source agreed to submit to the enemy's condition for an armistice. He would retain his Salka body and submit to imprisonment beneath the Ice. There he would suffer indefinitely as One Denied the Sky, while the evil Lights savored his pain and continued to oppress the Salka. Meanwhile, most of the vanquished Likeminded withdrew to the dark void between the stars, sunk in despair. They were immortal and immune to pain, since they lacked physical bodies, but their power shrank like the diminishing vitality of plants denied sunlight and water. Many of them forgot who they once had been.

A very few Likeminded, called the Remnant, remained on the periphery of the Sky Realm even though they risked being quenched by the Beacons. These good Lights stayed in contact with the Source of the Conflict and hoped that one day the situation might change.

Strangely, the triumph of the evil Beaconfolk was short-lived, thanks to an extraordinary human being. The Emperor Bazekoy invaded High Blenholme Island even as the two factions of Lights battled in the Sky. With the Beaconfolk game-players distracted and unable to guide them, the clumsy and slow-witted Salka were no match for a massive army of well-trained human warriors fighting on dry land. Not even their most powerful Great Stones could save them for long. They were ambushed by Bazekoy's troops and slain from afar by spears and arrows. They died by the thousands – and their sigils died with them, converted into useless bits of rock as the bonded owners perished.

The Salka survivors fled, some to the remote fens of Moss and some to the Dawntide Isles. Most of their Great Stones had long since been lost in futile skirmishes with the human foe. They continued to utilize their minor sigils only in a half-hearted way, and eventually allowed themselves to be duped by the human sorcerer Rothbannon, who took away their few remaining major sigils – including the Source's inactive Potency.

The frustrated Coldlight Army, now feeding on only meager amounts of pain, decided that the exiled Salka were a lost cause, unlikely ever to play the game again with their old enthusiasm.

So the Lights patiently began to target a new sort of pawn.

Cray the Green Woman now took up the tale from Thalassa as Induna and Deveron listened raptly.

The memory of the Old Conflict and the fate of the Source was for the most part safeguarded and passed from generation to generation by Cray's own people, who had resigned from the game long before Bazekoy's invasion. The Green Men, unlike the spunkies and Morass Worms, who also rejected the temptations of the Beaconfolk, had a culture that encouraged storytelling and the relating of racial history.

By and large, the first human settlers on High Blenholme had little interest in the Sky Realm, although they had a healthy fear of the demons who lived there. Very few of the newcomers possessed windtalent, so the sigils they sometimes found could never be empowered or bonded to them by the Beaconfolk.

Early on, the great human scholar of magic called Saint Zeth – one of the few talented associates of Emperor Bazekoy – made a special study of sigil sorcery and the uncanny power of the Boreal Lights. He deduced the danger posed by the moonstones and declared them anathema. The Mystical Order he founded would enforce this prohibition. Several centuries later, a certain Royal Alchymist of Cathra named Darasilo discovered a large collection of extinct sigils, together with two books in the Salka language describing their conjuration. He possessed talent but was too cautious to experiment with the moonstones, which he passed on to his successors as occult curios, along with a smaller book by an unknown sage which contained a partial translation of the Salka volumes into the Cathran language.

As humankind spread over the island, they mingled their blood with that of the curiously attractive and bewitching little Green Folk. These unions increased the number of talented humans, especially amongst the populations of Tarn and Moss.

Tarnian shamans were the first to travel successfully through so-called subtle corridors. In time – perhaps aided by the Green Men or the Likeminded Remnant – they learned the even more difficult art of soul-travel, which enables the practitioner to enter realms totally inimical to the human body. Thus they made contact with the imprisoned Source and began to help him. By doing so they put themselves in great danger; but the price seemed worthwhile when the Source explained that the Beaconfolk planned to shift the focus of their game from the Salka to human beings.

Thus the New Conflict was born.

'Some of your people enlisted freely in the cause,' Cray concluded. 'Other important humans, such as the Sovereign of Blenholme, Conrig Wincantor, were made use of without their knowledge, coerced by magic or otherwise influenced to act in a manner that would prevent the Beaconfolk from seducing humanity as they had seduced the amphibians. Conrig's unification of the island nations saved Blenholme from being invaded by Continental adventurers working in collusion with the criminally ambitious Conjure-King Beynor, a sigil-user himself. Certain persons close to Conrig – particularly *you*, my dear Grandson! – aided the Source significantly and set in motion the final phase of the New Conflict.'

Thalassa Dru took up the thread of the narrative.

'My nephew Beynor is afflicted with the unstable mentality that brought on the insanity of his late father. When the Lights realized they were backing a young lunatic who posed a danger to the Known World through wanton misuse of sigils, they first considered slaying him – just as they had earlier killed his imprudent mother Taspiroth. Instead, they contrived a way to use him.

'Cursed and deposed from his throne, Beynor was exiled to the Dawntide Isles. His persuasive schemes roused the Eminent Four Salka from their longstanding torpor and inspired them to begin a fresh war against humanity – which it seemed only Conrig and his Sovereignty could thwart. And this Conrig did. For sixteen years he held the monsters in check. But now the Source and the Likeminded Remnant sense a change in the offing. Triggered by Beynor.'

'It seems he's wormed his way into the Sovereign's good graces,' Deveron noted, pulling a face. He had finished both quail when Induna declined her share and now attacked a large bowl of honeyed porridge. 'But I can't believe the High King would trust the fealty of such a rogue magicker, nor put him into a position where he could influence matters of state.'

'Conrig hasn't done so yet,' said Thalassa in a bleak tone. 'But the one person who might have prevented that calamity – or even delayed it – has just died. Last night, just before Cray and I returned from our sojourn beneath the Ice, every adult person living in this village heard a singular shriek on the wind. Kilian Blackhorse perished of a broken neck at the hands of Beynor. Several of our more talented scriers traced the outcry to Boarsden Castle and observed the Conjure-King fling the corpse of his old crony into the moat. The body was recovered from the River Malle this morning.'

'God's Truth!' Induna exclaimed.

Thalassa nodded. 'Indeed. When I recovered sufficiently from my entrancement to be told of it, I bespoke Stergos, the Royal Alchymist, at the castle for details. He is a good friend of our cause who joined the New Conflict willingly. According to Stergos, the consensus among the distinguished guests of Duke Ranwing is that the Lord Chancellor was deeply depressed over a certain scheme of his that had come undone, and took his own life.'

'Kilian dead!' Deveron finished the last of the oatmeal and licked his spoon. 'I suppose King Conrig is overjoyed that his wicked old uncle is gone.'

'On the contrary,' said the Conjure-Princess. 'In late years, the chancellor was an ally of the Sovereignty and did his best to convince King Somarus not to rebel against it.' The sorceress related how the royal marriage was to have strengthened Didion's loyalty, how Prince Heritor Orrion came to be maimed and degraded, and how the Princess Royal herself had rejected Kilian's compromise that might have seen her betrothed to Corodon.

'Prince Orrion lost his sword-arm through Beaconfolk sorcery?' Induna cried in disbelief. 'How could this happen if he had no sigil?'

'He and his brothers hardly knew what they were doing when they climbed the Demon Seat hoping for a miracle. The entire summit of the mountain is an outcropping of raw moonstone mineral, and this was sufficient to channel sorcery from the Sky. But the true miracle that took place is one that none of the princes expected – for Orrion's rash petition was answered not by the evil Great Lights but by the Likeminded Remnant, who were thought to be too feeble to use the power conduit to the Ground Realm.'

Cray added, 'The Source was able to confirm that it was his benevolent allies who answered Orrion's misguided prayer. The Remnant were confused when the prince's petition reached them. But their intention was only to do good, to give Orrion the wife he wanted.'

'And instead they contrived to get the poor devil disinherited and disgraced,' Deveron observed scornfully, 'and they may have destroyed Conrig's Sovereignty to boot! Do you call *that* a miracle?'

'The miracle,' said the Green Woman with great patience, 'is that the good Lights are no longer impotent. The second Moon Crag may in some way enable them to resume the fight against the Coldlight Army. The Source is as yet uncertain how this might be accomplished, as are we. But we hope to learn more as time goes by.'

Deveron heaved a rather exasperated sigh. 'Meanwhile – what am I supposed to do? And Induna?'

'We have no instructions concerning your wife,' Cray admitted.

Thalassa Dru rose from her seat with easy dignity. Her head with its coronet of braids nearly touched the rafters of the low-roofed lodge. 'But *your* orders, Deveron Austrey, are to free a woman named Rusgann Moorcock, who has just been captured by the henchmen of the Lord Constable of Cathra and is being taken to Boarsden Castle for questioning under torture. Rusgann carries a secret letter. It is imperative that this missive be delivered to Prince Dyfrig Beorbrook, who will soon arrive at that castle after having concluded a military mission –'

'But we know this Rusgann!' Induna exclaimed in surprise. 'She was the dear friend of Princess Dowager Maudrayne during her captivity in Tarn. Deveron and I participated in the rescue of both women, together with Maude's little son Dyfrig.' Her face fell. 'But as I understand it, the princess took poison when King Conrig decreed that she would never see her boy again.'

'Princess Maude did not die of poison,' Deveron said. He explained how she had been spirited away by Tinnis Catclaw.

'That was sixteen years ago, however. I know not whether the princess still lives –'

'Oh, Maude's alive and well, all right,' Thalassa said with a sardonic grimace. 'Catclaw installed her in a luxurious hunting lodge of his, deep in the mountains east of Beorbrook Hold, and kept her as his willing captive and leman. Rusgann Moorcock was Maude's companion there until the princess sent her away secretly to deliver her letter to Prince Dyfrig. The letter contains information that the Source believes to be vitally important to the New Conflict. When the Lord Constable learned of Rusgann's escape, he realized that he was in deadly danger. He had told the High King that he'd killed Maudrayne years earlier, as Conrig had ordered. If she were found in Tinnis's hideaway, his own life would be forfeit. So he arranged to evacuate the place, leaving only the Princess Dowager behind. One of his men set the lodge on fire. It was intended that Maude should burn to death and her body be destroyed. But she escaped.'

'Thank God!' murmured Induna. 'What's happened to the poor woman?'

'The Source only told us that she was free,' Thalassa said. 'He seemed concerned mainly with the letter she'd written to her son.'

'Typical,' muttered Deveron. 'In his own way, the One Denied the Sky is as much of an inhuman puppetmaster and game player as his evil cousins, the Beaconfolk.'

Thalassa gave a sigh and stared at her hands, folded in her lap. 'There's some truth in what you say. Ansel Pikan was known to berate the Source for being coldly manipulative. But I think this time you must permit yourself to be coerced, Deveron Austrey. Save the woman Rusgann if you can. But you *must* secure the letter she carries and see that it reaches Dyfrig. In it, Maudrayne tells him he is the rightful heir to the Iron Crown of Sovereignty.'

'Good God,' Deveron murmured, his brow knit in thought. 'Could *that* have something to do with Ansel Pikan's deathbed statement?'

'I think it very likely,' the sorceress said. 'You should set out for Boarsden at once.'

'Our friend Baron Ising will furnish you with mounts from his stable,' Cray said. 'Eleven leagues south of Castle Morass lies the River Kelk, which is navigable. The Kelk flows into the Malle, which will carry you directly to Boarsden. The voyage is some two hundred leagues. Using the combined talents of you and your wife to augment the natural motive power of sail and current, I estimate that you might reach your destination in as little as eighteen hours.'

Deveron's hand strayed to the golden case hanging at his neck. 'But if Rusgann is captured and in danger of torture or death, it behooves us to travel in the quickest manner possible: using my Subtle Gateway sigil.'

Cray shook her head. 'Nay, Grandson. I think it most unwise for you to call upon Beaconfolk sorcery to assist you in this journey. Only recall the cruel trick they played on you the last time you conjured Gateway! You would have lost your life had Induna not been with you. I think there would be small risk in using your minor sigil, Concealer, on this mission. But it's best that you travel to Castle Boarsden by mundane means.'

'We'll need a trustworthy river boatman then,' Deveron said.

'Seek the advice of Ising Bedotha, the lord of Castle Morass.' A sly grin crept over the little woman's face. 'That old brigand knows the wilderness of the Great Wold Heath better than the palm of his hand.' She rose from her seat at the table. 'Have you and Induna had enough breakfast?'

'Yes, Eldmama,' the husband and wife replied in unison.

'Then come with me. I'll introduce you to the baron.'

*   *   *

'Recommend a boatman to take you to Boarsden?' howled the wild-eyed old man. 'Be damned if I will!' He gulped down the contents of a lidded beer mug and slammed the vessel onto a sideboard with a loud crash.

Deveron and Induna flinched and exchanged apprehensive glances.

Cray spoke sternly. 'Now behave yourself, Lord Ising. The request is harmless enough –'

Gangling as a scarecrow dressed in splendid robes, the elderly noble capered around the solar of his dilapidated castle laughing at the top of his lungs.

'No, no, Mistress Cray! You misunderstand.' He skidded to a halt before the visitors, cocked his head owlishly, and laid a knobby finger aside of his long nose. The sparse silver hair on his scalp and his straggling beard seemed to crackle with electric tension. His brilliant blue eyes bulged as though about to pop from their sockets.

Cray sighed. 'Explain yourself, my lord baron.'

'Your young relatives won't need a boatman,' Ising Bedotha proclaimed. 'I've been navigating Didion's rivers since I was a snottynosed sprog with mud between my toes. I intend to take them to Boarsden Castle myself! As it happens, I have secret business in the vicinity. And so does my liege lady, Queen Casabarela, who's a fair sort of river-rat herself. We'll all travel together.' He screwed up his face in a huge wink as his voice sank to a conspiratorial whisper. 'And likely these two outland magickers will help Casya and me as much as we'll help them. Tit for tat, eh?'

Deveron inclined his head in reluctant agreement. 'We have our own mission to carry out, but we'll do whatever we can to assist you both, my lord.'

The baron smacked his hands together in antic glee. 'Splendid! I'll tell Casya the good news. Now that her broken wrist is nearly healed, she's been champing at the bit, anxious to get to the Didion heartland where the army is camped out. Her grandsire, Duke Kefalus Vandragora, is there with his warriors. She thinks it's about time he met the Wold Wraith.'

Giggling wickedly, Ising Bedotha turned back to the sideboard, tapped a small keg atop a silver stand, and refilled his mug with beer.

Deveron shot a worried glance at his wife. What had they let themselves in for?

Induna only shrugged and said to the baron, 'When can we be off, my lord?'

'How about right now?' the baron replied, in a voice that was quiet and stone-cold sober. He sipped the brew and eyed them narrowly. 'No time like the present, eh?'

TEN

'It's too lovely a day to be sad,' Lady Nyla Brackenfield said, guiding her white palfrey closer to the tall bay gelding Orrion rode. 'And since I outrank you, sir, you must obey my command to speak only pleasantries as we journey to Rockyford Station.'

He lowered his gaze meekly. 'As you wish, my lady.'

'Put out of your head all thought of the future, sweetheart,' she said. 'We have these few precious days of travel together before you must be shut away in Stormhaven. Let's make the most of them. Who knows? Perhaps the Sky Lords of Demon Seat will find a way to repair their imperfect miracle before we reach our destination.'

'If it could only be,' Orrion said with a wistful smile. 'Still, the King's Grace did say I might petition him concerning our marriage once a year has gone by.'

'I'll be close to you, at Brackenley Manor, hardly forty leagues from the castle. An easy day's ride for a decent horse-woman . . . and I am one, be sure of it! Thank God I was not forbidden your company by the king. It's up to Father's discretion – and Mother has promised to intercede for me. So hope for the best and enjoy the sunshine. Brother Binon says we have days of fair weather ahead of us. Keep in mind also that the Sovereignty will soon be at peace, and perhaps your royal father's anger will cool.'

Small chance of that, Orrion thought. He was more aware of the political realities of the situation than Nyla. Still, his dear love was right: they'd see one another during his exile – and throughout this trip they'd scarce be parted, save when the party stopped for the night.

The cavalcade was not a small one. Besides the two lovers, it included twenty-two other riders and five pack-mules. The Lord Lieutenant and his wife preceded Orrion and Nyla; behind them came the family's elderly alchymist Vra-Binon – looking rather seedy and complaining of a sore throat, three Cathran knights belonging to Lord Hale's official household at Cala Palace, six men-at-arms under their command, and four young armigers in charge of the mules. Two more Cathran warriors brought up the rear, knights whose duty it would be to guard Orrion at Stormhaven Castle.

Additionally, riding at the head of the procession, were four Didionites: Count Egonus Cuva, the dour young widower who had been linked romantically with the Princess Royal, and three noble companions of his who were known to have abetted his illicit affair in defiance of Conrig's command. By order of the Sovereign, they were all banished from the court of Somarus for a year and confined to the environs of Dennech-Cuva, the ducal seat of Lord Egonus's powerful father Azarick.

It was the earl marshal who had suggested that the Lieutenant's party accompany Egonus and his men, to ensure that the royal command concerning the count was carried out. Dennech-Cuva lay in the far western reaches of Didion, within twenty-six leagues of the coast. From Boarsden Castle, the group might ride easily along the Wold Highroad to Rockyford and thence to Elderwold Town. There they would

turn west along the Shadow River track to Tweenwater
Fortress, and eventually reach Dennech-Cuva. After seeing
the count safely to his father's rustic palace, the Cathrans
would take ship from the port of Karum and sail directly to
Stormhaven, a voyage of some four hundred leagues.

Aside from the safe shepherding of the surly young count,
by taking this roundabout route Hale Brackenfield's group
would avoid an otherwise tedious journey through the rough
Cathran hill country west of Elk Lake, which the noble ladies
had not looked forward to. The Shadow River track was
lonely and wild, but at least it led over fairly level ground.
Before Somarus became king the region was a notorious
haunt of bandits and Green Men; but nowadays that part of
the wold was relatively safe . . . at least for well-armed travelers riding in sizable groups.

In the waters along the Desolation Coast of Tarn, the fog still
hung low and dense at midday. Sealady Tallu Ramis and her
husband Ontel Pikan stood on the quarterdeck of the frigate
Gyrfalcon, becalmed some thirty leagues off the mouth of the
Blue River. Both had their eyes closed and their minds open
to subtle traces on the uncanny wind.

No one aboard made the slightest sound. The crew had
their orders. But normal shipboard noises still disturbed the
near-perfect silence: the creak of planking in the hull and
decks, the squeaks and groans of the rigging, the soft slosh
of water in the bilges as the vessel rolled gently in long swells
coming from the east.

Tallu addressed her husband in voiceless windspeech. 'Do
you still detect the submarine currents of their passage?'

'Yes.' He responded in the same mode. 'Save for the fact
that they travel due north in huge numbers, they might be
whales. But it's the wrong time of year for pods of cetaceans
to migrate in that direction. And these creatures utter none

of the conversational noises normal to whales. We must draw the obvious conclusion.'

'If only we dared approach closer, so you could scry them underwater,' Tallu fretted. A stalwart, hatchet-faced woman whose greying rust-colored hair was cut short, she wore the curtailed jacket, easy-fitting breeches, and high boots of a mariner. Her only symbol of rank was a small golden badge pinned to the black silk scarf wound about her throat – the ancient winged escutcheon of Tarn's Company of Equals, who scorned the sumptuous trappings of the other Blenholme nobility.

Ontel, a shaman specializing in weather prediction, was a balding man of frail build, closely wrapped in a hooded cloak that almost concealed his birdlike features. 'My love, do you think it might be possible for our combined talent to move the ship stealthily through the water?' he asked. 'The swimmers are only a league or two distant. If we were very careful not to generate a significant bow-wave or wake . . .'

'We could try,' Tallu decided. 'I'll have to take the wheel. You point the way.'

She opened her eyes and moved noiselessly to the helm, motioning to the steersman to unfasten the lashed spokes. The sailor sprang to obey, then took his place beside the First Mate and two other petty officers who awaited the sealady's orders. Still bespeaking her husband on the wind, she said, 'Now.'

Both of them summoned propulsive magic and exerted pressure on the frigate's hull. For a long time, nothing happened. *Gyrfalcon* remained dead in the water, enveloped in fog as thick as wool. Ontel's eyes were also open now, although his gaze was unfocused. He stretched out an arm and pointed in a direction just off the starboard bow. Tallu increased her uncanny thrust and felt the massive ship resist – then suddenly stir. The bowsprit swung minutely as the vessel responded to the gentle coaxing of the rudder. An infinitesimal breath of air touched the sealady's parted lips. The billows of mist seemed to flow in a single direction now, rather than swirling chaotically.

They were moving.

Once inertia was overcome, the job was much easier. She told Ontel to belay thrusting, leaving it to her, and concentrate instead on the search. He nodded slowly, continuing to point the way in the white void. In this manner *Gyrfalcon* glided almost imperceptibly across the surface of the glassy sea, trailing an exiguous wake. Their motion was so gentle that the water slipped silently past the hull. For over an hour the ship crept further away from land, toward the source of the currents generated by the water-displacement of thousands of enormous bodies moving through the sea.

'I have an overview,' Ontel bespoke her at last. 'They are Salka – a vast column of them proceeding northward like a dark river, less than a league away. I see no beginning and no end to them. They stay two fathoms deep and never come up to breathe. Their skins act as gills, you know, extracting air from the water when their lungs shut down.'

'So the sloops sent out from Ice Haven were deceived,' Tallu observed sadly, also speaking on the wind. She left off pushing. The frigate slowed gradually and came to a stop. The fog was still so thick that nothing was visible beyond a distance of five or six ells. 'The monsters are not retreating to Moss. I think they intend to circumnavigate the island. Perhaps they plan to attack our capital! I'll send a warning to Zirinna at Fort Ramis, using the most guarded windspeech thread. She'll relay the tidings to the Joint Fleet admirals gathered at Ice Haven. But I fear there is no way Sovereignty warships can catch up with the Salka. Not in this cursèd flat calm . . . Do you have any notion of when the fog might lift and the natural wind rise to fill our sails?'

'Perhaps toward sunset, dearest one.'

'We'll follow then, using our magic to assist us,' Tallu asserted, 'keeping well out of their observation range. If they finally swing wide around the reefs at the tip of the Lavalands, we may be able to gain on them a bit by taking the cutoff through Needle-Eye Passage. It's a pity that we have no significant numbers of men o' war at Cold or Warm Harbors. There seems no way for our navy to engage the monsters until they approach the Firth of Gayle and –'

'Tallu!' Ontel spoke out abruptly with his natural voice. 'Bespeak the warning! Do it now! God of the Heights and Depths – hurry, love! The Salka know we're here. Numbers of them are leaving the main column and coming straight at us!'

She bowed her head and shut her eyes, launching a tightly aimed windhail at the shaman-farspeaker Zirinna, who was in residence at their principal stronghold along the Desolation Coast.

'Tallu cries a warning, Zerinna! Relay it to the Sovereign's brother Stergos at Boarsden. The Salka are not retreating as we believed. They swim north, perhaps to circle the island and attack Tarn along our western seaboard. There are many thousands of them – perhaps the bulk of their invasion force. Tallu cries a warning! Pass the word. Pass the word.'

Zirinna responds. I will pass the word, Sealady Tallu. Do you have further details of the enemy's movements?

'Later. I'll bespeak you later. Pass the word.'

She cut the windthread, opened her eyes, and saw Ontel staring at her with an ashen face. 'We have only a few minutes before they arrive, sweetling,' he said. 'At least six score of the devils. Too many . . .'

Tallu turned to the First Mate, who had stood by silently. 'Yavegin, call general quarters and ready the guns and tarn-blaze grenades. We'll give the slimy trolls something to remember us by.'

As the man shouted orders a tremendous splash sounded out in the fog. It was followed by another, and then by many more. The glassy surface of the water round about the ship was broken suddenly by a flurry of ominous ripples.

Invisible to starboard, a single Salka uttered a thunderous bellow. Tallu and Ontel swung *Gyrfalcon* to bear on the voice and a volley of cannon-fire blasted into white emptiness. But it was a futile act of defiance, for there was really nothing to take aim at.

'Ready the catapults with the bombs!' Tallu cried. 'They're closing on us fast! Range twenty to thirty ells!' Seamen dashed about the poop and foredecks, loading the war-engines with hissing tarnblaze grenades. Missiles flew into the fog, trailing luminous red arcs. The starboard battery fired again, the gun-barrels depressed to the ultimate notch. The air filled with smoke, worsening the already poor visibility.

And then the ship began to roll.

The oscillation was almost imperceptible to begin with, but gradually increased in intensity so that the crew were hard put to keep their footing. Tallu glanced at Ontel. His eyes had been closed as he scried beneath the water. Now he opened them and met his wife's gaze, shaking his head gently.

'They are upon us, darling. Clinging to the portside hull and rudder and using their great strength and the frigate's own mass to rock and capsize us.'

'All hands, leave off firing guns and grenades!' Tallu cried. 'Grappling irons to the port rails. Haul away and snag the brutes as best you can. Be alert to repel boarders!'

Ontel spoke to her on the wind. 'Can we fight them off? Is there still a chance?'

'No, my dear.' She gave silent reply.

'Then bespeak Zirinna one last time, giving her what information you can about the Salka tactics.'

'I tried,' Tallu admitted. 'But there was no reply to my

hail. The wind is strangely empty of any windthread, as though we were enclosed in more than fog – as though we were walled away from the world of life itself. It's strange . . .'

'Then all is lost,' the little shaman murmured.

The sealady took up a coil of hempen line. 'Dear husband, only this ship is lost. We who die on her can take comfort in knowing that our first warning was passed on. I shall so inform our crew. But first –'

She began to tie Ontel to the binnacle, the tall case holding navigation instruments that stood just behind the ship's wheel.

'I'll return to you immediately and lash myself in place,' Tallu assured him. 'From here you and I will direct *Gyrfalcon's* last battle.'

The memorial ceremony for Lord Chancellor Kilian Blackhorse was only sparsely attended. Lurking in the narthex where he had a clear view inside the chapel, Beynor counted only eighteen blackrobed Didionite wizards ranged around the simple open coffin, holding candles and chanting ritual praises to the deceased sorcerer. Neither Duke Ranwing nor any nobles from the court of Somarus had felt it necessary to pay last respects to the foreign magicker who had exerted such a powerful influence over their king.

Beynor had come to reassure himself that the body was that of Kilian, and that he was truly as dead as mutton. No suspicion had attached to the death, which was officially adjudged by the coroner to be accidental, and unofficially viewed as fortuitous. Rumors that the chancellor had schemed to unite Cathra and Didion under a single ruling dynasty had incensed the most powerful nobles of the northern nation and kindled fresh resentment against the Sovereignty.

When the service ended, Beynor stood watching impassively as pallbearers carried the now-closed coffin past him and down the steps into the outer ward. To his surprise, one of the wizards in the funeral procession broke from the line and approached him in a purposeful fashion, drawing back the hood of his robe. The man was well-built and quite good-looking, of no great age. He made a perfunctory bow and spoke without diffidence.

'Conjure-King Beynor of Moss, I presume.'

Beynor frowned at the fellow's over-familiar manner – but of course his own appearance was unique and striking. By now, the lowliest scullion in the castle kitchen would be able to recognize him. 'I am Beynor,' he admitted. 'Who are you, and why do you presume to address me?'

'Garon Curtling, at your service, Majesty. I was a close associate of the late Lord Chancellor Kilian. Like him, I am a Cathran and a former Brother of Zeth. If you could spare me a few moments, I have a proposal that might appeal to you.'

'Do you indeed, wizard? What sort of proposal?' Beynor moved out of the vestibule into the chapel porch and watched the cortege as it headed toward the watergate. The brief announcement of Kilian's demise that morning stated that his remains were to be sent downriver after the memorial service, to be interred in the royal cemetery in Didion's capital city of Mallburn.

The eyes of Garon Curtling revealed only a modest talent, but his attitude was that of a man with business to conduct. He glanced about to be sure that no one else was close enough to hear. A small bell had begun to toll the noon hour.

'Since I'm about to lose my special position and now face an uncertain future,' he said, 'I must do what I can to provide for myself. My late master kept a journal. I have it. It is written backwards to discourage ordinary snoops, but simply holding it to a mirror reveals the sense of it. It contains much that might interest one who has lived outside the higher social circles of the Sovereignty for some years – one who might be gratified or amused by an intimate view of notable personages as observed by a member of Didion's Grand Council. The journal is for sale.'

Beynor's mouth quirked and he almost smiled. 'By a thief?' he said without rancor.

'I only took it for safekeeping, after finding it discarded on the floor of Lord Kilian's bedchamber. It lay in a heap of other items from a ransacked iron coffer that the chancellor always kept locked. We – that is, I myself and Lord Kilian's other close confidants, Niavar Kettleford and Cleaton Papworth – always suspected that he kept his treasure in that box. I found no money or jewels. Since Niavar and Cleaton have disappeared, I fear they may have absconded from the castle with the valuables.'

'You did not raise a hue and cry over this?'

'No, Your Majesty. I can't prove anything was taken. Furthermore, my two fellow-wizards are highly experienced in conjuring expert spells of couverture. Finding them may be impossible for those having only moderate talent – and that description fits most adepts in Didion, including myself. I took charge of the journal, which has no obvious monetary value, because I'm sure Lord Kilian would have wanted me to have it as a souvenir of our years together. You see, I was the one who guided him over the trackless Sinistral Range on his escape from Zeth Abbey. In the ensuing years I've served him faithfully –'

'Ten gold marks,' Beynor interrupted the self-congratulatory gush with a laconic flip of his hand. 'Bring the journal to me at once and I'll pay you. I'll be walking along the esplanade. Don't let anyone catch you with the book or our bargain is void.'

Garon blinked. The sizable sum would buy a fine cottage, or ten superior horses with their tack, or keep a man in decent food, liquor, and feminine comfort for a year.

'All right, Your Majesty. I agree.' With no more ado, he hurried off to the Wizards' Tower, where the visiting magickers had their apartments.

'A self-confident sort of rogue,' the Conjure-King said to himself, 'And unemployed! A wastrel as well, unless I miss my guess. But he may have his uses.'

Beynor walked through the north barbican and over the moat's drawbridge to the long strip of gardens and parkland that formed an ornamental promenade along the castle's river side. The day was now pleasant and sunny, and many noble ladies and their male companions were taking the air. He strolled for nearly half an hour, using his keen windsight to survey the many military camps on the opposite shore, which were in a predictable state of ferment at the prospect of demobilization. At last he reached the western boundary of the esplanade, where the moat joined a natural stream that debouched into the great river. The main gatehouse of the castle was visible from this vantage point, as was the high-road leading to Boarsden Town.

Beynor took a seat on a stone bench and waited. There was no one else near by. Finally Garon Curtling reappeared in the distance, moving at a leisurely pace through the well-dressed gentlefolk, looking like a lone black crow amongst a colorful flock of finches and orioles. Beynor waited patiently for him and pretended to study boat traffic rounding the great bend in the river.

When the wizard approached and made a respectful obeisance, as though he were delivering some message, Beynor motioned him to sit down on the bench beside him. Garon obeyed and proffered a buckled leather dispatch case with bellows-sides.

'It's in here. When the case is opened wide, you may easily examine the journal without taking it out.'

'Excellent.'

They sat in silence for many minutes while the Conjure-King thumbed through the volume bound in worn brown pigskin. It was not easily deciphered, for Kilian had not only written backwards but also overwrote each page with vertical as well as horizontal lines, making a crosshatch that strained the eyes even in bright sunshine. Turning to the last entry, Beynor was able to read an account of the Lord Chancellor's disastrous final visit to Somarus. He chuckled aloud as he came upon Kilian's doleful speculations about the king's dreams of independence for Didion – dreams that Beynor himself had skillfully implanted.

'Do you find the journal good value?' Garon inquired.

'Yes, indeed.' Beynor refastened the straps of the case and took a purse from his belt. 'And here is your price.'

The other man reached out eagerly, but the Conjure-King kept the pouch just beyond reach. 'I'll be honest with you. This is sorcerer's gold – adequate tender only when the buyer will be quickly away and never again see the person who accepted it. The money is solid only for a single day and night, after which it vanishes like a blown-out candleflame.'

Garon's eyes widened with outrage. 'What?!' He tried to seize the dispatch case, but discovered that his arms were paralyzed. 'You cheating whoreson –'

Beynor laughed. 'Not at all. Hush! Be easy, Garon Curtling. No one will bilk you of your due. Didn't I warn you that the money was bogus?'

The younger man's anger melted into perplexity. 'But why?'

'Because I want more from you than just this journal – and I'm prepared to offer you a hundred times the journal's price, paid in coin of the realm, for your help in a certain venture. Plus one-tenth of whatever loot we recover on the job. And if you think it worth your while, I also offer you

a place as one of my men, at a generous stipend, for as long
as you wish to serve me . . . Now! If I release you, will you
sit still and make no rash move?'

'Yes.' The wizard shrugged. 'Why not? I have no chance
of besting one such as you in sorcery.' He eyed Beynor slyly.
'And neither did Kilian Blackhorse, I suspect. Did you slay
him?'

'Of course.' Beynor freed Garon from the magical restraint.
'We were once allies, then became mortal enemies. One of
us had to kill the other. I admit I was stupid not to have
considered that he'd have a treasure cached away. My mind
is too much befuddled by dirty politics these days.'

It was Garon's turn to laugh. 'Tell me about your venture,
and how it might concern me. Although I suspect I know
what you're about to say.'

'Do you, indeed! Well, it's obvious, isn't it: I want that
treasure. I need it if I'm to re-establish my kingdom. No one
can be a king without real money. Given time, I could do
this task alone. After all, I invented the superior spell of
couverture your larcenous friends are hiding under. I taught
it to Kilian before he taught it to *them*. They can't evade my
mind's eye.'

'Then why not nab Niavar and Cleaton yourself and take
away their goodies? They have only eight or nine hours'
start on you.'

'My time is limited and I have other vitally important
things to attend to. You know this precious pair of thieving
magpies from long association, and they know you. If you
approach them they won't be suspicious. At least, not at
first.'

'Perhaps,' Garon flashed a cynical smirk. 'But I won't bet
my life on it. My talents are no match for their combined
sorcery. They'd blast me to greasy collops with uncanny lightning. I've seen them do such a thing before, to a cutpurse

that was stupid enough to attack us in the back lanes of Mallburn Town.'

'You'll be quite safe if you use the spells I'm prepared to teach you.' Beynor looked away, distracted by a commotion of shouts and neighing horses over at the west gatehouse of the castle. The double portcullises lifted and a dozen or so mounted men, led by a knight bearing the guidon of the Sovereign, emerged at full gallop and headed toward the city.

'Spells?' Garon was intrigued. 'What kind of spells?'

'Wait!' the sorcerer commanded. He rose. His countenance was like wood and his dark eyes wide open but unfocused as he scrutinized the troop closely with his windsight. They were all Cathran knights and warriors save for one, who wore crimson leather with a hooded capuchon, the customary riding habit of ranking Brothers of Zeth. Beynor identified the Royal Alchymist, Lord Stergos.

'Well, well! . . . Garon, didn't King Conrig ride out earlier in the day to tour the military camps around Boarsden Town?'

'Such was the gossip among my fellow-wizards at breakfast. It was said he wished to inspect the condition of the men and mounts in the various companies before giving the official order to disperse. I believe the High Sealord accompanied him, and the Cathran Earl Marshal, and the new Prince Heritor – along with a gaggle of generals from all nations of the Sovereignty. But King Somarus was indisposed and stayed abed.'

Beynor uttered a bark of laughter. 'No doubt – after last night's bout of feasting and drinking.'

Getting up from the bench, Garon screwed his features to a gargoyle grimace as he windwatched the departing riders himself. 'I wonder whether some important report may have been vouchsafed to Lord Stergos, which he now carries personally to the Sovereign?'

'Doubtless we'll learn of it in good time,' Beynor said coldly. 'Meanwhile, other matters concern us. If you accept my offer and agree to track down your former mates, I'll instruct you in several types of advanced sorcery. You won't need to scry out Niavar and Cleaton – I'll find them for you. But you *will* have to defend yourself against whatever magic they're likely to throw at you. And ultimately, you must slay them.'

'I know.' Garon glowed with arrogant confidence. 'It won't break my heart. Both bastards despised me because I took time to enjoy life's pleasures, rather than serving Lord Kilian with blind devotion as they did.'

Beynor bit back the contemptuous remark that sprang to mind. An ascetic and sexless man himself, he despised those who were overfond of fleshly indulgence.

I've chosen another unworthy and venal henchman, he thought, even though he's hardly as vicious as the hedge-wizard Gorvik Kitstow. Still, the knave would probably perform his task adequately, especially if his smug self-confidence was rattled a wee bit. What a pity that the restrictions of Bazekoy's pearl were still in place!

'Once you have the treasure,' Beynor said, reaching out and placing his hands lightly on the other man's shoulders, 'you must bring it to me promptly. All of it! I'll know if you attempt any boneheaded trickery – or if you run.' He pinched both sensitive clavicle nerves, using somewhat less pressure than he'd exerted while torturing Kilian.

Garon screamed. But not a sound escaped his clenched lips.

'Do you understand?' Beynor inquired amiably.

'Yes! Yes!' The reply came on the wind.

'The punishment if you betray my trust will be more horrible than you can imagine. I'll find you, wherever you hide. The worst of it will be that you beg for death, but are unable to die.'

'Please – I won't play you false! I swear it.'

Beynor smiled. 'I think I believe you. You want the reward I've promised, and you shall have it if you carry out your task faithfully and well . . . Or would you rather just walk away, leaving me to secure the treasure myself?' Beynor's hands dropped from Garon's shoulders and he untied the man's tongue. 'You *can* walk away if you wish. I won't force you to serve me.'

Perspiration bathed Garon's brow and his attractive face had become grey and drawn. The choice was no choice: he either threw in with the terrible Conjure-King or he was doomed. He knew too much now.

'Swear you will never harm me again,' Garon said in a surprisingly steady voice. 'Not with sorcery, nor with physical weapons, nor with your own body's might and main. Swear you'll never command other persons or inhuman creatures or natural elements to harm me. Swear that a tenth of Kilian's treasure shall be mine to keep forever. I'll ask no other reward of you if you swear all these things, Beynor of Moss, on pain of eternal damnation.'

'I do so swear,' said the Conjure-King. His black eyes gleamed with reluctant respect. Perhaps this one was not so unworthy after all! 'And if I break this oath, may the Beaconfolk cast me into the Hell of Ice that claimed my poor mother.'

Garon let out a pent-up sigh of relief. To Beynor's astonishment, he managed a crooked grin. 'When do we begin the sorcery lessons?'

'Go to your rooms and wait. Gather what you'll need for travel. I want you on your way tonight. I'll come as soon as possible and teach you what you need to know. I hope you're a quick study.'

'When it's to my advantage. But wouldn't it be wiser to get on with this business without delay?'

Beynor glanced in the direction Stergos and his companions had taken. 'Do as I say without arguing! Now get out
of here. I need to concentrate if I'm to read lips at long
distance.'

'After the brief message of warning was received by the
shaman-farspeaker at Fort Ramis,' Stergos said to Conrig,
'nothing else was heard from Sealady Tallu and Ontel. Of
course, they may be keeping wind-silence so as not to be
overheard by the main body of monsters.'

'Do you really think they might have survived, Gossy?'

'No. I believe those two brave souls and all their crew
have perished.'

The High King and the Royal Alchymist stood beneath an
open-sided pavilion that served as an officers' mess and place
of ease for the battle company commanded by Duke Norval
Vanguard of Cathra. The sun was high and it was getting
very hot. Flagons of drink, along with platters of meat, bread,
and fruit covered with gauze to stave off the abundant clouds
of flies and wasps, had been laid out on trestle-tables for the
royal inspection party; but few of the battle-leaders were
partaking of it. They had gathered in a silent, baffled group
on the opposite side of the tent, along with High Sealord
Sernin Donorvale and his sons, Prince Heritor Corodon, and
Crown Prince Valardus of Didion. All wondered whether the
Sovereign intended to share the obviously urgent news just
brought by his brother.

Conrig's face betrayed nothing of the turmoil within his
brain. A fresh Salka assault aimed at Blenholme's west coast
had the potential for total catastrophe. The monsters might
come ashore anywhere. Tarn and Didion were equally imperiled. And his army was massed *here,* smack in the middle of
the island, hundreds of leagues from any likely point of
attack.

From what he'd seen on the morning's tour of the camps, neither the men nor the horses were ready for a lengthy forced march – especially one over mountains – all the way to the Western Ocean. Many of the nonprofessional levies were slack from the long period of inactivity. The conscripted Didionites, especially, had prematurely celebrated their dismissal and return home and were in a sorry state, hungover and insubordinate as they were formed up for inspection.

'Con?' The soft, anxious voice of Stergos broke the train of the king's thoughts. 'What would you have me do now?'

'Invite the High Sealord and Earl Marshal Parlian to attend me. Bid the others eat and drink and take their ease. Tell them we'll all confer together within the hour. Then bespeak Chumick Whitsand, Somarus's archwizard, and command him to bundle His Majesty of Didion onto horseback and whip his fat arse over here speedily, as though his life depended upon it.'

While Stergos went to fetch Donorvale and Beorbrook, the Sovereign collected five fieldstools and set them about a flat-topped military chest. On this he spread the marine chart of the island which the alchymist had brought with him, weighting the corners with stones.

'Plotting new strategy, my liege?' Sernin Donorvale bent down to peer at the map from his great height. He was half a foot taller than Conrig, a giant of a man with a full head of sand-colored hair pulled back in a short pigtail, and pale brows above eyes that were a changeable grey-green, like the Boreal Sea. He was pushing three-score-and-ten, but looked a dozen years younger.

'I have no revised plans yet, High Sealord,' Conrig admitted somberly. 'For that I'll welcome your advice – and that of others. Sit you down. There's fresh disaster brewing.'

'Oh, shite,' Sernin whispered. 'Not the Salka?'

Conrig gave a grim nod of assent. Earl Marshal Parlian Beorbrook had overheard, and he muttered a curse before taking a stool himself.

'My friends,' the Sovereign said, 'I've summoned Somarus as well, since he must participate in any decisions we make.' Pointing to the relevant spot off the Desolation Coast, he related how the monsters had been sighted by Ontel and Tallu less than an hour ago. 'It's likely that the Salka are planning another invasion in force. The message from the sealady and her husband estimated that there were many thousands of the creatures swimming northward. It doubtless means that they intend to circle around the island and strike somewhere in the west. No other possibility makes sense.'

'But it's too late in the season!' the earl marshal protested.

'Nearly two moons remain before the big winter storms begin,' the High Sealord said. 'It will be yet another moon before our northern ports ice up completely. I fear that the Salka have time enough to invade and establish themselves on land. They hibernate in winter, you know, burrowing deep into the mud of river or lake bottom where no human being can dislodge them.'

'Can they survive under sea-ice, my lord?' Parlian asked.

'I truly don't know,' Sernin replied. 'And I think it makes very little difference to our defensive strategy whether they can or not. What's imperative is that we set up naval patrols off the most obvious coastal targets. Safeguarding the Tarnian capital is feasible, using those of our ships still based at Yelicum. The Firth of Gayle is narrow and readily defended. Donorvale lies upriver and batteries of tarnblaze cannons protect its approaches. But the rich settlements of Shelter and Goodfortune Bays are another matter. The majority of Tarnian warships based in those areas were sent north when the Beacon River invasion was detected. Now they lie off Ice Haven with other vessels of the Joint Fleet.'

'I'll order Lord Admiral Hartrig to have the fleet up anchor and set sail at once,' Conrig declared. He looked down at the chart. 'Do you think the faster ships have a chance of catching up with the Salka horde before it rounds Cape Wolf and becomes an immediate threat to your larger towns?'

'Not a prayer, my liege,' said the High Sealord. 'The winds are fickle in northern waters this time of year, especially in the Icebear Channel between Blenholme and the Barrenlands. Salka are formidable swimmers. They're bound to beat our ships to the the Western Ocean, even if our shamans and the other wizards aboard lend magical propulsion.'

'Then so be it.' The Sovereign's tone was flat. 'But the Joint Fleet must move out anyhow and do what it can. Meanwhile, I can summon those Cathran men o' war still in southern waters to assist in patrolling your vulnerable ports.'

'There's no certainty that the Salka plan to invade Tarn,' the carl marshal pointed out. 'They could as easily continue southward, swarm into the Cathran harbors of Westley, and go up one of our rivers. Imagine the havoc they'd wreak – the panic among our people if the Army of the Sovereignty were not already emplaced to repel invaders.'

'The army!' Sernin Donorvale shook his head in dismay. 'Deciding how to deploy our ships is difficult enough. But who among us can say where the troops should now go?'

The three leaders fell silent, staring glumly at the chart. The truth was, without firm intelligence as to the Salka objective, the Sovereignty ground forces were all but helpless.

Stergos returned and said that Somarus was reluctantly on his way. 'I had to explain the urgency of the situation to Archwizard Chumick before he'd agree to waken the king. I doubt we can trust the man to keep quiet about this shocking development.'

'Everyone will know soon.' Sernin Donorvale was resigned.

Parlian Beorbrook had not lifted his eyes from the map. He now stabbed his finger down at a point on Blenholme's west coast where Tarn and Didion disputed the border.

'Here!' the old general said, poking the parchment again for emphasis. 'Right here is where I'd establish a beachhead if I were the Salka commander. In Terminal Bay, that stinking lair of pirates. Not even Duke Azarick Cuva, the nominal overlord of the place, can keep the local sea-wolves under control. They do as they please, and devil take the hindmost. With no solidarity amongst the various bands of corsairs, their resistance to a sudden massive Salka invasion might crumble rather quickly.'

'I'm not inclined to agree,' the High Sealord said. 'Tarn is the logical target. Our land is rich and the population relatively small.'

Beorbrook persisted. 'But look here: observe Terminal Bay's narrow entrance, all clogged with reefs and rocks, and its broad landlocked waters. If the monsters should ensconce themselves inside there, we'd have a hell of a time winkling them out with seapower. There's also an easy corridor to take them far inland: large rivers, swamps, puny little fortresses except for the one at Dennech-Cuva. Sire, I think we should give very serious consideration to Terminal Bay as a likely point of attack.'

Conrig seemed uncertain. 'You may be right, Parli, although I'm inclined to agree with Sernin. At any rate, we'll have to wait for Somarus before discussing defense of the place . . . Meanwhile, Gossy, relay my command to Lord Admiral Hartrig. I order the Joint Fleet to embark from Ice Haven at once and follow the presumed course of the Salka horde with all possible speed. Then bespeak our admiralty in Cala. The southern fleet is to set sail for Flaming Head and wait there for further orders.'

Sernin Donorvale said, 'Also be so kind, Lord Stergos, as to summon Grand Shaman Zolanfel to attend me here.' He eyed Conrig. 'We Tarnians will organize volunteer reconnaissance squadrons immediately – fast sloops that will range out from ports on the north and west coasts, scouting for signs of the enemy. Zolanfel can advise us on setting up relays of windspeakers, as well as secure means of communication.'

Conrig nodded approval and said to his brother, 'Take care of it all.'

'At once.' Stergos headed for a deserted corner of the pavilion, pulling his hood over his head as he went.

'What about the troops?' the High Sealord asked. 'Do we march them out of here right away to a new staging area? The cavalry and foot-soldiers of Tarn can be ready within a day or two, and I presume that the Cathran forces are also in good shape. But Didion . . .' He shook his head.

Parlian Beorbrok said, 'Sernin's point is well taken. As we visited the Didionite camps earlier, it was plain that the mood amongst their soldiers is touchy, even ugly. The vast bulk of them are yeoman infantry from eastern or central Didion. Few of them save the Elite Mallburn Guards are highly trained. They're eager to go home. Somarus himself must be the one to command his generals and their officers to respond wholeheartedly to this new threat. Otherwise, I fear we might face a mutiny.'

'There'll be no mutiny,' Ironcrown pronounced with merciless certainty. 'Not if Somarus hopes to keep his throne.'

Parlian blinked in astonishment. 'You wouldn't depose him! It would surely set off an insurrection.'

'I'd do it in an eyeblink to defend this island against the Salka,' Conrig said. 'And if the warriors of Didion revolted, they'd do it without their Crown Prince and generals and battle-commanders – who would remain confined right here in Vanguard's camp, under Cathran guard.'

The High Sealord's face wore a thoughtful scowl. 'Who would you put in Somarus's place, my liege – Crown Prince Valardus? He's not much of a warrior.'

'At least he's a political realist,' Conrig said with brutal candor, 'not a fat sot intoxicated by dreams of ancient glory. If the prince affirms fealty to the Sovereignty, I'll not hesitate to crown him.'

But would Valardus accept the crown? For all Conrig's bold talk, he knew that deposing Somarus by force was impossible. Another solution must be found.

A trumpet sounded distantly. The earl marshal glanced outside the pavilion, where a cloud of dust was rising near the camp's main entrance. 'I believe His Majesty of Didion has arrived. Will you see him alone, sire, or shall we three work together to make him see reason?'

'You and Sernin together, Earl Marshal,' the Sovereign said with a sigh. 'Somarus hates me, but he respects the two of you. Just remember that he's half off his chump. Appeal to his love of country and the warrior traditions of Didion. Do what you must to get him to accept your leadership. I'll . . . well, it's best that I keep strategically aloof, don't you think?'

The two older men chuckled uneasily but made no reply.

As the afternoon lengthened in Royal Fenguard castle, the Four Salka Eminences gathered once again to bespeak Beynor and ask whether he would agree to help them obtain moonstone mineral from Demon Seat. Nearly two hours passed before their combined hail was finally answered. They were fatigued and cranky but there was no helping it: they'd have to swallow their indignation and pretend friendship and good will.

'It's good to hear from you, Beynor,' Kalawnn said, ponderously jovial. The other Salka leaders were content to leave most of the negotiating to him, after having agreed how the human was to be handled. 'When we were unable to contact you at first, we feared for your safety.'

I'm fine. I was merely preoccupied with other affairs. No doubt you perceive that I'm situated in Boarsden Castle, where the leaders of the Sovereignty have been gathered in a Council of War. They've found out about your new Salka offensive, you know.

'Yes, that's a pity. We hoped to keep our intentions secret for as long as possible. But our valiant warriors had no choice but to obliterate the ship of the Tarnian spies, once they became aware of it. At least it was possible to muffle the further attempts of the human foes to bespeak information to their confederates before they were slaughtered.'

You were able to do that, were you? My congratulations! The spell of windspeech suppression is a complex one that I've never been able to master.

'It requires the concerted action of several hundred trained minds,' said Kalawnn proudly. 'We used a variant of the spell to blur the movements of our troops in the Beacon Valley, and we also use it when our main army communicates with the reinforcements moving around the south end of the island. But enough of Salka tactics. Shall I set forth the proposition we're prepared to extend in exchange for your help at Demon Seat?'

Master Kalawnn, I'm truly sorry. But at this time I can't undertake a long journey to Cathra, no matter what valuable considerations you offer. Conrig has accepted my claim to the throne of Moss. I'm once again its true king-in-exile and a loyal vassal of the Sovereignty of Blenholme –

'What?!'

Don't be dismayed. It's all a ruse to help me win Conrig's trust. This changes nothing between us, save that I'm now forced to postpone performing the favor you requested of me. The opportunities available here if I act immediately are stupendous. I can't ignore them.

'But – but you're willing to abandon us? When we offer our Potency to lift your curse – to say nothing of a myriad of other great gifts?'

I won't abandon you, old friend! Don't misunderstand. This is only a temporary change of plan, until I'm fully accepted by Conrig. Kilian is dead, you know. His passing leaves a useful power void that I intend to exploit. It's likely that I may now be able to assist your battle strategy as well. My great goal is to destroy Conrig – remember that! I'll do whatever I can to further your new invasion.

'We are greatly disappointed,' the Supreme Warrior grumbled. 'We had hoped for your assistance in obtaining raw moonstone, but there are other options open to us. Furthermore, we are in no way dependent upon your help to ensure the success of our new invasion –'

Where do you plan to come ashore, Ugusawnn? At Donorvale? . . . Or perhaps at Terminal Bay?

The Warrior concealed his dismay at the human's lucky guess. Or was it a guess? 'What makes you think we would choose either objective?'

I eavesdropped on the Sovereign's strategy session a few hours ago. Those two locations were picked out of a hat as being particularly vulnerable. You can count on their being heavily defended from the sea.

'What about from the land?'

Ah. That's another matter. Splitting up the Army of the Sovereignty is an option Conrig fiercely resisted, but his military advisers convinced him he had no choice but to do it. For the time being, their plans call for half of the troops to mass at Castle Direwold, near Frost Pass in the White Rime Mountains. If necessary, they'll undertake a forced march to defend the Tarnian capital. The other half will wait at the Lake of Shadows, near Elderwold, on the off-chance that you'll attack Terminal Bay. Either wing can reinforce the other once the point of attack is known for certain. However, Conrig is faced with an irksome dilemma.

'Indeed?' All four Eminences bespoke the query. 'What kind of dilemma?'

King Somarus is baulking at ordering any of his troops into Tarn. Conrig wants half the Didionite warriors to join the force at Direwold – an even split, as Tarn and Cathra agreed to. Somarus claims his men and the rest of the army as well are bound to be caught by winter weather in a far-northern country that won't be able to feed them. But he's really holding back for another reason: the worm has turned. He's sick of taking orders from Ironcrown.

'Ahroo!' the Master Shaman exclaimed. 'But has Somarus a choice in the matter?'

He stomped off in a fury after telling his generals they'd be executed if they ordered any troops into Tarn. The High Sealord and Earl Marshal Parlian will work with Somarus's son Valardus in an effort to change the king's mind. It's a rather droll battle of wills! I can hardly wait to see what happens next . . . By the way, where DO your people intend to land? You never answered my question.

'Nor do we intend to,' Kalawnn said equably. 'What benefit would accrue to us by doing so?'

I really think I'll be able to help you.

'Give us tangible evidence of that, Beynor of Moss, and then bespeak us again. For now, I bid you farewell.'

Kalawnn cut the windthread and regarded the other three Eminences with a resigned expression. 'That's that, colleagues.'

'But the Great Lights could not have lied!' The First Judge cried. 'They told us –'

'They told us to *ask* Beynor about obtaining raw material from the crag,' Kalawnn said. 'They never said Beynor was the only one who might fetch it.'

'But who else could do the job?' the Judge asked.

'I could,' Ugusawnn said.

'*Ahroo!*' the others exclaimed.

'Kalawnn's artisans have begun fashioning a Subtle Gateway sigil,' the Supreme Warrior reminded the others. 'If they are successful, the Great Stone might be used in more than one way . . . by a person who is prepared to accept the enormous pain-price. I've already told you I'm willing! It's my destiny as Supreme Warrior to carry Destroyer to our invading forces. But if it's the will of this group, I'll gladly travel first to Demon Seat and back, bringing whatever moonstone mineral I can prudently carry.'

'The triple pain-debt might kill you,' the Master Shaman pointed out, 'unless you postpone the third journey until you have sufficiently recovered.'

'I'll take the risk. If I perish, another warrior can bond to Destroyer. Our army must have that weapon! Victory depends on it. We've already agreed on that point.'

'True,' the Conservator of Wisdom noted.

'What if Beynor bespeaks us with a new proposal concerning the invasion?' the First Judge said.

The Supreme Warrior gnashed his crystalline fangs and suggested that the Conjure-King then be told to perform an impossible sexual act upon himself.

'No,' Kalawnn said, when the others had finished laughing. 'We'll listen. The Great Lights said that we have things to learn from him. And I, for one, intend to continue doing so.'

To keep the capture of Maudrayne's friend secret, Tinnis Catclaw had ordered Sir Asgar Beeton and his men to take her directly to a disused fowler's blind in the marsh behind Castle Boarsden, an isolated locale he was familiar with from hunting parties led by Duke Ranwing.

Late in the evening, after receiving word that the prisoner was secure there, the Lord Constable rode out along the dike track with the warrior who had brought the news. He had scarce paid any attention to Rusgann Moorcock during the years she'd spent as Maudrayne's companion at Gentian Fell Lodge. Indeed, the creature had been conspicuous only for her homeliness – and Lord Tinnis, like many other people who were fair of face, equated plain features with slowness of wit. He thought it would be an easy matter to ascertain whether the woman was carrying a message to Prince Dyfrig, and discover what dangerous information she might already have passed on to persons at the earl marshal's castle.

But Rusgann, whom he found sitting on the lattice-like duckboard floor of the hut with her wrists bound, seemed uncowed by her desperate situation. 'I ran away from captivity, my lord. That's all. I carry no secret message, nor did I steal anything from your lodge, as these men have claimed.'

The constable said to the stocky knight, 'Asgar, did you search her and her baggage thoroughly for letters or other clues to her purpose?'

'Yes, my lord.' Beeton grimaced. 'We tore her mule's saddle and tack to pieces and did the same with her bags, then stripped her bare – and a sight to turn a strong man's stomach *that* was! She carried no message of any kind, nor any other unusual thing, save a purse with nearly fifty marks in silver, which I have kept safe.'

Tinnis addressed Rusgann. 'So Lady Mayda caused you to memorize the message. Tell it to me at once, or you will be forced to speak.'

'There is no message,' Rusgann insisted again. 'My lady knew nothing of my intent to escape. I did it on my own, without her prior knowledge. You have no cause to blame her for anything –'

'Your lady is dead,' Tinnis Catclaw interrupted gently.

Rusgann went rigid, then gave a great wail of despair. 'No! You lie!' She burst into tears.

'The Lady Mayda perished this very afternoon when Gentian Fell Lodge was accidentally consumed by fire. It is a great tragedy.'

Rusgann screamed, 'You did it! You caused her death. But it'll do you no good, you murdering drab's-cunny!' And she spat in his face.

Sir Asgar struck her a great blow in the mouth with his fist, but she kept calling the constable obscene names and trying to struggle to her feet.

'Gag her, Asgar,' Tinnis said, fearing she would speak Maudrayne's true name next or reveal some other thing he wished kept from the guards. 'Tie her ankles as well. Then send your men outside to wait beyond earshot. Cut a number of osier switches and return to me. We'll soon make her talk.'

While his orders were carried out, he wiped the spittle away with a silk kerchief and studied the prisoner calmly. 'Rusgann Moorcock, I know you carry a message of some sort from the Princess Dowager to her son, Dyfrig. But your hope of meeting the prince is futile. He is nowhere near Boarsden. The Sovereign sent him on a mission deep into the Green Morass and it will be weeks before he returns. By then you will be as dead as Maudrayne – unless you tell me what message she entrusted to you.'

Rusgann shook her head violently. Her eyes blazed with hatred above the military neckcloth that stopped her mouth.

'You'll speak sooner or later,' he warned her. 'The only difference will be the amount of suffering you endure.'

She only glared at him in stony defiance until the knight returned, carrying numbers of flexible willow branches stripped of leaves.

'Lay her on her face and flog her,' Tinnis ordered. 'Thirty lashes to start with.'

Asgar ripped Rosgann's gown from collar to waist and fell to his work. But when the gag was finally removed, she only moaned and whispered, 'I know nothing. There is no message.'

'Thirty more,' the Lord Constable said without emotion. 'Leave off the gag this time. If she indicates that she will speak, stop.'

The scourging continued, but she only cried out curses and screamed like a wildcat. Finally the flesh of her back was a mass of oozing scarlet cuts and she was so weakened by pain and blood loss that she lost consciousness.

'Throw water on her,' Tinnis ordered.

The captain took up an old wooden bucket that stood at one corner of the hut and went outside to dip it into the pond that the blind overlooked. Returning, he flung the bucket's contents over the tortured woman. The scum-laden liquid drained away through the slots in the duckboard floor. Rusgann did not move, nor did she cry out.

'You haven't killed her, have you?' Tinnis said anxiously.

Asgar laughed. 'Not a bit of it, my lord. She's a sturdy old bag, but I don't think she'll revive for some time. What are your orders?'

'See that she's covered warmly and let her be. You and your company may return to Boarsden. Leave two reliable men to guard her – and warn them to pay no heed to any fanciful lies she may tell when she wakes. They may threaten her with fearsome punishments to come, but make them understand that she must not be otherwise mistreated. If she dies, so will those who guard her.'

'And in the unlikely event that she shows signs of failing, all on her own – what then?'

'One of the men must come to the castle and fetch me at once,' the Lord Constable said. 'Otherwise, she is to be given water and bread, if she'll eat it, and taken outside to relieve herself. I have unavoidable business to tend to during the day tomorrow, but we'll return and start again on her after nightfall.'

ELEVEN

The tall young girl who called herself Queen Casabarela finished her conversation with Ising Bedotha, who was manning the riverboat's tiller, and came forward to where Induna sat at the foot of the mast. They were passing through an area of brushy flatland where the River Kelk wound in sluggish braids before its confluence with the Upper Malle. It was nearly noon.

'Induna, Lord Ising says the boat has slowed down,' Casya Pretender pointed out, speaking in the imperious manner she seemed to adopt whenever things were not going according to her wishes. 'Are you and your husband faltering in your magic? We must keep up to speed if we're to reach Boarsden before the ninth hour tonight. It'll be impossible for me to enter my grandsire's camp after that. There'll be a military curfew. All of the whores will be shooed out, and my clever disguise will be useless.'

'Deveron is presently using his talent to search for Rusgann, the woman we're charged to rescue,' Induna said mildly. She refused to call the girl Your Majesty, as the rebel baron did, but made no issue of it. 'I'm filling the boat's sail with air all by myself for the time being. Deveron will rejoin me when his other uncanny work is done. Ordinarily, a person can exert only a single magical talent at a time.'

'That's not acceptable –' Casya started to say.

'Madam, our mission is no less urgent than your own. You made no complaint earlier, whilst my husband was scrying out Duke Kefalus's force amongst the many others emplaced about Boarsden Town and learning details of the new Salka threat. Be patient. We're really moving along at an excellent clip. Suspiciously fast, as a matter of fact, since the air is almost dead calm. Fortunately, there are only a few herders along shore to see us defy the laws of nature.'

Casya scowled. Then with the mercurial mood-change of youth, she grinned at Induna and plumped down on the deck beside her. Both of them were wearing male clothing and had their hair stuffed beneath knitted caps. 'I'm overeager. I admit it. To see Eldpapa face-to-face for the first time scares me and at the same time makes me wild with excitement. His letters have been few, but generally sympathetic. I pray he still believes in my cause!'

'Have you any reason to doubt it?'

'He's one of Didion's great timberlords, with rich holdings. If he openly supports my claim to the throne, Somarus could charge him with sedition and high treason and seize everything.'

'Why are you so determined to meet with Duke Kefalus now?'

'Ising has heard rumors. The first invasion of the Salka monsters strengthened Conrig Ironcrown's hold over the vassal states. Even free-minded nobles such as my grandsire found that their desire for an independent Didion softened in the face of the alien threat. King Somarus is an ineffectual leader, but he's ruled for years, leaning on men more clever than he, such as Kilian Blackhorse. But now that scoundrel is dead. Somarus's defiance of the Sovereign over

the Tarnian deployment will have bolstered his tattered reputation greatly amongst our people. You can understand why!
I need to know whether my own cause has any chance of
prevailing – or if I pursue an impossible dream, encouraged
only by a few fanatics like dear old Ising Bedotha.'

Induna looked away with a sniff. 'A strange thing to say
about one so loyal and devoted!'

Casya spoke with quiet authority. 'I'd be a fool if I didn't
know Ising's flaws. No queen can afford misjudgments based
on sentimental feelings.'

'What a cold thought,' Induna said. 'And prideful. How
can you even be sure you're really a queen and not some
poor foundling?'

'I am a foundling for certain,' was the surprising reply. 'I
was plucked from the River Malle by a wizard named Tesk
at the behest of Mistress Cray, who was commanded to rescue
me by the Source himself.'

Induna's mouth dropped open in astonishment.

'My nursemaid Dala was rescued with me. Dala and Tesk
became man and wife and raised me in a cottage hidden
deep in the Great Wold. I was given the education of a future
queen, although I did not realize it at the time. When I
entered womanhood at thirteen, Cray came to me again and
told me who my parents had been, and why they and my
brothers had been killed. At base, the deepest guilt lies with
Somarus. He knew what the evil sorcerers Kilian and Beynor
planned, but was so greedy for the throne of Didion that he
did nothing to prevent the atrocity.'

Induna stared at the girl with wide eyes, momentarily
forgetting to make the breeze blow. The sail fell slack.

'Oy!' cried Baron Ising from the stern. 'What're you silly
magickers playing at up there? More wind, damn your eyes!'

'Sorry,' Induna called. The sail bellied full. She turned back
to Casya, addressing her with fresh respect. 'So you learned

you were a queen without a country. Did Cray and your
other friends advise you how to regain the throne?'

'No,' said Casya. 'Up until now, almost all decision-making
has been left to me. If I am to rule this troubled land, I must
hone my wits and political skill and understand the obliga-
tions and perils of leadership. Otherwise I'll be unworthy to
wear Didion's crown – a puppet ruler controlled by others,
as Somarus is. And so, for three years I've traveled the wild
regions of central and western Didion, seeking out discontented barons and . . . others who are unhappy at the
situation in our land. I explained what I intended to do if
the throne were mine: what ancient wrongs I would redress.
A year or so ago, when Cray felt confident in my maturing
abilities, she went to Baron Ising and commanded him to
send a message to Duke Kefalus Vandragora – an old anta-
gonist of his who yet was a childhood friend – telling him
of my existence. Ising also sent my baby bonnet, embroidered with the regal crest, which I wore when the royal
barge foundered. It was not hard for him to convince the
duke that he spoke the truth. My mother Queen Bryse was
Vandragora's dearly loved only daughter . . . and Kefalus had
long suspected that Somarus colluded in the Salka attack that
killed her and my family.'

Induna said, 'What will you do after speaking to your
grandsire? Will you remain with him?'

'No, but I do intend to seek his advice and give it my
deepest consideration. The time is ripe for me to do so. Earlier
this summer, before the Salka invasion, I announced myself
to all the people of Didion and declared my intent to take
back the crown denied me by the usurper. Somarus named
me an outlaw and sent a company of soldiers into the wold
to seek me out and kill me.' Her mouth curved in a dark
smile. 'They failed. Instead, my warriors and I slew them
almost to a man. We left a handful alive to return to Somarus

and tell him what had happened. Other bands of searchers
met a similar fate. I became Casya the Wold Wraith, with a
huge price on my head. I had intended to gather my loyal
fighters into an army and march on Holt Mallburn, gathering more partisans along the way. But –'

'The Salka came,' Induna put in.

'Along with High King Conrig and his Army of the
Sovereignty. My followers were unwilling to pursue a rebellion then – not with a horde of monsters invading the Green
Morass and Ironcrown ensconced in the heart of our nation,
preparing to direct its defense. So Cray suggested another
plan to me, one of great audacity that I was able to pursue
only with her help. Now, with a second Salka attack
impending, I'm at a disadvantage once again. But I'm mulling
over an idea that may provide a useful weapon against the
monsters.'

'What is it?'

Casya Pretender rose to her feet without responding to
the question. 'I think I'll take a turn at the tiller and give
Ising a rest.'

'Thank you for telling me your story, madam.' Induna
inclined her head in respect. She could not help but be moved
by the girl's resolution and political astuteness. 'I wish you
good luck in your bold quest. Deveron and I will help you
as we are able.'

Casabarela Mallburn gave a condescending smile, as
though she had expected no less, and went aft.

She had hardly left when Deveron returned from the
stubby bow of the flatboat, wiping sweat from his brow. His
face was pale and he walked unsteadily.

'Love!' Induna cried anxiously. 'Is aught amiss?'

He busied himself obtaining a flask of Baron Ising's good
wine from the vessel's tiny cabin, then rejoined his wife with
a sigh and drank deeply from a wooden cup. 'I'm only

exhausted after two tough bouts of far windsearching. But I finally found poor Rusgann. She's in a duck blind or some such place in the marsh south of Boarsden Castle, guarded by a couple of men wearing the badge of Tinnis Catclaw. They've flogged her back severely.'

'Oh! God pity her . . . Do you think she betrayed Maudrayne?'

'I know she didn't.' Deveron was an expert reader of lips. 'She taunted the guards, using language to make a sailor cringe. Said they'd never find the letter Maude sent to Dyfrig, even if they minced her flesh and made soup from her bones. She's a brave wench, but the men said the Lord Constable would find a way to make her talk when he returns at nightfall. They made atrocious suggestions. Red-hot irons were the least of it.'

Induna flinched. 'Will we get to her in time?'

'I hope so. The Malle flows more swiftly than the Kelk, and there's usually a good breeze in its deep valleys. Once we drop off Casya and Ising at the army's landing stage, they'll be on their own. You and I will have to steal a light skiff somewhere, then go invisible with my Concealer sigil as we try to rescue Rusgann. This flatboat is too bulky and clumsy to take into the marsh.'

'Then we can reach this duck blind by water?'

'Creeks wind all through the area.' He dropped to the deck and rested his back against the mast. 'Bazekoy's Brisket! I'm knackered, love. Can you keep up the breeze for a little while longer without my help? I should do an oversight of Boarsden Castle itself and find out where Catclaw resides, but first I need to rest.'

'Just close your eyes,' she told him, and made the sail snap like the blow of an axe. The boat surged forward.

'That's a hell of a lot more like it!' Baron Ising yelled happily from the stern. 'Keep up the good work, you two!'

*   *   *

Using an ordinary spell of invisibility, the sort that merely distracts observers so that they pay no notice to the intruder, Beynor entered the rooms formerly occupied by Kilian Blackhorse and his three henchmen. It was mid-afternoon, and the tower where the visiting magickers resided was quiet. No one had even bothered to put a guard on the suite assigned to the late Lord Chancellor and his minions. The outer door that had been locked by Garon Curtling upon his departure posed no obstacle at all to the Mossland sorcerer's art.

Beynor was not there out of idle curiosity, but came in search of a needed reference tome and certain exotic ingredients he suspected might be found in the dead wizard's laboratory. Kilian had brought from the capital a large traveling library and collection of thaumaturgical materials and implements. After collecting what he needed, Beynor settled down at a worktable to concoct a certain potion. He'd never had much use for such a thing earlier in his career; but he now hoped it might facilitate his scheme to influence Prince Heritor Corodon in a manner so benign that the constraints of Bazekoy's blue pearl would not come into play.

He measured and mixed, seethed and distilled; and when the liquid was ready at last he infused it with the proper spell, decanted it into a small faceted crystal vial, and held it up so that a beam of late sunlight pierced it, causing it to glow like a liquid ruby.

'Beautiful,' he murmured in satisfaction, 'and the color and flavor will be fully compatible with red wine. The only potential problem lies in the administration. But with careful coaching, even a dolt such as Corodon should be able to do it properly.'

Smiling, he stoppered the bottle containing the love philtre, tucked it into his wallet, and began to clean up all evidence that he had ever been in Kilian's rooms.

*   *   *

Even though the suspicious jeweler at the Great Market of Beorbrook gave Maudrayne less than a third of its value, the sale of a silver finger-ring with a small amethyst stone provided more than enough money for her immediate needs.

At the stall of a dealer in second-hand garments she obtained a gown, smallclothes, and a cape for the little maid Chelaire, who had been forced to journey down from the mountains wearing the torn, inadequate garments she had escaped in. For herself she purchased a veil and wimple, which she donned immediately in order to disguise her unusual auburn hair. The rest of her clothes were dusty and rumpled after two nights of sleeping under the stars and still smelled faintly of smoke; but their superior quality was un-diminished, lending believability to her pretense of being an unemployed lady's maid dressed in the castoffs of her former mistress, come to Beorbrook in search of her sister.

Using this explanation, Maudrayne engaged a tiny private room at a run-down inn. Bedraggled Chelaire played the rôle of her daughter, who had supposedly suffered a fall on the highland track during the trip to town. By the time they had bathed and tidied themselves and eaten a meal of day-old duck soup and dumplings it was nearly the fourth hour.

'We have at least two more hours of daylight,' Maudrayne said to their hovering hostess. As yet, they were the only guests in the shabby little place. 'I mean to spend the time looking for my sister's house. Not that I'd be likely to spend the night with her,' she added hastily, seeing the innkeeper's eyes narrow. 'Ludine's husband and I were often at odds in former years, and he might not welcome us.'

'Well, you've already paid for your bed here,' the hostess pointed out tersely. 'There'll be no refunds if you do decide to stop elsewhere.' She eyed Chelaire, who was meekly finishing her small beer. 'And if you ask me, that little one of yours would be better off tucked in bed. She looks done in. And I've got some salve that would help her bruises and her poor black eye.'

Maudrayne rose from the table. 'It would be a kindness if you'd let the lass have the salve. But she's stronger than she looks and the bumps are healing well. It'll do her no harm to stay up for an hour or two longer. Isn't that right, Chelly?'

'Oh yes, my – my mother!' the girl exclaimed. 'I do so want to see dear Auntie!'

'Likely we won't find my sister today.' Maude said, continuing the charade with only a small wince at the maid's dubious acting ability. 'I don't even know what street she dwells on – only that her husband works as a fuller. His name is Olan Wadhurst. I don't suppose you know of him?'

'The dyers and fullers mostly live in the Mercers' Quarter,' the innkeeper said with a dismissive gesture. 'In the south end. If you intend to go there, you'd best be moving. It's clear across town.'

Maudrayne thanked the woman, then inquired whether she might have anything to write upon. 'I could post a note on the quarter's bulletin board if my inquiries bear no fruit,' she explained.

The hostess rooted through a chest and finally produced a piece of much-scraped and re-used parchment. For this, plus the loan of a pen and ink and a few smears of comfrey ointment from a clay pipkin for Chelaire, she charged Maudrayne a halfpenny, then went off about her business.

'I know you are aching and weary, child,' the princess whispered as she tended the girl's wounds, 'but if you will be strong and brave for one more hour, it may be that you and I will sleep in Beorbrook Hold tonight, rather than in this dreadful hovel.'

'It seems a nice enough place to me, Lady Mayda,' Chelaire said, 'but I'll do anything you want me to.'

'Good. While I write, go to our room and fetch the book of dried plants we carried away from the lodge. Wrap it in your old skirt.'

While Chelaire ran off, Maude composed a letter to the widow of Parlian Beorbrook's eldest son, slain in the Edict of Sovereignty massacre over two decades earlier. Of necessity, the message was couched in ambiguous terms. If the woman was able to decipher it, would she still feel sympathy for the former queen, a woman of her own nation of Tarn, whom she'd met only briefly such a long time ago?

Chelaire came dashing back, carrying a cloth-wrapped bundle. 'Here it is, my – my mother! Shall I carry it for you? It's not heavy at all.'

'Do so, Chelly. But take care not to drop it. Auntie would be very disappointed if our gift for her were damaged.'

The countess finished examining the extraordinary herbarium book that had been wrapped in dirty rags, closed it, and set it aside on her desk. With a troubled expression, she smoothed the grubby and wrinkled piece of parchment the footman had brought to her along with the book, reading it for a second time. The words were beautifully formed, for all that they had been set down with a quill having an ill-cut nib that left unsightly blots.

My dear Morilye,

A countrywoman of yours begs your help with the utmost urgency, and beseeches that you keep this message secret. I am one whom you met many years ago in Cala, while your dear husband still lived. At that time, you expressed a kindly interest in a pastime of mine which others thought foolish. And so I showed you other books such as the one that

accompanies this letter, which I had assembled with
my own hands. Do you remember?

In the goodness of your heart, would you be
willing to lend assistance to one who once was high,
but now is laid low? What was said of me is not true.
I was unjustly accused. Now I am here at the gate of
Beorbrook Hold, in danger of my life, with no one
else to turn to. I promise not to inflict my presence
upon you for long. I only beg you will let me rest
briefly, secure from those who would hunt me down
and kill me. Then I will leave.

If you cannot see your way clear to meet with me,
then send word and I will go away.

M – who was once Q

Countess Morilye reached for the bell that would summon
her footman, then thought better of it. Taking up a shawl
against the chill of the approaching evening, she hurried
through the corridors, halls, and inner ward of the massive
fortress, ignoring the curious looks of guards and servants,
and came at last to the main gatehouse and the small office
of the captain of the guard. He hastily rose from a desk where
he had been scribbling on a slate, clapped his helmet back
on his head, and knuckled his breastplate in salute.

'My lady! What brings you out here alone?'

'Riscodon, where is the woman who sent in the note to
me?'

'She and her little girl are in the guardroom being questioned by my sergeant. Did you know that there was an advi-
sory sent out several days ago concerning a tall woman who
had absconded from the custody of Lord Constable Catclaw?
We were told she might attempt to enter Beorbrook Hold
with mischievous intent. Even though this present visitor did
not quite fit the description, I thought it best –'

'Take me to her at once,' the countess commanded.

The captain inclined his head. 'Please follow me, my lady.'

They crossed the gatehouse to another chamber with a soldier on guard outside. The officer motioned him aside, then opened the door and bade Morilye precede him.

The countess halted with a small cry as she saw a woman standing furious and defiant, back to the wall, with a frightened young maid clinging to her skirts. The hair straggling from her grubby wimple was a richer red than Morilye's own greying tresses, and her eyes were blazing, full of haughty disdain for the hapless man who had attempted to interrogate her. At the sight of the countess, the woman's demeanor underwent an abrupt change. The anger drained from her features and she smiled as radiantly as sunlight bursting through stormclouds. She opened her mouth to speak but stopped short, a wary expression replacing the look of sudden joy, and waited in silence as the sergeant began blustering to his superior.

Countess Morilye broke in. 'Captain Riscodon, you and your man may leave us. Close the door behind you.'

'But, my lady –' the officer began.

'This woman and I are old friends. She cannot possibly be the one sought by the Lord Constable. There is no danger. Go now.'

He gave a curt nod and both men retreated.

Maudrayne put her finger to her lips as the door slammed. 'They'll be listening. Speak softly. So you *do* remember me?'

In answer, Morilye stepped close and enfolded the princess in her arms. Her voice was almost inaudible. 'I can't believe you're alive, Maude! How in God's name did this come to be? What are you doing here? Who is trying to kill you? What can I do to help?'

Maudrayne gently released herself from the other woman's embrace and spoke low. 'There's peril in it if you do help me. I give you fair warning. Tinnis Catclaw would have me slain without batting an eye – for he engineered my fictitious death out of besotted love, and has kept me prisoner in a mountain lodge near here for some sixteen years.'

'The lecherous brute! And him a married man with five children.'

'I forbore attempting to escape for one reason only: Tinnis would have had my dear son Dyfrig killed if I had defied him. All throughout my captivity I was forbidden any contact with my boy. He believes me to be dead, as do all other persons save the Lord Constable.'

For a moment, the countess was confused. 'Dyfrig? The earl marshal's adopted son? The royal bastard?'

'Whatever you have heard said of me, I swear he is Conrig Wincantor's true first-born son.' Maudrayne spoke through clenched teeth. 'And now that Dyfrig is a man grown, my only goal in life is to make certain that he knows it.' In a few brief words the Princess Dowager explained how she had sent a letter to Dyfrig through her friend, informing him of his heritage. 'But now I fear Catclaw's men have intercepted poor Rusgann and found the letter. Tinnis had the lodge set afire with me locked up in it. Obviously he wished to destroy all evidence of his treasonous perfidy, fearing that my friend might have told others of my existence. I barely escaped death through the good offices of this dear child, Chelaire, one of the maidservants in the place, who was left behind when the others fled the fire.'

The countess gave a gasp of horror. 'Distant smoke was seen from the Hold's towers a few days ago, but we thought it was wildfire in the highland forests.' Her face hardened. 'You asked my help and I'm prepared to give it – Tinnis Catclaw be damned! What is your wish? To be smuggled safely to your people in Tarn? I can arrange that –'

'Nay,' Maudrayne interrupted. 'I must go to Dyfrig, wherever he may be.'

'As far as I know, the young prince is at Boarsden in Didion with the earl marshal, attending the great ongoing Council of War called by the Sovereign . . . Are you aware that the Salka invasion has ended? The monsters are in full retreat! I've no doubt that Ironcrown's army will now disperse and Dyfrig will return home along with the other warriors led by my father-in-law. You can wait here for your son in safety.'

Maudrayne's face clouded at the news and she shook her head. 'I must go to Boarsden at once, regardless. Zeth knows what Tinnis will do next. He might try to harm Dyfrig. At any rate, I'm now determined that my son should know the truth from my own lips: that he is the lawful heir to the Iron Crown of Cathra and the next Sovereign of Blenholme.'

'Oh, my!' Morilye's eyes widened. 'There's something else you don't know. Prince Orrion was debarred from the succession after losing his sword-hand. The new heritor is his scapegrace twin, Corodon, and the High King is said to be livid with disappointment! Come – let's get out of this drafty place and go to my chambers and I'll tell you everything.'

She would have headed for the guardroom door, but Maudrayne took her arm and spoke urgently. 'Wait. I must know whether you will lend me a swift horse and a few trusted men, and see me off to Didion at dawn. I can pay well for their hire.' She pulled the gold-and-opal necklace that had been Sernin Donorvale's wedding gift from within the neck of her gown.

'No, no, I won't hear of any payment!' Morilye was distressed. 'My heart breaks at the thought of what you must have suffered. I'll lend you a fine horse. If you ride hard, you can reach Boarsden Castle in less than three days. My two young Tarnian cousins who serve here as armigers will ride with you. Tormo and Durin are strong, stouthearted lads, well versed in the warrior's art even though they are only fifteen and sixteen years old. I would trust them with my own life.'

'For their own safety, they must not know the truth,' Maude warned.

'We'll devise a suitable story and disguise you well.' She regarded the princess thoughtfully. 'You might dress as a man! You're tall enough. My late husband's coffers can provide suitable garb, just a little old-fashioned. You could even take some of his armor and weaponry if you choose, and I can outfit you with a surcoat bearing the device of a Beorbrook household knight. No one in the borderlands would challenge you if you wore it.'

'An excellent idea. And I know how to use both sword and shortbow, if it should be necessary.'

For the first time, the little maid Chelaire spoke up. 'I'll go with you, Lady Mayda! I can pretend to be a boy, too.'

Maude whispered, 'Oh, my dear brave Chelly!' She caught up the girl in her arms and hugged her, but her eyes met those of the countess and she shook her head imperceptibly.

'We'll talk about it inside,' Morilye said, giving the princess an understanding glance. The girl would be well taken care of. 'Chelly, do you like quince tarts, honey-poppyseed biscuits, and mulled wine with clove and cinnamon?'

The maid ducked her head shyly. 'Indeed, my lady, I've never had any.'

'You've a fine treat in store,' the countess said. 'Follow me, both of you.'

About an hour after sunset, following a simple evening meal taken with the Sovereign and the Tarnian leaders at the encampment of Sealord Yons Stormchild, which lay directly across the Malle from Boarsden Town, Prince Heritor Corodon went off for a solitary stroll along the riverbank, cursing his rotten luck. The sky was clear and moonless, spangled with bright stars. At supper, Grand Shaman Zolanfel had opined that the Great Lights might be visible tonight, for the first time since the spring equinox.

Corodon had spent a second long and exhausting day attending his father. The Sovereign was in the saddle from dawn to dusk, riding into every camp and personally addressing each company of troops, giving them the unwelcome news of the fresh Salka threat and the need to redeploy to staging areas more suitable to the defense of the west coast.

In spite of the pleas of his son, Crown Prince Valardus, Somarus had intractably refused to order his ground forces into Tarn; Conrig finally agreed to a compromise in order to stave off a ruinous confrontation.

The entire army was under orders to pull up stakes in three days and prepare to march to one of two new interim bases. All of the Tarnians plus two-thirds of the Cathran host, headed by Conrig himself, would proceed to Castle Direwold, where they would be in a position to move swiftly over Frost Pass if the Salka attacked Donorvale or another objective in western Tarn. The rest of the Cathrans, led by Earl Marshal Parlian, and the entire Didionite force under Valardus and Duke Kefalus Vandragora, would take a position on the shore of the Lake of Shadows, the first to respond if the monsters should come ashore at Terminal Bay, Puffin Bay, or Sorna in Didion – which seemed less likely.

To his disappointment and dismay, Prince Corodon had been assigned to this latter group, with the nominal title of Royal Liaison between the Cathrans and Didionites. It seemed all too clear that his father couldn't bear the sight of him.

'It's not fair,' the prince muttered bitterly, picking up a flat stone and shying it out over the darkening surface of the river. 'Everyone thinks the Salka will attack Donorvale rather

than those raggedy-arse pirate nests in Didion. I should have
been given a battle-company of my own to lead! As it is, I'll
straggle into Tarn days later with the Cathran rear guard after
the really exciting action is over and done with.'

Corodon sat on a rock, simmering with frustration. The
decision had been made. There was nothing he could do
about it.

Small watercraft were shuttling busily to and fro between
Boarsden Town and the camps. Some of them were the
bumboats of pedlars and victualers, while others were laden
with giggling female passengers whose trade was obvious.
The whores would do a roaring business tonight, the prince
thought gloomily. Small chance they'd be allowed to accompany the divided army to its new positions. Both Direwold
and Shadow Lake were austere outposts with scant facilities
for camp-followers. Corodon had already been warned by
the earl marshal that his high rank would bring no special
privilege in accommodation. He'd sleep in a tent like the rest
of the troops, eat pottage and bannock cooked over an open
fire, and endure clouds of biting midges drinking his royal
blood –

'Good evening, Your Grace. May I join you?'

Corodon swallowed a yelp of surprise and leapt to his feet
at the unexpected salutation. Conjure-King Beynor of Moss
stood there in the gloaming, wearing the simple tunic,
gartered trews, and dark cloak of a Tarnian land-warrior.
Despite the fact that the riverbank was a mass of slippery
pebbles, he'd approached without making a single sound.

'What a surprise to see you here, Majesty,' Corodon said
without enthusiasm. 'I thought the Zeth Brethren had you
confined to the castle with their sorcery. How did you
escape?'

Beynor laughed good-naturedly. 'No one keeps me where
I don't want to be. As far as the Brothers know, I'm safe

in my rooms. I'll return there after we've had a chance to talk.'

'Mmm.' Corodon felt a frisson of alarm. His older brother Vra-Bramlow had told him what he knew about the Conjure-King's ominous history – specifically that he was said to have been an ally of the Salka and a user of moon-stone sigils.

'I have a small gift for you,' Baynor said. He opened his belt-wallet, extracted a sack of wash-leather, and pressed it into Corodon's hand. 'When I witnessed your distress at the aborted betrothal feast, I realized that there was a simple remedy for Princess Hyndry's rejection of you. Go ahead! Open it.'

The prince loosened the sack's drawstring and drew forth a pretty little stoppered bottle that contained dark liquid. 'What is it, Majesty?'

'A most useful potion. Pour it secretly into a lady's cup of wine, and she will fall in love with the first man who touches her after she drinks.'

'Codders! A love philtre?'

Beynor nodded. 'It will cause her to forget her former lovers and diminish her hostility toward a new suitor. Princess Hyndry won't just fall at your feet, swooning in rapture. She's rather a tough nut – even for me to crack! But a hand-some young chap like you should be able to soften her up if you work at it.'

Corodon's eyes narrowed in doubt. 'Why are you willing to do me a favor? You don't know me or care about me.'

'You must learn to think like a statesman, Your Grace. This really has nothing to do with *you*. I'm certain, as your royal father is, that a marriage between the Prince Heritor of Cathra and the Princess Royal of Didion would be advantageous to the Sovereignty – of which I am now a loyal vassal. High King Conrig's plan to strengthen the bond between two mutually suspicious nations was brilliantly conceived and should not be thwarted by an unfortunate . . . accident.'

The sorcerer's black eyes seemed to enlarge. Corodon attempted to look away from that compelling gaze but found it to be impossible. 'What do you want from me?' he whispered desperately.

'Only the truth, and a little bit more. First: tell me if it was really an accident that cost your twin brother his sword-arm.'

To his horror, the prince found himself babbling everything about the Demon Seat incident. As he finished, he opened his own belt-purse and displayed the piece of raw moonstone he'd taken from the mountain, adding that he'd given a second chunk of mineral to Lord Stergos.

Staring at the Heritor in stunned silence, Beynor only barely managed to conceal his utter consternation. It was a cosmic joke! Three royal idiots had inadvertently discovered the second Moon Crag – *and drawn uncanny power from it.* But the sorcery had obviously not come from the Beaconfolk, but from their ancient antagonists in the Sky Realm.

I must find a way to use this knowledge, Beynor thought. But how? For the moment, his great intellect failed him. He'd have to take time considering the ramifications of what the prince had revealed. It seemed obvious that Corodon and his brothers had no notion who the 'demons' really were. But Lord Stergos might! As for the two pieces of raw moonstone –

Beynor blinked. Instantly the spell coercing the prince dissolved and the young man stepped back, furious with himself. 'What have I done?' he cried. 'What have you *made* me do?'

'Be at ease, Your Grace.' Beynor let soothing emanations flood the agitated mind of Corodon, forcing him to be calm, convincing him in spite of himself that all was well and no harm done. 'It was very clever of you to take bits of moon-stone from the mountaintop. You're quite right to believe that they are objects of wondrous power. But even more marvelous are the sigils the Salka carved from them.' He reached again into his wallet. 'Have you ever seen one?'

'No,' Corodon said in a trembling voice. He seemed ready to flee, and Beynor had to use a gentle restraining spell.

'Look here.' The Conjure-King pulled open a second little leather bag and drew out the individually wrapped amulets. He held up the translucent finger-ring. 'These are not ordinary sigils such as the Salka use. They are Great Stones, capable of exerting enormous power. This is a Weathermaker. Its use is obvious.' He replaced it and showed Corodon a second sigil. 'Here is Ice-Master, a tool to freeze water. Perhaps you think that a small thing: but remember that the human body is naught but a container of vital juices! . . . And here is the most awesome sigil of all, a simple little wand named Destroyer. Can you guess what it's capable of?'

Corodon shook his head mutely.

'Imagine the mightiest lightning bolt, the most appalling quake or avalanche, the strongest whirlwind, the stormiest sea. None of them compare with the overwhelming power of Destroyer.' He wrapped the rod again and tucked away the pouch of sigils. 'I own these miraculous magical tools, but you need not fear that I'll use them against the Sovereignty. Even though I am a great sorcerer – perhaps the greatest on earth – these sigils are forbidden to me. I know how to activate them, but I can never wield such things myself.'

'But, why not?'

'I'm under a curse, Prince Corodon. Once I used a Great Stone in a manner that displeased the Beaconfolk. They were merciful and spared my life, but I am now forbidden to use sigils ever again under pain of damnation to the Hell of Ice.

And so I have chosen to bestow them upon someone else who can make best use of them, safeguarding the island that we love from its many enemies and restoring my lost kingdom of Moss to me and my human subjects.'

'Who will you give the sigils to?'

'The ruler of High Blenholme, of course.'

'My father?' Corodon was so astounded that his response was a strangled croak. 'You'd give them to *him*?'

'They are to be the property of the Sovereign,' Beynor said with sinister emphasis. 'Whoever he may be.'

The prince's eyes widened in comprehension and he gasped. 'Do you mean I could inherit such things when I take up the Iron Crown?'

Beynor smiled. 'Now do you understand why I came to you tonight? You are in a position to believe what I say. You stood on Demon Seat and saw the power of the Sky Beings channeled to our Ground Realm. By myself, I'd never be able to convince the High King that I wish to become a great benefactor of Blenholme. He sees me only as the foolish younger brother of the woman who was once his mistress, a Conjure-King deposed and banished by his own sister, an obscure wizard come creeping back to beg of him a useless boon: the throne of conquered Moss. By myself, I can never drive the Salka monsters out of my vanquished kingdom. They wield sigil sorcery, which I can't withstand. But if your father Conrig used these three moonstone weapons against the Salka –' Beynor paused in a meaningful manner '– or, failing that, if another Sovereign did so, then my homeland would be released from a terrible bondage.'

'What do you want me to do?' Corodon's voice had steadied and strengthened.

'Show the High King the love philtre. Tell him who gave it to you and ask his permission to use it. After he has seen it work, tell him of my offer to be his benefactor, to give him

the three sigils and show him how to use them. All I ask in
return is that he help me rebuild Moss once the Salka
invaders are gone.'

'But how can I convince him you told me the truth?' The
prince was dubious. 'He – he's never really thought very much
of me. My brother Orrion was always the favored one, even
though he's a stodgy sort and nothing much to look at.'

Beynor's features took on a judicious air. 'I think, Your
Grace, that you'll have to tell King Conrig what really
happened during your adventure on Demon Seat. Let him
know just how far the worthy Orrion was willing to go to
thwart the Didionite betrothal. Show him your piece of
moonstone as proof. He'll know what it is.'

'Futter me,' Corodon murmured. 'Do I dare?'

Once again, the sorcerer's stare was implacably compelling.
'If you decide to tell him all this, you must make certain that
your father informs no one else – most especially Lord Stergos
– about the three Great Stones in my possession. If I discover
that others have found out about them, I'll quietly disappear. There are rulers on the Continent who would be eager
to consider my proposal . . . Now *think*, Corodon Wincantor,
and then decide! Are you worthy to be Prince Heritor,
someday the Sovereign, or are you too cowardly to take upon
yourself a great challenge?'

He wants to use me, Corodon said to himself. I know it!
He thinks me a credulous fool, too stupid to realize that he
has some hidden scheme that has nothing to do with
restoring the lost land of Moss. But how can I turn my back
on his offer? It's an open secret that Father used Ullanoth's
sigil sorcery to establish the Sovereignty. There's no doubt
in my mind that these three Great Stones can defeat the
Salka monsters, whereas ordinary weaponry might fail.
Beynor is surely a villain, but kings have worked successfully with villains all throughout history –

'Corodon. You must decide.'

The prince gave a great start as the soft voice broke into his frenetic thoughts. He turned away deliberately from Beynor and pretended to study the bobbing lights of the many small boats out on the River Malle.

'I'll show the love philtre to Father,' he declared at last, 'and tell him it's a gift from you, and that you wish to assist the Sovereignty with your magic. Doubtless he'll want to confer with you and decide for himself whether you're worthy of trust. This is as far as I am willing to go.'

Beynor chuckled. 'It'll do for now. Farewell, Your Grace. May you have joy of your lovely bride-to-be! But don't wait too long to administer the potion. The royal tart is already thinking about running away to join her banished lover, Count Egonus.'

Corodon whirled about to question the sorcerer further, but he had already vanished.

As the Tarnian shaman had predicted, the auroral Lights soon appeared in the northern sky, flickering beacons of red and gold and emerald that seemed to slash at the polar constellations like fierce, luminous swords. The nightwatch in the camps of the Army of the Sovereignty looked up at the magnificent sight – the Cathrans uneasy without knowing why and the warriors of Tarn and Didion apprehensive at what they knew was a dire portent indeed. A few of the latter claimed they heard a mysterious whispering sound when the eerie flashes of color were at their brightest.

The men did not realize that Great Lights were laughing. Beynor of Moss, the great manipulator, had been successfully manipulated by them in spite of himself. Perhaps very soon, his usefulness to them would end and the New Conflict could proceed with no risk of his skewing the outcome.

*   *   *

In the small private pavilion of Duke Kefalus Vandragora, Casabarela Mallburn sat at a glowing brazier with her grandfather and Baron Ising. A tear trickled unheeded from her eye, sparkling in the ruddy light, as the two elderly noblemen sipped from cups of metheglin and waited for her to speak.

'Your promise to stand by me secretly in spite of the renewed Salka threat fills my heart with great joy, Eldpapa. I thought I would have to argue my case to you long and hard. There was even doubt in my mind that you would believe that I had actually made friends with the inhuman ones and secured their promise to aid our struggle against the Salka . . . All I can say is, thank you for accepting me so unquestioningly. I never thought it would happen this way.'

'Great Starry Bear!' Kefalus said, wagging a set of long white moustaches. 'How could I *not* accept you? You're the image of your poor dead mother – my beloved Bryse reborn! But you've got a flame in your guts that my sweet daughter never had. You're not quiet and gentle, lass – you're a fighter like your famous ancestress, the first Casabarela Regnant. And I intend to see you on Didion's throne before I die.'

She rose up, youthful but regal in spite of the tawdry finery of her whore's disguise, and held out both arms to the duke in loving invitation. But Vandragora did not embrace her. Instead he dropped to one knee and kissed her hand, then looked up with a broad grin on his rugged features. 'Accept my fealty and homage, Your Majesty of Didion.'

'Willingly, my lord,' she replied grandly – then spoiled the solemn moment by drawing the tall old man to his feet and kissing him resoundingly on both cheeks. 'But what in the world shall we do now? I'm not such a fool as to think of proclaiming myself openly to the people and inviting them to rally round. Not with war impending once again. But I can't stand back while the Salka attack. There are ways I can help.'

'You've already helped,' the duke said, 'by convincing the Green Woman Cray to guide you to the Morass Worms. The creatures might not have fought the Salka so fiercely and cleverly if she had not told them that the monsters were coming in vast numbers and urged them to accept your tactical suggestions. But if you would now do more, order your outlaw human followers to join my force at Lake of the Shadows. They will be welcomed without condition. None of my officers need know what took place in the past. Your fighters will simply be fresh recruits from deep within the Elderwold.'

'But what of *me*?' Casya looked forlorn. 'I'm their leader!'

'My dear, I must speak frankly. It would be best if you went to my great citadel on Firedrake Water until the situation stabilizes. You know there's a price on your head.'

'But I want –' she began.

Kefalus Vandragora held up a monitory hand. 'You are a queen uncrowned with two mortal enemies – Somarus and his son Valardus. Your life is precious, perhaps vital to the future of Didion. God only knows what the next few weeks will bring. You must be patient. And when you're needed, you must be ready.'

'I'm ready now!' she wailed.

'It won't do, Granddaughter,' the duke said. 'If you think the citadel is too remote, then let me arrange for you to stay in another of my forts on Firedrake Water. There are several where you'd be quite safe from the henchmen of Somarus.'

'Firedrake,' she grumbled rebelliously. 'What a silly name. What does it mean – "Burning Duck?"'

Vandragora laughed. 'Far from it. It's a very old word for a mythical fire-breathing dragon. I suppose our ancestors named it after the Morass Worms, who once must have lived thereabouts until driven further north by humanity. Even our citadel's ancient name hints at that.'

'Oh.' Casya looked thoughtful and silence fell amongst the three.

Baron Ising Bedotha helped himself to more of the powerful honey-liquor, then cleared his throat in a meaningful fashion. 'If the Salka decide not to attack Tarn, as Conrig Ironcrown thinks they will, and come at Didion from a new direction instead, we could be deep in the shite. Ain't that right, Keffy?'

The duke gave his long-time friendly enemy a morose nod. 'I fear so. Too many of our troops are brave as tundra-lions but lacking in discipline. King Conrig claimed the bulk of the Cathran army's professional ranks for his northern force. And while Sealord Yons Stormchild's lads have an unlimited supply of sophisticated tarnblaze munitions and battle engines at their disposal, we're only equipped with hand grenades, crossbows, and blades – plus whatever matériel Parlian Beorbrook can pry loose from the Sovereign's tightfisted battalions.'

'Fighting in the bogs and thickets of the Great Wold could be a nightmare for our men,' the baron observed. 'Nearly as bad as the Green Morass.'

'If it falls to me to defend Didion from the Salka, I'll do it no matter where the monsters threaten.' Kefalus paused. 'I'm not at all sure that I'd do the same for Tarn, however. Somarus may be a fratricidal loony, but he's right on the mark when he refuses to send our warriors into that arctic wilderness with winter only just around the corner.'

Casya regarded him with a neutral expression. 'Then you are no friend of the Sovereignty, Eldpapa?'

'No, my liege lady,' he replied formally. 'Nor should you be, once the Salka monsters are defeated.'

Her eyes slid away from him and stared into the coals of the brazier. 'It's a subject I've not thought much about. Perhaps I should do so. It may help pass the dull hours I'll spend at Firedrake Water.'

'Ah!' Kefalus cried in relief. 'Then you'll go?'

She nodded in agreement. 'If my old friend Ising will be so kind as to escort me there. With one or two trusted men of yours, Eldpapa, to see us to our proper destination.'

The baron bestowed a long, searching look on her. 'Isn't this a rather sudden change of heart, lass?'

She shrugged. 'A prerogative of queens, my lord.'

TWELVE

'I hear something,' Induna whispered. 'Very faint. It might be an owl or some animal crying out at a far distance. The mist is so dense now that I can't scry anything beyond a stone's throw away. Are you able to see farther?'

The invisible skiff with its two invisible passengers slowed to a halt. At this time of year, before the autumnal storms began in earnest and the great river rose, the marsh below Boarsden Castle was an expanse of partially dried-out flats on which grew head-high stands of rushes, sedge, and coarse grass, along with scattered copses of scrubby trees. Many of its countless ponds had turned into mudholes, and only the deepest creeks still held water. Deveron and Induna were following one of these twisted streams in an old skiff they had commandeered after dropping off Casabarela and Baron Ising at the encampment docks.

Recalling his unsettling experience with the Subtle Gateway sigil, Deveron had at first been wary about conjuring Concealer. Would the Lights once again show their dis-approval of his intentions by pulling another near-lethal prank? Warning Induna to keep her distance, he had silently invoked the minor stone's sorcery – and vanished. Nothing

untoward had happened. He expanded the sphere of invisibility to enclose his wife and their bags, and bade Induna
cling to his jerkin as he prowled the docks looking for a suitable boat. Deveron selected one that was shabby but sound,
with no leaks, a shallow draft, and a very low freeboard. He
left a silver mark tucked behind the cleat where it had been
tied up – a grossly inflated price, considering the quality of
the craft. Then he spoke the words that rendered it as invisible as its passengers, and they set off unseen to the place
where Rusgann was held captive.

It was now about an hour after nightfall, and their progress
had been reduced to a crawl due to the sudden rise of the
mist. Both of them could see in the dark – a talent so trifling
that it did not restrict the use of a second uncanny power –
but the nearly opaque vapors limited their scrying ability to
a distance of only five ells or so. This was just slightly beyond
the radius of Concealer's invisibility spell. Deveron exerted
his windsight to the utmost in an attempt to pierce the murk,
but he was only minimally successful.

'I can see the stars overhead but little else.' He spoke
low, realizing how sounds carried under these conditions.
'The fog is much thinner above us. We're traveling in the
right direction and I'm certain this creek will take us to the
area where Rusgann is. I oversaw the way earlier, when
we were on the River Malle. But we dare not move too
fast in this maze of waterways, lest we miss a turning and
become lost or stuck in a quagmire. I'm also concerned
about the Lord Constable possibly getting there ahead of
us. There are other routes than this one from the castle to
the fowler's blind.'

'Listen!' Induna whispered. 'There it goes again.'

The second quavering shriek had a ventriloqual quality: it
could have come from any direction and it was much louder
than the first.

'Dear God, husband! That's no swamp creature. It's a woman in agony.'

He crouched in the stern of the rickety skiff, steering with the scull-oar while giving additional impetus with his talent. With all the other handicaps, invisibility made the task even more difficult; he himself could see neither the boat nor even his own body. Only his instincts and the faintly glimmering bow-wave enabled him to determine the position of the craft relative to the walls of vegetation encroaching on either side of the creek. In spite of his best efforts, they scraped against stems and spindly trunks again and again, making a considerable noise and flushing out sleeping geese and other waterfowl, which flew off squawking and splashing.

It made little difference, Deveron thought grimly. The pathetic moans and screams were becoming almost continuous, making it nigh on impossible for the torturers to notice their approach.

Induna was seated in the bow, hunched low, wincing at each new outcry. Forgetting that her husband could not see her, she began to wave her arms frantically just as they emerged from a thick reed-bed into the open black water of a sizable pond. The mist above it was torn by a breeze and floated like ragged swatches of gauze.

'Stop!' she called silently on the wind. 'This is the place. We've found them.'

Deveron halted the skiff. Faint golden ripples spread out from the indentation in the water's surface marking the position of the invisible craft. The scene was dimly illuminated by a lantern shining within a small structure resembling a crude hut that stood on the pond's opposite shore. Behind it rose an area of higher ground where four horses and a mule were tethered amidst a thicket of saplings. The fowler's blind was erected on pilings sunk in the water and connected

to the land by a short dock of log puncheons. The flimsy
walls of wattled twigs and withes facing the water had arrow-
slits in them rather than windows. A silhouetted form,
moving with ominous purpose, could be seen through gaps
between the woven sticks.

The sickening sounds of a lash meeting flesh mingled with
heart-rending cries. Then, suddenly, the tormented woman
fell silent.

A harsh male voice let out a furious curse. 'She only
pretends to have fainted! Prick the sole of her foot with your
dirk, Larus. That'll rouse the stubborn slut. You must make
her talk!'

'Sir, there's no response. She's senseless again.'

'Damn it!' another voice exclaimed. 'Use that old bucket
to throw water on her. Sir Asgar, get the smelling salts we
brought with us. Trozo, untie her hands and lift her head.
See if you can get some brandy down her gullet without
choking her.'

'What are we to do?' Induna spoke soundlessly. 'I scry
four men gathered about the poor soul, who lies on her back
with her wrists and ankles tied to the slatted floor. Those –
those arrant fiends have torn open her dress and beaten her
breasts and upper body bloody. We know that yesterday they
scourged her back. We've got to stop them before they start
in again!'

'We will,' Deveron responded on the wind. 'Calm yourself
and look closely at the place. Do you think its floor is high
enough above the water so that our skiff will slip beneath
with you inside?'

She hesitated. 'If I lie flat I can just make it. But I fear
you will be too bulky to fit.'

'It matters not. Now this is what I want you to do . . .'

Moments later, the low-riding invisible boat's bow was
nosed against one of the blind's outer pilings. The men inside

were arguing about whether it would be best to postpone
the inquisition until the morrow. The voice Deveron now
recognized as belonging to Lord Tinnis Catclaw resisted the
suggestion.

'I must know *tonight* what message she carries. It's imperative! A certain person is due to arrive at the castle soon,
and I must have the woman's information beforehand.'

Low mutterings ensued. Someone said, 'We should light
the brazier then, my lord. It's plain that flogging hasn't
worked.'

'Oh, very well,' Catclaw growled. 'Get on with it.'

Deveron bespoke Induna: 'Are you lying well down?'

'Yes.'

'When I'm four ells away from you, the sigil will be unable
to render you invisible. There's little chance of anyone seeing
you under the blind, but be very cautious. Remain in hiding
until I say it's safe to come out . . . What I must now do will
be messy and horrid, love, but you must be brave. For
Rusgann's sake I dare not leave any of these men alive.'

'Must it be so?' she asked, her voice heavy with dread.

'In truth, I shrink at the prospect with all my soul. But
mercy rendering them unconscious before rescuing the
woman will not serve. The Lord Constable is now a man
whose own life is in grave danger. He's doomed if King Conrig
discovers that he lied about killing Princess Maudrayne – and
even worse, kept her as his lover. Catclaw's men are equally
at risk as accessories. None of them can rest easy until they
hunt down and slay Maude and anyone who has had contact
with her.'

'And Prince Dyfrig, once he reads his mother's letter –'

'He, too, would know the constable's deadly secret. And
there's another thing, Duna: if Dyfrig *is* the Sovereign I am
to assist in the New Conflict, then no price is too great to
ensure his safety. We are at war, my love. The men inside

that hut are the foes of the Source and the Likeminded Lights just as surely as the Salka are.'

She knew he had killed before, but always in self-defense. Now he would be forced to go against the Tarnian Healer Oath he had pronounced after being taught shaman arts by her mother Maris, and slay in cold blood as a soldier must.

'Deveron, have courage,' she said. 'Do what you must do.'

All he said was, 'Later, I may have great need of your comfort.'

The boat rocked as he slipped overboard without a sound and waded toward the shore through lingering wisps of fog. She peeped over the gunwale and her heart leapt into her mouth as she realized that in spite of the sigil's sorcery his presence was all too obvious in the lantern's betraying light. Where his legs entered the water were peculiar dark 'holes', and the yellow-glowing mist tendrils swirled unnaturally around the moving mass of his body, giving it a faint human outline. But no one emerged from the hut and saw him. A moment later all traces of Deveron were out of her sight.

Then it happened.

She froze in terror. For a brief instant she and the boat popped clearly into view, no longer invisible, lit by the narrow beams shining through the gaps in the wattle. Then, blessedly, Concealer's spell embraced them again.

With trembling hands she gripped the crudely hewn floor-joists and pulled the skiff beneath the blind with infinite slowness until it was positioned near the pathetic motion-less body. Drops of bloody water dripped down from it. Through the cracks in the slatted duckboard floor Induna could see the brutes who had done the evil work. A nobleman dressed in a fine riding habit of midnight blue stood against one wall with folded arms and a scowl disfiguring his comely face. Two men-at-arms in mail shirts and hoods, whose livery bore the blazon of a wildcat's threatening paw, worked with a tinderbox at a rusty brazier. A fourth man, unarmored and wearing a knightly belt, stout of body and flushed with frustration, knelt beside the victim and ministered to her clumsily.

'My lord, the brandy runs from her lips,' this villain announced. 'She cannot swallow. If you wish us to continue, we'll have to wait until she comes around. Shall I cover her? It may hasten her revival if she's kept warm.'

'Oh, very well,' snapped the Lord Constable. 'Use her own cloak. And give that brandy flask to me. I need a drink worse than she does.'

'We'll warm her up soon enough!' said one of the warriors at the brazier, which had begun to smolder. His mate gave a coarse guffaw.

Induna's eyes filled with tears at the callous cruelty. How could human beings treat a helpless person so?

The duck blind's ramshackle door creaked slowly open. One of the warriors spun about with an oath. 'Who's there?'

An instant later, he crumpled with a bubbling cry, both hands clutching at his neck in a vain attempt to stanch the torrent of blood gushing from it.

Catclaw howled, 'On guard!' and drew his sword. But no enemy could be seen. The constable stood in helpless horror as the second warrior, who still knelt at the brazier, flung wide his arms and arched his head backward, exposing the bare throat above his mail hood. A gash opened miraculously like an additional gaping mouth, flooding the man's surcoat with scarlet, and he fell dying.

The Lord Constable slashed the empty air, shouting obscenities, until his voice soared in a piercing shriek. Induna saw blood pouring from the back of his right boot, just above the heel. An invisible blade, perhaps wielded by someone lying on the floor, had hamstrung Tinnis Catclaw. He staggered, dropping his weapon, and crashed onto the slats, where he

writhed and roared until his own sword rose up like a living
thing and smote off his head.

The spouting cascade of gore barely missed Induna in the
skiff floating beneath. She retched thin bile and impelled the
craft out from under the shambles into the open water of
the pond, rendering herself clearly visible. After she caught
her breath and cleared her mouth, she continued her resolute
scrying of the ghastly interior of the blind. When Deveron
needed her, she would come.

Sir Asgar, the corpulent knight, was on his hands and
knees, so dumfounded at the uncanny carnage that he had
yet to put hand to weapon. He scrambled toward the open
door on all fours, uttering a frantic mewling sound, struggled to his feet, and lurched awkwardly along the dock
toward the shore. Catclaw's flying sword plunged into his
unarmored back and found his heart. Still impaled, the bulky
body swayed, then fell into the shallows with a monstrous
splash. The mounts tied in the thicket screamed and plunged
in fear.

'BI FYSINEK. KRUF AH!' Speaking the Salka words that
cancelled Concealer's spell, Deveron stood on the muddy
shore, head hanging, splattered with blood, surrendering to
the sigil's pain-debt and the greater anguish afflicting his own
heart.

Induna sent the skiff speeding to him. She stepped out,
took hold of one arm, and led him to a place where the
ground was drier and grass grew. There she made him lie
down, bathed his face and hands with pondwater, kissed
him, and let him be. The sigil Concealer was a minor stone
and its price, at least, would soon be paid.

Taking her fardel from the boat, she entered the blind and
drew her small dagger, which served to cut Rusgann's ankle
bonds. The unconscious woman's wrists were already free.
After reassuring herself that the tortured victim yet lived,

Induna lifted the cloak covering the half-naked form and turned her carefully to examine the injuries. The fresh weals on her breasts and upper belly still bled copiously, while the older wounds on her back were scabbed and oozing.

Induna had loaded her fardel with medicines and bandages obtained from the healers at the Green village. Now, after cleansing the wounds with a solution of witch hazel and dilute spirits, she laid out squares of linen on sections of the floor free of gore and smeared them with thick unguents that would slow blood loss and promote healing. These she applied to the cuts, binding them in place. Then she wrapped Rusgann tightly again in the black woolen cloak.

Ignoring the dead bodies round about her, closing them off from her sight as though they were already enshrouded, Induna searched the small hut. She found another cape folded neatly in one corner, a rich and voluminous thing that might have been the property of the fat knight called Asgar. She made a pillow of it and eased this beneath Rusgann's head before beginning to chant ancient Tarnian invocations that she hoped might strengthen the sufferer and ease her pain.

Time passed.

Deveron appeared at the door, looking hollow-eyed and haggard, and wordlessly proceeded to haul away the remains of Catclaw and his men. She heard multiple splashes outside. When the grisly task was finished he used the old wooden bucket to sluice out the blind, sending bloody water draining through the duckboards. Finally he spoke aloud.

'How fares Rusgann?'

'Her color is not good, and her breathing is rapid and shallow, as is her heartbeat. She is in grave condition. In a moment I'll try to give her a potion, but she may be unable to swallow it.'

'I'll be just outside, sponging the worst of the gore off

myself. You'll want to clean up as well. I can dry our damp clothes with my talent. If we stink too much of blood, the horses may shy at carrying us. And ultimately, we'll have to be seen in public. I lack the strength to use Concealer again immediately, and three persons cannot readily be hidden by the distracting cover-spell.'

'So you intend for us to ride out, rather than use the skiff?'

He nodded wearily. 'We've still got to deliver the letter to Prince Dyfrig – or its content. I pray you can rouse Rusgann.'

'Her nether regions and legs seem unharmed, but I fear she is too feeble to sit a saddle or even ride pillion. She lost much blood.'

'I've found leather rain-capes in the saddlebags of the Lord Constable and the knight. I'll fashion a litter, using them and two poles, to drag behind one of the horses. She can lie in that, and you and I can ride ahead and behind.'

'The dead bodies –' she began.

'Stripped naked, bellies punctured to inhibit floating, and consigned to a part of the pond thick with rushes. Wild pigs, fitches, pike, and other swamp scavengers will dispose of them in a week or so. Their clothing, weapons, and other accoutrements are sunk in the pond. Let us hope the Lord Constable told few persons where he and his henchmen intended to go on this accurst night.'

He turned and went out the door.

'Accurst for some, may they freeze in hell,' Induna murmured, rummaging in her fardel for the needed tincture of burnet and tormentil. 'Blest for another – if she survives and is yet able to fulfill the important duty she was assigned.'

'If I don't live,' said a cracked voice very slowly, 'then you must carry my lady's message to Prince Dyfrig. You, Induna of Barking Sands! I remember you.'

'God of the Heights and Depths!' the healer whispered, nearly dropping the medicines in her surprise. 'You're awake!'

Rusgann's eyes were half open. Her discolored, unlovely features brightened in a triumphant smile. 'I still carry the letter. Hidden. They searched me. Stupid whoresons . . . stripped me but never found it.'

Induna bent low to hear the indistinct words. 'Where is it?'

Rusgann blinked. 'Folded very small and encased in a sealed gold locket without a chain. Hidden. Take it! Take it now.' Tears trickled from the corners of her eyes. 'The bastard Catclaw said my dear lady is dead. Burnt alive in a house fire. Alas – I prayed Dyfrig might free his poor mother from her long captivity. But at least he will have her precious letter as a remembrance.'

'Maudrayne dead?' Induna cried in dismay. 'But she lives, Rusgann! My husband and I were told by a friend of the Source – do you know who he is? – that she escaped from the Lord Constable's burning lodge. I know not where she may be, but she is certainly not dead.'

'Thank God! Then . . . give Dyfrig the letter. Take it from me now. It's a good thing you're a healer. A woman. No silly squeamishness.' Using an earthy term, she told where the locket was.

Induna gave a soft gasp. 'You mean –'

'The letter is safe.' Rusgann uttered a rattling breath. 'They said I was too old and ugly. Never raped me, so they never found it . . . damn . . . fool . . . *men*!'

'Oh, Rusgann, how clever of you!'

She smiled. 'Take it now. Take it! So glad . . . my lady lives.' Another hoarse sound come from her lips and then she was silent.

'Rusgann!' Induna took both of the woman's hands. They were like ice and utterly limp. 'Oh, no, no.'

She felt for a pulse, but there was none. The pupils of Rusgann's eyes were wide and black, staring into eternity. Induna shut the lids, blinking back her own tears. Then set about retrieving the locket. She wiped it and studied it closely in the lantern light. It was gold, very flat and no larger than a double-mark coin, engraved with an ornate initial *M*. Some sort of dark cement had been daubed along the seam and hinge to render it waterproof.

She tucked it into her belt-purse, then re-wrapped Rusgann's body in the knight's fine cloak. Closing her eyes, she began the Tarnian Incantation of Soul-Departure.

'Duna? Wife, can you hear me? We dare not tarry here any longer.'

She found Deveron standing over her. All physical traces of the necessary slaughter had vanished from his person, but his face looked more ravaged and pallid than she had ever seen it before.

'I was praying for Rusgann. I did what I could, but . . .' Induna shook her head. 'She still had Maudrayne's letter with her. Hidden in a locket.' She told her husband where it had been.

'Good God!' he murmured. 'Did you open the thing?'

'It's cemented shut. I think the locket can only be opened by destroying it. Perhaps we should deliver the locket to Prince Dyfrig as it is.'

'I'll think about that . . . We must locate him without delay. My deep-scrying ability is presently too weak to penetrate the castle walls, but he's probably somewhere inside. When we're closer to Boarsden I'll try again. I did manage to wind-search about the army encampment a bit. Casya and Baron Ising are no longer with Duke Kefalus or anywhere near the town. I'll look for them again later, when my strength recovers.'

'But where could they have gone?'

'Zeth knows. At least they weren't found out and clapped in irons. I did find out something of vital interest while eavesdropping on the nightwatch: the army is preparing to break camp within three days.'

'Are they disbanding, then?'

'Nay.' His countenance grew more doleful. 'The news is very bad. The Salka horde is swimming toward the Icebear Channel – perhaps to attack western Tarn. The Sovereign has been forced to split his force in two, not knowing where they might land. The larger North Wing, some twenty thousand experienced warriors of Cathra and Tarn led by Conrig and Sernin Donorvale, will follow the Wold Road almost to its end and wait there to cross Frost Pass and defend Tarnian cities if the necessity arises. The smaller South Wing, ten thousand Didionites under Somarus and his son Valardus, and five thousand Cathrans led by Earl Marshal Parlian, will camp at the Lake of Shadows, in case the Salka objective lies further south, on the coast of Didion. Once the enemy landing point is confirmed, both wings of the Sovereign Army will converge there. However, King Somarus has refused to send his troops to Tarn. Even worse, nearly half of them are only armed yeomen with no battle experience, whose resolve and discipline is dangerously shaky.'

'How many Salka might be in this new invasion?'

'No one in the camps seems to know. It was estimated that about fifty thousand of the brutes swarmed up the Beacon Valley. If that number assaults the west coast without adequate warning . . .'

'This is terrible! You must bespeak the Source at once, Deveron. Perhaps he can pinpoint where the monsters intend to go, and you can then inform Lord Stergos.'

Deveron's laugh was bitter. 'Duna, the Source is a supernatural creature trapped in a fleshly body, but he's hardly able to read Salka minds.'

'Oh. I – I'm being foolish.'

'You've just undergone a shocking ordeal. It's no wonder

that your thoughts are muddled. So are my own. But I do know that we must leave this place immediately and find somewhere to rest until morning. Pack up your things. We'll have to take Rusgann's body with us in the litter until we find a suitable place to bury her. I won't leave her in this bloody marsh.'

Induna nodded dully. She began putting the medicines back into her fardel.

'I kept two nondescript horses that were tied outside and drove away the knight's courser, Catclaw's stallion and the mule after removing their harness. Come, now. You take Rusgann's feet while I lift her arms.'

Working together, they carried the body out to the waiting litter. While Induna tied it securely, Deveron returned to the fowler's blind and flung more water about, removing the last vestiges of the awful deeds that had been done there and quenching the brazier. As a last gesture, he took the lantern that had been brought by the Lord Constable's men and threw it far out into the pond like a shooting star. It sank without a trace.

A few other objects, visible to his nightsight, still floated low in the black waters, but Deveron could do nothing about them. He only hoped that no one would come to this remote spot before they vanished, in the natural order of things.

The inn outside the small city of Twicken looked to be a congenial hostelry, crowded but not overfull, so the fugitive wizards Niavar Kettleford and Cleaton Papworth decided they might stop there without being conspicuous. They guided their horses down to a thick grove of birches near the River Malle, and after making certain they were not observed abolished the spell of couverture that had rendered them virtually unnoticeable during the flight from Boarsden Castle.

Both wore the garb of ordinary wayfarers of the middle class. The sorcery they had used to conceal their movements did not truly render them invisible; rather, it hid them efficiently from distant windsearchers and caused persons who were at least five feet away to pay no attention whatsoever to them and their mounts – a useful thing for thieves on the run, so long as they had no need for social interaction. But the enforced isolation had drawbacks if one desired to travel in comfort.

'I'd feel happier if we could keep the spell active,' Cleaton grumbled as they returned to the inn. Sounds of music and laughter coming from the place were audible at some distance, and a fine aroma of beef pottage carried on the breeze, 'By now our young friend must surely have raised a hue and cry over our absconding.'

His smaller companion gave a cynical chuckle. 'I rather think not. If I were Garon Curtling, I'd snatch up what likely loot I could find amongst our late master's effects and follow our wise example. He has no future in the court of Didion, any more than we did. And small reason to set the law on us if he does help himself to valuable magical items.'

'Well, I suppose it's all right,' Cleaton conceded. 'We're at least seventy leagues away from Boarsden. Not many Didionite wizards can scry that far. Garon certainly can't.'

'We'll be be safe enough unsorcelled for the short time it will take to have supper and hire a room. Don't fret, Clete. We can re-establish the cover-spell before going to bed.'

The pinch-faced wizard sighed. 'Zeth knows I'm ready for some hot food and a soft pallet. I didn't sleep a wink in that damp hedgerow last night. There were *creatures*.'

'Castle living has made you soft,' Niavar sneered.

'You're damned right it has, Squinty – hence my willingness to join you in the theft of Kilian's treasure. I look forward to a luxurious retirement on the Continent.'

In the inn's courtyard an ostler lad helped them dismount and unbuckle their saddlebags, which they insisted upon keeping with them. They were welcomed by the innkeeper, and after arranging for a small private sleeping-chamber were led to a table in the noisy taproom, where they sat down to eat and drink and take their ease. An hour or so later, after they had polished off big bowls of beef-and-parsnip stew, slabs of fresh bread slathered with nicely spiced lard, and three tankards of brown ale apiece, they were pleasantly replete and ready to retire.

'I can't think when I've enjoyed a meal so much,' Cleaton said rather wistfully. His sour features had relaxed and his expression was almost pleasant. 'All this music and jollity and the pretty women giving you the eye . . . one could easily get used to it, as Garon did. Perhaps our lives *were* just a bit over-austere. We were well-rewarded, I know. But I can't help think of what might have been.'

'Don't talk like a maudlin idiot,' Niavar said. 'Recall the gold you and I squirreled away over the years in Holt Mallburn. We'll pick it up on our way to the harbor, then take ship for Stippen. Along with Kilian's gemstone collection, we'll have enough to live like kings for the rest of our lives. The diamonds alone . . . Do you have any notion what faceted stones that size are worth? Thousands of gold marks each!'

Cleaton nodded. Then speculation wrinkled his brow. 'I've been wondering, Squinty. Those five dead minor sigils that we took from Kilian's workroom at the last minute? Do you really think there's a chance we might be able to re-activate them?'

'I don't know. There could be a way. The master was too afraid of the Beaconfolk to experiment, but of course he had other strong sources of occult power to draw on and didn't really need them . . . Well, no sense talking about it now. It's getting late. Let's go outside and find the necessarium. Be sure you don't forget your saddlebags.'

Cleaton grimaced as he rose from the table. 'Not bloody likely!'

They pushed through the crowd into the darkness. The courtyard was lit only by two lanterns near the entry-gate and by wan illumination coming through the inn's dirty windows. The stable and other outbuildings were deep in shadow and there was no moon.

'Where is the futtering thing?' Cleaton growled.

'Follow your nose,' Niavar advised. 'Probably over there.'

With the yoked saddlebags weighting their shoulders, they trudged toward a likely shack. Someone stepped out of the stable to meet them.

'Ho, lad,' Niavar said, thinking it was the young ostler. 'Well met! My companion and I will be setting out at dawn. I wanted to tell you to have our horses ready. Here's a half-penny for your trouble.'

'A halfpenny won't do, messire,' said a familiar voice. 'I fear your journey ends here.' The dark figure lifted its hand, from which a dim purplish glow emanated, and pronounced a single incomprehensible word.

Niavar and Cleaton halted in their tracks, paralyzed. Garon Curtling drew back his hood. He tucked the amethystine crystal into his wallet and relieved the stricken pair of their burdens, which he quickly buried in a nearby pile of straw.

'Now, into the jakes – both of you!' he said softly. 'Your feet will carry you there. But if you try to run, I'll strike you lame. It will be quite painful, and you'll still be forced to obey me.'

'How did you scry through Lord Kilian's cover-spell?' Cleaton asked as he stumbled along. 'And how were you able to catch us up when we had such a long head start?'

'With help. I have a new and very powerful master, who

cut through your spell like a hot knife through butter. A fast riverboat on the Malle carried me here ahead of you. My master bespoke me that you'd stop at Twicken tonight after reading your lips. He's very likely scrying you at this very moment.'

'A new master?' Niavar sputtered. 'In Zeth's name – who?'

Garon grinned proudly. 'He is Beynor, Conjure-King of Moss.'

'Bazekoy's Ashen Arse! You'd trust that Salka-lover? He'll discard you without a thought after he's used you. Throw in with us instead, man! There's plenty of booty for all.'

'We even have the five dead sigils with us,' Cleaton added eagerly. 'The ones the Salka palmed off on Kilian. Remember? A Concealer, a Stunner, an Interpenetrator, a Longspeaker, and a Wound-Healer. You can have first pick and we'll dice for the odd pair! Niavar thinks we can find out how to make them work again –'

'Be silent, you jabbering fools,' Garon said, taking out the amethyst again and brandishing it. The wizards felt their tongues thicken and cleave to their palates. Speech became impossible. 'Get in there, both of you. Now!'

They shuffled into the convenience, knowing they were dead men walking, and swallowed the poison he gave them as meekly as lambs.

When it was over, Garon lifted the lid of the four-holer, disposed of the bodies in the pit, and poured a generous amount of lime over them from the barrel that stood in one corner. Then he went to recover the saddlebags. As he dug them out of the hay, he glanced up at the starry sky.

'Are you scrying me from afar, Your Majesty?' he spoke on the wind.

Yes. Smartly done, Garon. You have the makings of an excellent professional assassin. Interesting – what Cleaton said about the dead sigils. I already knew about them, but I'd written them off as useless, just as Kilian had. Now I wonder . . .

Garon slung the bags over his broad shoulders. 'The two knaves were prepared to give me at least one of those moonstones. Will you be as generous?'

A laugh floated on the wind. *Why not? I once gave a sigil to another associate of mine. He made poor use of the gift, unfortunately, but you might have better luck. Hurry back to the castle!*

Holding high a silver candelabra with three tapers, Lord Stergos knocked persistently on the door of his royal brother's private bedroom. It was an hour past midnight.

'Con, let me in! This is very important.'

The door was finally unlocked and Conrig stood glowering in his nightshirt. His face was blotchy, his eyes were clouded with sleep, and his wheaten hair hung in sweaty strings.

'I'm sorry to have woken you after your long day –' Stergos began.

'I was having . . . a nightmare. You did me a favor. Bring the light inside. I need wine. My mouth feels like a muckraker's bootsole.'

'A nightmare?' The Doctor Arcanorum was immediately solicitous. 'Do you suffer from such things very often?'

'Often enough,' the High King snarled, pouring from a decanter on a side table and taking a deep draft. He wiped his mouth with his hand and headed back to his bed. 'Never mind. Why are you here?'

'Prince Dyfrig and his men have just arrived at the castle. He thought you would like to receive his report on the Morass Worms immediately. It seems he had a face-to-face encounter with one of the things. It spoke to him!'

Conrig sat on the edge of the bed and drank more wine. He did not look particularly pleased or excited at the news. 'So the creatures do exist, and they *are* intelligent.'

'Apparently so. I'll bring Dyfrig in and he can tell you the details. He waits in the anteroom.'

'Dyfrig,' the king repeated. He passed a hand over his face, as though wiping cobwebs from his brain. 'Never expected him to succeed. I hoped . . . never mind what I hoped.'

'And there's something else, Con. A little earlier, as I was preparing to retire, it suddenly occurred to me that we've been terribly remiss – not informing Lord Lieutenant Hale Brackenfield of our discovery that the Salka plan a new offensive against the west coast. I took it upon myself to bespeak the news immediately to Lord Hale's family alchymist, Vra-Binon, who accompanies his party.'

'Yes,' the king muttered absently as he emptied the goblet. 'That was well done. We'll need Hale's services in the new defensive operation. Once he reaches Karum and puts his women and Sir Orrion on a ship bound for Stormhaven, he must return to us for assignment. Did you so inform him?'

'I couldn't reach him at all, Con. I'm sorry.'

'What? Why the hell not?' Conrig muttered irritably.

'Old Binon told me that he fell sick on the day they set out. The Lord Lieutenant left him behind at Rockyford Way Station in the care of the resident alchymist because you'd urged the group to travel speedily. Binon was told to return home to Brackenley Castle by land, in easy stages, when he recovers. I then bespoke the adept Didionite at Elderwold Fortress thinking to catch Lord Hale there, but the windspeaker said the cavalcade arrived rather early today and decided to press on until nightfall. They must now be encamped somewhere on the Shadow Lake track – without a windspeaker. Shall I have a courier ride out from Elderwold with their adept and join Lord Hale? Otherwise, he'll be unable to communicate with us for several days.'

Conrig hesitated for some moments, seeming uncertain how to answer. Finally he said, 'Nay. Let be. It would probably be unwise to deprive Elderwold of its windspeaker now, with the army preparing to march through there on the redeployment. When the Lord Lieutenant reaches Tweenwater Fort or Dennech-Cuva, he'll doubtless avail himself of the local wind facilities and contact us.'

Stergos nodded. 'It's fortunate that the noble ladies and Orrion will be out of the region long before any Salka might come ashore there.'

'The monsters will attack Tarn, not Didion,' the Sovereign said in a tone that brooked no argument.

'Well, I won't argue,' Stergos said soothingly. 'Shall I fetch Dyfrig now?'

The Sovereign grimaced, almost as though he were in pain. 'Damn it, Gossy, I don't want to see him now. I feel like hell. Let him wait until morning.'

The Royal Alchymist's face fell. 'I'm sorry. Can I get you a calming potion –'

'No! Just . . . bring that flagon of wine over here.'

Concealing his disapproval, Stergos obeyed. It was no use going against the king when he was in one of these cross-grained moods. The matter of the nightmares would have to be looked into, however.

The alchymist plumped and turned the king's pillow, which was damp with perspiration. 'Come and lie down. Of course we can postpone your meeting with Prince Dyfrig until after breakfast tomorrow. It will give you time to decide how the brave lad should be rewarded.'

'Rewarded?' Conrig said harshly. The crystal decanter clashed against the rim of the golden goblet, spilling red wine onto the royal coverlet. The king ignored the mess and drank.

'You must agree he has performed his difficult mission remarkably well,' Stergos pointed out. 'He's sure to be hailed as a hero for confirming the retreat of the Salka, but you'll want to make some generous gesture to show your personal regard. Perhaps you might consider making him commander of one of our battalions defending Tarn.'

'Never!' Conrig shouted. 'I'll do no such thing! And futter you for presuming to shove the young knave at me! D'you think I don't know what's on your mind?'

Stergos went white and stood a step backward. 'I was only –'

Dropping the half-filled goblet, the king surged up and took hold of his brother's robe with both large hands and hauled him close. His dark eyes held the wild glint of an emotion that Stergos realized, to his consternation, was more fear than rage. When he spoke, Conrig's voice was thick and forced. 'Don't you realize that Dyfrig is my great enemy? And *you* want me to love him! Don't deny it. You've been taking his part for years, telling me what a stalwart fellow he was growing up to be. You frigging fool, he's the man in my nightmares! The faceless one!'

'Dyfrig is a fine, loyal –' the alchymist tried to say.

'He's the one who can destroy me!' Conrig hissed. 'Gossy – *he has no talent.* At first, I didn't recognize him in the dreams, but now it's perfectly clear.' The king spoke in a more normal tone, but his eyes darted about in agitation. 'He's the only Wincantor who can legitimately wear the Iron Crown. *Her son* – damn her to the Hell of Ice! We can't let him know I'm onto him. We must deal with him secretly. Just you and I! Do you understand?'

'Of course I do, Con,' Stergos said softly. 'Trust me. I'll help you take care of everything.'

And then the Royal Alchymist did a thing he had never done since he was a novice, five years older than the heedless little brother who gleefully threatened to open the stall of a dangerous stallion to prove that he was 'brave'.

Stergos used his powerful talent to strike Conrig senseless.

Standing over the crumpled figure of the Sovereign, his

face taut with shock, the Doctor Arcanorum tried to marshal his wits and analyze the bizarre words Conrig had spoken. He had to be suffering some sort of brainstorm – perhaps the unhealthy aftermath of a stressful day with the troops and wrangling with the Didionite generals, exacerbated by the nightmare.

Or might the king's malady be something quite different?

'I think it's time I bespoke Thalassa Dru,' Stergos said to himself.

He pulled pillows and covers from the bed and made his brother as comfortable as he could on the floor. Normally, the spell would wear off in an hour or so. But it seemed likely that the king would sleep through the night. When his servants found him in the morning, they'd cope discreetly, as always.

So you believe High King Conrig's dreams might have been invaded by my nephew Beynor?

'The villain is capable of it,' the Royal Alchymist said on the wind. 'You know that better than I, Conjure-Princess.'

Yes. The talent is exceedingly rare, but Beynor is adept at it. We don't know where he hid for the long years of his disappearance, but it might well have been close enough for the insidious suggestion about Dyfrig to be effective. Conrig's own petty talent would have been too weak to repel the malignant images projected. They would have had a profound effect upon his inner mind, influencing his attitude toward Dyfrig – which was already none too cordial, given his hatred of Maudrayne.

'Princess Thalassa, what shall I do? Tonight's outburst makes me fear for Conrig's sanity. And so much rides upon his leadership at the present time! Our island needs him desperately if we are to fight off the new Salka invasion.'

It also needs Prince Dyfrig. The Source has assured me of that. You must find a way to disarm Conrig's hostility towards the young man.

'I'll try, but it won't be easy. I made a bad mistake, urging the king to take Dyfrig as one of his field commanders. The lad's proper place is at the side of his adoptive father, Earl Marshal Parlian. I'll propose that to Con tomorrow. It should calm him down. If you can give me any other advice on dealing with his irrational moods, I'd appreciate it, It would be disastrous to army morale if the High King showed mental instability.'

Take heart, my son. The Source has promised help to the Sovereign of Blenholme in battling the Salka monsters. As for Conrig's night terrors, I believe everything will be forgotten by morning. But his true cure can only come about when the dream invasions cease.

'Lady,' Stergos gasped, 'are you telling me I must kill Beynor?'

I doubt that you are able, my dear son. But there are others who may have sufficient power. What you can do is urge your brother the king to send my evil nephew away. Far away. The closer Beynor is to the Sovereign, the greater his nefarious influence will be.

'I'll do my utmost. Con is rightfully leery of Beynor. It shouldn't be difficult to make certain that the Conjure-King doesn't accompany the army when it marches to its new staging areas . . . But tell me more of how the Source intends to aid our fight against the Salka horde.'

How that help will be expressed is unknown to me. There are two things I can tell you, however. First, Prince Dyfrig will play a decisive part in the war; Conrig must not be allowed to harm him. Second, Deveron Austrey, the former Royal Intelligencer, has been sent to you as the Source's agent. He will appear shortly. Trust his advice.

'Snudge! Great Zeth, I haven't thought about him in years.' Stergos paused for a moment. 'I don't know how the king will react to his resurfacing. There's still a price on Deveron's head.'

Then keep his presence a secret from your brother until a propitious moment presents itself. With the commotion of the army's march that should not be difficult. And now, my son, it's time that both of us were in our beds. Farewell.

'Farewell, Conjure-Princess.'

The windthread snapped and Stergos rose from his chair by the fire and padded slowly toward his own bed. The effort of bespeaking at a far distance compounded the deep weariness already oppressing him, but his mind still roiled with disturbing thoughts.

Thalassa Dru's opinion that Conrig's irrational fear of Dyfrig would be forgotten with the dawn struck Stergos as wishful and facile. The alchymist had not missed his royal brother's ominous reaction to the prospect of Dyfrig being acclaimed as a hero. The king was plainly furious that the so-called 'bastard' would be lionized by the military and the court, while Prince Heritor Corodon was still regarded as a subject of derision after being rejected by Hyndry.

A sudden thought struck him and he groaned aloud. Why hadn't he remembered to tell Thalassa about the two chunks of moonstone mineral brought from Demon Seat by Coro?

'What a fool I am,' he said. 'I'll have to bespeak her again tomorrow.'

He climbed under the covers, blew out the candles on the bedside stand, and settled in. He'd also have to tell the sorceress about Dyfrig's dragon-sighting, another matter that had slipped his mind.

What a curious thing that was! And the creature speaking of some mysterious woman who'd urged the Morass Worms to band together and fight the invading Salka . . . who in the world could it have been? Cray the Green Woman? Or perhaps Thalassa herself?

He'd have to ask her.

Eminent Warrior Ugusawnn! Please respond to Commander Tasatawnn.

'I'm here. What do you have to report?'

Our force lies at rest for the night, well out to sea from the bay holding the human settlement of Warm Harbor. We've made exceptional time, and the human fleet that pursues us is nearly becalmed in the waters above the Lavalands.

'Excellent news, Tasatawnn. My commendation to you and your warriors. Do you wish to revise your time of arrival at Terminal Bay?'

There is a storm approaching Cape Wolf, but it will have little effect on our progress. We might arrive at our destination in as little as seven days. This is four days ahead of our original fourteen-day schedule.

'Remarkable!'

May I enquire, Eminent One, how the reinforcement group of young fighters is coming along? The spell shielding their movements from oversight is so efficient that we're unable to scry them.

'They're moving a bit slower than you, having to keep well away from the island's shipping lanes. Regrettably, some of the immatures have had to turn back because of failing stamina. We must probably expect the rest to take the full two weeks getting there. But it shouldn't be a serious problem. We never expected the trainees to join in the initial battles.'

How many youngsters remain in the secondary force?

'More than twenty thousand all told, many with minor sigils newly acquired from the Great Fen Salka population. There will be ample numbers to secure Terminal Bay after the regulars press inland. I still plan to lead you in the first assault myself, Tasatawnn, traveling to the scene of action by means of our new Subtle Gateway sigil. Work on it is proceeding well, as is the manufacture of the Destroyer, which I'll bring with me.'

Will you wield that awesome weapon yourself, Eminence?

'Perhaps, if I'm not seriously disabled by use of Gateway.

If that should happen, another might be chosen to bond with Destroyer. There are also . . . other considerations that might preclude my own use of the Great Stone.

Ah. You mean the potential peril to the wielder.

'Exactly.'

Well, we should have no dearth of patriotic volunteers amongst my staff officers, Eminence.

'No. Of course not. Sleep well now, commander, and dream of the glorious victory to come.'

Good night, Eminence. Until we share the wind again.

THIRTEEN

Tormo and Durin Kyle, the young cousins of Countess Morilye, were handsome youths with freckled faces, sandy hair, and a shy demeanor. They were struck dumb when she introduced them to Maudrayne. Even attired in a household knight's riding garb, booted and spurred, with her auburn hair concealed by a capuchon hood, she was a magnificent sight.

It was nearly dawn and a light drizzle was falling. The murky cobblestone ward of Beorbrook Hold was torchlit, and black puddles with golden reflections gleamed everywhere. Maudrayne and the youths stood with the countess in the shelter of the stable porch with baggage at their feet, waiting for their horses to be led out.

'Now, then, lads!' Morilye spoke briskly. 'From now on, you must address this noble lady as *Sir* Maydal. He is a knight on his way to join his lord, Earl Marshal Parlian. You are his armigers.'

'Yes, my lady!' the boys chorused. Tormo, the elder at sixteen years, stuttered, 'B-but who will believe she's a man? She's too beautiful!'

Maudrayne laughed. 'When my face is filthy from riding

the muddy highroad to Great Pass, no one will look twice at me. But you and your brother must take care not to give me away inadvertently.'

'We'd never do that, my lady,' Durin protested.

'*Messire,*' Maude corrected him firmly. 'You must call me messire or Sir Maydal. My life is in your hands, boys. Never forget that.'

'No . . . messire,' Tormo said. 'The countess has explained that you are on a mission of great importance, and evil men would kill you if they could. We will defend you to the death, Durin and I.'

'Yes indeed, messire!' Durin exclaimed, his face solemn.

'Thank you.' Maude took the hand of one lad after the other and gave each a quick embrace. They were sturdy young fellows, not quite as tall as her own five foot eleven. 'I wish I could confide more to you, but my true identity must remain a secret for now. As for defending me, let us hope it won't come to that. But if we are forced to fight, be assured that I am not unfamiliar with weapons. I've killed stag, wild boar, and even a brown bear with my own hands. I'm Tarnian, as you are, and no cowering court damosel.'

'Here are the ostlers with your mounts,' the countess said. 'Lads, strap Sir Maydal's armor and saddlebags in place. Then you must be off to Castlemont.' As the armigers complied, she and Maude stepped aside for a final word. 'The news we received this morn, that the Army of the Sovereignty will not demobilize after all, has Beorbrook Hold in a furor.' Morilye spoke in a whisper. 'Every able-bodied warrior and yeoman in the borderlands, even the very young and very old, is likely to be called to arms this day because of the new Salka threat. We're still awaiting the final word from the earl marshal's windspeaker, but it's possible the army might march out of the Boarsden encampment as early as tomorrow. All manner of rough characters will soon be on the road. You

and my cousins should be safely ahead of most of them –
but take care, Maude.' She pressed a heavy purse into the
other woman's hand. 'Here, take this. No argument! You'll
need it, and you'll have no easy way to sell your jewelry for
what it's worth in the small towns up north.'

'Dear Morilye. Thank you from the bottom of my heart.
We'll take every precaution and move as quickly as we can.
Comfort poor little Chelaire. She'll be devastated when she
wakes and discovers that I've gone.'

'Don't worry. I'll find a good place in my household for
the brave child.'

Maudrayne's face within her hood was pale. 'Then
farewell, my dear friend. Pray for me. The thing that I must
now do is hard . . . so very hard. I will see that your young
cousins are kept safe – as safe as armigers can be in wartime
– but my intuition tells me that we two will not meet again.'
She turned away and swung into the saddle. Tormo and
Durin were already mounted. 'Farewell.'

Morilye lifted a hand as the three urged their horses
toward the Hold's massive gatehouse. 'Farewell, my queen,'
she said softly. 'God grant you success. And peace at long
last.'

Conrig broke his fast rather late that morning, at the ninth
hour, but the Lord of Chamber made no comment about it
– nor about the unorthodox royal sleeping arrangement –
and served the meal in serene silence. After tossing down
the restorative potion which Stergos had discreetly provided
for his pounding head, the Sovereign ate coddled eggs on
muffins and drank unhopped wheat beer, warmed and with
a modicum of ginger.

Touching his lips with a linen square, he finally sat back
with a sigh. 'I feel better now, Telifar. Clear the table. I'll
receive the morning's visitors right here.'

'Very good, Your Grace. The Royal Alchymist and Prince Dyfrig have been waiting in the anteroom for some time.'

'Have them shown in.'

Footmen scurried about tidying up, and drew two more chairs to the table near the tower window.

When the visitors entered, the High King spoke greetings in a forced, hearty tone. 'Good morrow! Sit you down, both of you. Now then! First of all, I want to hear about the dragon.'

The prince bobbed his head with a nervous smile, unwrapped a small parcel he had tucked in his jerkin, and handed over the yellowish crystalline tooth. 'My liege, this is the clue that first convinced me that our guide told the truth about our being shadowed by Morass Worms. You may keep it, of course.'

'Bazekoy's Brains! Look at the size of it!' Conrig peered closely at the glittering spike. 'Bit of the root, too, I see.'

'It was found broken off in the carcass of a large brown bear,' Dyfrig said. 'When our party's windspeaker, Vra-Odos, bespoke Lord Stergos news of the Salka retreat, we could only conjecture that the tooth belonged to a great worm, as our guide had insisted. But not long afterward, while we were on our way out of the morass, the fact of the creatures' existence was confirmed in a rather amazing way.'

He described how he had been awoken in the night by Morass Worms invading their campsite. 'It was not a dream, Your Grace. The three terrible beings were real. Their leader stood only a few ells away from me. He was at least twice the height of a man, in appearance very like the dragons of legend, save without the wings and not covered in scales. He spoke to my mind, not my ears. And what he said –' the prince shook his head in bewilderment '– I confess that I hardly understood. It appears that some woman *told* the

Morass Worms how to band together and attack the Salka most effectively.'

'Did the creature name her?'

'Nay, but when I told Lord Stergos the tale last night, he suggested it might have been a great sorceress called Thalassa Dru –'

The Royal Alchymist interrupted the prince. 'As you know, she is the sister of the late Conjure-King Linndal of Moss, but no friend of his nor of her nephew Beynor. I . . . became acquainted with Thalassa recently through the good offices of the Tarnian shamans, who esteem her as a mentor and friend.'

Conrig frowned in disapproval. 'A Mosslander witch? Why didn't you tell me you consulted her?'

'There was no reason to, Brother. She and I discussed Salka sorcery, but she had no useful new information to share. And she is *not* the woman who advised the Morass Worms on military tactics. I bespoke her this morning and asked her. She said she knows nothing at all about any such person.'

'Hmph!' snorted the king. 'Probably lied through her teeth.' He turned to Dyfrig. 'Did your dragon say anything further about the female tactician?'

'Only that she promised humanity would allow the Morass Worms to live in peace, in gratitude for their expulsion of the Salka. The creature then ordered us to leave its territory and never return.'

Conrig shrugged. 'Fair enough. When your windspeaker first told me of the brutes' existence, I was afraid we'd have to battle them as well as the Salka.'

'Oh, no, sire,' Dyfrig said. 'All the worms want is the Green Morass. Their leader also spoke of certain other things I could not understand.' He gave Stergos an apologetic smile. 'I neglected to tell you of this last night, my lord. Forgive me . . . The worm cursed the Great Lights, who use sigil sorcery. He said something about pain and power. And he also spoke of a New Conflict. But none of this meant anything to me.'

Stergos gave a sudden start, but said nothing.

'Never mind,' the Sovereign said. 'The Royal Alchymist will make sense of it if anyone can. You've done well, young prince. Very well.'

'Thank you, sire.' Dyfrig lowered his head. 'There is little more I can tell you.'

'I've heard enough. No doubt you've been informed that the Salka monsters didn't turn tail for home as we'd initially hoped. They may invade Blenholme's western coast. Tomorrow the army will begin its march to new positions in order to counter the new threat. I want you to serve under your father, Earl Marshal Parlian, in this redeployment. Can you be ready?'

'Of course, Your Grace,' Dyfrig said eagerly.

Conrig rose from his seat at the table. 'Leave us then, and prepare for the march. This evening you and your companions will be officially commended at supper. I'll see you there.'

'Yes, sire. Thank you, sire.' Beaming with happiness and quite unaware of the mental disquiet concealed by the Sovereign's cordial manner, Dyfrig withdrew.

Conrig turned a cold eye on his brother. 'You know more about this Mosslander witch Thalassa than you've told me, Gossy. Out with it!'

'There's nothing sinister about our relationship,' the alchymist insisted. 'She's a friend of the Tarnians who has lived in that nation for decades after quarreling with her late royal brother of Moss. Thalassa said she had no notion at all who might have advised the Morass Worms – and yes, she may have lied to me. But what difference does it make? Whoever contacted the creatures and advised them did us a tremendous favor.'

'I suppose so,' the king conceded with ill grace. He stared

at his own hands, which were partially clenched, the thumbs rubbing nervously together. 'Still, it disturbs me to learn that our island harbors yet another race of inhuman beings possessing uncanny talent.'

'Thalassa told me that her shaman friends are doing their utmost to scry the Salka out.' Stergos hastened to steer his brother's thoughts away from that uncomfortable subject. 'She herself has promised all the help within her power. As the amphibian host rounds Cape Wolf and enters the Western Ocean, it'll come within the scope of many more land-based Tarnian windsearchers than before. Others are taking to sea in fast small boats, patrolling offshore and scrying under-water. They'll find the monsters in time for you to organize our defenses, I'm certain of it.'

Conrig uttered a noncommittal grunt. 'Another thing: I was watching you when that boy mentioned something called the New Conflict. You know what it is, don't you.'

'Yes.' Stergos's eyes slid away. *That boy.* Not once during this morning's meeting had Conrig called his first-born son by name.

'Then tell me what the conflict is about, damn you!'

'Con, it's a – a mythical battle, not yet joined, that will supposedly pit the Beaconfolk and their malignant sigil sorcery against other Sky beings. Good ones. It's only a legend told by Tarnian shamans with no relevance to us.'

'No relevance? I don't believe you! Somebody – was it Ulla or Snudge? – said it was . . . Ah, God, I can't remember!' The king groaned and put his hand over his eyes. 'My head's throbbing again, Gossy. Do something.'

'I'll fetch another potion immediately. But listen to me, Con. I've been thinking about your disturbing nightmares. It's possible that they're not natural. You could be – someone might be meddling with your dreams through sorcery.'

'What!' Conrig looked up, his features a mixture of wrath and pain. 'Is such a thing possible?'

'Unfortunately, yes. Be calm. Now that our suspicions are aroused, we can take steps to prevent it.'

'Who's responsible? The damned Salka? Or is it some minion of that fat troublemaker Somarus?'

'I believe it's Conjure-King Beynor.'

'Beynor?' The king was incredulous. 'Nonsense.'

'You've got to send him away. The redeployment of your army provides a perfect diplomatic excuse. Ship him off to Incayo on the east coast, where his exiled countrymen have settled. Give him enough money to set himself up in reasonable style –'

'He only arrived a few days ago and the nightmares have afflicted me for months!'

'Your former Royal Intelligencer told me long ago that Beynor invaded *his* dreams and tried to exert insidious coercion upon him. This happened while Snudge was in Cala City and Beynor was voyaging on the high seas somewhere between Blenholme and the Continent. The Conjure-King has the ability to perform his sorcery over a considerable distance. He might have been working on you for a long time. We know he must have some self-aggrandizing plan up his sleeve, and attacking your sanity might be part of it. For all we know, he could be invading the dreams of other leaders as well. Somarus –'

Conrig gave a hoot of derisive laughter. 'That royal zany doesn't need a sorcerer mucking up his dreams to make him crazy. He's pickled his brain in ardent spirits all by himself.'

'Send Beynor away,' Stergos urged. 'Whether or not he's responsible for your nightmares, you know we dare not trust him.'

A memory of the latest dream flashed into the king's brain – the tall figure standing aside from the futile mêlée, telling

Conrig that he was using the *wrong weapon*. Had its voice been Beynor's . . . ?

'Very well, I'll order him to Incayo, as you suggested. He can leave before dawn tomorrow. There's no good reason to let him tag along after the army, but I'd thought – Never mind. Go and bespeak your Mossy witch friend, Brother. Ask her about remedies for dream invasion.'

Stergos rose from the table. 'Don't forget that Prince Heritor Corodon waits outside in the anteroom. He claims to have something important to show you. Will you see him?'

'Oh, very well,' Conrig growled. 'Send him in, but warn him that I have to confer with my Privy Council at the eleventh hour. He can have only a few minutes. And hurry with that headache potion!'

The Royal Alchymist went to the door and called out. Corodon appeared, dressed in a hunting habit of russet and gold and sporting a winsome smile. 'Good morrow, my liege! Thank you for seeing me.' He stole a glance over his shoulder to be sure that Stergos had closed the door behind him, then hurried to the table with a conspiratorial air. 'The most curious thing has happened. May I be seated, Father?'

Conrig made a fretful gesture. 'Be quick about your business, Coro. I have a long day ahead of me and I feel unwell.'

Corodon opened his belt-wallet and removed a small object, which he set on the table before the High King. 'This vial contains a love philtre. I'd like to slip it to Princess Hyndry – if you'll grant me permission.'

Conrig stared at his son, momentarily at a loss for words.

The prince continued hurriedly. 'I was given the philtre by Conjure-King Beynor. He advised me that it would cause the princess to look upon me with more favor if I could get her to drink it, even if she failed to fall instantly in love.'

'*Beynor* gave you this potion? In God's name, why?'

'He said that a new marital liaison between Cathra and

Didion was in the best interests of the Sovereignty. He said
he wished my rejected suit to succeed in order to prove his
loyalty to you.'

'Oh, he did, did he?' Conrig muttered.

'Father – it's worth a try. The fellow could hardly be
scheming for me to poison Hyndry. Everyone would know
he was responsible. He called the princess a tough nut to
crack, but if the love philtre doesn't work, we're no worse
off than before.'

Conrig began to laugh. He threw his head back and
bellowed with mirth, smacking the table with one hand so
that the tiny bottle tipped over and Corodon made a frantic
grab for it, lest it spill. Finally, when the paroxysm diminished, the prince spoke up again.

'Hyndry has been sulking in her chambers, ignoring my
friendly messages, but you could command her to go a-
hawking with me. I'll put the stuff in her wine as we have
our picnic lunch.'

'Do it.' Conrig wiped his eyes. 'A love philtre! Lad, you've
made me feel much better. Here, I'll give you a note to send to
the wench.' He rose from the table, went to his desk, and scribbled a few words, then melted wax and sealed the folded sheet
with his ring. 'She'll not ignore *that*.'

'Thank you, sire.' Having also risen, the prince tucked the
parchment in his wallet. 'And . . . there's something even
more interesting that Beynor told me, if you have time to
listen.'

'Well?' said the king.

Corodon hesitated, remembering that the sorcerer had
warned him not to speak of the sigils until after the philtre
had been successful. But the prince had hardly slept last
night, mulling over the stupendous potential of the three
Great Stones that one day might be passed on to him. The
temptation to tell his father about them now – to show that

he, Corodon, was instrumental in bringing the offer of these powerful weapons to the king's attention – was more than the young man could resist.

'Conjure-King Beynor took me into his confidence, sire. He told me he had been cursed by the Beaconfolk, that he could never again use the sorcery of their moonstone sigils himself without being cast into the Hell of Ice. But he has a few of the things in his possession, what he called Great Stones – not the minor kind of sigils owned by the Salka. These Great Stones are presently inactive, but he knows how to bring them to life. I wasn't supposed to tell you about this yet – but he wants to give them to you!'

Conrig felt his heart constrict within his chest. Was it possible? For years he'd dreamed of getting hold of one of the moonstone amulets. He'd even been tempted to do away with Snudge and seize the stones he owned – but activating the things was impossible without knowing the complicated incantation that infused them with power and bonded them to their owner. And Conjure-Queen Ullanoth, his former lover, who had known the activation spell and might have shared it with him, was long dead.

Killed by the accumulated pain-debt of the moonstones she had used in *his* service . . .

'What sigils does Beynor have?' Conrig asked, striving to keep his voice steady. 'Did you actually see them?'

'Oh, yes, sire! There are three only – a finger-ring called Weathermaker, a carrot-shaped little thing called Ice-Master that freezes water and living bodies containing water, and a small wand that King Beynor said was the most powerful sigil of all. Its name is Destroyer.'

'*Destroyer.*'

The tall figure in his dream had held such a wand, calling it the proper weapon to defeat all of his enemies . . .

Conrig turned away from the prince, his thoughts in

turmoil. What had Ulla told him of that stone? That a Destroyer was part of Rothbannon's original collection. That the first Conjure-King of Moss had deemed the thing dangerous, and used it only rarely. That Queen Taspiroth, mother of Ulla and Beynor, had dared to activate the Destroyer sigil and had given it an inappropriate command, whereupon the thing had slain her in a particularly horrid fashion and cast her into hell.

'Did Beynor say why he wanted to gift me with these perilous tools of sorcery?'

'Sire, he wants the Kingdom of Moss back. He believes you can defeat the Salka with the Great Stones. He also said he would expect you to assist him in rebuilding his ravaged homeland. It seemed reasonable to me. Again, why would he lie?'

'You are an ignorant child,' Conrig said with deliberate cruelty. 'Persons such as Beynor may have hidden motives you can't conceive of. The simplest might be to bring about my own death and break up the Sovereignty, so that he might gain some great personal advantage.'

'But what could that be?' the prince demanded. 'The Salka are his true enemies – not you! They occupy his country and threaten to overrun other parts of our island. How can you refuse magical weapons that would bring certain victory?'

'I can refuse because the sigils might not work for me!' the king roared. 'The Beaconfolk are evil and capricious. They feed on pain – do you know that? They slew Beynor's mother for God knows what reason. They could do the same to me!'

Corodon took a deep breath and gave voice to the audacious thought that had repeated itself in his mind thoughout the night. 'I understand why you mistrust the stones, Father. And you are the Sovereign. Blenholme needs you to rule and guide it in these dangerous times. So ask Beynor to bond the three sigils to me! Then command me to use them in your service. I'd willingly risk my life.'

'You?!'

'I'm not afraid.'

Conrig swallowed his fury at the prince's implication –
unwitting or not – that he himself *was* afraid to use the
stones.

Not noticing his gaffe, the Heritor dug into his belt-wallet
and drew forth the chunk of mineral he had brought from
the summit of Demon Seat. 'There's something else I thought
of. Look here, Father! I have this piece of uncarved moonstone, which I found on – on a mountain near Swan Lake.
I saw magical power come down from the Sky Realm and
work through larger raw stones just like this. So did Orrion
and Bramlow. And the power came not from the evil
Beaconfolk but from other Sky beings who bear no ill will
to humankind! Uncle Stergos said so.'

'*Others* . . . So my brother already knows where this rock
came from?' The question was ominous, but Corodon did
not seem to notice.

'Oh, yes. He has a second chunk of moonstone that I gave
him as a souvenir.'

'I see. Did these . . . benevolent Sky beings speak to you?'

'Well, first they said all three of us were worthy to ask
favors of them. Bram, Orry, and me.'

'Worthy?' Conrig whispered. 'Can that mean what I think
it does?' All three of his sons by Queen Risalla possessed
talent, as he knew well enough; but only that of Bramlow
was strong enough to be readily identified.

'It was only an unfortunate misunderstanding that led the
kindly Sky beings to blast off Orrion's sword-arm,' Coro went
on blithely. 'Father, why can't we ask these good Lights to
empower Beynor's sigils for us, rather than the Beaconfolk?
Perhaps they could do it in a way that didn't endanger the
user or even cause pain. I thought this idea over very carefully while I lay abed last night. It could work!'

The Sovereign stood stunned, unable to comprehend at first what the naive young fool had nattered on about. He took hold of the back of one of the sturdy oaken chairs, drew it out, and seated himself again at the table, then gestured for Corodon to do the same. He poured a beaker of beer and sipped it. It was many minutes before he spoke.

'Coro, are you telling me that your twin brother lost his arm as a result of Beaconfolk sorcery?'

'Nay, sire.' The prince was patient. 'Lord Stergos said it had to have been other Great Lights – antagonists of the ones we call Beaconfolk – who smote off Orry's arm. He asked them for a miracle, you see. That he might not have to give up Lady Nyla Brackenfield and marry Princess Hyndry. Bram had read some dusty old manuscript that said Demon Seat Mountain harbored supernatural beings who granted miracles to worthy persons.'

'Demon Seat – near Castle Vanguard?'

'Yes, sire. We three climbed the mountain – this year the deep snow has melted – and found the top was made of moonstone. Orry spoke his prayer. Not in any special way: he just asked politely. And the demons – the Lights, I mean – answered. A stroke of lightning took off Orry's arm and healed it instantly. Later, when we told Uncle Stergos about it, he said the mountain demons couldn't have been the evil Beaconfolk. They were too wishy-washy and confused, almost as though no one had besought a miracle from them for a long time.'

Conrig shook his head. His gaze had turned inward and when he spoke, he seemed to be talking to himself.

'A mountain of moonstone? Raw sigil material? . . . But of course it had to come from somewhere. We know the ancient Salka made the sigils themselves. All kinds, major and minor. But they have no Great Stones now, and not all that many minor ones, either – therefore they don't know

about the mineral deposit atop Demon Seat. But Gossy knew
and said nothing to me about it. Two factions of Lights, antag-
onistic to each other! Could that be the meaning of the New
Conflict? Yet my brother thinks the Conflict is irrelevant to
human affairs. Either he's a consummate fool, or –'

'Sire?' Corodon ventured. 'What do you think of my idea?
Of letting me use Beynor's sigils in the service of the
Sovereignty?'

The High King picked up the chunk of pale mineral. 'If
you had not showed this to me, and told me the truth about
Orrion's mutilation, I would have thought you had been
duped by Beynor. Now I'm not so sure.'

'I'm certain –' Corodon began.

'Silence!' thundered the king. 'The notion that a callow
youth such as you should be entrusted with overwhelming
magical power is ludicrous. Did Beynor suggest that to you?'

'No, sire.' The prince was sullen, pierced to the heart by
the Sovereign's ridicule. 'He only implied that I might inherit
the Stones from you some day.'

'And sent you to present his magnanimous offer – prematurely, as you admitted to me! Well, never mind that. It was
well that you told me everything. And you mustn't take too
seriously my harsh words to you. As I said, I'm feeling seedy
and my temper's on edge. Your feelings have been hurt, but
they'll mend soon enough. If that love philtre works, you'll
have your work cut out for you, wooing Princess Hyndry in
the short time before you march with my Northern Wing of
the army to the Tarnian border.'

'March with you, sire?' Corodon brightened. Had his father
really changed his mind?

But the king brushed the rhetorical question aside. 'I must
consider at length what to do about Beynor's sigils. He's a
wily shitepoke, make no mistake, and his schemes have only
one principal objective: to further his own ambition.

Remember that. And he's mad, Coro. Plausible, charming, but mad. His sister Ullanoth knew him better than anyone, and she convinced me of the fact.'

'If you say so,' the prince murmured. 'But he did not seem so to me.'

Conrig picked up the piece of moonstone and put it into his own belt-pouch. The prince tried to hide his dismay. 'We can hope that the potion he gave you will work. Go and administer it and romance the surly princess as though she were a battle objective and you a conquering general. If you can win her over, you'll do heroic service to the Sovereignty.'

'I'll do my best, sire. And what if Beynor questions me about our meeting? Shall I admit I told you of his sigils and the events that took place on Demon Seat?'

'Say nothing,' the king commanded. 'And see that you tell no one else what transpired here – most especially your Uncle Stergos, who would strongly oppose any use of sigil sorcery, even to save our people from the Salka.'

'I understand, Father. King Beynor also warned me not to tell Lord Stergos about the sigils. He threatened to take them to the Continent and offer them to another ruler if I did.'

Conrig placed his hands on his son's broad shoulders and looked him in the eye. 'The Iron Crown is a heavy burden, Corodon. The man who wears it must make terrible choices. Beynor and his sigils may indeed be the ultimate answer to the Salka menace, but I am the one who must decide what to do about them. Only I, The Sovereign of Blenholme. Now go and give the note to Princess Hyndry's lady-in-waiting, and ready yourself for the hawking party. Later, you and I will discuss your assignment in my army – but rest assured, you will ride at my side into battle.'

'Yes, sire!' Corodon rushed from the chamber in a transport of joy, forgetting to bow, and slammed the door behind him.

When the youth was gone, Conrig went to the window of the tower room and looked out on the vast inner ward of Boarsden Castle. The generals who lived in the encampments and their senior battle-commanders were riding in through the main gatehouse, gathering for the final council of war before the great march up the Wold Road. Less than an hour ago, the king had dreaded that meeting even more than the upcoming conference with his Privy Council, his self-confidence in tatters because of the dire dreams and the possibly disastrous necessity of splitting his military force in two.

Now, fingering the lump of mineral inside his wallet, he felt differently. Of course he could say nothing to the war leaders about Beynor's extraordinary proposal and Coro's other amazing revelations. But simply knowing of them bolstered his spirits and hinted at hopeful and exciting options. There existed more gracious Sky entities than the sadistic and fickle Beaconfolk, who might grant further miracles to a worthy petitioner. And raw moonstone lay on top of Demon Seat, beyond reach of the clumsy Salka, but apparently within easy grasp of ordinary humans.

Yet his beloved brother Stergos had kept that information from him – along with the second piece of raw moonstone.

Oh, yes, the king said to himself, I have much to think about.

He turned about to summon his Lord of Chamber and prepare to meet the council. But as he took hold of the bell-cord, the fine Didionite tapestry hanging behind it caught his eye. It was a hunting scene, with many small figures, richly dressed, in a woodland setting. One of the male riders he'd never noticed before had been imperfectly embroidered and was unfinished. The man lacked a face.

A notion struck Conrig like a sudden splash of cold water.

What if Dyfrig was not the faceless son of his dreams? What if the one he feared was another – the least likely he might suspect?

No, the idea was utterly ridiculous.

There came a distinctive double knock at the door. Conrig said, 'Come!'

The Lord of Chamber entered, bearing a crystal goblet containing a pale golden liquid. 'The potion for your headache, Your Grace, from Lord Stergos.'

'Put it on the sideboard, Telifar,' the king said. 'I may not need it after all.'

'There. That'll have to do.'

Deveron placed the last rock atop the cairn and stood back to survey the melancholy task he and Induna had finally completed. It was around the second hour after noontide and they were in a ravine north of the Boar Road, which connected Castlemont with Boarsden Castle and its adjacent town. The declivity was steep, with numerous rockfalls along its sides. They had found a suitable wide ledge beyond the view of travelers passing beneath, and there they had interred the body of Rusgann Moorcock.

They stood together with bowed heads, then Induna picked a small bouquet of wild asters and laid it amongst the heaped stones. 'Perhaps some day Prince Dyfrig will make her a more fitting memorial. She was a faithful and courageous friend to his mother.'

'Maudrayne,' Deveron mused. 'I must windsearch later and find out what happened to her. But not now, with the bulk of the great dividing range screening her from my mind's weary eye.'

They started down the slope to the dense stand of trees where they had left the horses, following an exiguous game-track that paralleled the ravine's meager stream.

'If your talent is still fatigued,' she said, 'perhaps I can windspeak Lord Stergos with news of the letter for Dyfrig.'

'Nay, wife. I must do it. Like many powerful adepts, the

Royal Alchymist does not usually leave his mind open to casual windhails. I'll bespeak him using his personal signature, and thus ensure that no one eavesdrops upon us.'

'You're thinking of Beynor.'

'Of course. His talent is formidable and we must not underestimate him. Nevertheless, he knows nothing of you and so has no motive to scry you out. As for me –'

'No one can scry you, my beloved wild-talented one!' she laughed.

'Beynor is still capable of invading my dreams if I don't throw up a mental wall to prevent it.' Deveron refused to be distracted. 'Once he discovers I'm still skulking about, I have no doubt that I'll hear from him. I'm rather interested to know what he'll say.'

Their mounts were undisturbed, peacefully cropping grass. He dismantled the drag-litter, removed the harnesses, and turned them loose. It would be too dangerous to ride into Boarsden Town on beasts bearing the Lord Constable's brand. Weary as they were, Deveron and Induna would have to walk.

While she set out a midday meal of hardbread, cheese, and the last of their ale, he sat on a fallen trunk and bespoke Lord Stergos. The reply was soon in coming.

Snudge! My dear boy, Thalassa Dru bespoke me that you were coming. Where are you now?

'On the Boar Road a few leagues west of the castle, near the junction with the town road. My wife and I have just emerged from the marshes after an unfortunate encounter with Lord Constable Tinnis Catclaw and his men.' As briefly as possible, he described how Maudrayne and Rusgann came to be held captive by the besotted royal official, how Rusgann escaped with a letter for Dyfrig, and how he himself was commanded to rescue the woman from Catclaw and make certain the vital message was delivered. 'The constable tortured poor Rusgann by scourging, trying to retrieve Maude's letter. I killed him and his evil minions but was too late to save her life. Before she died she passed on the letter. I have it safe.'

What does it say?

'It's contained in a sealed golden locket. I have not opened it and don't intend to if I can put the locket into Prince Dyfrig's hands without delay. I need your help to contact him and arrange a meeting place in town.'

Oh, Saint Zeth preserve us! Maude must have written to Dyfrig telling him the truth about his birth. He recently came of age . . . Snudge, you mustn't hand over the letter at this time! Not when the Salka are poised to attack our island again. Just think what an appalling uproar would ensue if Conrig's talent were revealed now and Dyfrig claimed the crown. Feribor Blackhorse would surely renew his own claim to the Sovereignty! And King Somarus of Didion –

'My lord, the Source himself ordered me to give that letter to Prince Dyfrig. I was also told that the young man is destined to play a pivotal rôle in the New Conflict.'

But –

'The Source also informed me that my duty was to assist the Sovereign in some vital manner. But Red Ansel, on his deathbed, said that the Sovereign I must aid may not be Conrig. Do you understand what I'm telling you?'

There was silence on the wind. When Stergos bespoke again, his windvoice was tinged with awe. *Are you certain of this?*

'I'm certain of nothing, save that I was charged to ensure that Maudrayne's letter was given to her son. You know how enigmatic the Source can be. Not even Thalassa and the Green Woman Cray can be sure what convoluted schemes that creature has in mind. But I'm not prepared to defy him . . . at least, not yet.'

And you say that Maude still lives?

'She does. She somehow escaped the housefire that was intended to kill her. I have no notion where she may be or what she intends to do. If I were she, I'd seek out Dyfrig. Before long, the Lord Constable's strange disappearance will be public knowledge. Maude's certain to hear of it and be emboldened.'

Catclaw was missed at a Privy Council meeting that just concluded. No one has seen him since he rode out last night with some of his men on a mysterious errand. He's being searched for – using mundane and uncanny means.

'Then what's left of him will probably be found sooner or later. It makes no difference. The world is rid of a depraved villain and Princess Maudrayne need no longer fear for her life.'

Snudge, that's not true. If you windsearch her out, you must caution her not to approach Conrig. Remember that he's the one who originally ordered Catclaw to kill her. For reasons that are as valid today as they were sixteen years ago.

'All right. That's understood. But what I need from you now is the name of a place where I can meet Dyfrig some time later tonight. My wife and I will have to walk to town and find a place to stay there. You must assure the prince that he can trust me and convince him to come.'

It will have to be late. Conrig is having a final dinner for the generals and high-ranking officers before the redeployment of the army, and Dyfrig is to be royally commended for a successful reconnaissance mission he performed. So let's say half before midnight, at the fountain in Chandlers' Square down by the riverfront docks.

'Very well.'

There's a tavern called Watty Peascod's across the square from the fountain. It's a notorious dive where even the gentry go to buy contraband goods smuggled in from Cathra, so no one will think it strange for us to loiter about. I'll bring Dyfrig myself, well disguised.

And don't you worry, Snudge – I'll spin a spell of couverture to get
us out of the castle and into town without being seen. These days,
the town gates are never locked.

'I'll be there with my wife Induna. Our clothes are shabby
and very dirty. I'm tall and nondescript and I wear a beard
now. She's a little thing, lovely as a day in May, with red-
gold Tarnian hair . . . And, by the way: I'm called Deveron
now – except by the Beaconfolk.'

I see. Deveron it is. We'll try not to be late.

'If you are, don't worry, my lord. Look first into the tavern,
and if you don't see us, just hang about the fountain and
wait for someone not-quite-visible to tap you on the
shoulder.'

Corodon and Hyndry rode side by side along the main marsh-
land track, leading the hawking party back to the castle. She
still carried her beautiful peregrine on her wrist, and praised
the bird lavishly for its prowess in killing six teal. Corodon's
borrowed goshawk had taken an instant dislike to him and
behaved badly, and was now consigned to the custody of the
castle falconer. But the prince cared naught for that.

The important thing was, Hyndry had drunk the potion.

The group of high-born young people – the Prince Heritor
and Princess Royal, two of her equerries, two ladies-in-waiting
– together with three hunt servants and the falconer, had eaten
their picnic on a pleasant wooded islet in the great marsh.
Corodon, playing the devoted suitor to the superciliously indifferent Hyndry, had simply poured the philtre into his own
solid gold goblet, filled it and the silver one belonging to the
princess with wine, and insisted that she drink from his and
keep it because only a golden vessel was worthy of her lovely
lips. The sentimental speech (and the obvious value of the
goblet) had made the ladies giggle and the equerries roar in
approval and insist that Hyndry accept the gift.

'One does not judge a horse by the faulty skills of its rider,' she said with a lofty smile, 'or a meal by the surly temper of the cook. So why should I despise this pretty cup because it belonged to a royal nincompoop? . . . I'll keep it.' She downed a hearty pull of wine while her companions applauded and Corodon pretended to be abashed by the insult.

He lay a gentle hand upon her shoulder before anyone else could touch her and made sheep's eyes. 'Every time you drink from it, sweet lady, please remember your broken-hearted, rejected suitor kindly.'

'I'll remember you one way or another,' Hyndry said, 'but it won't spoil my pleasure in using the cup.' She drank the rest of the wine.

There was much laughter at poor Coro's expense, and then they resumed the hunt.

At first, the prince saw no change in the older woman's manner toward him. She made snide remarks when his hawk refused to fly for him, and laughed in malicious delight when the bird tore apart the lone duck it had downed, instead of waiting for the hunt servant to retrieve it. But when the last bird was bagged and the party headed homeward, Hyndry surprised her ladies by commanding Corodon to ride beside her.

For a time she was silent, then she began questioning him about hawking customs in Cathra and other sports afield.

He thought: By God, she's weakening! The love philtre works! I wonder if I can get her drunk at dinner tonight?

They continued on, chatting more or less amiably, until one of the servants gave a cry. 'Ho! Look over there beside that creek – a fine horse loose with neither bridle nor saddle.'

'Oh, he's a beauty!' Princess Hyndry exclaimed. 'Avrax, we must catch him and take him with us.'

'Then all you royals and gentlefolk stand stock still,' the man said, quietly dismounting.

He muttered to one of his mates, who handed him an apple from the picnic hamper and a long strap from one of the saddlebags. Looping the leather through its buckle, Avrax crept up on the magnificent animal. It was a dark bay stallion with black points, splattered with mud and rolling its eyes skittishly.

Holding out the fruit and speaking soft and coaxing words, Avrax soon had the strap looped about the horse's neck. He patted its muzzle while the big yellow teeth crunched up the apple, then led it back to the waiting party, who gave congratulations in low voices so as not to startle the captive.

Avrax tugged his forelock to the princess. 'He's well-behaved, Royal Highness, and bears a brand that's unfamiliar to me. Cathran, I'd say.'

Corodon urged his mount closer. 'I know it. The wavy cat-scratches comprise the mark of our Lord Constable.'

The falconer spoke up. 'There was talk of how he rode out last night with a few of his men and never returned.'

'Well, it seems his horse might have been heading for the castle stable,' Corodon said. 'I don't like that its harness is missing. The beast didn't simply slip away from its rider. Are there brigands or other outlaws along this marsh track?'

'Never, Your Grace!' said Avrax indignantly. 'This is civilized country.' His glance shifted. 'But the bogs and mudholes can be dangerous to those who don't know 'em.'

'I doubt Lord Tinnis fell into a bog,' Corodon said somberly. 'Bring the horse, my man. We must hasten to the castle and report this to my royal father.'

'To both our fathers,' Hyndry added. 'Let's be off, Coro. A silver mark says I'll beat you to the postern gatehouse!'

By the end of the afternoon, Maudrayne and the two armigers had come through the steepest part of the downhill grade on the Didion side of Great Pass. Durin Kyle, the youngest boy, who had been riding ahead, abruptly wheeled about and rejoined the two others.

'I caught sight of Castlemont below us!' he cried eagerly.

'It's still at least ten leagues away,' his brother Tormo scoffed.

'I saw it, I tell you. My eyes are much better than yours. Another couple of hours and we'll be there! I've heard it's a fine place to spend the night. Real beds with feather pillows even in the less expensive rooms. Fine food and drink for those who dine in the hall.' He addressed Maudrayne. 'We will eat in the great hall, won't we, my la – messire? Can we afford it?'

'We can,' she replied with a smile. Mealtimes were the most important part of the day for growing boys. 'And both of you will do so. But it would be safer if I ate in my room –'

The sound of a horn echoed amongst the crags, along with shouts of warning. 'Make way! Make way!'

Maude swore. 'Off the track quickly, lads. Here comes another party in a tearing hurry.'

They pulled aside just in time. A cavalcade of three richly dressed individuals attended by a dozen retainers thundered by in a spray of muddy water.

'That's the fifth hell-for-leather bunch to overtake us,' Tormo remarked. 'What d'you suppose the great rush is about?'

Maudrayne went stiff in her saddle. 'God of the Starry Roads – I think I know. Do you remember the conversation we overheard while waiting at the frontier guardpost at the top of the pass? One of the wagon-train captains who'd passed through Boarsden said that the Army of the Sovereignty would begin moving out of there tomorrow, in the hours before dawn.'

Durin was puzzled. 'Why would that cause people to hurry?'

'Because the authorities will close the entire road to civilian traffic, you blockhead!' his older brother exclaimed. 'Any travelers spending the night at Castlemont will be stuck there for who knows how long – days, maybe! – until the troops and their supply trains pass by.'

Maude said, 'You're right. Persons with important affairs in Tarn – or even in the Didionite cities downriver from Boarsden – would want to pass through that section of the road while they're still able. And so must we, lads.'

They stared at her. Tormo said, 'Must we bypass Castlemont, then, and proceed directly to Boarsden? Messire, even if we change horses and carry torches we would not arrive until the middle of the night. Can you endure such a long ride?'

'I can,' she replied grimly. 'But we're not going to Boarsden. Unless I miss my guess, the army will make its first overnight bivouac in the vicinity of Rockyford Way Station. It's an exceptionally secure Wold-Road establishment operated by Cathra, not Didion, used mainly by diplomatic couriers, Tarnian gold and opal merchants, and others bearing precious cargo. It would be the perfect spot for High King Conrig and the other leaders to spend the night.'

And Dyfrig as well, she thought.

'Do you intend to press on to Rockyford tonight, then?' Tormo was confused. When she nodded, he said, 'May I ask why?'

'We'll sleep and eat there, then depart in the morning long before the first advance guard of the army arrives. But we won't go far. We'll find a safe place for you two to hide. But I intend to return to Rockyford after dark tomorrow.' A remote smile touched her lips. 'I have private business with one of the guests who will be staying there . . . or perhaps with two.'

Watty Peascod's tavern furnished Deveron and Induna with a good meal. When there was still no sign of Stergos and Dyfrig as the midnight bell tolled, Deveron gave coins to the potboy and said to Induna, 'Let's wait outside, love. Too many people are giving us the eye, knowing we've money on us.'

They slipped out the door, carrying pack and fardel, and immediately Deveron invoked the simple spell of couverture that would cause ordinary passers-by to ignore them as though they were invisible. Most of the square was still alive with people. The imminent departure of the Army of the Sovereignty had prompted the whores and sundry-pedlars to come out in force, seeking last-minute trade as Boarsden Town emptied of its temporary throng of visitors.

Induna sat on the parapet of the fountain's wide basin, into which six streams of water poured from the mouths of heraldic swine. She felt deathly weary after a hard night and day without sleep. They had arranged to stay at a small inn near the town gate, and she did not look forward to the prospect. The place was mean and miserable, but it had been the only hostelry with room for them in its communal dormitorium.

'Where can Dyfrig and Stergos be?' she muttered crossly, after another half hour passed and no one approached save persons filling water-jars or buckets or giving their horses a drink. 'Did you release the cover-spell so that they might find us?'

'Be patient, love. I think I scry them now. See? They're just coming out of that lane next to the tavern.'

The cloaked figures who approached were plainly dressed but beyond a doubt persons of quality. The scruffy crowd parted before them and importunate whores scattered like shooed chickens. One man was of slight stature, with a round, pleasant face that bore an air of deceptive youthfulness – save for the deep-set eyes with their gleam of powerful talent. The other was much younger and very tall. When Deveron magnified the blond-bearded countenance with his scrying ability he uttered a gasp of astonishment, for Dyfrig was the very image of the youthful Prince Heritor Conrig whom he had attended in the stableyard of Cala Palace so many years ago.

'Is something wrong?' Induna whispered anxiously.

'Not at all. The prince's resemblance to his father is extraordinary. I wonder that the pretense of calling him a bastard born of Maudrayne's adultery was able to be sustained.'

Stergos made no bones about embracing the former Royal Intelligencer wholeheartedly. 'Sir Deveron! Even after all these years, I would have known you anywhere. And you must be Sealady Induna, honored by Sernin Donorvale himself. May I present Prince Dyfrig Beorbrook.'

'Your Grace,' the two of them murmured in unison.

'I'm sorry we're late,' the Royal Alchymist said. 'Tonight's supper at the castle turned rather tumultuous when Didion's Princess Royal unexpectedly announced that she intended to entertain the suit of Prince Heritor Corodon after all.'

Dyfrig grimaced. 'Say it plainly, my lord: King Somarus was carried from the hall after collapsing in a spasm of apoplectic rage. His Majesty seems to be resting comfortably now, but a riot between Didionite opponents of the match and Cathran supporters nearly came to bloodshed before the Sovereign restored order by sheer force of his personality.'

'Let us speak no more of this,' Stergos said. 'I have already explained to His Grace why you wanted to see him, Deveron.'

The prince's face tensed. 'I believe you have a very important letter for me. From my mother, who was said to be dead. Is she truly alive and well?'

'I have been told that she escaped from the place in
northern Cathra where she was imprisoned. Other than that,
I know nothing of her movements, save that she will certainly
attempt to find you.' Deveron already had the gold locket
tucked in his glove. He extracted it and handed it to Dyfrig.
'The message from her is inside. You should know that this
was carried to Didion by a faithful woman friend of the
Princess Maudrayne, who was foully murdered by persons
who would have taken it away from her. Her name was
Rusgann. Today we buried her.'

Dyfrig responded in a low voice, staring at the locket in
the palm of his hand as though it were a harbinger of doom.
'God rest her. Lord Stergos has already apprised me of that
sad fact. Do you know what the letter says, Sir Deveron?'

'I have only a general knowledge of its contents, Your
Grace. Would you like to read it now? My talent can soften
the black cement that seals the locket shut.'

'I –' The prince turned to Stergos with a haunted expression. The Royal Alchymist simply lowered his eyes. 'Very
well,' Dyfrig said to Deveron. 'Please open it – although it
may be hard to read anything in this poor light.'

Without a word, both Induna and Stergos held up their
index fingers, from which little yellow flames suddenly
sprang. 'I forgot I was in the presence of talented ones,' the
prince said.

Deveron held the locket between his palms and warmed
it with magic to a point greater than blood heat. When the
resin finally lost its adhesive grip, he pried open the golden
case, removed the many-folded square with its dots of sealing
wax, and handed it to Dyfrig.

With difficulty, the prince read the lines of tiny handwriting
by the light of the two flames. When he finished, his face was
white and his hands had begun to tremble. He refolded the
missive, replaced it in the locket, and put it into his purse.

'My – my mother enjoins me to trust you, Sir Deveron. So does Lord Stergos, who believes you have been sent by – by certain powerful persons to help me through perilous times to come.' Dyfrig composed himself with a visible effort of willpower. 'If you and your lady will consent, I wish you to accompany me now to Boarsden Castle. Horses are waiting for us at a stable not far from here. We can enter the bailey secretly, beneath the cloak of Lord Stergos's magic, and we two will see you comfortably lodged for the night. I can tell you're in sore need of rest. Later . . . we'll talk of future plans.'

'Very well, Your Grace,' Deveron said.

'I intend to show this letter to my beloved adoptive father, Earl Marshal Parlian. He must advise me what is to be done about it.'

'You don't intend to share the letter's contents with me?' Stergos said.

'I think you must already know what it says, my lord.'

The alchymist sighed. 'I can guess.'

The prince turned an apologetic smile toward Induna. 'Leaving only you unenlightened, my lady.'

'It is none of my business, Your Grace,' she said equably, blowing out the flame at her fingertip. 'However, your offer of lodging in the castle is a boon from heaven that my husband and I accept eagerly. We've lived rough for the past few days. Shall we be on our way? I just felt a drop of rain.'

FOURTEEN

Induna remained sound asleep when the gentle scratching at their chamber door awakened Deveron. Scrying Prince Dyfrig standing outside in the corridor, he climbed out of bed, pulled a borrowed houserobe about his nakedness, padded barefoot to the door, unlocked it and cracked it open.

'What is it, Your Grace?'

Dyfrig held a single candle. In the dancing shadows, his face was a mask of conflicting emotions and his speech tinged with a strange excitement. 'I know it's late. Forgive me. But my father the earl marshal would like to speak to you. I would deem it a great favor if you would read the locket letter and affirm to him that it contains the whole truth. After that . . . there is a request we would put to you.'

Deveron felt his stomach sink with premonition. 'Shall I wake Induna? We work together in all things, but she was very weary.'

'Let the Sealady sleep, by all means. You can tell her everything tomorrow. Will you come with me now?' His eyes were pleading.

'Let me find a pair of houseshoes,' Deveron said with a sigh. 'These floorboards are like ice.'

As he admitted them to his apartment, Earl Marshal Parlian Beorbrook said, 'Maturity suits you, Sir Deveron Austrey. Somehow I could never take seriously a Royal Intelligencer named Snudge – no matter how lavishly your virtues were praised by His Sovereign Grace.'

'He has long since changed his favorable opinion of me, my lord,' Deveron said wryly. He followed Dyfrig inside.

'Which has only raised you in my estimation,' the earl marshal said. 'I'm a loyal servant of the Sovereignty still, but my heart was sorely grieved at the manner in which Princess Maude was first cast aside, then deemed to be a menace to the security of the Crown. Your efforts on her behalf – and on behalf of my dear son Dyfrig – were well and nobly done. I deplore the fact that you were dealt with so unjustly as a consequence . . . Come, let us be seated.'

The old general led them to a table crowded with dispatch cases and writing materials. A branched candlestick with three tapers gave the only illumination aside from the guttering logs in the fireplace across the room. Clearing a space, Parlian said to Dyfrig, 'Let Deveron read your mother's letter.'

The prince produced the tiny folded square from the locket that now hung on a golden chain about his neck and placed it on the table without comment.

After Deveron had read it twice over, he returned the parchment to Dyfrig. 'It is much as I expected. What the Princess Dowager says concerning the secret talent of the king is absolutely true. I myself detected his weak magical powers when I was a mere stableboy at Cala Palace. Rather than have me executed as a threat to his position, Prince Heritor Conrig made me his trusted man. And so I remained, until I saw my own trust betrayed.'

Parlian's piercing eyes searched Deveron's face. 'And *you* were able to recognize this feeble talent in the king even though none of the Zeth Brethren – not even Conrig's own brother Stergos – had any inkling of it?'

'I won't boast to you, my lord, but I'm different from other magickers. I can detect talent even in those who are clever at hiding it, and I can do certain other things that exceed the abilities of Zeth's alchymists.'

'And do you still possess your two moonstone sigils – the Concealer and the Subtle Gateway?'

'Yes. But I rarely use them because of their inherent dangers. My natural talents sufficed throughout most of my career as Royal Intelligencer for King Conrig. When he condemned me to death, I used the sigils to escape the Lord Constable's noose. Since then, I have used each of them only once.'

'Remind me of some of your inborn uncanny abilities,' the earl marshal requested.

'Only two of them might be considered extraordinary – but they were very useful when I was a spy. When I'm well rested and in good fettle, I can windspeak and scry over extremely great distances. But no other person of talent can scry *me*. My talents are called "wild" because they more closely resemble those of the more powerful Mossland sorcerers or Tarnian shamans than the abilities of Cathran or Didionite adepts.' His mouth moved in a suppressed grin. 'Princess Maude's letter speaks of the origins of talent – how humans came to possess it. I've discovered how mine was inherited. My great-great-grandmother, who is still alive and well, is a Green Woman who once seduced a human male. According to the custom of her people, her half-blood babe was given to the relatives of its father to rear.'

Dyfrig had been listening to Deveron's recital open-mouthed, but now he broke in with an apology. 'Forgive me, but we should stick to the matter at hand and save the tale of Sir Deveron's ancestry for another time. My mother's letter names you, messire, as witness to the truth of its contents. Father, will you accept his affirmation as proof of King Conrig's secret talent?'

'Yes,' Parlian Beorbrook said. 'Whether others would accept it is problematical. Technically, Sir Deveron is an outlaw. As for the bastardy issue raised by Maude – which Deveron cannot prove or disprove – I consider the matter moot. The official declaration that your mother was an adulterous wife is given no credence whatsoever by unbiased persons. One need only to look at you, Dyfrig, and then at Conrig to know that you are his natural son and the true first-born heir to the throne. That said, I remind you that you were named a bastard *by royal decree*, and placed behind Corodon in the succession only according to the royal pleasure.'

'I'm aware that the Sovereign could remove me from the succession at any time,' Dyfrig said without heat. 'But would he? He seems to think little of Prince Coro as a candidate for the Iron Crown.'

'There's something you should know about both Orrion and Corodon,' Deveron said, 'a fact known also by the High King and by Lord Stergos. Both young men possess the same nearly imperceptible portion of talent as does their father. Only you, Prince Dyfrig, are talent-free and thus eligible to sit the Cathran throne.'

The earl marshal groaned. Dyfrig looked stricken.

'But here is the dilemma, Your Grace: If you were to use your mother's letter – and my own witness to it – in an attempt to depose Conrig now, you would destroy the unity of the Blenholme Sovereignty. Tarn and Didion would withdraw their oaths of fealty at once. Even without the threat of a Salka invasion, such an action might precipitate civil

war in Cathra between your own supporters and those of
Prince Heritor Corodon . . . or Duke Feribor Blackhorse, who
stands next in the succession.'

'There seems only one choice open to me,' Dyfrig said. 'I
will not press my claim. I cannot. The consequences would
be devastating.'

Parlian said, 'Perhaps a time will come when changing
circumstances demand a different course of action, but I think
the time is not yet.' He glanced at Deveron. 'What is your
opinion, messire?'

'I agree heartily with you and Prince Dyfrig, my lord. But
there's another person who may feel differently.'

'Princess Maudrayne,' said the earl marshal, rolling his
eyes. 'Her letter leaves no doubt of her position. If she gains
the protection of her Uncle Sernin Donorvale . . .' He shook
his head. 'Conrig was able to discredit her allegations against
him once, but he may not be able to pull the same trick
twice! Sir Deveron, can you use your talent to help us find
Maude and convince her to remain silent?'

'My windsearch faculties are greatly diminished by severe
fatigue and by . . . the stress of recent events. You may know
that my wife Induna and I tried in vain to rescue Rusgann,
the woman who was charged by Princess Maude to deliver
her letter to you. And after that –'

'I have told my father how you were forced to slay the
Lord Constable and his gang of villains,' Dyfrig said. 'He has
agreed to keep silent about it.'

'And do you both understand why such harsh measures
were necessary? My strongest motive for taking their lives
was not mere vengeance. If the constable had lived, knowing
Prince Dyfrig had received the letter and was aware that his
mother had been a secret prisoner for years, Catclaw would
have killed the prince to save his own skin from the
Sovereign's fury.'

'True enough,' said Parlian in a voice gone flat and emotionless. 'And there's another point that needs making. My son, I'm sorry to tell you that Lord Tinnis is not the only one who might believe you better off dead. Only think about it! Why was the High King so willing to send you off on the perilous Green Morass reconnaissance – you, a brave but untested youth? Had I known your intention to penetrate Salka-occupied territory, I would have forbidden it. But Conrig leapt at your rash proposal.'

Dyfrig stared at him in shocked silence.

The earl marshal addressed Deveron. 'How long will it be, messire, before your talent recovers and you're able to scry Maude out?'

'I'll begin looking for her tomorrow. As I have already told Prince Dyfrig, *she* will certainly try to find *him*, even though doing so places her in the gravest danger.'

'What can we do?' the prince cried. 'I'd mortgage my soul to see her again.'

'When I know where she is,' Deveron said, 'and what disguise she wears, I'll attempt to find a safe way to bring you two together. No one save you will be able to convince your mother to keep her peace. I know her temperament all too well . . . Since you'll be riding with the army, a meeting may not be easy to arrange. But I'll manage it. I was once rather good at clandestine activity and I've already thought of a plan.'

Parlian Beorbrook's eyes narrowed. 'Indeed?'

'Making it work will require your cooperation, my lord, and also that of the Tarnian Grand Shaman Zolanfel. Since Princess Maudrayne is his countrywoman and a close relation to the High Sealord, her secret will be safe with the shaman. I propose that I disguise myself as a Tarnian windspeaker. You, Earl Marshal, can pass me off as a new member of your general staff, the official liaison between your

Southern Wing of the army and the forces of Sernin Donorvale in the Northern Wing.'

'Such a position is hardly necessary,' Parlian said. 'The Zeth Brethren on my staff can easily handle any necessary communication.'

'In military matters,' Deveron said, 'the commander can chose what officers he pleases. Who would dare gainsay him?'

'No one,' Parlian Beorbrook admitted.

'You must pretend to take me into your service so I can remain close to you and Prince Dyfrig – at least for the time being. This is necessary if my plan is to succeed.'

'I'll agree to the scheme,' Parlian said.

Deveron rose from the table. 'My wife, Sealady Induna, will assume the role of my apprentice.'

'But surely she'd be safer left behind!' Dyfrig protested.

'She's a talented magicker in her own right and I need her help, Your Grace. Reuniting you with your mother is not the only duty I've taken upon myself. I've also been charged to help in the war against the Salka. Perhaps we can ride together tomorrow and I'll tell you more.'

The prince nodded slowly.

'I would also like to know more about your . . . other duties,' said the earl marshal, 'and who laid them upon you.'

'Certainly, my lord.' Deveron stifled a yawn. 'I'll visit the Grand Shaman before I retire and get everything organized. The next time you see me, I'll be a plausible Tarnian. Where and when shall we meet tomorrow?'

'Go to Zolanfel's quarters around the eighth hour. I'll send my adjutant, Viscount Aylesmere, to collect you when the rest of my staff is ready to ride out with me and my son. It'll help validate your status if Aylesmere sees you with the Tarnian shaman. The viscount is a shrewd man, so have your cover-story well polished – and your alleged apprentice well disguised.'

Devron acknowledged the point with a tired smile, then turned to Dyfrig. 'Keep the letter safe, Your Grace. You may someday have great need of it.'

The Prince clasped the locket that hung around his neck with one hand and laid the other upon Deveron's shoulder. 'Whether or not my mother and I ever meet again, I intend to carry her letter next to my heart forever. Let me thank you again for bringing it to me. My debt to you can never be repaid – but anything you ask of me shall be granted if it's within my power to do so.'

'Perhaps we'll speak of that tomorrow,' Deveron said. He pulled the nightrobe tighter about his naked body. 'The only favor I need now is a warm bed, but I suspect I won't get one for a while yet.'

The night-muffled chime of the castle struck the second hour.

Accompanied only by his trusted chamberlain Telifar, Conrig Wincantor stood before the door of the tower room assigned to the Conjure-King of Moss. It was guarded by two fully armed Cathran knights and a senior Brother of Zeth.

'He is within, Vra-Polian?' the Sovereign inquired of the alchymist.

'Beyond doubt, Your Grace. He returned from the feast looking smug and self-satisfied and has not emerged since.'

'I will speak to him. Open the door.'

The Brother bowed his head, then knocked and announced the High King. One of the guards removed the iron bar securing the door and lifted the latch. Conrig waved back Telifar and the men, entered, and found Beynor seated by a crackling fire, toasting cheese on a fork.

The sorcerer lifted his gaunt head and smiled. 'I've been expecting you, my liege. Come in and take a seat. We'll share a little wee-hours snack.' At his gesture, the door to the chamber closed gently. 'No one will overhear what we say

or realize that you've been here. I've spun the appropriate
spells.'

'Fine. That cheese smells appetizing.'

Beynor took a bread-roll from a small side-table, tore off
half, and plopped the oozing tidbit onto it. 'Try this. Will you
also join me in a cup of the duke's honey-liquor? I intend
to take my metheglin mulled to warm my belly. It seems
those who prophesied continuing fair weather were badly
misled. You and your army will have an uncomfortable
march.' He thrust a red-hot iron into an earthenware mug.
Hissing steam and a sweetly pungent scent arose.

Conrig nodded and settled into a cushioned chair. Rain
was ticking steadily against the glazed window and the fire
felt good in the chilly room. He nibbled his bread and cheese
and sipped from the cup of hot spirits before speaking. 'You
know why I came, Conjure-King.'

Beynor pushed the mulling iron back into the glowing
coals. 'To congratulate me on the presumed success of Prince
Corodon's love philtre?'

'Let's not be premature. Princess Hyndry only agreed to
let my son pay his court to her. The minx might only be
toying with him.'

Beynor smirked. 'I think she's doing more than that – even
as we speak! But we can only wait and see. I hope that my
ploy met with your approval – in spite of King Somarus's
adverse reaction. He nearly died of tonight's fit, you know.
Only heroic efforts by his wizards and your Zeth Brethren
saved him from a fatal stroke.'

Conrig's features remained bland. 'I didn't know that. I do
know that his physicians have forbidden him to accompany
the Southern Wing of the army when it moves out. Crown
Prince Valardus is now officially Commander-in-Chief of
Didion's armed forces. He only accepted the post when his
father agreed not to supersede his authority.'

'There's one obstacle to victory tidily removed!' Beynor took a large bite of his cheese roll and chewed with enthusiasm. 'I wish I could take credit for it. But it was only a welcome but unforeseen side-effect.' When the Sovereign said nothing, he took the iron from the fire and plunged it into his own cup. 'And now you are here in the middle of the night, to question me about the sigils that Prince Corodon told you about.'

'The boy said you showed the moonstones to him.'

Beynor set aside his metheglin. 'You wish to see them for yourself? Very well.' He went to an oaken clothes press, opened it, and took a stained leather pouch from one of the shelves. Returning to the fire, he pulled the table with the food and drink between the chairs and laid out four small translucent objects after unwrapping each from its cloth covering.

Conrig found himself holding his breath. He recognized the Weathermaker ring: his dead lover Ullanoth had owned one exactly like it. The wand was the same as that he had seen in his dream. The sigil Coro had thought shaped like a carrot was actually an icicle. But what was the smooth disk?

He asked Beynor.

'This is not one of the Great Stones. You might think of it as a key, having the potential to activate the others. It works . . . in an irregular manner. It's preferable to bring the sigils to life through certain lengthy incantations to the Lights spoken in the Salka tongue, but I no longer possess the necessary reference books containing them.'

'And you are also forbidden to use the activated sigils yourself,' the king stated. 'So you require – shall we say – a surrogate. An agent.'

'Yes.'

'Let's stop playing games, Beynor. Do you actually intend to give these things to me?'

'Would you dare to accept them, my liege?' The sorcerer's black eyes danced with mockery. 'They can be very dangerous. And the one who uses their sorcery will suffer intense pain. I believe you already know this. But are you also aware that the stones will only bond to persons of talent? It's a fact known to very few. I only recently confirmed it myself. However, I suspect that my aunt, the Sorceress Thalassa Dru, may be aware of it . . . as well as the Royal Alchymist. If you wield these sigils, you put yourself in peril from more directions than one.'

'My brother Stergos already knows of my talent. He's known for years and kept quiet about it. And I'm prepared to risk and endure anything in order to save this island from being conquered by Salka monsters.'

'Are you indeed!' Beynor sipped his drink. 'Knowing how my poor mother died after attempting to use Destroyer, I was too cowardly to activate it – even though I might have thereby saved my crown. And made myself Sovereign of High Blenholme in your place.'

The blood drained from Conrig's face, but his voice remained calm. 'What was it that your mother asked of Destroyer that brought about her terrible fate?'

'I don't know. My father was driven mad by the hideous manner of her death and would never discuss the matter with me. Whatever it was, the Lights were so affronted by her command to the stone that they requited her no mercy. The worst of it is, her mortal mistake might have been a trivial thing! Who knows how supernatural beings think?'

'What did *you* do that made the Beaconfolk curse you?' Conrig asked suddenly.

Beynor scowled. 'That's none of your affair.' He began rewrapping the stones and restoring them to their pouch.

Before he could deal with Destroyer, Conrig laid a single finger on the wand. 'It's cool,' he remarked in surprise.

'Ordinary. Rather fragile. One could snap it with a sharp blow against the table's edge.'

'Only if it were not alive and bonded to an owner. A living sigil glows faintly green. If it's touched without the owner's permission, it burns flesh like white-hot metal. Try to break it then, Your Grace, and it will smite you like a thunderbolt, leaving only ashes behind.' He finished and tucked the pouch into his robe. 'You haven't yet asked me what I expect in return for the sigils.'

'Coro said you wanted me to defeat the Salka and give you back your lost kingdom. But I rather think you want more.'

'What I want – and what I might expect to receive and to keep – are two different things.' The sorcerer's voice was heavy with bitterness. 'If I activate the sigils and teach you how to use them, you must accept me as your chief adviser and do as I say in matters of sorcery. Moonstone sigils are not safely wielded by amateurs. You'll need expert coaching.'

The king made no reply. He'd see about that . . .

'I've also learned that the Salka are making two Great Stones of their own to use as weapons against you. One is a Subtle Gateway, like the sigil once owned by your Royal Intelligencer, and the other is a Destroyer. The source of the raw material being used to manufacture those sigils is now obliterated. But the Salka have located a second outcropping of the stuff on a mountaintop and plan to go after it as soon as possible.'

'Bazekoy's Burning Britches!' Conrig's hope that the Salka were unaware of the Demon Seat moonstone source was dashed. But would the clumsy amphibians actually be able to get hold of the mineral?

They would, he realized with an apprehensive chill, if they used that Gateway sigil they were making.

'Even if you defeat this invading army,' Beynor was saying,

'they'll make more sigils in the future and start the war all over again unless a way is found to deny them the source of moonstone mineral. It's a nasty situation.'

'Well, what the hell can I do about it?' Conrig growled.

'*We* can do a great deal – if you follow my instructions precisely and agree to abide by certain conditions when wielding these sigils.'

'Huh! What do you expect of me?'

'First, you must swear to use the Great Stones only under my guidance. Second, your brother Stergos must be removed from the position of Royal Alchymist and retired to private life – or otherwise disposed of. I won't brook his interference or hostility. And neither should you, as you pursue your ambition of emulating the Emperor Bazekoy and set about to conquer the Continent.'

'You know about that?' Conrig said in surprise.

Beynor got up from from his chair. Standing before the fire, he was a dark silhouette, the enigmatic tall image of the king's nightmare. 'I know everything about you – all your vainglorious schemes, all your hopes and fears and secret perfidies. We're more alike than you can possibly realize, Conrig Wincantor.'

'Liar,' shouted the Sovereign. He surged to his feet, sent the table and its contents crashing to the hearthstones, and would have taken hold of the taunting magicker and choked him senseless. But his muscles refused to obey. He stood helpless, with arms locked at his sides and fists clenched. 'Release me!' he groaned.

'Of course.' Beynor made a negligent gesture.

'Whoreson!' The king lurched as his body came alive again. He saved himself from falling only by catching hold of his chair.

Beynor chuckled. 'You're quite unscathed – as Bazekoy's blue pearl knows – which is why it ignored the little spell I just cast upon you. But even when the pearl's enchantment is nullified, after we leave this castle, you'll never be able to harm me. If I become your mentor in sorcery, the arrangement will be permanent. You won't break it through mayhem or murder. And if you try to use the sigils against me, I'll abolish their magical power, turn them into dead trinkets, and find a more compliant creature to wield them.'

'Cullion!' Conrig whispered in cold fury. 'Mind-futterer! How could I possibly have considered allying myself with an insolent conniver such as you?'

'Easily.' Beynor flipped one hand in dismissal. 'But you're free to do as Stergos advised. Send me away to Incayo. I won't stay there, of course. You can't confine me *anywhere.* Understand that! I'll leave Blenholme to you – and the Salka – and seek my fortune on the Continent. Is that what you want? Shall I depart this very night?'

Conrig's gaze shifted. His knuckles gripping the chair-back were white. 'No,' he said at last in a strained voice. 'Don't go.'

'You'll have to take me with you on the march to the Tarnian border and leave Stergos behind.'

'He could insist on coming. Use gammadion sorcery against me. Last night . . . he dared to smite me senseless. Me! His own brother and liege lord.'

'Then the situation with him is even more grave than I suspected. We may be able to conceal your secret talent – even your use of the sigils – from your war-leaders and the lesser magickers by subterfuge. But Stergos won't be fooled. He won't stand by helplessly while you draw power from the Beaconfolk. Your dear brother is allied with those on the opposite side of the New Conflict.'

'What . . . is the true nature of that conflict?'

'It's complicated. There's not enough time for me to explain it now. All that need concern you is the necessity of removing any threat posed by your brother. We can't use the sigils safely if he knows about them. You know that he's lied to you, held back vital information, consorted with inhuman beings and even pledged himself to their mysterious cause. His protestations of loyalty and fraternal devotion are nothing but a sham. He's one of your enemies, even if he's never appeared in your nightmares.'

But he loves me, Conrig thought. He's known about my talent but kept the secret all this time against the dictates of his conscience.

'Can't you cope with Stergos, Beynor? I don't think I'd know how.'

'Your brother has instructed his gammadion pendant to defend him against any sort of attack from me. Stergos knows I'm trying to sway you. He can't scry out my sigils – even the inactive moonstones are imperceptible to wind adepts. But he already knows that I've influenced your dreams.'

'Why did you do that?' Conrig demanded. 'You nearly unhinged my mind, damn you!'

'I had to warn you in a way you couldn't ignore. To make you aware of unsuspected threats. To prepare you for this meeting – this understanding between us. Do you remember the strange dead-black creature with the tentacular arms, one of the principal menaces you fought with in your nightmare?'

'Yes.'

'He's real. His name is the One Denied the Sky – but he is also called the Source of the Conflict. This entity is your greatest foe. The Source will stop at nothing to deprive you of the sigil sorcery I offer to you – merely because it draws power from his own ancient adversaries, the Beaconfolk. He cares nothing for the human population of High Blenholme Island. He even disdains the Salka! All that matters to this aloof creature is a longstanding war between factions of

supernatural beings including himself: the so-called New
Conflict. And Stergos is allied with this inhuman monstrosity.
If you doubt me, just ask him.'

'No,' Conrig said. 'I believe you.'

Beynor thought for a few minutes. 'What I can do to help
you, is prepare another sort of philtre. One you can administer to your brother, which I cannot because of his gammadion's protection.'

'You mean a poison.'

'It would be a quick and painless end. What most of us
hope for, after all. Stergos would fall asleep and never waken.
If you wish I'll make the philtre tonight, using chymicals in
the workroom of the late Kilian Blackhorse. I'll leave the
vial in your apartment anteroom, a crystal bottle containing
a colorless, tasteless liquid. What you do with it is up to you.'

The king's face was unreadable. 'Just like that.'

Beynor shrugged and changed the subject. 'Our sudden
"friendship" won't sit well with your more conservative
nobles and generals, but I'll try to be tactful while we're in
the field, stay out of the public eye for as long as it's expedient. When battle with the Salka is joined, however, I must
be at your side.'

'Can *you* tell me where the invaders will land?' The king's
voice was almost despairing.

'Not yet,' Beynor admitted. 'Scrying underwater is arduous
work, but I'll locate their main force eventually. Windsearching
their reinforcements may be more difficult because of the
greater distances involved.'

'Reinforcements?' Conrig cried.

'I've learned that a large contingent of Salka reserve
fighters from Fenguard are swimming around the south end
of the island to link up with the others.'

'God help us! How many?'

'I don't know. I'll try to find out. I'll also do my utmost

to assist your campaign using my own sorcery. I spoke less than the truth during our first meeting when I said my uncanny faculties are weaker than those of Stergos. They're far from it! You'll have a new Royal Alchymist – unofficially, of course – considerably more powerful than the old one.'

The old one! Conrig thought in despair. Oh, Gossy. Why couldn't you have remained faithful? Why did you abandon me? Now I have no choice. None at all.

Aloud, the king said in a dull voice, 'When will you activate the sigils?'

'When you need them. Not before.' The sorcerer paused. His narrow face had gone hard. 'Do you swear to abide by my terms, then? Without any mental reservation?'

Conrig Wincantor, Sovereign of Blenholme, lowered his head in surrender. 'I swear it by my Iron Crown.'

'Excellent. Then I suggest we part company and go to bed.'

Conrig turned away from the sorcerer and started toward the door. 'Yes. Both of us need peaceful sleep.' He looked over his shoulder and added, 'We should clarify one final point. There will be no more induced nightmares or other invasions of my dreams by you. Ever. Otherwise, our bargain is void.'

'The tactic is no longer necessary,' Beynor said with a smile. 'Goodnight, my liege.'

The six young Heart Companions waited impatiently for the Prince Heritor to join them at a pre-dawn breakfast. While they gobbled a hearty meal in anticipation of the upcoming day's ride to Rockyford Way Station in pouring rain, the young noblemen exchanged wild speculations concerning Corodon's whereabouts on the previous night. He had failed to return to his room in their communal apartment following the feast.

'He might have gone out with the search-parties looking

for the Lord Constable,' opined Lord Ilow. 'Coro helped find Catclaw's horse, you know. He hunts the marshes often and knows the area.'

'Or perhaps the Sovereign's still pissed off at our prince in spite of Hyndry's change of heart,' Lord Fentos suggested lugubriously. 'What if he sent poor Coro back to Cala Palace to sit out the war?'

'If old Somarus kicked the bucket last night,' Lord Alardon speculated, 'all the royals in the castle might have had to sit with the body overnight in some weird barbarian ritual.'

'Hsst!' Lord Rabidig whispered in alarm. 'He's coming.'

'Good morrow, Your Grace!' Lord Mardilan said brightly. 'Did you sleep well?'

Corodon shuffled into the room like a man half-conscious, garments wrinkled and imperfectly fastened, eyelids drooping, and lips curved in a sweet dreamy smile. Without a word to his disconcerted friends, he plopped into his regular seat at the head of the table, poured ale into a beaker with a shaking hand, and chugged it down in four heroic gulps. He belched, then emitted a deep sigh. The silly grin returned.

'Bazekoy's Buttocks!' cried Lord Jerek, who sat next to the prince. 'What in God's name ails you, Your Grace? Are you ill?'

'Nay, Jerry. Far from it.' He flapped a hand at his empty plate. 'Please. One of you dish me up some food. I'm famished. I'll faint in the saddle if I don't eat something now, and Father will poke fun at me. But I'm too wrung-out to lift a platter or crock.'

Uncertain chuckles greeted this remark. The six Companions had been told yesterday that King Conrig had ordered the Heritor not to accompany him, but to ride instead with Earl Marshal Parlian's smaller Southern Wing to the Lake of Shadows, along with the despised army of Didion.

Naturally the prince's band of Heart Companions would have to go with him and share his humiliation.

Corodon sensed their discomfort. 'What? Long faces? Ah – what a fool I am! I forgot to give you lads the happy tidings. My royal father has changed his mind. I'll ride at his side after all, with the Northern Wing of the army to the encampment below Frost Pass. And so will you!'

The young nobles broke into clamorous cheers while the prince picked up his tableknife and thrust it into the air as though he were leading a battle charge with sword on high. 'Forward!' he croaked. 'Bring on the monsters!' The others echoed him, roaring with laughter.

Count Ilow Woodhouse, the oldest of the Companions at nineteen and the most sensible, heaped Corodon's plate with bacon and scrambled eggs and fried bread, then poured more ale. 'Would you care to tell us what happened last night? We were concerned when you never came to bed. Did you spend the night with His Sovereign Grace?'

'I slept elsewhere,' the prince murmured, 'after conferring with my dear father . . . It was a night to remember!'

They stared blank-faced.

'And do you know what?' the prince continued. 'The bawdy old tales are right! I thought I knew it all, but I was wrong. God damn that Mossyback sorcerer and bless him, too – I'm fair destroyed. A husk of a man! But so very, very, very –' He giggled and slumped back in his seat, ignoring the food. 'Those tales. They're true, so true.'

'What tales, Your Grace?' Ilow inquired, mystified.

Prince Heritor Corodon cocked his head in blissful reminiscence. 'The stories about older women . . . Oh, lads, I'm so much in love.'

The dawn skies over the northern half of High Blenholme Island were ugly, and Cray the Green Woman studied the rushing clouds above the distant ocean with her longsight and shook her head. It was only days past the autumn equinox, and already the weather seemed to be slipping into a pattern more suited to the dreary Boreal Moon.

Rain sluiced the thatched roof of her snug cottage and poured in sheets from the eaves. She added more wood to the fire and swung the small kettle of milk on its crane to a spot above the coals that would heat it without scorching. Before long, the soul of her friend Thalassa Dru would re-enter her inert body, which lay fully clothed on Cray's bed. The sorceress would need restoring herbal tea and a bowl of milksops with cinnamon and honey.

After a short time had passed, Thalassa came to her senses, sat up with a grunt, stretched, blew her nose on a frayed old silk kerchief, and joined Cray at the table where the light meal was waiting. She had been entranced for less than an hour. Like the equally adept Cray, she no longer needed to perform a lengthy drum-ritual in order to visit the Source in his otherworldly prison beneath the Ice. The effects of the soul-journey upon her sturdy constitution were also minimal because of her magical expertise.

'Well?' the Green Woman inquired. 'Did you manage to obtain a remedy against dream-invasion for Stergos to offer his royal brother?'

The sorceress paused in the spooning of her pabulum. 'I have the spell. But, alas – it may be too late to help Conrig. The Source told me that Beynor has already offered the king his three Great Stones. And Conrig has agreed to use them according to Beynor's instructions.'

'Toadflax!' Cray exclaimed in consternation. 'Did the Source know when the actual bonding would take place?'

'The decision is entirely Beynor's. The king is apparently a willing puppet. His courage and self-assurance seem to be tottering and he fears – quite rightly – that the dubious strategy forced upon him by Somarus will cause a fatal delay in his army's response to the new Salka invasion. He's ready to grasp at any remedy. And you may not know this, but Ullanoth once told me that Conrig always had a secret desire to use sigil sorcery, as she and Beynor did. Not only against the Salka, but to further his ambitions of imperial conquest.'

'Did the Source have advice for us about coping with the situation? What if you and I popped through a subtle corridor and stole the sigils from Beynor? Or carried him off and marooned him in the Far East?'

Thalassa shook her head. 'I suggested something of the sort. The Source flatly forbade it. We are to inform Deveron Austrey of what's happened. Nothing more. When I protested, saying that we should take direct action to save Conrig from Beynor's evil influence, I was told that *events are unfolding as they must.* Really, I'm very vexed with our leader! He sees only his ineffable cosmic game-plan and spares scant sympathy for us groundling pawns.'

'Ansel dared to defy him,' Cray noted. Her gentle voice had a rebellious note. 'The Source is not infallible nor is he omniscient. Ansel single-handedly prevented the Salka from obtaining a large quantity of raw material for new sigils. What he did was justified, even if it cost him his life. Perhaps . . .' She trailed off, sending an unspoken question to her friend.

Thalassa Dru sighed and set aside her spoon. 'I'm afraid I lack Ansel's wisdom and invincible confidence. What if we inadvertently brought about disaster through meddling with Conrig and Beynor? It could happen. Even Ansel's victory was not total. The Salka salvaged enough flawless moonstone in the Barren Lands to manufacture two new Great Stones. The Source told me they're close to completing a Subtle Gateway and a Destroyer. Beynor might know about this. He could have used the fact to sway Conrig's decision.'

'Lousewort and pissabed!' Cray swore. 'What else did that blind black enigma have to say to you? Is there no good news at all?'

'The Source did have hopeful information from the Likeminded Remnant, although he wasn't certain what it signified. The exiled Lights – those who abandoned our world's Sky in despair, leaving only the Remnant behind – have made tentative contact with their old compeers. The exiles are finally willing to listen to the Remnant's plan for the New Conflict.'

'I suppose it's encouraging.'

'Do me a favor, dear, and bespeak Deveron Austrey this information while I eat a bit more. I think I need some of your jam tarts and a link of cold venison sausage to rebuild my stamina. This bowl of milksops didn't quite do the trick.'

The Green Woman nodded and fetched more substantial fare, including a flask of bilberry cordial to liven up the tea. Then she retired to a corner stool, scried out the present location of the former Royal Intelligencer, and windspoke him at some length.

When the silent converse was finished, she opened her eyes. 'Well! Hemlock and henbane – if this isn't a pretty state of things!'

'Whatever's the matter?' Thalassa cried in alarm.

'I understand now why the Source insisted that my grandson rescue the woman Rusgann Moorcock – but I can't say that I approve of it!' Cray related everything that Deveron had bespoken her about Rusgann's mission and her tragic death, as well as the delivery of Maudrayne's portentous letter to her son Prince Dyfrig.

Thalassa sat openmouthed with shock. 'Both the young prince *and* Earl Marshal Parlian now know that Conrig is Dyfrig's true father? And that the king possesses secret talent and sits the throne illicitly?'

'They know more than that. Deveron informed them that Conrig's twin sons by Risalla Mallburn are also attainted by slight magical abilities. In her letter, Maudrayne urged her son to claim the Iron Crown, since he is the only true heir. But Dyfrig rather sensibly shrank from the prospect, knowing it would throw the Sovereignty into chaos at this critical time. His adoptive father, Earl Marshal Parlian, agreed. And so did Deveron – until I told him of Conrig's alliance with Beynor and those three Great Stones.'

'Will Deveron now try to change Dyfrig's mind?'

'He hasn't decided,' Cray admitted. 'And I can't say as I blame him.'

Thalassa Dru's usual aplomb was badly shaken. 'Oh, my dear! Do you think Stergos knows about the letter?'

Cray nodded. 'He knows. He was present when Deveron delivered it and immediately divined what it must contain. He's always known the truth about Dyfrig and the king's secret talent.'

'I don't know what to say,' Thalassa murmured. 'Are we expected to somehow act upon this sensational information? The Source said nothing to me about it. Nothing, damn him!'

Cray got up from her stool, went to the cottage window, and looked out at the murky rainswept village. Most of the other dwellings were dark. 'Weather fit for Salka, that's what it is. Storms everywhere north of the dividing range, and it's getting colder as well.'

Thalassa finished the last of the sausage, washing it down with the fortified tea. 'That's better. My windtalents only needed a good stoking with hearty fuel. So now I'll bespeak Stergos directly and see what he thinks about all this. And I'll pass on a warning as well. The Source told me that Beynor ordered Conrig to get rid of his brother – send him away so Beynor would have a clear field. I must tell Stergos to take precautions. He could be in considerable danger.'

'And not only from Beynor,' Cray remarked. She reached for her cloak, which hung on a peg by the door. 'I need to do some work in the longhouse, so I'll leave you to your windspeaking. Poor Stergos! Why don't we invite him to join us here? Beynor's ascendance puts him in an untenable position with the Sovereign. And let's ask him to bring along that chunk of raw moonstone Prince Corodon gave him. We three might experiment with it.'

'So we might,' Thalassa said with a slow smile. 'I've been thinking about the old manuscript that inspired young Vra-Bramlow to propose the Demon Seat climb to his brothers in the first place. Its author claimed that the mountain was the site of miracles granted to worthy petitioners many years ago. Which must mean that the Remnant used uncarved moonstone mineral as a Sky-to-Ground magical conduit long before Prince Orrion's adventure! Maybe the good Lights don't require an entire mountaintop to do the job . . .'

'Did you tell the Source about Corodon's two souvenirs?'

'It slipped my mind.'

'Then let's keep it a secret from him for now, shall we?' The sweet inhuman face was sly. 'I wonder if the Prince Heritor still has his own piece? I don't suppose we can scry it.'

'No. It's imperceptible to wind-sensibilities, just as the finished sigils are. Hmmm . . .' The sorceress stood rooted, mulling new possibilities. Then she strode to the door and began to don her own cloak. 'I've changed my mind, Cray. We don't dare waste time sending warning messages to Stergos. We need to snatch him! Otherwise, he might do something very foolish.' She frowned. 'Or someone else might.'

'Snatch? Through a subtle corridor, you mean?' Cray's emerald eyes had gone huge.

'Yes. And I think both of us will have to go for Stergos in case we run into trouble. Spinning a corridor large enough for three will be hard on us, dear, but I think it's become imperative. We can build the portal in one of the empty long-house workrooms for safety's sake. Let's hurry. I have a fore-boding that urgency may be required.'

'Right.' Cray opened the door and a blast of wind-borne rain smote their exposed faces. 'Will you conjure the umbrella-spell, or shall I?'

Garon Curtling had bespoken his master several times during the night while hastening back to Boarsden Castle with the stolen treasure of Lord Kilian. Even though he could see in the dark, the rain had slowed his progress and he was in desperate need of rest. He had worn out two horses and pressed a third to the limit by the time he finally reached the Firedrake Bridge and let Beynor know that he was only an hour or so distant.

Windsearching across the River Malle as he urged his faltering mount to a last burst of speed, Garon oversaw that masses of troops in the great encampments were already on the march in the stormy dawn, proceeding west toward the Wold Road in endless torchlit columns, four abreast if mounted and six abreast afoot. Before long, he knew, the Sovereign and his generals, along with the battle-leaders of Tarn and Didion, would also quit the castle.

In their last wind-conversation, Beynor had informed Garon that he intended to accompany the Sovereign, but he said nothing about taking the younger wizard with him. Garon had prudently held his peace about the matter; he still hadn't made up his mind whether or not to accept the Conjure-King's offer of employment.

More important was Beynor's command that Garon meet him privately within Boarsden Castle as soon as he returned. The reason for the meeting had at first made the renegade Brother of Zeth wild with anticipation. Later, the momentary excitement was obliterated by a saddle-weariness that threatened to rob him of his senses.

Garon arrived at last in the teeming castle ward around the seventh hour of morning, feeling more dead than alive and splashed from head to toe with mud. Flinging the reins of his jaded horse to an ostler, he hoisted the weighty bags of treasure and stumbled into the vestibule of the Wizards' Tower where Beynor was lodged. The long climb up the winding staircase carrying the heavy burden almost finished him. His heart was bursting and he had to pause for breath at every landing. Fortunately, almost everyone he met was going in the opposite direction and paid no attention to him at all.

There was no one on guard in the corridor outside Beynor's room. Before he could lift his hand to knock, the door opened.

'Quickly, inside with you!' Beynor exclaimed. He locked the door behind Garon and re-established the cover-spell. 'Where are Kilian's inactive sigils?'

The younger man gaped at him. Beynor was wearing the riding habit of the Brothers of the Mystical Order of Zeth. An authentic-looking gold gammadion pendant hung from a chain around his neck. 'Speak up, man,' he snapped.

'In there,' Garon gasped. He dropped the saddlebags with a thud and pointed to one of them. 'Those bloody things must weigh over five stone, all told. For God's sake, give me water!' He would have collapsed, but Beynor's magic caught him and lowered him into a chair beside the door.

'Rest there, my friend,' Beynor said. 'I'll fetch something.' He returned in a few moments with a beaker of water and a small dish of confections. 'Suck one of these herbal pastilles. It will restore your strength.'

Garon relaxed as fresh vitality animated his spent body. 'Ah, that's better! Am I in time, master? The ward below is a turmoil of caparisoned horses and splendidly armed men.'

'King Conrig and the great battle-leaders of Cathra, Tarn, and Didion are gathering for a last-minute emotional rally before riding out to join their troops on the road. We have a good hour to spare. I'm very pleased with you, Garon. You've done exceptionally well.'

'Thank you, master.'

Beynor proffered the dish of pastilles again, popping one into his own mouth. 'Eat another of these. They're good for aches and pains as well as banishing fatigue. And divest yourself of those filthy things. I have fresh clothes waiting for you. There are two sorts: civilian garb if you've decided to go your own way, and a habit of the Zeth Brethren to match my own, if you choose to work with me. Take your pick. A tub of warm water stands before the fire behind that folding screen, along with soap, sponges, a towel and a razor.'

The haggard features of the besmirched magicker gained vital color and his sagging body straightened. He trudged away to bathe, peeling off his sodden garments and dropping them on the floor behind him.

Beynor put the saddlebags on a table and began unpacking them. Most of the weight was sacks of gold coinage, which the sorcerer set aside. The true riches were in four opaque steel-mesh bags with magical seals . . . and perhaps in a little wooden box tucked into an old oilskin sack. He broke the enchantment on the first mesh bag easily and found it packed full of luminous strings of large pearls. The second bag contained star-ruby cabochons and the third held quantities of square-cut emeralds as green as new grass. The last bag was crammed with faceted diamonds; none of them were smaller than pease, and several dozen were almost the size of hazelnuts. He'd never seen their like anywhere.

Beynor smiled in satisfaction as he pulled the drawchains shut again and ensorcelled their locks with the anti-theft spell. Finally, he lifted the lid of the small box and tipped out the five minor sigils. One was a thin-walled short cylinder that would fit a man's little finger. The other four were pendants: a square, a pentagon with a hole in its center, a tiny pyramid, and a delicate carving shaped something like a fairy-cap mushroom. All were devoid of the soft radiance of uncanny power.

Beynor examined each one with interest. They would be extremely useful if the Potency's abolition of their magic could be reversed. But prudence was called for.

He opened the purse at his belt and unwrapped the simple moonstone disk. Once it had been fastened to the cover of a book containing information about Great Stones and their activation. The book was gone forever but under certain circumstances the rondelle itself was able to summon the Great Light charged with the care and activation of sigils.

If the Sky being chose to respond.

While Garon finished restoring himself, Beynor lowered the wind-barrier guarding his room and cast about with his keen seekersense, overseeing the meeting of battle-commanders. It was unshielded by couverture and the leaders were taking turns making brave speeches asserting their courage and resolve. Even as the Conjure-King watched, the gathering dissolved and the more exalted participants scattered to various parts of the castle to bid farewell to loved ones and deal with other details of departure. High King Conrig led his brother Stergos into a small solar adjacent to the conference room and closed the door. Earl Marshal Parlian Beorbrook and Prince Dyfrig walked away conversing so discreetly that Beynor was unable to read anything from their lips.

'I'm ready, master,' Garon said. 'Shall we try to activate the sigils?'

Beynor snapped the windthread of his scrying and opened

his eyes to find his stalwart henchman standing there transformed into a Brother of the Mystical Order.

'I must warn you, Garon. There could be a risk to both our lives in this attempt, but I think the danger is small. If it does work you'll have five precious magical tools of your own – subject to the usual conditions of operation, of course.'

'Tell me what to do. I feel lucky!'

Beynor explained and had Garon rehearse pronunciation of the Salka-language responses to the Light's ritual queries. When the sorcerer was satisfied, he handed over the disk and the dead Concealer pendant. 'Try it, then. If the responding Light seems angry, separate the two stones at once and the contact between the Sky and Ground Realms should be severed, preserving you from any harm.'

The younger man pressed the two pieces of moonstone tightly together and held his breath, waiting for them to begin glowing and suffusing him with pain, the first signs that one of the Beaconfolk had taken notice of him. He waited for the inhuman voice to thunder the portentous questions inside his brain.

Nothing happened.

'Shite!' Garon moaned. He tried the Interpenetrator sigil, then the three others. The results were the same.

Beynor sighed. 'What a pity.' He took back the disk and replaced it in his purse. 'Keep the dead sigils if you wish,' he told the disappointed Garon. 'And don't look so downhearted. You still have your ten per cent of Kilian's treasure.'

Garon gripped the golden gammadion pendant at his neck. 'I suppose this is only a counterfeit without magical powers.'

The Conjure-King's reply was good-natured. 'Of course it is, you sodding blockhead! So is my own. Do you think I'd risk using real ones?'

'I suppose not,' the other said with a sigh. 'But I sorely

miss the gammadion's augmentation of my rather mediocre natural talent.'

'Do you also miss the ability of your former superiors in the Order to track your every move through the damned thing?' Beynor inquired snidely. 'Bah! Be my loyal man and I'll teach you more high sorcery than you ever dreamed of. Well – what do you say? Are you with me?'

'I accept your offer of employment and agree to serve you to the best of my ability.' Garon's eyes flickered. 'Until we decide that the arrangement is no longer mutually advantageous.'

'Done,' Beynor said. 'Now put on your raincloak and pack the gold into those new saddlebags, over there. I'll take charge of the jewels myself. We'll divide everything up later, when the royal entourage halts for the night.'

'Royal entourage?' Garon looked puzzled.

'We'll be riding with members of the Sovereign's personal staff and sharing his accommodation. I'll disguise our faces with a small spell so no one recognizes us or thinks to ask impudent questions. I don't think I can risk a genuine shield of couverture. One of the senior Brothers might detect it.'

'But won't Lord Stergos be suspicious if two extra Brothers join the group?'

The Conjure-King laughed. 'I don't think we'll have to worry about that.'

The summons had come to Vra-Bramlow Wincantor as he broke his fast at dawn with the other novices attached to the Cathran Court. It had been a sad meal, for Bram expected that he would not see his Brethren again for a long time; they were to ride out with the army's Corps of Alchymists today, while he would have to stay behind, attending his royal mother as the Sovereign had ordered.

The note from Queen Risalla only bade Bram to come at

once, so he left his food half-eaten and hastened to
Boarsden Castle's Octagonal Tower and presented himself
at her apartment.

'Please come in, my lord. The Queen's Grace is very
anxious to see you.' The lady-in-waiting who had opened
the door sank in a respectful curtsey to Risalla's eldest son.

'Thank you, Lady Sivara.'

The antechamber and large sitting room were crowded
with coffers, fully packed panniers, and other baggage, for
the queen and her retainers would be quitting Boarsden and
returning to Cala Palace as soon as the roads cleared. The
novice followed Lady Sivara through the small salon and into
the dressing room.

The queen sat on a stool, studying her reflection in a hand-
mirror. She was a small, plain-faced woman with brilliant
blue eyes and an air of quiet determination. Her hair, once
a lustrous honey-brown, was now almost entirely grey, even
though she was only one-and-forty. The elaborately bejew-
eled Didionite coiffure she had worn at last night's banquet
to please her brother Somarus had been transformed into
the simpler coronet of braids she had adopted as Queen of
Cathra.

Risalla rose, embraced Bramlow, and ordered the ladies
and tiring-maids to leave the room. She led her son to a
settee and drew him down beside her.

'Bram, dear, after giving the matter careful thought, I've
changed my mind. Rather than return to the palace with
me, I want you to accompany Corodon and his Heart
Companions as they attend the King's Grace in the defense
of Tarn. Your father has acceded to my request.'

He was unable to hide his surprise. 'But His Grace said
that Coro would have to go with the Southern Wing and
Earl Marshal Parlian —'

'My royal husband informed me this morning that he's

had a complete change of heart about about Coro's aptitudes. He says he misjudged the boy, found hidden depths to his character he never appreciated before. His Grace wants Corodon at his side. And I want *you* to stay close to your brother.'

'May I ask why?'

'I love Coro dearly, but I have no illusions about him. He is the Heritor now, for better or worse. But he doesn't understand that he might soon face dangers more insidious than the Salka monsters. To survive, he'll need your help. Magical help.'

'Mother, I'm sorry. I don't understand.'

Her voice was unsteady. 'Since the Salka invasion, your father has changed. There's a new darkness about him, something I can't express to you in words. It frightens me. And your brother . . . Coro is not an insightful person, Bram. He never looks beneath the surface of anyone, considering that they might be other than they profess to be. He has no idea how ruthless some people can be if they feel threatened.'

Bramlow took his mother's hand in both of his. 'Surely *Father* can't see Corodon as a menace! For all his faults, the lad hasn't a perfidious bone in his body. He idolizes His Grace.'

'That may be part of the problem.' The queen looked away, but not before Bramlow had seen a flicker of fear in her eyes.

'Just what is it you want me to do, Mother?'

'Safeguard your brother as best you can with your magical talent, even if this means scrying for perils in the most unlikely quarters. I believe Corodon is truly free of malice, but he might be tempted to make disastrous decisions, not realizing the evil inherent in them.'

Vra-Bramlow dropped her hand as though it had become red hot. 'Tempted by Father? Is that what you mean?'

But Queen Risalla only stared at the sturdy young novice

with unblinking eyes, then rose from the couch and went
to summon her women.

'Come and share a stirrup-cup with me before we go, Gossy,'
the Sovereign said. They were alone together in the solar
next to the chamber where the rally of battle-leaders had
taken place. 'There's something I want to ask you.'

'Con, what is it?' Stergos waited smiling.

The High King filled two silver goblets from a decanter on
the sideboard then turned, holding both cups without
offering the wine, a frown of deep concern darkening his
face.

'I've received some appalling news. Earlier this morning,
Beynor informed me that the Salka regular army of fifty
thousand strong is being reinforced by a large number of
reserve fighters sent from Fenguard.'

'Great Zeth! Our troops were already outnumbered. But
now –'

'This second force is swimming around the south end of
the island to join the others. I haven't yet told our people
since the fact can't be confirmed – nor do I wish to cast a
pall of hopelessness over our new campaign before we even
march out of Boarsden.'

'How did the Conjure-King learn about the reinforcements?'

'He didn't say, but it doesn't matter. The bad tidings just
serve to confirm a belief I'd entertained for some time: the
only chance we have of defeating this horde of fiends is
through sigil sorcery.'

Stergos took a step toward the king, his eyes wide with
horror. 'Brother, no!'

'Without Ullanoth's magic, I never would have been victorious in Holt Mallburn. You know that's true! And our navy
would never have defeated the Didionites in the Battle of

Cala Bay without the uncanny winds summoned by her Weathermaker.'

'Ullanoth is dead, Con. Her sigils are lost and so are the ones comprising Darasilo's Trove. Even if we had any of the devilish things at our disposal, we lack the means to bring them to life.'

'Gossy, Beynor has three Great Stones from the trove. I saw them.'

'No! It's some trick of his!' The Doctor Arcanorum clasped his gammadion pendant and besought the wind: Tell me this isn't true.

It is true, said the Source, *as it had to be.*

Conrig said, 'Beynor has had the things for years, apparently, and he knows how to activate them. I know the bastard can't use the sigils himself. But I can.'

The alchymist was silent, thinking about the wind-spoken affirmation for a moment before speaking in an incredulous whisper. 'Beynor has actually offered the stones to you?'

'Yes.' The king's gaze shifted. He still held the filled goblets close to his chest. 'I had to tell you, Gossy. To learn your reaction. One of Beynor's conditions for handing the stones over was that you resign as my adviser, retire from my service and not interfere as he teaches me how to use the sigils against our foe.'

Stergos felt as though his soul had fled his body. He seemed to float near the ceiling, looking down upon the two of them, seeing the brilliant red wine inside the silver cups. One cup of wine seemed to shimmer . . .

He gripped the gammadion tighter and knew. He said: Source, I can't stop him. His decision is adamant. He's wanted this for too long. Even if I revealed his secret he would not be stopped. Is this also true?

It is true, as it had to be.

When Stergos was able to speak, his voice seemed to belong to someone else. 'What sigils does Beynor possess?'

'A Weathermaker, an Ice-Master that can freeze water – including the fluids within living bodies – and a Destroyer.'

'A Destroyer.' Stergos was himself again, calm and unafraid. 'So you are determined to go ahead with this scheme, even though I beg you with all my heart to abandon it? And I do, Con, for the sake of your own soul's peace as well as the future of our beloved island.'

'Nothing you can say will dissuade me. Will you agree to go away – perhaps to Zeth Abbey – and do nothing to hinder me?'

'I cannot.' The reply was one of quiet resignation. 'It is my solemn duty to oppose you openly in this heinous thing.'

Conrig gave a small sigh. He was smiling gently. 'Well, I don't have the sigils yet, Gossy. And maybe that slippery viper never intended to give them up at all. This might only be a plot of his to drive us two apart, so that he can insinuate himself into my inner circle of advisers . . . At any rate, there's no need for us to discuss this matter further now.' He held out one of the goblets. 'Here. Drink with me. Then we'll mount up and ride out of this cursèd Didionite castle. We've tarried here fretting and twiddling our thumbs far too long. I must take action, Brother! I *must.* Try to understand.'

The Royal Alchymist accepted the cup. 'Are you certain that this is what you really want?'

'Yes,' said the Sovereign. He added in a low voice, 'I'm sorry.'

Stergos said, 'As am I. Nevertheless, I give you my blessing, Con, hoping that you may yet realize what it is that you do.'

Then he drank.

Thalassa Dru and Cray emerged from the interface of the subtle corridor into the reality of the castle solar and found him seated in an armchair next to the large leaded window, seeming to look out at the grey and weeping landscape with a serene face. There was no one else in the room.

'Too late,' murmured the sorceress sadly.

'For him and for Conrig Ironcrown as well, I'm afraid.' The Green Woman stood on tiptoe and closed the eyes of Stergos Wincantor. She then opened the wallet at his belt, searched it, and shook her head. Unfastening the neck of his riding habit, she found the golden chain of his gammadion. A longer thong of leather inside his linen shirt held a small cloth bag. Cray opened it. 'Empty.'

'Stergos must have hidden the piece of raw moonstone elsewhere,' Thalassa said. 'We'll never find it.'

'We'd better get out of here,' Cray said. 'His gammadion will already have signaled his demise to the other Brethren.'

'The Source might know where the bit of Demon Seat mineral is. Are you sure you don't want to tell him about it – and about Prince Coro's piece as well?'

'More certain than ever. Let's go back to my house. I *would* like to ask our esteemed leader why he didn't warn us that our poor friend was in danger of being slain by his own brother!'

'Why bother?' Conjure-Princess Thalassa Dru inquired despondently. 'We already know what he'll say: *Events are unfolding as they must.*'

The two of them re-entered the invisible entrance to the subtle corridor and vanished from sight.

FIFTEEN

Duke Kefalus Vandragora had quietly given orders to Baron Ising and to the three men-at-arms escorting Casya Pretender to his north-country fortress: they were not to let his grand-daughter out of their sight for a moment. She was a wilful and reckless creature, he said, capable of anything, with bigger bollocks than a man twice her age, an altogether worthy Queen Regnant of Didion – if she might only stay alive long enough to assume the throne.

There was no problem at the first night's stop, when they all bedded down in a cow byre in the open countryside. But on the second night, when the rain began, they stayed at a little inn on the shore of Firedrake Water where the hostess refused to compromise her notions of propriety. The girl would sleep on a pallet in a storage cubby next to the kitchen, *not* share a room with the men. A newly installed bolt inside her door would ensure that she slept safe and undisturbed. Since the innwife was a formidable dame with a moustache and muscular arms that could have snapped the spine of a hog, her will prevailed.

Casya went meekly to bed, but she did not sleep. Instead, when the establishment had settled down for the night, she slipped the bolt, crept out through the scullery, and crossed the storm-swept yard to the side entrance of the stable. A dim lantern hung from a cross-beam. In an empty stall she found the simpleminded old man who served as the inn's ostler, asleep in a pile of hay.

After rousing him with a none-too-gentle nudge of her boot, she knelt, held up a silver quarter-mark coin in front of his face, and whispered, 'Would you like to have this, my man?'

His bloodshot eyes opened wide. The silver would probably equal his wage for a month. 'Oh, yes, mistress!'

She rose and stood over him. 'Then saddle up the sorrel with the white blaze and the big dapple grey. Strap a sack of goodly feed to each cantle, and have the beasts ready to leave here as quick as you can hop.'

'But why, mistress?' the ancient whined. 'The night ain't half gone and it's pissin' rain fit to drown frogs!'

'Do you want this money or don't you?' she snapped. 'My dear uncle and I were abducted by the three warriors we rode in with. Those scoundrels want me to marry their lecher of a father who's thirty years older than I. But I intend to escape their evil clutches.'

The ostler chortled. 'Good for ye, lass!' Then his face clouded. 'But what happens t'me in the morn? At best, I'll get a beatin' for not raisin' the alarm.'

'Before we go, my uncle and I will tie you up and gag you gently and leave you to snooze in your nest. When you're found, say you were overpowered. Tell the warriors that you heard us say we were heading south, toward Boarsden.'

'Well . . . I could do that, I s'pose.'

'Do you have torch brands available?' she asked him.

'Aye, pineheart well plugged with resin. Won't be quenched easily in the wet. But –'

'I'll need four. Lash them to the grey's saddle with the feed. You'll get an extra two pennies for the lot and keep the change. I'll fetch my uncle now and be back directly.'

She left before he could object, re-entered the inn, and slunk up the stairs to the guest accommodation. Loud snoring covered the creak of hinges as she opened the door of the front room.

At the second tweak of his ear, Baron Ising came awake with a startled grunt. Before he could speak, a hand pressed firmly over his mouth.

'Not a word!' Casya whispered fiercely. 'Up with you. We're getting out of here. If you make a row and wake the others, I'll wring your scrawny old neck.'

His eyes, rheumy with sleep, could barely identify her in the darkness of the room he shared with the three warriors. She grabbed the baron's boots, indicated his bags and cloak with a peremptory gesture, and swept her thumb eloquently toward the open door.

A moment later they were both creeping through the deserted taproom toward the kitchen. He muttered, 'What the bloody hell d'you think you're doing, you daft wench?'

'Keep a civil tongue in your head, my lord. I'm not sitting out the Salka war in Grandpa's castle.' Casya thrust his boots at him. 'Put these on while I get my things.'

When she returned with her own saddlebags, dressed in male riding gear, he scowled at her. 'Your Majesty, you promised Duke Kefalus –'

'And I intend to break that promise to accomplish a greater good,' she stated in a wintry voice. 'Come on.' She went out the back door with him trailing reluctantly after.

'What greater good?' he demanded peevishly, stumbling through the mud. The rain was no longer torrential, but it still fell steadily. One of the tall stable doors was open now and the lantern inside swung in the cold east wind blowing off the big lake, casting moving shadows like spectres. Another lantern, giving much more light, hung at the entry to the inn courtyard just off the highroad. It was intended to guide benighted travelers to shelter, and one like it was required outside every public lodging by the law of the Sovereignty.

When Casya ignored his question, Baron Ising continued to chide her. 'No one's going to let you lead a troop of real soldiers into battle, you know! And by now, your gang of friendly brigands have scattered to the four winds. You aren't Casya the Wold Wraith anymore, luring Somarus's men on a merry chase through the bogs and moorlands. You're just a saucy chit waiting to be handed a crown on a platter.'

She gave him a haughty glare. 'I'm more than that, damn your eyes, and you know it! . . . So do the Green Men. And the Morass Worms.'

'Hmph. That was then,' he said obscurely. 'This is now.'

Inside the stable, The old ostler was tightening the knot on the final bundle of oats and torchwood. He knuckled his grimy forehead in salute. 'All ready, mistress. Quick enough for ye?'

She handed over the coins. 'Well done. Go lie down and I'll bind and muffle you.' She said to Ising, 'You strap on our bags and check the saddle girths.'

The baron was grumbling blasphemies under his breath when she returned. She said, 'The old fellow has promised to tell our guards that we went south. But I'm going west instead, to the track that follows the Upper Malle. Then I'll head north to Black Hare Lake. Where *you* go, old friend, is your decision. If you choose, you can even unsaddle your horse and crawl back to bed.'

Ising Bedotha hoisted his tangled brows. 'Black Hare Lake, you say? But you can't – not the Green Morass!'

'I did it before. With Cray's help, to be sure, and by a

different route. But I'll find other Green Men to help me re-
establish contact with the worms, or else hunt them down
myself.'

'Oh, lass, lass!' the baron moaned. 'What can you possibly
accomplish, even if the horrible things agree to confer with
you? The focus of the Salka war is completely different now.
The crucial battles will be fought in Tarn or on the far side
of Didion where the pirates dwell. Nowhere near the Green
Morass.'

'You don't understand how the worms fight.'

'And you do?' he jeered.

'I showed them how to use their uncanny powers to best
advantage. How to feint and bluff and hippity-hop about
and lure the foe into pincer-traps after the Salka sigil-bearers
had wasted their magical energies. Human military tactics
allowed the Morass Worms to halt the first Salka invasion,
even though they were greatly outnumbered. I promised
the creatures a territory of their own as a reward, and I
intend to see that they get it. Once I explain this new situation, they'll listen and do as I say, just as they did before.'

'What if they don't? What then, eh?' Ising's face had gone
crimson with frustration.

She mounted her spirited sorrel horse and looked down
at him with a smile of supreme confidence. 'They *will*
listen . . . I dare not tarry here any longer arguing. Will you
come with me, or not?'

He uttered a great groan. 'Great Starry Wain – what else
can I do?'

'Good. I'm very grateful, dear Ising.'

With difficulty, he hoicked his left foot into the stirrup,
then pulled himself up with painful slowness by gripping the
mane of the patient grey. When he finally settled into the
saddle, gasping and cursing, he bestowed a baleful glower
on her. 'It's the joint evil, Your Majesty. A bugger in the cold

and damp when you're a creaky old fart like me and there's no mounting-block.'

'I'm sorry,' Casya said, lowering her head. 'I didn't know.'

'Queens shouldn't apologize,' said Ising Bedotha. 'Chin up, lass! Now, let's ride out of here at a dead-slow walk until we're well away from the inn. Then we can light the first torch.'

At breakfast in Rockyford Way Station's common room, Maudrayne had learned from a fellow guest at their crowded table that the Army of the Sovereignty was redeploying in two wings. It was already on the march and would reach the station that very afternoon. By the time she and the two young armigers rode out of the place, heading north, she had worked out a tentative plan for meeting Dyfrig.

'Tormo, Durin, now is the time for us to part company,' she told the Kyle brothers. Their horses were wading the wide boulder-strewn stream that gave the nearby hostel its name.

'Oh, no!' both boys protested.

Tormo added, 'We promised Countess Morilye we'd protect you. We can't leave you alone. It would sully the name of the House of Kyle.'

'Follow me and I'll explain,' she said, turning off the high-road as they gained the other side of the brook. A narrow path alongside the bank led to a dense thicket of alder and sallow that gave shelter from the drizzle and hid them completely from the eyes of passers-by. Maude dismounted, but held up a hand to stop the squires when they would have joined her.

'I've learned that the Army of the Sovereignty is going to split into two parts because no one knows where the Salka invaders will land. King Conrig and High Sealord Sernin will lead the largest contingent to the vicinity of Castle Direwold, near the Tarnian border, where it will wait until there's news of the Salka. If it seems that the monsters intend to invade Tarn, then this wing of the army will hasten over Frost Pass to defend whatever Tarnian cities are threatened. I want you to join this force. You'll certainly find some of your Kyle kinfolk amongst the warriors.'

'But what will become of you, my lady?' Tormo's freckled face was pinched with worry.

She spoke in a low tone, so the younger armiger could not hear. 'A second wing of the Sovereign Army will be poised to defend the west coast of Didion. It will camp at Lake of Shadows. My son will surely be part of this group, since it is being led by his adoptive father, Earl Marshal Parlian Beorbrook. Meeting with Dyfrig is the reason for this journey of mine to Didion. It's vitally important for me to speak to my son before he rides into battle. We have not seen one another since he was four years old.' She began to unstrap the saddlebags, bedroll, armor, and weapons from her saddle. 'Now, I want you to return to the highroad. Take my horse with you. It might betray my hiding place.'

Understanding dawned on Tormo's stunned face. 'If you are indeed the mother of Prince Dyfrig Beorbrook, then –'

'Be quiet and listen to me,' she said. 'Ride north to Elderwold, which is sure to be the army's next stop tomorrow night. Wait there for the outriders to arrive and present yourselves to them as noble volunteers. You'll be welcomed, I'm certain of it. Tarn needs every swordsman it can muster. I'll remain here in hiding all day. Tonight, when the entourage of King Conrig and Lord Sernin sleeps at Rockyford, my son will be part of the group. I'll seek him out. He'll take care of me from then on.'

The older boy said, 'Are you sure you don't want us to stay?'

'It's more important for you to defend your homeland. I'm

in no danger now.' She handed the reins of her horse to Durin. 'Go along, my dear young friends. And if you should ever be presented to the High Sealord, pass on to him affectionate greetings from his long-lost niece – but do it secretly, for I have enemies in high places.'

'I understand, Your Grace,' Tormo said. 'And I shall make certain that my little brother does, too. Your secret is safe with us. It has been a great honor to serve you. Farewell.'

He turned his mount about and beckoned for Durin to follow, leading the other horse.

The royal herald dashed across the open ward of Boarsden Castle, heedless of the raindrops wilting his splendid tabard, and handed the Sovereign's message to the earl marshal even as he and the members of his general staff guided their mounts toward the gatehouse and prepared to take to the road.

Parlian Beorbrook turned aside and reined in beneath the overhang of the bakehouse, unrolled the parchment and scanned it, then called for the others to gather close. His face had gone wan with shock.

'My friends, here's melancholy news from the High King. I'll read it. *To the Earl Marshal of the Realm: Let it be known that my beloved brother, the Royal Alchymist Vra-Stergos Wincantor, on this morning suddenly and tragically departed this earthly life. The cause of death has been determined by my physicians to be failure of the heart. In his last words, as he expired in my arms, Lord Stergos asked that the departure of the Sovereign Army from Boarsden not be delayed for his obsequies. We will honor his request. Three days hence, when the road has cleared, a cortege of his fellow Brethren will carry my brother's body to Zeth Abbey for interment. I ask that you join me in praying a peaceful repose for this great and noble benefactor of our realm. From Conrig Wincantor, Sovereign of High Blenholme. Given on this Eighteenth Day of the*

Harvest Moon, in the Chronicle Year One Thousand One Hundred Forty-Nine.'

The stunned group of noble officers and aides murmured and shook their heads. After a moment, the old general said, 'We will obey His Grace's command. All of you – ride on ahead. Dyfrig, attend me closely. You too, Master Haydon, and your apprentice.'

Parlian let the group of two dozen or so riders precede him through the barbican and across the moat. Prince Dyfrig remained at his side along with Deveron and Induna, who were disguised as Tarnians.

The earl marshal said, 'This is a sorry day for the Sovereignty.'

The prince, who had hardly known Stergos, was more bewildered than saddened by his unexpected demise. 'The Royal Alchymist was only two-score-and-ten years old and seemed in excellent health. Who would have thought he had a weak heart?'

'No one,' Parlian said. He repeated himself in a dull voice. 'No one at all.'

'I felt his dying,' Deveron said unexpectedly, 'although I did not believe that it was my place to speak of it. It happened shortly before you joined our group, my lord. As the soul fled, I hid myself in a corner of the stables and used what talent I could muster to discover what might have happened to the Royal Alchymist. He was always very kind to me and I considered him a friend and a colleague in magic.'

'You scried the very death scene?' Dyfrig was astounded.

'Enough to come to a terrible conclusion, Your Grace,' Deveron replied. 'I regret to tell you that Lord Stergos perished not of heart failure, but of poisoning. There was – this is hard to explain to persons without talent – a distinctive aspect to the alchymist's fading life-aura, one that connotes a mortal affront to the body, an unnatural separation of the soul inhabiting it. The royal brothers had apparently been drinking wine together. Stergos did indeed die in the king's arms, and his mind windspoke a few final words that were perceptible to me. He said, "It doesn't hurt, Con. Don't be concerned."'

'Good God,' the earl marshal murmured. 'Then what happened?'

'I scried the king as he carried his brother's body to a chair. Then my trance was broken by the trumpet-call forming up your retinue outside the stable, and I joined you and my wife and the others.'

'But who could have committed such a despicable crime?' the prince cried. 'And for what motive?'

'One villain who comes readily to mind,' Parlian Beorbrook said, 'is Beynor of Moss. We all know how he must have resented the Royal Alchymist's conjuration of Bazekoy's pearl, which limited his powers. On the other hand, in a Privy Council meeting yesterday the High King told me that he intended to banish Beynor to some distant city on the east coast of Didion. Unless the Mossy bastard administered a very slow-acting poison during that damned feast last night, he had no opportunity to get at Stergos. He was kept under heavy guard all night and was to be taken away before dawn this morning.'

'My suspicions also fell upon Beynor,' Deveron said. 'I made a point of scrying his whereabouts, even though my windsearching faculty is not yet fully recovered. I didn't have to look far. He's still in Boarsden Castle.'

'Are you certain of this?' the earl marshal demanded.

'He's disguised his features with magic, but his distinctive talent is unmistakable to . . . one such as I.'

'Codders!' said Prince Dyfrig. 'We must warn the King's Grace!'

'I think he already knows,' Deveron said.

The earl marshal turned in the saddle. 'What are you trying to say, man?'

'My lord, I scried the two of them conversing alone together in the vestibule of the Wizards' Tower. Beynor wears the riding habit of the Sovereign's own Corps of Alchymists. I have no doubt that he'll soon be riding out as a member of the royal entourage.'

'But –' Prince Dyfrig was at a loss for words. Finally he blurted, 'What does it mean?'

'I don't know,' Beorbrook said. 'But I intend to find out.'

'My artisans worked all through the night in order to finish this first sigil. Colleagues, our new Subtle Gateway is ready to be empowered!'

The Salka Master Shaman held up the miniature door carving for the admiration of the other three Eminences. Beams of morning sunlight penetrated the audience chamber of Royal Fenguard Castle like bright omens of hope. The heavy squalls that had lashed the Darkling Estuary of Moss for the past two days had passed on to the west.

'Is it perfect?' the First Judge asked nervously. 'No inner flaws?'

'There are none,' Kalawnn said, 'and no imperfections in the crafting of it, either. If Ugusawnn is willing to take the considerable risk of overloading his brain with its pain-debt, the sigil can be used at once.'

'Ahroo! You dare to impugn my courage?' The Supreme Warrior bellowed his outrage. 'I told you that I'm prepared to go to the summit of Demon Seat and carry back as much raw moonstone as my tentacles can lift.'

The wizened Conservator of Wisdom uttered a testy sigh. 'No one doubts your bravery, Ugusawnn. Only your good sense! Our fighters will have great need of you in the upcoming invasion. But if your stamina is depleted by trips to and from Demon Seat, and then by a third lengthy journey to the Western Ocean before you even assume the leadership –'

'We agreed that I would do this,' the Warrior reminded the others. 'I'm confident that I can endure the necessary suffering and recover quickly. Several days remain before the first of our warriors reach Terminal Bay. I'll be prudent and only transport the best, most perfect pieces of mineral. Now that the tempest has abated, I can examine the samples on the mountaintop under a clear sky and return quickly, before the full impact of the pain-debt overtakes me.'

'If only we could scry the moonstone formations on the summit and advise you,' the Conservator said with regret. 'Then Kalawnn might be able to indicate in advance which specimens were most suitable.'

'Well, he can't do it.' Ugusawnn spoke with grouchy finality. 'The mountaintop is just as unscryable as sigils are. Shall we get on with the empowerment ritual, or continue dithering? Every minute wasted is one that can't be spent making more Great Stones.'

'He's right,' the First Judge conceded. He slithered off the dais, went to a golden cabinet ornamented with amber, and took from it a stack of thin ivory plaques closely inscribed with writing, strung together at one corner with a golden chain. 'Here's a copy of the incantation. Let him get started. It's not a short ceremony and we want him to have as much daylight for the search as possible.'

Out of respect (or perhaps as a precaution) the other three Eminences withdrew from the audience chamber, leaving Ugusawnn perched confidently upon his seaweed-heaped couch. He would bespeak them when the sigil was empowered. Kalawnn led the Conservator and the Judge down to the cavern of the lapidaries to show them how work on the Destroyer was progressing. Although the moonstone wand was not nearly so delicate an object as Gateway, its surface was more ornately engraved.

'But as you can see,' The Master Shaman said proudly, 'the carving is nearly complete.'

'How long?' the Judge inquired tersely.

'Three days at most,' Kalawnn said. 'It'll be ready when it's needed. Shall we go into my sanctum and have a small libation?'

The others agreed that a drink would be welcome. They sipped quantities of fermented squid-ink before Kalawnn felt emboldened to voice his secret concerns. 'Colleagues, I would never doubt the Supreme Warrior's greathearted valor for an instant. But it's our solemn responsibility to consider what course of action we might follow if he should become disabled through overuse of one or more of the sigils.'

The Judge said, 'I think it's obvious that we must appoint a deputy wielder. There is a spell of abolition that deactivates sigils safely, unbonding them from one person so that another may re-empower and use them. I also have a copy of that spell. If Ugusawnn overreaches himself and becomes incapacitated, the sigils must be taken away from him and bonded to another. I think you, Master Shaman, are the only plausible candidate. Our revered Wise One is too burdened with years to qualify and I'm too damned fat and sluggish to cavort about on a battlefield.'

'I concur,' said the Conservator of Wisdom. 'Kalawnn, you must agree that we cannot entrust the only Great Stones possessed by our race to an individual of inferior stature. The deputy must be an Eminence.'

The Master Shaman bowed his massive head. His crest had fallen in distress. 'This is a terrible onus you would lay upon me. I'm not a soldier, I'm a scientist and a scholar. I don't know the first thing about generalship –'

'You need not concern yourself with military tactics,' the

Conservator said. 'Our field commanders will do their duty. Your only real responsibility would be putting Destroyer to use. You have the good judgment to wield the terrible Stone properly and to best advantage.'

'Perhaps more astutely than the Supreme Warrior,' the Judge said under his breath.

They debated the matter for a long time, but in the end Kalawnn was forced to agree that no other person could do a better job. And he was, after all, the custodian of the Stone of Stones as well. It was fitting that he take on responsibility for Destroyer and Gateway if Ugusawnn were disabled or killed.

'Very well,' he said at last. 'I will agree. This means, however, that the Warrior will be forced to carry me to the scene of action.'

'Gateway is capable of transporting two Salka,' the Judge said.

'Just barely,' the Conservator added. 'But we have no –'

I have done it! The Supreme Warrior's triumphant windvoice rang in their minds. *The Great Stone is active and bonded to me. The presiding Light said he was gratified by our ingenuity in creating a new sigil of such delicacy and elegance.*

'Congratulations!' the three bespoke him in heartfelt relief. 'Will you wait for us to join you before transporting yourself to Demon Seat?'

Why bother? I'll go at once, taking a byssus-silk net to carry the rocks. When I finish sorting them, I'll bring the load to you in the audience chamber. How long can it take? I'll certainly be back in time for supper. Tell the cook I want dolphin in red dulse sauce and pickled tunnyfish!

But the Supreme Warrior returned long before that.

It was less than half an hour later that he materialized abruptly on the dais, sprawled like a giant sack of blubber across his golden couch, moaning in agony and disappointment. His slick dark hide was roughened and blotched with chilblains, crystals of ice rimmed his discolored mouth and swollen eyelids, and the tips of his tentacular digits were ominously pale. His net was empty. The Subtle Gateway sigil hung safely about his neck, however, alive and glowing.

'Denizens of the Black Abyss!' the Conservator exclaimed. 'What happened?'

'Snow,' Ugusawnn responded in a faint rasp. 'The entire cursèd mountaintop . . . shrouded in hardened snow and thick white ice.'

'Ahroo!' keened the Judge and the Conservator.

'The high altitude,' Kalawnn said. 'Alas, we never took that into consideration. Up there, not all the precipitation fell as rain.'

'Snow . . . not deep,' the Warrior whispered. 'Sunny there, but cold as hell and the ice . . . all the chunks of moonstone stuck together tighter than coral cementing lava blocks. Even exerting my talent to the utmost . . . spending all my bodily strength . . . I couldn't loosen a single piece. As fast as I melted a bit of ice, the wind and cold froze it solid again. *Ahrooo!* . . . Must pay the debt now.' His eyes closed and he fell silent.

'Summon the healers,' the Conservator of Wisdom said to Kalawnn. And to the First Judge: 'Fetch the spell of abolition. I wish to familiarize myself with it.'

The rain slackened after the earl marshal's party had been traveling for several hours. As Deveron and Induna crested a long rise in the land, leaving forested country behind them, they got their first clear view of the Army of the Sovereignty as it traveled along the winding Boar Road. The sound of thousands of hoofbeats filled the air with muted thunder, making normal conversation difficult.

Using windspeech, Induna exclaimed, 'What an awesome sight!'

A vast quadruple column of cloaked and armored riders, many with sodden pennons hanging limply from lances, stretched for leagues across the rolling heath as far as the naked eye could see. With all civilian traffic temporarily suspended, the cavalcade of warriors took up nearly the entire width of the road. Narrow lanes on the left and right flanks had been left clear to accommodate faster riders – dispatch carriers and the retinues of the leaders. It was in one of these that Earl Marshal Parlian, Prince Dyfrig, and their general staff were perforce trotting along single-file, until they reached the broader thoroughfare of the Wold Road at the Castlemont Junction.

Deveron bespoke a response to his wife. 'Even without the Didionites, the armies of Cathra and Tarn and the first supply train number over twenty-six thousand men, half of them afoot. Didion's force of eleven-thousand-odd and the second supply train will start out in three days. Since they are not as disciplined in close marching, it was thought best to postpone their departure until the forces of Cathra and Tarn were well on their way.'

'Overseeing only a part of the great encampment around Boarsden Town,' Induna said, 'I never appreciated how many men and horses had gathered together. How will they find shelter along the way?'

'The warriors and their knight-commanders will bivouac in tents along the wayside at nightfall. But our party and that of the Sovereign and Sealord Sernin – which should be coming up directly behind us – are more fortunate. We'll all sleep under the roof of Rockyford Station tonight, and tomorrow we lodge at Elderwold Fortress. But beyond that, for the foreseeable future, we'll camp out. It'll be a dreary affair, love, if this unseasonable weather continues.'

'I can bear it.' She said nothing for some time. Then: 'Have you tried to windsearch Princess Maude yet?'

'I made a stab at it shortly after we left Boarsden. All I'm certain of thus far is that she's not anywhere between here and Castlemont. I'll try again shortly.'

Conrig rode in a state of total distraction. The enormity of what he had done had finally sunk in, but instead of feeling any sense of guilt or sorrow, he knew only a petulant bewilderment and a sense of betrayal. Gossy was gone! The wise older brother who'd both pricked his conscience and counseled his uncertainties was no longer at his side. There was no one left to whom he might confide his deepest secrets.

He had convinced himself that Stergos's death was an unfortunate necessity. The welfare of the Sovereignty had depended upon it. The alchymist would never have agreed to let him use the Destroyer sigil against the Salka, even though it was the only weapon that could guarantee victory.

Why couldn't his brother have trusted him? Why had Gossy seemed to go willingly to his own doom?

From time to time as he rode, the High King lifted his hand in listless acknowledgment of scattered cheers from the sides of the road. Knots of civilian travelers stood or sat there, some with horses or mules or even wagons pulled up into the muddy verge. All had been forced to move aside and wait until the military passed by. The luckier ones who had heeded the warning of the advance scouts had found refuge in the local hamlets, while the laggards were stranded in the open with only cloaks to fend off the cold drizzle.

Their misery was irrelevant to Conrig Ironcrown. He was only concerned with his own.

Hunched in the saddle, his unseeing eyes and slack features concealed by his hood, and his mount led on a long rein by

Induna, Deveron Austrey soared the uncanny wind on the wings of his talent, searching.

He finally found his quarry in mid-afternoon. She was in a good hiding place and seemed settled in for a long wait. With a sigh he opened his eyes and uncovered his face.

'I have her, Duna,' he bespoke his wife. 'I'll take my reins now. Pass the word to Prince Dyfrig that I'm moving up to talk to him in a few minutes, as soon as I pull my wits together.'

Maudrayne Northkeep waited calmly for the long hours to pass. She had learned patience in a hard school. Her letter to Dyfrig had not told the whole truth about her confinement at Gentian Fell.

During the early weeks of captivity at the hunting lodge, when the truth of her predicament sank in at last, she became restless as a caged leopard. She rejected all of Lord Catclaw's blandishments, snapped and swore at the guards and servants, indulged herself with crying jags, refused food, and demanded quantities of ardent spirits to achieve the oblivion she craved. She neglected her body's care, turning herself into a repulsive harridan, and spent hours planning ways to end her life and thus wreak the ultimate revenge upon the man she hated.

As his fantasy of forbidden love turned to an ugly fiasco, the Lord Constable in desperation sought out the former maidservant of his prisoner, who had been left behind in the Tarnian capital city of Donorvale. Rusgann was not abducted or coerced. She willingly agreed to join her former mistress in exile and do what she could to help her.

Ignoring the screaming tirades and wild mood swings of the princess, the tall homely woman urged only one thing of Maudrayne: *Think of Dyfrig.* With dogged persistence Rusgann pronounced the same phrase again and again. And finally, Maude listened. Worn down by her friend's relentless love, she broke free of the shell of rage and humiliation that truly imprisoned her. Maude's fierce pride bowed to Rusgann's wisdom. She changed.

For Dyfrig's sake, she curtailed her surliness and fits of anger. For his sake she learned to smile again, to laugh, to make friendly conversation, to ask after the wellbeing of the lodge staff and treat them kindly. She thought of Dyfrig as she accompanied herself on the lute, permitted Rusgann to dress her hair and array her in pretty gowns, collected plants for her herbarium and wrote down salient facts about them. She thought of Dyfrig as she reared a peregrine eyas left abandoned in its nest and trained the powerful bird to hunt from her wrist as she and Tinnis Catclaw rode out on the mountainside.

In time Maudrayne even submitted to his embrace, fulfilling their original bargain. But as the constable lay with her she thought not of her lost child but of his father Conrig. When, at the finish of lovemaking, Tinnis Catclaw slept exhausted in the bed beside her, Maude wept silent tears – not from shame but from knowing that her body would not allow her to repudiate her first love. Seeing Conrig with her mind's eye, imagining his touch, she could endure anything.

How I hate him! she would think. Why can't I forget him?

In return for her complaisance, Catclaw had one of his minions installed in Beorbrook Hold, so that regular reports of Prince Dyfrig's progress might be forwarded to her. At long intervals there were even portrait sketches of the growing boy, rendered secretly by some itinerant artist.

So Maude learned patience and tranquility, and planned for the day when she would tell her son the truth about himself. And about her. And about his natural father . . .

Sitting by the side of Rocky Brook, secure beneath a tiny brush-masked shelter of dark oilskin that she had rigged from the branches of saplings with bits of cord, the princess watched the walled compound of Rockyford Way Station some two hundred ells distant. She had seen the arrival of the royal party and even recognized Conrig by the splendor of his black-and-gold panoply. She had not laid eyes on him for twenty years, but her breath faltered and her blood quickened involuntarily at the thought of his nearness. Furious at her betraying flesh, she tore her gaze away from the glittering figure and tried to search out Dyfrig in the throng pouring into the station courtyard. She found the Beorbrook guidon, but those who rode beneath it were so numerous and distant that it was impossible to tell one cloaked man from another as they dismounted and entered the main hostel building after the long day's ride.

She thought of her friend Rusgann. Where was she resting tonight? Had she reached Dyfrig safely and passed on the letter? Was it possible that she might even have accompanied the prince to Rockyford? What a happy reunion it would be if the three of them were together again!

Now the day was ending and the rain had stopped. The smell of woodsmoke and roasting meat was borne to Maudrayne's hiding place, causing her to sigh with yearning as she chewed a heel of rye bread and a knob of hard cheese. She wore her heavy coat of mail, her helmet, and the surcoat of a Beorbrook household knight. Her swordbelt with its varg blade and dagger lay close at hand, ready to be donned. When it was full dark, she'd think how to get inside the station.

A few advance companies of warriors and a single wagon train had crossed the brook after sundown and continued on toward Elderwold. But the main body of the army halted for the night along the roadsides on the opposite side of the water. As the broken clouds turned to purple and gold open fires begin to spring up, illuminating serried ranks of small canvas tents, the occasional knightly pavilion, and rows of picketed horses. Soon she could see thousands of them, extending back along the road to the south like a river of orange stars.

And the troops were not only encamped along the road, but also in the moorlands immediately surrounding the walled Rockyford compound. Hundreds of armed men were bedding down just outside the place. She heard a sergeant bellow orders to a night patrol.

Her heart sank. How in the world would she ever reach Dyfrig? She'd been a fool to think she could slip into the fortified hostel where the ranking leaders of the Sovereignty were staying. The situation was impossible. There was nothing to do but make herself comfortable, eat a bit more food, go to sleep, and stay hidden until the army moved on, leaving her behind. When it was safe, she could buy another horse at the station and make her way to Lake of Shadows –

What was that?

The soft, regular splashing noises were faint but her ears were extremely sharp. Someone was walking through the shallow brook. The increasing volume of the sounds seemed to indicate that the person was coming directly toward her hiding place. A dislodged rock rattled against another. Even though the daylight was nearly gone, she had a clear view of the water.

No one was out there. No animal, no man.

Feeling the hairs creep at the back of her neck, she reached for her shortbow and nocked an arrow.

'Please don't, Princess Maude. I won't harm you.'

She stifled a cry of surprise. The voice was close by, some-where on the near bank of the stream. She hissed, 'Who are you? *Where* are you? You won't take me without a fight!'

'Do you remember the Royal Intelligencer?' the invisible

man said. 'The wild-talented young knight who rescued you and your son from the stronghold on the Desolation Coast sixteen years ago and transported you to your Uncle Sernin's palace with magic? . . . I'm he: Deveron Austrey, once known as Snudge, outlawed by High King Conrig – but a faithful friend to your son, Prince Dyfrig Beorbrook, who has sent me to fetch you.'

'Great God of the Heights and Depths,' Maude whispered. 'Is it really you?' She lowered the bow.

'In the flesh – although not so anyone can notice. I don't want to show myself. There's still enough light left for a casual observer to spot me and wonder why I'm prowling abroad by night. We mustn't take chances. Are you ready to meet Prince Dyfrig?'

'Of course! But how –'

'I wear a moonstone sigil called Concealer. It uses Beaconfolk sorcery to render me, and persons near me, invisible. It will do so for you, my lady. Is there aught you'd take with you?'

She was taken aback, having despaired of seeing her son and now finding that hope rekindled in such an amazing fashion. But another thought came to her, more somber. 'Only let me remove this opal necklace and buckle on my swordbelt, Sir Deveron. I won't go unarmed into a place that harbors Conrig Wincantor.'

'There's no need to worry. I've already arranged things for the safety of you and the prince.'

But she armed herself anyway, tucking her gauntlets into her belt. 'Very well. Let us be off now.'

'I'm going to take your hand,' he said. 'Don't be startled.'

She could not help shuddering at the spectral grip of a damp glove. 'What must I do?'

'Only stay close to me, my lady, or risk popping suddenly into view. Here we go: FASH AH!'

One moment she was poised uncertainly with one hand extended, and then, as he pronounced the strange words, her own body vanished. She moaned. 'Oh, how queer a feeling! I'm bodiless, yet substantial. Sir – I don't think I dare move. I'd surely trip and fall.'

Deveron chuckled. 'Being invisible can be unnerving at first, but you'll soon get used to it. Here . . . take hold of this strap. It's fastened to my belt. Just let me draw you along. We'll walk slowly back to the road and use it to approach the station.'

'But what if the troops –' She broke off the protest, realizing the silliness of what she'd been about to say. 'But they *can't* see us!' A small bubble of giddy laughter escaped her lips.

'Not if you remain within four ells of me. It's not even necessary for us to touch – but safest, since you have no other way of judging where I might be. Remember, though, that we can still be heard and felt. We're not phantoms and we must still move with caution, especially when other people are about.'

He was pulling her after him, and she found herself tripping and stumbling and cursed her own ineptitude. It seemed as though she were detached from her legs, unable to control them. She felt humiliated and frightened at the abrupt loss of a function she'd always taken for granted. Panic began to paralyze her. If she bungled this strange magical business, she'd bring Sir Deveron into mortal danger as well as herself. And Dyfrig –

'I can't do it,' she wailed, overcome with vertigo. 'God help me, I feel as though I'll fall at any moment. I'm so sorry.'

They stopped. She heard his voice say gently, 'My lady, take my hand again. Close your eyes and trust me to lead you for a while. We'll go slowly. There's plenty of time.'

She tried it – and miraculously, all went well.

*   *   *

Saying that he was in mourning for his brother, the Sovereign ate in his sleeping room that evening rather than in the station's privy dining room with High Sealord Sernin, Beorbrook, and the other nobles and high officers. Only Vra-Bramlow and Prince Heritor Corodon shared his meal.

Lord Telifar Bankstead himself served up the roast beef and mushrooms, wild duck baked with pickled cabbage and apples, and mashed buttered turnips with raisins of the sun and walnuts, setting heaped stoneware plates before Conrig and his sons. There were also dishes of late greens dressed with verjuice, bacon-fat, and tarragon, and a platter of curd-cheese pastries. After pouring bumpers of the hearty brown ale that was the station's pride, the Lord of Chamber bowed.

'When you're finished, sire, if you summon the guards stationed at the end of the corridor, they'll carry the dishes away. I bid you good night.' He withdrew from the room.

Conrig and the young men fell to, famished after the long day's ride, saying little until they pushed aside their plates and started on the salad.

The king helped himself to more ale. 'You'll both be interested to know that the Brackenfields and your brother Orrion have arrived safely in Dennech-Cuva. The Tarnian merchant ship that is to carry them from Karum to Cathra has been slightly delayed, but it's expected to arrive within a few days. Lord Hale will see the others off, then rejoin my army. We'll have sore need of the Lord Lieutenant's services, with the constable lost to us.'

'It was a strange happenstance, that,' Bramlow observed. 'Certain Brethren in the Corps of Alchymists discussed it with me as we made our way here. Not only Lord Tinnis, but also his Guard Captain and two of his most trusted men have vanished. The Brother scriers who helped in the search found nothing new, save two horses with the Catclaw brand wandering at the western edge of the marshes, and a dead mule that had been disemboweled by a wild boar far back amongst the quagmires. None of the beasts had saddles or harness.'

'I think Catclaw and the others are slain,' the king said, frowning as he toyed with the leaves of cress and dandelion. 'But Zeth only knows by whom and for what reason. I've decided to appoint Baron Wanstantil Cloudfell as the new Lord Constable once the army reaches its new staging point at Direwold.'

'But he's such a fop!' Corodon grimaced in distaste. 'He adorns himself like a peacock, flaunting his wealth . . . and he's never taken a wife or leman. We know what that must mean.'

'Cloudfell is a brave and clever leader, esteemed by his knights and warriors,' Conrig said in a tone full of authority. 'He fought valiantly at my side during the Battle of Holt Mallburn, and his overlord, Duke Munlow Ramscrest, holds him to be unflinchingly loyal to the Sovereignty. If you are to be king, Coro, you must become a wiser judge of men.'

'Yes, sire,' the prince mumbled. 'I realize that I have much to learn.'

'If you know that,' the king said more easily, 'then your education is well begun.'

'I could help you, Coro.' Bramlow made the tentative offer, seeing an opportunity to remain closer to the Heritor and thus fulfill the plea of his mother. 'I tutored our brother Orrion in such things. An alchymist is schooled in the judging of character as an aspect of the healing arts. One cannot fully understand the working of the human body without also knowing that of the mind.'

'I'd welcome your counsel,' Corodon said with a sigh. 'And please begin by giving me insight into the quirks and crochets of women! After treating me in a most winsome and amatory fashion last night, Princess Hyndry looked down her nose

and refused me a goodbye kiss and a token to carry into
battle as I rode out of the castle this morning.'

The king laughed in spite of himself.

Bramlow said, 'Dear brother, I'm the last one to instruct
you in such mysteries. But perhaps the lady was vexed with
herself for having behaved in a manner she never would
have thought possible earlier. Don't be concerned. Her mood
will likely pass. My teachers at Zeth Abbey have told me that
mutability is part of the feminine temperament.'

'I gave Hyndry a love philtre I got from Beynor,' Coro
confessed to his brother. 'After first getting permission from
Father, of course. It worked a treat – but how will I know
whether its effects be more than passing, if the princess and
I are long separated by this war?'

'You can only wait and hope,' the novice said, hiding his
astonishment at the revelation. 'I should think, however, that
the Conjure-King would want to impress His Sovereign
Grace, and thus would provide you with the most powerful
potion in his grimoire.' His expression grew more thoughtful.
'It's rather a pity we can't question Beynor about its efficacy.
All the same, after hearing what the older Brethren said
about him, I confess I'm glad he was banished.'

'He is not banished,' the king said. 'I decided that his services might be required in the upcoming campaign. He travels
with us in disguise. I expect both of you to keep your mouths
shut about this. If certain of my lords were to learn of it,
there'd be trouble. Are we understood?'

'Yes, sire,' the princes said.

Bramlow saw a flicker of guilt cross Corodon's face and
thought: He knows something about this! I'll pry the truth
from him somehow.

They all began to nibble the flaky curd-cheese pastries.
The king poured small noggins of malt spirits for each of
them.

'My boys, I know you're weary, but I have a serious matter to discuss with you before you retire tonight.' Conrig opened his belt-pouch, took out the two pieces of raw moonstone, and held them up so that they glinted in the candlelight.

Bramlow gave a sharp inhalation.

'You both know what these are,' the king continued. 'One I took from you, Coro, after you finally told me the truth about what happened to Orrion on the summit of Demon Seat. The other I found upon the body of the late Royal Alchymist as I tried in vain to revive him.' He paused for some minutes, rolling the stones on the table in front of him while staring at them intently. 'Today, while I rode through the rain and contemplated the tribulations facing our army, my mind kept returning to these chunks of mineral. It was almost as though my dead brother were trying to tell me something about them. Finally, I realized what it was. If the Sky demons – who seem *not* to be the malignant Beaconfolk who empower sigils for the Salka – were willing to grant a favor to Orrion, channelling their magic through the outcropping on the mountaintop, then they might be induced to repeat their generous gesture to one who invoked them through these smaller stones. What do you think?'

'I supposed the very same thing, sire,' Corodon said eagerly. 'This is why I brought back the souvenir rocks in the first place.' He prudently kept silent about his earlier suggestion to the king that the benign demons might also channel power scathelessly through Beynor's sigils if they chose.

Conrig turned to Vra-Bramlow. 'And what is your opinion? As a Brother of Zeth, you should be more familiar with high sorcery.'

'Sire, I can only remind you that invoking the Sky beings cost Orry his sword-arm. The person who dares to ask the demons for another favor might also pay an unexpectedly great price.'

'The favor I would ask,' Conrig said, 'is to know whether the principal Salka host plans to come ashore in Tarn or in Didion. This information is crucial to the defense of our island. It would render unnecessary the division of our forces. Yet thus far none of our windsearchers can tell me anything of the brutes' whereabouts. Their progress is strangely unscryable, even to the most powerful Tarnian shamans. This is why . . . I'm inclined to take the risk.'

Corodon's face had gone still. In a halting voice, he said, 'Father, let me do it.'

The king let a small smile of satisfaction touch his lips. It was what he had expected of the impetuous Heritor. But before Conrig could speak, Bramlow surged to his feet.

'No! If anyone does this thing, it must be me. Forgive me, sire – but neither you nor Coro should endanger your lives, not even to obtain this vital intelligence. You're both too important to the Sovereignty. But I'm only a novice magicker, quite inconsequential. I'll invoke the Sky demons gladly. Right now, if you wish.'

'Perfect!' Corodon crowed.

The king said, 'Try it, then. But first ask them what the favor will cost. You may decide whether or not to pay their price.'

Bramlow nodded, realizing that his choice was no choice at all. He knew exactly how he'd been manipulated, just as Coro had. But for his mother's sake and that of his brother, he held out his hand. The king gave him the pieces of mineral and he crossed to the other side of the room. 'I'd rather do this outdoors, with you both at a safe distance, but I suppose that's not possible.'

'Nothing happened to you and me during Orry's miracle.' Corodon gave uneasy reassurance. 'Do you remember the words he used?'

'I'll never forget them. Now please be silent.'

The novice pulled the hood of his crimson leather chaperon over his head and gave a brief touch to his silver gammadion, even though it was not imbued with the fulness of Saint Zeth's power. Then he pressed the two chunks of moonstone together and began to speak under his breath.

Every candle in the room was abruptly extinguished. Corodon gave a great start and gulped back a cry of fear.

The Sovereign whispered, 'God's Teeth! The things are glowing.'

'The Demon Seat formation also glowed when Orry touched it,' the Heritor said. 'He later told us that it became unbearably hot –'

'Hush!' Conrig hissed. 'Have respect for Bram's bravery, if nothing else.'

Corodon subsided, eyeing his older brother with resentment. Later, Father would find out which of them was the braver . . .

The novice was motionless, a statue lit by eerie votive radiance. If he addressed the Lords of the Sky he did not use his normal voice. The only sounds in the room came from the blazing wood in the small fireplace and the creaking of the two chairs as Conrig and the prince eased their tense bodies.

Finally, after what seemed an endless time, the green glow winked out abruptly, leaving only firelight illuminating the room. Vra-Bramlow uttered a deep sigh, pushed back his hood, and returned to the table.

'Well?' the Sovereign demanded brusquely.

'They answered my questions. They asked no parlous penalty of me.' Bram placed the chunks of moonstone on the table and slowly sat down. 'I seemed to float in a vast blackness, and saw numbers of sad, ghostly faces shining dimly among the stars. They were Lights, but not the evil Beacons – just as Lord Stergos opined. They seemed hesitant but kind.'

'What did they tell you?' Conrig did not bother to hide his impatience. 'Where will the monsters land?'

'It was the first thing I asked. They replied that the Salka have contrived to conceal their movements and squelch the threads of their windspeech through a novel meld of talent. This is why our scriers can't find them. Also, since the Salka are beings with free will, who have a multitude of choices open to them, not even the Lights can determine what the creatures intend to do.'

Conrig groaned, 'No!'

'However, I *was* told where the principal Salka host is located at this precise moment, and I know their approximate swimming speed. They've rounded Cape Wolf and are moving southward very rapidly. They should arrive off the mouth of the Firth of Gayle within three days – perhaps sooner. The Lights were able to discern this information by studying aberrations in the currents of the Western Ocean itself, as well as movements of schools of fish preyed upon by the passing host. Now, as to the second Salka force –'

'A second force?' Corodon cried out in dismay.

Bramlow went on unperturbed. 'It's now entering the Dolphin Channel after skirting the Vigilant Isles, swimming westward. This army is slower than the first group and might approach Flaming Head within four days.'

'I already knew that the Salka were being reinforced,' Conrig said. 'This information is still very useful, even if it fails to answer my original question. Tell me, Bram: did you ask the Lights if they would continue to help us by following the monsters' progress?'

'I did. And they will – as best as they are able.'

'Oh, well done, Brother!' Corodon exclaimed, clapping his arms about the novice and pounding his back.

Conrig bestowed a curt nod of approbation, then took the stones and replaced them in his pouch. 'Inside of a few days, we should at least know whether the Salka intend to attack Donorvale . . . Bramlow, I'm promoting you to the position of adviser to my General Staff. From now on, you ride with me and the Prince Heritor.'

'Thank you, sire.'

Despite his show of gratification at Bram's success, Corodon was still feeling miffed. He thought: I could have besought the favor of the good Lights as readily as Bram did, if he only hadn't turned Father against the notion. Futter me for a fool! I should have insisted.

But he hadn't, and he was uncomfortably aware that his original offer to invoke the demons had been half-hearted. Even worse, he suspected that his father knew it as well.

SIXTEEN

The station compound's main gate was barred and heavily guarded by the time Deveron and Maudrayne reached it, but he explained that the postern would stay open for some time yet, so that the kitchen lackeys could carry rubbish to the midden-heap after the evening meal was finished.

'We'll enter easily by the back gate,' he whispered, as they paused momentarily on the road. 'If you and Dyfrig decide to come away together after your meeting, we may be able to get out that way also.'

'And if we cannot?'

'I have another plan in mind. But come, my lady. We should move along as quickly as possible from here on, and without speaking or making other noise. Do you think you can manage?'

'Don't worry,' she assured him. 'My earlier qualms have melted away. I've been following you with open eyes, clinging to the strap, for some time. Thinking about my son has helped focus my mind. I've dreamed of this reunion for so long, but never did I suspect it would happen so strangely.'

They began circling to the rear of the high stone wall topped with iron spikes, threading their way amongst clusters of small tents. Full night had now fallen. The myriad campfires surrounding the place were subsiding into embers as the exhausted warriors settled down to sleep. At the postern gate, two bored sentinels sat on empty kegs, sharpening their swords and gossiping. Deveron and Maudrayne passed through unnoticed, even though they threw faint shadows.

Rockyford Station had been built over two hundred years earlier, when lucrative land trade along the Wold Road between Cathra and Tarn was constantly under threat from Didionite brigands, and even the local castellans might succumb to temptation when particularly well-heeled foreign travelers sought hospitality. Under a longstanding treaty, this fortified hostel had always been staffed by Cathrans. Once it had housed a garrison that might, when times were especially dicey along the Wold Road, provide armed escorts to important persons and wagon trains carrying valuable cargo.

Since the advent of the Sovereign's Peace, Rockyford's clientele had greatly diminished. Most of the resident warriors were now gone, and two large timberbuilt annex wings of the structure had been closed off, leaving open only the original stone stronghouse with its kitchen, common room, private dining hall, and austere dormitorium chambers.

Deveron led the princess through the stableyard, where the station ostlers were still caring for the mounts of the privileged, and into one of the disused wings, accessed through a little storm-vestibule. He had already oiled the lock and door hinges and now used his talent to gain admittance. Inside, once the door closed, the place was as black as pitch because all the windows were shuttered. It smelt strongly of mildew and less savory things.

'Stay very close and hold my hand,' he cautioned her. 'I can see in the dark and I'll guide you. Keep your voice down and try not to stumble. The log walls of this passageway are coming unchinked in some sections and you might be over-heard by those out in the yard. Further inside, it'll be safe to speak normally.'

'IIow much time will my son and I have together?' she whispered.

'Dyfrig has told his adoptive father, who shares his room, that he intends to confer with me this evening. The earl marshal knows about your letter but is not aware that you're here. It would be best if your meeting with Dyfrig did not last much longer than an hour, but you may take whatever time you need.'

As they crept along, Deveron explained that she would wait in one of the old guestrooms while he brought her son to her under a pall of invisibility. 'You should decide your mutual future tonight. I've told Prince Dyfrig that I'm willing to summon friends of mine – Green Men – who will shelter one or both of you in a secluded Elderwold village until it's safe for you to go elsewhere. But it's probable that your son won't want to shirk his duty to the army.'

'Nor should he!' she replied with spirit. 'I want to remain with Dyfrig, keeping to my knight's disguise, if he'll have me. I won't be any bother, and if Parlian Beorbrook is the paragon you say he is, he should not object. After all, he and Conrig will be long leagues apart once the divided forces deploy to their separate positions.'

Deveron's response was cool. 'Such a course might still place both your son and the earl marshal in jeopardy, my lady. However, whatever the prince decides, I'll help to carry out.'

An inner door opened with a small rattle from the lifted latch. Deveron took Maudrayne's hand and guided her to a rough wooden bench, where he bade her sit and then intoned the words, 'BI FYSINEK. KRUF AH!' A moment later she saw him standing before her, a yellow flame like that of a candle springing from his index finger. Her own body was also visible again.

'I would not have known you, sir,' she remarked. 'With the beard and a certain deepening of your eyes with maturity, you are a different man from the young knight I once knew.'

He only smiled. 'This room looks out on the exterior stone wall, so there's no danger of anyone seeing light through cracks in the shutters or between the logs.'

He took up an oil lantern that stood on a small table and lit it. The chamber was about five ells square. Besides the bench, it held nine rude cots with rotting pallets, four stools, and a rusty brazier. Festoons of cobwebs hung from the ceiling, and pale fungi like obscene tumors bloomed here and there amidst the nameless litter on the floor.

'I regret the dampness and the musty stench,' Deveron said, 'but this is the best place I could find. Just down the passage is a door connecting this wing with a section of the station's stronghouse where the Sovereign and the highest nobility are quartered. The room occupied by Earl Marshal Parlian and Prince Dyfrig is very close by. Wait here. I'll return very shortly with your son.'

He left her and rendered himself invisible again. Using windsight, he looked through the thick connecting door to be sure no one was out and about on the other side. The stone corridor was deserted, lit by three torches in wall sconces. He knew a squad of the Royal Guard was posted around the corner at the far end, near where the chambers of the Sovereign and High Sealord Sernin were located, but at present the guardsmen were out of sight.

He entered the hostel silent as a ghost, hurried to the room occupied by Dyfrig and Parlian, which was next to that of the Tarnian leader, and scratched three times on the door. It opened immediately and the prince looked out. He wore an

unadorned woolen tunic and trews, an open budge waistcoat against the night chill of the moorland, and soft house
shoes.

'Are you here, Sir Deveron?' he hissed, looking about. An
unseen presence gripped his hand and he flinched.

'FASH AH!' a soft voice said. Dyfrig froze with shock as
his body disappeared and he was pulled through the door,
which closed by itself behind him. 'Just relax and hold onto
me, Your Grace. We must hurry out of here. Even invisible,
we cast a slight shadow in the torchlight.'

The prince let himself be drawn to the exit at the end of
the corridor that gave into the disused wing. It had apparently been fastened shut with a large iron hasp and padlock
and also barred with a stout oaken plank. But the lock opened
without a sound and the wooden bar had been twice severed
in an ingenious fashion and fixed back in place, so that the
door might swing freely open while it still seemed secured.

'Quickly.' Deveron urged him. 'Someone is about to
emerge from the Sovereign's room.'

In an instant they were safe on the other side, hastening
through the dark toward a faint thread of golden light glimmering beneath a closed door.

'BI FYSINEK. KRUF AH!' The words dissolved Concealer's
spell.

Before Deveron could stop him, Prince Dyfrig tore the door
wide open. He saw a fully armed knight wearing a surcoat
with the Beorbrook blazon seated on a bench, gingerly using
a dagger to pare dirt from beneath his fingernails. Lamplight
showed a face beneath the helmet's eyeguard that was pale
and beardless.

The prince glanced wildly about the dim room. 'Where is
my mother?' he demanded. 'What have you done with her?'

The knight stood up slowly, placing the dagger on the
table. He was almost six feet tall, with narrow shoulders and

a slender build. After lifting off his helm, he stripped away
the mail hood and untied the padded leather coif beneath,
releasing a coil of shining auburn hair.

'I am Maudrayne,' the knight said to the dumfounded
prince, 'come to you in this guise so my enemies would not
know me. But I'd recognize you anywhere, my dearest son,
for you are the image of your father when I first laid eyes
on him long years ago.'

She held out her arms. With an inarticulate cry, Dyfrig fell
to his knees before her and kissed her roughened hands,
bathing them with tears.

'I'll leave you,' Deveron said. 'I'll wait outside in the stableyard, invisible, near the storm-vestibule of this wing,
guarding your privacy from intruders. When you wish me
to return, knock softly three times on the outer door.' He
left them together.

Maude drew her son to his feet and hugged him with
mailed arms – which made him cry out in surprise, then
burst into laughter. She kissed his lips, his damp cheeks, and
his brow. 'You received my letter,' she said at length,
returning to the bench.

Dyfrig pulled up a stool and seated himself before her. He
drew the gold locket on its chain from the neck of his tunic,
and held it up so that it gleamed in the lamplight. 'I will
always wear it next to my heart, Mother, and pray peaceful
repose for the brave soul of Rusgann, who carried it so far.
If only she could have given it into my hands! . . . But it was
not to be. Sir Deveron brought this to me.'

'Rusgann is dead?' At his nod of acquiescence, her eyelids
closed and she uttered a wordless cry of woe. For a time she
sat with head bowed, her lips moving silently. Then she
looked up, wiping her eyes, and bade Dyfrig tell him of her
friend's fate.

Briefly, he related how Rusgann had been captured by

Lord Catclaw, scourged nearly to death, and rescued too late by Sir Deveron and his wife, Sealady Induna. 'Rusgann's body was buried by them among rocks. One day we'll make a proper tomb for her, Mother. Her courage will be celebrated by bards and the tellers of heroic tales.'

'*He* was the ultimate cause of her suffering and death,' Maudrayne murmured, her eyes gone flat and cold.

Mistaking her meaning, Dyfrig said, 'Her killers – including the Lord Constable – paid the ultimate penalty for their crime. Sir Deveron slew them to a man so none could report to the High King that Rusgann carried a message from you to me.'

'Were you surprised by the letter's contents?' she asked him.

He tucked the locket back into its hiding place. 'I was not surprised to learn that I'm the Sovereign's true first-born. The rumors about my paternity came to me early, and when I understood their portent I asked my father – my *true* father, Lord Parlian – what the truth might be. He would say only that I was declared a royal bastard by the High King's own decree, and this was done for the peace of the realm, and that he and his wife, the late Duchess Falise, loved me with all their hearts and wanted me to inherit the marshalship that was the pride of their family.'

'I was told this by my captor,' Maudrayne said, 'and took comfort in the fact that you had been adopted by noble and kindly persons. But . . . did you find other things in the letter that moved you?'

'Some of what you wrote was joyous news: that you lived and were in good health and that we might someday meet again. Some words shocked me profoundly: the Sovereign's unconscionable treatment of you, the knowledge that he possesses uncanny talent and by law cannot sit the throne of Cathra.'

Maude's sea-green eyes glittered and her speech became

almost breathless in its urgency. 'And what have you decided
to do about that dire knowledge? Will you confront Conrig
with it and demand justice, as is your right? I could stay
with you, disguised, and we two could plan how best to
overthrow the High King in the encampment at Lake of
Shadows.'

He caught her slender, grimy hands in his own powerful
ones, bowing over them. Again she felt his tears. 'Dearest
Mother, I've given deep thought to this weighty matter. I
also consulted Deveron Austrey, the witness you commended
to me, as well as my father the earl marshal. Amongst us
we have concluded that attempting to pull down Conrig
Ironcrown at this pivotal point in our island's history would
place all of Blenholme's people in grave danger.'

'Oh! But surely –'

'Please listen to me,' he broke in with insistent firmness.
'We are threatened not only by Salka monsters but also by
evil beings of the Sky Realm who are engaged in a mysterious Conflict of their own. Sir Deveron and his wife have
told me that the Beaconfolk enslaved the Salka and the other
inhuman creatures who lived on our island in prehistoric
times. They did this through dark sorcery. And now they
hope to enslave humankind as well, using Salka as their
agents.'

'What are you talking about?' Maudrayne demanded in a
voice of ice. She pulled away from him and climbed to her
feet. 'Are you foolish enough to believe that only Conrig
Wincantor is able to defeat the Salka horde?'

'He's the only leader strong enough to unite the island
nations.'

'That liar?' she cried in scorn. 'That heartless blackguard
who commanded that his own tiny son, the heir to his throne,
be put to death in order that his shameful secret not be
revealed? Who on Blenholme would follow Conrig Ironcrown

if the truth about him were known? No one! *You could lead the Army of the Sovereignty to victory yourself!* You, Dyfrig! This is your destiny. Seize it!'

'If I claimed the High Kingship,' he said simply, 'the great lords would not accept me outright. There would have to be a second trial proving Conrig attainted. He was acquitted of the charge once before.'

'But this time, I'm here to speak for myself! Sealord Sernin and the other Tarnian leaders, people who love and revere me, know the truth of my allegation. They can be given status to testify if the Lords Judicial of Cathra agree to it. And you also have Deveron and Stergos Wincantor, the king's own brother, as witnesses –'

'Lord Stergos is dead, Mother. This very morning he perished when his heart failed. And Sir Deveron has been an outlaw with a price on his head for sixteen years.'

'There must be a way!' She was near weeping with disappointment and rage as she saw her great hopes for him dissolving. 'I can't believe you'd give up your heritage! Seeing justice done for you has been my only reason for living. Was my sacrifice for naught, Dyfrig?'

'Never!' he exclaimed. 'And the day may yet come when I can claim Cathra's throne with a clear conscience. But not now. We're at war, Mother. If I attack King Conrig I only give a weapon to political foes who'd destroy the union that's kept Blenholme strong. Didion would repudiate the Edict of Sovereignty in a trice. Its shortsighted leaders think the Salka now only intend to attack Tarn, so they'd stand back while others defend that nation. And what would Conrig himself do if I proclaimed myself the true Sovereign? Do you really think he'd submit tamely and hand over his Iron Crown? . . . Nay, I think he'd slay me with his own hand, bringing on such dissension among the Cathran peerage that waging the war would become nigh impossible.'

'And you would not defend yourself if he attacked your person?' Her query was now almost wistful, for she knew the answer. Conrig and Dyfrig were not alike for all that they were mirror images of each other. Not alike in their hearts, nor in their souls. The father would readily kill his son in cold blood, but the son would be unable to harm his father.

'Mother, let it be,' he said softly. 'You must let it be.'

'You are the rightful Sovereign of Blenholme.' Her words were forlorn, pleading.

'If I sat the throne, the welfare of our island and its people would be my foremost concern. And so it is now, when I'm a mere bastard prince. My own rights must always come second in my mind. Believe what I say.'

She stared at him for a long moment before looking away and speaking in a toneless voice. 'I do believe you. And I understand your decision, while deploring it. You must do as you think best.'

And so must I.

'God be thanked!' He hastened to add, 'As I said, now is not the time for me to press my claim. Later, when the Salka are defeated . . .' He trailed off. 'Who can say?'

She sighed. 'Who, indeed.' She subsided back onto the bench. 'Sit down again, my darling boy. Please, be of good cheer. I'm sorry if my zeal, my burning desire to see you in your proper place, has caused distress at this difficult point in your life. Our reunion should have been a joyous thing and I've spoiled it.'

'Nothing can diminish my happiness at seeing you again.' He sat beside her on the bench, once more taking her by the hand. 'I saw your face often in my dreams, and you've not changed at all. Would you like to know my favorite dream of you?'

'Of course.'

'It's of the time we escaped those two rascally fishermen

who would have kidnapped us and killed Rusgann near the sea-hag's steading in Tarn. You fought so bravely and slew one and marooned the other. Then we all sailed away and were free for a while. I dream of you standing at the wheel of the lugger you took away from the villains. Your hair streams in the wind and your face is damp with spray and you and Rusgann are laughing. I'm a very small boy, snuggled down safely in a smelly old blanket in the bottom of the boat, and I'm happier than I've ever been before.'

'I remember,' she said, and sat in silence for a time. Then: 'But let's not spend our precious time reminiscing. Tell me of your life nowadays! You're a belted knight. Do you have special duties under your father, Earl Marshal Parlian?'

'You might like to know of an expedition I carried out recently,' he said, relieved that she seemed to have abandoned the thornier topic. He launched himself into a colorful narrative of the Green Morass, and the encounter with the great worms. When he concluded the account with his official commendation at the feast, they spoke about what she would do now that she had escaped Tinnis Catclaw's captivity.

Knowing now that he would never abandon his military duties even for her sake, she again expressed her wish to remain close to him during the upcoming campaign, disguised as a man. When he made no response, she broached reluctantly Deveron's suggestion that she might seek sanctuary with the Green Men. Dyfrig seized on it with an eagerness that bordered on the unseemly.

'Yes! That would be the wisest course, Mother. If you were to accompany me in the new deployment of the Southern Wing of the army, I'd worry constantly that your identity might be discovered. I long to have you near me, but the Sovereign has fanatic partisans, even among the forces of Earl Marshal Parlian. We can send letters secretly to each other, of course. As soon as it's possible, I'll come to fetch you. We'll find a permanent safe home for you in your Uncle Sernin's palace in Donorvale. No one but he and I and Sir Deveron and his wife need know who you are.'

Her reply was unexpectedly docile. 'I'll do as you want, knowing it will keep you from being troubled about my safety.'

'Thank you. It's the best thing for both of us.' He stood. 'And now we should say farewell for the nonce. If I don't return to our room soon, the earl marshal may seek me out.'

'Dearest son!' She sprang up and threw her arms about his neck. 'Seeing you, speaking to you, touching you again after so many barren years has given me more joy than you can conceive of. So kiss me one final time and then leave me. I'll summon Deveron when you're safe away and he'll lead me from Rockyford invisible, as he brought me.'

'Let me call him for you.'

'No.' Her face shone with tears. 'I wish to sit here for a few minutes more, regaining my composure.'

'Of course.' They clung to one another, then he guided her back to the bench, spoke a blessing, and took his leave.

She waited, listening at the door, until she was certain he'd gone. Donning her coif and mail hood again, she left the helmet on the table. It hid too much of her face and she wanted to be recognized.

After sheathing her dagger and slipping on her gauntlets, she departed the squalid chamber, having left its door open slightly so that light from the lantern relieved the inky darkness outside. The heavy door that led into the way station proper yielded to her touch and cracked open without a sound. She peered through, praying that Sir Deveron would remain at his post outside in the stableyard and not come looking for her.

Guttering torches revealed a stone corridor with six doors along the righthand wall, all so widely separated that they must lead to spacious quarters. The most distant chamber had stacks of dirty platters, dishes, and drinking vessels on the floor outside its entrance. No one was in view, but she heard the sound of voices echoing from the vaulted ceiling.

She eased through the door, closed it, and pricked up her ears. Guardsmen, on station out of sight around the far corner, were bemoaning their ill luck at having to stand night watch while their mates slept – as if anyone would dare break into this stronghold while it was surrounded by thousands of troops!

She wondered which room was *his*. Would he be sleeping alone?

Maudrayne studied the floor of the corridor, beginning with the stone paving beneath her own feet. Most of it was fairly clean; the mud tracked in from the outside by those entering the station's front door had been left in other parts of the building. But an obvious trail of filthy bootprints led from where she stood, at the supposedly barred portal of the disused wing, to the fourth door down. That, she deduced, must be the chamber occupied by Dyfrig and Parlian Beorbrook.

Would the next door lead to the High Sealord's room? And the one beyond that, with the discarded dinnerware outside, lead to Conrig's?

I'll have to chance it, she said to herself, and be damned quick about it, too.

Drawing her slender varg blade, Maudrayne went as lightly as she could. When she reached the last door, she rapped on it with the hilt of the sword.

'Who the bloody hell is it?' someone called out. It was a familiar voice – one that made her heart leap, her breath catch, and her resolution falter.

'It's Corodon, Father,' she said in slurred tones. 'I must speak to you.'

'I was asleep, you futtering young idiot!'

'It's very important. Please!'

There were growled imprecations from inside and a faint crash as some small object fell to the floor. After a few moments the door was flung open and he stood there in a loose woolen nightshirt and fur-lined slippers, his wheaten hair disheveled from the pillow and his dark eyes slitted with vexation. At the sight of her, his jaw dropped.

With the curved sword at her side, she spoke in a soft, rich voice, as she'd spoken to him long ago during their nights of blissful passion, when their love was fierce and strong, before his vaulting ambition and impatience for an heir turned him against her; before her wounded pride made her shrewish and vengeful.

'Conrig. Do you know me? I've come back to you, my husband. Maude, the wife whom you thought was dead.'

'No!' he gasped, taking two steps backward. 'Impossible!' But his expression betrayed him. He knew her.

She followed him, whipping the gleaming varg up and holding the tip an inch from his body, just below his breastbone. 'I've come for justice,' she hissed. 'For myself and for our son Dyfrig, who is the true-born Sovereign of Blenholme. You disowned him! You, a man stained by hidden talent. I begged Dyfrig to reclaim his heritage but he refused, out of a foolish misplaced loyalty. He wouldn't take your Iron Crown. So I shall give it to him.'

She lunged with all her might. He dodged but felt an explosion of agony as the sword raked his ribs and penetrated deep into the flesh along his left side. The voluminous nightshirt had defeated her thrust to his heart.

'Guards!' He bellowed. 'Help! Royal Guardsmen, to your king! Help!'

Conrig toppled, bringing her down with him, and rolled away with the blade still caught in his body. His bladder gave way. As he lay on the stones in a puddle of urine and blood, roaring and cursing, Maude leapt to her feet and yanked the varg free. Scarlet stained the long cut in his shirt but the wound was obviously not a mortal one; he was making too much noise.

Before she could strike again someone came pounding around the corner of the passageway. She whirled and saw a single member of the Royal Guard, armed with a long halberd. A deadly morningstar hung at his belt, its ball studded with iron spikes sheathed in a leather pouch. He swung the pole-axe at her wildly, striking the doorjamb a glancing blow. She ducked, hopped out into the corridor, and sliced open his unarmored shin with her sword. As he lurched, screaming and scattering the stacked stoneware dishes in all directions, she came at him and smote off his right hand. Blood fountained from the stump, splattering her from head to toe, and the halberd clattered to the floor. He was able to pull the morningstar from his belt before he collapsed, but lost his grip on it and sent the weapon flying across the corridor. As he writhed on his back, she sank her blade into his vulnerable throat.

Doors along the corridor were crashing open and the high-ranking occupants peered out, so befuddled with sleep and disbelief that at first they did little more than gawk and shout. A second guard came around the corner, brandishing a shortsword.

Maude dropped her varg and scooped up the long-handled halberd. Screaming at the top of her lungs, she ran straight at the warrior, then skidded to her knees in the gore, angling the weapon to enter beneath his mail shirt, and let him impale himself upon the halberd's pike as though he were a charging boar.

'No, no! For the love of God! Stop!'

She turned. It was Dyfrig's voice. Standing paralyzed with

horror a dozen ells away, he had recognized her. Another tall youth emerged from a door farther away, wearing only smallclothes. He began edging hesitantly toward her, followed by a second young man in the red robe of the Zeth Brethren. From around the corner, martial shouts announced the approach of more warriors. The sprawled body of the first guard partially blocked the king's doorway, so he could not shut himself safely inside his chamber. In spite of his wound, Conrig was fumbling at the corpse, trying to drag it out of the way.

I must finish him, Maude thought in desperation. She drew her dagger and reclaimed her varg blade, but suddenly her boot slipped in the widening pool of blood and she fell heavily to the stones, striking her head. A blaze of white pain blinded her for a moment; then she struggled up, having lost the dagger but not the sword. Moving forward on her knees, with trembling arms, she poised to swing the razor-sharp varg at the neck of the man who had been her husband.

Conrig crouched behind the dead guardsman. He smiled at her, but his eyes were dark pits of hatred. 'Can you kill me now, while I'm helpless?' he taunted her in a low voice. 'Would your son accept my Iron Crown from the hand of a murderess?'

She hesitated, aware of someone moving behind her: a jangling of metal links, an intake of breath that was almost a sob.

The king looked over her shoulder and his smile broadened.

Prince Corodon ripped the leather sheath from the morningstar he had retrieved, clutched the handle with both hands, and swung the heavy oaken ball on its chain down onto the crown of Maudrayne's head. Inch-long iron spikes penetrated the chain mail hood and the leather coif beneath, crushing the bones of her skull and the brain within. She was dead before her body struck the stones.

The Prince Heritor gave a great howl, like an animal. He flung down the weapon, staggered away, and vomited against the opposite wall.

Triumphant shouts came from the others; but before they could approach, Conrig stood up, taking hold of the morning-star. With his foot he turned over the corpse of his attacker, then struck the dead face again and again with the spiked ball until the features were obliterated. He would not stop until Earl Marshal Parlian and High Sealord Sernin Donorvale laid hold of him and wrenched the weapon away.

'For the love of God, sire!' the earl marshal cried. 'Desist! The villain is dead.'

'And now how shall we tell who he was?' the Tarnian leader said. 'Parli, he wears your household blazon.'

'But he's none of mine,' the old general retorted. 'I'd swear it. Only members of my staff are housed within the station tonight. All of my knights are outside, sleeping with the troops.'

Conrig eyed Dyfrig, who stood whitefaced beside his adoptive father. 'What about you, young Beorbrook?' the king inquired in an peculiarly incisive tone. 'Have you any notion who this vile assassin might be?'

'My liege, I can only believe the wretch was some madman,' the prince said. 'Who else would dare to attack Your Sovereign Grace in such an abominable manner?'

'Perhaps it was a deranged Didionite,' Donorvale's older son, Sealord Simok, suggested. 'One of those fanatics seeking independence with no thought of the consequences. He might have pretended to be one of the station servants earlier, to gain access to this place, then assumed a knight's disguise.' There were grim exclamations of agreement from some of the others standing about.

'But, sire! My lords!' cried the Captain of the Guard, 'I can swear on my life that no intruder passed by us and entered this corridor, which is a dead end.'

The Tarnian Field Commander, Yons Stormchild, said, 'Well, he got in somehow. What about that door down there?' Clad only in a linen bedsheet, the hulking battle-leader strode toward the portal in question.

'It's barred and locked from the inside, my lord,' the captain called. 'We checked it out early, before any of you great folk moved in. Hasn't been opened in donkey's years.'

But Stormchild hauled the door wide open. 'Like hell! It's been meddled with – and cleverly, too. Bring a torch, one of you.' In moments, the guards were rushing into the disused wing on the Tarnian's heels, shouting at what they found. Both of Donorvale's sons hared off after them.

Vra-Bramlow had been giving solace to his wretched brother Corodon while Dyfrig hovered near the body of his mother, as blank-faced and detached as a sleepwalker. Now the burly novice gave the Heritor into Dyfrig's care. 'Wash the puke and blood off him, Your Grace, dress him warmly, and give him a stiff drink.' Then he spoke curt orders to two of the remaining guards. The surprised men saluted and began hauling the corpse of their defunct comrade away from the door to the king's chamber.

Bramlow then approached the Sovereign. Conrig sagged in the arms of Sealord Sernin and the earl marshal, teeth clenched against his pain and features gone ashen with blood-loss. 'Sire, you're in great need of a physician. I've presumed to bespeak Vra-Garason, the most discreet healer in your Corps of Alchymists, and the Tarnian Grand Shaman Zolanfel. They'll be here to minister to your wound in a few minutes. That the bleeding is not more profuse bodes well. It's probable that none of the large blood vessels were severed.'

Awareness resurfaced in the king's glazed eyes. 'Bram. It's important that this be hushed up. And . . . a certain person must not learn of the attempt at assassination.'

Bramlow knew his father was speaking of Beynor. The

novice feared that the Conjure-King had already scried the mêlée; in fact, he was probably windwatching them at this very moment. But Bram was more worried about a different source of potential mischief.

The earl marshal had raised his eyebrows. 'A certain person, my liege? Who might that be?'

'The King's Grace is concerned,' Bramlow said swiftly, with a covert glance cautioning his father, 'that if this dead whoreson should indeed be a man of Didion, our Cathran warriors might be incited beyond endurance if this terrible incident became commonly known. Just think what altercations might ensue when Crown Prince Valardus and his army join with that of the earl marshal, at Lake of Shadows.'

Both Parlian and Sernin grimaced.

'So we must keep this as quiet as possible,' the novice said. 'The Grand Shaman and the Brother Alchymist will let it be inferred that His Sovereign Grace took a tumble and wrenched his left shoulder severely. The High King can ride with Zolanfel in his carriage until he's able to sit a horse.'

'The bodies?' Conrig said to his son.

'I'll send these guards for canvas and cord. They and the others can wrap the remains securely, weapons and all, and bury them deep in some remote corner of the station compound. The Captain of the Guard can give it out that the dead warriors were sent back to Boarsden on some mission. I'll personally see to it that this gory mess is cleaned up. I'll take care of everything, sire. Depend on me.'

'Yes,' Conrig said. 'I will . . . Parli, Sernin, take me into my room now. God help me, I've pissed myself. Help me into some fresh drawers before the doctors come. I won't have them think me a craven.'

'It's naught but an inadvertent loss of control, sire, and nothing to do with bravery,' Bramlow told his father cheerfully. 'Our bodies sometimes betray us thus when we suffer sudden severe pain. This I learned studying medicine at the Abbey. No one would ever think *you* craven.'

Conrig managed a wry chuckle. 'Thank you for the small comfort.'

The tall High Sealord regarded the novice with a bemused eye. 'What a pity you were born with talent, Prince Bramlow Wincantor. A great pity . . .'

The two great lords turned the king about gingerly. But when they would have carried him, he said, 'I can walk, damn you!' And he did, with their support.

Invisible, Deveron Austrey took a spade from the stable. Since both of the station's gates were now locked, he had no choice but to use the Subtle Gateway sigil to transport himself over the compound wall. The Great Lights vouchsafed the minuscule bit of sorcery with supreme indifference and the penalty was equivalent to that of a stubbed toe.

It was necessary for him to return to Maudrayne's makeshift camp on the bank of Rocky Brook to retrieve her necklace and bury the saddlebags and other things she'd left behind. No trace of her presence must remain. Trudging through the starry night beyond the outer limits of the army camp, flushing out the occasional night-roaming wild creature, he bespoke Induna. She woke from sleep in the small chamber they had been allotted and mourned the bleak tidings.

'Poor Dyfrig,' she said. 'To see his mother die so horribly before his very eyes and be helpless to save her. But at least he was able to enjoy a brief happy reunion beforehand. In time, it may give him some solace.'

'I confess that I scried the two of them while they conversed, reading their lips. For their own safety, I had to know their plans. Princess Maudrayne told Dyfrig she'd take refuge with the Green Men as I'd proposed, and I was greatly relieved. But alas, she lied. When the prince left her I shifted my wind-scrutiny to the postern gate, thinking I'd have to take her out that way. I only learned what she secretly intended when I felt the death-pang of the first guard. By then it was too late to intervene. Men were swarming about the passages like enraged hornets. And – and I think I harbored a secret hope that Maudrayne might succeed.'

'Oh, Deveron . . .'

'I know not where my loyalties lie nowadays, Duna. For certain they are not with Conrig! I know why he disfigured Maude's countenance: if her identity had been discovered, no one could have prevented the news from spreading. The scandal would be too blatant. But the king acted with such ferocity – as though taking vengeance on her beauty! Even Lord Parlian and the High Sealord were appalled. Wounded as Conrig was, those two strong men could hardly restrain him from battering her poor dead face.'

'Do you believe that her identity can remain a secret?'

'When I left the station, the disposal of the corpses was being supervised by the king's son, Vra-Bramlow, who showed rather unexpected presence of mind at the conclusion of the slaughter. He's an alchymist-in-training and a damned clever one. I wouldn't put it past him to scry through the canvas shrouding the princess, seeking clues. He'll doubtless ascertain her sex, at the least, and the distinctive color of her hair. My guess is that Brother Bramlow will eventually make the correct deduction. Whether he shares that knowledge with anyone else, or uses it against Dyfrig . . .'

'The prince is your charge, Deveron. Conrig must know why Maude sought his life. What will you do to protect her son from the king's wrath?'

'I've not had time to think it through. But the fact that Dyfrig did nothing to prevent his mother's death – and indeed cried out for her to cease her attack – may help stay the

Sovereign's hand. I know the temperament of the late Princess Dowager better than you. She was a woman of amazing courage, yet possessed of a fiery pride that could often obliterate common sense. Think how she tried to drown herself and kill her unborn child after signing the bill of divorcement! Conrig knows her impetuous nature. He may decide that Dyfrig deplored her attempt at regicide, rather than colluding in it.'

'We must both watch over the prince with special care, all the same,' Induna said. 'It will help that he accompanies Earl Marshal Parlian and the Southern Wing of the army, rather than the king's own force . . . Until you return to the station, I intend to oversee his security. My magic is not entirely non-aggressive. I can defend Dyfrig if need be.'

'Peace, dear wife! Scry the prince by all means. And it would be good for us to know Lord Parlian's reaction to tonight's terrible events. But the young man can be in no special danger yet. By now, King Conrig will have been rendered senseless by the healers to relieve his pain. And he is the only one who can order the arrest of a prince.'

Conjure-King Beynor had endured a tedious and uncomfortable ride that day, and when he and the other members of the Corps of Alchymists arrived at Rockyford, he took to his bed immediately after the unsatisfactory evening meal (overdone roast beef, mutton pie, underdone turnips in mushroom sauce, flabby salad, and cheat bread), served in the common room in the company of rowdy and half-drunken noble officers.

The wind-borne death-cries woke him and a few of the other magickers. Astounded, Beynor lay still on his cot in the cubicle he shared with Garon Curtling – who snored on oblivious – and scried the situation.

Unlike the aroused Cathran and Tarnian adepts in the

dormitorium, he made no effort to approach the scene of the carnage. He had observed that the Royal Guardsmen were fending off curious persons, even nobles and knights, admitting to the corridor only the two healers, who immediately erected a spell of couverture around the Sovereign's bedroom. But Beynor had already seen Conrig's wound, and the mutilated body of his would-be assassin. He knew the attacker was a woman but not her identity. While wind-watching the ensuing cleanup and disposal of the bodies with fascination, he thought about how he might twist this strange affair to his advantage, but no useful idea came immediately to mind.

Curiously enough, Prince Dyfrig Beorbrook sat slumped before the fire in the chamber he shared with his father, weeping as though the world had come to an end, while the earl marshal drank far more brandy than was good for a man of his age and cursed endlessly under his breath. Neither made any coherent remark, so their oddly over-wrought reaction to Conrig's close brush with doom remained unfathomable.

One other thing caught Beynor's attention. The wind-thread of oversight focused on Prince Dyfrig was well-spun and all but imperceptible, but nevertheless the sorcerer perceived it and traced it to its origin: the Tarnian shaman apprentice who was newly attached to Beorbrook's staff, whom he had seen at supper along with his nondescript master. Neither one of them had attracted his attention at the time. Beynor undertook a windsearch for the shaman called Haydon, but he was not in any of the station buildings, nor anywhere outside within three leagues of the compound.

Interesting – especially if the fellow should reappear in the morning! What had he been up to?

Master Haydon and his assistant would bear close

watching. They had been seconded to the earl marshal's service for some good reason. Certain Tarnians possessed formidable talent, even more powerful than that of Moss's extinct Glaumerie Guild. Might this Haydon be one of the highly adept? And if so, why was such a one so concerned with Prince Dyfrig?

Relaxing again in his bed, Beynor returned to his oversight of the young apprentice, observing him for a long time while a feeling of unease grew ever stronger in his gut. In spite of his youth, the lad seemed to possess exceptional windwatching skill. The stronghouse was of massive construction, and to oversee Dyfrig, one had to penetrate several interior walls made of granite blocks –

Icy Hell! The door to the Tarnian shaman's room was opening, then closing by itself.

Thunderstruck, Beynor watched the apprentice break off the surveillance and look up with an expectant smile. The lad rose from the stool where he had been seated. Speaking a single sentence, he extended his arms, embracing thin air, and lifted his pale, fine-featured face in what was obviously a kiss . . .

But by then Beynor had lip-read the apprentice's greeting: *Oh, husband, thank God you returned safely, using that treacherous thing.*

Not a lad, but another woman in disguise!

And one, by God's Teeth, who was married to an unscryable man. Beynor had encountered only one such person in all his life – the wild talent, that cursèd spoiler of well-laid schemes, who owned two active moonstone sigils.

King Conrig's renegade Royal Intelligencer, Deveron Austrey.

'Coro, you must take this draught of herbs. It'll calm you far better than ardent spirits and allow you restful sleep.'

Vra-Bramlow held out the cup of potion he had prepared after returning to the room he shared with the Prince Heritor and finding him maudlin drunk and still guzzling Didionite brandy.

'I see it still,' his younger brother moaned. 'Every time I close my eyes, I see and feel it: the awful spray of blood and brains, the sound of his skullbones shattering, that *sound*. God help me, Bram, I thought I had a warrior's heart. I have prizes for my swordsmanship! I've slain boar and bear and bull-elk with the lance. I wielded the star and mace and war-flail with skill when we rode at quintain, smiting the twirling mannequin. Why, oh why, should I then have disgraced myself by spewing my supper after killing the assassin? I'll never live this down. They'll dub me a mollymawk!'

Bram shook his head in reassurance. He pried the goblet half-filled with devilish plum lifewater from Coro's fingers and substituted the potion. 'Very few people will ever know what you did this night. For good reason, Father has commanded that the incident be kept strictly secret. Those whose opinion matters – and that includes His Sovereign Grace – will deem you a hero and attribute your distress to youthful sensitivity. Don't be surprised if certain important personages approach you in days upcoming, offering to share similar experiences suffered during their first battle-kill. And you *were* in a battle, Coro. A fight for our father's life.'

The Prince Heritor looked confused. 'Truly?'

'Truly. Now drink the herbal infusion. It tastes good and will do you good. There! What did I tell you? Finish it all.'

Corodon drained the cup and sighed. 'So you don't think Father and the noble Tarnians will laugh at me?'

'Did Prince Dyfrig laugh at you when he cleaned you up?'

'Nay. He was kind. He said I'd done a terrible but necessary thing, a deed of valor. He tried to put me to bed and take the flask of brandy away after I'd had a single dram. But I made him leave it –'

'And then you began to brood and conjure horrors.'

Corodon hung his head. 'There *were* horrors. They got the better of me. What if . . . in the war to come . . .'

'You'll be brave, Coro. It's your true nature, the thing that enabled you to do what you did tonight. Who cares what came after? Brother, trust me. All will be well.' He led the younger man to his bed. 'Sleep. In the morning you may have a whacking hangover, but you'll look at this affair with new eyes.'

He turned and headed for his own cot, shrugged out of his stained woolen houserobe, then cast it on the floor. 'Ruined. The blood has set and won't be washed out – and it was our sister Wylgana's birthday gift to me.' He blew out the candle and burrowed into bed naked.

After a while, Coro's voice came softly in the dark. 'Bram?'

'What?'

'If you could have saved Father with sorcery, would you have done it? It would have been so much easier . . .'

'What do you mean? Put up a protective magical shield? Struck the attacker unconscious? If I were a Doctor Arcanorum, I'd have certainly done one or the other. But I'm just a novice. I don't have such power.'

'No. I meant would you have slain the assassin outright – blasted him with lightning or stopped his heart.'

There was a long silence. Then Vra-Bramlow said, 'We Brethren are forbidden by the Zeth Codex to use sorcery to kill an untalented sentient being – human or nonhuman. There are no exceptions. Not even self-defense or defense of another would justify it. A powerful adept person has arcane spells at his disposal that spare the life of the normal-minded assailant and give him time to repent his wickedness and atone for it. A dead man cannot be sorry.'

'But the assassin was threatening our father. The Sovereign!'

'Coro, I know it may be hard for you to understand, and your wits are not at their sharpest right now. But I stand by my statement.'

'How about in wartime, Bram? What then?'

'The Brethren aren't warriors. We obey the Codex because lethal magic has such a huge potential for misuse. Ordinary warfare is terrible enough.'

'What if your enemy used deadly sorcery against *you*? Or against your country? Would you retaliate if you were able to?'

'Some men would,' Vra-Bramlow said. 'As for me . . . I don't know what I'd do. Now shut up and go to sleep.'

SEVENTEEN

Wrapped in cloaks against the moderate breeze, Lady Nyla Brackenfield and Sir Orrion Wincantor, Knight Bachelor, stood together at the stern rail of the Tarnian merchant brig *Gannet,* watching the tiny Didionite port recede astern. On a precipice high above the harbor and its settlement, the fortress of Karum stood shining and impregnable against a slate-grey morning sky.

'What a lovely-looking castle,' Nyla said in admiration. 'Much more attractive than the ducal citadel in Dennech-Cuva where we stayed. With those white limestone walls and turrets, it almost resembles a banquet subtlety fashioned from snowy marzipan.'

'A shame it's nothing but a lair of filthy pirates,' Orrion observed.

'Perhaps some very rich pirates! I wonder what the castle is like inside?'

'Pray you never find out. It's said that Rork Karum is the most vicious buccaneer and kidnapper-for-ransom on Terminal Bay. Only a handful of Tarnian ship captains seem able to do business with him. He and four others of his ilk control the bay waters like a private fiefdom. They give only nominal allegiance to their overlord, Duke Azarick, and prey on shipping in the open waters almost with impunity. Our captain admitted to me that the Sovereignty had to pay an exorbitant port fee of forty gold marks to Rork so he could enter Terminal Bay and pick us up. Getting the funds transferred from the Exchequer to a bank in Donorvale where *Gannet* is based is what delayed the ship.'

'I wonder why King Somarus allows such extortion?' Nyla said.

Orrion shrugged. 'My love, probably for the simplest of reasons: the pirates give His Majesty of Didion a kickback.'

'And your royal father winks at it?'

'Say rather that he concentrates on fights he thinks he can win. The Sovereign has troubles enough with the Salka without being concerned about this backward nook of Didion – except, perhaps, as it provides a convenient port of embarkation for an unwanted son.'

Nyla winced at his caustic tone. 'I'm so very glad we're on our way back to Cathra at last. The Dowager Duchess Margaleva was very cold to Mother and me during our stay at her palace. As if if were our fault that her grandson Egonus was punished for wooing Princess Hyndry!'

Orrion, the Brackenfield family, and the fifteen lower-ranking members of their party had cooled their heels in Dennech Palace for a sennight, awaiting the tardy arrival of their ship. During that time, windspoken tidings concerning the campaign against the Salka were only stingily relayed to them by Dennech's resident wizard. Even now, they knew little more than that the two wings of the army had been encamped at Lake of Shadows and the foothills above Direwold for a number of days, while the whereabouts of the Salka horde was still unknown. According to the palace magicker, the best windsearchers of Cathra and Tarn had done everything in their power to locate the monsters, but had failed . . .

As their ship sailed westward, Nyla and Orrion took what pleasure they could in each other's company and the un-expected beauty of the passing scene. Although the shifting breezes bore the brig along at a fair clip, the air was not very cold, for the waters of the nearly landlocked bay still conserved the summer's heat. Flocks of birds were every-where, feeding avidly on fish or sharing rocks and barren islets with basking seals. Larger islands, some having dramatic cliffs striated with black and white, were crowned with dark conifers and shrubs beginning to show flashes of autumnal gold or red. The mouth of the bay was as yet out of sight, a good seventy leagues distant. There the ship would have to thread its way cautiously through the shoals and reefs guarding the entrance to the pirate sanctuary. *Gannet* would not reach the open sea until sunset.

As had become their habit when alone together (the helmsman had his back to them and none of the other crew members were near), Nyla stood at her lover's left side, so that he might use his single hand to hold hers. 'How deeply I regret that my dear father could not accompany us,' she said. 'Mother is below in our little cabin, poor soul, over-come by sorrow. Both of us put up a brave front when we learned that he would have to return to the Northern Wing of the Sovereign Army and join the general staff, but in truth she and I were desolated – and for good reason.'

Hale Brackenfield, Lord Lieutenant of the Realm, three of his knights, their four armigers, and six men-at-arms had remained in Karum Port only long enough to see the *Gannet* and its passengers off safely. Then they rode out along a little-used track that would take them through the wilderness to Castle Direwold and the camp of the Sovereign. Only two knights were left to share the voyage with Orrion, Lady Nyla, and Lord Hale's wife Countess Orvada.

'Father is too elderly and infirm to fight monsters,' Nyla

went on, her face woeful. 'His duties have been mostly administrative in recent years, and he was able to fulfil them with efficiency and distinction. But wounds he suffered while serving as Master-at-Arms to old King Olmigon will bring him misery so long as he sleeps in an unheated tent, and he also has spells of shortness of breath that have worried our house physician.'

Orrion could say nothing to comfort her, only holding her hand tighter as he considered his own humiliating situation.

Many thousands of other men besides Hale Brackenfield would face discomfort and worse during the upcoming war. Yet here *he* was, fit and strong, forbidden to assist in the defense of the High Blenholme. Each night before sleeping alone he thanked heaven for Nyla, even though their marriage must be postponed indefinitely. But Orrion Wincantor could not escape the harsh truth. He had placed love before duty, and now the knowledge brought him sore pain.

The two of them stood together undisturbed for nearly an hour; then Sir Naberig and Sir Vashor, two good-natured older knights of Duke Norval Vanguard's cohort who had been assigned to guard Orrion, came onto the poop deck and saluted.

'My lady,' Naberig said to the young noblewoman, 'your mother the countess begs you to attend her below. She says the motion of the ship is making her feel unwell.'

Nyla left with an apologetic look over her shoulder, letting Naberig precede her to the aft companionway.

Vashor gave Orrion a sympathetic grin. 'Perhaps we can divert ourselves for a while with swordplay, sir. You'll need a lot of practice if you're to become proficient with a varg in your left hand. Why not begin during this voyage? There's a place on the maindeck, just forward of the two lifeboats, where we might whack at each other without annoying the crew too much.'

'You'd trust me with a blade, Sir Vashor?'

The older man winked. 'Even if you had two hands, you'd have a hard time besting me. And if I school you well, I hope you'll remember me kindly when your exile is ended and your rank restored.'

Orrion was taken aback. 'Do you think such a thing is possible?'

'When one is the twin brother to the Prince Heritor? I've no doubt of it, sir! Now let's find you a varg and get started.'

Thalassa Dru and Cray had guessed what Casya Pretender planned to do, and although they sighed together over the girl's reckless bravado, they decided it would not be appropriate to stop her. At seventeen, she was an adult by the laws of her kingdom and capable of deciding her own fate. If her dubious mission succeeded, it might speed the resolution of the New Conflict; if it failed, and her life seemed imperiled as a result, then a rescue operation might still be mounted. The sorceresses took turns windwatching and hoped for the best.

On this day, Cray was the one overseeing the progress of the uncrowned young queen and her companion through a nasty part of the morass west of Black Hare Lake. It was a trackless mire where horses could not venture and even small watercraft were hampered by the shallowness of the vegetation-clogged ponds and a dearth of streams connecting them. Casya and Ising Bedotha would paddle their skiff across one overgrown body of water, portage it through boggy ground to the next tiny lake, then repeat the process – over and over again. On good days they traveled eight or nine leagues. On bad ones, when the weather was especially bad or they had to fight off bears, the valiant pair did three leagues or less.

One saving blessing was that a single night of hard frost

had killed off the biting midges early on. Another was that old Baron Ising seemed to be getting stronger rather than weaker, the more hardship he endured.

Casya's goal was a small river, unnamed by human beings but called the Worm by Green Men, that flowed in a north-easterly direction. At its confluence with the Raging River was an outpost of the small folk, occupied only in summer, where the great dragons sometimes condescended to meet with Green traders and exchange valuables. The Morass Worms coveted various fragrant herbal unguents that they used in their mating rituals, while the Green Men esteemed the gemlike discarded teeth of the worms, from which they made precious jewelry.

Unfortunately for Casya, the post had been abandoned by its traders shortly after she and Cray used it to rendezvous with the reclusive worms in Thunder Moon, at the time of the first Salka invasion. The Pretender knew this, but she hoped to summon the huge creatures to another meeting there somehow, and present her new proposition . . .

Cray left off windwatching and opened her emerald eyes with a small grunt of satisfaction.

Thalassa, who sat beside her friend near the longhouse hearth, knitting a winter toque of muskox wool, put aside her work and prepared mugwort tea for both of them. 'Good news?'

'Casya and Ising have finally reached the trading post – and just in time, for there's a snowstorm rolling down from the Barren Lands. The first of the season, and much too early.'

'Hmmph. Well, in the place where they are, the air barely dips below frost-point at night, so any snowfall ought to melt soon enough. We're surely due a stretch of Redleaf Summer before the true deep freeze arrives. Here – have a nice cup of tea.'

Cray sipped in appreciation. 'Now that the two of them

are safe inside Morass Worm territory, we should bespeak Vaelrath and her clan and see whether they'll deign to meet with Her Audacious Majesty. Shall we explain to them the purpose of Casya's mission?'

Thalassa considered the matter, then shook her head. 'It's the girl's task to persuade the worms, as she did before when you guided her. We can be of help to her by summoning the worms, but we must not interfere. I don't think the Source would approve.'

No, said a silent voice. *I would not.*

Cray squeaked and slopped her tea. 'Black rue and cuckoospit! How long have you been scrying us?'

Not long, dear soul. I was about to pass along information recently given to me by my Remnant colleagues when I noted your oversight of the young queen and her elderly champion. So I waited.

'And do you approve what they're up to?' the Conjure-Princess inquired.

The plan is well worth a try. Conrig and his Sovereign Army are at an impasse, waiting for the Salka to strike. Would that I could advise the king, but I am unable to do so. It may interest you to know that the prince-novice, Vra-Bramlow, has used two raw chunks of moonstone to invoke the Remnant and ask about the Salka. The Remnant responded – as they did to his younger brother Orrion – but to less drastic effect.

'What happened?' said Cray.

Alas, my friends were able to vouchsafe only minimally useful information on the whereabouts of the Salka host to Conrig's son, which he then conveyed to his father. The amphibians have devised an ingenious new form of cover-spell to conceal their activities. Thus far, it is impregnable to oversight . . . Other tidings passed on to me by the Remnant were more felicitous: the majority of the exiled Lights have been persuaded to return to our world's Sky Realm. They are already streaming through subtle corridors toward the hiding place of the Remnant.

Cray and Thalassa exchanged a dubious look.

'Why do they come?' the Green Woman asked. 'Have they plucked up their courage at last and decided to fight?'

'And are the wicked Beaconfolk aware of this startling new development?' Thalassa added.

The return is being accomplished very stealthily. We may hope that the detestable Coldlight Army will remain . . . in the dark, at least for a time.

Thalassa's lips formed an astonished O. The Source had cracked a joke!

As to what may come of this, I cannot say. For now, the exiled Lights and the Remnant will only wait for the appropriate time of action. When it comes, all of us will know that the final phase of the New Conflict has begun.

'And what about us groundlings?' Cray said softly. 'Source, will you and your supernatural friends be able to help us in our own conflict? Or are you only concerned with the Sky?'

Victory will come to all of us when the channels conveying power and pain between our two Realms have been shut down. How this is to be accomplished remains an open question. You might think about it. Be of stout heart until we speak again, dear souls. Farewell.

The two women looked at each other.

'Enigmatic,' said Thalassa Dru.

'Infuriating,' said Cray. 'Let's think instead about how we might assist Casya's appeal to the worms, and leave the Source to his own devices. Frankly, I'm feeling very disappointed in him.'

The Eminent Four had gathered on the parapet of Fenguard's highest tower for the farewell. It was a soft afternoon, with misty drizzle resting most pleasantly on amphibian skin. Mighty Ugusawnn, the Supreme Warrior, was still convalescent after his Demon Seat ordeal; but he was confident of his ability to carry the Master Shaman safely to the place where the Salka invasion force was massing for its assault.

'My recovery from Subtle Gateway's pain-debt was gratifyingly rapid,' Ugusawnn reminded the others. 'One would almost think that the Great Lights were mitigating their price in order to encourage us in our great endeavor.'

'My own debt from the initial experiment with Destroyer surprised me with its leniency as well,' Kalawnn admitted. One tentacle digit stroked the innocuous-looking wand, which hung on a golden chain around his massive neck. The Potency rested safely within his gizzard. 'Of course, I only obliterated a sandbank at the mouth of the Darkling Estuary. Still, it was a most satisfying outcome, proving that the Great Stone would perform its sorcery at a considerable distance from the conjurer – and with precision.'

'Made a lovely bang and waterspout, too!' the First Judge remarked in approval. 'Still, you don't want to overstress yourself at the beginning of the campaign, Kalawnn. A measured use of the tool will best serve our purposes.'

Ugusawnn ground his crystalline tusks in suppressed frustration. He was still bitterly disappointed that he would be unable to wield Destroyer himself. 'The Master Shaman will use the sigil according to the instructions of Attack Force Commander Tasatawnn and myself. That is the agreement!'

'Of course,' the shaman soothed him. 'I would not dream of doing otherwise.'

The aged Conservator of Wisdom brought forth a sealskin sack attached to a baldric and gave it to Kalawnn. 'Here are the books of spells, colleague. Guard them as you guard the Stone of Stones. For if misfortune should strike either you or Ugusawnn, only these conjurations will enable your sigils to be transferred readily to another person. The great defeat of our people under the abominable Bazekoy resulted when

Great Stones held by dead warriors could not be quickly re-empowered.'

'It is understood,' the Supreme Warrior rumbled. He took hold of the delicate Gateway sigil and glanced up at the sky. Although the sun was shrouded in cloud, his talent perceived it and knew the hour. 'And now it is time for Kalawnn and me to go. The main force of our army is in position, and the warriors assigned to perform the Gayle Feint Maneuver are acting out their charade in the waters off Fort Kolm in Tarn even as we speak. The human Sovereign will learn of their presence shortly – to his eventual dismay – and lead the bulk of his army in the wrong direction.'

All four Eminences gave thunderous chuckles at the thought of the foe's upcoming abasement. Then the First Judge and the Conservator moved away from the other two, bowed their crested heads in salute, and murmured, 'Travel well, and may good fortune attend you.'

Kalawnn and Ugusawnn showed their glittering teeth in broad smiles. Then the Supreme Warrior intoned Subtle Gateway's spell, and both Salka vanished in a soundless flash.

The First Judge sighed. 'If only we had been able to obtain more raw mineral from the second Moon Crag! The future of our race for years to come rests on those two Great Stones – and their wielders.'

'Take a long view,' the Wise One urged. 'We endured defeat for a thousand years, and only now have we begun to reconquer our island. If there should be a setback . . . remember that winter gives way to spring. And snows, even on lofty mountaintops, can melt again.'

The air was windless and chill in the foothills around Castle Direwold that morning, and the thin skin of ice that had encrusted puddles and water-buckets in the great encampment of the Northern Wing of the Sovereign Army had melted quickly as the sun climbed. But the Brother of Zeth in charge of weather-divination warned the generals that a snowstorm was crossing the Icebear Channel, and a wind-shift might carry it toward Frost Pass.

It was now near noontide of the fifth day since Conrig had suffered his injury, and the first time he had felt well enough to ride out among the troops. The wound had not festered, the doctors claimed that healing was proceeding well, and thus far it seemed as though the true nature of the disability remained secret.

'I'm well pleased with the look of the warriors,' the Sovereign said, as he and Sernin Donorvale and their top officers completed their inspection tour of the army units. 'All seem warmly clad, full of enthusiasm, and with their arms combat-ready. I trust they're getting plenty of good food.'

'A surfeit, if anything,' said the High Sealord, who rode beside Conrig. 'Supply trains from Tarn arrive daily with ship-ments of oatmeal, salt cod, smoked salmon and char, goat cheese, and venison. This is, of course, in addition to the wide variety of victuals brought up from the south.' He hesi-tated. 'Of course, neither Frost Pass nor Great Pass has yet to receive any snow.'

Conrig lowered his voice. 'And what of supplies from Didion?'

'Precious little, my liege,' Sernin admitted, 'now that you're no longer in a position to coerce Somarus and his merchant-lords in person. What resources Didion has left after the long stalemate are being sent to its warriors at Lake of Shadows, where perforce they are shared with the earl marshal's men. It was probably to be expected. Be assured that Tarn won't stint its obligation to its defenders – what-ever their nation – so long as wagons or pack trains can breast Frost Pass. But I'd be remiss if I did not admit that severe weather could prove to be as great an enemy to us as the Salka.'

'I know,' Conrig murmured. 'And I hope to be able to do something about that problem very soon.'

Sernin raised one eyebrow. 'Would you care to elaborate on your remark, my liege?'

The king only laughed. 'I've got a surprise up my sleeve. I'll explain in good time.'

Sernin looked away and his response was wooden. 'Perhaps that time is already at hand . . . My field commanders and I have arranged for a special midday meal in the common mess tent we share with the Cathran general officers. I request that you join us today, my liege. There is an urgent question all of us must put to you.'

'Question?' Conrig frowned. 'What kind of question? Are you in some doubt as to my strategy? It's a little late for that!'

'Our concerns involve a wholly different matter. But let us suspend this discussion until after we've eaten.'

The Sovereign only picked at his food but consumed a quantity of mulled ale in moody silence, for the tenor of the High Sealord's earlier remarks had disturbed him more than he wanted to admit. Was it possible that Donorvale had found out the truth about Maude? What a catastrophe that would be! But who knew for certain that she was the would-be assassin aside from himself and Dyfrig? And the prince must know that his life would be forfeit if he opened his mouth . . .

Sernin Donorvale rose from his stool at the head of the U-shaped table, where he was seated next to Conrig, and prayed silence. After commanding the young armigers who had served the meal to leave the tent and keep everyone outside beyond earshot, the Tarnian leader looked down on the Sovereign and addressed him without diffidence.

'My liege, we thank you for visiting us here in camp, even though your doctors would have preferred you to remain within Castle Direwold until your injury is better healed. Let me go straight to the point. We of Tarn – and many great lords of your own nation – have recently learned a disturbing fact: that Conjure-King Beynor of Moss was not banished to eastern Didion, as we had been earlier informed. Instead he is here in disguise, sharing quarters in Castle Direwold with your own Corps of Alchymists. We cannot believe you're unaware of this. And so we request an explanation – with respect, but also with a firm determination to learn the truth.'

Sernin resumed his seat. The others at the table, Tarnians and Cathrans alike, were deathly silent.

Conrig felt a vast relief. Maude's identity, and the threat she still posed, remained secret. Beynor's presence, on the other hand, must necessarily have been revealed before long, as well as the uncanny weaponry he owned and had offered to share. So be it. He'd give the explanation that the leaders had demanded.

He rose to his feet with care, since his side was still exquisitely painful, and took a swallow of ale before speaking. 'High Sealord Sernin, my lords – Beynor is here at my invitation.'

Murmurs of disapproval came from many. The Sovereign ignored them and continued.

'On the very eve of our departure from Boarsden, he came to me with an astonishing proposal. Most of you are aware that Beynor lives under a curse. He offended the Beaconfolk somehow or other and was forbidden to use sigil sorcery on pain of being cast into the Hell of Ice. Nevertheless, the man is in possession of three so-called Great Stones – the most powerful of all moonstone sigils. He showed them to me. He *offered* them to me, saying he knew how to activate them. They would serve as very effective weapons against the Salka.'

Sensation! Shouted questions rang out from almost every throat until Sernin Donorvale's clarion voice restored order.

'Naturally,' Conrig resumed, 'I asked the Conjure-King what recompense he required. His only request was that I use the sigils to defeat the monsters – who had done Beynor a great wrong during the years when he dropped out of sight – and that I restore the devastated Kingdom of Moss and assure his position as its king, and the Sovereignty's loyal vassal.'

'You believed him?' the High Sealord said.

'I suspected he might want more – or even attempt some foul treachery, such as slaying me through the sigils. But as he explained their operation, my skepticism waned. Friends, you all know that I was once closely allied with Beynor's sister, the late Queen Ullanoth.'

Covert smirks and smothered chuckles.

'She helped me establish the Sovereignty, using her moonstone sorcery to control the weather and oversee the actions of my opponents. She told me how the magical amulets work – so I realized that Beynor was also telling me the truth about them. The sigils are inactive and useless until a certain spell conjures them to life. Then they are bonded to a single owner. No one else can use them. No one else even dares touch them, for they defend themselves with a fierce uncanny fire. Beynor knows the spell of activation, but he cannot use his three sigils himself. So he has offered them to me, believing I will use them in a right and just manner, as weapons against our common enemy.'

'What kind of sigils are they?' The question came from Duke Munlow Ramscrest, one of the most astute veteran battle-leaders of Cathra.

Conrig nodded affably at his old friend. 'There is a Weathermaker – which might do marvelous good service fending off heavy rain and snow, if these should threaten our success. Weathermaker can also conjure favorable winds for our warships. The second sigil, called Ice-Master, is able to freeze water – even the liquid humors within living bodies.'

'Can it freeze seawater?' asked Yons Stormchild.

'I presume so,' Conrig said with a shrug, 'but I have no notion of how broadly or deeply its scope might extend. In the past, neither Beynor nor Ullanoth owned such a sigil. I suspect the Conjure-King might not know just how it works – only that it will.'

'And the third sigil?' The new Lord Constable, Wanstantil Cloudfell, posed the query with deceptive insouciance.

'It's called Destroyer,' Conrig said, 'alleged to be the most powerful weapon ever fashioned by the ancient Salka. The human rulers of Moss had a Destroyer in their magical arsenal, but all of them except the first Conjure-King, Rothbannon, were afraid to activate it because the stone had such a terrible reputation. Finally the mother of Ullanoth and Beynor dared to bring the sigil to life. But Queen Taspiroth's command to it somehow enraged the touchy Beaconfolk. They killed her in an unspeakable fashion and damned her soul to the deepest of the Ten Hells.'

Sernin said, 'Our Grand Shaman Zolanfel has told me that sigil sorcery exacts an awful price upon the one who uses it.'

'Yes.' Conrig spoke in a matter-of-fact manner. 'Each time any sigil is used, the wielder suffers pain. The more powerful the stone, the greater the suffering. I'm willing to undertake whatever penalty the Beaconfolk demand in order to defeat the Salka. And if I should perish before victory is won, Prince Heritor Corodon will take up the sigils in my place.'

The prince's eyes widened for an instant as he realized the full import of his father's words. The pain-price was news to him! But he lowered his gaze at once and nodded in solemn agreement.

'This transfer of the sigils to another person is possible?'
said Sealord Hobrino Kyle.

'If Beynor is present, and able to pronounce the new
bonding spell.' Conrig let the meaning of that sink in. Then
he swept his glance across the assembly. 'Well, my lords, now
you know the truth. Certain home-grown opponents of mine'
– he stared at Duke Feribor Blackhorse and his cronies –
'have castigated me in the past for daring to make use of
sorcery in military tactics. Other warriors, more pragmatic,
have seen the magic for what it is: a weapon no more repre-
hensible than tarnblaze. The Salka possess quantities of minor
sigils and will certainly use them against us. Their moonstones are more numerous than those Beynor offers us, but
infinitely weaker in potential. Shall we refrain from fighting
the foe with their own kind of weapons because of some
traditionalist superstition?'

No one spoke.

Conrig's dark eyes narrowed and his mouth went hard.
After a pause, he said in a low voice, 'I'll be straightforward
with you. I am not requesting your consensus in this matter.
There is only one Sovereign of Blenholme! I have already
decided to accept the sigils that Beynor offers. I also intend
to have my alchymists and the most powerful Tarnian
shamans guard the Conjure-King like hawks – even
restraining him with Bazekoy's blue pearl if he threatens
mischief. But I don't believe Beynor is a danger to us. He
has too much to lose by betraying the Sovereignty. He's a
human being, for all his talent, and he wants to live in a
human world, not one ruled by Salka monsters. So do I. So
should you.'

The leaders were whispering amongst themselves, and
Conrig left them to it for some minutes, taking needed rest
on his field-stool and quaffing more ale. But finally he stood
up again and lifted his hand to gain their attention.

'And so, my lords, I'll know your minds right now, before you leave this tent. Those who oppose my use of sigil sorcery must depart the encampment at once, taking their followers with them. Their action will be judged not by me but by the people of High Blenholme, when the war is over . . . So indicate how you are disposed. Let those who support me rise to their feet.'

At first, nothing happened. Then Prince Heritor Corodon stood without saying a word. He was followed a moment later by Sernin Donorvale, his mature sons the Sealords Simok and Orfons, and the rest of the Tarnian commanders.

Munlow Ramscrest jumped up and shouted, 'By God, I'll follow Ironcrown to hell and back! Cathrans – are you with me?'

'Yes!' roared most of his compatriots, surging to their feet with upraised fists. Duke Feribor and the other recalcitrant Lords of the South who were present glanced sidelong at one another, then slowly rose.

When the cheers subsided, Conrig inclined his head and spoke a brief word of thanks. His face was noticeably drawn and haggard. 'It would be best if we kept knowledge of the sigil weapons secret from the rank and file for the time being. I leave it to all of you to decide which of your officers should be told. This meeting is now over.'

He beckoned to Prince Corodon and asked for help in mounting his horse. 'I want to ride out before the Brother Healer finds me and gets a notion I ought to return in a litter.'

'But, sire,' the prince said, 'if you're in pain –'

'To horse, damn you! No arguing!' He limped away, cursing.

The battle-leaders began to stream out of the mess tent after the Sovereign, conversing in subdued tones, while the crowd of armigers and Tarnian squires re-entered to begin clearing up.

Sernin Donorvale was one of the last to leave, after giving instructions to Stormchild and a few other high-ranking Sealords. As he lifted the tent-flap he felt a tentative touch on his elbow and turned to find two very young squires clad in tunics bearing the insignia of the House of Kyle.

'Please, my lord,' the older boy said. 'If we might be so bold, we bear greetings to you from a certain high-born lady.'

'Do you indeed!' The head of Tarn's Company of Equals smiled down from his great height. 'And who might you be?'

'My name is Tormo Kyle, and this is my younger brother Durin. We only joined the force of our cousin Sealord Hobrino back at Elderwold. Before that, we served as escort to a Tarnian lady on orders from another cousin of ours, Countess Morilye Kyle of Beorbrook.'

'Our lady's name is Mayda,' Durin piped up eagerly. 'She is a great noblewoman, fleeing from villains who sought to kill her. So she disguised herself as a knight! She's very beautiful, with red hair, but tall enough to pass for a man if the light is bad.'

High Sealord Sernin felt his heart contract, as though a spectral hand were squeezing the life's blood from it. 'Boys . . . did this lady give you any other message for me, besides sending greetings?'

'My lord,' Tormo said, 'she told us to tell you she was your long-lost niece.'

'Oh, God of the Vasty Firmament!' Sernin groaned. 'Grant that it was not she – not Maude!'

'Her name is Mayda,' Durin said again. 'She said her son is Prince Dyfrig, who lived in Beorbrook Hold as we did – although we hardly ever saw him except from a distance, at feasts in the great hall. The lady wanted to find her son. Do you know if she did?'

'Come with me,' the High Sealord said. 'You are excused from your duties here. I have many questions to ask you.' He beckoned for the squires to follow him and they left the tent.

The other noble youths who were left behind pulled envious faces, then carried on with the tedious scut-work of clearing the dirty dishes from the table.

'That was most interesting,' Beynor said to Garon Curtling. Both of them were imperceptible to the denizens of the camp, concealed beneath a strong spell of couverture. They had eavesdropped on the Sovereign's speech and also on Donorvale's conversation with the squires.

'It seems that King Conrig is well-disposed to trust you, master,' Garon said.

'Don't talk like a blockhead,' Beynor said sharply. 'He'll never trust me. But he realizes that I'm indispensable – which is just as good.'

'I don't understand,' Garon said. 'And what was all that about a disguised lady and Prince Dyfrig?'

'I'll try to explain as we ride back to the castle,' Beynor said. 'Let's get out of here. I'm anxious to resume wind-searching for the Salka. If I could only find them, it would enhance my prestige tremendously. I might then be able to sit openly on the Sovereign's general staff, rather than lurking hole-and-corner like an outcast.'

Garon was surprised that such a thing would bother the sorcerer, but wisely kept his own counsel as they returned to their horses.

Earl Marshal Parlian Beorbrook was sitting alone on a drift-wood log on the shore of the Lake of Shadows, toasting a sausage over a small open fire and thinking troubled thoughts, when the Tarnian apprentice shaman approached stealthily through the underbrush, avoiding the regular trail between the lake and the encampments of Cathra and Didion.

'My lord, I have important news for you. My husb – Master

Haydon Sympath has just received a windspoken message from Grand Shaman Zolanfel Kobee, who speaks for the High Sealord.'

'Come and sit down, Induna,' Beorbrook said. 'No one will disturb us here. I suppose Sernin and the other Tarnians have finally confronted the Sovereign about Beynor.' He began to eat, alternating bites of meat and rye bread. 'I wondered how long it would take them to act on the information I passed along back at Rockyford. Was there a flaming row?'

'Not at all, my lord. King Conrig replied rather calmly to the question posed by Sealord Sernin. He revealed to the entire group of battle-leaders that Beynor was present on his own sufferance. Furthermore, the Sovereign said that the Conjure-King had offered him three Great Sigils, which he intends to accept and wield as weapons against the Salka.'

Beorbrook almost choked on a bite of sausage. 'Swive me! And how did the generals react to that?'

'After some hesitation, they approved. They had no real choice. The king said he'd send away anyone who opposed his decision . . . But there's further news. Scalord Sernin has confirmed what you already suspected about the would-be assassin. Two young armigers who escorted Princess Maudrayne from Cathra to Rockyford revealed her identity to him.'

The earl marshal groaned and threw the rest of his meal into the fire. 'My appetite is ruined. I suppose Donorvale and the Tarnians are now contemplating secession from the Sovereignty – or worse!'

Induna shook her head. 'The High Sealord is deeply grieved at the death of his beloved niece but intends to keep the knowledge privily in his heart for the sake of the realm's security. He feels that Lady Maude should have come to him directly and requested protection from Conrig, rather than seeking bloody vengeance. He suspects that Prince Dyfrig warned his mother that he would not seek to depose Conrig at this time – again, for the sake of the realm – and that she acted without her son's knowledge.'

'Chaos,' Parlian muttered, staring into the flames. 'That's what Conrig's murder would have brought about. Maude didn't see it, poor deluded woman. But Dyfrig did.'

'The young man must be devastated,' Induna could not help but say.

The earl marshal shot her a stern look. 'His own hard decisions – to remain loyal to the Sovereign and repudiate his mother's folly – are worthy of a great prince. His sorrows will make him stronger. The only true comfort we can offer Dyfrig is to keep secret Maude's identity and the motive for her misguided action. Tell that to Deveron.'

'I shall, my lord.'

The earl marshal rose and began to kick apart the fire and push sand over the embers. 'Also, be so good as to inform my adjutant, Viscount Aylesmere, that I will have an immediate conference with all of my battle-leaders at Birch Grove Circle. Then bespeak the staff wizard of Crown Prince Valardus in the Didionite camp, asking His Royal Highness and his generals to also attend the meeting. We must discuss the Sovereign's impending use of the sigils. I want to nip any opposition in the bud.'

'Very well, my lord.'

'Does your husband continue to windsearch the coast, seeking signs of the invaders?'

'At intervals, but so far to no avail.' Her smile was one-sided with exasperation. 'It's enough to make one wonder whether the monsters didn't decide to return home to Moss after all – where they now loll in their caverns, laughing at the futility of our frantic preparations for war.'

*   *   *

Earlier, Vra-Bramlow had received permission from the Sovereign to consult the demons again, using the lumps of raw moonstone. At breakfast in the gloomy great hall of Castle Direwold, before leaving to inspect the troops, Conrig had given the novice the key to the small leaden casket where he kept the minerals.

'I'll order my chamber guards to admit you,' the king had said. 'The casket is hidden at the bottom of my armor coffer. Take care that no other magicker follows and spies on you while you invoke the good Lights. Most particularly, beware of Beynor! If he knew about the specimens Coro brought from Demon Seat, I doubt not that he'd try to take them from me. I trust you to ensure that this doesn't happen.'

'I'll do my best to safeguard the stones, sire,' Bram said, but his heart plummeted. He was well aware that his uncanny abilities were no match for those of the Mossland sorcerer. Still, he thought, it was not likely that Beynor knew of the stones' existence. A leaden box ought to thwart the windsight of even the best scrier.

'I'll be at the encampment for several hours,' Conrig said. 'Try to cajole the demons into searching for the Salka horde with special diligence this time – and for as long as possible.'

'I will, sire.'

After Conrig departed, accompanied by the Prince Heritor, his physician Vra-Garason, and half a dozen Royal Guardsmen, Bramlow went to the tower where the Sovereign had been installed by Direwold's ill-tempered Didionite castellan, one Baron Jordus. The novice cast about with his windsight as he climbed the tower stairs, finding no one in the vicinity save the two guards usually posted there. They admitted him to Conrig's chamber without a word. The place was stark and unadorned with any tapestries or arras – a sorry contrast to the luxury of Boarsden. The single bearskin rug in front of the small hearth was motheaten, and the sparse furnishings were more suited to a country cottage than the fortress of a Didionite lord. Only the tester bed, made up with the Sovereign's own hangings, linen, and coverlets, looked comfortable.

After fetching the leaden casket and unlocking it, Bramlow settled down in an uncushioned chair beside a narrow window with the box in his lap. He lifted the lid only enough so that his fingers could slip in, closed his eyes, and pressed the stones together without removing them from the box.

'Great Lords of the Sky,' he intoned in soundless wind-speech, 'here is Vra-Bramlow Wincantor once again, begging your favors if you would be so kind as to listen.'

He saw the sad, ghostly faces floating in a starry firmament. *We hear you. Do you still seek the position of the Salka invasion force?*

'Yes, and with great anxiety, for it seems certain that they must now be within striking distance of vulnerable cities on the west coast of our island.'

We see numbers of Salka, swimming so close to the surface of the sea that their bodies often break through the waves.

'Bloody hell! . . . Forgive me, great lords. I – I'd despaired of locating the enemy. Exactly where are they?'

We see the nation you call Tarn. We see a long arm of the sea trending east and north, with many human settlements along its shores. It culminates in a great river whereon boats of many kinds and large sailing ships float. Do you know this place, Vra-Bramlow Wincantor? We have no name for it.

'Tell me: is the entrance to this estuary very narrow, with a large island lying just south of it?'

Yes.

'It sounds like the Firth of Gayle. And the great river must be the Donor, which provides a water corridor to Tarn's capital city.'

The Salka hover in the waters just outside the entrance to this

Firth of Gayle. On a promontory nearby stands a human stronghold.

'Fort Kolm. Yes! Can you see how many Salka are present?'

We cannot. Some of them are clearly visible to us. But we believe that there are others in the vicinity who conceal themselves in an uncanny fashion, very ingeniously.

'Thank you, great lords! We humans thank you with all our hearts for helping us.'

The One Denied the Sky is also pleased with our action. We are not really sure why this should be. We will ask him. But listen! You must take the two pieces of raw mineral with you. Do not leave them in your father's possession.

'Why not?' Bramlow asked.

We do not know. But you must take them and keep them safe. This we are sure of, Vra-Bramlow Wincantor. Take them! And when you feel that catastrophe threatens your groundling race, use them to summon us.

The vision dissolved to blackness and Bram opened his eyes. With unsteady fingers he removed the chunks of mineral and concealed them within his jerkin. He locked the casket and replaced it at the bottom of the chest containing the Sovereign's armor and ran from the room, leaving the guards staring with puzzled expressions, and flung himself down the tower's iron staircase.

At the bottom he dashed through the corridors of the keep to the apartment occupied by the most important of the Tarnian shamans. The place was unshielded by magic, so Bram pushed aside the Tarnian warrior on guard and burst through the door without knocking. He found three men, handsomely dressed in gold-studded leather jerkins and gartered trews, sitting entranced at an ill-made round table. One of them was Grand Shaman Zolanfel Kobee.

'Masters!' the novice exclaimed. 'Leave off your scrying and listen to me. I know where the Salka are!'

Zolanfel was the first to open his eyes, and he was clearly peeved at the interruption. 'Young Prince Bramlow? What's that you say?'

The second shaman snorted scornfully. 'How can you possibly know where the monsters are? You – a mere novice in the Order of Zeth!'

The third shaman said, 'Let the youth explain himself.'

The table held a large-scale chart of Blenholme's western coast, much scribbled upon with leaden pencil to indicate areas under wind-scrutiny by the adepts. Bram indicated a location on the parchment. 'Right here. Direct your scrying to the waters off Fort Kolm and see for yourselves. The Salka are in these waters!'

'Colleagues,' the Grand Shaman said to the others, 'let us do as Vra-Bramwell says.'

In unison, they closed their eyes and sat stiff as wooden effigies. Tarnian magickers were never unseemly-looking when they scried.

Bram waited, fidgeting, as time passed with glacial slowness. At last Zolanfel relaxed and opened his eyes again, as did the others.

'You are correct, my prince,' the Grand Shaman said. 'We have seen members of the amphibian horde clearly, and have directed the battery at Fort Kolm to bombard the monsters with tarnblaze. I have also bespoken the Lord Admiral of the Joint Fleet, who will lead his warships to the vicinity, and alerted the Tarnian naval base at Yelicum. In good time, I will require you to inform me just how you were able to succeed in a task that eluded so many others more experienced in windsearching. But for now, I command you to accompany me and my colleagues to the stables. We will ride out at once for the encampment, to inform the Sovereign and the High Sealord of this development in person.'

*   *   *

Two dozen ells beneath the surface of the water, in a part of the open sea west of Terminal Bay where subterranean reefs gave birth to a confusing welter of currents, the main body of the Salka horde lurked, fed, and built up its strength. Nearly fifty thousand inhuman minds were seamlessly united in an immense shield of dissemblance that concealed their presence from oversight.

Kalawnn and Ugusawnn alone floated motionless off the shore of a small island, disguised as flotsam. They windwatched as the guns of Fort Kolm, 270 leagues to the northwest, began to fire into the sea. A few valiant warriors lost their lives in the initial feint before the Salka officers commanding the diversionary force gave the order to move up the Firth of Gayle to the next objective. There the amphibians would be more circumspect, allowing human lookouts in widely separated locations to catch only brief glimpses of them before they vanished into the depths and continued on to the next point of misdirection.

'The trickery will serve its purpose,' Kalawnn observed with satisfaction. 'By dawn tomorrow, enemy warships will converge on the Firth of Gayle, while the Northern Wing of the human army will be marching over the White Rime Mountains into Tarn.'

'And our fighters will already be ensconced within Terminal Bay, ready to come ashore,' Ugusawnn concluded. 'It is . . . well done.' He gave a soft groan.

'Do you feel able to continue the oversight for a while?' Kalawnn inquired. 'If the pain-debt is too severe –'

'No, I can bear it quite well. Pay no attention to my noise-making. It's most satisfying to see that our strategy is succeeding.'

The two of them did a careful scan inside Terminal Bay for another hour, counting armed pirate vessels and noting their position. Then, as the sun sank toward the horizon,

Ugusawnn used his minor sigil Longspeaker to bespeak Commander Tasatawnn in the depths below.

'It is time. Alert the troops.'

I hear and obey, Supreme Warrior! What are your first orders?

'Deploy the surface observers and elite attack forces. Any vessel, large or small, plying the open sea within scrying distance of the baymouth must be sunk. This is to be done in a manner so swift and devious that none on board suspect the cause of disaster. We must preserve secrecy as long as possible. Naturally, there must be no human survivors. Attack the shipping at your discretion, Commander.'

I understand, Tasatawnn responded. *We'll use the false-reef tactic and the boring augers . . . Warriors away! . . . Your next order, Eminence?*

'At present, the bulk of the pirate fleet lies at anchor or tied up at docks in their home ports.' He indicated their numbers and where they were gathered. 'Perhaps word of our mighty invasion force has spread this far and the humans are cowering in fear! . . . The tide is now on the ebb. We have detected only small craft presently moving about inside the bay. The single exception is an armed merchant vessel now moving slowly through the bay's lone deepwater channel toward the open sea. Strangely enough, it is a Tarnian brig, not a Didionite corsair. The Master Shaman will dispose of this ship himself using the Destroyer. He will also block the channel to prevent future encroachment on our beachhead by the enemy navy or homing pirates . . . On my command – but not before – order our warriors to enter the bay via the shoalwaters. Dispose of any bodies from the sunken Tarnian ship. Otherwise, make no assault on any humans or their watercraft. We will not strike until our entire battle-company – including the reserves – is gathered inside the bay. Is this clear?'

Very clear. I await your bespoken word, Eminence.

Ugusawnn's enormous eyes shone like monstrous rubies. 'And now, Kalawnn – it's our turn! Let's go.'

The two Salka leaders emerged from the cove of the island where they had been concealing themselves and swam toward the treacherously shallow and reef-strewn mouth of Terminal Bay, moving faster than any whale or great fish. In minutes they were within sight of their prime objective, a towering sea-stack marking the entrance to the sinuous channel that afforded the only water access to the pirate colony.

The Warrior licked his chops with his snaky purple tongue. 'Can you crack that rocky pillar all along its length, so that the falling bits and pieces demolish the ship and clog the channel at the same time?'

'Destroyer has only two commands, Ugusawnn: "smash" and "obliterate completely". I'm too inexperienced to fine-tune it. It's supposed to adjust its power output to the indicated command and to the target. If I attempt your two-at-one-blow ploy, I might end up accomplishing neither objective – and pay the pain-price for nothing.'

The Supreme Warrior gave an apologetic grunt. 'Well, then, topple the stack first. Let the humans know their doom is upon them! After that you can smash their ship so they tumble helplessly into the water. Our warriors have waited a long time for sentient prey.'

Kalawnn lifted the wand on its golden chain, pointed it at the spire, and intoned a command in the Salka language.

'BREESH TUSA ROWD SHEN!'

They saw a flash of white light; an instant later, a tremendous peal like a thunderclap rolled across the water, followed by a prolonged rumble. The tall pillar of greyish rock fractured into segments, which fell with a series of enormous splashes that temporarily hid the scene.

'Not as loud an explosion as the one that destroyed the

sandbar back in Moss,' the Warrior observed. 'Looks like it did the job nicely though, from what my rather incompetent underwater scrying can make out. The channel is now impassable to anything but small human boats . . . and us, of course!'

'When I blasted the bar in the Darkling Estuary, I used the more powerful conjuration,' the Master Shaman gasped, 'the one that orders the sigil to annihilate the target completely.' He bobbed in the water with his eyes closed, attempting to catch his breath.

Ugusawnn was solicitous. 'Are you in severe pain, colleague?'

'I'm still all right. But I'd better take care of the ship quickly, while I'm able to, before the captain does something unexpected.'

'Use the annihilation command this time,' the Supreme Warrior said. 'I've changed my mind about letting our warriors feed on human flesh. They'll have plenty of time to enjoy themselves later. Tarnian ships often carry a windspeaking shaman aboard, and we don't want to risk a premature revelation of our invasion, do we?'

'Of course not.' Kalawnn lifted the wand again with a quivering tentacle.

'Shall I steady you?' asked the Warrior.

'Yes, please. And if I require help swimming back to our rallying point . . .'

'Of course, colleague.' Ugusawnn braced his massive body against that of the shaman. 'Carry on! Destroy the ship utterly.'

The Master Shaman inhaled to fortify himself, then conjured Destroyer for the second time.

'SKRESS TUSA ROWD SHEN.'

Across the water, beneath the raging sky, a sphere of green flame swelled behind the stub of the broken rock pillar. Then came a deep roaring sound that smote the ears of the two Salka so painfully that they were deafened for a long minute. As the fireball quickly faded, the site of the explosion was enveloped in a spreading mass of fog that hid the scene.

The Supreme Warrior's windsight found no trace remaining of the ship. 'It's done. We've struck the first effective blow in the war against our human foe. Accept my sincere congratulations.'

The shaman only gave an anguished moan.

Ugusawnn was astonished to see a ruddy internal radiance swell beneath the skin of Kalawnn's throat. The Known Potency sigil that he kept within his craw had begun to pulsate regularly, like a silent heartbeat. The pale residual glow of Destroyer and Subtle Gateway mimicked the tempo of the Stone of Stones in uncanny synchrony.

'Kalawnn!' the Warrior whispered. 'Something strange is happening to our Great Stones. Look at them!'

But the Master Shaman only said, 'Take me down into the depths.' Then his huge form floated inert on the surface of the sea.

'At once. I'll summon the healers.' Ugusawnn took firm hold of Kalawnn, being careful not to touch the throbbing Destroyer. But before the two of them submerged, he commanded the invasion of Terminal Bay to begin.

Incredible! We are being interfered with blocked cut off.
  The conduits between the Realms . . . this is not possible.
    The Potency. Can it be responsible?
      Who knows who knows what mischief it is capable of?
MISCHIEF! Sky mischief! Warmlight mischief!
  Their doing? The Ones Exiled?
    No they are gone away rendered feeble and afraid.
      The Remnant then and the One Denied.
They are not powerful enough to block the conduits.

See – the phenomenon is gone! Power and pain flow as usual.
All is well all is well and all the Sky is well.
Perhaps not ... SCRUTINIZE CAREFULLY.

'Bespeak my orders,' Conrig told the Tarnian shamans, who had not even dismounted before delivering tidings of the Salka. 'Both the Northern and Southern Wings of the Sovereign Army are to break camp and prepare to march over the White Rime Mountains into Tarn at dawn tomorrow.'

EIGHTEEN

The master of the brig *Gannet* rose from the table and bowed to the three privileged passengers who had been invited to share wine and sweet biscuits with him in his cabin after the evening mess. For a Tarnian he was rather short in stature, leathery-faced and bald as a goose-egg; but his manner was supremely confident and the deep-set blue eyes beneath his silver brows sparkled with good humor.

'Countess Orvada, Lady Nyla, Sir Orrion, I've enjoyed our conversation greatly. But now I must join the helmsman. We're approaching the mouth of the bay, where the sailing is tricky because of the wind in our teeth, the strong ebbing tide, and the many shoals and rocks that obstruct the waters. We shall have to back and fill our way through the winding channel. Don't be dismayed when the ship drifts broad-side! . . . Might I suggest that you all take some fresh air on deck before retiring? It's not at all cold outside. There should be a magnificent sunset and a fine view from the bow.'

'I'd like my shawl anyhow, sir.' The countess nodded at Orrion. She wore a fine blue silk gown, while Nyla was garbed in fawn camlet.

'I'll fetch it, my lady.' He and the captain left together.

Orvada poured more red wine into her pewter cup and drank it down too quickly. Her eyes were hollow and her plump face, normally rosy and cheerful, was pallid and had acquired new creases about the mouth. When she reached for the decanter once again, Nyla gently slid the wine out of reach.

'Too much will upset your stomach and make your head ache, Mother.'

The countess pouted. 'You're afraid I'll get tiddly and embarrass you in front of your prince!'

'That, too,' Nyla admitted with a smile. 'And if you're prostrate with misery, who will nurse me if I should become . . . seasick myself? There are no other women on the ship.'

'You're never seasick, you saucy wench, no more than I, and at least you have your sweetheart's presence to comfort you. Now let me have another drop of wine. It will blunt my sadness and help me to sleep tonight.'

'Mother –'

'Don't fuss, daughter. I can't help feeling wretched about parting from your father, but from now on I promise to show a braver face. Stop treating me like an irksome child and think of the wine as a physick. If there was a shaman aboard, I might seek another remedy for my low spirits. But there isn't, and I am in great need of a surcease from my pain.'

Wordessly, Nyla poured a small quantity of wine into the cup as Orrion returned with the shawl.

'The western sky has turned the most amazing color!' he announced. 'Never have I seen the like – lines of narrow black clouds silhouetted against a blaze of flame, as though heaven itself were a raging inferno viewed through the charred siding of some enormous wall in the sky. Come and see! We're sailing right into the setting sun.'

Countess Orvada finished her wine, put the cup down with an unsteady hand, and stood up so that the young man could drape the soft wool about her shoulders. 'Let me take your good arm, sir. The stairway up to the deck is steep.'

Nyla rolled her eyes in chagrin. 'Mother!'

'One of the sailors is also missing a hand,' the countess said, unperturbed. 'He has fitted his stump with a very useful hook. Perhaps, Sir Orrion, you might consider getting one of those yourself.'

He laughed. 'I'll think about it.'

The three of them climbed the companionway steps and moved about cautiously on the deck to avoid scurrying sailors. The air was balmy, with a breeze from the Western Ocean, and the waters had only a light chop. A seaman at the forward rail was taking soundings and calling them out to the captain, who stood at the helmsman's shoulder. Other crew members clambered in the rigging performing various tasks. Only the topsails were set, and the brig followed a strange meandering course through an amazing seascape of black-shadowed rocks and smoldering scarlet water. As the captain had warned them, *Gannet* often drifted broadside as though she were out of control; but it was only an illusion caused by the backing and filling against the headwind. The ship remained in the middle of the channel, progressing slowly westward as the ebb tide took her.

The view from the bow was as remarkable as the captain had promised. The baymouth itself was unexpectedly broad, but rocks and exposed sand-flats were everywhere, littering the glowing waters so densely, especially to the south, that it seemed impossible that any large vessel could slip safely amongst them. Some masses of weathered stone barely broke the surface while others towered high, veritable islands with sheer drops on the seaward side and little beaches to landward.

Despite the mildness of the air, Countess Orvada shivered as she clung to the rail. 'No wonder the pirates dwelling in

Terminal Bay feel safe to flaunt the Sovereign's justice! Only a sailor intimately familiar with these waters would dare to brave these dreadful rocks and shoals. I think they must have named this bay Terminal because it's the last place any sensible person would want to go.'

The leadsman cried, 'By the mark, six fathoms.'

'Is that very deep?' Nyla asked Orrion.

'Nay,' he replied in a low voice as he peered over the rail, shading his eyes, 'only about twelve ells. But quite sufficient to float our brig. Don't worry, love. The captain knows what he's doing. And thank God for it, because the color of the water seems to indicate that this channel grows more and more narrow, the closer we come to its end.'

Ahead on their right loomed a notable formation resembling a tall crooked pillar, that stood half a league or so from the bay's precipitous northern shore. The captain had called it Rogue's Pricket and told them it marked not only the channel mouth but also the boundary between the bay shallows and the deep waters of the open sea. *Gannet* continued to drift toward it broadside.

There was a sudden dazzling flash and a concussion like a thunderclap. The Rogue's Pricket was partially enveloped in a shimmering veil of dust.

The women screamed and clung to Orrion in terror. As they watched with mouths wide open, the big pillar of rock shuddered and broke apart with an atrocious noise. The massive fragments fell, sending plumes of spray sky-high.

'Hold fast, hold fast, all hands!' one of the seamen screamed from the rigging. 'There's a bloody gallopin' wave coming right at us!'

Orrion pulled Nyla and her mother to the deck behind the bowsprit. 'Hang onto me and brace yourselves. The ship will roll on her side when it hits.'

Others were shouting and the boatswain's pipe squealed.

Then the wave was upon them. *Gannet* heeled violently on her ear until the deck was tilted almost vertically. A monstrous welter of water crashed over Orrion and the women. They tumbled together as helplessly as dolls. He felt the force of the deluge lift and fling him painfully against the bulwarks. With his left arm, he gripped Nyla's waist and clutched her belt with all his might. Water engulfed them both. He tried to hold his breath, kicking out with his legs when there was no longer any solidity beneath them. She was struggling, trying to break free while bubbles of precious air streamed from her mouth, but he kept hold of her as the water darkened. They were sinking to the bottom of the channel. No matter how strongly he kicked, they sank. He saw other forms moving in the roiled water, casks and other loose gear washed overboard from the ship drifting downward. Overhead was a great black shadow that had to be *Gannet* –

A stupendous burst of emerald fire flared at the surface.

The water turned to a raging maelstrom. He and Nyla cartwheeled. Something struck his head and he felt air stream from his mouth along with his howl of despair. Nyla's body had gone limp, but he still clung tightly to her.

Until I die, he vowed, I'll hold you fast.

And then his world went dark and silent.

Orrion vomited seawater, took a whooping breath, and felt a painful weight compress his back. Again and again it crushed him until he cried out in agony. He heard a voice say, 'Let be, let be, child! He's breathing again. Help me turn him over.'

He opened his eyes and saw a beloved face all streaked with tears. Her hair was undone and hanging in damp ringlets, but she smiled as she bent low to kiss him.

'Love?' he croaked, trying to sit up.

'Lie still, messire,' Countess Orvada commanded.

She knelt on coarse sand beside her daughter. They were on the beach of what appeared to be a small islet, surrounded by rocks that were partially awash and encrusted with seaweed and marine creatures. The sky was deep blue with mauve clouds, and a few stars were beginning to appear.

'What?' he asked. 'How?'

'Mother saved both of us,' Nyla said happily. 'She can swim! Isn't it a wonder? I never knew a woman could do such a thing.'

'A lot you don't know,' the countess muttered. She rummaged in Orrion's sodden wallet, which she had detached from his belt. 'Great Zeth, messire! What a lot of useless rubbish you carry. At least there's a table-knife here. But don't you have a tinderbox?'

'I'm sorry, my lady. I have yet to learn how to strike fire one-handed.'

'Well, we must try rubbing sticks or some such thing. I think I remember how to make a fire-drill. We can use one of the laces from my corset. Nyla, go search for some fine dry stuff that'll serve as tinder. There are a few pitiful plants growing here and there. Gather some driftwood as well. Without a fire we have no hope of attracting rescuers. And before long it will be cold.'

'I'll see to it, Mother. Don't let Orry come after me. He must rest awhile.' She went off among the shore rocks and was lost to sight.

Orrion pulled himself up to a sitting position and took stock of himself. No bones seemed to be broken, although his head and back ached abominably and every breath was a rasp of pain. He still wore all his clothes and his sturdy boots. For the first time, he noticed that the countess had lost the right sleeve of her flimsy silken gown and most of her overskirt and petticoat. Her feet were clad only in torn scarlet stockings.

'My lady, how were you able to save us?' he asked, averting his eyes from her bedraggled form. He began to unbutton his wool jerkin, intending to give it to her.

'I was tossed overboard along with you two,' Orvada said calmly, 'and taken down into the depths. I saw you both sink together like stones, dribbling air. I went down more slowly, since I'm fat, and I kept my breath. Then came the damned green flash and a surge of current that slammed me to the bottom of the channel. I thought I was finished. But no! I kicked off my shoes and got rid of what clothes I could and started to push off for the surface. Then I saw the pair of you twined together and drowned. You'd managed to wrap Nyla's belt around your wrist so tightly you were impossible to separate. So I towed you both up, made it to the side of the channel, and dragged you into the shallows. This little barren island was not far away. I revived Nyla first. After all, sir, she is my daughter! Then both of us worked on you. You seemed dead to me, but she wouldn't give up pushing on your ribs. Finally you breathed – and that's that.' She grinned in satisfaction.

'But the ship –' he started to say.

The countess's face sobered. 'It was still light when I got you out of the water. Sir Orrion, you must believe me when I tell you that not a single trace of the *Gannet* was to be seen anywhere! Nor have I noticed any broken pieces of her drifting about, only a few things that might have been cast overboard by the wave, just as we were.'

He was aghast. 'There were no other survivors? None at all? I'm sure I saw other bodies sinking in the water.'

'As did I,' she replied. 'When we came ashore I called out, but no one answered. If anybody else found safety, they're too far away to hear.' She picked up a stick and snapped it in half to ascertain its dryness. 'Do you have any idea what might have destroyed the Rogue's Pricket and the ship?'

'No, my lady. If lightning struck the rock pillar, it came from a sky with the wrong kind of clouds. As for the green flash, which I perceived while underwater, I know not what to make of that.'

But an uneasy thought came to him even as he spoke: he'd seen strangely colored light once before – or something closely resembling it – at the time his right arm was smitten by the demons. Was it possible that Sky Realm sorcery had destroyed the brig? . . .

Nyla reappeared, emptyhanded but smiling. 'On the land-ward side of the island is a sort of sandy nook above the tide-line where we can be out of the wind. I gathered wood and found some dry seed-heads that might do for tinder. Orrion, Mother and I will help you to walk.'

'I can do it on my own,' he said, hauling himself to his feet. But he staggered and would have fallen if the women had not borne him up. A few minutes later they were ensconced in the sheltered area.

Countess Orvada accepted Orrion's jerkin and went out of sight to remove her corset. She returned with a strong linen lace, which she cut with Orrion's table-knife and tied to the ends of a green stick, fashioning a small bow.

'Can such a thing really make fire?' Nyla wondered.

The countess settled down near the heap of driftwood. She used the knife to gouge a shallow depression in a slab of dry pine, then whittled fine curls of wood and heaped them around the little hole, along with the seed heads. 'I've seen fire-drills used by the shepherds near my childhood home of Craketop Manor.' She selected a sturdy stick less than a foot long and sharpened one end to a point, then twisted it neatly into the bowstring. 'One sets the pointed stick-end into the hole, presses down firmly on the other end of the stick with a cupped stone, then saws back and forth with the bow – thus – causing the stick to spin as a drill would.'

'And friction makes heat within the hole,' Orrion said, 'which should ignite the tinder.'

'Correct.' The bow-and-stick contraption slipped out from under the weighting stone and fell apart. Orvada uttered a colorful curse. 'There's a trick to it. I'll get it right if you two stop watching. Go somewhere else.'

'We'll look for signs of life on the mainland,' Nyla said, drawing Orrion down to the water's edge. They began scanning the north shore, which was not too far away, but saw no lights. It was now almost full dark.

'There was a chart of Terminal Bay on the wall of the library at Dennech Citadel,' he recalled. 'I seem to remember that this side of the bay had only a few tiny settlements. The pirates have their strongholds and port villages further east and on the south shore.'

'Someone will surely see a fire and come to investigate,' she said quietly. 'If only Mother can make the drill work.'

'She seems a changed women, not at all the drooping, despondent soul who embarked weeping from Karum.'

'Adversity can bring out unexpected virtues in some people, Orry.'

'I hope that's true,' he said. 'God, how I hope it's true!'

They went back to the countess after a time and found her sawing away feverishly with the bow. 'It smokes,' she said through clenched teeth, 'but the tinder refuses to catch fire. I blame the damp air.'

'Perhaps if I blew on it gently,' Orrion suggested. He dropped flat on the sand and inched close to the plank with the seeds and shavings. 'Let me steady this piece of wood with my hand while I breathe on the charred bits.'

Nyla said, 'Can I do anything to help?'

'Pray,' said her mother tersely, and began to work the bow-drill again.

A minuscule wisp of smoke rose from the hole and Orrion

found himself following the countess's admonition and praying for a flame. Their lives depended on making fire. Without it they would die of thirst and exposure on this desolate rock. A flame. Please, God and Saint Zeth, a flame –

'Booger me blind!' The countess gave a start of fear and dropped the bow-drill.

Nyla uttered a soft scream. 'Your finger, Orry! Oh, no! It's burning!'

That was not quite the truth. His left hand steadying the board with the drill-hole had a small yellow flame emanating from the tip of its index finger. Wide-eyed, he lifted the hand. The flame danced, not quite touching the fingernail. There was no sensation of his flesh burning.

'Magic!' Countess Orvada gasped, staring at him as though he'd sprouted a second head. 'You possess uncanny talent, Orrion Wincantor, just as your royal father was alleged to do at his trial long years ago. He was acquitted of the charge, but some believe –'

'Oh, who cares?' Nyla shrieked. 'Orry, light the tinder!'

He touched the little pile of wood-curls and fluffy seeds. It flared up instantly. Nyla fed it with twigs and sticks.

'Small stuff, small stuff first!' the countess said, her mind snapping back to the only matter of importance. 'That's right, let it catch well. And now something a bit larger . . .'

Bemused, Orrion watched the finger-flame snuff itself as he bade it. He knew the rumors about his father. And not only him! Corodon was suspiciously adept at conjuring tricks. And of course Bramlow's uncanny abilities were obvious.

'But if I possess talent,' he said, 'why didn't the Brothers of Zeth find out – and bar me from Cathra's throne?'

The countess looked up at him, her fear and revulsion giving way to another emotion. 'It would seem that your talent is undetectable but nonetheless real. And since it may save our lives, I bless you for possessing it, dear boy.'

'I knew nothing,' he whispered. 'I never suspected a thing.' But then he recalled what the demons had said as he begged a miracle on top of the mountain.

AT LEAST YOU ARE WORTHY, AS ARE THE OTHER TWO WHO COWER NEXT TO OUR CRAG.

Nyla pulled up a sizable broken spar and positioned it so it might be pushed into the flames as it was consumed. Then she piled more sticks on and stepped back to revel in the warmth.

'Oh, wonderful! Now we can dry ourselves. Orry, take off your boots and stockings. I'm going to strip to my smalls and hang my gown and petticoat on a tripod of sticks.'

'Daughter!' the countess huffed.

'Orrion and I are to be married,' Nyla said with a toss of her head. 'My things will dry much faster this way.'

'Oh, very well.'

'And we must keep Orry's talent secret, Mother, so the Zeth Brethren don't claim him. What difference does it make if my darling can do magic? He can never be king.'

Orvada had drawn away as the fire grew. Now she gave a little wry smile and extended her feet toward the blaze. 'I will say nothing of your talent, Sir Orrion, unless you grant me permission. A loyal mother-in-law elect can do no less.'

Orrion scrambled over to her and kissed her cheek. 'Thank you. Now let's concentrate on drying off, then make this fire as large as we can.'

Hours passed. They all fell asleep, waking as the fire sank to embers and cool air chilled them. After donning their dry things they set out to gather more driftwood.

It was then that Orrion saw the light on the water. It was yellow, like an oil lantern, and bobbed gently as it came closer. The fat crescent moon was about to set behind the Cuva Hills far inland, but there were millions of stars in the clear sky and it was possible for him to make out a small dinghy being rowed toward their island. The light hung from a stanchion at the bow.

'Hello!' he called. 'Hello, the boat! We're three shipwrecked souls begging your help.'

'We be coming,' a pair of high-pitched voices said in unison.

Orrion had dropped his burden of wood. The two women came running. 'I think they're children,' he said quietly. 'What in the world are they doing out on the water at this late hour?'

'Fishing, I don't doubt,' the countess said. 'Poor folk aren't as sentimental about younglings as you royals. Our peasants at Craketop Manor put the little ones to work gleaning and caring for fowl and gathering potherbs and such when they were five years old.'

'They come of pirate stock,' Orrion warned. 'We must be cautious dealing with them. If they turn us over to Rork Karum, he'd discover our identity by despicable means and hold us for ransom. Ladies, I beg you to say nothing. Let me cope with these young rescuers.'

Countess Orvada grumbled under her breath, but fell silent as the dinghy scraped the sand. It had a mast, but the sail was furled in the calm air. Orrion waded out, took the painter, and hauled the craft up as the two small rowers shipped their oars and leapt out to help. They were a boy and a girl, large-eyed with astonishment, scrawny and no more than ten or eleven years old. They had lank flaxen hair and wore tunics of woven wool with cord belts, hooded capelets of tattered thin leather, and stout open sandals with no stockings.

'Starry Dragon!' the boy exclaimed, eying the scruffy adults warily. 'Did ye come off t'ship got blasted by lightning, then?'

'That's right,' Orrion said with a friendly smile. 'What are your names?'

'Turrible thing that was,' the girl said with gruesome relish. She seemed the older of the pair. 'A course, it were only a Tarnian ship.' She gave a nervous laugh. 'We'uns ain't too friendly with Tarn. I's Ree and he be m'little brother Klagus.'

Orrion hunkered down, sensing their apprehension. 'We're not Tarnians. We're people of Didion, just like you. We're cold and hungry and we want to go home to our people in Dennech Town. Do you know where that is?'

The boy shrugged. 'Somewhere inland. We'uns don't know inland.'

'Were you out fishing by yourselves?'

'We gotta,' the girl said. 'There's only us and Ma and t'brat at home.' She screwed up her face. 'And no food t'spare, either, less'n ye wanna buy summa our fish at fair price. They's grimmels. Good and juicy if ye grill 'em.'

'What's a fair price to feed us, and your mother to cook up the fish?' Orrion inquired briskly.

The fishergirl scowled, pursed her lips, and finally said. 'A silver penny. No less!'

'Done,' said Orrion, and held out his left hand.

She put her cold, grimy one into it, noticing his missing limb for the first time. 'It's good luck, meeting a one-handed or one-legged man. Wotcha gonna do t'morrow? We'uns can't keep ye in t'hut. No room.'

'Can your boat sail to Karum Port? We want to go there as soon as possible. I'll pay you three pennies and buy you both a nice meal at the tavern there. From Karum, we can find our way home to Dennech.'

Ree looked at her brother. 'Wotya think, Klagus?'

'Yar,' he said with a laconic nod to the adults. 'Sea wind'll rise agin after midnight. We'uns can take our catch in early t'market. Ye, too, if ye don' mind sittin' nigh baskets o' fish.'

'We don't mind at all,' Nyla said sweetly. 'We just love fish. Let me help you to board, Mother.'

'Say *nothing*,' Orrion reminded the women in a tense whisper.

When they were seated in the bow and the girl took her place on the mid-thwart, Orrion and the boy pushed the dinghy off and hopped in. In a minute both children were rowing strongly. Orrion had more sense than to offer his help. The fishers were proud of their skill, smirking sidelong at each other at the thought of the windfall of real money that was soon to be theirs.

He thought: Perhaps the children's mother would part with some old clothing if I offered another penny. And when we leave for Karum, I'll hide a gold half-mark coin in the hut where someone will be sure to find it later.

But it would never do for the fishers to find out that his wallet was full of gold. Young as they were, Klagus and Ree would sell the three of them to the pirates in the blink of an eye . . .

Nyla and the countess were silent, heads together. After a time, they seemed to have fallen asleep.

Orrion spoke low to the children. 'Were other folk from the wrecked ship found?'

'None we'uns know,' the boy said. 'Not many out fishin' t'night. This be a lonesome part o' t'bay. All shoalwater and reefs. All we'uns seen was Old Tig's boat early on . . . and later mobs o' great big seals cavortin' in t'moonlight. A sight, that was! They was jumpin' clear outa t' water – like it was one uvum's birthday or some such happy thing.'

'Seals?' Orrion felt a tingle of trepidation. 'How large were they?

The girl said, 'Monstrous! Biggest we'uns ever saw. Red eyes they had, shinin' in t' dark like hot coals. So scary wee Klagus there like t'browned his britchclout, but they didn't do us no harm. Too busy with dancin' or whatever.'

'How – how very curious.' Orrion could not keep the tremor out of his voice.

The mystery of *Gannet's* demise was solved. And he, Orrion Wincantor, was perhaps the only one who knew the place where the Salka horde intended to invade High Blenholme.

What am I going to do? he asked himself. Do I dare wait until morning to carry this terrible news to the authorities at Dennech Citadel? And if I do inform Duchess Margaleva and her people, will she believe me and take action before it's too late?

Numb with horror, he sat in the stern of the dingy. The two wiry children plied their oars, sending the dinghy racing toward the shore. The crescent moon was down, but peeping over the northern highlands were a few faint beams of green and crimson radiance, like ghostly beacons among the stars.

The Lights.

The demons.

YOU ARE WORTHY . . .

I have talent, he thought. Is it possible for me to speak on the wind, as the other adepts do? I've never tried. I never imagined such a thing was possible. But I must attempt it now. God help me, I must!

Who to call? Bramlow was certainly talented and to be trusted. But perhaps he'd have better luck bespeaking the person who had been closest to him from the day of their birth eighteen years ago: his twin brother, Corodon –

The two children giggled shrilly. The girl said, 'Man, ye look like ye swallered a spoilt clam! Feelin' poorly, then?'

'A little,' he said. 'I'm going to try to sleep. Wake me when we reach the shore.'

He closed his eyes and set out to find the wind.

The bell of Castle Direwold struck the hour before midnight and Conrig muttered an imprecation. 'Where is that damned sorcerer? I told him to come at ten! Coro, put more wood on the fire. Bram, see if you can scry the rascal out.'

Baron Jordus's little solar was drafty, and two huge smelly wolfhounds who had been ejected earlier by the servants had crept back in somehow and now lay sleeping before the hearth, making weird noises and twitching as they dreamed.

The High King paced restlessly about the shadowy room while the Prince Heritor and Vra-Bramlow sat at a table lit by tapers in two tarnished candelabra. A matching silver tray held an ornate ewer full of inferior ale, some dented cups, and a plate of dusty sweetmeats. No one had touched the refreshments. Corodon, armed with broadsword and dagger, tossed several billets of wood on the dwindling flames and stirred the coals with a poker. The novice, who had been stroking the golden reliquary that held Bazekoy's blue pearl, left off rehearsing its incantation and covered his head with his hood to attempt the windsearch.

Conrig had ordered his sons to attend him during the ceremony that would activate the sigils, but rejected urgent requests from the senior Zeth Brethren and the Tarnian Grand Shaman that they also be present. The king wanted no one save those of his own blood to know the formula that brought the Great Stones to life.

Bramlow pushed back his hood. 'Beynor comes, sire. As you commanded, he is alone.'

'Both of you take stools beside the hearth,' the king said. 'Be vigilant for treachery! Bram, you are my prime defender.'

'I understand, sire.' The novice took the reliquary and tucked it into the sleeve of his robe, knowing that Beynor would surely be aware of its presence. But would the pearl's benign power be sufficient to shield the Sovereign from Beaconfolk perfidy? None among the Brethren or the Tarnian shamans knew whether Bazekoy's talismans had ever been thus tested.

I must not fail my father, Bram thought. But another notion gnawed at him: Had he already failed Conrig by acquiescing in his intention to use the terrible sigils?

'Good evening, my liege.' Beynor stepped into the solar and closed the door behind him.

Conrig nodded. 'Your Majesty of Moss.'

The sorcerer had put aside the spell of disguise as well as the garments of Zeth's Order and now wore a simple robe of dark green, cinched with the ornate belt of Moss's Sword of State. 'As you can see, I have left the royal blade itself and its scabbard behind in my room. Your valiant sons need have no fear for your safety.'

'Good,' Conrig said. 'Produce the sigils and tell me how to activate them. We'll need them at once. We've located the Salka horde.'

Beynor frowned at the king's peremptory manner. 'Indeed! Very well, I have the stones ready. It would be more respectful to the Great Lights if you knelt –'

'No. I'm the Sovereign. I'll stand before the Beaconfolk as I stand before God himself.' He rose to his feet.

'We can only hope that the Lights will understand royal protocol.' Beynor opened his belt-wallet, removed a small pouch, and tipped its contents onto the table. He unwrapped each moonstone from its covering and laid them out in a row. 'Which stone would you empower first?'

'Destroyer, of course.' Conrig's dark eyes flashed.

'Of course.' Beynor smiled thinly. 'Just remember that using it safely will require a certain technique that only I can teach you. Any attempt on your part to –'

'I'll never harm you unless you play me foul, Conjure-King. Get on with your instructions. I'll need to activate all of the sigils.'

Beynor's glance flicked to the two watching princes. 'Are you certain you want these young men to witness the empowerment?'

'*No one* will witness the empowerment,' Conrig stated adamantly. 'Once you've taught me how to conjure the spell, I intend to take the moonstones out onto the balcony and say the words under the stars, alone. Whatever will be, will be. But only I will speak to the Great Lights.'

For a moment, Beynor was taken aback. Then he shrugged. 'As you wish.' He began to rehearse the king in the questions the Keeper of Sigils would ask and the proper responses he must give in the Salka language.

'But why must I address these Beaconfolk in an alien tongue? I thought they were infinitely wise. Don't they understand the language that all of us on the island speak?'

'I can only tell you what was written down by Rothbannon, the first Conjure-King. He emphasized that proper pronunciation of these Salka words was vital. Speak them imperfectly and you may pay with your life. Now – have you everything memorized?'

'Yes,' Conrig growled.

'Be careful to touch the disk to only one sigil at a time. You may expect to suffer a certain amount of pain during the activation. It's the Lights' way of testing your resolve, your willingness to pay the price for their sorcery.'

'Huh! I'll pay any price to save the Sovereignty.' He swept up the three sigils and dumped them back into their pouch. The disk he carried in his hand. 'Stay inside, no matter what happens. My sons will see that you obey.'

'Your excessive caution is quite unnecessary,' Beynor said with dignity. 'But suit yourself.' He sat down in one of the chairs beside the table and helped himself to ale from the silver ewer. One of the wolfhounds gave a gruff snort, then settled back into slumber.

The door leading to the balcony had only a small glazed window. In truth, Conrig wanted no witness to his first attempt at high sorcery because he was afraid he might botch it and suffer another public humiliation like the one at Rockyford.

I'd rather perish in a bolt of astral lightning, he thought, than have that snotty bastard and my boys behold me in ignominy!

The moon was down and the sky was diamond-spangled. Even better, the aurora borealis had appeared right on cue, exceptionally splendid for so early in the autumn. It had to be an omen . . .

He removed Destroyer from the pouch and placed the other sigils on the balcony railing to wait their turn. Then he pressed the little wand firmly against the gold-framed moonstone rondel.

The stones felt icy cold. As they began to glow, a sudden pang of agony lanced his heart and he gasped aloud. The pain swelled and he felt his vision of the castle battlements and the surrounding dark countryside dimming. He hung suspended in the starry void. Only the Sky remained, with a single irascible face painted upon it in crimson Light.

CADAY AN RUDAY? The being roared in his mind's ear, asking what he wanted.

Conrig bellowed the words he'd learned. 'GO TUGA LUV KRO AN AY COMASH DOM!' Which meant, 'May the Cold Light grant me power.'

A frightful stab of pain smote him and he almost lost hold of the stones. The face seemed to snarl as it asked him, *KO AN SO?* Wanting to know who he was.

Using all his strength, he straightened his racked body and cried out the reply. 'CONRIG WINCANTOR, CALLED IRON-CROWN, THE SOVEREIGN OF HIGH BLENHOLME! AND WHO THE DEVIL ARE YOU?'

The Light's face appeared to swell with rage. And then it began to laugh. The sound was shattering, like a gigantic bell tolling, and the stars seemed to cringe and pale before its force. Then the Sky entity fell silent, staring at Conrig, and the stars regained their brightness.

'Well?' the king said in resignation. 'Have I insulted you? I didn't mean to. But go ahead, strike me dead for impudence if you must. The Conjure-King will instruct my son to address you with the proper deference when *he* tries to empower these sigils.'

WE WILL NOT STRIKE YOU DEAD. NOT THIS TIME. WE HAVE WAITED LONG FOR A HUMAN OF YOUR POTENTIAL TO APPROACH US. AS A SIGN OF OUR FAVOR, WE WILL ADDRESS YOU IN YOUR OWN LANGUAGE . . . YOU ASK WHO I AM, BUT WE HAVE NO NAMES AS YOU GROUNDLINGS DO. I AM THE STONE-KEEPER, THE ONE WHO ACCEPTS OR REJECTS THOSE WHO PETITION TO SHARE OUR POWER.

'Well then, Stone-Keeper, do you accept me? Will you let me wield Destroyer and the other two Great Stones against our Salka enemies? You may squeeze what pain you must from me in payment –'

WE WANT MORE FROM YOU THAN THAT.

Conrig felt himself go numb; all sensation fled, leaving him with the terrible impression that his soul had been extracted from his body. 'Am I dead?' he asked. 'Have you slain me?'

CERTAINLY NOT. WE ONLY WISH TO HAVE YOUR COMPLETE ATTENTION. WE ESTEEM YOU AND OTHER STRONG PERSONS OF YOUR GROUND REALM. WE WISH NUMBERS OF YOU TO EMBRACE SIGIL SORCERY WHOLE-HEARTEDLY, AS THE SALKA ONCE DID. OF LATE, THE GREAT AMPHIBIANS HAVE DISAPPOINTED US. THEY HAVE BECOME TIMID AND APATHETIC, HESITANT TO MAKE THE NECESSARY SACRIFICE REQUIRED TO OBTAIN THE GREATEST

POWER. AND SO WE TURN TO YOU AND YOUR KIND, OFFERING OUR GIFTS.

Conrig was thunderstruck as the Light's meaning became apparent. Finally he said, 'But if you give sigils such as Destroyer to many human beings, we'll end up fighting each other to the death! We're not a peaceful race, Stone-Keeper.'

YOU MISUNDERSTAND, CONRIG WINCANTOR. CERTAIN GREAT STONES ARE FIT ONLY FOR GREAT PERSONS TO WIELD. THEY ARE NOT FOR THE STUPID, THE VAIN-GLORIOUS, OR THE VENAL – NOR ARE THEY FOR PERSONS WHO PLACE THEIR GOALS ABOVE OUR OWN. THERE ARE HUNDREDS OF DIFFERENT KINDS OF MINOR SIGILS YOUR LESSER PEOPLE MIGHT EMPOWER AND USE: LONG-SPEAKERS, HEALERS, BEAST-BIDDERS, SHAPECHANGERS, FLAME-STONES . . . SO MANY MORE. AND YOU WOULD BE THE ONE TO BESTOW THEM ON YOUR TALENTED ONES – AT THE APPROPRIATE TIME, OF COURSE. BUT HUMANS MUST FIRST PROVE THEMSELVES MORE WORTHY THAN THE SALKA, MORE WILLING TO . . . PARTICIPATE IN A CERTAIN CONTEST WE LIGHTS ESTEEM.

'Can you explain your proposal further?'

LATER. AFTER YOU, CONRIG IRONCROWN, PROVE YOUR-SELF TO BE TOTALLY WORTHY.

'What happens now? I've already asked you to grant me power. Do you intend to accept my petition?'

THASHIN AH GAV. WE ACCEPT. THE THREE GREAT STONES ARE ALIVE AND BONDED TO YOU ALREADY. CONJURING THEM WILL REQUIRE NO SALKA INCANTATION. SIMPLY COMMAND THEM TO DO YOUR BIDDING. THERE WILL BE A PROPORTIONAL PAIN-PRICE – BUT PERHAPS NOT ONE SO SEVERE AS WE HAVE DEMANDED OF OTHERS. WE WISH TO ENCOURAGE YOU.

The Light went on to explain the functions of the different stones and their limitations. Conrig could hardly believe his good fortune. Beyond any doubt, these three sigils alone would enable him to rule the world. And the raw material for making more of them was now easily within his grasp . . .

'Thank you, Stone-Keeper. MO TENGALAH SHERUV.'

WE HAVE ONE LAST ADMONITION FOR YOU: DO NOT TELL THE ACCURST ONE OF OUR BARGAIN – AND DO NOT RETURN THE MOONSTONE DISK TO HIM. HE IS A DANGER TO YOU AND TO US.

'Beynor may be cursed by you Lights, but he's still a powerful sorcerer. He'll force me to hand over the disk, retaining power over who inherits them upon my death.'

NO, HE WILL NOT. WE HAVE BONDED THE DISK TO YOU, AS WAS DONE SEVEN HUNDRED OF YOUR YEARS AGO WITH THE ORIGINAL THREE DISKS VOUCHSAFED TO THE FIRST HUMAN TO WHOM WE PROPOSED THIS BARGAIN, ONE VRA-DARASILO LEDNOK. THAT MISERABLE COWARD! ULTI-MATELY, HE WAS AFRAID TO USE THE TROVE OF SIGILS WE GAVE HIM. HE ONLY WROTE BOOKS ABOUT THEM – THE FOOL – AND WHEN HE DIED, SO DID THE BONDING OF HIS MOONSTONE DISKS. WE OFFERED DARASILO A SHORT CUT TO POWER. HE REJECTED IT. WE HOPE YOU ARE WISER.

'Be assured that I am. You have given me what I longed for all my life. I'll use the sigils well. Bonding the disk to me was a master stroke.'

WE THOUGHT SO.

By allowing Conrig to command the sigils in his own tongue, and making it impossible for Beynor to seize the disk, the Beaconfolk had effectively barred the Conjure-King from exerting any significant influence over the Sovereignty. Beynor no longer had any leverage to impose his will.

Conrig said, 'Will you allow me to return to my own world now, and fight my war?'

YOU ARE DISMISSED . . . UNTIL THE TIME WE MUST

SPEAK AGAIN. THEN WE HOPE TO HAVE AN EXCELLENT NEW HUMAN ALLY FOR YOU.

'Who?'

YOU WILL KNOW HIM WHEN YOU SEE HIM.

The eerie face of Stone-Keeper vanished, and the king realized that his own body belonged to him again. He stood on the balcony and felt no pain. A cold breeze blew from the north and the air smelled of approaching snow – but he had the remedy for that! The finger-ring called Weathermaker glowed with subtle life on the railing, as did the equally useful Ice-Master sigil lying beside it.

But the Great Stone that Conrig most coveted was safe in his hand: Destroyer, the key to victory against the invading monsters. He lifted the fragile wand, wondering if he dared to test it.

Not here, he thought with a smile. Inside, while that whoreson Beynor watches!

He put the disk and the sigils into their pouch and re-entered the solar. Beynor looked up, his gaunt face without expression. 'And so, my liege, have you empowered the sigils?'

'Didn't you scry me through the doorway – or overhear my conversation with the Light?'

'I could perceive nothing,' the Conjure-King replied coldly. 'Indeed, I feared you'd been snatched away in some tragic uncanny mishap. I attempted to go to your aid . . . but your sons restrained me.'

Bram and Coro stood on either side of the sorcerer. The Prince Heritor held a drawn broadsword and the novice had the reliquary lifted high in both hands.

'I invoked the "All Harmful Spells Avaunt" command, Father,' Bramlow said, 'and Coro restrained the Conjure-King physically.'

'Good lads,' the king said. 'You may stand down now. His Majesty means me no harm.'

'Certainly not,' Beynor said easily. But his fists were tightly clenched at his sides.

'Father, the sigils –' Bramlow ventured.

Conrig strode to the table. One by one he took the three small carvings from the pouch and laid them out. The princes gave cries of awe.

'They glow. They're alive!' Corodon exclaimed, extending his hand.

'No!' Conrig shouted, seizing the lad's wrist. 'Touch a living sigil that's not bonded to you without the owner's permission and it will kill you.'

The Prince Heritor staggered back. 'I didn't mean –'

'I know. It's all right . . . and I have one more piece of moonstone to show you.' He extracted the shining disk from the pouch and held it up for Beynor to see. 'A special favor was granted to me. This empowering disk, which summons the guardian Light when touched to an inactive sigil, is now also bonded to me. No one else may control it.'

'No!' Beynor cried. 'The Lights wouldn't do that!'

'But they did,' the king said. 'It seems that they don't trust you, Conjure-King. I was commanded not to give the disk to you.'

'But, my liege! You will still need my help to use the sigils safely, and you swore –'

'The oath is void. The Light who talked to me explained how each sigil works. Furthermore, I am allowed to conjure their power using my own language – not that of the Salka.'

'Would you care to prove that, my liege?' The question was insolently delivered, but Conrig only gave a gracious nod.

'Baron Jordus Direwold has an appalling taste in silver hollow ware, don't you think? That ewer is particularly ugly. And the ale is sour.' The king pointed the moonstone wand at the container. 'Destroyer, obliterate that thing, but harm nothing else.'

There was a sharp explosion. A cloud of luminous green steam with a pungent odor bloomed, then dissipated to nothing. The two wolfhounds sprang to their feet and began to howl their hearts out.

Conrig laughed. After a shocked instant, the princes joined in.

Beynor made a sharp gesture that quieted the dogs. Then he spoke in a strained voice. 'Do you mean to say that you are repudiating our agreement to use the sigils to mutual advantage?'

'Not at all.' The Sovereign began to gather the moonstones and put them into the pouch. 'You shall have the throne of Moss, as you requested, but I no longer require your services as a royal adviser. You and your crony must leave this camp tomorrow at dawn. Horses will be placed at your disposal. Go to eastern Didion. Find your former subjects who have settled around Incayo and the adjacent towns. Ingratiate yourself so they will accept you as their leader.'

'That will be difficult –'

'Hardly. The Mossland expatriates are poverty-stricken, while you are well-supplied with treasure, are you not? It was reported to me that the material assets of Didion's late Lord Chancellor disappeared on the night he died. Kilian's two elder henchmen, the likeliest suspects in the theft, fled from Boarsden. Shortly afterward, Garon Curtling also disappeared. The bodies of the older men were found in a tavern privy near Twicken, and Garon returned to the castle and was taken into your service. Need I go on?'

Beynor said nothing.

'So long as you continue to render fealty to me, I'll support your claim to Moss's throne. In time, the Salka will be cast out of your country. The Sovereignty will assist all of its loyal vassals to rebuild towns laid waste by the monsters. Will you be one of those vassals?'

For an instant, black fury glared from the eyes of the thwarted sorcerer. Then he bowed his head. 'I will, my liege.' *Until there is a new Sovereign more amenable to my persuasion.*

'Very good. Now you may go.'

The Conjure-King turned and went out the door without another word, closing it behind him.

Conrig tucked the pouch of sigils into his wallet. 'My boys, sit with me for a few minutes. Then we all must go to bed, for the army marches to Tarn on the morrow to meet the foe. But I want to share my great vision of the future with you now, so that you may dream of how the wondrous events upcoming will affect your own lives. What I have obtained tonight from the Beaconfolk is more than the means for victory over the Salka. So very much more!'

Grinning in eager anticipation, Bramlow and Corodon seated themselves and listened to what their royal father planned to do. By the time Conrig had explained, the smiles of the two young men had gone glassy.

'You do see how the scheme comes to full fruition, don't you?' Conrig said. 'The key is Ice-Master, the sigil we thought was the least significant of the three. But that's because Beynor didn't understand its function. The Light named Stone-Keeper told me that the sigil not only freezes – *it also thaws.* Even if the summit of Demon Seat is once again shrouded in winter's ice and snow, the sigil can melt it and make the raw mineral available to us. Think what this means, lads. Just think of it!'

The princes could only stare at him, speechless.

'I can see you're both overwhelmed,' Conrig said kindly. 'And no wonder. We'll talk about this later, when you've had time to take it all in. Goodnight, my dear sons. Sleep well.'

They nodded, saying together, 'And you, too, sire.'

As the brothers went to the chamber that they shared, Coro finally found his tongue and began to chatter giddily about the glorious scope of the Sovereign's vision.

Bramlow cut him off. 'Be silent! Don't you understand what's happened to Father? Are you a complete idiot?'

'Look here, you've no cause to speak to me like that!' the Heritor blustered. 'What the hell do you mean? A miracle has occurred and you act like it's some terrible disaster –'

Bramlow broke in. 'The Beaconfolk threw out an irresistible lure and Father swallowed it! They gave him power, Coro. Power that will give them control over him. But the Lights don't only want the High King. They want all of us.'

Deep beneath the permanent Ice of the Barren Lands, the One Denied the Sky groaned in ineffable sorrow.

'He has fallen. I knew it must happen, but how bitter is the actuality! Ironcrown will bring about his own ruin . . . but will the rest of humanity on the island also perish? Tell me, my friends!'

We see only paradox, said the Likeminded, *and no clear inkling of the outcome. But the Conflict in the Sky Realm has now begun. We must all be vigilant – whatever happens on the Ground.*

'Nevertheless,' the Source said, 'I think I must attempt one last intervention, using the groundling soul called Snudge.'

Conjure-King Beynor lay rigid in his narrow bed, ranging on the wind in search of Deveron Austrey's dream. It took him half the night to find it, and more hours to gain entry, for the wild-talented one had greatly matured and his mental barriers were much stronger than they had been in earlier years.

Appealing to the former intelligencer was an act of utter desperation on Beynor's part. He was loath to admit it to himself, but he could think of no easy way to kill Conrig and thus regain control of the sigils and the disk. Not with Bazekoy's blue pearl once again safeguarding the king from malignant sorcery, and the companies of magickers and guards armed to the teeth who would henceforth defend the royal person from physical assault.

There was also the most sinister realization of all: that Conrig Wincantor was clearly the Chosen of the Lights. Even if Beynor were able to kill the Sovereign, the Beaconfolk might then slay *him* in retaliation.

Another would have to do it. One with the ability to penetrate Conrig's various defenses, who might yet be willing to strike a bargain.

The only person who came to mind – improbably, but that was the irony of it! – was the former Royal Intelligencer. Deveron Austrey must certainly be bent upon vengeance against his former master. Why else had he suddenly emerged from hiding after sixteen years? Beynor thought it likely that Deveron had instigated the failed assassination attempt at Rockyford, and he had once wielded sigils. Perhaps he might be tempted to regain the power he had evidently lost. The gamble was a risky one, but it had to be chanced . . .

He invaded the ex-intelligencer's dream, using his unique natural talent, and laid out the facts of the situation, showing in detail how the death of Conrig Wincantor might redound to their mutual advantage.

When you wake, Deveron, you might think this dream was only fancy. In this you would be wrong. Bespeak me on the wind tomorrow and we'll arrange a place to meet. I'll be traveling on horseback, southbound on the Wold Road from Castle Direwold with a friend. Conrig has commanded me to return to my own exiled people, thinking he has no more need of my services. He has no notion of the Beaconfolk's plan for the subjugation of the human race. My

ancestor Rothbannon was able to outwit the Lights and prosper.
Together, you and I can do the same.

'You've misjudged me, Conjure-King.'

I don't think so. Do you deny you returned to Blenholme to take
revenge on Conrig? Do you deny you organized the failed attempt
at assassination? I know you were prowling about the station that
night!

'You know nothing about me or my intentions. Nothing!
And you're a fool to think I'd ally with you in an attempt
to take control of the High King's sigils through murder. In
fact, I intend to notify his alchymical advisers of your evil
scheme, so they can protect him.'

. . . I see.

'I'll guard my dreams more efficiently from now on,
Beynor. Don't bother trying to invade them again. My answer
to you will always be NO.'

Then perhaps we'll meet again someday in hell, Deveron Austrey.
May you arrive sooner than I.

Prince Corodon woke with a startled shout, leapt from his
bed, and began to shake his brother's shoulder. 'Bram! Bram!
Wake up!'

The novice, who had spent most of the night wallowing
in sleepless dread, was slow to rouse. Seeing in the dark was
not one of his stronger powers, but there was minimal light
from a few living embers in the fireplace. 'Coro? It's not even
dawn –'

'Bram, I heard Orry! He spoke to me, clear as a bell, whilst
I was half-dozing.'

'Codswallop. You were dreaming.'

'No, listen! I think he talked to me on the wind. You know
as well as I do that I've got some sort of puny talent. Suppose
Orry has it, too? And what he told me . . . Bram, he said the
Salka are invading at Terminal Bay in Didion! He said they

used sorcery to sink the ship he and Nyla and her mother were on. They also knocked down a tall rock pillar at the entrance to the bay.'

Bramlow groaned. 'The good Lights told me the monsters are coming ashore in Tarn, at the Firth of Gayle, not in Didion. Go away!' He pulled his pillow over his head.

Corodon ripped the pillow off his brother and flung it onto the floor. 'What if the sighting in Tarn is some sort of a ruse?'

Bram pulled himself up onto his elbows. 'What am I supposed to do? Run and tell the other magickers that you can hear windspeech? *Reveal that you're ineligible to sit Cathra's throne?*'

The Prince Heritor was taken aback only for a moment. 'Tell Father! Say that *you* received the windspoken message from – from some dying person on Orry's ship. Or from the demons themselves! That might convince him to order the Brothers to do a windsearch of Terminal Bay. Perhaps they'll see the broken rock pillar, if nothing else. Bram, for God's sake! You have to do this.'

'Right. And when all comes to nothing, then I'm a silly ass who took a nightmare seriously.'

'But –'

'No, dammit, no!' Bram shouted. 'Stop pestering me and let me sleep. Tomorrow, I'll go to the Tarnian Grand Shaman and ask him to scry the bay as a special favor to me before we march out. Perhaps he will. Now hand me my pillow and go back to bed before I perform some magic that we'll both regret.'

Corodon did as he was told. 'I did hear Orry's voice,' he muttered, slouching back to his own cot. 'I didn't imagine it and I didn't dream it.' He threw himself down, hauled the blankets to his chin, and lay there sleepless, staring into the dark.

Vra-Bramlow's robe, hanging from a wall peg, was made

of heavy wool, and there were many folds of cloth covering the inner pocket where the two lumps of moonstone were hidden. So neither prince noticed when they began to shine with a pulsating greenish glow.

NINETEEN

The dinghy pulled up at the quay in Karum Port in the hour before dawn. The place was oddly silent and deserted, with small boats of all kinds tied at sagging docks and seven tall-masted corsairs moored in deep water. Only a few of the waterfront buildings had lighted windows, but flame-pots lined the battlements of the clifftop castle that reared up against the wan pink sky.

Little Klagus dropped the sail while Ree neatly guided the craft to the landing. Orrion jumped ashore and helped the boy tie up. Roused from sleep, the two women emerged from beneath the worn and filthy blanket that had sheltered them and peered about uncertainly in the half-light.

'Orrion, have we arrived?' Nyla asked.

'Yes, love. I'll help you to disembark.'

Ree held out her hand to him. 'The fare first,' she demanded.

He smiled. 'Well done. Here are the three silver pennies I promised. Will you have your meal right away, or after you unload your fish?'

'After,' the girl said, shooting a look at her brother, who had probably been about to say something else. ''We'uns'll hafta wake up t'fishmonger. Market not be open yet. But tavern lights're on, so ye can go feed yer faces.' She pointed the way.

'Thank you for your kindness,' Countess Orvada said, alighting with some difficulty as her bulk rocked the boat. She still wore Orrion's jerkin, but had acquired a too-short tattered skirt and a pair of wooden clogs from the children's mother.

Nyla also murmured her thanks. Ree and Klagus paid no attention to her and went trotting off together into a dark lane between the buildings. 'Poor things! Orry, perhaps we should have hidden more coins in their hut before leaving.'

'That which I did leave is a small fortune to folk such as these. If I'd left more, it would only be an incentive for some rogue to cheat or harm them when they tried to spend it.' He stared out over the dead-calm water. 'My ladies, we must secure horses and hasten away from this place with all speed. I don't like the feel of it.'

'But not before we have some hot food,' the countess insisted. 'I hope the tavern-keeper will also be able to sell us some warmer clothing. Both Nyla and I are chilled to the bone. So must you be, sir, without your jerkin.'

'Follow me,' he said tersely. 'I have good reason for wanting us away from the waterfront.' He set off for the tavern, which was at the far end of the harbor, and the women stumbled after on the rough cobblestones of the narrow quayside street.

'What reason?' Orvada demanded. 'Explain yourself!'

'The Salka are coming,' Nyla said in a low voice. 'Do as he says, Mother. I heard him and the children speaking of the creatures last night, whilst lying half-asleep.'

The countess gave a gasp and seized Orrion's left arm. 'Is it true?'

He stopped and turned with a face gone grim. 'Yes, madam. The young fishers didn't realize what they had seen earlier in the evening. They thought the monsters were huge seals leaping about in the water. I didn't disabuse them for fear they'd refuse to carry us to Karum. But the presence of Salka sorcery is a logical explanation for the demolition of the sea-stack to block the channel, as well as the uncanny green flash that seems to have annihilated our ship without leaving a trace.'

'But there's no sign of the Salka having landed here,' Nyla said.

'They're biding their time,' he told her. 'Probably waiting for their entire force to get into the bay before sinking the armed pirate vessels and swarming ashore in a massive strike. We've got to get to Dennech and convince Duchess Margaleva to have her wizard raise the alarm and summon the Sovereign Army. Come along now.'

'What about the poor people in this village?' Nyla said as they started out again. 'Shouldn't we warn them?'

'They'd laugh us to scorn if we tried,' the countess predicted cynically. 'Backcountry yokels like these mistrust strangers.'

'Nevertheless,' Orrion said, 'I'll try to tell them there's danger. But only after we've secured horses. If they take me for a madman, God knows what they'll do.'

When they reached the tavern, Orrion's heart sank. He'd paid scant attention to the place when they'd passed it by yesterday on the way to the moorage of their Tarnian ship, not realizing the structure was a public accommodation. It looked more like a derelict farmstead, with a stable half in ruins and the main building canted sideways on a subsiding foundation. But the fading sign above the front door proclaimed WOLF & LAMB, and ominously depicted the latter in the jaws of the former.

'Wonderful!' the countess said in disgust. 'I suppose this is the only hostelry in this benighted hole?'

'It is,' Orrion replied, 'and keep your voice down, my lady. If they turn us away, we'll walk fasting the twenty-six leagues to Dennech. Now remain outside in the courtyard until I tell you it's safe to enter.'

Two rawboned nags and a mule hitched to an empty cart were tied up in front of the tavern. The place had guests. Orrion pushed the door open and entered a deeply shadowed and malodorous common room, which yet had the attraction of being both warm and dry. Three poorly clad men were seated together at a table spooning up some sort of seafood pottage and drinking beer. They stared at him in astonishment, as did the leather-aproned host who was tending a cauldron at the smoky fire. Orrion announced himself in ringing tones before any of them could speak.

'I'm a shipwreck victim off the Tarnian brig that sailed from here yesterday morn. She foundered and sank on a reef at the baymouth and I was picked up by a fishing boat. Who can help me reach my cousin, the good Duchess Margaleva Cuva at Dennech? Besides myself, outside are two high-born ladies who were also cast away. The duchess will pay a generous reward to the person who brings us to her citadel.'

'Shipwreck?' the host exclaimed. The three patrons began to babble all at once until he yelled, 'Pipe down, ye loudmouth pizzlers!' And to Orrion: 'Who might ye be, then? No man o' these parts, by t'sound of ye.'

'I'm Sir Nocarus, from Mallburn in the east. Will you help me and my women or not?'

The landlord scowled. 'We got no horses t'hire. Best I can do is send one o' my lads afoot up Dennech Town with word that yer bidin' here. Then duchess can send people to fetch ye . . . if she pleases.'

'But that could take all day!' Orrion exclaimed in dismay.

'That's as may be. Bring yer ladies in outa t'mornin' chill

if ye can afford breakfast. Ha'penny each for a bowl and cannikin.'

Orrion said, 'We can pay. Let me –'

Outside, there were shrill screams and the sound of a loud male voice issuing an order. The prince whirled about, tore the door open, and murmured, 'Oh, shite.'

Three hulking ruffians, much better dressed than the ragtag clientele of the tavern and armed with daggers and short-swords, stood there grinning. Two had hold of Nyla and Countess Orvada, who struggled to escape without success. The third, who sported a vivid red beard, stepped forward into the tavern, seized Orrion's left wrist, and twisted his arm up behind his back in an expert and painful restraint.

'Welcome t'Karum,' Redbeard said in a jovial tone. 'Lord Rork'll be real happy t'meet ye. Come along nicely now. We don't wanna upset t'ladies, do we?'

'Swive a swine, you stinking cullion!' the countess spat.

'Don't hurt them!' Orrion pleaded. 'We'll do whatever you say.'

'Mother, it's no use,' Nyla said, letting her body relax. 'Let be.'

'That's a sensible lass.' Redbeard eased up on Orrion's armlock and called out to one of the tavern patrons. 'Ye there, Maff Deepwell! His lordship has need of yer cart. Get yer tarse outside and haul these fine folk up t'castle fer us right now.'

Grumbling bitterly, a little old man tossed down the last of his beer and followed Redbeard and Orrion outside. After a bit of fussing, the prisoners were bedded down in straw and the driver flicked the mule with his whip. With swords drawn, the three bruisers followed the rumbling cart on foot up the steep track to the pirate-lord's castle.

'What will become of us?' Nyla asked Orrion in a tremulous voice.

'I think that will depend upon the Salka,' he said softly.

The last thing they saw as they left the village behind were the diminutive forms of Ree and Klagus skipping up to the tavern door and going inside to enjoy their delayed breakfast.

'But you've already admitted that the Tarnians oversaw nothing in Terminal Bay,' the Sovereign said to Vra-Bramlow.

'I also asked them to windsearch for the brig carrying Orrion and the ladies, sire. They were unable to find it. Surely –'

'That's not proof that the ship came to grief. It could be hidden in a fogbank.' Conrig pulled on a linen undershirt, concealing the small pouch containing the sigils that he now wore on a chain around his neck. He was dressing without assistance, and none too pleased about it, because Bramlow had pleaded for a private word.

'At least consider postponing the army's march into Tarn until the Brethren and the shamans do a more thorough windsearch of Terminal Bay,' Bram pleaded.

'I've a better idea. Fetch those magical rocks from my armor coffer and ask your good Lights to look the place over.' Not noticing Bram's stricken expression, the king muttered, 'I wonder if I should wear an extra pair of woolen socks?'

The novice moved to the coffer on the opposite side of the room, opened it, and knelt down as if to rummage for the small leaden casket. He extracted the two pieces of mineral from their hiding place inside his riding habit and pretended to take them from the box.

They shone with a pulsating greenish glow.

Bram gave an astonished cry and the Sovereign said, 'What's the matter?'

'The stones – I've never seen them do this before.' He held up the slowly throbbing moonstones.

'Bazekoy's Biceps – just get on with it, boy!'

'Yes, sire. Of course.' And he tried to bespeak the bene-volent demons, but there was no response. Instead, the pale chunks only blinked more rapidly, and the novice threw a bewildered glance at his royal father. 'The Lights don't answer. I don't know what's wrong.'

'Put the rocks back in the casket,' Conrig commanded, exasperated. 'No, wait – don't return them to the coffer. Put them on the table there. I'll want to keep the rocks with me. Now leave.'

Bram's face was desperate. 'But –'

'Once and for all,' the king bellowed, 'I have no intention of postponing our march into Tarn because of your silly dream! I gave you my reasons. Now get out of here and send Lord Telifar to help me with my boots!'

'Sire, there's one other matter.'

'What, dammit? . . . Hand me that woolen waistcoat.'

Bram proffered the requested garment. 'Very early this morning, I was bespoken an urgent warning about King Beynor. The message came from Deveron Austrey, your former Royal Intelligencer.'

Conrig froze in the act of buttoning up the vest. 'Good God! That miserable traitor has returned to Blenholme?'

'Sire, he told me that Beynor attempted to draw him into a conspiracy to kill you and take back the three sigils. Austrey refused to have any part of it. He told me he respects the way you've defended the Sovereignty from the Salka over the years and – and he offers to serve you again if you'll have him.'

The king's face flushed with rage. 'If I'll *have* him! That – that faithless whoreson –' And then he fell abruptly silent, the anger draining from him as he recalled what the Stone-Keeper had said to him:

WE HOPE TO HAVE AN EXCELLENT NEW HUMAN ALLY FOR YOU.

'Futter me!' Conrig murmured. 'Could he be Snudge? If he still has the Concealer and the Gateway –'

'Beg pardon, sire?' The novice was mystified.

But the king only made a dismissive gesture. 'Son, you've done well to bring me this message from Austrey. I'm sure he's telling the truth about Beynor's murderous proposal. It's just the sort of ploy that smarmy viper would concoct.' He strode to the table, where writing materials were set out, and began to scribble. 'Here's a message for the Captain of the Royal Guard. Give it to him immediately. I want a squad of warriors to keep a close eye on Beynor. They're to make certain that he leaves the castle.'

'I understand, sire.' Bramlow took the folded note.

'And you yourself are to bespeak Deveron Austrey on my behalf. Give him my heartfelt thanks for the warning. And tell him he has my leave to come and speak to me in two days when the Southern Wing of the army rejoins my main force on the other side of Frost Pass. Keep this information about Austrey to yourself, Bram.'

He bowed. 'Of course, sire. I'll send Lord Telifar in to serve you at once.'

When the door closed Conrig corked the inkpot with a thoughtful little smile. 'Snudge my "excellent new ally"? Well, stranger things have happened . . .'

Welcome, welcome, our long-exiled friends!

> *We rejoice at the unification. Do They show signs of having taken note of our surreptitious return?*

We think not – although They are concerned because the pain-power channels between Sky and Ground showed momentary interruption. Was this your doing?

> *We exerted tentative disruptive action as an experiment when we became aware that two groundling persons used Destroyers. The action was not very successful. We were discoordinated. To be truly*

effective, we require the talent of the One Denied the Sky to direct
us. He did not respond to our query. What is his situation?
He is still enchained beneath the Ice with a single fetter. Loosing it
and freeing the One will require the abolition of significant sigils.
The groundling helpers do not have access to such as yet. The One
is doing his utmost to assist the helpers. Meanwhile, They scrutinize.
It cannot be long before They know you have arrived –
WE KNOW. AND THE NEW CONFLICT IS JOINED.

Shrewd little Ree had heard Nyla address Orrion by name.
When this was whispered to Rork Karum by Redbeard, after
he and his men brought the captives into the sumptuous
castle hall, the pirate-lord realized he had been gifted with
a goldmine in the shape of the son of the Sovereign of
Blenholme.

'Welcome to my modest abode, Your Grace!' Rork sprang
up from his seat of presence and sketched an extravagant
bow. 'And you, too, noble ladies! I never dreamed that the
Tarnian brig was picking up such distinguished passengers.
They told me you were mere Cathran diplomats fleeing the
turmoil around Boarsden.'

'And so we are,' Orrion said.

Rork gave a hearty laugh. 'Oh, I think not! Please accept
my deepest sympathy at your terrible misfortune, my dear
prince. It's a shame those brave seamen perished, but how
lucky you are to have survived the disaster. The Gods of the
Heights and Depths have smiled on you – and on me! –
bringing you safe to my home. Your stay here will be as
comfortable as my simple means allows . . . and as brief as
High King Conrig chooses to make it.'

'Baron Rork –' Orrion began.

The pirate winced delicately. 'Your Grace, the lords of
Karum have been styled as *duke* from time immemorial. It's
sadly true that King Somarus attempted early in his reign to

degrade my dignity and foist an overlord of his choosing upon the free corsairs of Terminal Bay. But happily, he saw the error of his ways. I pay him tribute, and his old friend Azarick Dennech-Cuva is perforce content to control the territory beginning ten leagues inland, leaving me and mine to carry on our customary maritime activities without interference.'

'Piracy,' Countess Orvada snapped. 'Holding prisoners for ransom!'

Rork smiled at the bedraggled noblewoman and resumed his seat. He was a tall thin man with dark hair and a saturnine mien, handsome in spite of a long lantern jaw, and possessed of brilliant white teeth. He wore a scarlet sarcenet shirt embroidered with gold, trews of fine dove-colored wool, folded black seaboots, and a cloth-of-gold sash. On his left hand was a massive ring inset with a ruby the size of a cherry.

'I ply a trade, my lady, as did my ancestors before me. May I know your name and that of the young damsel? It will facilitate my negotiations with the Sovereign.'

'I am Countess Orvada Brackenfield and this is my daughter, Lady Nyla, who is affianced to Sir Orrion.'

'You mean, to the Prince Heritor,' Rork corrected her, glancing at Orrion in surprise. 'But I heard that Your Grace was betrothed to Crown Princess Hyndry.'

Orrion lifted his truncated limb. 'That was called off. Having displeased my royal father by losing my sword-arm, I've been reduced to the rank of Knight Bachelor.'

'A pity.' Rork smirked. 'Still, I reckon Ironcrown will still want you and the ladies safely home in Cathra rather than languishing on these lonely shores. He paid handsomely enough to have the Tarnians pick you up. I'll just triple that tariff! When he pays, we'll ship you off to some little port down south, and all's well that ends well.' He cocked his head winningly. 'How's that for a fair deal?'

'My lord,' Orrion said somberly. 'The deepwater channel connecting your bay to the open sea has been blocked by Salka invaders.'

'Whaaat?' Rork drawled.

The three village bullyboys burst into derisive laughter. After a moment, so did the collection of henchmen and servants gathered about the pirate-lord's dais.

'It's true!' Nyla exclaimed shrilly. 'They sank our ship with their sorcery and blasted the tall rock pinnacle at the channel entrance to pieces.'

'Topple Rogue's Picket?' somebody scoffed. 'Never!'

Nyla persisted. 'The two children who rescued us and brought us here even saw some of the Salka. They mistook them for huge seals –'

'And you saw these invading monsters yourselves?' The pirate-lord lifted a skeptical eyebrow.

'No,' Orrion admitted. 'We saw the sea-stack destroyed. The falling rock caused a gigantic wave that flung us off the deck of the brig. Under the water, we saw an uncanny green flash above, and the ship vanished utterly.'

'You'd better listen to us, you saucy rascal!' the countess said. 'Don't you know that the Sovereign Army expects the Salka to invade the west coast of our island at any day now?'

Rork flipped a languid hand. 'We heard rumors that the Salka might attack Tarn. As a precaution, I called in our fleet so they wouldn't be endangered. But why should the monsters bother with our insignificant little enclave when the rich cities of the Sea-Harriers offer such superior targets?'

'My lord, you're thinking like a human being,' Orrion said.

Redbeard took a furious step toward him with a fist upraised. 'Mind yer sassy gob, Cathran, or I'll shut it fer ye!'

'No! Let him speak!' Rork said. And to Orrion: 'Explain what you mean.'

'The Salka care naught for human riches, my lord. All that

interests them is reclaiming the island from which they were expelled a thousand years ago by humanity. They took Moss and were emboldened. They tried to invade Didion from the north coast and were forced to retreat. Now they're trying to come in from the west. The Sovereign's advisers believe there might be as many as sixty thousand of them out there.'

'Great Starry Dragon!' muttered one of the village rough-necks.

'As to why they'd invade at Terminal Bay rather than in Tarn,' Orrion resumed, 'it makes sense if you look at a chart. The bay is landlocked and full of shoals. Its human popula-tion is fairly small. If the single channel is blocked, the Sovereignty naval forces can't enter . . . but the Salka have easy access. If they come ashore in a massive assault, they can go up the rivers and through the wold wetlands faster than any horse can gallop. Even if our army engages them, the amphibians have the advantage because of the poor roads in the region. The only fortress of any size is at Dennech, and it can easily be bypassed.'

'That's a crock o' shite!' someone yelled. 'We only got this Cathran's word. He's tryin' t'pull a fast one, lord duke!'

'Where's real proof t'Salka be here?' Redbeard demanded. 'Two sprogs what found t'castaways said their ship sank sundown yestereve. They said she were hit by lightnin'. If Salka did t'trick with sorcery, why ain't we heard of 'em attackin' ships and towns in t'bay?'

A chorus of assenting voices rose.

Rork smacked his fist on the arm of his gilded chair. 'Quiet, you poxy lubbers! . . . Paligus, go fetch the wind-speaker. If he's drunk, sober him up! We'll find out the truth one way or another.' One of the retainers dashed out of the room.

The pirate-lord said to the three villagers, 'You lot go with Captain Erkitt. He'll give you your reward for bringing up

these hostages. Then go back down to the port. Spread the
word along the quay to keep an eye peeled for anything
strange out on the water – but no boats are to leave the
dock. Anybody sights a Salka or something looking like a
giant seal, sound the tocsin bell –'

Orrion interrupted. 'And tell all the folk to hasten up here
to the castle.'

'Ye mean, *run away?*' Redbeard was incredulous. 'Not fight
t'slimy boogers?' There were scornful mutterings from some
of the others.

'Have you ever seen a Salka?' Orrion asked quietly.

Silence.

'I have not seen one in the flesh myself,' the former prince
said, 'but I've spoken to certain of our fleet captains who
fought them in the Battle of the Dawntide Isles. They are at
least twice the height of a man, but many times more bulky.
In body form they are rather like seals, with broad flippers
instead of legs and two thick tentacles tipped with clawed
fingers. They can wriggle along rather quickly on land and
they swim faster than any other creature. Their heads are
large and set on their shoulders without necks. They have
glowing red eyes like saucers and wide mouths that open
something like those of frogs. But unlike frogs, they have
teeth: crystalline teeth like daggers made of glass. Each tooth
is longer than a man's hand.'

'Futter me blind!' somebody said.

Another guffawed. 'He's spinnin' a yarn!'

'Tryin' t'scare us into lettin' him go! T'creeturs be but
animals!'

'Salka look like beasts out of a nightmare,' said Orrion.
'But they are intelligent beings possessed of uncanny talent,
like wizards. They can use windspeech and perform many
kinds of magic. Even worse, some of them possess moonstone amulets capable of high sorcery. I believe that one of

these amulets was used to destroy the Tarnian brig and block the channel leading into this bay.'

'Be that as it may,' Rork Karum said, 'we have yet to prove that these monsters threaten *us*. My magicker will scry the bay. I'll also have him bespeak the shamans at Tarnholme north of here to see if they've heard anything. The Tarnians don't usually share news with the likes of us, but perhaps they'll make an exception this time.'

'I ask that you have him bespeak Duchess Margaleva's wizard first,' Orrion said. 'She'll relay your ransom demand, of course. But also beseech her to inform my royal father of my belief that the Salka are here.'

'Oh, I think I'll wait awhile before doing that.' Rork's face bore a sardonic look. 'I've heard there's some sort of Cathran army encamped up at Lake of Shadows. We wouldn't want them nosing around here if your Salka invasion turns out to be Boreal Moonshine, would we?'

Orrion said nothing.

Countess Orvada took a step toward the dais, her plump face white with indignation. 'Do you mean to say, sirrah, that you do *not* intend to warn the Sovereign that the monsters are here?'

'When I know it for a fact, my lady, I'll certainly do so. But not until.' Rork Karum snapped his fingers and a retainer wearing a steward's chain and keys stepped forward.

'Yes, my lord duke?'

'Andalus, have our guests escorted to comfortable chambers. Let them bathe and don fresh garments. Provide them with food and every comfort. And see that they are kept safe and secure. Very secure.'

'Yes, my lord.'

Rork said to Orrion, 'We'll meet again anon, Your Grace. Do I have your word that you and the ladies won't abuse my hospitality?'

'You do, God help you – and help us all! For if I am not mistaken, we are all of us doomed by what you have here and now decided.'

Prince Heritor Corodon was waiting in the keep vestibule of Castle Direwold with the pile of baggage belonging to the royal party when Bramlow returned from the the Sovereign's rooms. The novice's downcast manner told his brother all he needed to know.

'Father didn't believe you,' Corodon stated, rather than asked.

Bram shook his head with a dispirited sigh. 'He insisted that I must have been dreaming about Orry. There've been numbers of other wind-reports of the monsters swimming up the Firth of Gayle, and he's absolutely convinced that's where the invasion is starting. He told me our navy is closing in, and the fleet admirals believe they can bottle the Salka up in the estuary before they reach the mouth of the Donor River and slaughter them with cannon-fire. The chain barriers are already going up to protect the Tarnian capital and the big naval base at Yelicum.'

'Didn't you get the shamans to windsearch Terminal Bay?'

'They did it as soon as it was full light – and found nothing. The broken rock spire was there, but Zolanfel said the thing could have collapsed from natural causes.'

Corodon's face twisted in a grimace of frustration and he bunched his fists and knocked them against his skull. 'Curse it – maybe I did imagine Orry's call! But it seemed so real . . .' His expression brightened. 'The demons! Couldn't you consult them again?'

Bram glanced about in consternation and pulled his brother into an alcove. 'Shhh!' A few lords-in-waiting, household knights, and others belonging to the royal entourage were supervising removal of the bags to the stables, but no one seemed to have noticed Coro's indiscreet words.

The novice spoke in a whisper. 'Father commanded me to do that very thing. I had to slip the rocks out of my shirt and pretend they'd been in their leaden casket all along. The moonstones were blinking in a strange manner! Zeth only knows what it means, but I don't like it. If only Uncle Stergos were still alive –'

'Well, he's not.' Corodon's retort was brusque and more than a little fearful.

'I don't dare ask advice from any of the others in the Corps of Alchymists,' Bramlow said. His normal confidence seemed to have evaporated.

'So we'll do nothing,' the Prince Heritor decided, 'at least for the time being.' He paused. 'Bram, It certainly looks like snow is on the way. It's colder than hell outside and I heard some of the men talking about it. Do you know whether Father has used the Weathermaker sigil yet?'

'I don't think so. Perhaps he intends to wait until he has no other alternative. I know that's what I'd do.'

'I wonder how much it hurts?' Coro said hesitantly, meeting his brother's eyes. 'You know – to use a Great Stone.'

'Those damned sigils hurt people in more than one way,' the novice muttered, 'and bodily pain is probably the least thing Father has to worry about . . .' He took a deep breath. 'Well. They'll be expecting us at the High Table for breakfast. Let's eat.'

'Kalawnn? Can you hear me?'

The Master Shaman stirred inside the submarine grotto where he had been resting and opened his eyes. Their gleam was feeble in comparison to the slowly pulsing luminescence of the Known Potency, which the Salka sorcerer had temporarily removed from his gizzard and placed on the organism-encrusted rock surface beside him. Destroyer and his minor sigil Scriber, which hung about his neck, blinked in synchrony.

'What is it, Ugusawnn? Have the young reserves finally arrived?'

'Soon, soon, my friend!' the Supreme Warrior said. 'They spent last night amongst some lonely islands off a tiny human settlement called Puffin Bay, feeding and recuperating from their last sprint. Their vanguard should be here tomorrow around noontide. I'm debating whether to attack at that time or wait an additional day. I hesitate to say it – but the decision rests with you. Would you feel able to wield Destroyer tomorrow?'

'Yes, I believe so. Removing the Potency has hastened my recovery, I think. While I carried it within me, I had a strange feeling that it was exerting a negative influence on me. Never before have I experienced such a sensation.'

Ugusawnn proffered two enormous golden salmon, freshly killed. 'Here's food. This region has an amazing abundance of sea-life.' He hesitated. 'Have the Beaconfolk bespoken you concerning this?'

'No, nor have I had the heart to query them. I'll try tomorrow when I feel better.' He eyed the small Potency with apprehension. 'This stone is still an unknown factor, Ugusawnn. There's so much about it that I don't understand – its paradoxical abolition of the pain-price was hardly advantageous, since sigils thus treated were then good for only a single use afterwards. Neither our archives nor Rothbannon's writings mentioned this undesirable effect. And yet the human Beynor seemed to believe that the Potency would be of great benefit to us!'

'Beynor was a liar,' the Supreme Warrior growled. 'Untrustworthy. Accurst! But the Lights themselves commanded him to bring the Potency to us, so we dare not dispose of it.'

The shaman toyed with one of the fish. 'True. Yet I have decided no longer to carry it within my body. Instead, we'll encase it safely in gold and chain it to my tentacle wrist.'

Ugusawnn nodded in approval. 'An excellent idea. Now eat, my friend. Build up your strength for our great triumph tomorrow.'

Beynor was more taciturn than usual as he and Garon Curtling shared their morning meal with an assortment of other magickers in a corner of the great hall of Castle Direwold. The Conjure-King had had only two hours of sleep following his failed attempt to lure Deveron Austrey into a conspiracy. He was absorbed in considering his next course of action, and at first he ignored the urgent whispering of the man seated beside him.

'Master? I know I'm not imagining things. Those guards – the ones loitering near the main door of the hall – are keeping us under close surveillance.'

'What?' When Garon repeated himself, the sorcerer pretended indifference, reaching for another bread-roll and dipping it into his bowl of cheese-and-onion soup.

But he discovered that the other wizard was quite correct. Six members of the Royal Guard armed with pikes and swords had their eyes locked on the table full of junior alchymists and lower-echelon shamans at which the two of them had been seated by a shifty-eyed servitor. Garon had not seemed to notice his master's abrupt plunge in status, but Beynor's stomach had clenched in fury when he was told that a chair at the High Table was unavailable and he would have to eat with the man he regarded as his servant.

And now Conrig was taking steps to see that the two of them were escorted off the premises and sent packing as soon as they'd broken their fast!

Beynor swallowed his resentment. It was only to be

expected. Deveron Austrey had probably wasted no time passing on a warning, and someone in authority had taken it seriously. The warriors had doubtless been told to be circumspect and not make a scene.

'What do you make of it?' Garon was still only mildly concerned.

'I think perhaps those warriors are standing by to ensure our safety,' Beynor prevaricated.

'But who would wish to do us harm, master?'

As yet, Garon knew nothing of Beynor's abrupt dismissal. The sorcerer was leery of how his new associate might react to the devastating news and had considered unceremoniously abandoning him. The renegade Brother's loyalty was by no means wholehearted, and Beynor firmly believed that he who travels alone travels fastest. Still, he'd decided to keep Garon with him for a little while longer. The burly wizard did have his uses.

If that usefulness ended, it would be easy enough to dispose of him. And only prudent to prepare for the contingency . . .

'Some persons strongly disapprove of my having given King Conrig the moonstone sigils,' Beynor explained glibly. 'To disarm their hostility, His Grace and I have agreed on a temporary change of plans. You and I are riding south this morning, rather than north into Tarn with the Sovereign and his army. I've been given a special mission.'

Garon's brow wrinkled in puzzlement as he considered what his master had just said. 'But surely the Sovereign will need you near him now that the sigils are empowered. You said you were indispensable – that he couldn't wield the stones properly without your help.'

'That's true,' Beynor said. 'But we won't be gone long. I've already instructed His Grace in how to use Weathermaker to fend off snow or other dangerous conditions when he leads the army through Frost Pass. He won't need the other sigils for days yet.'

'How can you be sure?' the wizard persisted. 'What if he tries to experiment with the stones and harms himself? He's only an untrained amateur, after all.'

Beynor glowered at him. 'Are you questioning the Sovereign's good judgment?' he hissed. 'Or mine?'

'No, master.'

Garon subsided with apparent meekness, asking no more questions, but his aura betrayed his continuing unease as they finished their meal, took their bags to the stable, and finally mounted and left the castle. The squad of Royal Guardsmen watched their departure stolidly, but made no move to follow them across the moat's drawbridge.

The Wold Road outside Direwold Village was thronged with riders and pack-trains heading north toward the mountains. Without a word to Garon, Beynor turned his mount in the opposite direction and spurred it to a canter. Having no choice, Garon followed suit. After less than a quarter of an hour, they had the highway all to themselves. Beynor let his horse slow to a walk and beckoned for Garon to ride beside him.

This part of the Great Wold was a desolate plateau with sparse vegetation, its monotony broken only by the occasional quaking bog or copse of twisted small trees. Overhead, the clouds were low and threatening. Even if Conrig did manage to fend off snow in the mountains with his sigil, it seemed all too likely that the wold country was in for an early taste of winter weather.

'I'm expecting important messages on the wind,' Beynor said. 'They will come from a considerable distance, and I must listen for them intently as well as think over my future plans. Please take my lead rein while I cover my head with my hood and concentrate. If anything unexpected happens, break my trance at once.'

'Yes, master.' The wizard accepted the long strap and urged his horse ahead.

Garon Curtling brooded over the situation as several hours dragged by. He was not a quick-witted man, but his long years as a subordinate of Chancellor Kilian Blackhorse and his two villainous cronies had honed in Garon a keen instinct for self-preservation. He was now almost certain that the Conjure-King had lied about the purpose of this journey. If all was well between him and the Sovereign, Beynor would be ebullient and charged with his usual boldness; instead, he seemed withdrawn and apprehensive. Furthermore, those guardsmen in the castle hall had not acted like protectors. Their attention had remained totally focused upon him and his master rather than being alert to any external threat – almost as though the two of *them* constituted a danger.

Had something gone terribly wrong with the sigil empowerment ritual last night? Had the Beaconfolk refused after all to bond the moonstones to the Sovereign, just as they had earlier refused to re-activate Kilian's five minor stones whose power had been drained by the Potency?

If that's what happened, Garon thought, then Beynor's hopes of manipulating Conrig and gaining a position of political power were as dead as those useless sigils. And if the Conjure-King was now an outcast from the Sovereign's court, he'd already be thinking of how he might cushion his fall from grace. The money and jewels Beynor carried in his saddlebags would help; but the cushion would be even plumper if it were augmented by Garon's own share of Kilian's treasure . . .

Oh, no you don't! he said to himself.

It wouldn't be done easily, or even safely. But Garon Curtling had long since hatched a plan to save his own skin from the likes of the Conjure-King of Moss. And it was time to put that plan into operation.

He glanced over his shoulder. Head bowed and hooded, Beynor swayed listlessly in his saddle.

Good enough. Garon reached down and unstrapped one of his own bags, rummaging deep within it for something he'd kept safe since disposing of Niavar and Cleaton. Yes – it was there, wrapped in a rag inside his wash-kit, the stopper resealed with wax. Garon extracted it and tucked it into an inner pocket of his heavy tunic, then studied the landscape ahead with his windsight. The road was ascending a broad hill, on top of which was a grove of pines and junipers that would provide shelter from the cold.

A good place to pull off the road and rest, he thought. And brew a nice pot of bearberry tea while he waited for his master to emerge from his trance.

When he was unable to bespeak Master Shaman Kalawnn at Fenguard Castle, Beynor scried the much-changed old royal seat of Moss as meticulously as he could, hoping to ascertain whether his former Salka mentor was in residence. It was hard work, penetrating stone walls at such a distance, but he persisted with a strength born of desperation. The amiable monster who carried the Known Potency within his craw was his last hope.

But Kalawnn was nowhere to be found within Fenguard – nor was the irascible Supreme Warrior, Ugusawnn. The only Eminences in the half-deserted castle were the First Judge and the Conservator of Wisdom. There was no helping it: he'd have to bespeak one of them, abase himself, and try to work his way back into their good graces.

'Here is Beynor of Moss, beseeching one of the Eminent Two to graciously respond.'

Beynor? The Judge seemed astonished to hear from him. *What do you want with us? Aren't you Ironcrown's vassal now, claiming a kingdom that no longer exists, in a part of the island*

that we have liberated and made our own? And haven't you treach-
erously turned a Destroyer and two other Great Stones over to our
enemy so he can use them against us?

Uh-oh . . .

'I don't know who told you those foul lies, Eminence, but
I assure you I've done nothing of the sort. Conrig and his
alchymists stole those stones from me –'

The Great Lights say differently. They say you freely gave the sigils
to Conrig, thinking to withhold certain knowledge of their functions
from the king and maintain a controlling hold over him. The Lights
say that it 'pleased' them to grant this human ruler use of the stones!
They say they are disappointed in the Salka. Their capricious new
game is to pit our two races against each other, with sigils used on
both sides. For this atrocious abrogation of our ancient privilege we
blame YOU, Beynor of Moss, and we declare you abominable in our
eyes forever. And be sure that humankind will not prevail on High
Blenholme. Soon this island will belong to the Salka again, while
you and all others of your ilk perish. Think about this and despair!

Beynor opened his eyes and began to cough as a gust of
smoke blew into his face. 'God of the Depths, Garon – are
you trying to suffocate me?' The bay gelding he rode tossed
its head and stamped its hooves, backing away from the
crackling blaze in front of it.

'Not at all, master. Let me lead your horse to a more comfortable position.' The wizard reached up and took hold of the
reins. 'Would you like to dismount? The weather was deteri-
orating and I thought it best that we pause here in this little
wood. I kindled the fire a bit overzealously, wanting it to be
burning well by the time you recovered from your trance.'

'Hold this brute still while I climb down,' the sorcerer said,
swinging his leg over the bay's broad back and dropping to the
ground. 'You can tie him over there with yours.' He groaned.
'By the Ten Hells – I ache all over!'

Garon gave him a cheerful smile. 'I'm going to make us a hot drink. I trust you received the wind-message you were expecting.'

The sorcerer laughed harshly. 'I got the message, all right.' He went off to relieve himself among the junipers.

As the fire settled down, Garon filled the small pot from their waterskin, added a good pinch of dried bearberries, and put it on to boil. He set out the flagon of honey from their mess bag and two tin cups. 'Would you care for an oatcake, master?'

Beynor opened one of his own saddlebags and groped inside. 'Let's have some of these apple-nut turnovers instead.' After some fumbling he extracted two of the small pastries he had saved from breakfast and gave one to Garon, who was crouching as he poured honey into the cups. 'Don't make my drink too sweet.'

The Conjure-King stood staring silently into the flames for some time, fingering the handle of Moss's Sword of State. Finally he said, 'I'm afraid I have some bad news.'

Garon looked up with an expression of concern. 'What is it?'

Beynor lowered himself to the ground and began to eat his pastry, fixing a melancholy gaze on the wizard. 'My friend, I've discovered that King Conrig has betrayed my trust. I have just bespoken a certain person in the Didionite camp at Lake of Shadows, whither we were bound. As you probably know, Crown Prince Valardus declined to join the Cathran contingent of the Southern Wing as they marched out this morning on the way to Tarn. He and his army have vowed to remain at the lake until King Somarus gives them express permission to leave Didion.'

'I was aware of that, master.' Garon poured tea into the two cups and handed one of them to Beynor. 'Let it cool a bit, but not too much. There's more when you want it.' He sat down opposite the sorcerer and began to eat his own pastry and blow on his cup.

'My so-called mission,' the Conjure-King went on, 'was to persuade Valardus to reconsider. But now I've learned from my confidant in the Didionite camp that Conrig made a perfidious deal with the Crown Prince. I was to be set upon and killed in ambush by the prince's men because Conrig fears I'll interfere with his wielding of the sigils. In return for thus engineering my demise, Conrig promised not to retaliate against Didion for refusing to defend Tarn from the Salka.'

'Oh, master! That's appalling!' Garon spoke with his mouth full.

Beynor took a deep swallow of his bearberry tea. The drink was aromatic and soothing. 'Giving Ironcrown the sigils was a foolish mistake on my part. I see that now. I believed him when he promised to restore my kingdom. But he lied.'

'I'm – I'm sorry.' Garon flinched as he took a gulp of tea. 'Damn. My guts are starting to gripe. Maybe I shouldn't have eaten so many pickled herring at breakfast.' He finished the cup and poured more with a shaking hand.

Beynor felt perspiration start out on his brow and an uneasy feeling in his own stomach. 'Needless to say, I don't intend to continue on to – to Lake of Shadows. Instead, I – I –'

His eyes widened and the cup fell from his hand. 'No. You didn't.'

Garon's face was bluish-grey and contorted, but he still managed a painful chuckle. 'I did. And so, evidently, did you!' He convulsed and fell onto his side, narrowly missing the fire.

Beynor clutched his belly with both hands and began to gasp out an incantation in a strangled voice. But he was on the point of collapse. As he slumped to the ground his lips continued to move, although no sounds emerged.

You poisoned the tea, he bespoke his dying minion. *With the tincture I gave you for Niavar and Cleaton.*

Saved some, Garon replied. *Thought ahead. Like you.*

For all the good it did us.

Beynor ash Linndal, Conjure-King of Moss, gripped his Sword of State with all of his strength, vowing that not even death would loosen his fingers, and watched the world dissolve into darkness.

There was silence on the uncanny wind, while the pines began to moan and sway, the campfire crackled, and the two horses whinnied with fear and jerked at the reins that fastened them to the spindly juniper bushes. After a long time they broke free and galloped southward across the heath, away from the approaching storm.

Casya Pretender stood looking out of the tiny window of the trading post at the ground leading to the river. The rain was coming down harder now and by morning the new-fallen snow would be gone.

'It's getting dark, Ising. They must know we're here – especially after we shot that reindeer this afternoon and butchered it. Why haven't they come?'

The old man used a fork to turn the collops of liver and tenderloin broiling on the crusty black gridiron. 'Maybe the Morass Worms suspect what you're here for and don't want to be dragged into another fight.'

'But they *won* the last time, thanks to me! If I hadn't showed them what to do – how to flank the Salka battalions before emerging from the subtle corridors – the silly things would have charged head-on and been crushed by the sheer numbers of the monsters.'

'Ah, but the worms did win, didn't they? Their own territory is secure. Why should they be concerned with what happens on the west coast of the island?' He drew his hunting knife, sliced off a bit of liver, and popped it into his mouth. 'Mmm! This is done. Hand over the plates and get the salt and pepper. We'll give the loin cutlets a little more time.'

She did as he said, also bringing the mugs and filling them from the pot of mint-and-spruce-needle tea that steamed on the hob. They sat companionably before the fire on stools, eating the tender liver, watching the venison sizzle, and sipping their drinks.

Ising said, 'Just because the snow that fell last night is melting, it doesn't mean that we can afford to hang about here for very long. A genuine blizzard will come soon and we could be trapped. Two days I'll give 'em. If the worms don't come by then, lass, they never will. We'll have to head back to civilization.'

'No!' she wailed. 'We only got here yesterday.'

He took a taste of the tea and pulled a face. 'Better than hot water, and it'll fend off scurvy, but I'd sell my soul for a beaker of mulled wine. Too bad there's naught to sweeten this stuff.'

'You can leave here if you want,' Casya growled. 'I'm staying.'

'Now listen to me, Your Majesty! You said it yourself: the worms know we're here. If they don't want to talk, we can't make 'em. Two days, Casabarela Mallburn! Then we go.'

She scowled and retreated into a sulk, saying not another word as they ate the rest of the meat and emptied their cups, setting aside the remainder of the beverage for tomorrow. After going outside for a few minutes Ising returned, wrapped himself in blankets, and lay down on one of the bare cots. He started to snore within minutes.

Anger and resentment had made Casya wakeful. She combed and replaited her hair, donned a dry pair of socks and hung the sweaty ones she'd removed in front of the fire, then slipped on her boots and left the cabin to use the ramshackle convenience. The rain had diminished to a light drizzle and the morass was very still except for the murmur of the river. Most of the snow had disappeared.

Casya stood still, eyes straining to see into the dark forest.

Where are you? she called without speaking. Why won't you come and talk to me? Don't you know that this island belongs to all of us? I'll never be Queen of Didion if the Salka overrun my country. I won't be able to fulfil the promise I made to you! We have to help each other. Oh, please come!

Nothing happened. She waited only a short time until the cold and damp drove her back inside the shelter of the trading post. Taking one last look out the window before going to bed, she gave a gasp as she caught a brief glimpse of something sparkling high among the trees across the water. But it was only there for an instant before it winked out.

The sky's clearing, she realized. It was probably only a low-hanging star. She turned away and lay down fully clothed. As she pulled the blankets around her ears, one last question posed itself:

But are stars green?

She was too tired to bother thinking of an answer. After a time Casabarela Mallburn slept, and a spectacular display of the aurora borealis raged all across the heavens, scarlet and gold and violet banners and spears of Light like the clashing of radiant armies on a star-spiked battleground.

TWENTY

Their mutual fear was as yet unspoken; nevertheless, Deveron and Induna made love that night as though it were to be their last time together. Afterwards they lay in each other's arms inside the tiny military tent that they shared, listening to the gentle rustle of cold drizzle on the waxed canvas.

At the Sovereign's command, the Southern Wing of the Cathran army – all of them mounted, some on commandeered Didionite horses – had left Lake of Shadows and started north to rejoin the main force on its march into Tarn. Earl Marshal Parlian's force, including Deveron and Induna, was now bivouacked for the night along the highroad some thirty leagues below Castle Direwold, while the cavalry led by Conrig and Sealord Sernin had halted halfway up the steep zigzag track to Frost Pass. The riders of the Northern Wing intended to cross the pass late in the morning, while most of its foot-soldiery and war-engines, now commanded by Lord Lieutenant Hale Brackenfield, would require another day or more to scale the height. If all went well, Parlian's army would overtake and bypass the slower-moving contingent and reach Conrig's camp in Tarn late on the morrow.

But Deveron Austrey could not wait that long.

'It's time for me to leave you now, Duna. It must be nearly midnight. The camp is finally settled down to sleep.'

She clung to him. 'If I could only change your mind, love! Don't use Subtle Gateway. Ride with us to Tarn instead. Conrig doesn't expect to meet with you until tomorrow night, at the earliest.'

'The uncanny premonition prompts me to go to him now, without delay, even if it means using my sigil. I have to do this. The distance to be traveled isn't great, as the crow flies. The pain-penalty should not be too severe.'

She buried her face in the crook of his arm and he felt her body shudder. 'It's not the pain I worry about – it's the Beaconfolk themselves. When you used Gateway to journey from Andradh to the Green Morass, they sent you where you wanted to go – but they intended that you should die on arrival! It's obvious now that they didn't want you to rejoin the New Conflict. Who knows what they might do now if they suspect you plan to dissuade King Conrig from using sigil sorcery?'

'It's a chance I must take.'

'Could you not consult with the Source first? Perhaps your premonition is false.'

'I tried to bespeak him, sweetheart, but he didn't reply. For all I know, the feeling of dire urgency comes from him – or from those good Likeminded Lights who are his allies in the Conflict.'

He disentangled himself from the cocoon of blankets and began to dress. The golden case with the owl blazon that held his moonstones hung from a chain around his neck.

'I shall pray unceasingly for your safety,' Induna said. 'You must be on guard every moment you're with King Conrig. If he possesses a Destroyer, as Prince Bramlow said, he could slay you in an eyeblink if he perceives you as a threat.'

'I think he'll want to ask me a number of questions about sigil sorcery first. In fact, I'm counting on it. With both Lord Stergos and Beynor gone, the king has no one else to consult save the Beaconfolk – and he might be having second thoughts by now about their unexpected generosity. Conrig has coveted moonstones for years. I'm only too aware of that. But he also knows what they did to Ullanoth – and to her mother before her. I must convince him not to use the stones, help him to understand how deadly dangerous they are, not only to him but also to all the people of our island.'

'Ironcrown is not known for sweet reasonableness and a tender conscience,' she said with asperity. 'Princess Maude would tell you that if she were still alive! Deveron, I'm afraid of the man. His arrogance and ambition are unbridled and he may not be entirely sane.'

'I hope to gain a better idea of the king's state of mind by talking to Vra-Bramlow first. When he spoke to me on the wind earlier today, he appeared to be intelligent and genuinely concerned for his royal father's wellbeing.'

'Do you really believe Bramlow can give you valid insight? Few children can be objective about a parent.'

'With luck, I'll be able to cajole Conrig himself into revealing his intentions concerning the sigils.' He smiled and kissed her lips lightly. 'Remember, in Andradh I was known as Haydon the Sympath. One of the most useful tools a healer can have is the ability to pry the truth out of patients who would rather keep their secrets hidden.'

'I still don't understand why you're willing to leave Prince Dyfrig. If he's destined to become the Sovereign –'

'I don't know that for certain. I only assumed it because of Red Ansel's dying words and Cray and Thalassa's belief that the old shaman may have been right. For some reason, it never occurred to me to put that question directly to the Source himself. Now I wonder why! Perhaps his original message to you was the correct one after all, and *Conrig* is my true charge.'

'Then heaven help you.' Her voice broke. 'For I think he sees himself as Bazekoy reborn! But the emperor didn't use sorcery to conquer, he hated and shunned it and barred men with talent from the Cathran throne and most positions of great power. Bazekoy ordered that the dead sigils found on the bodies of slain Salka be smashed to bits. Every Tarnian shaman knows this, although modern Cathrans seem to have forgotten.'

'Which is why I must go to King Conrig and enlighten him . . . and you, my love, must ride with Prince Dyfrig and Earl Marshal Parlian tomorrow and do the same.'

'What do you mean?'

'They'll ask where I've gone. Tell them. Explain why Conrig can't be trusted to wield those Great Stones, and why I'm going to do my utmost to stop him. Tell them all about our work for the Source. Tell them of the New Conflict and how it threatens humanity, how the Beaconfolk want to use us as they used the Salka, as pawns in a depraved super-natural game.'

'But will they believe me?'

'Dyfrig may have trouble grasping it all, but I think old Parlian will understand. Especially about Conrig's dreams of world conquest using sigils. Inform Dyfrig that the Source said that he himself is to play a vital role in the defense of this island, but don't suggest that he may become the next Sovereign. We don't know that for certain, and the very idea of it might distract the prince at a time when he'll need all his wits about him.'

'Very well.'

'Stay close to Dyfrig and the earl marshal on the march tomorrow. Be ready to relay to them any windspoken message I may send you. Part of my premonition is that strategic matters are coming quickly to a head. We'll know before long where the Salka are.'

'When . . . will you return to me?'

He reached out for her in the dark and drew her close against him. He was fully dressed now in a winter hunting habit, a hooded raincape, and stout boots. He wore no armor and carried only a shortsword and a dagger, but the two sigils were now free of their case and nestling against the bare skin of his chest, ready to be called upon.

'I don't know how long this mission will take. I'll bespeak you after I reach Conrig safely, then again as soon as I have something important to report. Now kiss me farewell, my dear. Come into my mind and rest there. Know that I'll always love you, always be with you. Do you believe me?'

'Yes,' she said as his lips tasted her tears, and let him go.

He slipped out of the tent and made his way toward the outer perimeter of the elongate encampment, which was bisected by the Wold Road. The only fires were at scattered watchposts, but he rendered himself invisible with the minor sigil Concealer so none of the prowling sentries would delay him. This part of the heath was open and mostly devoid of trees, cut here and there by brushy streambeds carrying small torrents. He descended into one of these so that his uncanny departure would be unnoticed, then voided the spell of invisibility.

Reaching into his jerkin with an ungloved hand, he took hold of the Great Stone Subtle Gateway and closed his eyes. He intoned the command 'EMCHAY MO' and instructed the sigil to transport him to the pavilion of Prince Heritor Corodon and Vra-Bramlow, on the trail leading up to Frost Pass.

He felt no pain, only a sudden great chill. Soft inhuman voices whispered inside his mind: *WHAT DO YOU WANT?*

Stricken with dread – for this same thing had happened to him once before, when he first attempted to use Gateway – he opened his eyes. He was surrounded by starless black space. Limned against it were innumerable glowing faces depicted in colored Light. They spoke to him in unison, repeating the same question, and he realized to his astonishment that they addressed him in his own language, not that of the Salka.

So he replied in kind. 'I want you to transport me where I asked to go.'

WHO ARE YOU?

They almost caught him off-guard. But he recovered in time and said: 'Snudge. I'm Snudge.'

THAT IS YOUR NAME AND IT IS NOT YOUR NAME. TELL US YOUR TRUE NAME SO WE MAY KNOW YOU COMPLETELY. THIS IS NECESSARY FOR THE ULTIMATE FORGING OF THE LINKAGE AND OUR VICTORY IN THE NEW CONFLICT.

'My name is Snudge, Great Lights.'

At that, a commotion broke out amongst the spectral visages. The Beacons began whirling around him. Some of them kept their composure while others roared or howled in a swelling crescendo of fury until a shattering hiss silenced them. Then, as before, Snudge heard the Beaconfolk arguing – although it seemed they were unaware that he was able to listen.

Snudge is not his name it is his JOB again he plays with us defies us.
He insults us he should be cast into the Hell of Ice.
Into hell! Into hell with this trickster!
No. We need him. We must cajole him.
Coerce and bribe him as we bend him to our will.
He is the perfect ally for the World Conqueror.
No no no no kill him punish him drink his pain to the end!
Kill the rule-twister.

Yes!

  Conrig needs him and we need Conrig.
  The Conflict rages! The Sky is aflame!
  CONRIG AND SNUDGE ARE THE KEYS TO VICTORY.
Ohhhhh . . . Human keys not Salka? The irony the strangeness!
  Show Snudge the bribe. Let that decide the matter.
    The bribe yes the STUPID bribe for a STUPID human!
    It is done.

Deveron Austrey heard spectral laughter and experienced a flash of chaotic brilliance. So it was the Beaconfolk who had instilled the sense of foreboding in him, compelling him to use the Great Stone that would place him in their power! This thing about his true name . . . why had they still been unable to discover it?

Because you did not tell them, another voice said.

'Source? Is it you? Speak to me! I have so many questions –'

But there was no response. Then he felt himself falling, landed on solid ground with a bone-jarring thud, and opened his eyes to almost impenetrable conifer-scented darkness and a deluge of rain. It took a moment for him to exert his talent and focus his mind's eye to render the night scene visible.

He was in a woodland clearing. At his feet were the drowned remains of a campfire and on either hand lay the motionless bodies of two men. Their saddlebags were nearby, unbuckled but otherwise undisturbed, along with the homely implements for tea-making.

One of the men, a strapping fellow well but plainly dressed, lay on his back. He had died hard, for his face was frozen in a terrible grimace of agony and his lifeless eyes were wide open and weeping raindrops.

Deveron had never seen him before.

The other victim, who had fallen on his face, wore more expensive garb – including an ornate belt with a splendid scabbard and sword. Deveron felt his breath catch. He knelt and turned the body over, whispering an oath. The features were smeared with mud, but this man was undoubtedly Beynor of Moss, the one who had invaded Deveron's dreams. His eyes were closed and his expression tranquil. One of his hands held the sword pommel in a grip of iron. His body showed no obvious marks of violence.

Deveron climbed to his feet again and set about scrying the entire scene. Hoofprints, partially washed away by the rain, marked the ground. A pile of manure and the torn branches of adjacent juniper bushes suggested that horses had been tethered there but had later broken free. More extensive windsearching revealed that the small grove of pine trees stood atop a hill adjacent to a principal highway traversing a desolate moorland. It had to be the Wold Road.

There was no trace of the Sovereign's army anywhere in the surrounding countryside. In fact, Deveron could discern no living soul anywhere within five leagues.

'Why the devil did Gateway bring me here?' he asked himself.

SHOW HIM THE BRIBE . . . THE BRIBE.

He felt ice at the base of his spine and a terrible surmise stole into his mind. Withdrawing from the windsearch, he bent over the saddlebags of the victims and examined them. The first pair held the usual spare clothes and equipment of a common traveler, plus two leathern pouches of medium size, affixed with padlocks which Deveron's talent opened easily. One pouch was full of gold coins, while the other held precious gems in small cloth sacks, along with a little wooden box.

Inside the box were five inactive minor sigils.

'Codders! Well, now it's plain that no brigand attacked

Beynor and his companion . . . Let's see what the Conjure-King carried.'

In addition to travel gear and a sack of food, the handsomely tooled bags yielded peculiar metal-mesh containers secured with enchanted locks. Rather than spend time deciphering their spells, Deveron simply scried the contents. He was not surprised to find a much greater quantity of gold and a large collection of gemstones. In fact, the diamonds alone were probably worth enough to purchase a sizable castle.

'This then is the bribe,' he murmured, 'intended to convince the "stupid human" to throw in his lot with Conrig . . . and the Beaconfolk.'

The response came softly into his mind: *THIS AND MUCH MORE.*

Shite! They were watching him.

And what would they do if he scorned the dead men's treasure?

He felt a strange sensation at his chest and opened his jerkin and shirt, heedless of the persistent downpour. Both Concealer and Gateway were brightly aglow – but their light was throbbing in a manner he had never seen before. Paralyzed by fear, he wondered if the sigils were somehow being commanded to annihilate him. Every instinct urged that he cry out to the Great Lights on the wind, beg mercy, and accept their dark bargain . . . but he held back.

Was it possible that he could outwit them? Convince them that he had taken the bribe, while yet repudiating it within the sanctuary of his own conscience?

He let out a long exhalation, willing his body to cast off terror. With steady hands he pulled together his shirt, hiding the disquieting pulsation of the sigils. He emptied the mundane contents of Beynor's saddlebags onto the ground and transferred into them the riches that had belonged to the other man – save for the five extinct sigils, which he put inside his owl-case. Then he went to the Conjure-King's body, unbuckled the Sword of State, and girded it about his own waist. After lifting the heavy bags to his shoulders and re-arranging his clothes to fend off the rain, he took hold of the Gateway sigil, closed his eyes, and repeated his request to be transported to the tent of Prince Corodon and his brother Bramlow.

Again, no pain accompanied the translation. When he opened his eyes an instant later, he found himself standing beneath the front canopy of a smallish pavilion with a royal blazon stitched on the closed flap. It was pitched amongst rocks in an alpine meadow, surrounded by others of its kind and a multitude of more ordinary military shelters. Watchfires burned nearby and a few flakes of snow were falling.

An astounded knight standing guard with three men-at-arms uttered a curse and drew his sword. 'You there! Stand fast or die! Don't move! Who the hell are you and how did you get here without a challenge?'

'I am the expected guest of these princes,' Deveron replied. He lifted one hand, smiling, and the four Cathran warriors halted in their tracks as though turned to statues. 'I mean no harm.' He called out the names of the princes and announced himself.

The tent flap opened and Vra-Bramlow poked his sleep-disheveled head outside, saying, 'Sir Deveron Austrey? A bit premature, aren't you? Well, I'm glad you got here safely. Come inside and I'll stoke the brazier and wake Coro. I suppose you want to see our father right away.'

'First, I need to confer with both you and the Prince Heritor.'

'Very well.' The novice blinked as he noticed Moss's Sword of State for the first time. 'How the bloody hell did you get *that?*'

Deveron sighed. 'It's a long story. Just let me disenchant these poor warriors, and I'll tell you about it.'

Many leagues to the south, atop a storm-lashed wooded hill, a man lying on the wet ground stirred and lifted his head. It was a long time before he came fully conscious, and even longer before he was capable of cogent thought. His first feeling was one of elation.

'I'm alive! So the antidote spell was effective after all . . . Was ever a man so blessed by fortune as I?'

When his talent recovered to the point that he was able to scry his surroundings and understand his situation, he uttered a deep groan. 'Was ever a man so accurst?'

There was no answer to that, so he used his talent to dry his soggy garments and weave a rough dissembling spell that would cause any uncanny observer to believe that he still lay dead in the mud. Then he commanded the missing horses to return to him, even though he had no notion at all of where he might go.

Orrion Wincantor sat by the window of his 'guest' chamber in Karum Castle and watched the riding lights of the seven pirate ships moored below in Terminal Bay. Sleep refused to come to him that night, and he had spent many hours vainly attempting to bespeak someone – anyone – who might pass on a warning about the presence of the Salka.

He had called out on the wind to both Coro and Bram without success, tried those Zeth Brethren of the Royal Corps of Alchymists whose names and faces he could recall, even attempted to communicate with Grand Shaman Zolanfel of Tarn, who was said to be the most sensitive windspeaker in all of High Blenholme.

No one had responded.

So he gave it up, and tried to think how best to take care

of Nyla and her mother when the monsters attacked the castle. It was probable that there were batteries of tarnblaze cannons to defend the place, but what good would such things be if the Salka used the awesome weapon that had blasted Rogue's Picket to pieces and obliterated the brig *Gannet?*

Earlier at supper, an extravagant feast apparently intended to impress the captives, Rork Karum had announced that his house-wizard had heard from shamans at Tarnholme that the Salka were invading the Firth of Gayle. All of the Tarnian frigates from the southern port were speeding to join the Joint Fleet's attack on the monsters. The wizard also found no evidence that the bay's exit channel was blocked by fallen rock from Rogue's Picket. Of course, the magicker's mediocre talent was unable to scry underwater, so Rork had dispatched a fast cutter to take soundings. With only light breezes prevailing, the boat was unlikely to arrive at the channel before dawn.

In the face of these discouraging tidings, Orrion could only implore the pirate-lord to be on guard. Laughing, Rork had said he'd command his cannoneers to stockpile extra tarnblaze shells in the bayside batteries that night, just to calm his royal guest's faint-hearted fears . . .

Now, thinking about this, Orrion realized that it was precisely the wrong defensive tactic to employ. If the flesh-devouring brutes came ashore, only a different, paradoxical course of action might save the inhabitants of the castle and numbers of villagers from a ghastly death.

But how could he convince Rork Karum to accept his plan?

Vra-Bramlow slipped out of the Sovereign's pavilion into the blustery night, where Deveron had waited for at least a quarter of an hour, attended by a squad of the Royal Guard.

'I suppose you were scrying Father and me and reading our lips.'

The former intelligencer only smiled. 'See that *you* don't attempt the same thing whilst I'm with the king, Brother Bram. I'll know if you do, and it'll go ill with you.'

The novice pretended haughty disdain. But he was in awe of this strange man who had questioned him and Coro so incisively about the mental health of their royal father and the manner in which Conrig had acquired his sigils. It was plain that Deveron Austrey knew every ramification of the dangers posed by Beaconfolk sorcery – especially if it was conjured by the Sovereign of Blenholme.

'I didn't mean to threaten you, Brother,' Deveron added. 'But the situation is delicate enough without inadvertent interference on your part. All of us will suffer if the king refuses to listen to my advice.'

'I believe Father's really willing to give you the benefit of the doubt,' Bram said. 'Your news of Beynor's death was a great boost to his spirits. He's taken his sigils from their hiding place and laid them out for you to see, along with those two raw lumps of Demon Seat mineral I told you about. He says that earlier this evening he tried to use the rocks to ask the good Lights why his sigils were blinking so weirdly. They gave no answer and it worries him. Tomorrow he wants me to try contacting the Lights myself – but only while he supervises.'

Deveron wagged his head in frustration. 'I wish there was some way you could get those pieces of moonstone away from the king. The Likeminded wanted *you* to safeguard them. They must have had a good reason.' He squared his shoulders. 'Well, I mustn't keep His Grace waiting any longer. One last thing: if this visit goes badly and I am slain, I ask that you bespeak the tidings to my wife Induna, who travels with the army of the earl marshal.'

The novice gasped in horror, as if such a thing had not occurred to him. 'I'm sure – I trust that –'

'Never mind,' Deveron said, and pushed past Bramlow into Conrig's tent.

It was not much larger than the one shared by the two royal brothers, with the only warmth provided by a charcoal brazier perched on a base of tiles. The Sovereign, swathed in a heavy robe of sheared beaver trimmed with black fox, sat on a field-stool at a portable table. A single oil lamp hung from the pavilion's peak. Its flame was pale compared to the throbbing greenish glow of the moonstones that rested on the table before the king, giving his features a spectral cast.

'Come and take a seat,' Conrig said in a neutral tone.

Deveron inclined his head in respect. 'Your Grace.' He unbuckled the Sword of State and leaned it against a coffer, then drew up a second stool. 'I'll leave Moss's royal weapon in your charge, if I may.'

The king stared at him without speaking for some time before saying, 'We meet again under ominous circumstances, sir. So that you may be reassured, know that I've just signed and sealed a royal writ rescinding your condemnation for treason and the decree of outlawry.' He nodded at a folded sheet of parchment on the table. 'Examine it if you care to. Also, I would once again welcome you into my service, restore your knightly honors, and be glad of your good counsel.'

'Sire, I offer you my counsel wholeheartedly and herewith pledge my loyal service to the Sovereignty of High Blenholme.'

'To the office, but not the man?' Conrig gave a wry chuckle. 'So be it. In a moment you must tell me why you insisted that we two confer in the wee hours of the night, rather than at a more civilized time. But first –' He pointed to the pulsating moonstones: three major sigils, the disk that had empowered them, and two irregular chunks of mineral. 'What in hell's the matter with these bloody things? Have my sigils lost their power?'

Deveron reached inside his jerkin and drew out the chain with Concealer and Subtle Gateway. They blinked in unison with the king's stones. 'It's my belief that all of these tools of sorcery are somehow being affected by a great war now being fought in the Sky Realm. The beings that we call Beaconfolk are but one faction of a supernatural race. They are opposed by others of their kind.'

'Do you meant the so-called good Lights? But I thought they were relatively powerless.' The king scowled. 'Except for wreaking well-meant mayhem on my luckless son Orrion! I admit they've also been of some help in our war against the Salka. They gave Bram news of the monsters' entry into the Firth of Gayle. But now they refuse to talk to me when I invoke them.'

Patiently, Deveron explained almost everything he knew about the Old and New Conflicts, holding back only the manipulation of human beings by the Source and Conrig's own involuntary conscription into that entity's service.

'Particularly worrisome, sire, is a certain recent discovery of mine. The Source of the Conflict has made known to me that the Beaconfolk are actively seeking to ensnare all of talented humanity in the sorcerous game which has long enslaved the Salka. In ancient times, the evil Lights reveled in a feast of pain willingly vouchsafed by the foolish monsters in exchange for magical power. Bazekoy's conquest, and his destruction of so many sigils, deprived the Beacons of much of the unholy pleasure to which they had become addicted. They then attempted without much success to entice human beings into their game. A century ago, Conjure-King Rothbannon outwitted both the Salka and the Beacons and contrived to employ sigil sorcery in a way that was fairly harmless to himself and his realm. More recently the Lights transferred their hopes to Beynor. When he disappointed them, the Lights turned to you.'

Conrig extended his hand and touched the Weathermaker sigil on the table in front of him. For an instant, its glow intensified. 'They think to *use* me?' he said in a voice that was ominously soft. 'To control me to advance their own ends – as that Mossbelly whoreson Beynor hoped to do?'

'Yes, sire.'

'Why, then,' the king said, slipping the moonstone ring onto his index finger, 'I shall simply emulate the cunning Rothbannon and beat them at their own game! The first Conjure-King used sigils and managed to prosper. Cowardice and bad judgment brought down Rothbannon's successors. I shall not make the same mistakes.'

Deveron felt his heart contract. 'Your Grace, the sigils are insidious. The most powerful ones, such as the three you possess, are almost irresistibly tempting. Recall how Queen Ullanoth sold her soul, betraying her subjects and her nation and perishing miserably, just so that . . .' He could not bring himself to say it.

'So that she might prove her love for me.' Conrig's retort was cynical. 'But you have two sigils of your own, my Snudge, and you've used them to the endangerment of your life. Yet your soul seems quite intact, as is your body! Am I not right?'

The last words were flung out like a gauntlet of defiance, and Deveron could only lower his head and say nothing. How could he explain to Conrig Wincantor the way that the two of them differed?

The king pressed on. 'Can I not use my sigils as prudently as you do? As Rothbannon did? If course I can! I'll prove it in the upcoming battle with the Salka, those dimwitted tubs of blubber. And when I've conquered them, I'll find other good uses for the moonstones, paying their pain-price willingly for the sake of my people.'

'Sire, the Beaconfolk cannot be trusted to deal with you fairly. They don't follow our moral principles – or even our logic. If they think you insult or threaten them, if they believe that you're using your Great Stones in a manner they disapprove, they're capable of torturing you to death and condemning you to the Hell of Ice. The mother of Ullanoth and Beynor suffered such a fate, and the horror of it drove her husband King Linndal insane –'

'That's enough!' Conrig smacked his hand onto the table and made the stones jump. 'Queen Taspiroth was a silly woman. God knows what idiotic command she gave to her sigil that provoked the wrath of the Beacons.'

'Sire, the moonstones and the sorcery they channel are evil. I'm certain of this. The Source has assured me of it – and he is the very one who invented the perverse game of power and pain in the first place, and started the first war in the Sky Realm in a failed attempt to put an end to it.'

'What do I care about mysterious battles fought amongst the stars? My rôle is to save my people from the Salka!'

'If you use sigils against them, you'll endanger not only yourself but also every human being living on our island. When Emperor Bazekoy conquered the monsters he had his warriors destroy every sigil they found on the dead bodies of the foe. The Beacons probably tempted the emperor to join their game, too –'

'Codswallop!' the Sovereign bellowed, leaping up from his stool. 'No one's tempted me. And *you* flirt again with treason, Deveron Austrey, to insinuate such a vile calumny. You imply that you yourself can be trusted to use sigils wisely, and I cannot!'

'Not at all, sire. If I could get rid of mine, I'd do it in an instant. But the Source commanded me to keep them for the time being, so I've obeyed. And in truth, Concealer and Gateway have small potential for bringing unwitting harm upon others. The same is not true of your own Destroyer sigil.'

Conrig had thrown off his heavy fur robe and was pacing back and forth, scowling. 'It's a weapon. Any weapon can be misused. I'm not a fool. Rothbannon of Moss wielded a Destroyer to establish and secure his kingdom. He died in his sleep with a smile on his face and his mistress beside him under a swansdown quilt.'

'But he used Destroyer only sparingly. He was also a sorcerer of vast experience who knew the quirks and vagaries of the Beaconfolk. Forgive me, sire, but you are untrained in the magical arts – and your sons told me the sad news about Lord Stergos, so you no longer have him as a guide.'

'I have *you*.' Conrig extended the hand that bore Weathermaker. 'And when you entered my pavilion, you had snowflakes melting on your shoulders. So begin your service to the Sovereignty by instructing me how to use this ring to fend off snow in the pass above us. The Beaconfolk said that all I need do was command it like a trusty servant. Were they telling me true or not?'

Deveron's response was resigned. 'Perhaps. Only use common sense, sire. Make the sigil's job as easy as possible to accomplish. Say something like, 'Deflect all snowstorms from the pass until my army has gone safely through.' It would be imprudent to say, 'Let sunny skies and warm breezes prevail in Tarn until I command otherwise.' Such weather is not natural for northern latitudes at this time of year. As for the army's march from the pass to the Donorvale estuary, the sigil might indeed obey a command to produce a long interval of clement weather. But only at the price of debilitating pain that would render you incapable of leading your troops for many days. Conjure-Queen Ullanoth was so afflicted when she changed the weather drastically during your campaign against Holt Mallburn, and again at the Battle of Cala Bay. Surely you recall this.'

'I'm going to use the sigil anyhow,' Conrig said. He had stopped pacing and now lifted the finger wearing the ring. In a voice that was quiet and resolute, he repeated Deveron's first suggested command.

Weathermaker flared momentarily, like an emerald struck by a bright sunbeam. Then it dimmed to its former slow blinking. The king regarded it with bemusement. 'Do you suppose it worked?'

'I – I would think so. Do you feel any pain?'

'Not a bit. Is that usual?'

'No. But in my own experience, the primary pain-debt is extracted when one sleeps.'

'Well, shite,' muttered Conrig with a grimace. 'As if I didn't have enough to contend with, having the damned night-mares – and the latest this very night, just before Bram woke me to meet with you. But if Beynor is dead, how can such a thing be?'

'Sire?' Deveron was mystified. 'You suffer from bad dreams?'

The king's expression changed and he seemed to stare at something at a far distance, speaking in a strange slow voice that made Deveron's skin crawl.

'My sleep has been uneasy for many years. Every sort of shadowy enemy torments me – seeks to seize my Iron Crown and destroy the Sovereignty I have dedicated my life to preserving. Some of the dreamfoes are Salka. Some are human. There is also a dark fiend lacking eyes, impris-oned in some distant glacial chasm, who seeks to take my crown by guile rather than by might and main. In earlier nightmares I fought all these opponents with my sword and talent and won . . . until the coming of the traitor prince, the greatest enemy of them all.' The king closed his eyes and was still for some time.

Finally Deveron said, 'Sire, you intimated that Beynor provoked these phantasms. I know he is capable of dream-invasion, but –'

Unseeing, Conrig spoke again with the same eerie detachment. 'This disloyal son of mine has no face. The only weapon that can prevail against him is the sigil named Destroyer. In one dream, Beynor showed me that much. Later, when we spoke face-to-face, he admitted he'd used nightmares to seize my attention. He tried to convince me that I was incapable of using sigil sorcery safely without his close guidance. But the Great Lights told me otherwise. They'd cursed Beynor! Why would they permit that curse to be circumvented? And now the Conjure-King is dead. Defeated. But the traitor prince remains, held at bay only by Destroyer. I thought I knew his name. Now I'm not certain who he is. But I'll find out.' The king smiled. 'With your help.'

Deveron stiffened. 'You expect me to spy on the Heritor and Vra-Bramlow?'

Conrig's eyes refocused, dark and effulgent. 'I expect you to watch them and fend off any attempted perfidy on their part. And when Dyfrig Beorbrook joins our host in a day or so, you'll watch him as well. Only if you swear to do this will I permit you to serve the Sovereignty.' He removed Weathermaker from his finger and set it down. His hand hovered close to Destroyer.

'Very well, sire. You have my oath on it. I'll carry out this duty to the best of my ability. Am I dismissed?'

'Not yet. You were always an exceptional long-distance scrier, Snudge. Do you still retain this skill?'

'If anything, I'm better at it than ever.'

'My sons Corodon and Orrion . . . both have a tiny

modicum of talent, as I do. I think you already know this. Can I trust you to keep their unfortunate secret?'

'I'll do so as my conscience permits, sire.'

'I have a reason for bringing the subject up. Last night, Bram thought he heard his brother Orrion bespeak him across many leagues. Is this possible?'

'It might be.'

'Orry is supposed to have reported that the Salka are invading via Terminal Bay in Didion, rather than in Tarn as Sealord Sernin's shamans have confirmed. Orry was supposedly cast away when the brig he sailed on from Karum Port was sunk by a single explosion of green light. Another such explosion is supposed to have blocked the single channel into Terminal Bay.'

'Great God – but the Salka are only supposed to possess minor sigils! None of them could wreak such havoc.'

Only a Destroyer could . . .

'In my opinion, Bramlow only fancied that his brother bespoke him. The Tarnians scried no wreckage or bodies. They insist that any blockage of the channel must be due to natural causes. But I want you to scry Terminal Bay for me now, before you leave. Perhaps you might notice something that the shamans missed.'

'I'll try, sire. However, the windsenses of Sealord Sernin's magickers are probably keener than mine.'

Offering no apology, Deveron went to the Sovereign's own camp bed. He lay down atop the fine mink coverlet without removing his muddy boots, and hid his face in his hands.

Time passed. Conrig paced the uneven floor of the tent, stony soil thickly padded by sheepskin rugs. He ventured to peer outside. It was still very cold but the snow flurries had stopped. Bramlow and the guards huddled around a small fire talking in low tones and failed to notice him. Closing the tentflap, the king poured a small noggin of brandy into a handled pewter cup and held it over the coals in the brazier until the fragrant fumes rose and filled his head. Then he drank, returned to his stool, and waited.

After an interval that seemed endless, Deveron sat up, swinging his legs to the ground.

'What did you see?' Conrig demanded.

The intelligencer shook his head. 'Nothing. Nothing at all unusual in Terminal Bay save the vessels of the pirates tied up at docks or in deepwater moorages, the castles of the local lordlings with sleepy sentinels walking the battlements, and the dwellings of the common folk shut tight against the night. Smoke rises peacefully from their chimneys in the dead-calm air.'

The Sovereign turned away with a sigh. 'Very well. My son Bramlow awaits you outside. He'll find you a place to sleep. Tomorrow at dawn we'll start out for Frost Pass.'

'Very well, sire.'

Deveron inclined his head and left the royal pavilion without wishing Conrig a good night, since that eventuality was unlikely. The novice came to meet him, and the two of them silently made their way back to the princes' tent.

'Will you tell Coro and me how went your meeting with His Grace?' Bramlow asked rather nervously. 'Or do you deem it none of our business?'

'He conjured Weathermaker and asked that there be no snow in the pass. The sigil seemed to obey him in a surprisingly docile fashion. The rest of our conversation I must keep confidential. That situation may change. But for now, I require you to tell me everything you know about those two pieces of uncarved moonstone that His Grace keeps with his sigils.'

The Lights fought.

The manner of their contention was incomprehensible to

beings of the Ground Realm, and since clouds had spread
over most of High Blenholme Island, only a few humans
abroad on that night witnessed the shocking auroral displays
that tore the Sky asunder. Soundless death-flares blazed
brighter than miniature suns until they shrank into dark
oblivion. Again and again the Likeminded Exiles and their
Remnant fellows assaulted the conduits of pain and power,
but the breaks were only momentary and insufficient. Many
good Lights were extinguished and more were gravely weakened; some retreated to rebuild their strength.

The Coldlight Army suffered the battle's toll as well, but
unlike their antagonists they were able to drew fresh suste-
nance from the hundreds of Salka warriors on the world
below, who worked and suffered throughout the long night.

A disciplined force of amphibian engineers, imperceptible
to the few watchmen aboard the pirate vessels, utilized certain
minor sigils to drill scores of holes into the hull of each sizable
vessel in Terminal Bay. The work was done both delicately
and quietly, so that the oaken planks were almost – but not
quite – perforated in a broad circular pattern about an ell in
diameter. None of the boats and ships sank. That would only
happen the next day, when Attack Commander Tasatawnn
gave the order, and Salka warriors used the power of their
great bodies to rupture the weakened hulls.

Whereupon every important sailing craft in the pirate
colony would go down at the same time.

Beneath the Ice, the One Denied the Sky knew nothing of
these Salka activities. The spell of deceit woven by the
monsters was too well-made for him to see through.
However, the Source was all too well aware of the continuing battle being fought in the heavens. He knew that his
Likeminded colleagues needed his help desperately, but being
creatures of the Sky Realm, they could not reach into his

prison below the Barren Lands and break the blue-ice manacle that still held him fast.

Only groundlings have the power to free me, the Source told his frustrated friends. *I require many minor sigils to be immolated in the abolition ceremony – or else a single Great Stone. Tell my human and Green helpers of my need. Beseech them to hurry! I find I can no longer bespeak them directly because of the Conflict's turmoil.*

Unfortunately, the Likeminded were also incapable of communication with humans enlisted in the New Conflict, because the conduits between the realms were under heavy attack. The two pieces of mineral from the summit of Demon Seat that might have opened one of those conduits rested inside a leather pouch hanging about the neck of the sleeping Sovereign of Blenholme, along with his sigils and their empowering disk.

Conrig clutched the small sack as he dreamed. He success-fully fended off the latest onslaught of the prince without a face just before the Beaconfolk began to exact their pain-price in earnest.

Dawn came, cold and overcast but with the bases of the clouds above the crest of the White Rime Range. The Cathran armies and the force of High Sealord Sernin Donorvale broke their respective camps and resumed their march toward the Tarnian rendezvous, a deep valley on the opposite side of Frost Pass, where the climate was milder and there would be green forage for the horses.

Conrig was in a thunderous mood as he swung into the saddle, ignoring the greetings of his sons, his General Staff, and the reinstated Royal Intelligencer. He'd slept very badly and his head pounded as though he'd overindulged in the infamous national beverage of Didion. Two windspoken messages delivered to him as he broke his fast with poached eggs and dry toast had not helped his recovery.

The first came from Archwizard Chumick Whitsand, speaking for King Somarus. The monarch was adamant that his countrymen would not cross into Tarn and risk being trapped there for the winter. Crown Prince Valardus had been ordered to demobilize his men and send them home from Lake of Shadows on the following day.

The second disturbing piece of news came from Lord Admiral Hartrig Skellhaven, commanding the Joint Fleet which now stood at the entrance to the Firth of Gayle. Tarnian patrols from Yelicum and other ports along the vast estuary had reported that only small numbers of Salka had been met with and dispatched. The most authoritative shamans at Donorvale, the capital city, insisted that there was no way fifty thousand monsters could conceal themselves from the myriad of seagoing scriers probing for them at the water's surface. No spell of couverture was strong enough to hide such huge numbers of swimmers from scrutiny at close range.

High Sealord Sernin, stonefaced and adamant, had told the Sovereign that he was now forced to conclude that the amphibian host was not invading by way of the Firth of Gayle after all. The creatures who had been seen and killed there earlier must have been participants in a suicide mission, a daring feint that had successfully deceived humanity.

After a brief discussion with the Tarnian leader, Conrig told the crestfallen assembly of generals that he had agreed to divert the Joint Fleet from the firth and send it southward. Meanwhile, windsearchers of Tarn and Cathra would renew their search of other potential invasion beachheads at Shelter Bay, Foul Bay, and Goodfortune Bay in Tarn.

And most especially at Terminal Bay in Didion.

Casya Pretender walked along the bank of the little subarctic river, watching greyling rise to sip a late hatch of little winged insects and wondering if she'd be able to catch any fish for lunch. After two meals of venison and hardtack in a row, she was heartily sick of reindeer. The iridescent purplish fish with their lovely sail-like dorsal fins and delicate flesh that tasted faintly of thyme would be a welcome change.

She located a likely pool at last and set about preparing. A trimmed sapling made an improvised pole; her belt-wallet yielded a coil of line, a hook of sharpened bone, a cork bobber, and a fatty piece of leftover meat, which she cut into pieces. Greyling weren't finicky feeders. These big ones who lived in the far north even gorged themselves on mice . . .

Greetings to you, Casabarela Who-Would-Be-Queen.

She gave a small shriek and dropped the hook she was baiting. Not four ells away from her the fantastically orna-mented head of a Morass Worm hung in the misty air as though it were decapitated, almost resembling one of the demon-shaped box kites that the Green Men used in their Spring-Welcoming ritual.

'You startled me!' she admitted. 'Is it you, Vaelrath?'

The rest of the great female dragon's body emerged from an invisible subtle corridor and settled into a coil on the riverbank. The worm's mental voice was gratified and her fierce mouth expanded into what might have been a smile.

So you do recognize me. Too many of your kind – and the Green Ones as well – think we all look alike.

'That's ridiculous. You're particularly beautiful.' Casya set aside the fishing gear and came closer, extending her open hand. The worm's tongue caressed it lightly. 'Did you hear me calling out to you in my mind?'

We knew you were here, came the ambiguous reply. *Up until now, there seemed no good reason to acknowledge your presence.*

'Oh.' The girl tried not to let her hurt feelings show. 'Well, I'm very glad to see you. I have a very important request –'

We know that the New Conflict has begun, Vaelrath interrupted.

We know that the Salka have once again mounted a great invasion, coming ashore on lands you should rightfully rule, which are nevertheless at a far distance from our own cherished home. We are willing to listen to your plea for help, and then decide whether it should concern us.

'Thank you, Vaelrath,' Casya said humbly.

The Morass Worm rose to her full height, towering over the young woman. Moving slowly backward, so that her sinuous tail and hindlegs vanished through the unseen portal, Vaelrath extended a forelimb armed with terrible claws. *Take hold of me. We will go to my people.*

'But a human friend accompanied me here, a dear old man who waits in the trading post –'

He must continue waiting until the decision is made. Will you come?

'Yes,' Casya said, and stepped forward, and disappeared.

The warning bell down in Karum village began to ring not long after the noble prisoners had finished the midday meal served to them in their comfortable prison. The sound came faintly through the thick glass of the casement, but its ominous nature was unmistakable. Nyla dropped the book of Didionite tales she had been reading aloud to Orrion and started up from her chair, her face drained of blood. 'Oh, no!'

Trailed by Countess Orvada, who was still finishing her wine, the young lovers rushed together to the window that overlooked the harbor and the settlement at the foot of the cliff. The docks, the quayside, and the twisting lanes were crowded with the tiny figures of frantic people, but at first no obvious cause for alarm was to be seen.

Then Orrion said quietly, 'Look at that large schooner and the three sloops tied up at the third slip. Their decks are awash and they're listing. Sinking!'

'Some of those fishing smacks also seem to be going down,' Nyla noted in consternation. 'People are cutting loose the mooring lines from the bollards. Why would they do that?'

'To keep the entire dock structure from being torn apart,' Countess Orvada suggested. 'But I fear it's too late. Look how the slips are starting to disintegrate! Every boat of size seems to have mortal damage. They're all settling to the bottom.'

'Great Zeth!' Orrion murmured. 'Those seven great pirate vessels anchored out in deep water – they're foundering, too.'

The tall masts of the frigates tilted crazily. Some ships subsided at the stern while others sank bow-first faster than seemed possible. The few seamen left aboard on watch tried without success to launch lifeboats, then plummeted into the water where they splashed and struggled for a few minutes before being pulled under, perhaps by the suction of the doomed ships, perhaps by something else . . .

The bell continued its melancholy tolling.

Nyla gave a cry that mingled fear and pity, turned away from the horrid sight, and burst into tears. Orrion ran to the locked outer door of their apartment and began to pound on it, shouting, 'Guards, open up for the love of God! The Salka monsters are here. They'll come ashore any minute now and start their slaughter. Open up! I have a plan to save us. Summon Lord Rork before it's too late!'

Nothing happened. The countess took her sobbing daughter in her arms. She said to Orrion, 'Do you think we've been abandoned, sir?'

He left off hammering the door and gave her a despairing glance. 'I hope not. Our host seemed to have a certain vestigial chivalry tempering his venal nature. But he won't be able to defend his castle against the Salka using conventional tactics. I've got to convince him to –'

The door was flung open abruptly and Rork Karum stood

on the threshold wide-eyed and carrying a sheathed longsword. He tossed the weapon to Orrion, who caught it awkwardly. 'Use it to defend your women, my prince . . . or to grant them merciful release when the devouring devils fall upon us.' His teeth gleamed in a fatalistic grin. 'And now you may rightfully say, "I told you so!"'

Orrion placed the sword on the dining table. 'My lord, there may be a way to save all inside this castle without the use of weapons.'

Rork laughed. 'Not bloody likely! My house-wizard has received desperate messages on the wind from resident magickers in the other corsair castles ringing Terminal Bay. All of them report that their tall ships and larger sailing craft are sinking because of huge holes that appeared inexplicably in their hulls. The Salka must have done it slyly in preparation for their invasion. But at least we can die fighting! Shall I help you buckle on the sword?'

'Nay – only listen to me. This plan of mine could save us. First, you must have your wizard notify Dennech-Cuva of this attack. Implore the duchess to order her windspeaker to relay the tidings to the Sovereign without delay.'

The pirate-lord shrugged. 'Very well. My ransom scheme's a goner anyhow. But what's your plan?'

'It's simple. Barricade your castle entrances, shut up its windows and gunports, and let no living person be visible on the battlements when the Salka horde comes ashore. All inside the castle must remain quiet. Make no defensive move. None at all! Shoot no arrows at the Salka if they ascend your precipice. Fling no tarnblaze firepots at them with your catapults. Above all, don't use your cannons. If you make no resistance at all, I believe the monsters might pass us by.'

'But my castle is crammed with booty!'

'Their primary goal is to gain as much ground as possible before encountering significant human opposition from the

Sovereign Army. As I told you, the Salka don't seek plunder. They relish the taste of human flesh, but I fear they'll find victims aplenty amongst the unfortunates left outside your stronghold gates.'

'But what about that terrible weapon of theirs you described?' Rork protested. 'The thing that annihilates with green fire! Why wouldn't they use it against us whether we fight back or not?'

'I believe the Salka weapon is a magical moonstone of great power,' Orrion said. 'Doubtless it's capable of bringing down your castle walls about our ears. But I know for a fact that such high sorcery is not without peril to its user – who must pay a price of atrocious pain each time the moonstone is wielded. In my opinion, the Salka will not call on this weapon except in cases of absolute necessity. If we don't provoke the monsters, they may let us be.'

Beads of sweat had sprung up on Rork Karum's brow. 'What if you're wrong?'

'Hope that I'm right,' Orrion retorted.

Countess Orvada, who still stood at the window with Nyla, looking outside, turned and said, 'Numbers of village people are running up the cliff track toward the castle. Women and children are among them. You must give those poor souls safe refuge, my lord.'

The pirate frowned and set his jaw stubbornly, whereupon Orrion said to him, 'Such an act of mercy would redound to your credit when the forces of my royal father come to our rescue.'

'And when will that be?' Rork sneered. 'And how will it be accomplished?'

'In truth, I don't know,' Orrion replied. 'What I am sure of is that we have no chance of survival at all unless you hold off attacking these invaders and instead prepare to endure a silent siege. What's it to be?'

'Listen to him, my lord,' Orvada urged.

At the window, Nyla gave a soft moan. 'Look! They're coming. Rising from the water and swimming toward shore. The bay is alive with Salka as far as my eyes can see, thousands upon thousands of hideous monsters . . .'

Orrion, the countess, and Rork Karum came to look over her shoulder in shocked silence. The ships that formerly lay at anchor had disappeared and the once calm surface of the water was a shimmering mass of sleek bodies, as though some titanic rock had been lifted to reveal a squirming nest of noxious dark grubs beneath.

The first wave of Salka reached the quayside and surged ashore. The true size of them only became apparent as they pursued their terrified human prey and brought them down. Moving with astonishing speed even on dry land, they easily overtook people running for their lives. The panicked fugitives were plucked screaming from inadequate hiding places. Locked doors delayed bloody death only for brief moments as the enormous amphibians demolished the walls of cottages and warehouses by using their massive bodies as battering rams.

'Come away,' Orrion said, gently herding Nyla and her mother from the appalling scene. Both wept helplessly.

Grey-faced, the pirate-lord called to one of the guard officers who still waited outside in the passage. 'Captain Seba, mark my words well: Hasten with your men and tell the gunnery commander that no cannons, missiles, or arrows are to be fired at the Salka attackers. Anyone who disobeys will be thrown down to the monsters. Prepare the castle for a silent siege.'

The man saluted and went off at a run. Rork beckoned to Orrion. 'My prince, I think you'd best join me whilst I give other necessary orders. Then we'll find my wizard and you can dictate the wind-messages he must send. As for your women –'

Nyla stepped forward. Her face was still wet with tears but a new look of determination brightened her eyes. 'If it please you, my lord, my mother and I will take charge of the refugees from the village. Some at least will be able to make it here safely.'

Rork Karum swept her a deep bow. 'Come along, then. There's not much time left, but we'll get as many of them inside as we can.'

The Supreme Warrior and the Master Shaman crouched together on a flat rock, one of several that rose out of the harbor waters at the mouth of the broad, slow-flowing Dennech River. To the north the ruined port village lay beneath a pall of smoke. The remains of its buildings and wharf still smoldered from the attack by troops armed with Firestarter sigils. Not a human inhabitant was left alive. A few scavenging ravens and gulls flew about, but there was little for them to find but cracked and scorched bones.

Kalawnn still suffered the ill effects of Destroyer's double pain-debt. He watched the swimming warriors speed by on their way up the river with only an occasional comment. Ugusawnn, on the other hand, was in a transport of joy over the success of the initial assault, and now and then he uttered loud whoops of encouragement to the fighters or urged them on with windspoken cheers. A scant three hours had gone by, and already nearly five thousand Salka had penetrated inland all the way to the confluence of the Dennech with the Rime River, which drained the high mountains dividing Didion from Tarn.

'Our lads will reach the large human town called Dennech-Cuva before sundown,' Ugusawnn enthused. 'Then we'll show the miserable groundlings what we *really* can do!'

'I still wonder whether it was wise to transfer bonding of the Destroyer sigil from me to Commander Tasatawnn,' the

Master Shaman said. 'If he should overreach himself and become badly disabled, we will have lost our finest tactician before the war has hardly begun.'

'It had to be done, my friend.' The Warrior was solicitous. 'And our Eminent colleages concurred. It was plain this morning that you aren't yet strong enough to wield the Great Stone yourself. This way, you have many additional hours to recuperate, whilst Tasa's strike will demoralize the foe utterly! King Conrig will expect us to bypass Dennech-Cuva and invest the weaker fortress at Tweenwater. Instead, we'll eliminate the most formidable enemy stronghold in all of the west country.'

Kalawnn's ruby eyes closed for a moment as he ventured forth on the wind. 'Ah . . . Our second force moving up the Shadow River proceeds steadily, if more slowly because of the rapids, as we expected . . . My windsight also shows that our brave reserves are doing a fine job cleaning out the lesser pirate castles and villages around Terminal Bay.' His eyes reopened.

'All the youngsters had to do was scry the assault on Karum Port to see how the good work is done.' Ugusawnn lifted a fresh haunch of man-meat from the bed of rockweed that had been keeping it cool and proferred it to his colleague. 'Would you care for something to eat? I'm feeling peckish myself.'

'No, but thank you. I wish to oversee that white castle on the clifftop again. I'm still not certain we should have let it be.' After an interval, he said. 'The humans inside continue to appear strangely torpid, lying about almost as though they were sick – or paralyzed by fear. Certainly they show no inclination to use their weapons. It's rather unnatural.'

'We've terrified the cowardly runts into a stupor, that's what!' The Warrior chortled and began to gnaw flesh from the bone. 'Delicious. Exceptionally sweet and tender. Are you sure you don't want a taste?'

'A salmon diet will better speed my recovery.' Kalawnn's digits plucked a piece of fish from the baldric that also carried the ivory plaques of the reference books. The blinking minor sigil Scriber still hung about his neck, and the sight of it caused him much concern. Ugusawnn's Subtle Gateway and Longspeaker stones also pulsed in an identical disturbing rhythm. The Potency was still hidden away in the golden case fastened to the Master Shaman's wrist, and he had no desire to see what it might be doing; he was only happy not to be carrying it inside his gizzard any more. What good had the enigmatic little thing ever done the Salka? He wished he could get rid of it altogether but didn't dare. Not yet . . .

'The throbbing of our sigils still bothers you?' the Supreme Warrior inquired.

'Very much, as does the continuing silence of the Great Lights. I wish that the clouds would lift so that we could again see the Beacons in the night. Something important is happening in the Sky Realm. Why won't the Lights talk to us about it?'

Ugusawnn shrugged. 'So long as our sigils work, why worry?'

'I wish I had your soldierly confidence!'

'You'd be wise to stop fretting and conserve your energies, Kalawnn – especially if you're still determined to reclaim Destroyer from Tasatawnn after he demolishes the citadel at Dennech-Cuva.'

'It must be done. Your Gateway will transport us to his position as soon as the job is completed. He'll be weakened and in no humor to resist our demand. I feel strongly that we must abolish Destroyer without delay and re-bond it before Commander Tasatawnn decides he's entitled to keep the sigil and use it as he pleases. He's a brilliant and courageous fighter, but not always willing to . . . bow to the wisdom of higher authority.'

'Well, I agree we must keep close control of the situation. Matters are going to get interesting very soon. Conrig must be marshalling his armies against us even as we speak.'

Kalawnn nodded somberly. 'And without advice from the Great Lights, we have no notion of what he might do with the three Great Stones Beynor handed over to him. Don't forget, Conrig has a Destroyer, too. If only we could target him with ours before he uses his own against us!'

'The idea makes perfect sense to me,' said the Supreme Warrior.

'You forget what the Lights told the First Judge in their last communication: it *pleased* them to give Beynor's three Great Stones to King Conrig. They've inaugurated a new contest that pits us against humankind, with sigils used on both sides. The Sovereign of Blenholme is a principal game-piece. The Lights would hardly countenance our precipitate removal of him. It would spoil their play! Remember Queen Taspiroth's blunder . . .'

'Curse it!' Ugusawnn said. 'You're right, of course. We daren't risk it.'

The Master Shaman sighed. 'We remain subject to the rules of this damnable game. Fortunately, so does King Conrig.'

TWENTY-ONE

Vra-Odos Springhill was the keenest long-distance wind-speaker in the Royal Corps of Alchymists. Still, he almost missed hearing the feeble generalized hail from the Dennech-Cuva wizard, passing on tidings of the calamitous events that had occurred in Terminal Bay. Once the truth of the message was confirmed, Brother Odos spurred his mule through the column of mounted warriors descending the western slope of the pass until he finally reached the king and his party. Immediately a command went out for the entire army to halt until His Grace heard what news the alchymist had brought.

'The invasion took place four hours ago?' Conrig roared in disbelief. 'Why wasn't I informed earlier?'

The Sovereign, his General Staff, half a dozen or so of his most trusted battle-leaders, Corodon, Bramlow, and Deveron sat their saddles in the lee of a great rock alongside the moun-tain trail. Clouds of steamy breath from the animals filled the frigid air.

'We crossed over the pass around noon, Your Grace,' the little windspeaker pointed out with pedantic patience. 'The relatively weak voice of Duchess Margaleva's house-wizard was for some time blocked by the bulk of the White Rime Range lying between us and Dennech. It was only by a fluke that I perceived one of his hails at all. But I assure you that the details of the message from your son, Sir Orrion, are correct. I bespoke Grand Shaman Zolanfel and asked him to verify the information by setting up a relay to Karum Castle, whence came the original warning, via a colleague situated in Tarnholme, on the coast. This person complied. He learned that the port town has been laid waste, whilst its castle remains oddly unscathed. Sir Orrion and the noble ladies with him are unharmed. They are said to be the "guests" of the local pirate lord.'

Somebody spoke up in derision. 'We know what *that* must mean.'

Conrig called for silence and bade Vra-Odos to continue.

'The shaman at Tarnholme is a most competent adept. He windsearched the shores of Terminal Bay. The devastation was obvious but no Salka warriors were visible to his mind's eye. The monsters are surely concealing themselves with powerful sorcery, just as we suspected.'

'Curse them!' Conrig groaned. 'Too bad Karum's idiot magicker never thought to send the news to Tarnholme in the first place, rather than Dennech. The Diddly blockhead! We should have learned of this earlier.'

'I think the man might have done his best under most trying circumstances, sire,' Vra-Odos said mildly. 'Another point: the spearhead force of the Salka horde will likely fall upon Dennech-Cuva sometime before nightfall. I was told that the civilian inhabitants are fleeing and the old duchess and her grandson Egonus are preparing the citadel for an attack. The place is very well defended. This is all I have to report.'

The Sovereign sat his tall stallion, eyes hooded and lips pressed into a tight line, as if he were fending off both anxiety and physical pain.

'Sire, what are your orders?' inquired the new Lord Constable, Wanstantil Cloudfell.

'We go back, Wanstan.' Conrig's reply was colorless. 'There is no alternative.' He turned to Vra-Odos. 'Brother, please relay this command to High Sealord Sernin, as well as to Earl Marshal Parlian and Lord Hale Brackenfield: Every unit of the army must return to Direwold at a forced-march pace. Once there, we'll reconsider our strategy.'

The military windspeaker bowed, then urged his mount into a more sheltered position to send the orders.

'What about Valardus Mallburn?' Rugged old Munlow Ramscrest's harsh voice dripped contempt. 'His Diddly army is still lounging at Lake of Shadows. King Somarus won't weasel out of fighting the Salka *this* time! Not with monsters pouring into his country via the back door.'

'But would it be wise to order the Crown Prince to march against the Salka ahead of us?' Corodon ventured somewhat shyly. 'Valardus is no tactician and yet he refuses to cede authority to his wiser generals. He'd likely make a balls-up of any action and his troops would end up butchered to a man.'

'The Prince Heritor makes an excellent point,' Cloudfell stated. 'I propose that we instruct Brother Odos also to bespeak Chumick Whitsand, the Archwizard of Didion. He's a person of some sense – which is more than one can say of Somarus and his son. Let Whitsand apprise Somarus of the grave situation. Only His Majesty of Didion can order Prince Valardus to hold off attacking the Salka until we decide the best way to counter their advance.'

The others spoke their agreement and Conrig said, 'Well thought. We can't afford to waste the life of a single warrior – not even Diddlies.'

The grim laughter that came from the group was almost drowned out by an increasing clatter of hooves and irritable snorts and whinnies from their horses. One of the generals remarked, 'The animals are restless at having to stand still in this bitter cold. We should move on soon, sire, before their blood – and our own – freezes solid.'

Deveron Austrey raised a diffident hand. 'Your Grace, may I make a suggestion?'

'Speak.' Conrig's voice was almost a whisper. His weariness and discomfort were all too evident, and Deveron was not the only one who realized that at some point the king would have to be persuaded to rest – at least for a little while.

'Once we reach the pass's summit again, our alchymists will be in the best possible position to scry conditions in the vicinity of Terminal Bay directly, rather than through a relay of Tarnian adepts. Altitude enhances the ability to windsearch. Might we not halt briefly at the derelict frontier post up there? It could be extremely important for us to observe what the Salka do when they reach Dennech-Cuva. If they make a fight of it, perhaps the enchantment that conceals their numbers and their route of penetration from our oversight will falter or even be temporarily extinguished. Information on the disposition of their troops is vital to our future planning.'

'I'll say,' growled Ramscrest. 'What if the filthy great boogers intend to advance on more than one front?'

'Sire, after the windsearchers have ascertained the situation,' Deveron continued, 'you and your general officers can perhaps discuss potential defensive action for a time, giving you all a welcome hour or so of respite from the saddle and the cold.'

For a time, Ironcrown said nothing. Then: 'My lords, I think we should do as my Royal Intelligencer suggests . . . Wanstan, Munlow, get my army moving again. Duke Norval, be so good as to remain here until Brother Odos completes his windspeaking. Request that he also send an additional message to the Didionite Archwizard, setting forth the Lord Constable's idea of holding back the force of Crown Prince Valardus. All the rest of you, follow me to the top of the pass.'

She had no idea where Vaelrath had taken her, nor that such a place even existed in Didion – or anywhere else on the island.

The cavern was so large that its upper reaches were lost in shadow. From its puddled floor rose a forest of pinkish stalagmites striped with fawn and dark green like the pillars of some fairytale palace. Their wet surfaces gleamed like polished marble in the radiance cast by thousands of pairs of emerald eyes.

The conclave of Morass Worms surrounded Casya on every side. The uncanny gaze of the creatures never left her as she perched on an outcropping of dry rock that was covered with the thick pelt of a tundra-lion, beseeching them to join the Sovereign of Blenholme in his war against the Salka.

She pleaded with all the eloquence she could summon. The issue was not Conrig Wincantor's intent to use the despicable sigils, she said, it was the deliverance of their imperiled land from an onslaught of a merciless foe equipped with the same evil weapons. If the Salka defeated Conrig's army and drove humanity from High Blenholme, would the great amphibians allow the Morass Worms and the Green Men – and even the Small Lights – to live in peace?

Many minds responded: *If we are attacked directly, we will defend ourselves as we did before. But we will never form an alliance with a depraved human sigil-user. Never.*

She tried other arguments but was unable to shift the great dragons from their intransigent position. A Watcher among them had perceived Conrig using Weathermaker. Before long, he would surely call upon the ultimate abomination. He would use Destroyer, just as the Salka had.

'But if he doesn't?' Casya entreated the worms in desperation. 'You told me the Sovereign Army hasn't yet engaged
the Salka in battle. Can you not postpone your decision, at
least until you're certain Conrig intends to wield that infernal
thing?'

The vast assemblage of creatures stirred, considering the
matter, and finally the answer came.

Yes. We can do that.

As tears of relief sprang into her eyes, she heard Vaelrath
say, *The armies will clash very soon and we will know the truth.
The Salka spell of dissimulation does not conceal them from OUR
mind's eye! You may remain here with us in good hope, Casabarela
Who-Would-Be-Queen, until Conrig shows himself to be beyond all
redemption. Then, with sadness, we must return you and your aged
traveling companion to the shores of Black Hare Lake and look to
our own affairs.*

Attack Force Commander Tasatawnn and his principal aide
Omawnn studied the looming human fortress on the opposite bank of the Dennech River. It was about half a league
away. Its numerous heavy guns and missile catapults were
trained on the water, ready to rain tarnblaze on any Salka
who were detected swimming to the attack. The cover-spell
that hid the amphibian host from distant windsearchers was
quite ineffective at close range, so the defenders of Dennech-
Cuva knew well enough that the enemy was out there,
waiting.

The humans were also waiting – for the Salka to make
the first move.

The citadel was fairly new, dating to the time sixteen years
ago when Somarus had assumed the throne of Didion after
Salka raiders killed his older brother Honigalus and his family.
At the time, Azarick Cuva was naught but an outlawed
robber-baron, the close crony of a disreputable prince who

was little better than a brigand himself. Somarus rewarded Azarick with a generous amount of treasure and a 'paper' dukedom – a vast tract of the sparsely settled west country that was only nominally loyal to the Crown. The true rulers of the region were the ruthless corsairs of the coast; but Azarick was told by the king that the fiefdom was his if he could keep it.

The newly minted duke assembled an army of ferocious misfits as land-hungry as himself and built a fortress that was huge, unlovely, and impregnable. Using it as a base, Azarick terrorized the pirates into ceding him dominion of the hinterlands, while they retained control of the shore.

Field Commander Tasatawnn knew nothing of Dennech-Cuva citadel's history, only that it was one of the largest fortifications he had ever seen, rivaling the Salka race's own lamented stronghold in the Dawntide Isles, which had been blown to rubble by the cannons of the Sovereign Navy some years earlier. Bringing the place down would not be easy, even with the Destroyer.

'Respected leader,' the aide Omawnn pointed out, 'this is a formidable target indeed – perhaps too formidable. If you command your Great Stone to annihilate it, the occult energies required could well cost you your life, or demand a pain-price that would leave you a helpless invalid.'

'It's certainly a lot more of a challenge that I thought it would be,' the commander grumbled. 'However, if I spare myself by using Destroyer's lesser demolition command – the one Kalawnn employed to topple the sea-stack at the mouth of the bay channel – I might break through the walls, but leave enough of the fort's weaponry intact to kill thousands of our troops. Tarnblaze bombs are hellish things. No sorcery can deflect or quench them. Now I understand why our strategic advisers at first wanted us to bypass the citadel.'

'We could still do that, respected one. It's perhaps the wisest course.'

'But it would greatly slow our advance, Omawnn. Our force would have to move through the dense surrounding forest rather than easily through the water.' Tasatawnn's burning carbuncle eyes flared with audacity and his mouth split in a defiant grin, showing teeth like diamond carving knives. He clasped the paradoxically delicate wand that hung on a chain about his neck and erected his head-crest.

'Bespeak my field officers,' he enjoined Omawnn. 'Let all our intrepid warriors assume positions of safety, then prepare to fall upon the town and raze it to the ground after the fortress is reduced.'

The aide nodded. After an interval: 'I have obeyed. And . . . if you should become disabled?'

'You know what to do. Now take cover.'

As the staff officer retreated behind nearby shore boulders, Tasatawnn enveloped the slender sigil completely with the digits of his right tentacle and visualized the target. Then in a loud voice he intoned the spell of annihilation.

'SKRESS TUSA ROWD SHEN!'

Omawnn cringed in stupefaction as a monstrous green ball of light obliterated the edifice across the river. A split second later came a sound louder than any thunder and a tornadic blast of wind. He fell shrieking with pain onto the stony riverbank, thinking, 'He's killed both of us!'

But he was alive. A pressure wave rolled across the water, washed over him with soothing coolness, then receded. Faintly, his mind heard the ecstatic shouts of thousands of Salka.

'Respected leader?' Omawnn called. His ears registered no sound. He was completely deaf. Weak as a newborn seal pup, he squirmed toward the unmoving body of his commander.

Tasatawnn's saucerlike eyes were glazed and lifeless. His

flesh felt strangely icy to the touch. The sturdy golden chain of Destroyer had snapped in his death-convulsion, flinging the brittle rod onto the rocks and breaking it in half. The fragments were milky-grey, possessed of no internal radiance whatsoever.

Numb with the terrible knowledge of what had just happened, Omawnn screwed up his courage before bespeaking the Eminent Kalawnn. Out on the river, the waters swarmed with triumphant invaders who swept ashore into the doomed town, praising the name of Tasatawnn to the highest Sky.

Vra-Erol Wintersett, Chief Windsearcher of the Cathran Army, Deveron Austrey, and a handful of other powerful Cathran alchymists who had been capable of overseeing the disaster at Dennech-Cuva, stared in wordless shock at one another.

'Tell me!' Conrig raged. 'Tell me what happened, damn you!'

So they did.

There were some twenty men gathered with the Sovereign in the disused frontier post at the top of Frost Pass. The building had been officially abandoned years earlier at a time when Tarn and Didion disputed the border along the White Rime Range. Travelers still used it occasionally as a storm refuge, but every stick of furniture, every floorboard and wood partition, and every piece of interior framing had long since been burnt for fuel. Only thick stone walls standing on bedrock remained, enclosing a windowless chamber the size of a ballroom. It had an iron door and a timber roof weighted with rocks against the mountain gales. A few blocks of hewn granite served as seats and sleeping platforms, and others at the room's far end made hitching posts for the horses. The place was dreary, dark, and as cold as the lowest of the Ten Hells.

The magickers of Cathra had conjured fire in the crumbling hearth and a row of dancing flames along the mantel for illumination. Conrig sat on a rough stone bench, wrapped in furs and sipping hot buttered malt laced with honey. His generals crowded closely around him, as if willing their own vitality to strengthen their debilitated Sovereign. They listened in silence as each scrier in turn submitted his disheartening vision of the destruction of the citadel at Dennech-Cuva.

Vra-Erol discussed the death of the impetuous Salka commander who had become visible to the mind's eye after he perished. Others of the Corps of Alchymists concurred that the citadel had certainly been consumed by the sorcery of a Destroyer. The Great Stone itself, like all sigils, was unscryable whether dead or alive; but Erol had deduced what must have happened.

Deveron, being last to speak, pointed out a phenomenon that had eluded the others, who had been too engrossed in the sigil's amazing performance to take note of any side-effect.

'At the moment of the explosion of green light, there was indeed a disruption of the closely woven spell of couverture that has thus far hidden the Salka host from our oversight. I discerned two great streams of invaders. Their principal route of advance is up the Dennech River, as we suspected. The second force is moving up the smaller Shadow River, somewhat to the south.'

'How many?' the Lord Constable asked.

'The Dennech host includes at least thirty thousand monsters,' the intelligencer said. 'Another twenty thousand invading via the Shadow will approach the small settlement of Tweenwater tomorrow night. The fort there is little more than a den of bandits that won't delay the Salka for an instant. Above Tweenwater, the river provides a direct route

to Lake of Shadows . . . and ultimately to the lower Wold
Road. The Dennech River route followed by the larger force
snakes through uninhabited moorlands and bogs. Its head-
waters rise near the *upper* Wold Road, approximately fifty
leagues south of Castle Direwold. The Salka may intend to
follow its entire length, so as to cut the highway in two
places. Or, perhaps less likely, they might cut overland after
reaching a great bend in the river and attack Lake of Shadows
from the northwest.'

Norval Vanguard inquired, 'How fast are they capable of
moving up freshwater streams?'

'Very fast,' said Brother Erol. 'When they invaded the
Green Morass, it took them less than a sennight to move
from the sea to Beacon Lake. The distance from Dennech-
Cuva to either of their presumed objectives on the Wold
Road is much less.'

'Saving a miracle,' Ramscrest observed, 'there'll be
naught to oppose them other than that poor devil Valardus
at Lake of Shadows. Our troops and animals will be spent
by the time we retrace our steps to Castle Direwold. They'll
be obliged to rest. Then it's at least two days' hard ride for
warriors with remounts to reach the lake and reinforce the
Didionites. Our slower riders, foot soldiers, heavy ordnance,
and supplies will take a couple of days longer. More if it
rains or snows.'

'Not good enough,' said Duke Norval, who had been
consulting a small map. 'The distance from Tweenwater to
the western end of the lake is only eighty leagues or so.
Unless they run into serious trouble, the Southern Wing of
the Salka force is almost certain to reach the lake ahead of
us. We won't roust them out of deep water easily, even with
tarnblaze. They'll be able to strike, then fall back into the
lake to recuperate over and over again.'

Duke Nettos Intrepid, the only Lord of the Southern Shore

in the group, had been peering over Norval's shoulder at the map. He gave a gruesome chuckle. 'And if the northern mob of monsters come all the way up the Dennech headwaters to the Wold Road, they'll be in a position to wriggle right up the arses of our rear echelons! Unless we want our marchers to be caught in a pincer-trap, we've no choice but to send a goodly part of our army into the heath, to meet the Dennech Salka head-on.'

'But that's the larger enemy force,' Deveron reminded him, 'and the region is a forbidding wilderness – less accessible to heavy cavalry than one might suppose from looking at a map.'

'I've heard that section of the Great Wold is friggin' track-less,' warned a one-eyed general named Chokar Bogshaw, 'a maze of tangled brush and thickets and quagmires. It's impossible for wagons or wheeled war-engines, and deadly dangerous even for our mountain-bred horses, who can move cross-country far easier than the pampered padnags of the Southern Shore.'

'*Pampered padnags?*' howled Nettos Intrepid.

'Silence!' Conrig shouted. He had risen from his bench and stood in front of the leaping magical flames, which had a peculiar bluish cast. 'You've all forgotten one factor crucial to our battle-planning: my sigils.'

The dank chamber went silent except for the snuffling and stamping of tethered horses and the constant low rumble of the unending column of countermarching troops passing outside. The Lord Constable finally asked the question. 'What do you propose doing with the stones, my liege?'

'I'm not sure, Wanstan,' the Sovereign admitted. 'You may not all be aware of it, but these three so-called Great Stones can be effective at some distance from the conjurer – who is myself, of course. The tactical implications are exciting.'

A softspoken younger general named Pasacor Kimbolton

cleared his throat. 'I'm obliged to point out, sire, that you have as yet had no experience wielding the moonstones. The – er – effective range of the sigils surely cannot be infinite.'

'And there's the accumulating pain-debt,' Deveron said.

Conrig ignored him. 'I know for certain that Weathermaker is capable of exercising its power virtually anywhere around our island. Both Beynor and Ullanoth demonstrated it. I'm willing to wager my life that the Destroyer sigil will operate in a similar manner. And perhaps Ice-Master as well.'

No one seemed eager to comment on that.

The king said, 'At this time, you can see that I'm not at my best. I'm saddlesore like everyone else, my healing injuries still hurt like the devil . . . and I'm also paying the price for using Weathermaker last night to keep snow from dumping on us whilst we crossed the mountains today.'

Exclamations of astonished and mildly obscene admiration greeted the last point, which Conrig had kept secret from most of them.

'The sigils do work, my lords. At a cost I'm willing to accept. Now, this is what I intend to do. I must sleep here for a few hours and regain my strength. My sons and the Royal Intelligencer will attend me. The rest of you continue down to the wold. By all means confer amongst yourselves and consider what strategic options are open to us.'

There were murmurs of sympathy and concern as the king subsided onto his bench again and drew his furs around him.

The Lord Constable provided a tactful deflection from Conrig's evident discomfiture. 'My lords, very soon we must convene a new council of war that includes the Tarnians, the other Cathran generals, and perhaps even Valardus and his battle-leaders. Two important matters must be researched as quickly as possible. I hope our Brother Alchymists can work on them as they ride down the mountainside, saving precious time.'

'Be assured we'll do our utmost,' said Vra-Odos.

'My first question,' the constable said, 'is this: Is it possible that denizens of Castle Direwold or retired outlaws of that town would know of secret paths through the Dennech head-waters heath? Remember, in the old days the region at the foot of Frost Pass was prime brigand country.'

'And Baron Jordus Direwold was in league with most of 'em!' someone said.

When the laughter subdsided, Wanstantil Cloudfell continued. 'I also request that our alchymists undertake urgent windspoken consultations with the scholars at Zeth Abbey and Donorvale College of Shamans. We *must* find a way to puncture the Salka cover-spell – perhaps by an effort of conjoined talent. We can't fight the slippery whoresons if you magickers can't scry their troop movements.'

Vra-Erol said, 'I have a good idea who may be able to help us, Lord Constable.'

'Excellent!' said the Sovereign. His enthusiasm was clearly forced. 'All of you must now be on your way. Later, when my mind is clearer, I'll think about how best to use the sigils. I may even be able to discuss the matter with you all as we return to Direwold, using Sir Deveron as my windspeech communicator.'

The king's gaze lingered briefly on each person in the group, and even through his face was clouded by fatigue and pain, the others knew that he would brook no opposition. As he had told them at an earlier meeting, *he* was the Sovereign of Blenholme.

It was full dark by the time the leaders, the adepts, and their mounts left the frontier post and joined the torchlit procession of warriors heading back into Didion. When the Royal

Intelligencer closed the iron door on the last of them and barred it, Vra-Bramlow said to the king, 'Sire, will you have Coro and me make up a bed for you now?'

'No,' was the surprising reply. Conrig straightened from the drooping posture he had previously assumed and rose to his feet. 'I have no intention of sleeping. Nor am I quite so decrepit as I led you to believe. That was only a ruse to get rid of the others, whilst I do what I have now decided to do, without interference.'

He took the pouch of moonstones from its hiding place beneath his heavy clothing, opened it, and let the things pour slowly out onto one of the granite benches, chuckling at the astounded reaction of Corodon, Vra-Bramlow, and Deveron.

For the stones had changed.

The glow of the sigils, the empowering disk, and the two fragments of the Demon Seat Moon Crag no longer pulsated steadily or in unison. The throbbing of their magical heart-beats now fluctuated wildly, as did their brilliance. The raw pieces of mineral seemed moribund, while the Great Stones shone stronger than ever; but brightest of all was the simple flat rondel framed in gold. The disk had become a veritable beacon, whose flashing beams lit up the farthest corners of the bleak chamber, seeming to magnify the intense cold with their awful promise.

Conrig said to Deveron, 'Does our new Royal Intelligencer know the history of the two uncarved pieces of moonstone?'

'Your sons told me where they came from, sire, as well as your plan to use Ice-Master to obtain more of the mineral. I understand that you intend to fashion numbers of new sigils and activate them with the disk.' He did not confess his appalled reaction to the scheme.

Conrig's expression was satisfied. 'That's all right, then. If it becomes necessary, you must assist my boys in the project.

Your own sigils will help defeat the efforts of the Zeth Brethren to put a stop to it. As they are certain to do.'

Deveron's mouth tightened, but he merely lowered his eyes, hoping the king would take it as a gesture of assent.

'Father –' Corodon began in an uneasy tone.

'Any questions must wait. Now listen to me, my sons. Since the deed I now contemplate may have a fatal outcome – as was the case with the unfortunate Salka commander – we must make provision for the future. For passing on ownership of these special sigils and the disk in case of my death.'

'Oh, no!' both of the princes exclaimed. But their faces showed differing emotions.

'Corodon, you are my rightful successor. Will you now swear to me that you will take up and use these stones in the defense of the Sovereignty if I'm unable to do so?'

The Prince Heritor took a step backward. His skin took on a sickly pallor and his eyes were wells of fear. 'Father, I – I –'

'Don't agree,' Bramlow said in a voice of steel. 'Don't do it, Coro. The vile things can bring nothing but disaster on our people, turning us from free human beings into minions of the Beaconfolk. The evil Lights tempted Father with sigil power and he gave in to them. You must not – whatever the cost.'

Conrig turned his attention to the novice Brother of Zeth. There was no anger in him, only a sort of offhanded surprise. 'So *you're* the one! The faceless traitor prince. Who would have thought it?'

Corodon's lips trembled and it seemed he might be wavering as he said to his older brother, 'But Bram, if the sigils are the only way to defeat the Salka . . .'

Vra-Bramlow addressed the Royal Intelligencer, who stood aside with his head bowed. 'Help me convince him, sir! You know I speak the truth.'

'He must decide for himself,' was the reply. Nevertheless, Deveron Austrey lifted the golden sigil-case from around his own neck and placed it beside the king's stones. 'But here and now I renounce use of my own moonstones and the high sorcery of the Beaconfolk.'

Conrig's jaw dropped and his face darkened with shock and fury. He took hold of Destroyer and pointed it at the impassive intelligencer. 'So you'd also forswear me, Snudge?'

'I remain loyal to the Sovereignty, sire, as I avowed when I returned to your service.'

A cruel smile lifted the corners of the king's mouth. 'I won't waste Destroyer's pain-debt on you. The Great Lights will crush you like a maggot. I'll see to it.'

'Perhaps not, for the Beaconfolk don't know my real name. I never told it to them, thanks to Red Ansel's warning. But I dare say they know who *you* are.'

'Bah!' growled the Sovereign. 'To hell with you . . . Coro! Are you my true son or not? Are you worthy to wear my Iron Crown, or are you craven like these others?'

Corodon's glance flickered. His breathing was audible and a single tear on his cheek sparkled in the uncanny beams of the disk. After a moment of anguished hesitation, he declared, 'Father, I'll activate and use your sigils if I must, when I am Sovereign.'

The novice turned away with a grunt of disgust but Conrig nodded in benign approbation. 'Watch what I do, Corodon. In the future, don't be afraid to emulate me if the need arises. Your Sovereignty will face many enemies, as mine has. Never give in.'

The Prince Heritor's stricken gaze was locked on the pulsating glow of the small wand. He stood mute.

The king lifted Destroyer high. 'It seems evident to me that we must surely go down to defeat in this conflict if we rely upon the tactics of conventional warfare. We know now

610   JULIAN MAY

that the Salka possess a Destroyer. God only knows what
other Great Stones they may also have in their arsenal – but
that weapon alone is capable of ensuring their victory. I will
not allow this to happen! Therefore, I now command this
sigil to instantly annihilate every single Salka who threatens
the Sovereignty of High Blenholme.'

'Sire!' Deveron cried.

But the wand had already exploded into blinding Light,
as did the tall figure of the king. The two princes and the
Royal Intelligencer were thrown to the stone floor, covering
their faces and crying out from the sudden agony in their
seared eyes.

They clearly heard the voices speak the Sovereign's name.

*CONRIG WINCANTOR! YOU ARE A CONSUMMATE FOOL.
WE REPUDIATE YOU AND DECLARE YOU DAMNED, AS WE
DID CONJURE-QUEEN TASPIROTH OF MOSS, WHO MADE THE
SAME IMPIOUS REQUEST OF HER OWN DESTROYER. HOW
DARE YOU COMMAND THE DESTRUCTION OF OUR CREA-
TURES – THOSE WHO ARE ESSENTIAL TO THE GAME? THE
SALKA ARE IMPERFECT BUT THEY STILL BOW TO OUR RULE
AND FREELY OFFER THEIR PAIN. THEY ARE MANY AND YOU
ARE BUT ONE. NOW ENDURE THE PUNISHMENT YOU
DESERVE. SUFFER LONG IN YOUR WRETCHED GROUNDLING
BODY UNTIL YOUR SOUL BREAKS FORTH AND PLUMMETS
INTO THE HELL OF ICE.*

Deveron opened his eyes. He was still bedazzled and his
vision was excruciatingly painful, for the chamber was alight
as if with a million candles.

The Sovereign of Blenholme burned.

His tortured body writhed in uncanny fire that seemed to
devour him from the inside. The bones that framed him and
gave him human form dissolved slowly while his flesh
endured and fed the flames. His skull was incandescent and
becoming shapeless, surely incapable of any utterance; but

Deveron could see the mouth wide open and hear the king screaming in the wind. Screaming without ceasing.

The intelligencer recalled that Queen Taspiroth had lingered in such a state for two weeks. He saw the two stalwart young princes huddled together like terrified babes, their arms about each other, moaning and with their eyes tightly shut. But both of them possessed talent and both would hear their father's unbearable cries with the mind's ear . . .

'Source!' Deveron called out. 'There must be an end to this. Help us.'

Take the pieces of moonstone mineral, press them together, and declare your human race's peril and need.

He crept closer to the blazing king. No heat emanated from his melting form, only a cold as profound as that in the abyss between the stars. The sigils on the stone bench held no uncanny radiance; they were already dead. But when Deveron took hold of the pale rocks from Demon Seat and clutched them tightly in one hand, they were instantly suffused with warmth and shone with a steady luminosity.

He saw the tentative, kindly faces floating in darkness and sent his wind-borne plea: Mercy, for all of them.

The Likeminded Lights seemed surprised. *WE CANNOT PREVENT THIS KING'S DESCENT INTO THE NIGHT OF ICE, BUT IT IS POSSIBLE TO END HIS SOJOURN IN YOUR GROUND REALM.*

The thing that had been Conrig Wincantor was extinguished abruptly, vanishing as if it had never existed. Destroyer lay on the rock floor, a small wand intricately incised with the phases of the moon, harmless.

'Thank you,' Deveron said.

WE HAVE SUMMONED THE HELPERS. THE DETESTABLE LINKAGE IS WEAKER. THIS IS ENCOURAGING.

The auroral images winked out and Deveron was left blind

for a few minutes. He was unable to summon his night-vision or even a finger-flame.

Then he saw an ordinary brass lamp hovering in mid-air, its burning wick casting a mundane radiance about the chamber. A plump arm in an olive-colored velvet sleeve materialized, holding the lamp, and then the rest of Thalassa Dru's stately form emerged from the subtle corridor, followed closely by the Green Woman.

Cray exclaimed, 'Oh, poor Grandson! Let me heal your wounded eyes.' The small woman knelt beside him and touched his forehead. His damaged vision cleared instantly. She went to give similar solace to Bramlow and Corodon, who sat apart on the bedrock floor in dazed silence, squinting through swollen lids.

Thalassa scooped up all of Conrig's defunct sigils and put them into her belt-wallet. The disk she wrapped in a lace-trimmed handkerchief and tucked into her bosom. Her round face was flushed with happiness. 'We'll take these to the Source at once. They'll set him free at last. I'm sure of it!'

'What about those two Demon Seat rocks?' Cray said. 'And the case with Deveron's sigils in it?'

Open the case, dear soul.

The intelligencer and the women froze. Corodon glanced about the chamber fearfully. 'Did you hear that?'

'It's the Source, Your Grace,' Deveron said. 'A friendly Light – like your demons.'

Cray handed over the owl-embossed little golden container. 'You'd better open this, Grandson.'

He unfastened the tiny latch and cried out in wonder. 'Gateway and Concealer are dead! Just like these five inactive sigils I recently took from Beynor's henchman. See?'

Cray and Thalassa studied the stones. 'Five more minor sigils?' The Green Woman was puzzled. 'Beynor must surely have known about them. Why didn't he keep them himself and turn them over to King Conrig, along with the others? The disc could have empowered them –'

No, dear souls. Those minor sigils have been abolished by the Potency – the Stone of Stones. They can never channel power and pain again. Bring them to me along with those of the late king. They represent the first true victory for us in the New Conflict.

'We're on our way to release you from the Ice right now,' said Thalassa Dru. She began to close the owl-case, intending to take it with her.

Wait. Deveron, take back your Concealer and Subtle Gateway. Touch them to the Demon Seat rocks.

'But I've renounced sigil sorcery!'

Do it. The One Denied the Sky commands it.

With a small sigh, he obeyed. Subtle Gateway and Concealer rekindled, as did the pieces of raw mineral; but this time their radiance was a soft white. 'God's Blood! Have the *good* Lights empowered my sigils? For what reason?'

Because you have work to do – and so do Cray and Thalassa. Keep the two sigils and the pieces of Demon Seat, dear soul. I will tell you what to do with them shortly. Inform the human military leaders that the Salka no longer possess a Destroyer. When the one who used it rashly died, he dropped the inactive wand and it broke into pieces. It can never be mended.

'Bazekoy's Ballocks! Can it be true?'

But Deveron's question went unanswered. The Source had withdrawn.

Cray had helped the recovering Corodon and Bramlow to their feet. 'Grandson, take the new Sovereign of Blenholme and his Royal Alchymist down the mountain and present them to Earl Marshal Parlian Beorbrook, Prince Dyfrig, and your dear wife.'

'I'm not worthy to be Sovereign,' Corodon protested. His countenance was full of shame. 'I have secret talent, as my father did. And I was willing to do as he asked: use

Beaconfolk sorcery even though I knew in my heart it was wrong.'

Conjure-Princess Thalassa said, 'And if I placed those inactive sigils and the empowering disk into your hands this minute, would you ask the Coldlight Army to bring them to life?'

'Never,' he whispered in a voice full of loathing. 'I'd rather the demons struck me dead!'

Cray laughed and patted his shoulder. 'There, dear. It will all go well. We know you're a different man from King Conrig.'

'All the same,' Coro said, 'I'm not fit to be Sovereign nor to command the army – even though the monsters no longer have a Destroyer. I'm too young and scatterbrained. I can use a sword well enough, but I'm no leader of men. You know that full well, lady, and so do the generals.'

'And I'm not even an ordained Brother of Zeth,' Bram appended gloomily. 'How can I become the Royal Alchymist?'

The Green Woman smiled at both of them. 'You can learn. Both of you will find many good persons eager to teach you . . . High King Corodon, my grandson Deveron will now transport you by magical means to Earl Marshal Parlian, the man who will lead your human army against the Salka and instruct you in kingship. As to your secret talent, I advise you to admit to it before the Cathran Tribunal when peace returns to High Blenholme – but not before. Let the judges of your own nation decide your eligibility for the throne. Meanwhile, both you and Bramlow should get to know your brother Dyfrig.'

'He's the true Prince Heritor,' Corodon said, unable to disguise his resentment. 'Most of Cathra and Tarn know it already.'

'As does Dyfrig Beorbrook himself,' Deveron said. 'Nevertheless, he assured me he would never claim the throne if by doing so he would destabilize the Sovereignty. So take heed of Mistress Cray's excellent advice, Your Grace: let the matter be. Accept the Iron Crown while acknowledging your youth and inexperience, and surround yourself with worthy counselors.'

'Will *you* serve me, Sir Deveron?' Corodon asked, not daring to meet the older man's eyes.

'Of course. And my first service will be to carry you and Brother Bramlow away from this melancholy place.' He took the Gateway sigil from the owl-case, which now also held Concealer and the Moon Crag rocks, and refastened its chain about his neck. 'Let us resaddle our horses and mount. I shall transport us with this stone's magic.'

As they set about the task, Deveron threw a questioning look at the little Green Woman. 'Will simple commands given the sigil in our own language now suffice, Eldmama?'

'Try it and find out, Grandson. But I think we can trust the Likeminded not to play ridiculous games as their evil relatives do.'

A moment later, Cray and Thalassa stood alone.

The sorceress sighed and retrieved the guttering oil lamp. 'We should be on our way through the subtle corridor as well, dear. The Source is impatient to be free.'

'Then what?'

Thalassa Dru cocked her head and frowned. 'He'll return to the Sky Realm, of course, to lead the Likeminded in the Conflict that he himself started ages ago. As for those of us here on the Ground . . . who can say whether he'll have time to bother with us? His own concerns are so much more important.'

TWENTY-TWO

Ullanoth, who had once been Conjure-Queen of Moss, waited patiently in Thalassa Dru's home, situated in the mountains high above Tarnholme. Her natural talent allowed her to scry most of the events unfolding in the world outside the eyrie, and she had shared some of her knowledge with her devoted companion Wix. But when the Salka finally mounted their second invasion, butchering the people of Terminal Bay and Dennech-Cuva, she held back the sad tidings out of compassion for the old man's feelings.

She had clearly overseen Conrig's force as it crossed Frost Pass, only to turn back. His ghastly fate – deserved though it was – wrung her heart and so overwhelmed her with grief that she was forced to escape the sight of it. She had loved him so much, if so wrongly. She would have willingly sacrificed her own life to save him from the prideful trap he'd built, then fallen victim to.

The choice had been his own, but she knew that she shared his guilt. The years of atonement had never given her the peace she yearned for . . .

It was very late and the night sky was clear. She sat before a window in the cozy sitting room, looking out. The incredibly tumultuous auroral display continued overhead, making the snowy landscape almost as bright as day. The celestial clash between the Beaconfolk and the Likeminded had heightened, but she had no way of knowing who was winning or losing. The Source had told her nothing, even though she remembered the sea-hag Dobnelu saying that there was a vital role for her in the New Conflict's resolution.

'But how could that be?' Ullanoth sent the question out on the wind with scant hope of receiving an answer. 'I belong to the Ground and your battle rages in the Sky. I've lost most of my uncanny talents, save for windspeaking and scrying. What good can I possibly do you?'

You would have sacrificed yourself to redeem your lover, Conrig. Is it possible, dear soul, you might also be willing to give up your mortal life to secure peace in the Sky? And for yourself as well?

'Is it you?' she whispered, lifting her head. Her sense of despondency gave way to faint hope. 'But your windvoice is different. And . . . can it be coming from a different place?'

I'm no longer imprisoned beneath the Ice. The last shackle is broken. I've cast off the blind black body they confined me in and returned to my own aspect and my own kind.

'How marvelous!' she cried. 'You're no longer denied the Sky!'

True. Once again I am attempting with all my power to sever the perverted Linkage between our very different worlds. Long centuries earlier, when I first realized the great sin I had committed, I took upon myself a Salka body so I could create a special tool. Its purpose was to break the Link and close the channels of pain and power. But when I realized that wielding the tool might only worsen an already chaotic situation, I set it aside. The evil Beacons seized it during the Old Conflict. Not long afterward they captured me and chained me beneath the Ice. If I had not submitted willingly to their thrall, they would have extinguished the Light of my defeated colleagues.

'Princess Thalassa told me about this. The tool –'

You knew it as the Unknown Potency when it was one of the Seven Stones of Rothbannon. Now the Salka Master Shaman, Kalawnn, who was the friend of your poor father Linndal, has it. Kalawnn is a most interesting person. Of all the current Salka leaders, he is the only one who has dared to question the morality of the Great Lights' game. Kalawnn brought the Potency to life but has no notion of its true purpose.

'And what is that?'

He told her, then asked if she would be willing to carry the Stone of Stones to the appropriate place and conjure it there. This could only be done by a being of the Ground Realm. Even then, there was a small risk that the Link would not be completely severed.

And you would lose your mortal life, for both the wielding and its venue are deadly to fragile human persons.

'Ah,' said Ullanoth.

Do not feel compelled to agree, dear soul. There are others I could call upon: Cray or Thalassa or Deveron Austrey, for instance. But the Green Woman is greatly needed by her own people, and the Conjure-Princess has been chosen to revive the lost kingdom of Moss. As for the wild talent, Snudge –

'I'll do it. Of course I will! Don't even think of offering the task to another.' She spoke resolutely, as though no other course were conceivable.

Thank you, dear soul.

'There are some difficulties to be overcome. Here I am, snowbound in Tarn, while the Potency is in the possession of a Salka Eminence surrounded by tens of thousands of his fellow-monsters. Even if I can get hold of the stone, how can I take it to its proper place? We can't endanger Cray or Thalassa by asking them to carry me through subtle corridors, nor can you teach me this form of travel yourself. I was told by them that the learning process takes years of practice.'

The problems are solvable. Will you wait until I bespeak you again? You have my permission to share what I've told you about the Potency with Deveron Austrey. But no one else must know until the time of consummation is at hand.

'Of course.' She settled back in her chair, and soon realized that the Source had returned to the Conflict. For a while she watched the shifting colors in the Sky. Then Wix poked his head around the doorframe of the sitting room and asked whether she would like her usual solace – a nice cup of tea.

'What a grand idea! And bring one for yourself, my friend. There's important news, and I'm able to tell you about some of it, at least.'

Old Baron Ising Bedotha buckled his pack and surveyed the interior of the trading post for the last time through tear-blurred eyes. There was no helping it. He'd already waited for her a whole extra day. The Morass Worms must have taken her. (Any other thought was intolerable!) If she lived, the frightful creatures would bring Casya back, perhaps through the mysterious corridors. But he had to leave this place. His duty was to return to his longtime friendly enemy, Kefalus Vandragora, and report what had happened to his courageous and headstrong granddaughter.

Ising hoisted the pack and bedroll onto his back. His crossbow was lashed on with special knots that could be undone in a trice. He took up his walking staff, checked that his sword was loose in the scabbard and ready to be drawn swiftly, and left the log cabin. The ground was crunchy with frost beneath his boots as he started down the exiguous trail that eventually led to Black Hare Lake. If the ponds and bogs froze solid, the return trip would be easier. It was bound to snow before long, but he'd used the extra day of waiting to fashion 'bear-paw' snowshoes from strips of reindeer hide and flexible withes. He'd make it out of the Green Morass if his heart didn't wrack up.

But Casya . . .

'Curse it! If that silly chit has got herself killed and eaten by wild beasts I'll never forgive her. Dragging me away from my nice warm castle! Lying to her honest grandsire. Thinking she could charm Morass Worms into fighting her battles. Queen Casabarela? My arse! She's just a pigheaded little girl, and I'm a romantic old fool.'

He trudged on for hours, frightening himself with thoughts of the war that might even now be raging between humanity and the Salka, somewhere down south. Talking out loud to the unheeding spruces and dwarf williows, he wondered what he'd do if his own dilapidated stronghold was attacked by enormous slimy brutes with long tentacles and glass tusks and moonstone amulets that smote you with black magic.

'What would I do?' he yelled at the louring sky. He was negotiating a frozen bog, very tricky, but he was in no mood to abandon his self-pitying soliloquy. 'I'd hide under my damned bed like a cowardly old fart, that's what! And pray for that tyrant Conrig Wincantor to come to the rescue.'

What a very curious notion. And futile as well, for that Sovereign is dead.

'Eeeah!' Ising spun about in terror as the unexpected voice spoke behind him. He lost his footing on an icy puddle, his feet went out from under him, and he fell onto his backside.

The baron saw Queen Casabarela Mallburn standing there, doubled over with mirth. The Morass Worm named Vaelrath, who had only emerged partially from a subtle corridor, gave an impatient hiss.

'You're back, sweeting!' he mumbled in happy disbelief. 'You're safe.'

'And I've brought the dragons,' Casya said. She took hold

of his arm and hauled him upright. She was stronger than she looked.

Ising's eyes darted about in bewilderment. 'Where are they? I only see one. It won't be much help fighting the ravening Salka horde.'

The rest of us are waiting, elderly human. No more dithering. Come.

The Morass Worm never touched him, but Ising Bedotha felt himself flying forward into spinning blackness shot through with crimson sparks. He gave a screech and crashed to the ground again, temporarily stunned. When he came to himself, Casya was kneeling beside him and they were somewhere else.

He heard her chiding the worm. 'You didn't have to be so rough with him.'

It was vexing, having to hunt him down. He should have stayed at the trading post. At any rate, he's quite unharmed.

Ising found himself on an open hillside with the queen and Vaelrath, in a desolate scrubby moorland that looked for all the world like the Great Wold Heath. All around them, as far as his bleary eyes could see, were thousands upon thousands of Morass Worms, their sinuous bodies coiled in a compact manner but with their astonishing great heads held upright and their beautiful emerald eyes lucent in the twilight.

Casya helped Ising to get up. 'It's time for us to meet with the Sovereign of Blenholme and his battle-leaders. Do I look all right?'

Broken! the Conservator of Wisdom said sadly. *The sheer banality of the catastrophe is perhaps enough to break one's heart as well.*

'Not so!' the Supreme Warrior said with stubborn vehemence. He and Kalawnn were resting in a backwater of the

Dennech, conferring on the wind with their Eminent colleagues back in Moss. Two days after the razing of the Didionite citadel, the army was forging eagerly ahead in the river's mainstream. A gentle rain fell, not too cold. It was perfect weather for Salka.

Explain yourself, Ugusawnn, the First Judge demanded. *How can you believe that the loss of Destroyer is anything short of a calamity?*

'Allow me to point out that the Great Stone accomplished several crucial military objectives before its demise. Thanks to its sorcery, our army has successfully gained a secure hold on human territory. The channel into Terminal Bay is blocked, so that warships of the Sovereign Navy may not enter and threaten our rear guard. The single important human stronghold that might have served as a center of resistance behind our lines is gone.'

You have not yet entered a pitched battle with the humans, in which Destroyer could have been the deciding factor, the Conservator said.

'It's by no means certain how effective the sigil would have been in actual combat conditions. Humans seem to fight in separate groups, Wise One, not in a massive concentration which Destroyer might have targeted. Think how numerous squadrons of warships pounded our home in the Dawntide Isles, beetling about in all directions. It would have required dozens of strikes by the Great Stone to defeat them . . . True, it's theoretically possible to reactivate a sigil again and again if its previous owners perish or become too weak from pain-debt. But using the spells in Kalawnn's book is not a speedy process.'

There is that, the Judge said. *A Destroyer sigil is most effective in limited catastrophic strikes. It's not a glorified cannon.*

Ugusawnn sensed he had won a convert. 'Exactly! Now, our valiant warriors are advancing deep into Didion on a two-pronged offensive. The force led by me and Kalawnn is well on its way up the Dennech River. No threat requiring the might of Destroyer stands in our way. Commander Rikalawnn's army will reach Lake of Shadows tomorrow, at about the same time that our host attains the critical river bend. Patch your broken heart, Wise One! We have a tough fight ahead of us, but victory will be ours. May I remind all Eminences that we were willing to invade the Green Morass without a Destroyer? Our courage, sagacity, and over-whelming numbers will win the day. There's no reason to be concerned.'

Kalawnn spoke for the first time. 'If that's true, why are the Great Lights still silent? And why is our oversight unable to locate Conrig Wincantor? Furthermore, this morning I detected an anomaly in the fabric of our dissimulation spell. Human adepts may be meddling with it.'

'What does it matter if they can oversee us?' the Supreme Warrior scoffed. 'Our advance is now no great secret. Before long, the foe will view us with their own puny eyeballs! Be confident, colleagues. Anticipate triumph. This island will once again belong to us.'

Caped and hooded against the early morning rain in white leather emblazoned with his nation's heraldic black bear, Crown Prince Valardus Mallburn reviewed the ranks of his hastily reorganized army. He went afoot, unarmored, striding through the muddy pools of water dotting the rough parade ground, trailed by his senior generals and exuding invincible confidence, as a proper warlord of Didion should. He lavished honest praise upon the battleworthy and skewered sullen or slovenly troops with a blistering glare as his aides made note of offenders. These were not so numerous as they had been a few days earlier.

Nearly a thousand yeoman infantry of the prince's force

had faded surreptitiously into the dense forest south of Lake
of Shadows when word reached camp that the Salka had
invaded at Terminal Bay and were charging inland. The
much-hailed demobilization had been abruptly cancelled. Not
long afterward, a short, testy directive from King Somarus
bade Valardus henceforth to follow the leadership of Earl
Marshal Parlian Beorbrook without question. This prompted
a second wave of midnight flits – mostly amongst horse-
soldiers and knights from the lesser baronies, who hated the
Sovereignty even more than the Salka.

Livid with mortification, the Crown Prince had the abscon-
ders hunted down by Holt Mallburn's much-feared Palace
Guard. A dozen of the most flagrant miscreants were hanged,
cut down alive, and drawn and quartered. Others were dealt
a few lashes, deprived of their warhorses, fined two silver
marks, and returned to the ranks. But large numbers of men
had escaped without a trace, and the Army of Didion had
been reduced by another twelve hundred fighters.

Earl Marshal Parlian Beorbrook reacted to the news with
a message of withering contempt.

So Crown Prince Valardus decided to show the Cathran
whoreson a thing or two about Didionite bravery . . .

'The men look fit enough, considering,' he remarked, as
he and the generals completed their review and dismissed
the parade so the men could eat a quick breakfast. 'With the
warped spears repaired and blades honed to a fresh edge,
they're as ready as they'll ever be.'

'Some certainly are,' Duke Kefalus Vandragora said. 'I'm
confident that the commands of timberlords such as myself
and the forces of Boarsden, Riptides, and Mallthorpe are
ready to meet the foe and acquit themselves with valor.
Others are more problematical. I urge you, Highness, to
reconsider your decision.'

The prince beckoned the noble officers to follow him into

his tent, where he set about to serve them mulled mead with his own hands. 'No, Lord Kefalus. My mind is made up. A host of devilish monsters is coming straight at us up the Shadow River. Beorbrook himself admitted they may arrive before his army can reinforce us.'

'A strategic retreat back to the Wold Road makes sense,' said Fano Boarsden.

Duke Azarick Dennech-Cuva, even his armor blackened in mourning for his murdered son and mother, disagreed. 'Should the Salka take control of the lake, they'll turn it into an underwater stronghold. If we keep them away from the shore until reinforcements arrive, we'll improve the odds for ultimate victory.'

'Beorbrook all but called us cowards,' Crown Prince Valardus said in a low, fierce voice. 'He impugned my own leadership ability. He has spit in Didion's face, demanding that we fall back rather than mount a holding action against the Salka. Even more damning, his strategy is wrong.'

'Yes!' said most of the others.

The prince drained his cup. 'We march in one hour.'

The vast encampment surrounding Castle Direwold was in a ferment on the morning after the great meeting. Already shaken by the death of Conrig, many of the Cathran generals had cavilled at the proposal of the tall, imperious girl known as Casya Pretender, believing an alliance with Morass Worms too outrageous to be tenable. Large numbers of the rank and file were even more dubious.

Fight beside dragons? . . . Entrust their lives to hideous carnivores even more frightful than the Salka? Creatures with uncanny talents that human alchymists and shamans knew nothing about? How could the Morass Worms be trusted? What if they turned on humanity?

'I trust them,' Casya had said to the assembled battle-leaders.

'They don't want the territory where humans live, only the most remote part of the Green Morass, their natural home. I've promised that when I'm Queen of Didion, they shall have it.'

'How do we know you're the heir to Honigalus?' Duke Nettos Intrepid had jeered, and many other Lords of the Southern Shore had echoed his skepticism. 'You're the Wold Wraith! Somarus put a price on your head.'

'I have ways of proving my claim to the Didionite succession – but not now. There's no time to waste. The Morass Worms trust my leadership because it was successful at Beacon Lake. They're willing to fight the Salka down here as well, but they can't win the war alone. We must work together with them. Will you do it or won't you?'

In the end they agreed. But only because the young hero, Prince Dyfrig, declared that he was ready to fight at Casya Pretender's side and would willingly entrust *his* life to the dragons of the Green Morass.

'You've just come back to me, and now you must go again,' Induna said, squeezing her husband's hand. Her eyes were dry but she wore a wistful, one-sided smile.

Deveron looked down from the saddle. 'I'm always with you, just as you will always be a part of me. You shared your soul and restored my life. All I can give you in return is my unending love.'

The two of them were in the midst of a great mass of mounted warriors. The sun had come out after the rain and shone on a scene that was not as confused as it might have seemed. Three hundred Knight Commanders of Cathra and Tarn were poised and ready, each heading a closely grouped company of twenty men armed with lances six ells long. Also part of each group were gun-crews comprising ten grenadiers mounted on massive destriers, who towed compact tarnblaze mortars on wheels and small carts loaded with munitions.

They waited.

Meanwhile, numbers of their fellow-warriors not involved in the operation were gathered in a great mob at a safe distance, eager to watch the dragons take their mates away. How this maneuver was to be accomplished was known only to the nine thousand volunteers of what had been dubbed The Pretender's Army.

Thus far, only Vaelrath had come into the sprawling Direwold encampment. Impressive as her appearance was, many of the men were disappointed that she had no wings. How, then, would the great dragons carry off the troops? Bets (some of them bizarre) were being made . . .

Casya, Dyfrig, and the battle-leaders sat their mounts in a small group at the edge of the formed companies, waiting for Deveron to deliver the windspoken message from Vaelrath signalling that the worms were on their way. The Royal Intelligencer and Induna had withdrawn out of earshot for a final conversation.

'If this action is successful, it won't take long,' Deveron said to his wife. 'But Vaelrath has warned me that we might have to lie in wait for hours in order to attack the foe most effectively. Keep alert for my windspeech. It may be faint if the Salka try to block it. You are the only one I can trust to inform Marshal Parlian of the outcome of this first encounter. I dare not let another adept have access to my mind. I know too many secrets, love, and my mental defenses are not as strong as I would like. My newly empowered sigils don't exact a pain-price, but they do take a toll on my physical strength and the keenness of my talent. Whatever tidings I send you, no matter how dire or welcome they may be, you must tell Beorbrook and him alone.'

'He's concerned about Prince Dyfrig,' she said. 'But very

proud, I think, that his son convinced our warriors to go with Casya and the dragons.'

'His earlier experience with the Morass Worms gave credibility to Casabarela's assertions.' Deveron looked away as a worrisome thought struck him. 'I wish our alchymists and shamans had been able to crack the Salka cover-spell. Still, the dragons seem to know where the brutes are, even if they can't predict what they intend to do.'

Induna said, 'The earl marshal was also disappointed that his agents were unable to discover useful tracks through the heath, aside from the overly perilous game-trail the Lord Lieutenant and his men followed in their shortcut from Karum Port to Direwold. The heavy cavalry could never travel that way. He told me we now have no hope of outflanking the enemy without the help of the worms.'

'It galls Earl Marshal Parlian, I think, that our strategy must rely so heavily upon such strange and fearsome creatures. He's an old-fashioned warrior who would much prefer to fight in the good old-fashioned way.'

'Tell it to the Salka!' she said.

Both of them laughed. Then Deveron gave a sudden start. 'Leave me now, sweetheart. It's about to start.'

She ran off without another word. He kneed his mount and rode up to the Pretender, who was in close converse with Prince Dyfrig, and saluted them and the noble officers. They all wore helms and tough boiled-leather cuirasses but no mail, as did most of the troops. Vaelrath did not wish to overburden her people.

'Here they come, Your Majesty,' the intelligencer said. 'I've heard them on the wind.'

Casabarela Mallburn gave a command in a surprisingly resonant voice. 'Sound the horn!'

One of the aides lifted a silver trumpet. As the distinctive musical notes echoed over the heath, the watching crowd fell silent. Then thousands of throats uttered an earth-shaking shout as the Morass Worms abruptly appeared, gorgeous and frightful, a dozen or so of them suspended in the air above each company of human beings. They drifted to the ground as lightly as thistledown, opened the invisible portals to the subtle corridors that they had frequented from time immemorial, and gently shepherded the mounted warriors and their equipment inside.

The process was swiftly done. Last of all, Vaelrath manifested herself above Casya and the officers.

'You're certain the Salka won't see us coming?' Prince Dyfrig asked with some sharpness.

The Morass Worm laughed. *Did you?*

She descended and pointed to the portal. When every human had disappeared the dragons followed suit, leaving an empty expanse of barren moorland and a strangely subdued throng of onlookers.

A few minutes later other horns began to sound assembly. The troops of the Sovereign Army who were not already marching down the Wold Road toward Lake of Shadows began to break camp. Two hours later, they were on the way south.

Ugusawn and Kalawnn swam or slithered as little as possible to conserve their stamina. Taking advantage of Eminent Privilege, they skipped short distances up and down the long column advancing up the Dennech, making use of the Subtle Gateway worn by the Supreme Warrior. The pain-debt was very small. In this way they were able to supervise the troop movement closely and make certain that the spell of dissimulation stayed firm. The earlier interference had ceased.

This wing of the army, like the smaller one moving up the Shadow River, was in splendid shape, moving at top speed except during the infrequent rest stops. Adjacent wetlands supplied the Salka with plenty of fish and waterfowl. They had gorged themselves on man-meat as they overran Dennech-Cuva, but until they reached the Wold Road and engaged the Sovereign Army, they had to make do with less appealing fare.

It was late afternoon when the force reached a big bend in the river that was a relatively short distance from that great lake where a few thousand human warriors still tarried. At this point, a crucial decision would have to be made. Before long, the river would curve back to the west into empty country, then trend more directly northward again. The Eminences took their ease in a large marsh that spread along the eastern bank of the bend and discussed the situation. Thousands of warriors were already resting there.

Kalawnn wanted to continue to follow the Dennech for another two days, all the way to its headwaters near the upper Wold Road. If the Salka took possession of that all-important highway and the surrounding countryside, slaughtering what-ever stragglers of the human army they encountered, it seemed likely they could force the human leaders to divert significant numbers of their men from the upcoming Battle of Shadows. If the humans swallowed the bait and came north again, their diverted warriors would be led a fatal chase into the bogs.

Ugusawnn, on the other hand, favored going overland to Lake of Shadows immediately, linking up with Commander Rikalawnn's army and forcing a climactic confrontation with the humans without any delay. To reach the lakeshore, the Salka would have to cross the marsh, then ascend a ridge that was mostly gravel and glacial till, sparsely covered with sedge clumps, low-growing herbs, and patches of heather. It was raining again and the Warrior's windsight seemed to show that the going would not be too arduous.

He and Kalawnn argued the pros and cons amiably for a

short time before it occurred to them to scry a bit further up the lake and see what the small human army encamped there might be doing.

'Ahroo!' Ugusawn gave a howl of incredulous delight. 'I don't believe it. They're on the march – toward the foot of the lake where the Shadow River outflow begins!'

'Indeed,' Kalawnn concurred. 'How unexpected. Some are afoot and some on horseback, with a pitiful quantity of little wheeled tarnblaze cannons to augment their spears. Rikalawnn's force outnumbers them by better than two to one. Still, the humans might be able to slow him down long enough to cause a bit of bother. Unless –'

'Man-meat.' The Supreme Warrior licked his slimy lips. 'We give Rik's bunch some help, he'll have to share. And then, on to the great affray! What do you think?'

'I won't be able to climb that ridge,' the Master Shaman admitted.

Ugusawnn clasped Subtle Gateway. 'I'll whisk us to the top of it. There's a single copse of small evergreen trees up there. We can squat amongst them and watch while the column crosses over. Thirty thousand of us . . . the vanguard will just about get to the lakeshore as the rear starts out of the marsh. You tell Rik we're on our way, and I'll bespeak our officers with the change of route.'

Assume your assigned positions, Vaelrath said. *Be as quiet as possible, although it matters little whether they hear you now. We will keep you hidden from them. They will be unable to understand what is happening until it is too late.*

The cloudcover had broken and the rain was over. Auroral pandemonium flashed and swirled in the clear portions of the Sky and illuminated the land below, where a broad stream of huge dark forms approached the highland summit above Lake of Shadows.

The Pretender's Army had waited impatiently up there for most of the day, concealed by the talent of the Morass Worms. Only Casya herself displayed no surprise when thousands more of the great dragons joined those who had led the mounted humans to this strange battleground.

Two Salka – persons of importance from the comparatively large size of them and the gold and ivory accoutrements that adorned their bodies – had also stationed themselves atop the ridge, about two hundred ells from the place where the humans had picketed their mounts and waited in ambush. Deveron had scried them continuously, wondering whether they were Salka leaders. He had briefly considered using Concealer to approach them unseen, but in the end he decided that it was too risky.

'What was that?' Kalawnn said, his head swiveling apprehensively. 'I thought I heard something.'

'Of course you did,' the Warrior grunted. He rolled his glowing red eyes in exasperation. 'It's the sound of thousands of our warriors advancing. Look: the first of them have reached the top of the ridge. Shall we go to meet them? It's a glorious night.'

They emerged together from the partial shield of the evergreens and watched proudly as the head of the column came into clear view. The troops came on twenty abreast in close ranks, wriggling easily over the gravelly ground and humming a deep-pitched martial air.

'I think –' Ugusawn began.

Before he could say more, the first of the tarnblaze bombshells arced through the air like a low-flying meteorite and exploded with a stunning detonation amidst the advancing host.

'Impossible,' Kalawnn said, falling back in horror at the sight.

Ugusawn could only curse and groan as he clutched the Gateway sigil. A second bomb exploded and then a third. After that, both of them lost count of the coruscant balls of death raining down upon the hapless troops. The things could not be deflected with talent. Some of them did not detonate, but instead gushed fountains of bluish-gold fire that clung to any flesh it touched and could not be quenched.

The symmetry of the march disintegrated as frenzied Salka broke formation and began to flee in all directions through the roiling smoke. Shattered bodies lay on the ground in pools of blood that appeared black beneath the pitiless Light of the aurora. The wounded howled and cursed. A few courageous fighters brandished minor sigils, clashed their teeth ferociously, and cried out in frustration. 'Where are they? Where is the foe?'

'Where indeed?' Kalawnn croaked. He was sidling along at some distance from Ugusawnn now, trying to avoid the flailing wounded who would have taken hold of him in their agony and pulled him down. 'Use your windsight, colleague!' he entreated the Warrior, bespeaking him because the noise of the bombs and the screams of the dying and the panic-stricken made normal speech impossible.

'I continue to do so – and yet there is nothing. Nothing!'

A sudden lull in the bombardment made it possible for the Eminences to gain an oversight of the rest of the column. The march had come to a precipitate halt. On the steeper slopes, scores of gigantic bodies crashed into one another and tumbled about in helpless confusion. Valiant officers on the flanks tried to restore order amongst knots of struggling troops and guide them into a proper retreat. They bludgeoned and hauled and roared commands, and in some areas it seemed that the chaos might be calming.

And then the dragons appeared out of nowhere. Their eldritch shrieks and nightmarish appearance sowed fresh terror in warriors who had never encountered them before, and despair in veterans of the skirmishes around Beacon Lake. Taller than the great amphibians and infinitely more agile, their appalling tactic was to rend the tentacles of their enemies, leaving them helpless and bleeding to death. If a worm was cornered by superior numbers, it simply vanished.

Last of all came the humans led by Prince Dyfrig, mounted on their warhorses and armed with long spears tipped with sharp steel points. They darted about dispatching the fallen and pursuing Salka who fled downhill. If the lances broke, the humans took up crossbows that shot deadly broadheaded bolts, or fought with two-handed swords as long as a man was high. Their clever mounts wheeled and dodged and kept the riders balanced in the saddle as they hacked Salka to bits.

The carnage became so overwhelming that Kalawnn could no longer apprehend it. He called on the wind, pleading for Ugusawnn to fetch him and carry him to safety with Subtle Gateway, but there was no response.

'Are you dead, colleague?' he wailed. 'Have they struck you down and drained your blood or slain you with fire? We have lost this battle. I think we have lost the war as well! The Great Lights have abandoned us, even though the insignificant minor sigil I wear still glows.'

It was the end. If humans and great worms united in assailing the Salka, how could they ever hope to prevail in the new game? Their opponents could strike at them anywhere, when they least expected it. The Salka could only howl in pain and die. Or was there another choice?

'Might we be allowed to return in ignominy to Moss?' he whispered. 'Humans will deny us the prime areas, but perhaps they'd let us keep the Great Fen and the Hungry Sands. No one else wants them . . .'

Kalawnn began to laugh.

After that, thinking gave way to a vast apathy. The Master

Shaman viewed the scene on the ridge-slope as if it were taking place beneath murky water, and the fighting merely a kind of stylized dance. Even that slowed down to a quietus after a while. The human warriors and the worms went away.

He stumbled to a heap of boulders and took shelter behind them. He slept without dreaming, and when he woke, a man was standing over him.

'I've come for the Potency,' Deveron Austrey said.

Casya Pretender sheathed her broadsword and waved to Prince Dyfrig. He guided his mount through the bodies of the fallen monsters and saluted her by raising his bloody lance. The aurora was paling as the first light of dawn brightened the eastern sky.

'Your Majesty of Didion, I think the field of battle is ours. The Salka are retreating full-tilt back toward the Dennech Valley, harried by Morass Worms. The very sight of our terrible allies seems to have broken their spirits.' He reached behind his leather cuirass and produced a small velvet sack. 'If you'll permit, I wish to give you a token of my admiration. Never have I seen such bravery as yours.'

She removed her gauntlets and opened the sack. At the sight of the necklace with its three great opals set in gold, she gasped. 'Your Grace – Dyfrig – I cannot –'

He closed her fingers over the gift. 'You must. You deserve to be adorned as a queen, and this necklace once belonged to another royal lady of great courage. She's dead now, and one day I hope to tell you her story. But believe me when I say that she would want you to have this.'

Casya lowered her helmeted head and fastened the catch behind her neck. 'Then I accept it with heartfelt gratitude, my prince.'

'There's something else I must tell you. It concerns your future in Didion. My father, the earl marshal, has in his safe keeping a considerable treasure that was stolen from your country by Kilian Blackhorse. It consists of gold and precious jewels, taken from Kilian by Beynor of Moss, that were finally retrieved from that villain by Sir Deveron Austrey. The treasure belongs to the rightful Queen of Didion. I pray it will help you regain your throne.'

She looked at him aghast. 'I know not what to say . . . except thank you.'

'What shall we do now? I confess that I've not seen any of our warriors – or the Morass Worms – since dawn began to break. I suppose they're in hot pursuit of the Salka.'

She frowned. 'We shall have to consult with King Coro and his generals before deciding upon the next course of action –'

An acerbic voice spoke out of thin air. *Better to consult with ME.*

'Is that you Vaelrath?' Casya called.

The leader of the worms materialized, tall and awesome, her emerald gaze brilliant with triumph. *I have commanded my people to carry your cavalry and grenadiers back to the Wold Road, where they may await the arrival of the Sovereign Army. A few score humans were wounded and eight men died. This we regret.*

Dyfrig said, 'Thank you for your concern, Vaelrath. Will you now carry us away also?'

If you wish, said the dragon. *You must be very weary.*

'Not I,' Casya said, her eyes shining almost as brightly as the opals around her neck. 'I could fight on all through the new day at your side, if you'd have me.'

We would lief have your good counsel, Casabarela, rather than your sword. This country is strange to us. The second Salka force has abruptly halted its advance up the Shadow River. Their leaders are uncertain what to do. They have taken note of our presence and they are afraid. It's an opportunity not to be missed.

'I'll gladly advise you. New tactics will be called for, since

you'll be fighting the Salka in forested country. Prince Dyfrig
–' She shot a tentative look at her companion.

'Let me help, too, Vaelrath. My generalship is hardly the
equal of Her Majesty's, but I've been tutored in warfare by
Cathra's Earl Marshal of the Realm – as well as leading skirmishes against border bandits for half a dozen years.'

The worm nodded and made a gesture. *I have opened the
subtle corridor. Shall we go?*

'Only please let Earl Marshal Parlian know where we've
gone,' the prince said.

I will bespeak one of the Zeth Brethren accompanying him.

'Tell Crown Prince Valardus's wizard as well,' Casya added
with a wicked grin. 'Inform His Highness of Didion that I
look forward to our meeting – when the battle is over.'

Rork Karum and his guests were eating their evening meal
when the stout little house-wizard dashed into the great hall
and made a stumbling obeisance.

'My lord duke, there's astonishing news on the wind!
Every magicker on the island is bespeaking the tidings. The
Salka are indeed in precipitate retreat, as was rumored earlier
today. In fact . . .' He lowered his voice in portentous
emphasis. 'One can see the brutes from the battlements!'

Shouts went up from the diners.

The pirate-lord sprang to his feet, pushing back his chair.
'Show us, man!'

The wizard dashed off, with Rork and most of the castle-
dwellers and servitors pounding in his wake. The village
refugees sitting at the low tables hesitated for a moment,
then shuffled off in pursuit. Only Orrion, Nyla, and Countess
Orvada were left in the hall. Even Rork Karum's hunting
dogs had run away, baying with excitement.

'And so it ends, my ladies,' Orrion said. 'The Joint Fleet
will be awaiting the monsters outside Terminal Bay. Only by

scattering can the Salka hope to escape. I wonder where they'll go?'

'To hell, one would hope,' whispered Nyla.

'Morass Worms!' Countess Orvada shook her head. 'Led by the Wold Wraith and Dyfrig the royal bastard. It's passing strange. And if the rumors be true, only a handful of our brave warriors actually engaged the enemy – aside from speeding their withdrawal.'

Orrion took Nyla's hand. 'Shall we also go out and watch them, love?'

'If you wish.'

He asked the countess, 'Will you also come, madam?'

Orvada sighed as she reached for the crystal wine flask. 'You young people go. I'll stay here and celebrate. I've seen enough Salka, thank you very much.'

Strangely somber, the two of them went off – not to the keep battlements, as Rork Karum, his retainers, and the surviving villagers had done, but to the castle's eastern turret, which overlooked the mouth of the Dennech River.

After they had gained the top, they stood side by side in silence for a long time, watching the dark tide of bodies emerge from the river and disappear into the sunset-tinged waters of the bay. From their high vantage point, all they could hear was the soft moaning of the wind.

'Look at them,' Nyla said at last. 'They seem so tiny and ineffectual. But they would have eaten us alive if it had not been for you. *You* saved us, Orrion. Only you.'

He said nothing.

'What will become of us now?' Her tone was almost forlorn. 'Rork Karum has said he'll let us go, but must we return to Cathra where you will be imprisoned?'

'We'll not be separated. Last night I had a dream. Whether or not it's a true portent or merely a fantasy remains to be seen. In the dream, my twin brother Corodon spoke to me.'

Her eyes widened. 'Do you mean, *he spoke on the wind?*'

'I don't know. Perhaps I can ask Lord Rork's wizard to confirm the truth of it by bespeaking my older brother Bramlow in a relay through a Tarnian shaman.'

'What did King Corodon say in the dream?'

'He seemed to tell me that he'd rescind my banishment. Restore my rank.'

'Oh, if it could only be true!' she cried.

'There was more. He said he was too weak a man to rule the Sovereignty on his own. He's afraid he'll make a botch of it. He – he wants me to share the throne. He said he'd force the Lords Judicial to repeal the sword-arm law and accept me – else he'd abdicate and turn the Iron Crown over to Dyfrig Beorbrook.'

She was speechless for a long moment. 'What if it's true?'

'There's still the matter of our covert talent,' he admitted. 'Only you and a handful of others know of it – including Dyfrig himself and that strange fellow, the Royal Intelligencer. In the dream, Coro said that all have pledged to keep the secret.'

'Oh.'

He took her hand. 'So if, albeit improbably, this thing should come to pass, will you be my queen, Nyla Brackenfield?'

'I'll be whatever you want me to be, dear heart.' They kissed and she sank into his embrace, wondering why she suddenly felt an icy finger of fear touch her heart.

Ullanoth clung to Deveron's neck as they arrived at the summit of Demon Seat. From horizon to horizon the night Sky was clear of clouds, velvet blackness alive with angry whorls, slashing beams, and violent explosions of colored Light. Below, the mountain slopes lay deeply buried in snow.

Gale winds had blown the terrace formation clean, and the Seat itself had only a thin mantle of rime encrusting it.

Behind it, a climbing staff wedged among moonstone rocks still carried a tattered scrap of frost-stiffened red cloth that had once been the banner of the Sovereignty of Blenholme.

'You may put me down, Snudge,' she said. 'Then depart at once, for I think a human body can endure here only a few moments.'

'And this is truly where you want to be?' he asked her.

'Yes. But no more speaking. It hurts to breathe the cold air.' She smiled at him.

'Farewell, Conjure-Queen,' he said. His gloved hand still held the sigil as he gave the command that would take him from her.

When he was gone, she drew off the fur mitten that covered her own right hand, revealing a strangely twisted little ribbon of carved moonstone that had but a single surface and a single edge. It glowed steadily and scathelessly because it bonded to no one and belonged to everyone, to every thinking creature in the Ground Realm in danger of being drawn into a seductive and soul-destroying game of power.

Are you ready, Ullanoth?

'Tell me what to do.'

Touch the Potency to the Seat. The finality of it is easy and the peace is sweet.

Deveron had transported himself to a valley at the mountain's base where autumn still prevailed, rather than to the place where the Source had told him to go – a large pavilion pitched amongst many others on the verge of the Wold Road, where the Sovereign and Vra-Bramlow, Earl Marshal Parlian, Prince Dyfrig, Casya Pretender, and his wife Induna waited for him.

But they must wait. It was necessary for him to see what happened.

He scried the mountain and saw her, tranquil and unafraid.

Then his windsight unaccountably failed him and he was left only with the witness of his eyes.

The Moon Crag formation at the tip of the peak blossomed for an instant into a new blue star brighter than any he had ever seen.

The furious aurora vanished. In its place, enduring only for a heartbeat, were a myriad of ghostly faces. Some were smiling and some were outraged. All of them flowed together into a wide iridescent arc that spanned the Sky like an enormous moonbow.

'Are the evil Beaconfolk dead, then?' he asked.

Good and evil endure, but the Conflict is over. A minute portion of the Link has unfortunately survived. It is not easy of access, however, and power will flow between the Realms only with great difficulty now. There is no need to fear.

The Concealer sigil had faded to extinction even before he took Ullanoth to Demon Seat, but he still held his Great Stone tightly in his hand. He opened his fist and gasped. Subtle Gateway's Light was dead.

'Source!' he cried indignantly. 'After all this, must I walk back to my poor wife?'

An inadvertent oversight. Forgive me, Snudge. All sigils empowered by the Lights have been abolished with the end of the game. But of course I'm prepared to do a special favor for a friend.

Gateway's blue-white internal radiance rekindled.

'Take me to Induna,' Deveron said.

EPILOGUE

The Royal Intelligencer

There is more to the story, of course, but I may not be able to finish it after all. I've grown so very tired, and there are no genuine happy endings. Not in a place as paradoxical as High Blenholme Island, with its races of human and inhuman souls, and not elsewhere either, unless I miss my guess.

It is sufficient, I think, to relate a few outcomes.

The Salka offensive collapsed after both Kalawnn and Ugusawnn were found alive and taken prisoner by the Sovereign Army. They joined the other Eminences in calling for an end to hostilities and an armistice was declared. The great amphibians eschewed their dream of reconquest and did indeed withdraw to the Great Fen of Moss. However, the Eminent Four could never convince their people to enter into civilized relations with humanity, and the Salka were finally content to be left alone.

After King Somarus suffered a fatal stroke of apoplexy when informed of his niece's heroic role in the war with the Salka, Duke Kefalus Vandragora led an uprising that saw Casabarela Mallburn installed as the true Queen Regnant of Didion. She did give the Morass worms their homeland.

Orrion Wincantor married Nyla Brackenfield, and after a

brief interval of legal wrangling became co-Sovereign of
Blenholme with his twin brother. Corodon Wincantor
married Hyndry Mallburn in spite of strong advice to the
contrary. Their disastrous union, fortunately childless,
contributed to the destabilization and ultimate collapse of
the Sovereignty. Tarn, Didion, and the renascent Conjure-
Kingdom of Moss, ruled by Thalassa Dru until she died at
the age of ninety-nine, declared their independence.

Cathra endured a brief but messy civil war instigated by
Duke Feribor Blackhorse, who murdered Corodon and
Hyndry, drove Orrion and Nyla to exile in Didion, and seized
the Iron Crown. His coup was frustrated on the same day
that it was accomplished when he died in agony of a surfeit
of peaches and newly fermented cider at a celebratory
banquet.

At the urging of the demoralized Cathran peerage and the
Zeth Brethren, the Royal Alchymist Vra-Bramlow Wincantor
assumed the throne as interim ruler. In a series of brilliant
and ingenious compromises he restored calm and prosperity
to Cathra and mended relations with the former vassal states.
He abdicated by his own choice and his younger sister
Wylgana was acclaimed High Queen after the archaic law
barring the female sex from the succession was repealed. Her
first official action was to have the Iron Crown melted in the
forge of the royal blacksmith. The resulting lump of metal
was cast ceremoniously into Cala Bay, along with a wreath
commemorating her revered grandfather, King Olmigon.

At his own request, Dyfrig Beorbrook was relieved of his
office of Earl Marshal of the Realm by Queen Wylgana. He
married Queen Casabarela of Didion. The couple had three
children and ruled the northern kingdom together – although
this fact was never officially acknowledged – until their deaths
at a ripe old age.

I myself served each succeeding Cathran ruler in turn as

Royal Intelligencer, to the best of my wily ability in trying times. When High Queen Wylgana decided to revise the history of the kingdom to show her father Conrig, her pathetic brother Corodon, her great-uncle Feribor, and the late Sovereignty of Blenholme in a more favorable light, I protested the futile deception too loudly. The queen dismissed me for my pains, commanded me to leave the island, and provided me with a pension dependent on my good behavior. I lived quietly for many years on the Continent until, as is only too apparent, my instinct for troublemaking got the better of me.

Beynor of Moss was never heard from again; but three decades ago I received an engraved invitation to attend the coronation of the new self-styled Emperor of Stippen. A handwritten postscript said: *This time, it'll be better.* I sent regrets.

The Lights still shine. Some of them may be contemplating mischief. I'm too old to care.

As for my dearest Induna . . .

My memories of her are none of your business.